GOTHIQUE

A VAMPIRE NOVEL

KYLE MARFFIN

DESIGN IMAGE

THE DESIGNIMAGE GROUP, INC.

This book contains a work of fiction. Names, characters, places, organizations or incidents are used fictitiously and are only the products of the author's imagination. Any resemblance to actual events, locations, businesses or persons, living or dead, is purely coincidental.

Inquiries may be directed to:

The Design Image Group, Inc.
PO Box 2325
Darien, Illinois 60561
www.designimagegroup.com

ISBN:1-891946-06-4

First Edition

DESIGN IMAGE
THE DESIGNIMAGE GROUP, INC.

Printed In The U.S.A.

10 9 8 7 6 5 4 3 2 1

For my three M's

Cafe Caveat

Twisted Tales

Author's Open Mike Series

Every day Night – 9:00 PM

Start the week off right with creeps 'n coffee: your favorite local horror writers reading their most vile, twisted tales. This month's special feature: "Nosferatu Noir's". For more info, visit Cafe Caveat on the web at www...

Chicago Police Department

Youth Crimes Division

Report # 9903

Subject: R/MP Projections, 2nd Quarter '99

Confirming MIS tally, 32% increase in runaway and juvenile missing persons reports for YTD. Cook County Social Services corroborates stats with similar 34% increase in 1st quarter vs. same quarter last year. CC: HQ Homicide, HQ Vice, HQ Domestic Violence, All Precinct Community Watch Coordinators...

Chicago Night-Files, May 4

HOT SPOTS

Here's a way to get over hump day. Club Dominae has added "Fetish night", bondage boys & girls, so be there, be square (knotted) in your loveliest lycra and leather for Guest DJ Bad-Bobbie Ball-Gag spinning the finest techno-pop and whip crackin' dance tunes. $8 cover, dress code required. Meetcha there after...

A Wishin' And A Wantin'

ONE

The darkness emerges and it descends from the east.

And with the darkness, they awake.

The darkness emerges, creeps above the eastern horizon and then rolls across the wide expanse of blue water.

The darkness falls like a black curtain, igniting sparkle light explosions in the windows of the skyscrapers flanking the water's edge and in the neat rows of unassuming houses behind, where the blinds slam shut, the drapes draw close. The darkness emerges, descends from the east and the sky bleeds red while the city cringes.

Another night.

Another night, and they awake.

The children of the dark crawl out of their dens to embrace the night.

They awake.

Awake in their bungalow bedrooms, their rehabbed industrial lofts, their fourth floor walkup flats, their high rise penthouse suite perches. They awake in their anonymous workstations, their ergonomic cubicles, behind cash registers and Formica counters after cowering all day under the fluorescent dayglow brightness in greasy spoons and quick-prints, used CD outlets and comics shops, bookstores and flashy trashed second hand chic boutiques lining the desperately hip but still seedy side streets or struggling for survival in off-the-main-drag strip malls.

Another night.

Now they turn away from their computer screens, their chat rooms and websites. Put away their comics, their graphic novels, their used paperbacks, their magalogs, their ink-jetted 'zines, their multi-volumed sourcebooks and shared world figurines. They shut down their keyboards, unplug pawn shop guitars, pack up their plastic PC percussion sets and their MTV wet dream garage bandstanding. They flip off the man on their way out of detention, they flip off the jocks and cheerleaders on their way past the gym, flip off the frigid matrons behind the library desk, flip off the boss hiding in his corner office, flip off the parents enduring the mom 'n dad dinner thing. They tear off their pink and orange donut shop smocks, their chain store logo T's, their green plaid uniform jumpers and their faux French maid diner waitress aprons. For the moment, if only for tonight, they'll forget their never-to-be-finished software schemes and their adolescent dreamin' love-is-pain poems and novel fragments, their hand scribbled screenplays, their loose leaf doodled felt tip frescoes and stolen, scanned and bit-mapped digital art for the new ages, leaving all those roads to hopeful hells paved with obscure works in progress.

Darkness has descended on the city, and now they're awake.

Alive.

Free.

Free to be, in twisted rules of their own rigid conformity.

The rituals commence: time honored, savored, relished as much or more for all their eager apprehension. A wishin' and a wantin' that tonight it will all be different.

Be real.

That it will all come true this time. Tonight, maybe. Something more than pretend 'n play in the 7-11 parking lots and multiplex lobbies, in their coffeehouse booths, their basement and backporch-backseat groan & gropes.

The night descends outside their shrines and sanctuaries, painting their windows black while they mug for dresser mirrors, preen in grimy bathroom stalls, vainly ogle their vanities, swaying along with their headphone and bookshelf-speaker sturm und drang soundtracks.

Now they rummage through underwear and sock drawers and backpack pouches for their mail-ordered pewter skulls and headshop batwing rings, their genre-con chromed plastic ankhs, velveteen chokers and studded vinyl dog collars. They paint their chewed-to-the-tip nails all red, black, then decaled. They flounce on Whitechapel whorehouse blush, drag Cray-Pas creamy green, blue and smoky sable across their eyelids — rub it in, smear it in, mash it in, line it all with rims of black. Grip their drugstore pro model makeup brushes, gobbed with gooey purple and rich ruby red gloss, and paint their lips all shiny-sexy wet, paint them all seductively slow and autoerotic and as sensuously as any wet tongued kiss. Heroin chic faces, haute cocaine couture, gaunt and painfully pale and oh so creamy-hot-hard-wet, oh so sex-is-death-is-love — they wish.

They wish.

Frederick's Of Hollywood fishnets and military surplus hardware, back of the film mag prosthetics and filched antique shop costume kitsch, Victoria's Secret sale rack scanties and flea market dumpster gems — it all comes out now from the closets locked tight against mom and dad inquisitions, sis and bro tattletales, from Biff and Judy's snickering scorn and dormies' disapproval.

Now feel it. Feel the fingerless gloves against their soft, skinny, pale hands. Feel the rough sewn seams inside the mall store lace, the freshly painted nails clawing shiny sleazy nylons into gauzy black cobwebs, feel the uniform jett black tights snap into place around anorexic hips, feel the corset straps slide over bony white shoulders, feel the Harley Hog leather shimmy over gangly legs.

Listen — hear the artfully shredded jeans and leather pants and vinyl skirts slide and crinkle into place, hear the crisp satin capes flap, hear jingle-jangle bike jacket zippers, hear combat boots and fetish heels clomping below their black lycra'd legs. Painfully preened and primped, they emerge — dark and gleaming with that so-hard-to-achieve freshly molested look.

They're out.

Where the cool night air bathes their greasepaint faces, sneaks underneath the peekaboo skirts, ripples the salon outlet dyed and bleached and tortured tresses.

They're out.

Out and outed in the dark where it's all alive and a rush and just — just — just *better.* Where the costumes work like medieval armor against a passerby's scowl, like kevlar shields against the dopey dismissive straights who just don't have a clue driving by in their soccer-mom vans, standing behind USA Today's at the bustop, at the El platform, at the taxi stand, on the streetcorner. The sanctimonious suits and secretaries vanish with the dark, taking their wingtips and pinstripes, their sensible mall store suits and sensible mall store pumps and scurry off to sensible suppers in sensible suburbs with comfortably homogenized anonymity in fern bars, faux-Italian bistros and franchise coffeebars, the great proletariat unhip, vapidly content with sitcom soufflés and vinyl sided split level dreams.

Because now it's dark.

Now it's night.

Now the streets are *theirs.*

Theirs for the taking. For their fanciful games and promenades. Carnivale. Festivale. Mardi Gras every night, The Day Of The Dead, Walpurgis Nacht. Fêtes worse than death.

They congregate in their cults, their cadres and covens, in their *non*-franchise coffeehouses with authentic bare brick walled, mismatched cupped bohemian legitimacy, the elders arguing Siouxsie Sioux and Bauhaus and Maplethorpe, Gautier and Shelley and LeFanu, preaching to the newly converted, to the fledglings who are all flushed and cyber'd up to the minute with their Brite's and Rice's and the latest LARP led craze. They line up at sticky tables in dingy converted storefront bars and converted warehouse clubs and yet-to-be-converted gangways and alleys, licking the tips of their acrylic dental delusions, licking the rims of their gooey goblets of gore, licking their lips, licking themselves, licking each other, licking their wounds, wounds still bleeding from the sores of their days' discontented dreams. Needles gleam under the streetlights and strobelights, double blade Gillette's parcel out powdered portions of bravado, liquor cabinet rejects are uncorked, poured, guzzled along with the stinky, cloying, fruity smoke from countless colored cigarettes hovering around them like graveyard fog.

Yeah, like fog.

Like graveyard fog — oh, that would be cool.

Drug addicts, drag addicts, gender bent, hell bent, all of them post adolescent hands-in-her-pants, hands-in-his-pants, hands-in-*your*-pants dreaming.

Dreaming.

Wishing.

Wanting.

Desperately waiting and hoping.

Hoping for it all to come true.

Tonight.

Yes, maybe tonight.

The movies. The songs. The videos. The paperbacks. The CD's, the comix and the zines, the rulebooks and the games, the websites and chatrooms, the clubs, the con's and the costumes — all of it, *oh please,* if it could only be real, could happen for real, could erase the daylight blandness, could all be true, just be true, be real, oh please, *please* become *real.* Become fog shrouded savage sacrileges, become moonlit crystal goblets of warm-thick-red-*real,* be under-my-power, do-my-bidding *real,* welcome to my house, come into my room, climb into my bed, slither under my sheets *real,* be real and touch me — yes, touch me for *real* — there, yes, oh right there and don't stop, there — kiss me there, yes, there — bite — yes, bite me, bite me there, it's okay, bite me, no for real, make it *real,* like that, just like that, oh just like that and be *real.*

Be real.

Be *real.*

Oh, please be...

Chicago Business Monitor
June

Local Media Mogul Mauls Competitors In Expansion Moves

Chicago Whitestar Media Group, Chicago's second largest media conglomerate, controlling several midwestern metro television and radio stations along with a growing number of regional periodicals, completed its hostile takeover of the troubled BBX Entertainment, Ltd. theater chain. Whitestar has dabbled in the local entertainment scene for nearly two years now, with small stakes in several prominent Chicago theme restaurant chains. Whitestar spokespersons offered no comment on their immediate plans for the BBX properties, however...

Southwest News-Herald
Friday, June 9 – Section 2, Page 4

Second Body Found In Marquette Park Lagoon

8th District police discovered another body in the Marquette Park lagoon Sunday morning. A police spokesperson reported only that the deceased was a white juvenile female, that there was evidence of sexual assault and that she appeared to be a homicide victim. This is the third body discovered in remote locations in southwest side parks in the past three weeks, though only one has been identified so far, that being 20 year old Jonathan M...

Charade Magazine
June Fashion-Watch

Paint It Black All Summer!

There's no need to stash your beautiful blacks for the short lived Chicago summer. Look for lightweight linens in black on black gracing all the better Oak Street salons. New, kicky, ultra-thin black leather skirts are as cool as your own skin, even in the steamiest dance floor frolics, and devilishly desirable when mated to the new microfibre black opaque hosiery for a long and luscious silhouette. Plus, this year you'll simply die for Eulenaire's elegant ebony accessories, including...

Megan's Legacy

TWO

As soon as she'd ducked into the elevator, Megan Russell was certain she gave Nicky the slip.

Her ears popped twice on the ride up to the Hancock Building's ninety sixth floor, her stomach doing flip-flops all the way. But then, her stomach had been doing flip-flops ever since she fled from her condo the first thing this morning. All day, in fact, even though she'd somehow managed to stay one short step ahead of Nicky at each stop.

So when she'd spotted him down on Michigan Avenue, sprawled across a bus bench, peeking at her from behind an upside down Sun-Times and just smiling that sleazy little grin of his, Megan thought she'd throw up right on the sidewalk.

Instead, she ran.

Melt into the crowds on Michigan? Easy. A movie just let out at the multi-screen in Water Tower Place, so Megan navigated her way through that mob with only a quick glance over her shoulder. She saw Nicky toss his newspaper in the trash and cross Michigan, heading her way. Then he vanished into the evening traffic.

That's when Megan flitted in between two taxis and ducked into the revolving doors of the Hancock Building.

The lobby was empty. There wasn't even a security guard manning the front desk. Her Folgolio pumps clicked across the marble like firecrackers as she made for the elevators. It took forever for those elevator doors to close, and before they did, she poked her head out for one last glance in the lobby. But she didn't see Nicky. Didn't see anyone at all.

90 seconds: that's all it took for the elevator to whisk her up to the ninety sixth floor. The doors silently slid open on Megan brushing windblown hair off her forehead, wiping cold sweat off her skin. She took a deep breath and stepped into The Ninety Sixth Club.

"Good evening, Miss Russell." The hostess eased out from behind her podium, a two foot long leather menu cradled in her arm. "Another late night at the magazine?"

"Evening," Megan said. *Bonnie? Or was it Bunny?* Megan never was any good with names.

"Little late for dinner, Miss Russell. The kitchen closed at eleven. I'm afraid the chef's gone for the night. But I could — "

"No, I just popped in for a nightcap." Megan swung her purse around. Her fingers were still slick with sweat as she fumbled with the Prada's clasp, a sudden shiver shaking her whole body. Down on Michigan Avenue it had been a muggy June night, but up here in the Ninety Sixth Club, it was air conditioned cool.

"Here, let me take your things, Miss Russell."

"No!" Megan stepped back, clutching the purse to her chest. Calmer then, "No, thank you."

"Well, can I get you a table then? You can have your pick." Bonnie or Bunny, or whatever her name was, gestured towards the interior of the club: row after row of empty tables and booths.

A young couple held hands at a table for two by the windows, the glittery expanse of the Chicago skyline hovering outside their window like a picture postcard. In the center of the club, the bartender slid a drink to a middle aged man in a suit who was busy eyeing up one lone woman, four stools down.

Megan inventoried the place: the hostess' practiced politeness, the bartender glancing at his watch, the wedding ring glistening on the hand of the man at the bar as he reached for his drink, the woman winking back at him and elaborately crossing her legs while she toyed with the hem of her too-fancy dress. The young couple standing up from their seats and carefully counting out a tip to leave on the table.

And no Nicky.

"Have a Chivas on the rocks at that table in the corner." Megan pointed to a secluded booth tucked under one of the Hancock's immense diagonal crossbeams that dissected the panoramic view. "Make it a double. I'm going to freshen up." She finally got her purse opened and pulled out a five dollar bill.

Bonny-Bunny took the tip and nodded with a well rehearsed smile while Megan whisked away.

The bathroom was empty.

Doors dangled half open on four stalls. But Megan peeked inside each one just to be sure. Evidently the attendant was gone for the evening; the Ninety Sixth wasn't much a late night spot. Megan splashed cold water on her face, then helped herself to a spritz of perfume from the neat row of bottles lined up along the marble vanity. She touched up her makeup, a dash of eyeshadow here, a dab of lipstick there. There wasn't any need for blush. Her cheeks were red enough already. Running around Chicago all day and night — especially a hot and muggy June day like this had been — could do that.

Particularly when you were scared for your life.

Megan's short, frosted hair looked less frazzled once she dragged a brush through it. The makeup helped, but her face still looked tired. A thirty-five year old overworked executive tired, a not in shape for criss-crossing-the-city-like-amadwoman tired. Her Donna Karan blazer — a crisp, linen eggshell gem just this morning — was a wrinkled mess now. Little crescents of perspiration seeped through the underarm seams. She slipped the jacket off and sneered at the giant half moons of sweat staining her silk blouse. That blouse cost two twenty at Neiman's, and no dry cleaner was going to get those stains out now.

Tired face.

Tired looking clothes.

Tired and scared.

Megan eased one foot out of its shoe, almost sighing at the cool touch of the marble floor on her bare foot. The cream colored Folgolio's always looked smashing when she strutted back and forth across the Charade Magazine conference room, feeling all tall and in control. It was tough enough staying on your toes while the world nipped at your heels. But she usually slipped the Folgolio's off once she got back to her office and could keep her feet tucked under her desk. Those feet hurt like hell now, but then she'd been running around downtown all day in these three inch heels. It was a wonder she wasn't crippled.

Her foot was reluctant to squeeze back into the shoe, but it did, and she tossed her makeup case back into the purse. Megan pawed through the clutter inside: keys, Waterman pens, a gold Colibri lighter without any butane, Charade Magazine employee ID badge. Wallet stuffed with every dollar she could lay her hands on today.

The travel agent's folio, plane tickets all ready to go.

And the envelope.

The stamped envelope, addressed:

Whitestar Media Group
211 East Fairmont Court
Chicago, Illinois 60611
Attn: Jeff Stancheck,
Art Director, Charade Magazine

An envelope with no return address.

Megan stared at the envelope. Stared and thought about the floppy disks inside. Thought about the files on those disks. She thought — no, plotted, actually.

She'd drop the envelope in the mail at the airport and only if she absolutely had to. She could always intercept it at the office later. If everything worked out all right. Oh, Jeff would think she was crazy if he actually read any of those files. He'd think she was popping into the nose candy store again. But she could fix that, just tell him it was all a joke. Notes for a book, maybe. Sure — or a screenplay. Everyone at Charade had a script or a novel in the works. Jeff would buy that.

Jeff was awfully trusting that way.

Jeff, God love him, was trusting to the point of dumb sometimes.

Yes, there'd be time at the airport. She'd mail it there. Once Nicky gave up

"Yeah, I suppose you're right. What would be the point?" Nicky shrugged his shoulders. "Like they'd believe you." He leaned across the table, his whisper conspiratorial now. "But that's just what I don't get. You're so fucking smart, you know the cops wouldn't believe you. No one would believe you. So, why bother?"

"Nicky, someone *has* to — "

"No they don't. No one *has* to anything." He leaned away. "So, your place was clean. You must have it on you, that it? Let me have your purse."

"Nicky, there's nothing in my purse. I don't have anything on me. I don't even *have* what you think I have. What *they* think I have. I never did."

Nicky shook his head and sighed. "So fucking smart. And so fucking stupid." He fumbled under his jacket, then slid one hand under the table. "Megan, you know what a 'pistol whipping' is?"

She wiped the tears off her cheeks. "A...what? A pistol whipping? You think you can just beat me up in here? In the Ninety Sixth Club? You think they won't just call security and toss your ass right down to Michigan Avenue?"

"Megan, I didn't say I was gonna. I just asked if you *knew* what a pistol whipping is."

Puzzled, she answered. "Okay, sure. Sure, I know what a pistol whipping is."

"Really? Well, there you go. You really *are* smart. See, I never actually knew. I mean, you hear about it all the time. But, what actually happens? How does someone 'whip' you with a pistol?" Nicky laughed, a squeaky kind of a giggle, and it made Megan's stomach turn. "But smart as you are, I bet I'm still one up on you."

"Nicky, what are you getting at? "

"Do you know what a 'bullet fucking' is?"

Megan flinched. Suddenly she felt cool metal push against her knees, pressing them apart. Then slowly sliding up along the inside of her thighs, right between her legs. It stopped halfway under her skirt. "N-no, Nicky. I never..."

"It's my own thing, bullet fucking. See, what you've got there between your legs is a 9MM Mauser. Pointed right at your snatch. I pull the trigger, and it's going to make a brand new hole. Probably make a mess of those fancy panties you like to wear." He winked. "Well, I did have to go through *all* of your things this morning."

Megan squirmed, certain she was going to throw up.

"Easy, sweetheart," Nicky cooed. "I wouldn't move around too much. Just takes one shot, Megan. One shot and that bullet will bounce round and round inside of you till it makes meatloaf. I bet you can hear the little sucker pinging off your bones while you die." He giggled again, and then his lips twisted into a sneer. "So just give me the fucking purse."

She slid her purse across the table, urgently scanning the whole club. But the couple that had been at the other table was gone now. The old guy at the bar, the call girl eyeing him up — both gone. She couldn't see the bartender or the hostess, couldn't see anyone except an old Latino cleaning lady heading for the bathrooms with her cart.

"Megan, you weren't trying to leave us without saying good-bye, were you?" Nicky flipped open the travel agency folio. "Let's see here, tickets to LA, motel reservations, rental car." He looked back up at her. "Honey, maybe you could duck out on me, but you think *they* couldn't track you down?"

"No, Nicky, it's magazine business. I just — "

"Magazine business, huh? Oh, and lookee here, the tickets are made out in someone else's name." Nicky shook his head. "Megan *Smith*? That's the best you could do?" He scanned the travel agency receipt. "And paid cash too? Nice try, really."

Megan craned her neck, wondered if she could get away with hollering for another drink, anything to get someone over here. She spotted the cleaning woman again, feather dusting the planters along the hall by the bathrooms now. The woman squatted and picked something up.

Stared at it.

Stuffed it into her apron.

The envelope?

"And speaking of cash..." Nicky whistled as he pulled out her wad of bills. "Jesus, one thousand, fifteen hundred, two grand — you weren't planning on coming back for a while, were you?"

"No, Nicky, you have it all wrong. That's just — just a travel advance. I'm telling you, I have a business trip. A photo shoot on the coast, and — "

"Will there be anything else, Miss Russell?"

It was Bonnie — or Bunny — suddenly standing there beside the booth, and right now Megan wished to God she knew the girl's name.

"We're closing up now, Miss Russell, but I could probably sneak a last round."

Before Megan could answer, Nicky pulled a hundred from the bills in her purse and slipped it into the hostess' hand. "No, thank you. Miss Russell and I were just leaving." He tucked the rest of the money in his pocket.

The hostess hesitated. She looked directly at Megan. "Are you sure? Are you...sure you don't need anything?"

Megan glanced at Nicky. She felt his gun wiggle between her thighs.

"No," she said. "I really do have to go."

✦

Nicky swore under his breath when he found the service door next to the elevators locked. He looked over his shoulder, saw that the corridor was empty, then pulled something out of his pocket and poked around in the lock. *Click-click,* and the door opened. "Nimble fingers, ain't they?" He tapped Megan's back with his gun. "Come on, let's go."

They headed up a dark stairwell: unpainted concrete walls, metal steps, bare metal banister. "Where are we going?" Megan asked. She could hear machinery rumbling somewhere deep behind the concrete.

"Just walk." Nicky slid the gun up her back and pressed the barrel against her neck.

Two flights. Three. At the top of the fourth, they came to another locked door, and Nicky picked the lock just like the first. "Go on," he said with another shove of the pistol.

Warm, humid wind slapped Megan's face as she stepped through the door.

"Jesus," was all she could manage.

"Top of the world, Ma," Nicky shouted. He saw Megan didn't get the joke, and kicked the door shut. "Hundred stories up, Megan. Ain't it beautiful?"

With the gun at her back, Megan stumbled across the roof of the Hancock Building, the Chicago skyline twinkling all around her. It made her dizzy for a moment — out there in the open, strong winds tugging at her clothes, no windows or railings between her and the rest of the city far down below. She glanced up and saw the Hancock's huge twin antennas swaying in the wind, felt a swirl of vertigo and almost fell down.

But Nicky grabbed her by the arm and ushered her along. "The 'Top Of The Cock', I call it. Get it? The Han-cock?"

Megan didn't answer. Her throat had gone desert dry. But her eyes were spilling tears again as Nicky prodded her towards the end of the roof.

"Okay, far enough." Nicky halted just three feet shy of the very edge.

Megan started to turn around.

"No, don't turn around. I want you to keep looking down there. Long drop, isn't it?"

"Nicky, why are you doing this?"

"Shut up." He gave her back another shove with the Mauser — just a nudge, just a tap, actually. But Megan screamed anyway.

"Okay, now take your clothes off."

"What?" *Is that all this was about? Sex?* Megan decided that Nicky Kolitzky really was just a nobody after all. And here she thought...thought he was going to...thought they'd make him...

"I said, take your clothes off. Now."

"Nicky, if all you wanted to do was fuck me, why didn't you just say so?" *Could she give him the slip again, or would she have to screw the slimy punk?* "I know you've wanted me all along. I've seen the way you look at me. But not here, Nicky. Let's go back to my place." *She pictured the Mauser laying on the nightstand beside her bed, out of Nicky's reach while she got him off. Felt it all cold and metallic and heavy in her own hands, saw it pointed at his shriveling little dick.* "Or we could get a room. There's a hotel on every corner downtown, we could —"

The Mauser cracked her across the back of the head. Megan screamed, lost her balance and lurched forward towards the edge of the roof.

Nicky grabbed her.

He pulled her back.

"Now, just shut the fuck up, Megan, and take off your clothes."

Megan slipped off her blazer.

"Just hand them back to me," Nicky said before she dropped it.

She unbuttoned her blouse, feeling the wind on her chest and her belly, so cool, even though it was warm out, so cool the way it blew across the sweat on her skin. Megan's mind was still racing, but confused now. She reached back and unzipped her skirt.

Jacket, blouse, skirt, bra — item by item, she took them off and handed each back to Nicky. Finally, she stood there in just her panties and the Folgolios, the pumps crunching gravel imbedded in the roof tar.

"Now what, Nicky?"

"Take everything off."

Megan clenched her teeth, and stepped out of her panties.

"Shoes too, come on."

"Nicky, the gravel."

"Take the fucking shoes off."

Once she handed the pumps back, the gravel dug into the soft soles of her feet. She could feel the day's heat still baking in the tar.

"Okay, now you can turn around."

She did.

Nicky stood right there with a foot planted on top of the pile of her clothes, the wind tugging at them and trying to tear them loose. In one hand, he still held the pistol, pointed right at her. In the other...

Megan choked.

With his other hand, Nicky raised her ivory lace panties to his face, sniffed them like they were a fresh flower, and smiled his sleazy smile. "These, I think I'll keep." He stuffed the panties in his blazer pocket.

"So what now, Nicky?"

"Now?" His eyes crawled across her naked body like worms. "Now I give you one last chance to tell me where it all is."

"Nicky, I've told you. I don't have whatever it is you think I have. What *they* think I have." She was crying again now, big, raspy sobs that muddled her words. Megan's mind wasn't scheming anymore. She couldn't imagine that Mauser in her own hands anymore. She just felt naked. And scared.

Really scared.

"No, Megan. I don't think you're listening. I'm going to give you *one* last chance."

"Nicky, I got rid of it. Everything. I knew no one would believe any of it anyway, so I dumped it all, every goddamn file. I swear to God, I did."

Nicky shook his head. "You've got it, you don't. It's all at home, it's all gone." He raised the pistol and pointed it directly at Megan's forehead. "Fuck it. That was your chance."

Megan threw her hands up in front of her face. She instinctively took half a step back, remembered where she was, and froze. "N-Nicky, I swear, I really do. I got rid of it, all of it, everything I dug up. It's gone. I'll never tell anybody. You can tell *them* that. They'll believe you, they'll — "

"That's enough, Megan." He cocked the Mauser. Now...jump."

Her face went white. "W-what? *Jump?*"

"You heard me. Jump. Now. Over the edge."

"I'm not going to...Nicky you can't be serious, you..." Her voice went hysterical now. Nicky, and the gun, and her clothes and the antennas and the twinkly skyline all swam in watery blurs in front of her eyes while the tears cascaded down her cheeks. "Nicky, for the love of God, don't do this. Don't —"

"Jump, Megan. Jump, or I'll just have to shoot you."

"Nicky, please — "

"Either way, you're not going to see tomorrow."

"Nicky, oh please, Jesus-God-Jesus, I'm begging." Megan fell to her knees, hot gravel slicing into her skin. "Please!"

"Jump, Megan."

"No."

The tears stopped. Megan Russell looked up at him, eyes suddenly defiant, teeth clenched. "No," she repeated.

Nicky took a cautious step closer. He lowered the Mauser till it rested on her right temple.

"Shoot me," Megan seethed. "Go ahead and shoot me, then. Shoot me while I'm staring right up at you." She felt the barrel quiver on her forehead. Saw Nicky's fingers clench and unclench on the grip. "You don't have the balls, Kolitzky."

Nicky hesitated.

He lowered the gun.

"You're right, Megan. I guess I don't."

She closed her eyes and let out a gush of held breath.

And that's when Nicky Kolitzky's boot kicked her hard on the shoulder.

Megan spun around — head, arms, and torso dangling over the edge of the roof for an amazingly long moment. Her mind reeled at the sight of the little cars and streetlights a hundred stories down.

One more kick, this time at her legs, and Megan went flying over the edge, hovering in mid air with flailing arms and legs for a millisecond, then plunging down, straight down into dark, freefall nothingness.

The wind gusted up and swallowed her screams.

Nicky carefully inched closer to the edge of the roof, just in time to glimpse Megan's naked body catch the gleam shining out of the skyscraper's windows like a strobelight as she fell.

He turned away before she even hit the sidewalk. Nicky scooped up Megan Russell's purse and clothes.

THREE

Jeff Stancheck smacked his mouse three times, the last time with his fist. A telltale crunch of plastic on circuitry told him that he'd ruined another one. But sometimes walloping these little rodents was the only thing to do when the twin bank of G4's crashed on him. That's why he kept a drawer stuffed full of replacements.

Sometimes a good wallop on the mouse was all that was needed.

Sometimes. *This* time, the computer crashed anyway, and he lost pages 47 and 48 of Charade Magazine's July issue.

The issue that was headed to the printer tonight.

Jeff ripped out the mouse, tossed it into an overflowing trash can behind him, then pulled a brand new clear plastic-cartoned one out of his desk drawer. He just started to pry the blister pack open when Blair poked her head in the door.

"Meeting in five, Jeff."

"I'm kind of in the middle of something here, Blair."

"Quick one, I promise. Megan's office." Blair Armstrong, Charade Magazine's Assistant Managing Editor, was gone before he could argue.

Jeff plugged in the new mouse, waited a minute for the file to reappear, then started to search for pages 47 and 48. When he couldn't locate them right away, he swore at the screen, grabbed his empty coffee mug and glanced at the imposing stack of Zip disks and CDR's still waiting to be approved: one hundred and twenty eight pages of the July issue, to be picked up by the printer promptly at five o'clock, and here he was only on page 47. Sneering at the computer, he thought wistfully of the good old days of rubber cement and paste-ups and type galleys. *They* never evaporated into cyberspace.

Outside his office door, the Charade Magazine Art Department roosted in all its sloppy best, with stacks of layouts and mounds of unfiled photos, heaps of computer disks and every conceivable kind of proof rolled, unrolled and just cluttering the artists' workstations. Scanners, inkjets and banks of servers hummed a white noise workday sonata.

"Volunteer needed," Jeff called out. Every head ducked below the cubicle walls, as if on cue. "My computer crashed. Again. I lost 47 and 48, so someone needs to check the disks or locate them in the system."

Still no answer.

Jeff peeked over a cubicle wall. "Gabrielle, thanks for volunteering."

Gabrielle took the phone away from her ear and pressed it against her chest, glaring at him from behind a long drape of Adams-Family-black hair and thick gobs of mascara. Jeff couldn't tell if she glared at him for interrupting another in an endless stream of personal calls, or for the extra assignment. More likely, she bristled at the way he mispronounced her name; it was *Gah-BRAY-el*, she always insisted.

But Jeff just glared right back at her, wondering once again if the kid had ever been eight years old, ever rode a teeter-totter, ever played with Barbies, slid into home plate, answered to *'Hey, Gabby'*? He glanced at today's black on black on black wardrobe and Gabrielle's spoiled blueberry lip gloss.

Nope, probably not, he concluded.

"But I'm meeting someone for lunch, Jeff," she whined.

"It's only eleven thirty. You'll have plenty of time."

"But — "

"Sorry, Gabrielle. Meeting in Megan's office. Got to run."

Now there was a kid determined to go barefoot through a world of no shoes-no-shirt-no service signs, Jeff thought, shaking his head but smiling to himself while he left the Art Department. He filled up his coffee mug on the way to Editorial. Taking a sip as he walked, he immediately grimaced: cinnamon. And something else. Nutmeg? Time was that regular and decaf were the only options in Charade's coffee stations. Now whenever he brought a cup to his lips, it was a spice rack surprise.

Charade Magazine had moved into the sixteenth and seventeenth floors of the Whitestar Media Group building on Fairmont Court three years ago. Sometimes Jeff missed their old digs in a warehouse loft west of the Chicago Loop. *Way* west. West to where urban renewal hadn't segued into 'gentrification' yet. He'd spent seven good years there, and missed having a window that really opened, missed the free parking right on the street, and especially missed the reliably edible Italian Beef at the Westside Grill.

But he had to admit that this new faux marble and green glass eyesore had air conditioning that really worked, elevators that went up and down without threatening a five story drop, and the only rodents lurking here plugged into computers instead of building nests behind them.

On the other hand, parking was going for a $335 a month here in the Streeterville neighborhood, those few blocks of office skyscrapers, luxury high-rises and the occasional brownstone tucked between Michigan Avenue and the Lake. And Jeff hadn't found a satisfactory Italian Beef in three years.

Well, there was a passable Polish with mustard and grilled onions to be had at the carryout off St. Clair.

Jeff navigated the carpeted hallways between contrasting carpeted cubicles in Purchasing, unaware of the secretaries and data entry clerks glancing up from their terminals to give him the top-to-bottom once over. It would have left Jeff as red faced as surprised to find out that half of Charade Magazine's female staffmembers — single and otherwise — found him attractive. If anything, he was usually self-conscious about his too-casual style and perennially five years out of date clothes. After all, these days Charade Magazine *was* Chicago's current arbiter of all that was 'in'. And Jeff was Charade's Art Director. But that *was* one of Charade's own charades, just one of the many skeletons in a glitzy publishing closet that was practically an entire boneyard.

He took another sip from his coffee, remembered it was gooey flavored slop, and spit the cinnamon nutmeg concoction back into the mug. Or tried to. Instead, he dribbled a mouthful on the front of his white oxford cloth button down and across the front of his jeans, the last few drops speckling his cowboy boots. A secretary noticed and had to stifle a giggle from behind her terminal. Jeff scowled at her, then realized how silly he must have looked and his scowl melted into a smile. He shrugged his shoulders, the secretary winked back, and he stepped into Megan Russell's command center, the Managing Editor's palatial corner office.

No Megan.

Instead, Blair Armstrong perched in Megan's plush leather desk chair, squeezing the arms like she was trying it on for size.

"I hope Megan's not running late again, Blair. We have an issue due at the printer today, you know." Jeff plopped down in an armchair on the visitor's side of Megan's enameled desk.

"Couldn't tell you, Jeff. I haven't seen Megan in days."

Jeff lurched forward in his chair. "What do you mean you haven't...then who called this meeting?"

"I did."

"You? Since when do you call me to meetings? Did I miss something here? Me — Art *Director*, you — *Assistant* Managing Editor. I still have that right, don't I, Blair?" Jeff hated office politicking more than cinnamon nutmeg coffee, but he loved to bait Blair. She lived and died by the power struggles, the comings and goings, the gossip from Whitestar's upper floors, the organizational charts and the disciplinary memos.

Blair spun the huge leather chair in a full three sixty, showing off a crisply tailored summer double-breasted suit and long legs. She snorted when she circled back to face him. "*I'll* call you to a meeting when Megan's out and we have to make a change in the July issue."

Jeff chuckled. "No, you must mean the *August* issue." He grabbed Megan's desk calendar. It was still opened to three days ago. He flipped ahead to today, Wednesday, June 12th, and slid it back across the desk. "Look at the dates, will you? You *do* know what today is, don't you? 'Final Art' day. 'Art-to-the-printer' day. Not 'major change' day."

"Can't be helped, Jeff."

"Is this Megan's idea?"

"Well...no, actually."

"Who's then?"

Blair squirmed. "It's sort of a joint effort between Sales and Editorial."

"Meaning you cooked this up," Jeff said. "But Megan approved it, right?"

"Look Jeff, I told you I haven't seen Megan in days. No one has, as far as I know."

Jeff leaned back in the chair. "That's weird. I mean, it's not unusual for her to be out of town for a few days, but never on Final Art day. It's been a tradition with us. Megan and I always go over the pages one last time before they leave for the printer."

"Well, nothing against the boss, Jeff, but don't you think Megan's been acting a little, well...preoccupied lately?"

Jeff did think about it. And the more he did, the more he realized that Megan Russell had been more than just inattentive the last few weeks. She'd barely been around. "I try not to poke my nose where it isn't wanted," he finally said. "Maybe Megan has something going on in her personal life."

"Megan doesn't have a personal life," Blair said. She fussed at her blonde hair with her fingers, tipped with manicured nails. "Charade *is* her personal life. Come on, Jeff, you've worked with her since she was just a staff writer and you were a paste-up punk. Ten years now, right? You know, all those glory days the two of you always get all nostalgic about? When Charade was the Second City's cheap imitation of the Village Voice? Remember, before your 'Second City' dropped to third place?"

Jeff nodded. "It'd have done you good to be working here then, Blair. Charade was the first place people turned to for the latest topical writing, exposes, undercover stuff." He turned away from her and gazed out the windows at Lake Shore Drive. "Always got the best essays, the best book excerpts, the best fiction. Saul Bellow. Studs Terkel. Robinson, Mailer, you name it, and — "

"And barely turned a profit," Blair said, leaning forward over the desk. The plunging lapels of her double-breasted suitcoat flared out, drawing Jeff's eyes to a wisp of lacy something underneath. He quickly looked away.

"Jeff, don't go off on one of those ex-hippie things on me now. Nobody cares about 'The Days Of Rage' anymore."

"Look, even *I* don't care about The Days Of Rage," Jeff said. "I'm not even sure when The Days Of Rage were. Hell, I was probably still marking time in St. Bartholomew's grade school during The Days Of Rage." Jeff assumed that Blair was crossing and uncrossing her legs under the desk. His ears tingled with subtle sounds of nylon on linen.

"Whatever," she said. "What we have to worry about right now is adding three pages."

Jeff blinked. *Three years,* he thought. *Three years she's been here, and she still doesn't get it.* "Blair, let's track through this one last time, just so you'll remember when you get to sit in that chair for real. Pages are done in multiples of four, like a book. And Charade's printed in multiples of sixteen. It's called a 'signature', remember? *Sig-na-ture.* And that's how every major magazine in the world is put together."

"I know all that," she said.

"Then you know that we can't add *three* pages." Even with the summer sun glaring through the windows to silhouette Blair in the big leather chair, Jeff could see her face screw up into a familiar little girl pout.

"Can't we just add a foldout or something?"

"Let's back up," Jeff said. "What exactly am I trying to squeeze in?"

She opened a manila folder, spreading photos and typed copy drafts on the desk. At first glance, Jeff curled his lip.

"*Them* again?" he said. "Didn't we just — "

"Yes, 'them' again. Sales just clinched a four color ad with 'them', a two page spread no less. And a four page paid PR fluff piece. The ad art's on its way over from their agency now." Blair lowered her voice. "Though the word on the street is that it's the last assignment for *that* agency. I hear they're looking for someone new. So *you* get to lay out the fluff piece."

Jeff flipped through the photos. More trendy Helmut Newton knockoffs: anorexic, pale skinned teenagers, graveyard gloom and doomed, all gaudy S&M masquerading as haute couture. 'Highbrow kink', and all of Chicago's nightclubs and boutiques were into it these days.

Blair sensed his reaction. Maybe his sneer gave him away. "Oh, I suppose if it was an expose on the Chicago Transit Authority, you could make room? Maybe some ditzy short story that won a literary prize from some backwater college, then it'd be okay?"

"No, it's not that, it's just — "

"Look, Sales has been schmoozing their agency for months now. And God knows I've dropped enough free teasers in my column. So this is the payoff. They're talking about committing to a monthly two page spread for a year, quarterly color inserts. And some more PR pieces. Maybe even have us sponsor some kind of theme night. Do you realize how much revenue we're talking about?"

"All right," Jeff said. "Stop trying to convince me. The three pages go in. *How* is another matter altogether."

"Why can't you just add some more pages?" Blair asked. "Fill in with some junk?"

Jeff shook his head. "The issue's budgeted. The paper stock's contracted months ahead of time. Press time is already scheduled." He rubbed his chin. "Unless you want to call up to Whitestar? You could ask for a budget variance."

They both looked at each other.

Charade Magazine had been launched as a free weekly back in '71 by two

Northwestern University dropouts who actually *were* ex-hippies. They sold out to Whitestar Media Group three years ago for seven figures each, and supposedly were starting a gourmet popsicle company now. It was Whitestar that moved Charade into the slick space on Fairmont Court. It was Whitestar that computerized the Art Department. Based on some severely inflated credentials, it was Whitestar that hired Blair Armstrong away from Interview Magazine, where she'd actually been a glorified administrative assistant. It was Whitestar that turned Charade into the trendy fashion & nightlife glossy that it was today.

And it was Whitestar Media Group that would fire the both of them for pestering about a budget variance.

"Nah." Jeff and Blair both said it at the same time.

They smiled at each other, and for the moment at least, declared a truce.

"You could chop out some of the photos on that Taste Of Chicago piece," Blair offered, her voice a notch less caustic. "And I'll check with Sales and see if we can't just kill that full pager for Krowne's. I hear they haven't paid their bill in six months."

"So, a little snip here and a little trim there?" Jeff said.

"Sounds good to me." Blair glanced at her Rolex. "Look, I was supposed to be waltzing into LaStrada for lunch ten minutes ago. You get your Picassos working on this, and I'll swing by later this afternoon to see what's happening. Who knows? Maybe Megan will finally be in by then."

Jeff pulled himself out of the chair. "Whether it's you or Megan, better plan on looking at the changes later than this afternoon. I'd guess around eight, nine maybe. Presuming we get that ad art soon."

Blair scooped the photos and copy back into the manila folder and slid it across the desk towards Jeff. "That late?"

"*That* late."

But she was already around the desk and headed for the doorway now. "Well, we'll have to play it by ear then. Maybe you can fax me something at home."

And with that, Blair was gone.

Her perfume lingered in the office, though.

Jeff sniffed the air and smiled. The sound of Blair's suit swishing against her legs still whispered in his ears.

He shook his head to erase the smile and chase away the scents, then reached for Blair's folder. The project name was already neatly typed across a stick-on index tab.

GOTHIQUE.

FOUR

Wednesday's heat and humidity just got worse all day. Everything seemed to be congealing, even the air, till the garbage in the dumpsters below the Morse Avenue El platform was ready to bubble over.

Prodded down the platform and onto Morse by rush hour commuters, Colleen Russell could feel the asphalt sticking right to the soles of her clunky loafers. Or was it just bubblegum melting under the hazy, late afternoon sun? Colleen gripped her portfolio in one sweaty hand, and kept the other tight around her purse. Everyone was talking about the rash of muggings around the El station. Chicago's far north side wasn't what it used to be, the Rogers Park neighborhood in particular.

Hell, it probably never had been anyway.

She stopped in the Korean grocer a block down Morse and splurged on a cold soda, lingering at the refrigerator case just to feel cool air blow through her wrinkled cotton suit. She'd have to steam iron it again tonight, she realized as she headed back out into the heat. There was another job interview in the morning, still another right after lunch, and this beige cotton blazer and skirt were the closest things she had to legitimate business clothes.

She trudged along on Morse with the five o'clock sun beating down on the back of her head and toasting her long, red hair. It would have been a good day for a barrette, or even better, a headband - anything to keep those red bangs off her forehead. But she hadn't thought of either this morning.

She turned left up Sheridan, where the sun switched to her left cheek and tried to parboil her skin - creamy, fair skin that had been dotted with freckles clear through her sophomore year in college. Sometimes Colleen could still detect hints of them lurking there under her cheeks, even now, six years later.

The air hummed from hundreds of fans and air conditioners in the two flats and courtyard building windows. Those that were lucky, at any rate. In the others, windows just hung open and their sun bleached drapes flapped in the feeble breeze, dusted with soot from the car exhausts and smelly bus diesels roaring up and down Sheridan. But that breeze finally felt a little less hot, if not any less humid, when Colleen passed Loyola Park. There the ball fields and the tiny sliver of sandy beach hugged Lake Michigan.

Her loafers felt like they were lined with gravel today, their coarse insoles chafing her feet. But what could she expect? She bought them to go with the interview outfit at Buy-For-Less-Shoes on Broadway, all plastic and paper and man-made materials. Colleen was tempted to slip them off and do the rest of the walk home barefoot. But one glance at the sidewalk, polka-dotted with spit out gum, broken bottles and the occasional used rubber, changed her mind quick enough.

Five blocks up Sheridan, then right onto Chase Avenue, a short street lined on both sides with apartment buildings of various sizes and indiscriminate designs, canopied with old maples and dead ending at the Lake. On stormy nights, waves crashed right over the breakers and drenched any cars illegally parked there. In the winter, the spray from the churning waters could make an ice sculpture out of a sedan in an hour. But today the Lake just lolled along the concrete barriers, too hot and tired to make a stir.

Colleen made for the last building at the end of the block, a four story courtyard box seriously in need of tuckpointing and looking like it was ready to tumble into Lake Michigan with the next gale. She passed the gate that no one ever closed, passed the stubby patch of courtyard lawn that no one ever mowed, in through the door that no one ever locked, where she started up the stairs to the fourth floor.

After a five interview marathon day, it was a long climb.

Five interviews: one at nine, another at eleven. Three more in the afternoon, and all downtown, where everyone else scurried in between stores and offices on urgent and important business. Everyone but Colleen.

She knew five minutes into each of the five interviews that there wouldn't be a job offered in any one of them. In the last at 3:30, the art director spent more time probing her personal life than her resume. He barely glanced at her portfolio, though he certainly spent enough time leering at her legs, and they were nice enough legs, Colleen knew that, but *still.*

Maybe if she'd bothered to wear nylons today, maybe the lech would have been more...

No, the man was a sleaze and it was simply too damn hot to even think about wearing —

Goddamn.

Colleen dug in her purse as she stepped towards her door.

God damn it. Kleenex, pens, receipts, change, tampons. Wallet, matchbooks, a Walgreen's compact and a vinyl makeup pouch, most of that empty.

But no keys.

God damn it. Colleen dropped her two by three foot portfolio on the landing and rummaged through her jacket pockets. *Jeez, I hope Cass is still home.*

She was ready to give up knocking when a litany of clicks and snaps unlocked the deadbolts, security chains and safety latches on the other side of the door. It swung open and Cass stood there, hair shower-wet, a black towel wrapped around his waist, another tossed across his bare shoulders.

He dangled her keys in one hand. "Forgot something this morning, did we?"

Colleen grunted and lumbered past with one hand extended. Cass tossed the key ring in her palm. She dropped the portfolio beside the door, her purse on the floor, herself on the couch.

"Well, you look like you've been through the wringer today, sweetheart," Cass said. Colleen grunted again while she peeled off her wrinkled blazer. "Shirt looks familiar, Colleen. Except for the sweat."

"Sorry," she said. Colleen kicked off her loafers. They clunked on the hardwood floor with a man-made materials *thump*. "You were still asleep when I got ready this morning. I didn't have anything clean." She glanced down at the patches of perspiration soaking through the white T-shirt. "I'll wash it, Cass. In fact, I'll do the laundry tonight."

"The hell you will. You, a washing machine, and my things? I might as well donate them to the Salvation Army now." He ran the towel through his hair, the close cropped sides drying already, the lush, long bleached blonde bangs still wet and glistening. Cass threw his towel at Colleen. "You look like you need this more than me."

"Thanks." She caught it and ran the damp towel over her neck and face. It felt good, felt cool, and for a moment, the hot moist air seeping through the tiny living room's open windows didn't seem so foul.

"No luck today?" Cass plopped into the easy chair across from the sofa, unaware or not caring that the other towel wrapped around his waist flapped half open.

"Nope, more of the same." Colleen stole a peek at his lean hips, then quickly looked away. "Who was it that steered me towards graphic design? I know it wasn't my parents. They're probably still rolling over in their graves because I didn't go to nursing school."

"No," Cass said, "Pre-Law."

Colleen shook her head. "CPA."

"Education." Cass raised one eyebrow. "Grammar school teacher. *First* grade."

"As long as it's a Catholic school," Colleen added. "No point bothering with the publics and the pagans."

"And find yourself a nice fiancee *before* graduation. Rock on the finger by finals. Business major, maybe. Not one of those eggheads cocking around with a graduate degree." Cass bounced off the couch and cinched his towel up before it fell off. "Hate to tell you, love, but I do believe it was you, only you, that latched onto this designer stuff. Don't you remember? Artists who choose to eat choose graphic design."

Colleen nodded like he'd just let her in on some vital secret.

"And speaking of cocking around, I'm late." Cass grabbed his other towel back from Colleen and bounded out of the living room.

She tugged at her T-shirt collar and blew down her chest, raising her eyes to watch Cass scamper down the hallway, with his lean build, with those long, slender legs and their barely-there coat of light brown hair. With that firm little butt twitching under the towel. With that skin of his that was even fairer than hers. When Cass turned into the bathroom, she caught one last glimpse of his face, almost too perfect to be a man's.

The bathroom door shut, and she hefted herself off the couch, shaking her head.

All the real lookers were gay, weren't they *just*?

Colleen padded off to her room.

✦

With the wrinkly suit off, Colleen felt better. Once Cass vacated the bathroom, she washed the city grime off her face and hands, thought about a shower, then decided it was too much work. So she scrounged the kitchen instead.

The courtyard building had been built in the twenties, 'back when they knew how to build them', with thick doors that weighed a ton and real lathe-and-plaster walls. But the doors and the walls weren't sturdy enough to keep Cass' music from rocking the plates and glasses in the kitchen. 'More of that awful gotterdamerung stuff,' Colleen thought while she checked the last two slices of Wonder Bread for green spots. *Screaming Dead, The Cure, Christian Death, Lords Of The New Church, Dark Theatre, Alien Sex Fiend*... goddamn, it was all that boy ever listened to. Colleen slapped baloney that was a smidge too shiny to be safe onto her bread, making a mental note:

Never room with a Goth-rocker.

Juggling the sandwich and some stale corn chips on a paper plate with one hand, the mail and a soda in the other, she headed for the living room. As she crossed the hallway, Colleen spotted Cass just inside his opened bedroom door, swaying his lanky body in time to the crypto-rhythms, naked except for a pair of shiny black briefs. She hoped they weren't hers. He liked to pilfer her underwear drawer before a night out. But then, she *had* copped his T-shirt without asking this morning.

Fair's fair.

Cassidy 'Cass' Lumbach pressed his face closer to the full length mirror hanging on his door and carefully darkened his lips with burgundy-black lipstick. His eyes were already shaded with mascara and gray eyeshadow. Colleen knew he kept clear of *her* makeup stash; way too plain for his taste.

Colleen made one more mental note before she curled up on the window seat:

Never room with a gorgeous queer.

She inhaled her sandwich. *Never*....unless it was with Cass.

Roomies for almost a year now, Cass was her confidante, her banker when she was low on cash (which was most of the time), her all too eager but frustrated wardrobe consultant, her love life advisor and sometimes art critic. And most of all, her very best friend, which Colleen didn't take lightly. She couldn't think of a another soul in Chicago she could really call her friend.

Certainly none of the bubbleheads working the register at Groshman's Art Supply, where she'd part timed till last month.

And certainly none of the girls who shared her dorm room at U of I's Circle Campus. Not the theater major who turned their cramped quarters into a round the clock repertory. Not the physics major who kept her drugs in the mini-fridge and stole Colleen's stereo when the stash ran short. Certainly not the Gender Studies major who always insisted on haranguing Colleen right there in the showers about leg shaving being just one more example of the patriarchy's subjugation of women. *Try some shave gel, chick, you'll look better in shorts,* and the last of the corn chips vanished into Colleen's mouth.

She looked out the windows at the haze drifting off the lake. She'd watched it on a lot of hot and muggy evenings like this, and knew that by the time it was dark, she'd barely be able to see the apartments across the courtyard. Cass would like that, she figured. He'd like that foggy, gloomy thing. Probably why he picked this fourth floor rathole.

"And what are *you* doing, girl?"

There he was, resplendent and gaucho-gaudy in black leather pants and a frilly cuffed shirt, unbuttoned down to his belly to reveal his nearly hairless chest. He tossed a black trenchcoat over his shoulder.

"I'm finishing my dinner," Colleen said. "What are *you* doing? Don't you know it's like a hundred degrees out there?"

"Get your butt off that window seat and get ready," Cass said. "I thought you were coming out with me tonight?"

She slumped against the window frame. "Out? Back out there? You've got to be kidding."

Cass sat down on the back of the sofa. Perspiration already shined on his twenty-something face and his chest. Colleen stared at the gleam on his skin where his lacy shirt hung open. He wore that goofy medallion again, dangling from a black leather strap around his neck, that little gold-plated coffin with the clear plastic lid. It was filled with dirt. Another one of Cass' tacky treasures, mail ordered from the back of one of his gory Goth-rock mags, or discovered at one of those horror movie conventions he always traipsed off to. She lowered her eyes to the crumbs on her paper plate.

"Colleen, I am not going to allow you to sit here in this steampit all night. You had another shitty day of shitty interviews. Come on out and have some fun."

"Cass, it *was* another shitty day and they *were* shitty interviews, and tomorrow's going to be more of the same. So if it's all the same to you, I'm going to mope around in my underwear all night and stuff my face with ice cream."

"I ate all the ice cream for lunch."

"Then I'm just going to mope around in my underwear."

Cass set his trenchcoat aside and slid down into the cushions. "Colleen, I know you're going to tell me to shut up and mind my own business again, but you know perfectly well that you don't have to schlep that portfolio around to a bunch of third rate A.D.'s who are just trying to figure out how to get in your pants."

"Cass, don't start."

"No, you listen to me, sweetheart. If you'd just call your sister, you know you'd have a job tomorrow. And a good one, I bet." He pointed at the pop can in Colleen's hand. "Maybe then we could stop buying generic soda."

"I like generic soda," Colleen said with unintended petulance. "And there's no way I'm calling Megan to beg for a job at Charade Magazine."

"And this is because...?"

"Cass, I have my pride. Can't you understand that?"

"Actually, no. I think I forgot about all about pride the first time the jocks beat the shit out of me in high school. Having *fag* spray painted on your locker in an all boys prep school kind of plants the seeds for some self-esteem issues."

"Look, I'll find my own job, and a good job too, you'll see. I've been on my own all through college and ever since," Colleen said. "Megan was pretty busy with her 'career' when Mom decided to skip through the pearly gates, and she wasn't looking for a tag-along sister to clutter up her life in the fast lane. I mean, she's a lot older than me, Cass. It's not like we played Barbies together as kids. Hell, she was already in college and doing a column for some lit mag when I *was* still playing with Barbies." Colleen set her empty plate and soda aside, stretched her bare legs across the windowseat. "Though I have to admit, she did buy me some bitchin' Barbie stuff."

"I don't think you give her enough credit," Cass said.

"And I don't think it's any of your fucking business." It wasn't exactly what she meant to say. "Sorry, Cass. Enough about Megan, okay?"

"Okay."

"So, where *are* you headed? Ghoul Boys In Bondage Night?"

"No," he said, suddenly sounding sheepish. "There may be a new group forming. We're going to see if we can...well, maybe start up a new session..."

Colleen groaned. "Not more of those role playing games. What's it called again? The *Canolli*?"

He glared back at her.

But Colleen still wanted to tease. "The *Carmilla*? The *Chamomile*? The *Amarillo*? *Amaretto*?"

Cass reached for his trenchcoat.

"No wait, I'm sorry, Cass. *Again.* I'm not poking fun at whatever it is you're into." She hesitated. "Okay, I am. But don't you ever get tired of this whole...whole *thing*? Monster magazines, monster movies, monster conventions."

"You make it sound so silly."

"Hey, you said it, not me. Doesn't all that monster stuff get you down?"

"No," Cass said. "And it's not 'monster stuff'. It's a lot more than that."

"Call it what you like, Cass, but the clothes, the music, the people you hang with. It's all so morbid. And those role playing games...I mean, you'd really like Bela Lugosi to give you a hickey?"

Cass rolled his eyes.

"Oh, excuse me, what's his name then — Christopher Lee?"

"You just don't get it, Colleen, do you?"

"Okay, okay. Tom Cruise, then."

Cass smiled to himself.

"Gotcha," Colleen said. "Come on, you really like to pretend that — "

"Never heard of fantasies, Colleen?"

She looked at his frilly shirt and the makeup. "Cass, I never thought you were short on fantasies."

"Call it a lifestyle then," he said.

"I thought you already had a 'lifestyle'."

"Colleen — "

The phone rang, and it was just as well. They'd had this conversation before and never got anywhere. Anymore than they could get over Colleen's obstinate refusal to ask her sister Megan for a little help. Cass jumped off the couch and reached for the phone.

"Ooo, better hurry," Colleen said, giggling. "Maybe one of your friends caught his cape in his coffin."

He shot her a look that said 'Enough' and answered the phone.

Colleen was still working up her next line when she noticed Cass' face. He looked puzzled at first.

Then serious.

"Colleen, it's for you."

"Who'd be calling me?" She swung her legs off the windowseat. "Guess one of my interviews just couldn't wait to tell me I didn't get the job, huh?"

"No," he said, handing her the phone. "Actually, it's the police."

Cass dropped back into the sofa and watched Colleen. She answered into the mouthpiece with hesitant yes's and no's for the most part. But she started to shake when she said, "Yes...Yes, I have a sister...Here in Chicago, yes...Yes, Megan. Megan Russell..."

Colleen hung up the phone and just stood there staring into space for a minute.

"So, what did they want, Colleen?"

"What?" It took a moment to register. "They...it's Megan. Th-they want me to come down. Right away."

"Is Megan in some kind of trouble? They want you to come down to the police station?"

"Huh?" Colleen turned around and faced Cass. Her eyes looked glassy. Then a tear rolled down her cheek. She looked scared. "No, not the police. I mean, no — not at the station."

"Colleen, where?"

"The morgue."

FIVE

From his recliner, Frank Hoelevich watched out the front window while Libbie stacked dinner dishes back in the kitchen. He'd have been happy with a sandwich on a scorcher like today, but Libbie insisted on a full dinner. Round steak, boiled potato and sliced beet smells still lingered in the apartment.

Frank offered to help Libbie with the dishes, like he always did, and she shooed him out of the kitchen, like she always did. It had been a nightly ritual for over fifty years now. He'd peck Libbie on the cheek and pat her on the behind and she'd scoot him into the living room and his recliner by the front window. The only difference these days was that he couldn't light up a cigar once he sat down. The doctor said no more smoking, and Libbie was a damned good enforcer.

Frank loosened his belt a notch and untucked his short sleeve shirt. Bakery bread with slabs of butter were no longer on the menu in the Hoelevich household. And there were no more home baked *kolachki* for dessert. More of that kid cardiologist's suggestions. Not that Frank had to lose weight. At seventy four, his pant size was only two inches wider than it was when he got out of the service back in '46, and not too many guys could make that claim.

Cabinet doors shut in the kitchen.

Nails clicked across the linoleum, and then across the hardwood floors in the living room.

Sox gave up *his* nightly ritual once Libbie rinsed out the sink and set the garbage out back. The caramel and white sheltie always hovered in the kitchen while Libbie cleaned up, eyeing the trimmed off fat and stray potato chunks sliding into the garbage bag. But Sox knew that once the dishes were put away and the garbage set on the back porch, any hope of a snack had passed.

Frank was pretty free with the treats. Libbie, on the other hand, made things clear the day Frank brought Sox home from the pound — the very day the animal was going to find out if all dogs really do go to heaven. *"You brought him home, Frank, you take care of him. And if you think that mutt's dining from the butcher shop, you're mistaken, Mister. It's dog chow for him."* Of course, there hadn't been a real butcher shop in the neighborhood for years, and Libbie bought their meat at the giant Jewel supermarket just like everyone else, though she always complained that it just wasn't the same.

And Libbie gave in a lot more than Frank ever knew, sometimes letting Sox lap up leftover pork roast and kielbasa on the sly while she finished the dishes.

But, no round steak tonight. Libbie only bought two cuts, and she and Frank polished those off.

Sox wasn't starving, anymore than Frank was wasting away without his kolachki. Seven years old — born the same year Frank finally closed down their little hardware store downstairs, right below their apartment — at seven, Sox was a sheltie and a half, topping fifty five pounds. Libbie always said it proved he wasn't a purebred, that some real collie had been nosing around the sheltie pen somewhere back in Sox' ancestry. "Nosing around and more", she'd say, and then feel her cheeks go all red, as if she'd just had an impure thought and would have to confess it to Father Silverez come Saturday.

Frank turned away from the window as Sox sidled up to the recliner. The dog looked up at him with those round, brown, anxious eyes that always seemed to be saying 'now what?'". Frank gave him a pat on the head. Then he turned back to the window and poked a finger through the venetian blinds to peek across the street.

"So who are you spying on now?" Libbie untied her apron as she stepped into the living room. She eased onto the couch and wiped the balled up apron across her forehead. "Frank?"

"Just looking outside."

"What's so interesting on Damen Avenue that you haven't seen a million times?" Libbie pulled the TV Guide out from between two cushions and started to scan the Wednesday night listings. "Frank?"

"Nothing. Just looking at a car."

"A car?"

"Nice convertible," he said. "White Olds. '71, '72, maybe. A real beauty."

"Oh, and a sexy young blonde behind the wheel, I suppose?"

"Don't be silly, woman." Frank leaned closer to the blinds. "No, just a couple of punks from the looks of it. Just sitting there in front of The Palace."

Libbie closed the TV Guide and got up to turn on the set. On her way back to the couch she looked over Frank's shoulder and out the window. "The Palace?" She shook her head as she took her seat, while a Columbo rerun lit up the screen. "Frank, it's been almost fifteen years since that theater's been 'The Palace'."

"Maybe so," he said. "But it will always be The Palace to me." He turned away from the window and set his eyes on his wife. On her brown hair that was only lightly grayed, unlike his that had stayed thick, but had gone white when he turned sixty. He looked at her cotton housedress, the kind the women always wore back when they got married, after the war. Libbie looked hot.

She looked tired.

She looked old.

And to Frank Hoelevich's eyes, she looked every bit as beautiful as she did on their first date. "You remember how it used to be there? The ushers in their fancy uniforms, with their penlights? Those velvet seats? The spic 'n span aisles? Do you remember going to the show every week to collect the free silverware?"

"Of course I remember, dear. Rogers 1847 pattern, just like they used to advertise on Ozzie & Harriet, and I wish we still had it." Libbie was already becoming engrossed in the Columbo mystery, but she locked eyes with her husband for a moment and smiled. "I remember, Frank."

"Wouldn't it be swell to get all dressed up some night and take in a picture there across the street?" Frank said. "Maybe Ida Lupino and Bogart? Robert Mitchum and Deborah Kerr? Just like the old days?"

"I'll take Olivia DeHaiveland and Errol Flynn, thank you. Frank, the only pictures you could see there now...well, just be glad they aren't showing them anymore." Libbie frowned, recalling The Palace's last gasp in the mid-eighties when it featured a triple-X bill and live dancers on stage. That was before it switched hands a dozen times, before it tried rock & roll concerts one year and talk of turning it into a mall the next. The last few years, The Palace just sat vacant.

"Yep, '72 I think," Frank said. "That Olds. Now where would a couple of crummy looking punks like those two get a beautiful car like that?" He squinted through the blinds. The sun perched just above The Palace's roof, dull and ochre-orange through a layer of Chicago smog. The two fellows in the convertible parked down on Damen were listening to loud music. Frank could half hear it all the way up here through the closed window. They both puffed on cigarettes, cork tipped jobs, Frank thought. His eyes were in great shape just like the rest of him, if you didn't count the reading glasses.

Frank got up from the recliner with a groan, and Sox perked up immediately. "Well, think I'll walk dinner off."

"Frank, on a hot night like this?"

"Have to walk the dog, Libbie," he said as he leaned over to kiss her cheek. "Should I wake you when I come back?"

"You won't have to. I want to stay up for the news, see if we're going to get a break from this heat."

Frank smiled on his way to the kitchen, where he grabbed Sox' leash. He knew perfectly well that Libbie would be dozing on the couch long before Columbo ever confronted the murderer, much less make it to the news. Sox stamped his white paws at the back door. Frank looked at the leash, down at the dog, and back at the leash. He could have swore the dog nodded.

"Frank," Libbie called. "Just walk your dinner off with two beers tonight, all right?"

He exchanged glances with Sox. "How does she know what I'm thinking even before I do, boy?" Sox cocked his head and looked back with his 'let's get going' eyes.

"And Frank, no beer for the dog. He'll have gas all night. Promise?"

✦

The Cutlass convertible was a '71, and it was off-white, actually. Nicky Kolitzky had the chop shop down on 63rd repaint it from the original puke orange.

Nicky flicked a half-smoked Kool onto Damen and drummed his fingers on the steering wheel for a moment. Then he reached across the dashboard and grabbed another cigarette. Some old Guns N' Roses blared on the radio, the bass lines vibrating the convertible's seats. The Mexicans who used to sell Nicky his coke lifted stereos on the side, and he had them install giant sub-woofers in the trunk. They were as big as small TV's, and could rock the doors off the car if they wanted to. But right now, Nicky *didn't* want them to.

"Joey, turn that crap off, will you?"

Joey Fortuna just sat in the passenger seat and didn't make a move.

"Joey, I said, turn that fucking crap off." Nicky leaned over and shut off the radio.

"What's the matter with you, Nicky? Don't you like good music?"

"Yeah, I like *good* music. Not that shit you listen to."

"So, what's 'good' music? Elvis? Disco? Your cousin's polka band?"

Nicky didn't answer. He just slid his sunglasses down his nose and gave Joey a look, and that was enough to shut the kid up.

Joey had been getting on Nicky's nerves lately. Just little things, like the music. Joey was only twenty one, ought to show a little more respect. But he didn't. Nicky only hooked up with the kid because he'd assumed Joey Fortuna was Italian. He knew he dealt a little drugs, stole a few cars. It stood to reason that he was connected. Six months later it came out that Joey was half Mexican and half PR, and the little punk didn't know any real wiseguys any more than Nicky did.

But that didn't matter anymore. Hadn't mattered in months.

Not since Nicky hooked up with *them.*

"Hey Nicky, look." Joey elbowed Nicky and pointed across the street. "It's fuckin' Lassie."

Frank Hoelevich stepped out of his gangway beside the two-flat. He squatted beside a row of geraniums and fished around for a minute. When he stood up, he had a fat cigar clenched in his teeth. He turned south on Damen, with Sox straining at the leash, white paws padding the hot sidewalk.

"Oh, Lassie," Joey called. "Lassie!"

Nicky slugged him in the shoulder. "Shut the fuck up, Joey."

Frank looked their way, clenched his teeth tighter on his cigar, but he just kept walking. As if Sox would have let him stop.

"Joey, you ever hear of being discreet?"

"Nicky, you ever hear of fucking yourself?"

"Stupid spic."

"Polak," Joey shot back. 'Notice I didn't say *stupid* Polak, 'cause that goes without saying." He pulled a twelve pack up from the back seat. Three cans were gone already, the others were slick with condensation. He popped the top on a can and downed half in one gulp. "You want one, Polak?"

"No," Nicky answered. "Believe me, I'll be ready to get drunk *after* the meeting."

"So, about this meeting...how come I can't come in with you?"

"Trust me, Joey. You don't want to."

"Yes, I do."

"Well, you're not ready for them."

"Oh, big shot Nicky Kolitzky. You're ready for the big time, and I'm not?"

"That's not it, Joey. You're just...I just need you to stay down here in the car. Keep an eye on things."

"Things? What things?"

"Just things," Nicky said. "Just in case...just things."

They sat there for a while without talking. Not exactly in silence, with Nicky lighting one Kool after another, and Joey slurping his beers.

But no sound came from The Palace.

It loomed up over them, four stories tall. The marquee was draped in a black tarp, and the hot breeze was too weak to even ripple the plastic. The rows of windows on the top floors were either boarded up or painted over, but shut tight either way.

The building was immense. It took up half the block, the shuttered two-flats and storefronts on the other half completely dwarfed by its mammoth size. The entire facade of dark gray stonework had been sandblasted only a week ago, even all the arches over the windows and the creepy gargoyles lurking in their shadowy niches. It looked just like a castle, at least some deranged Disney-on-drugs Hollywood-esque version of a castle, a fake medieval monstrosity dumped right here on Damen Avenue. Wires dangled out of the sockets above the marquee, where the sandblasting still left traces of *The Palace* in curlicue script. Directly in front of Nicky's Cutlass, a huge dumpster squatted on the street with heaps of cracked plaster, old cloth-insulated wiring and ripped theater seats overflowing onto the curb.

"So, Mr. Bigshot, are we going to just sit here forever?" Joey asked. "When's this important meeting?"

Nicky didn't look at the clock in the dashboard. And he didn't check his wristwatch.

Instead, he looked up at the sky.

"Not yet."

Joey Fortuna grumbled, and went for another beer.

Nicky glanced across the street at the two flat with the vacant storefront on the first floor, the building on the east side of Damen Avenue, the building where the old man with the dog came from. The bottom half of it was painted with shadow, while the top still glowed orange from the sun.

"I'll know when it's time, Joey."

The old theater building wrapped its shadow blanket over the two of them in the convertible, and the shadow slowly crept up the face of Frank and Libbie Hoelevich's house across the street, as sunset neared.

SIX

Jeff Stancheck cleared the passable polish and curly fries off his desk to make room for the revised page printouts Kelly Feeny, his Assistant AD, just brought in.

"Does Blair need to see all the changes?" Kelly asked, sounding worried.

"Of course she does, but she's not going to." Jeff smiled. "If Blair wants to practically redo the entire issue in a day, then she might consider popping in for a peek, you think?"

"Maybe we could track her down? I have her secretary's home number."

Jeff shook his head as he scanned the spreads. "*I'm* not spending the rest of my Wednesday night skulking around every snooty bistro in town to find her for an approval. And neither are you, Kelly. Anyway, it's after eight, and the printer's driver will be here at nine sharp. Screw it."

"Excuse me." Gabrielle hovered in the doorway, looking beat and dragging page spreads in each tired, black lace gloved hand. "Here's mine." She tossed them on top of the spreads Jeff was just about to initial.

Kelly slid Gabrielle's two outputs aside. Jeff chuckled to himself and finished scribbling J.S.'s in the corners of the first stack.

"Now *those* are way hot," Gabrielle cooed, peering around Kelly's shoulder. "Who got to work on *those* pages?"

"Jeff did them," Kelly said. "Who do you think?"

"Jeff?" Gabrielle looked at Jeff, looked down at the pages, and back at Jeff again. "You...*you* did these?"

"I'll never be as quick on a computer as I used to be on a drafting table," Jeff said. "But yes, I did manage to get some work done while you were yakking on the phone all day."

Gabrielle edged Kelly aside and leaned over Jeff's desk, staring at the spreads.

The first was a gloomy duotone photo of a starkly pale, naked girl with pitch black hair and eyes made up to match. She knelt on top of a casket, a bouquet of drooping lilies clenched in her hands. The logo art that had been in the envelope Blair gave Jeff earlier today seemed corny looking. Evidently someone else thought so too, because there was writing all over the art, in elaborate penmanship, and done with a fountain pen, no less. *'Seems trite. Can we do better?'* Jeff recognized a dissatisfied customer, and took it upon himself to massage the graphic before he dropped it into place on the spread.

"Jeff," Gabrielle said, "That logo, it's...it's..."

"A cliché?"

"No, it's...vicious."

"So, that's good, Gabrielle?"

"It's great. *'GOTHIQUE.'"* She said it slowly, like she was reading it, reading each letter, tracing the sharp tipped serifs and flourishes. *"'GOTHIQUE. All night. And forever.'"*

Gabrielle just helped herself to the pages. Jeff leaned back in his chair, winking at Kelly.

The other ads and the P.R. fluff pages were splashed with photos as artsy and weird as the first spread. A boy and a girl with devil-clown makeup, the usual assortment of kitschy jewelry, tattoos and ripped leather gear, dry-hump dancing in fake fog.

Two bare chested boys with Duran Duran hair, hands tied behind their backs with rosaries, their chests pressed together, faces close but not touching, tongues lolling out for a French kiss.

A girl in torn black tights and nothing else, except for a crown of thorns in her hair, with a trickle of blood dribbling down her forehead...another girl's black nailed and disembodied hand reaching from behind to cup her breast.

"So, these pages *are* okay with you?" Kelly's sarcasm was lost on Gabrielle, who stopped drooling over the photos and started to mumble her way through the text.

"Huh? Oh sure, absolutely. *'Gothique, so much more than a nightclub, it's an entertainment complex that's even more than a state of mind. It's a lifestyle...'"*

Jeff clicked off his computer and grabbed his keys from his top drawer.

"...Gothique — dance club extraordinaire — opening this Fall.'" Gabrielle's raccoon eyes drank in the photos one more time, then she smiled at the closing headline.

"'Gothique. You'll just die.'"

Kelly snatched the spreads off the desk. "So, I assume it's okay to give these to the printer, Gabrielle?"

The mascara rings narrowed on Gabrielle's eyes. "Yes, Kelly, I approve." She turned to Jeff, and her sneer softened. A bit. "Sorry. I didn't mean — "

"No problem." He picked up his briefcase and tossed his corduroy blazer over his shoulder as he rounded the desk. "I'm glad you like them."

"But I don't want you to think that I...I mean, I just didn't think that you...."

"Gabrielle, quit while you're ahead." Jeff smiled and patted her on the black lace shoulder. She flinched. EEOC commissions and harassment suits flashed through his mind. Jeff yanked his hand away immediately.

Kelly rolled up the pages and followed Jeff out of the office.

"Okay, get everyone to archive their files before they leave, Kelly."

"No problem, Jeff. Everything should be wrapped up in hour, easy."

Jeff glanced at his watch. "Good. It'll be just in the nick of time. Again."

Neither of them noticed Gabrielle tagging along behind, a black shawl over her shoulders, and dragging her luggage sized purse. "Uhm, Jeff? I forgot to mention it before, but I can't stay to copy my files."

"Gabrielle," Kelly started, " You knew we were all working late — "

"But I made plans."

"We all had plans," Kelly continued. "You left early twice last week. You took a two hour lunch today. Now someone else has to — "

"Let her go," Jeff said.

Gabrielle sauntered out of the Art Department without any goodnights, other than the sneer she twisted her licorice whip lips into when she breezed past Kelly.

Jeff made the rounds, showing the two department interns — Tim and Ivy — how to save their classifieds pages for the archives, answering everyone else's last questions, while Kelly followed behind jotting down notes. "So, you see? We really can build a whole issue in less than a day," he said. "What do you say we take next month off and just show up on 'Final Art' day?"

Chuckles and groans wafted out of the cubicles. Tim and Ivy threw markers at him.

"Good work everyone, really," Jeff said as he walked out of the department. "The overtime's vouched for. And I promise to personally murder Megan Russell tomorrow morning for letting Blair get away with this.

✦

Jeff hit the turn signal and swung his red '78 Trans Am off southbound Lake Shore Drive and onto the Stevenson Expressway.

The Stevenson was empty. Evidently all the other workaholics left downtown already.

He gunned the Trans Am up to seventy, shooting due southwest through the city. Behind him, the skyline was just a twinkly toy town shrinking in the rearview mirror. Ahead, a sliver of orange hugged the horizon under the darkening sky. He cruised past miles of aging, vacant industrial parks and domino rows of two-flats working hard on tenement status. On each block, the streetlights haloed photo opportunities for a piece on the decaying rust belt.

Ten miles out of downtown, Jeff eased over to the right to exit at Pulaski Road.

But then he tapped the brakes and slowed to a crawl, staring ahead at a billboard along the expressway.

Red type, stark against a black background.

Just plain red type. Garamond Italic, by the looks of it.

Red type: *All Night. And Forever.*

Coming This Fall.

A car beeped from behind, and Jeff floored the Trans Am past the sign and up the exit ramp.

Heading south on Pulaski, he ignored the traffic, thinking instead about that logo he took it upon himself to redesign, those photos he played with all day. Not his kind of stuff, that Helmut Newton—Deutschen Vogue-dance club kink. Not his taste at all. But Gabrielle certainly seemed to like it, the way she drooled over those pictures. Gabrielle — in her second hand shop chic, her Maybeline-meets-Movie-Macabre makeup. Gabrielle — the department's expert on looking busy while she was just surfing the net, on trimming eight hour days down to six and not getting anything done in those. Gabrielle — stumbling over her words, *'You...you did these?'*

He was going to have to do something about Gabrielle, and soon. Jeff hoped Charade Human Resources would let her off easy.

But it wasn't just Gabrielle. Jeff pictured Blair smirking at him from behind Megan Russell's desk, too comfy in Megan's chair, all at ease in that summer double-breasted that probably had a designer label on the inside, jingling her treasure chest of jewelry with every flick of the wrist. *'Don't go ex-hippie on me now, Jeff.'*

He looked at his arms stretched out to the steering wheel. Looked at the ho-hum white button-down shirt (complete with cinnamon-nutmeg coffee stain), sleeves rolled up over a plain old analog Timex. He glanced down at his favorite cowboy boots, scuffed, but clean, and disappearing under the cuffs of comfy Levi's.

Jeff couldn't help himself. He twisted the rearview mirror his way. Blandly light brown hair curled around his ears and tickled his collar, gel-free, mousse-free and hopelessly out-of-style. His face still looked thirty, instead of his real thirty-seven, anchored by blue-hazel-brown eyes that he called gray on his drivers license.

The car. The hair. The shirt, the jeans, the boots. If fashions had expiration dates, he knew he'd be long overdue. "You are in the wrong business, Mister," Jeff said out loud, as he turned on to 49th Street.

Rows of bungalows and boxy raised ranches lined every block, each house with its little patch of front lawn, each with its solitary maple on the narrow parkway, its trimmed hedges next to the front steps. He made a left off 49th onto Karlov, a one-way, southbound, tree-lined bungalow row like the rest. Jeff slowed the Trans to a quiet crawl so the 400 horses wouldn't neigh too loudly for the neighbors. As he approached the end of the block, he halted right in front of his house.

Blair Armstrong leaned against the fender of her Silver Lexus, flicking at a piece of lint on her skirt. She looked up and waved.

✦

"Slumming?" Jeff asked as Blair followed him into the bungalow's eat-in kitchen. He dumped his briefcase on the counter and flicked on a light.

"Not exactly. Have anything to drink?" Blair opened the refrigerator. "Anything other than beer?"

Jeff flipped through the mail. There was nothing important other than the mortgage statement: another forty payments, and the brick bungalow would be his. "Second shelf, behind the milk. I think there's a bottle of wine there. And I wouldn't mind a cold one myself."

Blair found the wine bottle and snickered at the screw-on cap. "A little something for Auntie Sophie when she drops by?" She handed Jeff a beer, then started to poke through his cabinets.

"Actually, I had an Aunt Sophie. Died two years ago. And she preferred boiler-makers." Jeff took a gulp from the cold beer. "Third door over, Blair."

She took a wineglass from the top shelf, held it up to the light, then blew in it and wrinkled her nose when dust sifted out. "Hey, what's this?" She pulled out a plastic Winnie The Pooh bowl and matching mug.

"Mementos. Put them back."

Blair rinsed out her glass and poured herself a white wine. "I got corralled into dinner with Benny from Sales. NYC Fashion Consortium was in town, wanted to hear all about our big plans for next year, editorial tie-ins, that kind of crap." She leaned against the sink and sipped her wine. "We just poured their Marketing Liaison onto a plane at Midway half an hour ago. I figured since I was in the neighborhood..."

"If you think I have copies of the new pages with me, Blair, you're out of luck. They should be in the printer's hands any minute now."

"Did Megan see them before they went out?"

"No sight of her," Jeff said. "I approved the pages myself."

"Well, we can copy her tomorrow," she said. Blair drained her glass. "Mind if I use the little girl's room?" She grabbed her purse. "Pour me another, Jeff, will you?" She disappeared down the dark hallway.

Several minutes passed while Jeff loaded last night's dinner dishes and this morning's coffee cup into the dishwasher. It was still nearly empty. He'd turn it on tomorrow. "Hey Blair, are you okay?"

No answer.

Beer in hand, he walked down the short hallway to the bathroom. The door was open, the lights off, the room empty.

Blair's suitcoat hung on the doorknob.

A couple more steps down the hallway, and Jeff stumbled over her shoes.

At his bedroom door, he saw the streetlight slicing through the mini-blinds, saw in the semi-darkness that Blair's skirt was draped across his footboard.

Blair was draped across his bed.

"Where's my wine?" she asked, smiling as she reached back to unhook her bra.

Jeff held out his beer.

"I'd rather have wine."

"I'll get it," he said.

Blair tossed her bra away and snatched the beer, ran the cold, damp bottle over her neck and her chest, then took a sip. She set the bottle down on the nightstand. "Don't. I'd rather have you." She started to peel off her pantyhose.

Jeff pulled her hands away and wrapped them around his neck. He kissed her, slipping his fingers inside the nylons.

"Let me."

✦

On the other side of town, shadows continued to ooze off The Palace Theater, bleeding across Damen Avenue and up the Hoelevich house, till they finally merged with the darkening sky. The streetlights came on, one of them right above Nicky Kolitzky's convertible, which he didn't like at all. He started the car up and moved a couple spaces till it was out of the ring of light.

"Hey Nicky, check it out," Joey said as he emptied another beer. He pointed down the block, where the silhouette of a short skirted girl headed their way. "Looks like some sweet meat even from this far."

When she walked beneath a streetlight, Nicky could see that Joey was half right. She was tall and leggy in high heeled granny boots with lacy socks poking out the tops. Mini-skirted under links of heavy duty chains that coiled around her waist, her breasts bouncing under a blackish, see-through blouse.

Joey crunched his beer can and tossed it on the street. "Hey, sweet meat, come here. Yeah, you. Come — "

"Shut the fuck up, Joey." Nicky slugged him in the ribs. "I told you before, we're trying to be kind of low key here." The girl passed right by without a glance, then stopped in front of The Palace Theater's blackened glass doors. "Probably a junkie anyway, Joey. Look at her."

Up close, the girl's heavy makeup made her look like a nightmare mime: white face, red smeared in the hollows of her cheeks, lips painted bloody crimson, bullseye rings of eyeshadow around her vacant eyes. She pulled a piece of paper out of her little purse. Looked at it, looked up at The Palace.

"Junkie, monkey, hooker, I don't give a rat's ass," Joey said. "I'm bored, man. We've been sitting here forever. When is this big, important meeting?"

"When it's time."

"And when the fuck is it going to be 'time', Nicky?"

"It's time when I say — " Nicky stopped and nodded towards the theater's front doors. Joey turned around.

One black glass door slowly swung closed, just as a glimpse of lacy, white socks ringing the tops of black granny boots vanished inside.

"Pretty soon, Joey. Pretty soon."

Nicky got out of the Cutlass and opened the trunk. He looked up and down the street, saw no one, then took out a canvas duffel bag and carried it back. He stopped by the driver's door to light another Kool. Exhaling a cloud of smoke that dangled around his head in the breezeless air, he slipped the pack and his lighter back into the inside pocket of his blazer. As he reached for the door handle, he glanced back at the theater.

And he saw them.

Lurking in the shadows underneath the marquee — two of them there, dressed all in black, almost shadows themselves.

Nicky whirled around when he detected a movement from behind the dumpster. Another two stared at him with those creepy eyes of theirs. There was no sound, just a kind of walking darkness, and then two more stood there not twenty feet away — girls, he thought, but you couldn't always tell, they all looked so fucking weird anyway.

One of The Palace's glass doors opened. Nicky thought he saw a pale hand slowly waving to him. Thought he saw a white face hovering in the darkness inside.

He squeezed his arm against his side, felt the heavy hardness beneath his blazer, felt the leather shoulder holster and the Mauser 9MM press into his ribs. It was hot as hell tonight, even now that it was dark out. Too hot for a jacket. But it covered the holster, mostly, and right now the gun felt kind of comforting.

"Joey, you wait in the car like I told you," Nicky said, his mouth suddenly gone dry. "I think it's time."

SEVEN

The phone ringing in the kitchen woke Jeff up.

On the third ring, he leaned over the side of the bed and felt around in the dark for his jeans.

"Jeff, don't," Blair mumbled, her face half covered by the sheet. "It'll just be the printer with a bunch of stupid questions." She reached for him, but patted an empty mattress instead.

Jeff was already out of bed and climbing into his jeans. On the fourth ring, he could hear the answering machine click on. Blair mumbled something else, then buried her head under her pillow as he walked out of the bedroom.

Jeff paused at the kitchen doorway, squinting. Once his eyes adjusted to the bright overheads, he took a fresh beer from the refrigerator and listened to the answering machine playback. As soon as he heard the voice on the machine, his hand tightened around the bottle.

He checked his watch. 11:30 here.

9:30 there.

He swore under his breath, and dialed Encino.

Through the first few rings, he half hoped another machine would answer. But he changed his mind when he heard a bright, bubbly "Hello?".

"Hi, Jacks. School's out for summer, and *you're* home?"

"Dad!" Jacqueline 'Jacks' Porter-Stancheck (the hyphenated last name was her mother's idea) just about screeched into the phone. "Hey, thanks loads for that Bulls Jersey you sent. Is it for real?"

"Right off Michael Jordan's back, honey. The sweat was still fresh on it."

"He must be like ten feet tall, Dad. I wore it to the pool today, and it went down to my ankles. Well, almost."

"I hope it's not all you wore." Life was a lot simpler when Jacks' wardrobe was mostly Sesame Street T-shirts and Cinderella costumes. Once she turned ten, Jeff butted out and let her mother take over.

Once Jacks turned thirteen, it was a moot point.

Because one week after her thirteenth birthday, Jacks and her mother moved to California. The copies of the final divorce papers hadn't even arrived yet. Four years ago? It flew by so fast.

"Chill, Dad. Of course it's not all I wore. But those Lakers' fans were sure giving me the evil eye."

"Just jealous, Jacks."

"So, kind of late back there, isn't it? I suppose you want Mom?"

"Yeah, I guess so. What's the matter now? She sounded upset on her message."

"I don't know," Jacks said. "She's been major edgy since she lost...*OOPS.* I'm guessing the cat has officially left the bag. I don't think I was supposed to — "

"Did she quit this time, or get fired again?"

"Little of both, I think, Dad."

Jeff said nothing. Anything he wanted to say couldn't be said to Jacks. "Well, I'm sure you have better things to do than listen to the old man, Jacks. Hot date tonight?"

"Dad, *please*," she groaned, mortified like only a seventeen year old girl could be. "For your information, I don't have a date tonight, haven't had one since I broke up with Bobby March, and I've already done the obligatory swing through the mall. Some friends are coming by later for a sleep-over. No boys, don't worry."

A hand curled around Jeff's chest. He turned around and there was Blair, sleepy eyed, blonde hair tousled into a yellow fur ball. She had his white shirt draped over her shoulders. Blair ran her fingers over his chest, just playing, starting to plant soft kisses on the back of his neck.

Jeff held his finger to his lips, but she smiled back at him and kept on kissing. "Well, why don't you get your mother, Jacks."

Blair's playful smile drooped. She grabbed the beer out of Jeff's hand and stomped out of the kitchen.

"Jeffrey?"

Jeff flinched, just like he always did when he heard Elaine Stancheck-now-Porter- again's voice. At least, like he always did these past four years.

"Thanks for calling me right back," Elaine said. "It's late back there, isn't it?"

"Well, I got home from work pretty late anyway."

"Still playing Charades?'

"I think that one got a little tired even when we were married, " Jeff said. "So, what's up?"

"I need a couple favors."

"How much, and what for?"

"Jeff, you don't have to be such a prick about it."

Why not? He wasn't sure if he just thought that or said it out loud.

Jeff hadn't contested anything in the proceedings, even though it was Elaine who surprised him with the divorce late one night when he crawled home from a fourteen hour day at the office. *'Here's my lawyer's card, Jeffrey. Call him tomorrow. I'm leaving for Los Angeles.'* Like it was a done deal.

Still, Jeff didn't fight over the details, didn't want Jacks to see Mom and Dad kickboxing over the china and the checkbook.

Alimony?

Name a figure, he'd told Elaine.

Split their assets fifty-fifty?

Hell, make it sixty-forty, he'd said. Seventy-thirty, make it anything you want.

Just don't take my daughter away from me, Jeff had pleaded. Please, Elaine, don't take Jacks, please...

Jeff got half the house.

Elaine got Jacks.

"Elaine, I'm not being a prick. But you already get $1,100 a month in child support, and — "

"Jacqueline's your daughter too, Jeffrey."

"Wait a minute and let me finish," he said, trying to stay calm. "You know perfectly well I don't argue about a single penny for Jacks. Just like you know I didn't want to lose custody in the first place." He paused, trying to compose his voice. "What I was starting to say is that you've been getting $750 a month for your half of the house, $1,100 a month in child support, and you were only supposed to get alimony for the first twenty four months till you got settled. It's four years now, and you've still got me on the hook for $950 a month 'maintenance'."

"It's always money with you, Jeffrey, isn't it? You make enough with your fancy job. And you have no idea what it's like being a divorced woman in her thirties, trying to raise a teenage daughter all alone."

No, but I'd like to, he thought. *The last part, that is.* "Elaine, you're the one who wanted 'room to grow'. So, fine. Grow. Grow all you want. I'm just wondering when I can stop watering the garden."

"The cost of living is just a little different out here, Jeffrey."

So who told you to pack my daughter off to California? "Look, we can argue some other time," Jeff said. "I'm too tired. So back to my original question, how much and what for?"

"Three thousand."

"*Three* — Elaine, what the hell do you need three thousand dollars for?"

"Well...I quit my job last week."

"Gee, and here I thought this was going to be 'the one'," Jeff said. "Let's see, you were on this job — four months, right? What was it again, 'Management Trainee' in a record store?"

"*Record* store, Jeffrey? Assistant Merchandising Coordinator for Plum Multimedia," she corrected. "But Jeffrey, the manager was barely older than Jacqueline. There was simply no room for dialog about any of my ideas."

"Okay, so you need some extra to tide you over," Jeff said. "But, three thousand?"

"Actually, I already have another job."

"Then what's the problem?"

"Well, I'll be on the road a lot. And I won't get my first commission check for sixty days, and — "

"Wait a minute, what kind of job is this one?"

"I'll be the Assistant Regional Sales Administrator for New Dimensions Ltd. The whole region, Jeffrey, and — "

"Slow down, Elaine. What is 'New Dimensions Ltd.'?"

"Oh, you probably haven't heard about them back in the midwest, but it's absolutely the most impressive self-empowerment program I've ever encountered, and after I took the program myself, Calvin said that I was a born communicator, and —"

"Hold it." Jeff just had to interrupt again. "Who's Calvin?"

"Calvin? Calvin is the Program Director for Southern California..."

Elaine went on.

And on.

And on and on.

After a while, Jeff just tuned her out. Sure, she was excited. But Elaine was always excited about her next night school psych class, her next spirituality seminar, her next part time job that wouldn't pan out. He'd offered to pay her way to finish her degree but just ended up footing the bill for a string of community college fluff courses. Now he knew better than to offer advice. Maybe if she didn't resent him so much? Maybe if she didn't blame Jeff for getting her pregnant when they were still in college?

Maybe if she didn't decide to drop out altogether when Jacks was born?

Too many maybes, and all water under the divorce bridge now.

"...and he thinks I can definitely go places, Calvin does, and that's why he'll be training me personally at first, and..."

Jeff finally cut her off. "Whatever, Elaine. It sounds like a racket to me, especially the part about fronting the money for your own presentation samples. But hell, if *Calvin's* convinced, then who am I to argue? I'll drop a check in the mail later this week."

"Well, actually I was sort of hoping you could wire it to me or something like that?"

"What's the big hurry?"

"Weren't you listening, Jeffrey? You weren't, were you? God, you can be such an ass. I told you, I start training next week. I'm leaving for Ft. Worth Monday morning. I need the money right away."

It took a minute.

"Ft. Worth? Monday?" Jeff paused. "And where the hell is Jacks while Calvin's empowering you in Ft. Worth?"

"Well, that's the *other* favor I was going to ask about."

"I'm listening."

But once Elaine started to explain, Jeff *didn't* really listen. Not to the details, at least. He was too excited. *Jacks, spending the rest of the summer with him!* "So how does she feel about this, Elaine? I mean, her friends, her — "

"Oh, I haven't told her yet. I was hoping you'd tell her, Jeffrey. Position it like you *want* her to come stay with you."

He aimed a fist at the wall, but just punched air instead. Two sleazy divorce lawyers tried to out-sleaze each other for three months over the custody issue. Jeff lost, and had to pay both attorneys' bills in the end. And now, this?

"Elaine, I don't have to 'position' anything to her. I *do* want her here, I'd like her here all the time, and you know that. But I think you owe it to Jacks to tell her what you're up to."

"Don't tell me what I owe Jacqueline, mister. Don't try to make me feel guilty about taking what could be my last chance for a real opportunity. Something special for *me*..." Elaine paused, ready for Jeff to shoot back at her.

He didn't.

"Jeff?"

"Elaine, I'll talk to Jacks tomorrow. I'll straighten everything out just fine."

"Good. Now Jeffrey, what I think you should tell her is — "

"I said, I'll take care of it, Elaine. Look, I'm really beat. I'll go over everything with you tomorrow after I've talked with Jacks, okay?"

"Okay. But don't forget to wire that money."

Jeff hung up, not sure whether he wanted to swear or smile.

Another three thousand dollars.

Jacks for the whole summer!

So he did both on his way back to the bedroom.

Blue light flickered out of the bedroom door. He stepped in and saw that the TV was on. It was after eleven thirty, but the late news was still going. The Cubs must have played a double header. Blair left the sound off.

She sat on the edge of the bed. She'd taken his shirt off, but had her underwear back on. Right now, she jutted out her lower lip as she held up her nylons. "Jeff, next time, let me, okay?" She balled them up and tucked them in her purse. "They're not gym socks, you know."

Jeff sat down beside her. "What are you doing?"

"I'm getting dressed."

"Why?"

"So I don't get arrested for driving naked."

"Blair, you don't have to go."

"Oh yes I do." She picked up her skirt, but just held it on her lap. "Jeff, it's very weird being the 'other woman'."

"Elaine is not my wife, Blair. She's my *ex*-wife. Very 'ex'. They don't come any more 'ex'."

"Actually, I didn't mean Elaine."

"Oh." He looked away. Jeff glanced at the soundless news on the TV. "Jacks is coming to stay for a while."

"I heard." The skirt knotted up in her hands. "I kind of eavesdropped. So, I guess this means our tawdry little affair has to go on hiatus?"

"No, we just..." Jeff pulled the skirt out of Blair's hands and laid it out nice and neat over the footboard. "No, but one of these days you and I ought to have a talk about our 'tawdry little affair', don't you think?"

"Like what?"

"*Like* — what exactly is it? Like, this getting together, your place, my place, just sex..."

"Jeff, the sex is very good." Blair reached around him and snatched her skirt back off the footboard. "Correction: The sex is more than good. Anyway, it's not just sex."

"No? What, then?"

"Jeff, we're...pals."

"Pals, huh?"

"Look, I'm not shopping for trousseaus," Blair said. "And I don't think you have an engagement ring squirreled away either. Unless you still have Elaine's, in which case, I don't want it." She shook out her skirt and dipped one foot inside.

"Actually, Elaine never gave back the engagement ring. Or the wedding ring. I assume she sold them, eventually."

"So, there." Blair slipped her other foot into the skirt. "We wouldn't do things like that, 'cause we're pals."

"Blair, stay. It's late. You're tired."

"And I have a writers' meeting at nine."

"I'll make you breakfast."

"Fruit Loops and instant coffee. No thanks, Jeff."

"I'll *buy* you breakfast."

"Eggs Benedict? The Hyatt Rotunda maybe?" Blair's skirt halted halfway up her legs.

Jeff pulled it all the way down. "Actually, I was thinking more like the diner on Archer and Pulaski, but — "

She leaned over and kissed him. Just a peck at first. Blair's blue eyes stared into his grays, and they kissed again, soft and long. When their lips finally parted, Blair hugged Jeff close, her head on his shoulder. "Okay, mister, but I get the shower first this time."

"Deal."

Jeff stood up and unzipped his jeans. He glanced at the television again. A reporter on location silently prattled on about something. The minicam cut away from her talking head and panned up the full hundred stories of the Hancock Building. Jeff looked around for the remote to shut the TV off.

Behind him, Blair unsnapped her bra, then peeled off her panties. "God, I hope I have a decent suit at the office. I wonder if I'll have time to stop at home?" She crawled to the edge of the bed. "You know, the only problem with the morning after is climbing back into last night's clothes. Don't suppose I've left any underwear here? Spare nylons, maybe? Barely-Beige would be nice, preferably without runs, but I'm not fussy." She dug her fingers into the waistband of Jeff's jeans, and pulled. "Didn't think so." Blair wrapped her arms around him and pressed her breasts into his back. "Hey, I didn't change my mind so we could watch television. Jeff?"

But Jeff was staring at the screen. Staring wide eyed as the news cut back to the studio and the anchorman. "Where's the remote?"

"Jeff?"

"Where's the goddamn remote?"

"Jeff, what's —" Blair's words caught in her throat when she looked at the screen.

Jeff found the remote buried in the tangled sheets. He punched the volume button, then fell back down on the bed next to Blair, still staring, staring at the photo inset floating behind the anchorman's head.

Blair's hand inched across the mattress toward his. Their fingers locked.

'...spokesperson for Whitestar Media Group, Charade Magazine's parent company, stated that they had no comment about the Managing Editor at this time. However, a source in Area One Violent Crimes has reportedly said that while suicide is the likely scenario, the investigation is continuing. Coming up next, Steve Peterson with the highlights from that amazing double-header...'

Jeff punched the off button.

The bedroom went dark, except for the faint streetlight filtering in through the blinds.

Blair snuggled up close to Jeff. She was shivering. "Jeff, that photo. It was...did I just see what I thought — "

"Yes." He wrapped his arms tight around her. "That was Megan Russell."

EIGHT

Nicky Kolitzky tripped over a pile of coiled conduit on his way through The Palace's rundown lobby.

The old theater was in the midst of a complete makeover. At any rate, the materials were on hand. PVC and copper pipes twisted into snakepits on the lobby floor. Two by fours and aluminum studs were stacked beside the old refreshment counter. He passed through a set of double doors, into what used to be the theater itself, groping through the darkness and keeping an eye on the figure gliding along ahead of him.

"Falling a little behind schedule here, you guys?" Nicky's voice echoed in the cavernous hall.

The skinny androgynous figure leading the way just ten feet ahead didn't answer. Didn't even turn around. Just slithered along with a swish-swish of black leather pants.

The theater was huge. The Palace looked immense from the outside, but it seemed even bigger in here, especially in the dark. The arched ceiling rose high overhead. The mezzanine balcony was a story and a half above and behind them.

But it was a mess.

The whole place was a mess. Dark as it was, Nicky could see that. Tattered curtains dangled in shreds where the silver screen used to be. Drywall was stacked a mile high in every corner, scaffolds fenced the walls. Rows of old theater seats were still bolted to the floor, others were piled in stained velvet mountains. Colorless carpeting, ripped up like so much torn skin, was rolled into giant tubes and propped up against the stage waiting to be thrown out.

Nicky wrinkled his nostrils and coughed. The place stank. Barf and piss and rat shit and more barf. *'Opening this fall'*, he thought. *'Oh yeah, right.'*

"I think maybe you oughta have me talk to your contractors," Nicky said. "Kick some ass, huh?"

The skinny weirdo in the black clothes ignored him, just flitted along, disappearing through a doorway beside the stage. Nicky stepped up his pace and hurried behind, then up a dark stairway. "Only reason this joint's still standing is that the termites are holding hands," he muttered to himself.

Second floor, third, all the way up to the fourth.

The back stairwells were even darker and smellier than the rest of the theater itself. Nicky could almost hear the paint peeling, and he could definitely feel the plaster dust sifting down on his head with each step. Ahead of him, boy-girl glided up the stairs silently and crossed a dark hallway on the fourth floor, where a door creaked open. Nicky slipped past him-her, feeling cold breath on his face.

He could have sworn the freak sniffed him before vanishing into the darkness. Nicky stepped into the room, and the door shut right behind him.

Except for the girl's body on the floor, the room was empty.

She lay there in a twisted heap on the dirty linoleum, that pasty faced junkie whore from down on Damen Avenue. One overhead bulb shrouded in cobwebs shined down on her see-through blouse, which was ripped wide open. The chains that had been wrapped around her waist were coiled tight around her wrists and ankles now. Her black miniskirt was hiked up over her hips.

Rings of smudged mascara circled dead eyes that stared wide and open at Nicky — at anyone — with a surprised look of profound disappointment, as if to say, *No, it's not supposed to be like this, this isn't like in the books, isn't like in the songs, isn't what I thought, isn't...*

Nicky looked away from those dead eyes, looked at the gashes on her wrists just above the chains. The rip across her throat. Her knees were spread wide open and Nicky looked at the mauling her white thighs took, ugly wounds edged in shredded skin, pockmarking her flesh all the way up to the bloodied panties.

He looked at the two, neat punctures on one of her pale breasts, just above the nipple.

Looked away.

Hiked the duffel bag higher on his shoulder.

Patted his ribs and felt the Mauser under his blazer.

Lit a Kool.

Nicky walked over to the window and pulled up the dark shade. Tugged with his fingertips, tugged still harder, till finally, the window opened.

The glass was painted over on the inside. All opaque, flat black.

The sound of a car horn blared somewhere outside in the real world. A jet made its way high overhead to O'Hare. The sluggish breeze smelled of Damen Avenue smells and, faintly, of the Lake a mile east. It smelled like pure oxygen compared to the dank, stuffiness of this room.

Nicky smoked his cigarette. And he smoked several more, leaning against the open window, looking down on Damen, down at his Cutlass, down on Joey Fortuna, down and out on anything. He just didn't want to look at that dead chick lying there behind him.

Eventually, he saw that same old man, the one with the little Lassie dog, strolling down the street. The old guy paused by a flower pot in front of his two-flat, the one with the vacant storefront on the first floor. He tucked something under the flowers, then looked across Damen, at Joey dozing in the convertible. The old man frowned and let the dog lead him down their dark gangway.

Nicky almost lost track of time. Fifteen minutes? An hour? The pack of Kools was almost empty, but Nicky lit one more and dragged deep.

"May I have one?"

Nicky whirled around.

And there they were.

Four of them.

Marek and Arianne.

Drake hovering behind them.

Still another behind him, that freaky boy-girl that guided him up here.

"Don't be stingy, Mr. Kolitzky," Marek said. He leaned in close, too close, his lips an inch from Nicky's cheek.

Nicky took a step backwards. His cheek felt hot and cold at the same time, touched by dry ice. "One of my...? Oh yeah, sure. Here."

Marek took the Kool and ran it under his long nose. His nostrils flared. "Mint?" He licked the filter tip. "No, *pepper*mint. Camphor. Oh, of course — menthol. Dreadful what they put in tobacco these days."

Nicky clicked his lighter and held it close to the cigarette. But Marek smiled, shook his head and tossed the cigarette out the open window. Nicky did the same with his, hoping it dropped on Joey's head and woke him up.

Marek shut the window with a flick of his wrist.

Nicky looked around, squinting to see in the anemic light from that one, lonely bulb. He looked at them, at Marek, tall and regal, dapper in his black suit and black collarless shirt, shiny dark hair swept straight back over a pale forehead.

Arianne leaned against the opposite wall, devastatingly beautiful as always, and looking completely disinterested, as always. Long, wavy hair, as black as panther's fur, framed her slender, little girl's face. She had dark eyes, opal eyes, *old* eyes, and full, pouty red lips. Arianne wore a fancy dress, like a cocktail dress, with skinny shoulder straps, stiff gauzy layers, black as her hair. It hung on her slender frame and made her skin seem all the more shockingly white. Nicky remembered a porcelain ballerina his Ma kept out of reach on the mantle, and Arianne's skin looked just like that — like porcelain. She was bare legged and bare footed, lazily tracing her toe across imaginary lines on the floor.

The pale faced boy-girl in the black leather pants squatted beside the dead whore's body. He-she started giggling, and then Nicky could tell by the laugh that it was a he, and one sick, fucked up he at that. Nicky didn't know it, but *he* called himself Fonda, and honestly couldn't remember his birth name anyway. Fonda leaned over the dead girl's body to peel her torn blouse back further, and still giggling, poked at her nipple. He poked it again, and a little bubble of blood oozed out of one of the wounds on her breast. The freak dipped his finger in the blood, brought it to his lips, and —

Drake kicked the freak's hand away from his mouth.

Drake, the one who looked like a refugee from an 80's hair band, which he was, actually: blonde streaks in his long, dark hair, a torn sleeveless-T showing off skinny muscles and tattoos, torn black jeans revealing more of that creepy, white flesh. Drake lifted his lizard skin boot and took aim again, but Fonda slithered off into a corner.

Arianne crossed her arms over her chest, and just looked impatient.

"Please excuse them," Marek said, gesturing towards Drake and the freak. "Some children have no manners. So, Mr. Kolitzky, what news do you bring us? All went well?"

"Fuck the news, Marek," Nicky said. "Give me my money."

"How very mercenary of you."

"Mer — merciful, shit. The bitch is dead. So give me my money."

Marek smoothed his hair back. Fussed with his shirt cuffs till they were just so. "Perhaps you might tell us how things went with Miss Russell first?"

Nicky threw the canvas duffel bag on the floor, right at Marek's gleaming loafers. "*There's* how things went. See for yourself."

Marek turned to Drake and Fonda. Said something wordless, and the two dove at the bag.

Megan Russell's clothes tumbled out on the floor.

Nicky told them everything, from the search-and-destroy at Megan's condo, to catching her cold in the bar at the 'Top Of The Cock'. He even put in a good word for Joey along the way. If he managed to conveniently skip over the part about Megan's bundle of cash, well...that was for expenses. Nicky positively beamed when he told them about the pistol jabbed between Megan's thighs, when he told them about her pleading and stripping, pleading and naked at the edge of the roof a hundred stories up, told them about Megan Russell's screams as she plummeted over the side.

Or, more correctly, he told Marek.

Arianne didn't appear to be listening.

Drake was busy ripping apart the linings in Megan's blazer, blouse and skirt. Then he emptied her purse and sorted through all the contents.

Fonda was just as busy. After he sniffed and licked the insides of Megan's pumps, he tried on her bra right over his own shirt. It couldn't make it around his skinny chest, so he just held it in place and giggled to himself.

"Nothing," Drake said. He slapped Fonda across the face. The freak snarled, but dropped the bra. "Plane tickets, hotel reservations, the fake name, all like our little hired gun says." He smirked when he said 'hired gun', and glanced up at Nicky. "But there's nothing in her stuff."

"Nothing?" Marek said. "Papers? Photocopies? Disks, tapes, microfilm? Nothing?" He turned to Nicky, brows knotting over dark eyes. His condescending smile faded. "Nicholas, please don't let me think that you're — how would you put it — 'holding out' on us?" His eyes drilled into Nicky's, his voice sounded even more lethal than usual. "Please don't let me think that.

Not even for a moment."

"Don't give me that voodoo-eye shit, Marek," Nicky said, trying to sound tough, but suddenly feeling small and awfully vulnerable. One hand instinctively lifted towards the shoulder holster under his blazer, but he forced it back down. "What you got is what I got. There's nothing to hold out. Anyway, what's the difference? She's dead. Hamburger city on the sidewalk. She can't hassle you anymore."

Arianne rolled those opal eyes of hers, and for a second, Nicky could have sworn that they flashed red, just like brakelights. She slid down along the wall, all the way to the dirty linoleum floor, and crossed her white legs, mumbling to herself.

Marek wrinkled his lips at her. They were sensuous lips. Cruel lips. "What are you complaining about now?"

"I told you," she said. "I simply cannot believe that you allowed this Slavic twit to handle this business."

"Arianne — "

"You and your grandiose plans. You and your 'minions'."

"Arianne, please. Let's not quarrel in front of the help."

She shrugged her skinny shoulders and turned away.

Nicky tried to follow their conversation. But the fact was, half of it was spoken, and half if it was...what? Just thoughts? Just soundless words he'd eavesdropped on? "Look, Marek," he said. "I brought you everything Megan Russell had on her. She's dead. Gone. What's the problem?"

"Yes, Mr. Kolitzky, she's dead," Marek said. "But your errand was not to kill her. Or at least, not until you obtained what we wanted."

"And what's so fucking important that she had anyway?" Nicky said. "Maybe I should be asking double for this job?"

"Maybe you — " Marek bristled. "Maybe you will be lucky to leave here alive tonight."

Nicky didn't stop his hand from reaching under his blazer this time. He whipped out the Mauser and stepped back from the four of them.

Arianne laughed. Ice clinking in a glass, that's what it sounded like to Nicky. "Oh Marek, I do believe your gangster is a bit uneasy." She pulled her long legs up and leaned her chin on her knees. Then she smiled at Nicky. "Don't you understand, you imbecile? You're so very proud that you killed her. You are, I can feel your pride. But Miss Russell died without giving you what we wanted. It could be anywhere now, Mr. Kolitzky. She could have given it to anyone. You could be reading all about us on the front page of the newspaper tomorrow morning."

The Mauser shook in Nicky's hand.

"Pathetic," Arianne hissed.

Marek stepped closer to Nicky, ignoring the pistol. "Nicky, Nicky, Nicky. You've done poorly. And I'm very disappointed. I'd hoped to get more from this escapade than some new underthings for Fonda to play with."

"M-Marek, just stay where you are," Nicky stammered. He jerked the gun back and forth at the four of them. But Marek still approached.

"What exactly do you think you'll do with that gun, Nicky? Shoot me? Kill me?" Marek's eyes began to flicker. The black irises faded and then glowed red, fixing on Nicky. "Painful, of course. But kill me? You know better than that by now, don't you? And after all, there are four of us." He smiled, an ugly, malevolent smile that revealed his sparkly teeth.

"No, Marek. Don't," Nicky begged. "I don't want to have to — "

"To what, Nicky? What do you think I'm going to do?" Marek's grin widened, a serpent's smile, a cobra's leer.

"You can't possibly think I'd like to have you with us forever, can you? After how you've bungled this? No, Nicky, I'm afraid not."

Nicky aimed the Mauser at Marek's chest. His finger tightened on the trigger.

"Nicky, you are not going to shoot me," Marek said.

But what Nicky actually heard was, *'Nikolai, you are not going out tonight.'* It was his mother's voice, whining inside his head. *'Nikki, no, you will not.'*

"Nicky," Marek said, his voice low, forceful, commanding. "You will put the pistol in your mouth, please."

And a different voice throbbed in Nicky's ears — Tyrone, the black bull that ruled section six in the County lockup, *'Come on, Nicky-Dickie, put it in your mouth, that's right, just like suckin' on a licorice whip, ain't it, white boy?'*

"N-no, Tyrone, I don't wanna." Nicky held the Mauser with both hands, and both hands shook uncontrollably. "Marek, no. Don't do this to me." The barrel quivered an inch from Nicky's lips.

"Now, now, Nicky, open wide. That's it. Wrap your lips around the barrel, Nicky. Ahh, yes, just like that."

Nicky's teeth clinked on the oily metal barrel. "Mmmph-M-Marek, no." He gagged on the pistol as it slid back in his mouth.

"Now, pull the trigger, Nicky."

Drool glistened on the Mauser's barrel.

A tear dribbled down Nicky's cheek.

"Nicky, pull the trigger. Now."

The blast was surprisingly loud.

It echoed for a couple of seconds in the room, long enough to cover the wet sound of a chunk from the back of Nicky's head flying across the room and smacking against the wall behind him. By the time Nicky's body fell to the floor, that little clump of blood clotted bone and hair started to slide down the wall.

Fonda giggled on the other side of the room. He crawled away from the whore's body and the pile of Megan Russell's designer clothes. Crawled to Nicky. He looked over his shoulder at Arianne, but she just curled her red lips at him and hissed. Then he looked to Marek, who nodded back.

Drake looked at Marek too, a question on his face, a red glow simmering in his eyes. Marek nodded at him as well, and Drake kicked Fonda aside, then knelt down beside Nicky.

Arianne listened to the wet, oozy, sucking sounds for a moment, then abruptly stood up. "Pathetic," she sneered. "Utterly pathetic, all of you." She glared at Marek, then shook her head. "Clean this mess up when you're through." She stomped through the door.

"Yes," Marek grumbled once she was gone. "Of course, Arianne." His eyes flashed angry red.

He walked over to the window and flipped it back open with one finger. Sniffed the damp, night air. Looked out on the hazy skyline, looked down on Damen Avenue.

"Drake, when you're done there, be a dear and go downstairs to fetch Mr. Kolitzky's companion. I think I'd like a word with this Joey Fortuna."

Chicago In-Site, July 9

Personals/Other

Evil cabal seeks same for LARP, clubbing and more. Only truly imaginative need apply, costuming mandatory. Overweight or over 30, don't bother. No Trekkies! Fri/Sat nights only. NW suburbs. Own trans. a must. Response #INSP007555

Daily Southtown, July 11

Police Blotter

Willow Woods police responded to a report of vandalism in southwest suburban Sacred Heart Cemetery and discovered several tombstones overturned, grave markers defaced and two mausoleums broken into and burglarized. Willow Woods Police Sgt. J. Renwikci provided no confirmation on reports that several vaults in the mausoleums were actually broken open and the bodies disinterred. This is the fourth reported incident of cemetery vandalism in the last...

WMKK FM

Mad Mad Mattie's Morning Madhouse

July 14, 8:30 AM

"...And coming up after the break we'll talk to Leticia Lividna, self proclaimed 'Chicagoland Queen Of Darkness', with the very latest on where you'll want to get mean and be seen in the darkwave scene this weekend, along with Livvie's own...uhm, fashion tips...for all of you...Look, just what the heck are all of you out there? But first, here's the traffic from..."

If Rimbaud & Baudelaire Only Knew...

NINE

"A double espresso, two glasses of merlot, a —"

The girl behind the counter didn't even blink as she breezed right by Colleen Russell. Maybe she was deaf.

No, couldn't be deaf. The girl tapped her fingers on her thighs, keeping time with the music droning out of the speakers.

Blind, maybe?

Now that was a possibility. If not blind, Colleen thought, then unable to move her eyes. The waitress' pale foundation, deep red blush, thick eyeliner, purplish lips, her dark eye shadow — they all looked like they were inexpertly ladled on with a paint roller. If the girl blinked, her face would crack for sure.

Colleen forked two fingers, stuck them in her mouth, then whistled as loud as she could, surprising herself when she heard it over Gene Loves Jezebel's "Sweet Rain" blaring out of tower speakers. The counter girl halted, sauntered over at a snail's pace and glared at Colleen.

"A double espresso, two glasses of merlot, one dark Java Supreme, a — "

The waitress shook her head. "I won't be able to remember all that."

"Okay," Colleen said, "Get me what you can remember, and then I'll tell you the rest."

The girl mulled that over for an impossibly long minute. "Well, all right. I suppose that'll work."

Colleen sat down on one of the mismatched stools lined up along the bar. She spun around, surveying *Rimbaud's Cave.* If memory served her right, six months ago the gloomy spot on Elston and Wolcott had been a pseudo-beatnik coffeehouse called 'The Unseemly Bean', and a neighborhood tavern catering to the biker crowd six months before that. Now it was 'Rimbaud's Cave'. Colleen vaguely remembered Rimbaud as some kind of writer. A poet maybe, the kind that Cass and his new friends probably had memorized and were reciting to each other back at the table.

'Not a chance, sweetheart.' Cass said when she plopped down on the couch after work this evening. 'This recluse thing is getting a bit old. Even widows hang up the veil after a suitable mourning period.'

'Cass, this has nothing to do with Megan's death. It's been a tough week at work,

I'm tired, and I definitely don't like the sound of a place called Rimbaud's Cave.'

The waitress appeared with the first drinks. Colleen enunciated carefully as she ordered the rest, then twirled the stool some more, checking out Cass' latest hot spot.

She had to squint. Rimbaud's Cave favored strings of blue Christmas lights and a few track spots on dimmers dialed *way* down. They lit up a thick layer of smoke hovering four feet off the floor, just like fake horror movie fog. But that smoke stank to high hell from skinny fruit-scented cigarillos, the obligatory clove cigarettes and an occasional pipe loaded with who knew what.

Thrift shop reject sofas hugged the bare brick walls, where the serious Goth contingent and the new romantics lounged in their black leathers and white lace, sipping on flavored coffees and mismatched glasses of red wine, trying to appear aloof to the stray yuppie fringe and the Gap refugees that sometimes wandered in and just as quickly, wandered right back out. A few tables were scattered in the center of the room, where more pasty faced kids dangled elaborate smokes from the tips of their black gloved fingers, held court on the latest bands, the newest zines, the hottest websites. Here and there a group scanned rulebooks for their role playing games. From the sound of things, everyone was an artist, or a writer, or a musician, a filmmaker or a web designer or various combinations of all of those.

By the front windows, a makeshift plywood stage was mercifully empty just now. In fact Colleen had bolted for the fresh round of drinks as soon as the last act ended: two vampi-dykes doing an extemporaneous poetry slam while they nibbled each others necks and bared breasts, splashing stageblood (Colleen hoped) all over each other.

Performance art.

The waitress finally returned, but she stared at the coffees and wineglasses lined up on the bar like they were alien life forms sprouting up out of the sticky wood. "Okay, that's, uhm...wait, I think I need my calculator."

"That's okay, you can use my abacus." The waitress just waited, as if she actually expected Colleen to whip one out of her purse. She almost seemed disappointed when Colleen dug out a twenty, and laid it on top of the ten dollars already sticking to the bar. "Just keep the change and call it even, okay?"

The waitress eyed up the bills suspiciously, certain she was being ripped off.

"Look, you'll come out ahead," Colleen said. "Trust me. If I shorted you, you can make me wait tables or something. I'm sitting right over there." Colleen pointed. "Now, could I get a tray or something?"

"A tray of what?"

"A tray for...oh, forget it."

Fortunately, Cass appeared at her side just as Colleen started to stack saucers on top of cups. "Let me get some of those, Col." He dropped a black papered cigarette on the floor and ground it out with his boot. Poured into skintight black velvet stretchpants and sporting a flouncy ruffled white shirt —

along with the usual collection of oddball pewter finger rings, earrings, 'other' rings and makeup — Cass looked right at home in Rimbaud's Cave.

Colleen, on the other hand, had to endure half an hour of Cass tsk-tsk'ing at her closet door before they left the apartment. *'This stuff is strictly K-Mart meets Old Navy, girl. You know, they might hit you up for a double cover charge just for wearing those tennis shoes. Now that you have a real job, why don't I take you shopping?'* Once they'd stepped into Rimbaud's Cave, she felt like she'd shown up at a costume ball, sans costume.

Cass lifted one of the coffees out of her hand and wrapped his fingers around the wineglass stems. "I sense you're not exactly enjoying yourself."

"It shows?"

"Only in that 'Cassidy, I'm going to murderlize you when we get home' look. Do you want to leave?"

Colleen shrugged her shoulders. "No, you want to play with your friends." She wasn't sure it sounded convincing enough. "Sorry, Cass, but Rimbaud's Cave isn't quite my style."

"My friends are too weird for you, right?"

"Cass, I *live* with you. What could be weirder? Actually, most of your friends are okay."

"Which is a surprise, I gather. But that qualifier did not go unnoticed. *Most,* I believe was the operative word there," he said. "Colleen, I haven't known these guys that long myself. All she ever told me was that she got fired a while ago. *Where* she got fired from didn't come up. We don't spend much time chatting up our day jobs. I suppose you've noticed that a lot of people check the real world at the door when they come here."

Colleen glanced at the door when he said that. A sign hung there, badly painted medieval script on fake black marble.

'Where the children are cold
and do not sleep
and are afraid...'
RIMBAUD

"It's a little awkward for you, isn't it?" Cass asked.

"It's a lot awkward. It's major awkward. I took her damn job, Cass."

"Well, you didn't know it at the time. Now let's get these drinks back to the table before they all start drooling." Cass juggled cups and wineglasses. "Anyway, her bark's worse than her bite. Just don't let Gabrielle get to you."

✦

Over a month of precious Chicago summer had passed since that night at the Cook County Medical Examiner's building.

It hadn't been what Colleen expected.

No white sheet pulled back off a corpse. No black rubber bag to unzip.

Not even a video monitor showing the body from another room.

Because once they explained things to Colleen — how Megan died, or how they were guessing she died — she understood. There wasn't much of a body left intact after a hundred story fall.

It was just by accident that the police discovered it was Megan Russell.

There were no ID's. No clothes at all, Colleen learned. But with a tumble from a skyscraper, the police started their canvas at the top, where a hostess mentioned that Megan Russell had been in late the previous night, acting strange and with an even stranger guy. By the following morning the cops had talked to Whitestar Media Group. That afternoon they identified Megan Russell through dental records that matched what was left of her jaw, and by that evening they found out Megan had a sister living in Chicago.

The *why's* behind Megan's hundred story fall on a Tuesday night in June...*those* they didn't manage quite so well.

Megan's employee life insurance policy could pay more than enough to cover a decent funeral, a grave and a tombstone. But with the police investigation still pending, and the circumstances of her death so peculiar, no checks were going to be cut for a long time. Between them, Colleen and Cass couldn't have paid for an economy model cremation urn. But Whitestar stepped in and covered everything.

And so for all of Colleen Russell's obstinacy, big sister Megan ended up getting her a job at Charade Magazine anyway.

It was at the wake, actually.

As Megan's only relative — there were some second cousins somewhere in Pennsylvania, but Colleen wasn't sure — she found herself in a second hand shop black dress that Cass produced like magic, standing next to a ten thousand dollar casket in one of downtown Chicago's plushest funeral parlors. There she shook hands with a steady stream of Charade Magazine coworkers, Whitestar corporate types, fashion models, writers, photographers, editors, reporters and the whole of Chicago's media elite. The city's beautiful people were as perfunctory as they were visible with their grief. Mostly they just filed past the closed coffin without a glance, exchanged an awkward hug, dabbed at an invisible tear or two, nodded to Cass hovering behind Colleen, and whisked out of the chapel as quick as they could. Evidently the beautiful people didn't like dealing with death, even under a closed coffin.

Except for Jeff Stancheck.

He was different. He seemed genuinely touched by the whole business, genuinely sorry about Megan's death, even stifling a couple legitimate sniffs and tears when he first knelt down at the coffin, and Colleen pegged Jeff Stancheck as the kind of guy that didn't shed tears with ease. He stayed, spending the entire evening at Colleen's side to put names on the strangers' faces for her.

It was Jeff that offered Colleen the job, mentioning in passing that one of his staff was on the way out.

Colleen never asked about specifics, didn't ask what the job paid or what the hours were. She just knew that this man stayed with her throughout the whole depressing affair, took her and Cass out for something to eat after, then drove them both home. And that Jeff Stancheck didn't seem like the type who'd be chasing her around the water cooler.

With Cass elbowing her the whole time, Colleen said yes and thanks, and was sitting in Charade Magazine's personnel office filling out a W-2 three days later.

✦

There were six of them at the table, not counting Cass and Colleen.

There was Frostbite, aptly named and sporting a bleached-to-bone-white shag with skin to match, so pallid that Colleen wondered if he was an albino. But no, his brows and lashes were brown, or they seemed to be under his makeup. He shared his drink with his girlfriend, Gem, the one with the hennaed pudding bowl hair and the shiny velveteen catsuit under her black see-through shift. They fronted a darkwave band, or so they said. 'Kill Dance' was on it's sixth incarnation as bandmembers kept insisting on splitting for jobs that paid actual money. Frostbite was rhythm guitar. Gem did keyboards on a ESP30 digital set, proudly explaining to Colleen that she couldn't really read a note of music to save her life, but had ripped off an old boyfriend's stash of pre-programmed disks back in her groupie days, and those did all the work.

There was Brandon and Fitch, two guys who may or may not have been together, and rarely joined in on the conversations, mostly keeping their heads buried in their gaming mags, unless they looked up to snicker at someone's clothes or makeup that didn't make the grade. Their own getups tread the thin line between garishly hip and girlishly weird, even for this crowd.

There was Chelsea, a bit too fleshy to do the pale, anorexic look justice, but trying to make up for it with wild black hair, a black mesh see-through blouse that showed her jiggly breasts off to everyone, and a perverse gallery of tattoos on her flabby arms.

And then there was Gabrielle.

Gabrielle, brushing Chelsea away like a pesky fly when the pudgy girl persisted with her girlie giggles and conspiratorial whispers and dramatic pecks on the cheek.

Gabrielle, leaning forward over the table, with her chin resting in her lace gloved hands.

Gabrielle, busily flicking her long black hair off her face, curling her lips into an insincere smile while she glared at Colleen, too busy to listen to the conversation as the fresh drinks were passed around.

"So, I hear you're part timing at Dark Mystique Books," Cass said, sliding a glass of merlot in front of Gabrielle.

She tore her dark eyes away from Colleen. "What? Oh, right. Yeah, just for something to do. I figure I spend so much time in there browsing books, I might as well get paid for it. But it's not like it's a *real* job. I'm done with that whole commerce scene."

Cass shrugged his shoulders. "Sounds real to me. I've applied there twice."

"Well, guess you'll still be bending over in alleys for the rent then, won't you?" Gabrielle sipped her merlot. "No, it's just a couple evenings a week. Now that I'm not wasting so much time doing the job thing, I can really focus on my painting. You have heard about my show here next month, haven't you? No? Oh, they just love my stuff, couldn't wait to make room for it. They've already got one up."

"They do?" Cass asked, twisting his head. "Where?"

"Over there." Gabrielle pointed to the back of Rimbaud's Cave. "See."

"No, where?"

"*There.* Past the last couch."

Like Cass, Colleen followed Gabrielle's gloved finger pointing to the back of the room. Finally she spotted an unframed stretched canvas, hanging crooked on the wall right next to the mens room door. It was even darker back there than the rest of the club. All she could make out on the painting were some leering white faces and a trickle of blood.

"But enough about me," Gabrielle said. She turned back to Colleen. "I'm just *so* glad to meet *you.* How often does a girl get to meet her own replacement, huh?" She smiled away with those ribbon lips of hers, shining like wet, spoiled grapes while she pointed at Colleen's brown bottle. "Gee, I didn't even know they served beer here. Looks like the proletariat's moving in, gang. Next thing you know, Rimbaud's Cave will be playing Shania Twain and hosting wet T-shirt nights." Gabrielle peeled off one of her lace gloves, then gestured at Colleen's black T-shirt. "Oh, but you're all ready for that, aren't you? Oooo, black. How very...bohemian."

Cass slammed his coffee mug down in the saucer. "Come on, Gabrielle, lay off."

Brandon and Fitch buried their heads deeper in their 'Children Of The Grave' rulebooks. Chelsea seemed annoyed at all the attention Gabrielle paid to the new girl. Frostbite and Gem licked their lipsticked lips and got more interested.

Colleen just tapped her fingers on her bottle.

"Now Cassidy," Gabrielle said, rummaging through her knapsack sized purse. Don't go all paternal on us. There's no need to protect your little friend. Most fag hags can fend for themselves." She pulled out a jackknife, then smiled at Colleen again. "Don't worry, red, it's not for you."

"Look, I'm sorry you lost your job at Charade," Colleen said. "But believe me, I had nothing to do with it. The way I hear it, you were on the way out already."

Gabrielle flipped the blade open. "Uh-huh. I guess I got Cassidy's introduction all wrong before. It is Colleen *Russell,* right? As in *Megan* Russell,

Managing — OOPS, I mean *ex*-Managing Editor? That didn't grease the wheels a smidge, huh?"

"Gabrielle, stop," Cass said.

Colleen leaned across the table till her face was just inches from Gabrielle's. And just inches from Gabrielle's jackknife. "You got a problem with being fired, call a lawyer. You have a problem with me, then you can fuck off. Clear?" She leaned back in her chair and took a big gulp from her beer.

Gabrielle still smiled at Colleen, but her eyes turned to black ringed slits. She held the jackknife over her own palm and drew the blade across the skin. Immediately, a thin stream of red appeared. Gabrielle held her hand over her wineglass and let the blood drip into the merlot, holding Colleen's gaze the whole time. "Clear," she said, clicking the knife closed, then slipping her glove back on. "Like crystal." Gabrielle sipped her blood-wine cocktail.

Colleen started to say something, then shoved her chair away instead and stomped out of the club.

"I'll be right back," Cass said, jumping up and following behind.

"Don't bother," Gabrielle sneered.

"Come on, get off Cass' case. He's okay," Frostbite said. "His friend's just kind of straight."

"Maybe," Chelsea chimed in. "But I think she's cute."

"Another remark like that," Gabrielle said, "and you can fuck yourself tonight, queenie."

Quite out of character, Gem decided to be the peacemaker. Someone had to most every night. They knew they were a bitchy bunch that thrived on catfights more than merlot and scented smokes. "Everyone chill out. Cass will be back and be his old mincy-wincy self once his roommate's safe in a cab and back on her way to the world. So let's talk about *important* stuff." She turned to Gabrielle. "Like, where are these great new guys you met at Dark Mystique? And are they really as cool as you've been making them out to be? This better not all be hype, Gabrielle."

"Yeah, are we going to the cemetery tonight?" Frostbite asked. "Because if we are, we better get going. Gem and I should really practice tonight."

"Yes, we're going," Gabrielle said between sips from her wine. "And don't worry, these guys are the coolest. You'll just die when you meet them."

TEN

Whitestar Media Group was *not* a lateral organization.

The pyramid of power came to a peculiarly sharp point, and at its apex there was room for only one person, and that was Roberta Whitehead herself.

Roberta never felt a twinge of guilt over the way she'd parlayed her late husband's oil money and agridollars into a media and publishing conglomerate. Not a twinge — certainly not over the fact that just fifteen years ago she was still going by the name *Starr Roberts,* still doing the bump 'n grind in one of Phoenix's better 'gentlemen's clubs', even though she was pushing thirty two at the time (but palming herself off as an experienced twenty five), and certainly not over the fact that she made ends meet by pocketing a little extra on the side by going down on some of those same gentlemen in between sets.

Not a twinge of guilt.

Because that's how she met Hamilton Whitehead after all, though she had a mouthful of his seventy year old dick when Hamilton finally got around to introducing himself, not that the old coot's name would have meant anything to Starr Roberts at the time. But two crisp thousand dollar bills pressed into her palm along with his card certainly made an impression, and three months later, Starr Roberts strolled down the aisle in virgin white, arm in arm with old Hamilton, and became Roberta Whitehead.

The only surprising twist in the time honored tradition of savvy-stripper-sometimes-whore-marries-rich-old-fool was that no one contested Hamilton Whitehead's will when he died a short two years after the honeymoon. And Roberta never felt a twinge of guilt about that, over dear old Hamilton's demise, especially since she did everything she could to egg it on with twice-a-day rolls in the imported satin hay, till Whitehead's old head was worn out and blue.

Roberta had her own private bathroom adjoining her twenty seventh floor office suite in the Whitestar Media Group corporate headquarters. And right now, she gripped the Carrera marble vanity in that private bathroom, gripped it good and tight because she was afraid that if she let go, she'd just get dizzy again and end up on the floor.

One finger at a time, she took her hands away from the slick marble, then cautiously lifted the strap of her white silk slip back up her shoulder. There was nothing to be done with the lace bodice; it hung in tatters, just loose threads twisting into cobweb patterns, dissected by rips and tears. Just sheared, shiny silk, dappled with red stains.

That's where Roberta's blood had dribbled all over it.

She ran her fingers through her bleached silver hair, but it was a mess and there was no salvaging it either. Roberta splashed her face with cold water, splashed some on her neck and let it trickle down her chest, over her breasts, right over the purplish bruises ringing her nipples. She cupped one hand under the gold faucet and ladled a palm full onto the side of her throat. That stung, and she bit her lip. Of course it hurt, but it hurt *so good.*

The bruise there on her throat looked even worse than those on her breasts. That bruise on her throat had little gashes in the middle, and they still oozed red blood.

Just looking at it in the mirror made Roberta squeeze her legs together. Made her feel all warm inside, made her feel moist again. She toweled off the blood and water, tried to steady herself, then padded back into her office suite.

Marek stood by the floor-to-ceiling windows, evidently drinking in the glittery nighttime view down Fairmont Court.

Roberta fell into a curved couch that formed one half of a conversation pit, all plush Milanese leather, a spot she usually reserved for brow-beating toadies even when they were being fired, all those little corporate ferrets who's eyes invariably drifted towards her shapely legs crossing and uncrossing over the edge of the cushions. Sure, one or two might salvage their jobs there, but the Queen of Whitestar Media only offered mercy to the freshest faced MBA's doing their first stints in the real world, and only if they could stay hard and stay long enough and could ignore the battle scars on a forty seven year old body that had been tucked, sucked and sutured ten ways to hell.

Marek, however, didn't care for the Milanese sofas. As if he knew that Roberta felt in control there.

Tonight he'd taken her right up against the floor-to-ceiling windows, and that made it doubly exciting for Roberta — as if everything Marek did wasn't exciting, wasn't nasty and wicked and more deliciously dangerous than anything she'd ever seen in the back rooms of the strip clubs. Marek just ripped her Paris haute couture right off like it was a whiff of gauze, just pawed and mauled and scratched and bit — yes, bit, that was the best part, wasn't it? He bit her, and had Roberta wondering if her spiky pumps slamming the windows could break the glass, could send her flying twenty seven floors down to Michigan and Fairmont.

Just like...

"Could you fix me a drink?" Roberta sprawled across the soft leather. "Marek?"

He turned away from the window. The shaded lamp on her desk only lit up the lower half of his body, just his black suit pants and jacket. His face was still veiled in shadow. Even so, Roberta could detect how pale it was, how his eyes still seemed to glow.

"Marek? Please?"

He didn't budge. Roberta felt his eyes glaring at her from out of the shadows, felt them drilling holes into her head. "S-sorry," she mumbled. She crawled off the sofa and shuffled over to the wet bar.

The scotch burned its way down her throat. *Especially on that one side, that spot where Marek clamped his icy lips down on her neck, where Marek licked her flesh with that cold, velvety tongue of his, where he pressed his teeth against her tender skin, and...*

"Well Roberta, I must be leaving soon." Marek pulled her chair out from the desk, an impossibly huge chair that was more like a throne on wheels, tailor made for the impossibly huge desk. "Come now, we have work to do."

"Marek, please. Not tonight. Can't we just...?"

He patted the chair.

She refilled her scotch, looked at the glass, then left it on the bar. "Marek, please. I — I need...need more." She took the whole bottle with her.

"What you need is not really important."

"Marek, the things you say." Roberta smiled hopefully, then swigged from the bottle and leaned against him. But he pushed her away and into the chair.

She took a moment to focus on the contracts and forms spread out across her desk.

Marek slipped an onyx and gold pen into her hand. "Don't read, love. Just sign."

Her eyes darted back and forth from one paper to another. She dropped the pen. "I — I'm not going to sign these." She picked up one contract. "1.5 *million*? Are you insane." Roberta pointed at another. "Minority interest in *another* nightclub? You haven't even opened the first one yet."

"Simply planning ahead, Roberta. I'm an entrepreneur. An empire builder, like yourself. That's the American way, isn't it?" Marek picked up the pen and stuck it right back between her fingers. "Start signing. I have places to go tonight."

✦

It was a damn shame about Nicky's Cutlass. That convertible was cherry.

But Joey Fortuna didn't feel so bad about dumping the car in the Cal-Sag Channel once they gave him the keys to this brand new, black Mercedes. The car was huge, a real cruiser, and once Joey saw the sound system inside, he figured he could forget about Nicky's Cutlass *and* Nicky's bloodless corpse stinking up the Oldsmobile's trunk just fine.

Joey figured he could forget about a lot of things now.

Staring across the Fairmont Court sidewalk, Joey punched a button and advanced the CD to the next track. He turned up the volume, and *Type O*

Negative's stadium-gloom-rock droned out of the speakers full blast.

Yep, Joey Fortuna could dig it now, so long as he got to tool around in a car like this, so long as the cash kept coming in, so long as he got all the strays when *they* were done with them.

The Mercedes' back door opened, and Marek slid in silently, tossing a stack of papers on the seat.

"Turn that off, Joseph," Marek hissed. "Immediately."

Joey advanced the CD changer to another disk. Cellos started pensive notes. It was Shubert's Symphony No. 8, 'The Unfinished', not that Joey Fortuna knew who the hell Shubert was. He just knew that he heard Marek listening to it in the theater one night, remembered that even Arianne hung around and listened, and *she* never seemed to like anything.

"Where to now?" Joey asked.

"Home."

It wasn't late, barely nine thirty. Traffic was heavy on Michigan Avenue, heavier still on Lake Shore Drive. But the black Mercedes cruised along at an even seventy, soundless, sliding right by any other cars doing the forty five limit. Joey didn't care. He had five one hundred dollar bills clipped to his drivers license. If a cop wanted to stop them, six months of beer and bowling money went into the officer's hands with the license. And if a cop was ungrateful enough to go all law and order on them...well, Marek had a way with people.

He could be *very* persuasive.

Joey left the Drive and the lakefront behind, but traffic just got worse. "So, everything go all right with your meeting?"

"Yes, Joseph. Just fine. In fact, I have some papers here that you'll need to drop off with the attorneys tomorrow."

"*Which* attorneys?"

Marek smiled. "Yes, things are getting more complex, aren't they? I'll mull that over."

"Anything else up for tomorrow?"

The Mercedes turned onto Damen Avenue. "Actually, yes. Ms. Whitehead informed me that someone in the Liquor Licensing Bureau is still holding up the final approval. You *did* deliver all the envelopes as instructed, Joseph? None of them 'disappeared'?"

Nicky Kolitzky's blood-drained body with the gaping hole in the head flashed before Joey's eyes. "Absolutely. Five grand a pop. Handed them over personally. *And* at the Ward Office. *And* Streets & San'. *And* at the Police —"

"Very well, Joseph, I trust you. Nonetheless, we have to do something about this Assistant Commissioner fellow."

"You want him to kind of...disappear?"

Marek shook his head. "Joseph, Joseph, you simply refuse to let go of those strong-arm tactics of yours. I thought we were all done with that once your friend Mr. Kolitzky chose to leave us."

"Well, I just meant that — "

"Joseph, you will simply ask the Assistant Commissioner to drop by for a visit tomorrow evening. Say, about eightish?"

"Well, okay. If you want to deal with — "

"And Joseph, I believe you will find that this obstinate fellow happens to have a daughter. An impetuous young thing, I'm told. Nasty drinking problem. Nastier heroin habit. Just see that she is also at the theater tomorrow evening. It is not particularly important if she *wants* to come."

Traffic backed up on Damen. North Side streets were always backed up.

Marek handed the contracts over the seat to Joey. "I'm quite certain that the girl's presence will be enough to 'motivate' our reluctant Assistant Liquor License Commissioner."

Joey nodded. Tomorrow was shaping up to be a busy day. "So where do I find this chick?"

"Talk to Drake before you leave tonight. I'm sure he can give you all the details."

"Can't," Joey said.

"Come again?"

"I can't talk to Drake. He went out just before we left. Him and Fonda," Joey said. "Arianne, too."

"Arianne?" Marek leaned over the seat. His cold hand grabbed a hold of Joey's shoulder. "Out where?"

Joey shrugged his shoulders. "Hunting, I guess."

✦

Jeff Stancheck cursed the north side's crowded main drags. He didn't know any swear words good enough for its bewildering maze of one way side streets.

He zigged and zagged the red Trans Am east and south. Maybe the Cubs were playing a night game? Maybe there was another lakefront festival tonight? At almost nine-thirty, it certainly wasn't leftovers from rush hour. *Just get me to Lake Shore Drive. The Kennedy. Anything moving.* He gave up on Montrose, and turned south on Damen Avenue.

Working late was nothing new for Jeff. Actually, it was a way of life. But lately, he'd been checking his watch come five o'clock, suddenly anxious to head home.

Because for the first time in a long time, there *was* someone to come home to.

Jacks had moved right in to her old room a month ago. And when Jeff would come home from work, Jacks was just as likely to be standing in the kitchen as she was to be out digging up old friends — standing in the kitchen with an apron incongruously tied around her cut off's, something good simmering on the stove. *'You could have called, you know. Dinner's probably ruined now.'*

It was like music to Jeff's ears.

She wasn't a kid anymore. Hell, Jeff had even tossed her the keys to the Trans Am a couple times, even though she didn't have an Illinois license. She was talking about college, teasing him that she was considering design, maybe even here in Chicago. They'd been up to the wee hours more than once, sharing a gallon of chocolate-chocolate chip and feeling like a family again. So what if Jacks had turned the bathroom sink into a miniature cosmetics department, and if her music grated on his nerves till he bought her some headphones, so what if he had to remember all over again to dodge air-drying bras on the shower rod...so what?

Jeff was in heaven.

But the memo Blair had brought in a few weeks ago was as clear as it was unusual, and it came from Roberta Whitehead herself: *'...extend the full cooperation of Charade Magazine's resources — staff, writers, purchasing, production, and especially the art department — to Gothique management. Marketing synergies are being negotiated which will...'*

Memo?

It was a mandate.

So, working late. Again. Another press approval at a north side printer. Another day cooped up with fawning sales reps and burly union pressman, fussing over that all too familiar red on black logo, getting the pallid hues just-so on more photos of those anemic fashion ghouls.

Another Gothique mailer.

It was starting to feel like the magazine was just a sideline.

Jeff tailed a long, black Mercedes that looked as out of place on this stretch of Damen Avenue as he felt. The street might have once been a thriving neighborhood shopping district, all little storefronts and scattered two-flats standing at attention along the sidewalk. But the storefronts were closed or boarded up now. The two-flats had *For Rent* signs in their dirty windows, and the signs looked awfully old.

The Mercedes gained a block on Jeff while he gawked at the bleak buildings. Then its brake lights flashed red, and the black sedan pulled over to the right.

Jeff tapped his brakes too. Then he slammed them to the floor, and stared.

There it was.

There was that red on black logo, that same emblem he'd cobbled together on a whim over a month ago, that same logo he'd been staring at nearly every day now.

GOTHIQUE.

He blinked, and realized that it was a sign. A huge red on black marquee. There was the club itself.

GOTHIQUE.

Jeff gaped at the old building towering overhead, till another car pulled up behind him and beeped. He looked for someplace to pull over. That black

Mercedes had pulled into the only vacant spot in front of the theater. The rest of the curb was blocked with overflowing dumpsters. Jeff cut across the northbound lane and parked on the other side of the street.

GOTHIQUE.

An old theater, by the looks of it, one of those movie palaces from the thirties, done up in a quasi-medieval castle motif: gables, turrets, alcoves complete with gargoyles, arched window frames, the glass dark and opaque like shaded eyes.

This nightclub-entertainment complex with the countercultural veneer had been driving him crazy for weeks now — all the extra work, the way it had Blair running on about how this was going to be just the coolest thing to happen to Chicago in ages. Even Jacks had been asking about it, said that all the kids were talking nothing but *Gothique.*

But he had to admit, his logo looked pretty impressive fifty feet long in metal and acrylic across on the old marquee. Even if he didn't get one red cent for the extra work. Jeff remembered his Polaroid in the trunk and decided it would be a good idea to take a picture now. Chicago nightclubs and 'entertainment complexes' lasted about as long as Chicago summers.

While he popped off three pictures, the back door opened on the black Mercedes parked across the street. A man got out, then leaned back in and said something to the driver. He was tall — late thirties, early forties, Jeff guessed, wearing a fancy, black double breasted suit, black shirt, slicked back black hair.

Through the camera's viewfinder, Jeff saw the man slam the Mercedes' door shut, then look right across the street, staring straight at him. The shutter clicked, the little motor inside whirred, and another snapshot slid out of the front of the camera.

Jeff lay the film on the roof of the Trans Am, then looked up. But the man was gone. One of the dark doors under the Gothique marquee slowly closed.

The Mercedes pulled away from the curb and drove off southbound on Damen.

Suddenly, Jeff felt something behind him, and froze.

Something behind, and *below* him.

He heard a snort.

Jeff backed away from his car, and slowly turned around.

Looked down.

Sox stared up at him with his big, brown eyes, giving Jeff his patented *'Got a treat, mister'* look.

"Don't worry, he don't bite." Frank Hoelevich stood in the shadows of his gangway. "He's just saying hi. Dumb dog's always on the prowl for a handout. He'd go up to anybody."

Jeff leaned down and patted the sheltie's head. Sox leaned against his leg and lowered his ears, inviting more. The caramel and white fur was shaggy and unbrushed, but soft as mink anyway.

"Come on, Sox, quit bothering the man."

"No problem," Jeff said. "I'm a sucker for dogs myself. Had a pound mutt when I was a kid. Wish I could have one now."

Frank called the dog over and hooked a leash to Sox' collar. "Careful what you wish for, you just might get it. Care to walk this fellow every night?" Sox strained at the leash. "So, you a photographer or something?"

"Me? No." Jeff looked down at the camera in his hands. "No, I was just taking some snapshots of the theater across the street."

"Yeah, I noticed."

"It's an unusual looking place," Jeff said. "I did some work for them. I'm —"

What? Jeff usually stumbled when he tried to explain what he did for a living to anyone outside the business. *An artist? Art Director? Designer?* "I'm in publishing."

"Shame about that old place," Frank said. "'Gothique'. Now what the hell is *that?* Whatever it's going to be, it doesn't sound good. Say, you ever been there when it was still 'The Palace'?"

"No, actually I'm from the other side of town. But I bet it was a real showplace."

"It was." Frank started down the sidewalk, with Sox a few feet up ahead and sniffing everything his black nose could reach. Then Frank stopped. "Funny, though. There's something about that place now. Sounds goofy, I guess, but it doesn't seem...wholesome." Sox tugged on the leash. "Well, good night to you."

Jeff watched them go. He thought about the photos in the Gothique brochure he press-approved today. All those macabre models, anorexic kids fresh from a horror movie set. Or a dominatrix den. "You don't know how '*un*-wholesome' it is," he muttered to himself.

He grabbed the snapshots off the roof and hopped back into the car. The pictures were developed now, and Jeff gave them a once over.

Then, a twice and three times over.

Strange.

He squinted at the photos. There was the old theater building. There was the marquee, there was his logo, practically filling the frame. There was that Mercedes at the curb.

Even the theater's dark glass door was half open, blurred in the photo, but clearly there.

But that man, the man in the black suit...

He just wasn't in the photos. As if he hadn't been there at all.

ELEVEN

Gabrielle just *knew* that Brandon and Fitch would chicken out.

Even Frostbite and Gem hemmed and hawed and made excuses about band practice, though everyone knew they had a better chance of getting hit by a bus than landing a paying gig. Without a percussionist, a lead singer (only Gem's Liz Phair-on-Drano screeching) a P.A. or an ounce of talent, they were doomed to play to their empty apartment.

Gabrielle left them at Rimbaud's Cave with their noses buried in their wineglasses and gaming zines. Brandon and Fitch, Frostbite and Gem — the four of them just creeped out when Gabrielle's new friends showed up. *'Some people seemed to think it was all about Maybeline and fishnets and memorizing Anne Rice,'* she thought as she waltzed out with her new clique.

The big, black Caddie barely quivered as it sped over the potholes on Clark Street. In the back seat, Gabrielle was stuck in the middle, with her legs splayed over the hump on the floor and Chelsea squirming on her lap. Beside her, Cass stared out the window, or pretended to anyway, watching the Lincoln Park yuppies transform into Clark Street hustlers as they headed north. Cass wasn't talking, at least not to Gabrielle, and she figured he was still pissed at her for the verbal slice 'n dice on his fag-hag roomie.

But she wasn't done with Colleen Russell yet, not by a mile.

"Man, I just adore this car," Chelsea said, stroking the tufted velour. "It reminds me of a hearse or something."

Gabrielle rolled her eyes and wished Chelsea would just shut up. But the girl kept prattling on. "I knew some guys who had a hearse once. No, for real. But it was really old and scuzzy and hardly ever ran. Not like this thing at all."

Gabrielle shifted in her seat, trying to find a comfortable position, but Chelsea kept squirming on her lap. It was wrinkling holy hell out of Gabrielle's skirt, making it ride way up her thighs, right over the tops of her black opaque stockings and the black garters laying stripes across her pasty thigh. Gabrielle would have happily hiked the skirt up over her head if she thought it would get a rise out of anyone. But she glanced at Cass on her left, Fonda on her right, and stifled a laugh. Cass was trying to look all casual, trying not to be too obvious about doggie drooling over Drake up front.

While Fonda had *his* eyes on Cass.

Drake? He kept his on the traffic buzzing by on Clark.

And Arianne?

Gabrielle didn't know what Arianne was looking at. That one was all ice, not that Gabrielle knew any of them that well. But Arianne seemed to be elsewhere, even though she was just an arm's reach away in the front seat.

"Funny I haven't seen you guys before at any clubs or shows or readings or anything." Chelsea kept on gabbing. "So you met Gabrielle at Dark Mystique, huh? That's so cool. I keep begging her to get me a job there, you know. I mean, it is *so* lame waitressing, I can't even begin to tell you. A fucking uniform, my tits practically hanging out, flinging pizzas to yuppie scum, can you believe it?"

Gabrielle shoved Chelsea halfway off her lap onto Cass, just enough to get the girls' rat's nest of over-moussed hair out of her face. "Chelsea, put a cork in it, will you?"

"Here, put this in it instead." Fonda handed a bottle of sloe gin to Chelsea. She smiled at him, batting fake eyelashes as she guzzled.

"So Drake," Gabrielle said, "What cemetery are we going to?"

But it was Fonda who answered. "Graceland, darling."

"Oh. Right. I've been there before. I paint there sometimes. I just love those old mausoleums and the statues and everything. It's so...*authentic.*"

"*Authentic* what?" Drake said from the front seat. Those were the first words he'd said all night.

"Oh, you know, 'authentic'...like...'Gothic'," Gabrielle said. "Like Shelley and Coleridge and Whitby and *Les Innocents*. You know."

"No, actually," Drake said.

"Well, just like...like the atmosphere. The vibes. All those lagoons, the willows, the monuments. I think it's what Highgate Cemetery must be like. You know, in England?"

"It's a sty."

It was Arianne. Everyone in the car looked her way.

"What's a — "

"It's not like you see in the magazines," Drake said. "You can't even go into most of the old, interesting parts of the cemetery, where all the famous poets and artists are buried. Too dangerous." He turned the Caddie off Clark and onto a side street.

"Wow, you've been there?" Gabrielle said, first to Drake then turning to Arianne. "But isn't that where Bram Stoker got, like, all his inspiration? I mean, for Lucy's tomb, and — "

"Rubbish." It was Arianne again. Just a word, that was all she said. Just a word, but it silenced Gabrielle. Arianne's voice was so odd — low, yet musical. Like a viola. Or an oboe. Or both. There, yet somehow distant at the same time.

Cass turned away from the window he was pretending to look out of. "So, are we going to set some rules before we get there? I don't know what clan you guys are supposed to be, what characters you are, what traits you have. Maybe we should have brought one of Fitch's gamebooks?"

"We don't play," Fonda giggled. "Not role-playing games."

Drake pulled the Cadillac into a dark alley. Across the street, Graceland Cemetery loomed somewhere in the darkness behind a barely visible wrought iron fence. "We're just going in for a stroll," Drake said as he shut off the car. "Just to drink in some of that 'authentic' atmosphere."

Fonda giggled again. He giggled a lot. "Yeah, some of those 'vibes', man. Drink 'em in."

Drake turned around and leaned over the front seat. "Come on now, Cassidy, don't tell me you really go in for all those silly role-playing games? You?"

"N-no," Cass mumbled, eyes locked with Drake's opal irises. "No, but I just assumed..."

Drake shook his head and smiled. His teeth seemed to sparkle, even in the dark interior. "It's really kind of kiddie comic book stuff, don't you think? I'd say when it becomes a TV series that can't last a season, it's time to call it passé, right?"

"R-right, Drake."

"Absolutely, Drake," Gabrielle butted in. "All that gaming shit's just gotten so...suburban. I figured we just came here to party." She turned to Arianne. "*I* knew — "

But Arianne was already out of the car.

She stood by the curb, summer breezes buffeting her long dark hair, licking at the edges of her short, flimsy white dress.

She didn't look at Gabrielle. Didn't look back at the car. She looked straight ahead into the dark, and set off across the street towards the cemetery fence.

"All right," Drake said. "Let's party, then."

✦

The two 23rd district cops were royally pissed off when the call came over their belt radios. Hajih just brought out fresh crullers from the back, the double iced ones with gooey glaze all over, and thick chocolate on top. And they hadn't even peeled the lids off their extra large's with cream and sugar yet. They were mighty pissed that they had to pass on the donuts and hop back in their squad.

"Screams in fucking Graceland again," one cop said to the other as they peeled away from the donut shop. "Wait. Just you wait till October. Come Halloween, Hajih will have to deliver the goddamn donuts to us there, because we'll be baby-sitting tombstones all night."

The call came in on 911 from an apartment across the El tracks on

Kenmore. Another unit would swing by to check out the caller's story and would probably write up some neighbor with a TV on too loud and the windows open. It was summer, for chrissakes, couldn't people turn the volume down one goddamn notch on their slasher movies? Sure, another unit would pop over later. Later, after *they'd* eaten Hajih clean.

A rent-a-guard let the squad through Graceland's ornate iron gates on Clark Street. He hopped in back and rode with the cops up and down and all around the cemetery's winding lanes. *He* hadn't heard a thing, but then he'd been blaring his radio in the office all night.

They made two rounds, and it was a big cemetery. The squad's spotlight roamed across the fancy mausoleums and creepy statues, lighting up familiar Chicago names like Pullman, Armour, Marshall Field, Mies Van der Rohe.

But no freshly painted graffiti. No overturned tombstones. No neighborhood punks stuffing beer cans into their jackets and hightailing it for the fence.

"Bet your ass some bimbette just lost her cherry by the lagoon and hollered before it started to feel good," the cop who was driving said, midway through the second round. "Bet your ass that's all —"

"Stop the car," the other cop said. He actually laid his hand on his partner's arm.

The rent-a-guard in the back seat pressed his face right up against the window, his eyes following the spotlight stream as it sliced through the ground fog and darkness into the tombstone maze. All he could manage was a hoarse "Holy shit."

The squad pulled over. Both cops unsnapped the clasps over their revolvers. The rent-a-guard felt along his belt and wished he was licensed to carry.

The driver swung the spotlight back and forth, saw nothing move in the darkness, but saw what he saw, saw what the other two saw, and he knew it would be hours before he and his partner would get anywhere near coffee and fresh crullers.

"Holy shit is right," he said, reaching for the door handle and unholstering his .38. But it was going to take a lot more than donuts and coffee, it would take double shots at O'Bannion's after the shift to wash away the grisly sight just fifty feet away from the car, glistening under the spotlight beam.

✦

Gabrielle tried to keep up with Drake and Fonda.

They dashed through the dark and the fog towards the fence, but every dazed step sent her careening into another monument as they raced out of the cemetery. Finally Arianne glided up from behind, took her by the hand, and suddenly they were both up and over the iron spikes. It all happened so fast — the black Caddie fired up and spun out of the alley with screeching tires. The back door flew open, and Arianne shoved her inside. As the car roared down the street towards Clark, Gabrielle climbed up the back seat and looked out the rear window. She caught a glimpse of red and blue mars lights flashing deep inside Graceland Cemetery.

"We're...w-we're just going to leave them there?" Gabrielle said.

Fonda turned around and leered at her. His pallid face was splattered red. His grinning lips shined wet. "You want to go back? Drake can drop you off at the gate, precious."

Drake slapped Fonda on the back of the head. "Leave her alone, man."

"Why? She wanted to drink in some vibes. She wanted authentic atmosphere," Fonda giggled. "Well, you got 'authentic', Gabby-girl. How'd you like it?"

Drake ran the Caddie through a yellow, then let go of the wheel and twisted Fonda around. "Just sit quiet."

"Why?"

Drake jerked his eyes back towards Arianne.

"Oh." Fonda shriveled in his seat and stared straight ahead.

"Just play with your toys," Drake said. Fonda nodded, not giggling for once. But as he started to paw through Chelsea's rhinestone purse and Cass' wallet, his giggles erupted again. Dollar bills, keys, loose change — Fonda sniffed each item, then tossed them out the window.

In the back seat, Arianne draped a long, cool arm around Gabrielle's shoulders. "You are troubled?"

Gabrielle shivered. "N-no, I...I just...I — "

"The girl, she was special to you?"

"Chelsea? No, she was just...well, I mean, yeah, sometimes we...well, you know. Chelsea was just..."

Chelsea was just ...*what?*

Chelsea was just teetering on her tiptoes at the edge of a tall tombstone one moment, guzzling the last of Fonda's gin, laughing, drunk, flirting with Drake. Flirting with anyone willing to watch. Gabrielle ignored her, too busy traipsing through the grave rows. Fonda lounged beneath the pillars flanking a mausoleum doorway, doing his best to scoot closer to Cass. But Cass slinked away. His eyes were riveted on Drake.

One moment Chelsea was up on tiptoes at the edge of that tombstone, posing there like a tipsy ballerina, with the pint dangling in her hand. Maybe too much merlot and sloe gin got the best of her. Her face turned green right under the rouge slashes and eyeshadow. Chelsea wavered, laughed, started to slip off the edge of the stone, laughing some more.

That one moment Chelsea was laughing.

The next, Chelsea squealed. She tumbled off the tombstone and belly flopped on the grass.

Hard.

And that's when Drake pounced.

Chelsea's goofy squeal turned into a scream when he jumped on top of her and started to rip off her clothes.

Cass sat up on the mausoleum steps. Gabrielle stepped away from Arianne.

"I told him to stop," Gabrielle said. "I thought...I thought he was trying to rape her."

Arianne nodded and drew Gabrielle closer.

"I thought he was...I thought..."

"Hey, man, lay off," Gabrielle shouted, "She doesn't want to — "

But Drake's head spun around and froze the words right in Gabrielle's mouth. She saw his face, and it wasn't like the movies, wasn't like the magazines, wasn't like the books or gaming mags or CD covers, wasn't like anything she ever saw before. Drake's eyes glowed red hell fire in his dark sockets, and blood dripped like black syrup from his mouth. He snarled at her, then plunged his head back down to Chelsea's naked breasts, and bit down. Bit down hard. And Chelsea screamed again.

"Oh just shut the fuck up," he gurgled. But she kept on screaming. Till Drake swiped at her throat with clawed hands, and Gabrielle heard a sickening sound, a snapping, mushy, wet sound. Chelsea stopped screaming then. She just made awful, little bleating sounds, flopping there on the wet grass under Drake.

"You will miss her, this girl?" Arianne asked, running her long, white fingers through Gabrielle's hair. The Caddie turned right off Clark. Warm breezes blew through the open front windows. Up front, Fonda torched drivers licenses and ID cards with a cigarette lighter, watching each one flame, then tossing them out the window.

"Chelsea? Well...I..." Gabrielle leaned her head into Arianne's breasts. The white dress was so silky, so cool on her cheek. And Arianne was so soft, so calm underneath that smooth white dress. "No. I won't miss her."

Cass leaped off the mausoleum steps, but Fonda was on him in a flash. Gabrielle saw Fonda's face light up just like Drake's, red coals burning in dark rings, white skin tinted pink by the glow. His mouth gaped open, and he lunged at Cass' throat. They fell back down on the steps. Cass struggled at first. He punched and kicked and squirmed. But then he stopped. His arms just flopped onto Fonda's back. His hands tugged at Fonda's shirt, pulled him closer, and Cass just moaned and whimpered like a little boy sleeping through his first wet dream.

"And the other, the young man?" Arianne's cool fingers traced delicate lines down Gabrielle's neck, across her chest, slid under her dress and drew lazy circles around and around her breasts. "You wished to save him?"

"I don't know, I..." Gabrielle squirmed as Arianne's hand roamed under her dress. She curled up on the tufted velour seat and nestled in Arianne's lap. Another cool, white hand stroked her leg, danced over the top of her black stocking and up over her bare thigh. "I hardly knew Cass, I...only met him a few...mmmm..."

"So it does not trouble you?" Arianne's hand slid under Gabrielle's garter strap, crawled up inside her panties.

"Mmmm, no...I..."

"But there is something," Arianne said. One cool finger slid through warm, wet folds, fluttering with a feather touch. "Something, or *someone* else?"

"Some...no." A face flashed before her eyes — red hair, a black T-shirt, an angry stare, white tennis shoes stomping out of Rimbaud's Cave. But Gabrielle's' thighs clenched and unclenched on that cool hand. "No, nothing...no." She grabbed hold of the velour seat and sucked in her breath.

Chelsea's screaming stopped. Cass' moaning stopped. For a moment, the cemetery was as quiet as a cemetery at night should be. Then Drake stood up from the mess that was left of Chelsea, wiping his pale hand across his mouth and licking his sticky wet fingers clean. He ambled across the grass and knelt down by Cass and Fonda.

And all the while, she just stood there, Gabrielle just stood there. Didn't scream, didn't cry, didn't try to run. Just stood there, feeling Arianne's presence behind her, feeling that cool, soothing presence right behind her, bathing her, enveloping her.

Then she felt Arianne's touch, felt those cool, cool hands on hers, leading her across the grass, stepping right over Chelsea's naked, bloody body.

Arianne led her to Cass.

Drake pulled the Cadillac to a stop at the curb. "So, where to?"

Arianne slowly slipped her hands out from under Gabrielle's dress. "This will be fine, thank you."

Fonda jumped out of the car and opened the back door. Arianne slid out, then leaned back in with one hand held out to Gabrielle. "Come," she said. Gabrielle hesitated for a moment, then straightened her dress and stepped out onto the sidewalk. The warm, night air slapped her in the face.

The red dripping from Drake's and Fonda's mouths looked black in the pitch dark cemetery. Fonda looked up at Arianne, and Gabrielle heard a question, even though his lips never moved. "Yes," Arianne answered, "Go ahead."

Fonda smiled and bit down on his own wrist. He lowered it to Cass' mouth, and Gabrielle watched the blood ooze out, dribbling all over Cass' face, all over his lips.

Cass still twitched a little when Fonda was done. Tremors shook through his body every few seconds. His beautiful black velvet pants were pulled halfway down his legs, revealing pallid skin and shredded black briefs and streaks of blood. His beautiful ruffled shirt was splashed with red, his hairless chest shimmered with dark wetness. Hoarse whispers of air wheezed out of his open mouth. He looked up at Gabrielle, his eyes pleading. She thought she saw him shake his head, but it was so dark, she wasn't sure, it could just have been shivers.

"Go on, child," Arianne said. "It's what you wanted. What you've dreamt about. Isn't it?" Arianne clutched the back of Gabrielle's neck and pushed her down over Cass. "Go ahead. Taste."

Once the Caddie pulled away, Gabrielle let Arianne lead her across the sidewalk. If Arianne let go, she was sure her legs would buckle, sure she'd fall flat on the concrete. Gabrielle looked up, then smiled.

The huge marquee loomed overhead, the streetlight's glow reflecting on the red gothic letters and the black background.

GOTHIQUE.

Arianne drew Gabrielle close, tilted her head up. Black eyes, the blackest eyes, like black diamonds, drilled into Gabrielle's. Arianne leaned forward and kissed her. "I can still taste him on your lips, child. Can you?"

Gabrielle ran her tongue over her lips. She tasted Arianne there, but she tasted more.

She tasted sin and sex and death and lies and all the savory flavors of a thousand secret wishes. She could still taste Cass' blood on her lips, the blood she tasted from his throat while he died on the damp grass in a dark graveyard on a muggy Chicago night.

"Yes, I can still taste him."

"And how does it feel, child?"

"It feels..." Gabrielle turned away from Arianne's black eyes. She glanced back at Damen Avenue, at the streetlights, the two-flats and storefronts, at a geranium bed blooming along a gangway, a mailbox on the corner, a rusted out car parked down the street. She turned back to Arianne. "It feels...it feels just fine."

Gabrielle followed Arianne through the door.

TWELVE

"Read 'em and weep, Padre." Frank Hoelevich fanned his full house out on the table, and treated himself to another gulp from his glass of beer. "I warned you, I felt lucky tonight."

Father Silverez looked at his measly two pairs. "I still think you're cheating. It's the dog, isn't it? You two have a code? He spots the cards and winks to you, right?"

Frank leaned over to pat Sox on the rump. "Nah, pinochle's his game." Sox ignored him, busy below the table wrestling with a ham bone half his own size. "What do you say, one more hand?"

The priest checked his watch and his empty glass. "One more, sure." He shuffled the cards while Frank slid the last hand's winnings to his side of the table — seventy three cents. "Hey Mike, another over here?"

The bartender filled two pilsner glasses of Blatz and brought them around to their table, neatly sidestepping Sox. "I was gonna use that ham bone in the split pea soup for tomorrow. But I guess Sox'll enjoy it more," he said. "Hell, I'll just toss in some more bullion. Here you go, Father."

"Thanks," Silverez said. "Remind me not to order split pea tomorrow." The priest dealt a fresh hand.

It went fast, and Frank only needed a pair of nines to collect the buck-twelve ante.

Though Sox gnawed the ham bone pretty clean, Mike the bartender wrapped it in foil anyway and stuck it in the fridge for the next visit. Frank and Father Silverez bid their goodnights and let Sox lead them out of the air conditioned bar. Taking a moment to readjust to the muggy night air, they paused below the *Mike's Tavern* sign — trilingual these days, mindful of the neighborhood clientele — *Cold Beer* on top, *Zimne Piwo* in the middle, *Cerveza Fria* more recently added to the bottom.

Sox strained at his leash like it was his mission in life, nosing sidewalk trash and hydrants as they headed north on Damen. Frank Hoelevich's two-flat with the long shuttered hardware store on the first floor was four blocks straight ahead. St. Alstantius' Parish, where Father Gilberto 'Gil' Silverez was the Pastor (and these days, the only priest) was just a little further and around the corner on Montrose.

"All this loose change will drive me crazy," Frank said. "You take it, Padre."

"You won every hand but one tonight. That dog *can* read the cards for you."

"Seriously, Gil. What am I going to do with nine dollars in coins?" Frank looped Sox' leash around his wrist, then emptied the change from his pockets. He cupped the coins into his hands and pushed them at the priest. "Go on, I'm not spending an extra hundred years in Purgatory just for gambling with the Pastor."

"If you do overtime in Purgatory, buddy, it'll be for skipping Mass every week." But Father Silverez loaded the change into his pants pockets. "There, I'm nine up on last week's collection already. You know, if you showed up sometime other than just Easter and Christmas, maybe you could convince your wife to stop coming to the 10:30."

Frank shook his head. "Not likely. Libbie's gone to 10:30 Mass every Sunday since we moved to the neighborhood in '48."

"But it's in Spanish, Frank. The 10:30's the Latino Mass, you know that."

"I know, and Libbie knows it too, but it used to be the Polish Mass till...well, until a few years ago. Anyway, Libbie says she kind of likes the Mexican Mass. It reminds her of the old Latin. Sounds pretty much the same."

They waited out a red light at the corner. Pointlessly, though — no traffic scooted by either way. Damen and the sidestreets were quiet as a graveyard.

"You'd have liked it around here back then," Frank said. "Back in '48 I mean, when Libbie and I first moved here. Every one of these storefronts was a nice little shop, you had your friends sitting out on their front porches on hot nights like this, even this late. Just talking, sharing a cold one. Right over there, that was Buddy Yulkowski's place. He used to make his own slivovitz — plum wine, you know — could burn the tongue right out of your mouth. Mix that up with 7-Up on ice, now that went down smooth on a hot summer night. Up there, that's where Stan Lemovicky had his appliance shop. Bought our first TV from Stan. He used to go deer hunting up in Wisconsin every fall, made his own deer jerky and it was as good as any Slim Jim, let me tell you. And over there..." Frank looked at his faint reflection passing by in a dirty storefront window. "Well, things sure have changed. But you'd have liked it, Gil."

"Maybe. I don't know how your old friends would have liked me. My Polish is about as good as your Mexican."

Now Frank caught Father Silverez' reflection in the next vacant shop's cracked glass. The priest's wide neck strained at his clerical collar. Under a close cropped brush of salt 'n pepper hair, his light brown skin shined with sweat. Father Silverez was a burly fellow, looking robust for his even sixty years, looking a lot more like a dockhand than a priest. He laughed like a regular guy, joked like a regular guy. Even drank his Blatz like a regular guy, and that's what Frank liked about him.

'Course, he still played poker like a priest.

"In my book, it doesn't matter whether you go for enchiladas or kielbasa, so long as you're good people. No, they'd have liked you round here just fine. Anyway, you're a priest. And a vet. What's not to like?" They passed a rusted out station wagon up on blocks, a stack of sunbleached parking tickets tucked under its broken windshield wiper. "See, now that — *that* never would have been here back in '48, Gil."

"Course not. It's a '91 Toyota."

"You know what I mean. The cops would have had that hulk towed right away." Sox lifted his snout from the sidewalk and let out a half interested growl. Up ahead, Frank spotted a lonely figure bouncing off lampposts. "And *that* — well, you never would have to worry about a bum hanging around, about getting mugged, about walking down your own damn street at night."

"Want to move to the other side?"

"Why? I got my guard dog here."

"Sox would be sniffing the guy for handouts while he rolled you."

"You underestimate my pal here, Padre."

"Well, just don't go all brave on me, Frank. I'd like to give my Sunday sermon without a shiner to explain."

"Oh, you worry too much. Anyway, you were a Marine, what's to worry about?"

"A Marine *chaplain,* Frank. It's not like I was in the Special Forces or anything, you know?"

The figure drew closer, till Frank and the priest could see it was just a kid, drunk or stoned or both. He passed right by without a word, clutching his neck and bouncing off more lampposts as he disappeared down Damen.

"You never talk about it, do you?" Father Silverez asked.

"About what?"

"You know what. About the service. About the war. Mike's told me that —"

"Mike wouldn't know his ass from a ham bone. Don't be listening to stories Mike tells."

But Mike had plenty.

He opened his bar the same year Frank and Libbie started their hardware store. Mike told Silverez how you'd never guess it by Frank Hoelevich's quiet ways, by his gentle smile, told the priest how Frank had seen the very worst that World War II could show a kid from Chicago. The 1st Division under General Stormin' Norman Cota was in the first wave on bloody Omaha at Normandy on a gray morning in June of '44, hit the Siegfried Line near St. Vith, took it on the chin in the Hurtgen Forest, and was overrun by SS Panzers in the Battle of the Bulge. But the 1st survived, and marched into Germany in the spring of '45.

Not that Frank Hoelevich saw that last march.

He took shrapnel in the arm bright and early on D-Day morning. Got patched up and was hit again at Ouren in December, this time by a black uniformed Waffen SS guard with a burp gun, who giggled like a little maniac when he mowed down a group of American prisoners; a lot of that went on in

The Bulge. Frank had bullets in his leg, his left lung and his hip, but he played dead till the bastards left, and crawled off in the snow, dragging a wounded corporal — a kid even younger than himself. Crawled four frigid miles till he reached an American column, crawled — thinking the whole miserable time about a sweet young thing named Elizabeth that lived off Montrose and Hoyne who liked to go by Libbie, just like the canned vegetables, and who he'd only kissed once and that was at Union Station before he shipped off.

When they found him, Frank was still dragging that corporal. The kid was frozen solid. And dead.

Mike knew plenty of stories about Frank. About how Frank dived on top of a German potato masher to save his buddies, and when the grenade turned out to be a dud and they hauled him up, poor Frank had pissed his pants, but the troopers stole a clean pair from the C.O. they were so grateful. About how Frank could core an apple at fifty yards if the sight on his M-1 could be trusted. About the Purple Heart and the Distinguished Service Cross stashed somewhere in the flat above the old empty hardware store. Mike was a field commissary sergeant in the 1st himself, so he knew plenty.

"You know, Frank, if you ever want to talk about anything, I am a priest."

"Yeah, I know." Frank didn't say anything as they passed another shuttered storefront, then a weed choked vacant lot. "There's nothing to talk about. 'Talking about' it, that's a — a modern thing, you know? Not for me." They drew up to Frank's two-flat. "Gil, I saw a lot of things over there that nobody in God's whole universe ought to see. And I don't want to see anything like that ever again."

"Amen."

Sox halted.

His tail shot up just as his ears flipped back on his head. The dog peeked into the gangway and started to growl. A real growl this time, his caramel and white furred snout wrinkling to show his fangs.

"What the hell? Sox, what is it?"

But Frank and Silverez saw soon enough, dark as it was in that gangway.

They saw two silhouettes moving beside the two-flat's brick walls. They saw a skinny punk in shiny leather gear pawing at an even skinnier girl, one hand ripping her blouse off while the other tugged at her skirt. The punk had his head bobbing between the girl's bared breasts.

Sox started barking and wouldn't stop. Frank could barely hold on to the leash.

The punk in the gangway looked up.

And damn if it didn't look just like his eyes glowed, like they turned red as stoplights.

"Jesu Maria," Silverez said, crossing himself.

Sox kept on barking. Finally he gave a good tug, and pulled the leash right out of Frank's hand. The sheltie lunged into the darkness.

"Sox, no — " Frank ran after him.

The punk in the gangway stepped away from the girl, and she slid down to the sidewalk. A booted foot shot out and clipped Sox across the back, sending the dog flying right into the opposite wall, all fifty five pounds of him. The punk's face was white as a ghost, but he didn't look scared as he shoved Frank aside and bolted out of the gangway. He paused when he flew past the priest, but even then, only for an instant, and for that instant his pale face almost *did* look scared. But just for that instant. Then the punk smiled at Gil Silverez mouthing another 'Jesu Maria', laughed, and vanished somewhere in the darkness across Damen Avenue.

"Frank, are you okay?" Father Silverez dashed into the gangway, where Sox was still barking and Frank was helping the girl up.

"Yes, I'm fine. Help me with her, Gil."

But the skinny girl with the ten dollar hooker's makeup pushed Frank away. She kicked Father Silverez with a stiletto heel and stood up on her own. "What the fuck are you doing?" She stood there with her skirt halfway down her thighs, her stockings shredded and her torn blouse flapping wide open in the muggy breeze. She didn't even look at Frank or the priest. Instead, she looked right past them and out the gangway, out to Damen Avenue and across the street.

"Frank, maybe we could bring her inside, call the police?"

"Sure, Gil." Frank turned to the girl. "Come on, straighten yourself up and we can go — "

"Go to hell, old man." She stomped right past them and out of the gangway. There, she paused to yank up her skirt. Her dignity back, she turned around. "Why the fuck did you butt in?" Then she was gone.

Frank got hold of Sox' leash and quieted the dog.

"Maybe we should call the cops anyway?" Silverez said.

Frank shrugged his shoulders, staring down the gangway. The Palace loomed up across Damen Avenue. Frank could see a slice of the marquee from here. Just the red 'G-O-T-H' of GOTHIQUE. "Maybe." He turned back to Silverez. "Maybe. They're both gone. I guess she didn't want any help, huh?"

"No, she didn't."

"Maybe what I *should* do is walk with you to St. Alstantius? Me and the dog, what do you say?"

Silverez shook his head. "No, you'd just have to walk back alone. Or we could escort each other back and forth all night. No, I'll be fine, Frank. Whatever that punk was up to, he's gone now."

"Still — "

"Frank, I'll be fine. It's only a couple blocks." Silverez started up the gangway. He stopped when he reached the front sidewalk, and turned back. "Frank? Did...did you see her..."

"Her — her chest? Yep. There was blood all over."

Father Silverez nodded.

"So what the hell was that sicko doing to her?" Frank said. "And why was she letting him?"

"I'm not sure, Frank, but I'd have to say he was *biting* her."

"Biting her? Biting her — her boobs?"

"And I'd have to say she *wanted* him to." Father Silverez turned onto the sidewalk. "Frank, you get your ass to Church Sunday."

THIRTEEN

The Park Stratford wasn't a particularly tall hotel, at least not by downtown Chicago standards, where buildings under forty stories somehow didn't count. It wasn't actually in a park, though there were some trees and grass surrounding the landmark Chicago Water Tower across the street. But if it did seem to cower in the shadows of the marble and glass canyons, the Park Stratford's twelve stories commanded an impressive view nonetheless, overlooking Michigan Avenue's ersatz town square at the intersection with Chicago Avenue.

The charming view was lost on Blair Armstrong.

She had the blinds and the drapes both shut tight in the small but plush room on the Park Stratford's eleventh floor. Though the morning had been overcast, and the afternoon promised rain, it would still be too bright for a lunch hour romp otherwise. Anyway, all those skyscrapers looming over the hotel had an awful lot of windows, and all of them seemed to stare right at this eleventh floor room.

Blair already ordered bottled spring water and ice from room service. She almost forgot the sodas for Jeff. The bellhop was just wheeling his cart back into the elevator when Jeff got off on the eleventh floor. He knocked at Room 1115, and Blair opened the door, standing there in her black half slip, her bra, and a smile.

She didn't stand on ceremony. Blair went right to work on Jeff's clothes. Blue blazer, loafers, socks, khakis and boxers were off almost before the door closed. While Blair fumbled with his shirt buttons, Jeff waltzed her through the drawn drape dimness, back to the bed. They didn't manage to get Jeff's shirt off, or Blair's slip off, didn't manage to get her bra off, didn't even pull back the comforter. The sex was urgent, but then she'd spent the entire morning making eyes at him across a conference table back at the office while the other department heads droned through monthly budget reports, with Roberta Whitehead herself presiding. That's where Blair slipped Jeff the note, neatly typed on a Charade Magazine memo: *Park Stratford. Room 1115. Noon. Attendance Mandatory.*

The sex was as quick as it was good as it was loud, and after they were done, Jeff and Blair finally stripped off the last of their clothes, pulled back the comforter, poured soda and a Perrier on ice, and stretched out on the king size bed.

"Well, that's been overdue," Blair said, rubbing the cold room service glass over her forehead. She snuggled closer, her shoulder length blonde hair clingy and damp, spreading across Jeff's chest.

"It has been a while."

"Six weeks, mister. And yes, I have been counting."

"So, why have we been on hiatus? I know I've been putting in a lot of extra time handling all this ghoul-graphics garbage, but so have you. Long hours never stopped us before."

Blair shrugged her shoulders. "Things are different."

"Oh?"

"Jeff, don't pretend you don't know what I'm talking about."

"You mean Jacks?"

"Of course I mean Jacks. You're into this whole father-daughter bonding thing all of a sudden."

"You sound jealous."

"Maybe I am, in a way. I never had to share you with anyone." Blair sat up on the bed. "Except the magazine."

He sat up next to her and massaged her back and shoulders. "All right, I'm not sure I want to be doing overnights at your place while Jacks is here for the summer. She may be all grown up, but not so grown up I want to leave her home alone at night. Come to think of it, maybe she's *too* grown up to leave home alone at night." Jeff wrapped his arms around her. "But there's a simple solution. You just have to trek down to the provincial south side more often."

"Would it be a huge surprise if I pointed out that I'm not much for the bungalow and backyard barbecue scene?" Blair reached for her bottled spring water. "Anyway, maybe you shouldn't be rubbing me in your daughter's nose."

"I think Jacks can handle ol' Dad having a girlfriend."

Blair sank back against him. "A *girlfriend?* Hmmm, you've never called me that before. So, you think of me as your 'girlfriend' huh?"

"All right, what did I say wrong? *Woman*-friend? *Adult-female*-friend?"

"Pals."

"Oh, right. I forgot. Well then, 'pal', why don't you come over for dinner tonight? And plan on staying."

"You think Jacks is *that* grown up?"

"Something tells me Jacks has seen her share of overnight guests and more back in Encino," Jeff said.

"Okay, it's a date, mister." Blair leaned back against Jeff, knocking him down onto the mattress. She spun around on top of him, hair tickling his face, legs gliding around his. Smiling, she reached down and drew Jeff back into her.

"You think we really have time for this?" he said.

Blair peeled her watch off her wrist and tossed it on the nightstand. "It's been six weeks." She kissed her way up his chest and over his neck. "We'll make time."

Afterwards, they rinsed off with a quick shower, then poked around the dimly lit room for their clothes. Thunder rumbled from behind the drawn curtains. Jeff buckled his belt around his khakis and drew back the drapes.

"Hey, I'm still getting dressed," Blair said, climbing into a black skirt.

"Don't worry. No one's going to see in here. Look at the rain." The office and apartment buildings up and down Michigan Avenue were just fuzzy shapes behind the downpour. Jeff plopped down on the bed and buttoned his shirt. He grabbed Blair's blouse off the footboard and tossed it to her. The black silk fluttered into her open arms.

Blair smoothed her skirt down over dark nylons, then slipped the blouse on. Once Jeff found his loafers, he brought Blair's black blazer over. "So, whatever happened to 'summer white'?" He reached around from behind and helped her button the blouse.

"Summer what?"

"Your wardrobe just seems to be a little on the dark side these days."

Blair wiggled into black suede boots. "Well, you know how all creative types adore black. No, I guess you don't. Anyway, why don't you just go with the flow? It wouldn't hurt you to trade in some of those chinos and jeans for something a little more..."

"More *Goth?"*

"No, Jeff, that's not what I meant." She chuckled. "I could just see you dandied up in black leather and a ruffled shirt. A little eyeshadow maybe?" Blair slipped on her black velvet blazer.

"Not likely. They haven't got to *me* yet."

"Oh God, don't start with all that stuff again." She lowered her voice, mimicking him, *"There's something not quite right about that place. I can't put my finger on it, but something —"*

"Well, there *is* something funny about this whole Gothique thing." Jeff took a last drink from his soda and followed Blair to the door. "Haven't you looked at those snapshots I took yet? I'm telling you, that guy was standing right there, and then he doesn't show up on the pho — "

Blair silenced him with a kiss. "Enough about Gothique," she said once their lips parted. "I don't think the devil's setting up shop on Damen Avenue, Jeff." She reached behind her and opened the door. "Now come on, or we're never going to get a cab in that rain."

The thunder shook the Park Stratford's windows as they headed for the elevators.

✦

Jeff and Blair were still shaking rain off their jackets when Colleen Russell knocked on his office door. "Excuse me, Jeff? Got a minute?"

Blair practically leaped away from Jeff and plopped into a visitors chair.

"Sure, Colleen. What's up?"

"We finished up the preliminary layouts for the September issue already. Do you think it would be okay if I cut out early today?"

"I don't see why not," Jeff said, scanning his phone messages. "Is everything okay?"

Colleen hesitated. "Well...actually, no. It's my roommate. He hasn't been home in days, and I'm really getting worried."

"This is — Cass, right?" Jeff said. "That guy who was with you at...at your sister's wake?"

Blair hopped out of the chair and threw a sympathetic arm around Colleen's shoulders. "What's happened?"

Colleen shrugged. "I don't know. He just disappeared. I haven't heard from him in almost a week, and that's just not like Cass."

"You've asked around? Friends? Family?"

"I don't think Cass has any family," Colleen said. "I thought I might try to track down some of his friends today, and Cass has some pretty weird friends."

Jeff put the messages down on his desk and turned to Blair. "It turns out that Cass hangs with a crowd that includes none other than our own Gabrielle."

"You mean the girl you — "

Jeff nodded. "The Gabrielle I fired."

"The Gabrielle whose job I took," Colleen said. "Actually, the last time I saw Cass we were with a group of his 'friends'. Gabrielle included."

Jeff raised an eyebrow. "Is there anything we could do to help?"

"Thanks, but I don't think so."

"Have you considered..." Jeff paused. "Have you thought about calling the police?"

Colleen nodded, biting on her lip. "The last time...the *only* time I've had to deal with the police was...well, you know. I dread it. I keep hoping he'll just be there when I come home from work, and I can brain him for scaring me." She looked ready to cry. "I guess I will have to call them."

Blair gave Colleen's shoulders another squeeze. "You take all the time you want, sweetheart. Right, Jeff?"

"Absolutely. And seriously, if there's anything we can do to help, just holler."

"Thanks, you guys. You've been so good to me, I don't know what I'd —"

The mail cart squeaked into Jeff's office and cut Colleen off. Pulling a rubber banded bundle from the cart was one of Charade's new faces: another androgynous kid dressed in the obligatory black, pierced everything, and made-up eyes only half awake under a mop of dyed hair.

"I'll take it," Colleen said.

"Okay," the kid handed over the bundle of mail. "But I just want you to know that top one isn't my fault."

Colleen glanced at the envelope on top of the bundle. It looked innocuous enough, addressed like most of the department mail:

Whitestar Media Group
211 East Fairmont Court
Chicago, Illinois 60611
Attn: Jeff Stancheck,
Art Director, Charade Magazine

Innocuous enough, at first glance. "So what's so special about this one?" The envelope *was* dirty. A little torn. And it *was* hand addressed, that was a little unusual. Colleen stared at the envelope, stared at the handwriting.

Something...

"Look, I just started in the mail room last week," the kid said. He pointed with a long nail polished finger at the postmark. *June 13th.* "I found a whole bag of mail behind a cabinet yesterday. Probably been there over a month. But don't blame me, it's not my fault."

Colleen looked at the postmark. Looked back at the address. *There was something about that handwriting.* She shrugged her shoulders and handed the mail to Jeff.

"Sorry, Mr. Stancheck," the kid said. "I hope it's nothing important. But like I said, I just started last week, so it's — "

"Not-your-fault" Jeff said. "Got it. Thanks."

The kid backed his cart out of the office, just as Kelly Feeny poked her head in the door. "I'm heading out for lunch, Jeff," she said.

Jeff was busy frowning at the envelope and just waved at her.

"I could be a little late," Kelly added tentatively.

Not really listening, Jeff waved again, and she disappeared.

"Feels like disks," Jeff said, still looking at the envelope. "Oh well, if it didn't cause a crisis for all this time, it can't be too important." He popped open his briefcase and tossed the envelope inside. "You go ahead, Colleen. If you need more time off, just let me know."

"Thanks, Jeff. A lot." Colleen glanced at Jeff's briefcase before she left, still picturing the handwriting on that old envelope.

"Well, back to the real world," Blair said. She winked at Jeff from the doorway. "So, dinner at my place tonight, right?"

"Your place? Oh, right." Blair sauntered out of the office.

Jeff craned his neck to watch Blair sashay down the hall towards editorial. He smiled to himself, and finally stopped watching when Colleen blew past his door, calling "Hold that elevator!"

✦

Colleen and Kelly rode down together.

"Hot date?" Colleen asked.

"It shows, huh?" Kelly looked down at her brand new sleeveless black mini dress.

"Too slinky for a job interview or a press approval, Kelly. You look terrific."

"It's not really me. I just bought this last night." Kelly shifted from one foot to another in black patent leather flats that looked brand new too. She ran a brush through her blandly brown hair, but a rainy July day made it pointless. "You think it's too fancy fór lunch? Get me out of jeans and sweats, and I'm lost."

"I'd bet a guy would prefer to get you out of *that* than jeans and sweats," Colleen said, managing a smile.

"I suppose I shouldn't get too worked up. I mean, it's just lunch. But hey, the big three-O's just around the corner for me. I've been doing bad dates for so long, you'd think I'd at least be doing a bad marriage by now."

The elevator doors opened, and they walked across the marble lobby, Kelly's shiny new flats clicking like tap shoes.

"This must be some guy," Colleen said.

Kelly nodded. "He is. At least, I think he is. We've only gone out once. Well, actually, we didn't really 'go out'." She returned her brush to her purse. They could both see the rain drenching Fairmont Court as they approached the glass doors. "He was at that Gothique poster shoot yesterday. Took me for a drink afterwards. I mean, there were all these fashion models prancing around half naked, and he asked *me* out for a drink. That has to count for something, doesn't it?"

"You never know what lunch can lead to," Colleen said.

"There's his car." Kelly beamed, pointing to a big, black Mercedes sedan idling right out front.

"So what's Mr. Wonderful's name?"

Kelly stepped out into the downpour and popped open her umbrella. "Joey," she called as she dashed to the Mercedes.

FOURTEEN

After getting soaked running from bustops to El platforms, Colleen opted for a taxi after she left Dark Mystique.

Not that it was easy flagging one down this late on a rainy afternoon. Rush hour started early today because of the weather. And this was no summer shower, but a full-blown thunderstorm with ominous clouds, lightning aiming for every rooftop antenna and factory chimney, even a tornado watch for the boonies.

It took almost two hours just to zigzag through the steel and glass canyons of Michigan Avenue, through Old Town's and Lincoln Park's yuppified lofts and brownstones, finally to NewTown, bastion of the trendy six-flat, and to Dark Mystique. Her umbrella was useless against winds that buffeted the rain into nearly horizontal sheets while she hiked still another six blocks from the Ravenswood El stop on Belmont. And as it turned out, the two hours were wasted.

The Morticia-clone behind the counter in the tiny occult bookstore with the Gothrock veneer wasn't particularly interested in looking up from her latest issue of Propaganda to answer questions. At least, not until Colleen leaned over the Siouxsie Sioux And The Banshees retrospective that Ms. Personality was so engrossed in. Colleen's tangles of dripping red hair showered rainwater all over the magazine spread, and that elicited a response. But the girl's snippy answers left Colleen all the more worried: *Yes, she vaguely remembered a swishy gay guy called Cass. No, she hadn't seen him around. No, she hadn't seen Gabrielle either, and if Colleen knew her, she should tell her to pick up her check because she was fired.* Gabrielle hadn't shown up for work all week.

Colleen left Dark Mystique, almost grateful to be back in the rain, if only to wash off the stink from the bookstore's pungent incense. She started back up Halsted, rain pelting her face, thunder booming overhead like a soundtrack from one of Cass' countless horror videos, and decided to look for a cab.

The taxi's patchouli oil air freshener was worse than Dark Mystique's incense, and Colleen heaved a sigh of relief when the rickety green and yellow Checker Marathon finally pulled up in the fringes of urban pioneering land at Elston and Wolcott. The driver grunted at her fifty cent tip, and was already putting the cab in gear while Colleen fumbled with her umbrella for the dash across the sidewalk to Rimbaud's Cave.

Gray and overcast as it was outside, it still took a minute for her eyes to adjust to the day-is-night gloom inside Rimbaud's Cave. The place was nearly empty. It was only 4:00; evidently the Goths and gamers didn't rise till sunset. She ordered a black coffee and headed to the ladies room while that same desultory waitress she'd dealt with on her last visit glared at the two empty pots on the Bunomatic.

On her way down the dark corridor to the bathrooms, Colleen passed Gabrielle's painting, still hanging crooked on the wall next to the men's room door. Pine cleaner and piss potpourri wrinkled her nose while she stared at the picture: an unframed, store-bought, pre-stretched canvas, awkwardly gobbed with dirty colors. It was a bad homage to that same pansexual-graveyard-chic that was always staring back at Colleen on the Charade Art Department computer screens, just more pasty faced, naked figures in various kinky couplings, dribbles of bright cadmium red dabbed across every mouth and neck and breast and wrist. It may or may not have been set in a cemetery; with a little more talent and a little less chic, maybe Gabrielle could have let a viewer know for sure. Or maybe Rimbaud's Cave just hung the painting because they couldn't hang the artist.

Inside the filthy bathroom, Colleen crouched under the hand dryer, blowing rain out of her long hair while she read graffiti that pre-dated Rimbaud's Cave, all the way back through the shabby club's yuppie coffeehouse and biker tavern days. When the hand dryer started to spark, she decided to settle for uncomfortably damp, and squished-squished in wet tennis shoes back out to the bar.

Some non-descript 90's British angst-rock droned out of the speakers while the waitress slid a giant mug of coffee across the bar. Colleen paid and looked around Rimbaud's Cave. Two girls lounged on a threadbare chaise, their black tighted legs intertwined like twisted licorice whips, passing a long cigarette back and forth. A dripping wet boy, couldn't be a day over sixteen, flipped through a bondage magazine at a table by the window, sipping chocolate milk from a wine glass and twirling a finger through the nipple ring shining from inside his black satin vest.

Colleen snapped the strap shut around her umbrella, took a sip from the coffee mug and checked out the foursome huddled together on two sofas in a dark corner. She recognized Frostbite's white shag right away. Then Gem's hennaed pudding bowl hair. The two guys with their heads buried in paperbacks had to be Brandon and Fitch. Just then Gem looked up, recognized Colleen and waved.

"No, we haven't seen him either...Colleen, isn't it?" Gem took a Bi-Di's from Frostbite's pack and lit it, making a big deal of blowing the cloyingly sweet smoke at Brandon and Fitch. "Not since that night Cass brought you slumming among the glitterati. Surprised to see you back here. Hey, me and Frostbite just finished some lyrics for a new song, it's really a killer. Tell us what you think." Gem held out a spiral notebook.

Colleen sat down at the very edge of the sofa. The two boys reluctantly inched over to leave some room. "Um, maybe later." She took Gem's notebook but set it down on the couch. "Look, Cass is good for the occasional all-nighter, but it's just not like him to disappear for this long. Not without calling or something."

"Well, he isn't one for the nine to five routine, is he? Not that we've known him that long," Frostbite said. "Maybe he latched on to some comfy boy-toy-for-hire gig?" He noted Colleen's brows knotting up. "Hey, don't go all innocent on *us*. You want to do the fag-hag scene, you have to — "

Colleen grabbed her umbrella and stood up. "Do you creeps practice being annoying?" She thought about tossing the hot coffee on their elaborate black satins and lace. Better yet, on Gem's notebook.

She just stomped out of Rimbaud's Cave instead.

Once outside, she regretted leaving. It took all afternoon just to make these two stops, and the thunder still boomed and the rain still poured down. Getting a taxi to drop her at Elston and Wolcott was one thing. Finding another to get her home was unlikely. Colleen popped open her umbrella and started off down Elston. There was a bus stop a few wet blocks away.

Back inside Rimbaud's Cave, Gem watched her go from the window then returned to the sofas. "Well, that was a nice chat, wasn't it?" She grabbed her notebook, then eyed up Colleen's still steaming mug of coffee and slid it over her way. "Suppose we should have told her?"

"Told her what?"

"Told her about Gabrielle? And Chelsea? How we haven't seen them either?"

Frostbite shrugged. "So maybe they've all gone straight? Maybe they're holed up somewhere fucking each other's brains out?"

"Maybe," Gem said. "Gabrielle *would* fuck anything that wore black." But she didn't sound convinced. "Not Cass, though. He's confirmed Rive Gauche. And Chelsea? She wouldn't know what a dick was if she grew one herself."

"If Chelsea grew one herself, they wouldn't need Cass." Frostbite whisked the coffee mug away from Gem and downed half.

"No, something's up," she said. "It was those...others."

Frostbite looked back at her from behind the mug. "What about them?"

"I don't know, but they gave me the chills, man. They had some kind of...like an aura, you know?"

"Uh-oh. Going to break out the crystals now?"

"Fuck you, Frost. You know damn well what I mean. You sensed it too. There was some agenda there that I don't want to know about."

The thunder boomed and shook the bare brick walls of Rimbaud's Cave. Even Brandon and Fitch looked up from their paperbacks.

✦

"They're ready, Dad." Jacks put the lid back on the pork chops and untied the apron she wore over her baggies and T-shirt. "Actually, they were ready half an hour ago."

Jeff checked his watch. Almost 7:00. "She should be here soon. Traffic's probably awful with the storm." He set a bottle of white zinfandel out on the table, then took two wineglasses out of the cabinet and rinsed them in the sink.

"Hey, where's my glass?"

"Where it'll be till you're twenty-one, kiddo."

"So, are you sure you don't want me to leave early for the concert?" Jacks said. "Wouldn't you guys prefer a quiet dinner alone? You know, candlelight, soft music..."

"...pork chops, eating in the kitchen." Jeff dried the wineglasses. "No, actually. I miss enough dinners with you with all the extra hours I'm putting in. And you're only here for another month. Anyway, I want you to meet Blair."

Jacks checked the salad bowl and gave the greens another toss. "I've done this drill before, Dad. Mom usually prefers to entertain without me cluttering things up. Like she's afraid I'll eat Spaghetti-O's with my fingers or something." She set the salad bowl on the table, shaking her head. "Parents and dating. Someone should make a guidebook."

By 7:30, they started to eat. Jacks kept Blair's two chops in the oven under foil, and a salad in the fridge.

By 8:00, Jeff was loading the dishwasher. Jacks hovered in the kitchen. "Shouldn't you get ready for your concert?" he asked.

She shrugged her shoulders, handing him a plate. "I suppose. Maybe I should cancel? We could hang out together."

Jeff got the plate Jacks made up for Blair and emptied the chops and veggies in the garbage. "Thanks, kiddo, but don't worry about the old man. Now go and get ready. You smell like pork chops."

Jacks bounded off to her room, and once Jeff cleaned up the kitchen he took his briefcase and headed for his makeshift home office — the bungalow's little third bedroom — where his drafting table and markers still held the prize spot, and an already outdated computer was tucked into a corner. He sat in his desk chair, wondering if he should call Blair, reaching for the phone several times, but never dialing.

"Dad, my friends are out front, I really have to go." Jacks appeared in the doorway.

Jeff blinked at her. The baggies and T-shirt were gone. "You're going out like *that?*"

"Like what?" Jacks looked down at her outfit. "I thought I looked kind of cute."

What Jacks looked like was one of the new hangers-on at Charade: head to toe black, strategically ripped in all the right places, her long, straight brown hair moussed and teased out into a furball, makeup layered on thick and dark.

"You don't like it," Jacks said.

"I hate it," Jeff said. Then he laughed. "God, I sound just like my old man. Yelling at me to get a haircut, and how he was going to burn those pinko-hippie bell bottoms of mine."

"What's a pinko?" Jacks said. "Just kidding. Dad, you're an art director. And for the hippest magazine in town. I expect you to be a little more with it."

Now Jeff looked down at his khakis and loafers, his button down shirt. "That's me, the Chicago creative community's resident sore thumb."

"Are you going to be okay?"

"Sure. Why not?"

"Because you got stood up."

Jeff winced. "It sounds worse when you say it out loud. But I'll be fine, honey. I'm just going to catch up on a little work."

Jacks ran up to her father and gave him a bear hug. "Well, if you ask me, Blair Armstrong doesn't know what she's missing. The coolest guy in town...and my pork chops." She let go and started to back out of the room. "I'll be home at two."

"Midnight," Jeff hollered.

"One thirty?"

"One."

"Deal." She turned to go.

"And Jacks?"

"Yeah, Dad?"

"I really hate those clothes."

She ran back up to him and slugged him on the shoulder. Then Jacks' fishnets and combat boots disappeared through the doorway.

Jeff smiled. "Oh, for the days of PeeWee League and Bunny Ballet class," he said out loud as he turned on his desk lamp and opened his briefcase.

The old letter that the mail room ghoul dropped off that afternoon lay right on top. He tore open the envelope and three floppy disks fell out. There were no labels on them. Jeff glanced at the postmark on the envelope again. *June 13th.*

The day after Megan Russell died.

He turned on the old computer.

Once the machine booted up, Jeff inserted one of the disks. The screen went blank. He tried it again, with the same result. Finally, a message appeared: *This disk cannot be read. Please reformat or try again.* Jeff ejected the disk.

He tried the other two with the same result. Jeff looked them over: there was a crack on one disk's shell, the sliding shield was bent on another. More than likely, the files were corrupted. That envelope had been pretty beat up. He tossed the disks back in his briefcase. "Probably just more Gothique junk anyway," he muttered to himself.

Jeff forgot about the disks and plunged into the piles of papers overflowing from his briefcase. Mounds of changes were routed from Editorial in the late afternoon, but Kelly never brought them in.

In fact, Kelly hadn't even come back from lunch.

✦

Frostbite's pack of clove cigarettes was empty, so he mooched a Marlboro from a kid at the bar while Gem headed to the ladies room.

They'd just finished pleading with the manager again for a gig at Rimbaud's Cave, anything, even a weeknight, even for free. It pained them to grovel at the asshole's feet — the manager was an aging yuppie doing the whole darkwave thing just to get into pretty boys' pants. Gem whispered into Frostbite's ears that maybe he should consider it, but before he could reply, the manager told them to come back when they actually had a band; duo's groaning bad poetry over a pawn shop Strat and a computer programmed keyboard were a dime a dozen.

Frostbite made a face as he passed Rimbaud's Cave's front window. The rain still fell in torrents, if anything, worse than this afternoon when they arrived. He plopped back down on the sofa across from Brandon and Fitch and lit his Marlboro with the last match in a crinkled matchbook. "So what are you reading?" Fitch didn't even look up from his dog-eared Poppy Brite, but Brandon held up his used paperback copy of Baudelaire's *The Flowers Of Evil.*

"Any good?"

"De son empire si nos efforts te delivraient," Brandon started to read, *"Tes basiers ressusciteraient —"*

"Hold on there, Pepe LePeu." Frostbite grabbed the book out of Brandon's hands. "Save your Paris Coven routine for the gaming sessions, okay?" He scanned the page. *"'Though one of us should be the tool...to save thee from thy wretched fate, Thy kisses would resuscitate...the body of thy vampire, fool!'* Hey, this is cool shit. It'd make bitchin' lyrics."

"Baudelaire was like the original Goth, man," Brandon said. "You should read him. You know, he dedicated *Les Fleurs du Mal* to Theophile Gautier."

"Uh-huh. And?"

"Theo Gautier," Brandon said, rolling his eyes. "'The Dead Leman'? 'Clarimonda'? 'La Mort Amoureuse'?"

Frostbite shook out his white shag with a flourish. "And aren't those all just the same story? Sorry, buddy, I'm just in it for the tunes and the scene. Give me more *Lost Boys* and Marilyn Manson. I don't have the patience for all that Victorian crap."

Brandon shook his head and returned to his Baudelaire. But Frostbite was bored without Gem fawning at his side. He flicked some lint off his black velvet pants, then knocked the book out of Brandon's hands with his boot. "So, what do you think about all this?"

Brandon picked up his book and brushed off the wrinkled, pre-owned paperback cover. "All what?"

Frostbite shrugged. "All this weird shit, bookboy. Like, disappearances. Like, Cass' fag-hag telling us he's gone AWOL. Like Gabrielle and Chelsea just vanishing."

"I hadn't really noticed," Brandon said, looking for his page. "Maybe they got real jobs. Maybe they got pinched for public indecency and they're all detoxing in County?"

"Okay, so what about that weird crew Gabrielle brought in that night? Did they give you a chubby in the silkies Fitch makes you wear, or did they just scare you pissless? Me, I went with the scared pissless."

Gem waltzed out the ladies room then, and Brandon gratefully returned to his book. Frostbite hopped over the back of the sofa and took Gem's arm. "Shall I usher you to our coach, precious?"

"Don't you want to try the manager one more time before we go? We really need a gig," Gem said. "Offer him your pretty little ass and he'll go for it. Better yet, offer him Brandon's and Fitch's."

Frostbite pondered that for a moment. Then he shook his head. "They'd never go for it. To the coach, darling."

Gem tucked her umbrella under her arm and dug through her purse. "Well, unless you have another buck-fifty, Frost, the coach leaves the bus stop without us."

He guided her to the door. "All taken care of. I already pocketed some of Fitch's change."

"Aren't we going to say goodnight?"

Frostbite looked back at Brandon and Fitch, curled up on the couch and squinting in the dark at their books. "No, Fitch might miss his money." They left Rimbaud's Cave, black lace gloved hand in hand under Gem's umbrella, dodging puddles as they ran down Elston. Velvet pants and artfully torn tights were drenched long before they reached the bustop. The streetlights were already on along Elston Avenue, haloing Frostbite and Gem's silhouettes as they disappeared behind windblown curtains of rain.

Once they were gone, the rear door opened on a black Cadillac that had been sitting at the curb just two doors up from Rimbaud's Cave.

Gabrielle stepped out, oblivious to the storm, wind lashing her clothes and dyed hair, rain pelting her face. She looked back inside the car and nodded, then walked into her old hangout, wondering who'd care to go for a ride.

✦

Kelly Feeny pressed the button on the side of the Mercedes front seat, and it eased back like a recliner. She slipped off her patent leather flats and stretched her legs out, resting her bare feet up on the dashboard. Her dress rode high up tanned legs. "Wow, what a night. What a day. This has been too much."

Joey Fortuna kept one eye on an empty rain drenched Damen Avenue and another on Kelly's legs. He reached over and patted her thigh. "Hey, Joey knows how to show a lady a good time."

"I'll say." Kelly shifted on the soft leather seat as Joey's hand gently crept higher. She lay her own hand on top of his, but didn't stop it from sliding under her dress. "Lunch in Greektown, drinks at Excalibur, dancing on Rush Street. Man, they are going to kill me tomorrow at the office."

"Nah, you deserve some time off for a little special handling." Joey's fingers crawled a little higher. "And I'm the man for special handling."

Kelly glanced at the digital clock on the Mercedes' walnut dashboard. "Two o'clock! I'm never going to get up for work tomorrow. But I almost hate for this night to end." She looked away from the clock and let her eyes track back and forth with the windshield wipers. It was hypnotic, just like Joey's fingers on her bare skin, then under her dress, now dipping inside her underwear.

"So who says it has to end?" Joey pulled the Mercedes over to the curb.

Kelly sat up. "Where are we?"

Reluctantly, Joey slipped his hand out from under Kelly's dress. "Well, look for yourself."

Kelly squinted, trying to see through the rain splattering the windshield. Finally, she made out the huge black marquee with those familiar red letters, looming right overhead. "Oh man...Gothique!"

"Put you one up on your coworkers, huh? Bet none of them have ever been inside."

"Inside? For real? Can we, Joey?" Kelly was already slipping her feet back into the flats.

"Hey, I told you, I'm connected, sweetheart." He leaned over and kissed Kelly, wet and sloppy and all tongue, his hand straying back to the hem of her dress, pausing, then sliding away. But Kelly kissed him back, just as sloppy, just a little drunkenly.

"Race you, baby."

She didn't even grab her umbrella. The rain still plummeted down, but the huge Gothique marquee almost reached to the curb. Kelly wiped raindrops off her bare arms as Joey reached for one of the black glass doors.

"Joey, don't you need a key or — "

He held the door open for her. "Nah, not for me. I'm kind of what they consider a VIP."

Kelly let him take her by the hand. Once the door shut behind them, it was pitch black inside. "Joey, are you sure this is okay?"

"Sure, come on." He led her through darkness, through a pair of swinging doors, and into more darkness.

"Joey, how can you see where you're going?"

"I practically live here, babe. I know the way with my eyes closed." He guided her to a wooden chair. "Look, you sit here, and I'll go fix us a drink."

"No, wait." Kelly gripped his hand. "Don't leave me here in the dark."

But he pried her fingers off. "I'm gonna get the lights, don't worry."

"Joey, I don't think I need another drink." But he was gone. She could hear his shoes padding away across carpet, growing fainter, then nothing.

Kelly sat there in the dark, fidgeting, crossing and uncrossing her legs, no longer thinking about how warm Joey's hands had felt on her thigh, or how anxious she felt when his fingers slid beneath her underwear.

Instead, she felt a sudden draft, and rubbed her bare arms. They were damp. Kelly rubbed them again, but it wasn't the rain anymore. It was sweat. Cold sweat. A droplet formed under her arm and slowly slid down her side underneath the dress. "Hey Joey, I don't think I really want anything to...Joey, I think I want to go now. Joey?" Kelly heard a rustle somewhere in the darkness. She felt another draft, like a cool breeze brushing by, kissing her cheek, raising gooseflesh on her skin. That cool breeze smelled floral and sweet — sickly sweet, like fruit gone bad.

"Joey? Joey, I really want to go, okay? Would you turn on the lights? Joey, please?"

There was a loud click from above and behind, and a spotlight flashed on right overhead. Kelly jumped off the chair, knocking it over onto the burgundy carpeting. She stood there in the middle of the spotlight glow, blinking in the brightness, wringing her hands together.

Trembling.

"J-Joey?"

A shuffle. Somewhere in the darkness. Kelly leaned forward, squinted past the light. But she saw nothing.

Then, a whisper. Behind her. She spun around, but there was only blackness outside the spotlight circle. Blackness and shadows. But the shadows almost looked like...like they moved.

"Joey? This isn't funny, okay? I really want to go now."

A giggle, then. Murmured words, and a distant laugh. Disembodied sounds, lurking in the darkness.

A hiss.

"Joey...p-please?"

Kelly yelped when a cold finger poked her bare shoulder.

She started to turn, mad now, fingers balled into fists, ready to sock Joey Fortuna in the chops for scaring her this way.

But her fists opened, her fingers started shaking, her whole body went limp when she saw the little pairs of red eyes flare in the darkness all around her. Saw those shadows bleed into the spotlight glow, but they weren't shadows now, they were figures slithering across the burgundy carpet, figures in black, pale skinned figures cloaked in leathers and lace, velvet and chiffon, painted nails clawing the floor, clawing their way towards her.

Red eyes simmered in their dark sockets.

Ugly, malevolent eyes.

Hungry eyes.

A cold, white hand shot out and grabbed her ankle. Another flew out of the darkness and wrapped its clammy fingers around her arm. Still another seized Kelly's hand.

Suddenly, there were icy fingers everywhere, pawing her, poking her, gouging her flesh. Pale hands clutched her brand new dress and tugged till the black cotton ripped.

Kelly dropped to her knees. "J-Joeeey!" The figures dragged her down, where their faces hovered only inches away, dead white faces, smiling red lipped smiles, sinister white teeth glistening under the spotlight.

One of them lunged and clamped its mouth down on her leg, and Kelly started to cry then, a frantic, choking crying from the pain searing her thigh and the fear racking her entire body.

Another bit her arm. Still another tore open her dress and dived for her breasts. She tried to struggle, but the shadows just came alive, and more black figures materialized in the light — giggling, hissing, drooling, grunting, dragging her down into their twisting heap of cold white hands and burning red mouths and sharp, grinning teeth.

Kelly screamed then, a desperate, terrified shriek that echoed in the darkness.

And it still echoed in Gothique's shadow caverns long after a leering mouth bit down hard on her throat, silencing Kelly Feeny forever.

FIFTEEN

The Charade Magazine Art Department was always chaotic. A little anarchy was almost expected from creatives, after all.

But by midmorning, chaos had turned into bedlam. The usual clique of freelancers, photographers, printers reps and salespeople waited to see Jeff and fought over the three visitors chairs in the tiny waiting area outside the artists' cubicles. Tim's and Ivy's computers crashed, and the two department interns took it in stride like real pro's, heading out for coffee instead of trying to fix their machines. But then everyone knew that Tim and Ivy were dating on the sly and took every chance they could to 'sneak off for coffee', even if that meant a locked stall in one of the bathrooms. The rest of the staff scrambled with the changes Blair Armstrong had sent over yesterday afternoon.

And all the while, the phones rang nonstop.

Jeff slammed down *his* phone after leaving his third voice-mail this morning for Blair. He turned back to his computer screen just as Colleen knocked on his door. "I have the outputs on those changes, Jeff."

"Good. So, how are you holding up today?"

Colleen shrugged her shoulders. "Okay. All this work keeps my mind off of things."

"Then, no luck yesterday?"

She shook her head. "Hey, at least I didn't drown coming in today." The thunderstorms blew over the lake during the night and presumably were pummeling Michigan by now. They left cloudy skies behind while Chicago dried off.

"Well, let's see what you have there."

Colleen watched Jeff plunge right in to the changes with his red pen. She took a seat. "So, is Kelly sick today?"

"Kelly is — God love her — Kelly is in trouble, is what she is," Jeff said. "She didn't come back from lunch yesterday afternoon, didn't call today, and she's not answering at home. I've been trying her since nine thirty."

"Doesn't sound like her."

Jeff looked up from the pages and locked eyes with Colleen. "No, it doesn't, does it?" The phone rang again, then another line started ringing, then a third. Jeff answered the first call, rolled his eyes, and held the phone against his chest. "Colleen, you better get the other calls. This one's going to take a while." She gave a thumbs up and dashed back to her cubicle.

Jeff took a deep breath. "Morning, Elaine."

"Don't put me on hold, Jeffrey," Elaine Porter-Stancheck snorted. "It's rude."

"I didn't put you on...so what's up? I'm really pretty busy here."

"You're always busy. But don't worry, this won't take long, Jeffrey. *I'm* rather busy today myself."

So Jeff listened.

And listened. Elaine never could get to the point. After several minutes of round-about rambling, he cut her off. "Houston, Dallas, Southwest Region, Calvin, roadtrips...Elaine, what exactly are you getting at?"

She didn't respond right away. But finally after a long pause, she said, "Jeffrey, do you think it would be possible...that is, do you think...would Jacqueline be very upset if she had to stay with you a while longer?"

His heart leaped. "How much longer?" He knew a perfectly stupid looking smile was widening across his face.

Elaine didn't answer.

"Wait a minute, Elaine. Jacks has to be back in school in another month, doesn't she? This'll be her senior year...prom, yearbooks, ACT's, college applications, all that stuff. We shouldn't screw around with school. How much longer?"

Elaine answered, and she didn't. Instead, she launched into another protracted ramble that left Jeff more confused than before. "So, let's cut to the chase, Elaine. What I'm hearing is that Calvin must be an especially good lay and you want to be living out of suitcases with him until this whole 'Empowerment Program' scam catches up with him a year or two from now, when I'll have to wire you some more money to get you home from wherever he dumps you in backwater Texas." Jeff's voice grew louder with each word. "Meanwhile, after ruining our daughter's life — and what the hell, *my* life too — with an awfully expensive guided tour of the entire Cook County Family Court System, you suddenly want Jacks to have more 'quality time' with her Father. To leave her friends, leave her school, screw up her senior year. Does that about sum it up?"

"Jeffrey, you really are a cruel, insensitive bastard. I can't believe I was actually married to you. If it wasn't for Jacqueline — "

"If it wasn't for Jacks, you'd have gotten someone else to knock you up just so you could blame *him* for the rest of your life." He was shouting now, but didn't care.

On one hand, Elaine's surprise was more than he could have hoped for.

On the other, he didn't want to uproot Jacks in her last year of high school. "Save the psychobabble for Calvin when he's empowering you in the Waco Holiday Inn. Let's figure out what to do about Jacks." Jeff stepped out from behind his desk and stretched the phone cord to the limit so he could reach his office door. The rest of the conversation was bound to get louder.

Colleen peeked over her cubicle when Jeff's door slammed shut. She blew off another photo lab salesman on line three, and punched the hold button to get back to her other call. "Sorry," she said. "Now, you're name was...?"

"Detective Shepherd, Ms. Russell." The woman sounded pleasant enough. Almost chipper. "Terri Shepherd." But still, she was a detective.

Detectives.

Police.

Megan.

Cass.

Colleen knew she sounded nervous, but she couldn't help it. She twirled a lock of her red hair into a knot. "And...what's...uhm, what is this about?"

"I believe you reported a missing person last night to the 14th precinct?"

"Cass? Y-yes, I did."

"A Mr. Cassidy Lumbach, that's right. And you said that he's been missing for a week now?"

"Yes, almost a week. So? Is he all right? Is Cass in some kind of trouble? Is everything — "

"I just need to ask you some additional questions, Ms. Russell. Do you think there's any chance you could stop by here today?"

"Gee, I guess so. It's a madhouse at work today. Maybe at lunch time, but —"

"I could come to see you, if that's more convenient."

"Here at work? The police?"

"All right then, I can see you *after* work, if you prefer. Let's see, you're in Rogers Park, right? I have your address here somewhere."

They settled on 6:30. Colleen just hoped she'd be home in time. If this morning was any indication, the afternoon would be insane. And it was going to be hell concentrating on type changes while she thought about Cass. And meeting with this Detective Shepherd.

✦

Joey Fortuna parked the Mercedes in the alley next to Gothique. If it was anywhere else, he'd never consider leaving the black beauty under a fire escape. Pigeons would crap all over it.

But for some reason, pigeons never roosted around the old theater, the way they just moved right in on most buildings. Not a one.

Joey's breakfast made his stomach rumble just as he popped the trunk. He looked over his shoulder to be safe, saw that the alley was as empty as he should have known it would be, then hefted out a heavy corrugated box. The box was dirty, so he held it away from his sky blue blazer and white slacks. His old pal,

Nicky Kolitzky, taught him about that, about always wearing a jacket, even on hot summer mornings. After all, a shiny Mercedes, a silk shirt and a wad of cash tucked in your back pocket went a long way in a jam. But you couldn't parade around town in a shoulder holster without some cop asking a question or two.

Joey went in the back way today, carefully keying in the security code and unlocking the deadbolts. Anyone could wander in at night, nothing was locked then. Not that anyone stupid enough to wander in would ever come back out.

But never during the day.

Gothique was always locked up tight during the day. Joey locked all the doors and set the alarm himself last night. This morning, actually. It *was* almost dawn before they were finally through with her. They really took their sweet time with Kelly Feeny. That girl was clean: maybe a few too many margaritas, but no drugs, no diseases, and that must have been a real treat.

They all would have been tucked in for the day by the time Joey dumped Kelly's body in the Lake. He did it way down on the southeast side this time, right in the turning basin off Calumet Harbor. No one saw him, and no one would have butted in if they did. It was a pretty tough area, and anyone out there that early had their own agenda to hide.

Kelly had been roughed up pretty good. Her pale, naked body was a patchwork of mauled bruises, torn skin and ragged punctures. But there wasn't a lick of blood on her skin. Not a lick.

Because it had all been licked clean.

Kelly's body had floated on top of that scummy water for a moment, till Joey tossed in the two cinder blocks he'd tied to her leg. Those dragged her down feet first, and the last thing he saw of Kelly was her dead face sinking under an oil slick, eyes bugged out like she'd gone crazy when she slowly died.

Joey figured she probably had.

He locked the back door behind him, that heavy box straining one arm while he tucked the keys back into his jacket. Joey was trusted with all the keys. He navigated the maze of dark hallways towards the main hall, flipping on lights as he went along. The back corridors were still a mess of construction materials, remodeling dirt and old Palace Theater crap waiting for the dumpster. But as he approached the main club rooms, everything looked a little more finished. Some things were finally nearing completion. And none too soon. Gothique's grand opening was scheduled for the first week in September.

Joey entered the cavernous hall that had once been the theater itself, but the rows of seats and the silver screen were gone. It was all transformed into a nightmare dungeon of fake medieval buttresses arching to nowhere, backlit stained glass, dark alcoves with booths and sofas and conversation pits. Giant speakers and gelled lights dangled from overhead piping. Huge video screens hung from the walls like blank canvasses framed in black. The narrow platform that once rested at the foot of the movie screen had been enlarged into a huge stage, framed by an immense, ornate proscenium that rose into the shadows, seventy five feet above.

Joey found the main switch panel and hit the lights.

"Thanks."

He dropped the heavy box, and it's contents banged and jangled. Joey whirled around, one hand on the pistol strapped under his blazer.

"Don't wet your pants, Joey. It's only me." Gabrielle perched on the edge of the long, black marble bar that ran nearly the whole length of the club's main hall, her dark legs crossed and dangling a spiked suede pump off the tip of one foot. She smoked a Gitane, elegantly clenched between the very tips of two long nailed fingers. "Who the hell did you think it would be?"

"You shouldn't surprise me like that," Joey said, stooping to pick the box up. "It's a good way to get killed."

Gabrielle flicked her long, dyed hair off her face. "Oh, I don't know. I bet there's a lot better ways to get killed."

"Yeah? Maybe we can look into them someday." He set the box on the bar. "So what are you doing here anyway?"

She shrugged, and her lace shawl slipped off her shoulders. "I stayed here last night. I didn't feel like going home. There's nothing there for me anymore. Fact is, I was thinking of just moving in. "

"That so? *They* know about these big plans of yours?"

"Actually, yes. Arianne said it would be a good idea. She said it would be nice to have someone with brains here during the day."

"She said wh — well, Marek might have something to say about that."

"Marek?" Gabrielle snickered. "You really aren't plagued by a lot of insight, are you?" She dragged on the Gitane and lifted her head to snort the smoke out of her nose, right at Joey. "Typical macho shit. That's just how an imbecile like you would read their whole dynamic. Oh, just go do your chores. I didn't join up just to make small talk with a greaser pimp like you."

"Oh? Your pimp's not a greaser?"

"No, he was a...Hey, fuck you, Joey." She twisted around on the stool and criss-crossed her black legs, watching to see if Joey looked. He didn't. "It's pretty lame the way you just assume Marek's in charge because he's 'the man.'"

"No, I just know which side my bread's buttered on."

"Well, they can butter your balls for all I care. I'm not here for the money, or the leftover pussy, like you."

"Really?" Joey smirked. "You only like it fresh, huh?"

Gabrielle flicked her cigarette at him. Joey dodged it, and the cigarette landed on the floor, quickly burning a little hole in the burgundy carpet.

"Oh shit!" Gabrielle shrieked. She leaped off the bar, picked up the cigarette and smashed the smoldering burn with her heel. "Now look at what you made me do! Why the hell do they want carpeting in a nightclub anyway?"

Joey laughed as he picked his box up off the bar. "Remind Marek about their whole dynamic when he sees that, babe." Joey sauntered away, his laughter echoing in the cavernous hall.

"Hey Joey, you won't tell him I did that, will you?" Gabrielle scooped her cigarettes and her lighter into a little black velvet bag and traipsed after him. "Joey, please? C'mon, I'll give you a blow job."

He paused by a service door at the back of the hall. "No thanks, I don't want to be wiping off blackberry lipstick this early in the morning. But if you could stop being such a bitch for five minutes, maybe you could help me out here."

"Sure, Joey. Sure, anything."

They followed another maze of corridors and staircases, flicking on lights where there were any, and inching through darkness where there weren't. Down into the basement, where a brand new gas furnace had been installed just last week, down into the sub-basement, where an all-new plumbing system was completed at the end of June — signed and approved with a seal by the City Inspector — just before Drake and Fonda bent the mope over a row of freshly soldered copper pipes, where they ripped his throat out and shared sips from *his* plumbing. Down one more narrow staircase, deep into the dark bowels of the old building's foundation. The concrete and quarrystone walls were pitted and mildewed down here. The air was old, as old as the building itself. If any rats remained alive in the place, this is where they roosted.

"You're not going to bother *them,* are you?" Gabrielle asked, hovering right behind Joey as they passed one door after another in the dark corridor.

"I thought you're the one who's so into all their 'dynamics'. How could I bother them this time of day?" Joey halted in front of the last door in the corridor. He tried to juggle the heavy box while he fished in his pocket. "Get my keys, will you?"

Gabrielle did and unlocked the deadbolt. The door squealed on rusty hinges and they stepped into the pitch black room.

"Get the switch. On the wall right behind you."

Gabrielle flicked the switch, and one, lonely overhead bulb flashed on under a blanket of cobwebs. "Oh, coooool."

The room was about twenty by fifty feet of ugly gray mortar and seepage. The floor was more dirt than cement. That one lonely bulb dangling from the ceiling cast its feeble light on rows of old fashioned cast iron cots, like dormitory beds, their headboards and footboards just bent piping. There were twenty four of them in neat rows, each with a skimpy, grayed mattress, each of those more torn and stained than the next.

Right underneath the lightbulb, Brandon and Fitch were curled up on two of the beds — stark naked, with silver duct tape wound around their wrists and their ankles, another strip across their mouths.

"So this is where they brought them," Gabrielle said. She followed behind Joey as he carried his box to the two beds. "They let me watch last night. These two put on a real show, going down on each other upstairs. But once Drake pounced...well, Fitch there, he started screaming like a baby with a diaper full, so Drake and Fonda just dragged them off somewhere. I tried to follow, but they told me to wait upstairs." She sat down on the edge of Brandon's cot and poked him in the ribs. "I figured they just drained them dry." Brandon kicked back at her with his knees, but Gabrielle easily scooted away.

"This one's out cold," Joey said. He felt Fitch's wrist. "Still alive, though. Sort of."

Brandon moaned from behind his duct tape gag.

"Yeah, I got all these cots from a guy in County Purchasing," Joey said. "I think they used be in the 26th street lockup, or something. Like, a million years ago, maybe." He dropped his box on the floor and ripped it open. Gabrielle peeked over. It was filled with handcuffs, brand new looking by the way they caught the glimmer from that feeble bulb. "Now *these* I got from our boys over in the 17th district. Regular Police Issue." He matched keys to cuffs and opened two pair. "All it takes is the right amount of cash in the right hands and this whole fucking city's in your pocket, Gabrielle. Marek sure figured that out. Keep that in mind when you're deciding who's who around here."

Joey reached into his blazer's pocket and whipped out a switchblade. The knife clicked open with a lethal sound.

"What are you going to do to him?"

"I don't know, " Joey said. He ran the six inch blade along Brandon's chest, down his belly, and into the ring of hair below. "Maybe cut his balls off. That'd be how you prefer your guys, right?"

Gabrielle's eyes gleamed, riveted on that silver blade stroking Brandon's skin.

Brandon started to cry. The tears ran down his cheeks, but his sobs were muffled by the duct tape.

"Don't worry," Joey said. "I wouldn't touch your little marbles. I might catch something." Instead, Joey jammed the switchblade under the tape binding Brandon's feet, tugged, and sliced it open. Immediately, Brandon started kicking, but Joey grabbed a leg and slapped one end of the handcuffs around his ankle. He locked the other end around one of the footboard's iron spindles.

"Give me a hand, Gabrielle."

She held Brandon's arms while Joey sliced the tape off his wrists and cuffed him to the headboard. "Okay, there's more keys in the box. Lock one end of the handcuffs to each of the footboards and each of the headboards. And leave the other end of the handcuffs open, so it'll be easier to slap 'em on once there's more...guests." Joey proceeded to cut away tape from Fitch's wrists and ankles, then cuff him to the bedframe. Fitch didn't struggle, didn't even flinch. He just wheezed when Joey rolled him over. Once he was finished, Joey, took out more handcuffs and began to lock them onto the other beds.

But Gabrielle still sat next to Brandon. First she looked at the blue-black bruises on his arm. Then the meaner, scabbed wound on the side of his throat. She ran her nails up Brandon's thigh, while he squirmed on the dirty mattress, cuffs clinking against the metal bedframe, the whole thing squeaking like a pack of mice. She stroked his limp penis with one long, black polished nail — stared at the pink nub trying to hide in its wreath of hair —scrutinized it, then flipped it aside and leaned closer to examine the two punctures hidden in Brandon's crotch. "Ooo, what have we got here?"

"What's that," Joey called from across the room.

"A dick, I guess." She giggled. "Only smaller."

She stroked Brandon's crotch, tracing her fingers around the wounds. The holes were still slick with oozing blood. She daubed her finger in the red trickle, and smeared it across her lips. Gabrielle smiled, and her raccoon eyes winked. "Now *that* had to be Fonda, am I right?" She gave Brandon another pinch, and he tried to squirm away across the mattress, tears soaking his cheeks. "Little different from make-believe time at Rimbaud's Cave, isn't it, sweetheart?"

"Quit playing with him," Joey said from across the room.

"I can't help it." Gabrielle giggled. "Look at him, he's getting a boner."

"What do *you* care?"

"Okay." She left Brandon wrestling on the filthy mattress, straining to reach his cuffed hands to the duct tape across his mouth.

When all the handcuffs were finally locked onto the bedframes, Joey and Gabrielle stood by the door, surveying the dingy room. Fitch was still out cold, and Brandon still thrashed on his cot. Joey switched off the overhead bulb and the room plunged back into darkness, and that started Brandon jerking at his cuffs even harder.

"Reminds me of a dormitory my parents sentenced me to," Gabrielle said. "Girls' school up in Wisconsin. Had a special way with behavioral problems."

"That where you turned into a dyke?"

Gabrielle glared at him. "No, Joey. That was the only thing that made my little vacation there bearable."

"Well, it reminds *me* of prison."

"You've been?"

"Short stay. I don't plan on returning." Joey stepped out of the dark doorway. "So you're thinking of becoming one of *them,* huh?"

"You kidding? Soon as I can. If they'll let me. And they better."

He gestured at her clothes. "So, what's with this whole...*thing?* This whole 'Goth' scene. Where the fuck did that all come from?"

She shrugged. "I don't know. Aren't you into — "

"I'm just here for the money."

"Oh, yeah. I forgot. And the leftover pussy."

Joey clenched his fists and took a threatening step towards her. Gabrielle's sarcastic grin drooped. She was suddenly aware of just how tall Joey Fortuna was. How his arms bulged inside the sleeves of his blazer. How his shoulder holster poked out from underneath.

But then, he stopped. "Look, I know you think I'm just some stupid fuck," he said. "And I'm not too revved up on you, either. But what do you say we both play it cool, huh?" Joey closed the door on Brandon's muffled shrieks, then locked the deadbolt. "I don't know about you, but I'm not looking to end up cuffed to one of those beds. Now you can wear all the black dresses you want, and listen to any music you want, and read all the books you want, and paint your face any goddamn way you like. But we both know that all it would take is one fuck-up, and either of us could be crying in the dark like that little fag in there." Joey returned the keys to his pocket. "What do you say? Truce?"

Gabrielle glanced back at the locked door. They could still hear Brandon's handcuffs clinking on the spindles.

"Deal."

SIXTEEN

Detective Terri Shepherd looked more like a kindergarten teacher than a police officer.

There she was at Colleen's apartment door promptly at 6:30, just like they'd agreed. Colleen nervously rushed around the living room picking up cast off clothes, old newspapers and several nights' dirty dishes. "You'll have to excuse the mess, Detective. I've been working some crazy hours this week."

"No problem, Ms. Russell."

"Call me Colleen."

"Okay. No problem, Colleen." Detective Terri Shepherd not only looked like a kindergarten teacher, and an awfully young one at that, but she sounded like one, too. Her voice was on the high side, but that fit her: all of five foot four, slim, with pixieish brown hair that was windblown and humidified into a tousled mess right now. Alert brown eyes hid under those brown bangs, and her nose was a little on the long side, giving her face an almost elfin air. 'Cute' was the word that would immediately come to mind to anyone glancing at her.

But it was more than that.

She didn't even dress like a detective. Or, however Colleen imagined detectives should dress. Colleen had only met two real detectives in her whole life, both of them in their late forties, both homicide detectives, both bungling their way through their questions when Megan died. They fit her assumptions about cops to a T — paunchy, balding, favoring shiny elbowed, colorless sportcoats, undone ties and cheap wingtips.

But Detective Terri Shepherd really looked like she was ready to announce *'Good morning, class'* to a bunch of five year olds.

She wore a khaki skirt, not too long and not too short, with a striped man's styled shirt tucked in the waistband, brown penny loafers. A pair of plain aviator sunglasses dangled from her shirt pocket. She carried a slender leather attaché that overflowed with papers. Colleen whisked a stack of dirty plates into the kitchen, wondering where the Detective hid her gun. Or if she even carried one.

"So, wouldn't you like to check my identification?" Detective Shepherd asked once Colleen returned to the living room.

"Well, okay. If you think I should."

The detective flipped open a brown leather wallet and held it in front of Colleen. There was her badge and her picture ID: Detective Sergeant Terri Shepherd, Inter-Departmental Division.

"I always thought it was 'I-A-D'," Colleen said. "Like on all the cop shows." She gestured towards the sofa, and they both sat down.

"That's 'Internal Affairs'. I don't work in that department. I did three years there, though."

"Really? You don't look — "

"I know. I don't look old enough to have worked *anywhere* three years." Detective Shepherd smiled. "Don't be embarrassed, I get it all the time. But I've been on the force for six years now, since I graduated from law school." She could see that Colleen was studying her even closer now. "I'm thirty two, Ms. Russell."

"Wow, you don't look a day over — "

"Twenty one, I know. If I had a dollar for every time I heard that." She laughed. "Weird, isn't it? Women my age are already going into bankruptcy at the cosmetics counter at Fields, and here I am wishing I could get a couple wrinkles just so the guys at work would give me a break." She opened her attaché and pulled out a manila folder. When she did, Colleen saw that Detective Shepherd did indeed have a gun, a big and mean looking one at that. It was buckled into a clip-on holster inside the attaché.

"So, what does the 'Inter-Departmental Division' have to do with me?" Colleen asked. "More importantly, what's this have to do with Cass?"

The detective flipped open the manila folder and scanned some notes and forms. "Mr. Cassidy Lumbach. That's your roommate?"

"Right."

"Male, Caucasian, approx. 6 foot, hundred fifty pounds, brown hair bleached to blonde in sections..."

"Yes, that's Cass," Colleen said. "I don't like the sound of this."

"Ms. Russell, you reported your roommate missing yesterday evening. But you said he's been gone for five days now. Why the wait? Most people call right away. We can initiate a search after an adult is missing for 48 hours."

"I —I don't know." Colleen was sweating. Talking to the police brought back fresh and still painful memories. And as usual, the apartment was oppressively hot. She hopped off the couch and opened the living room windows. A damp breeze blew in off the Lake. "Cass and I are close, you know? But we don't always socialize together. I mean, he has his scene and I...well, I don't really have a scene. He has been gone overnight before, though. I just figured...I guess that I..." Colleen trailed off as she sat down on the window seat. The breeze blew her long red hair off her face and started to dry the perspiration. Her eyes wandered towards the lake; fog was building along the breakers, and just beginning to creep into the courtyard below.

"So Colleen, you were out with your roommate when you last saw him, correct?"

"Yes. But we didn't go home together."

"Is that unusual?"

"A little. I wanted to split. Cass was ready to come with. But he was with his friends, and I didn't want to ruin his night out."

The detective made some notes. "By any chance would you recall what your roommate was wearing that night?"

"Sure. But I told them all that when I called last night."

"Sometimes I can barely make out the writing on these forms," Detective Shepherd said. "Cops are worse than doctors when it comes to penmanship. Tell *me.*"

Colleen shrugged, thinking. "Let's see, Cass had on black slacks...make that black velvet slacks. A white ruffled shirt." She made eye contact with the policewoman. "Sounds weird right? But Cass is kind of an unusual dresser." She closed her eyes and thought some more. "The ruffled shirt, and black Beatle boots...uhm, lots of jewelry, like neckchains and earrings and..."

"This is an unusual question — or maybe it's not. Was he wearing any facial makeup?"

Colleen chuckled. "No, not unusual at all. You'd have to know Cass." She nodded. "Yep, Cass had the old Max Factor ladled on pretty good that night. He usually does when he goes out. Like I said, he's an unusual dresser." She pulled her legs up on the window seat and tucked them underneath herself. "Look, Detective — "

"I'll call you Colleen, you call me Terri."

"Okay — Terri. Then let me know what this is all about. You're going to tell me something really bad, I know it. And what's with this Inter-Departmental stuff?"

Detective Shepherd closed her folder. "As I said, I'm an investigator for the Inter-Departmental Division. I deal with cases that may involve multiple branches of the Police Department. Or other municipal departments, for that matter. Colleen, did your roommate have a girlfriend?"

"Cass and I kept a few secrets, but he was definitely not a cop, he definitely wasn't working for any 'municipal departments'. And he *definitely* did not have a girlfriend. That much I'm certain of."

"Got it." Terri Shepherd paused, looked around the living room, noted the framed movie posters hanging on the walls: *Razor Blade Smile, Lost Boys, Dance Of The Damned.* She took a deep breath. "Colleen, I'd like to tell you that your roommate is just drying out in a cell, or doing thirty days for solicitation or something like that, but I can't."

"He's dead." Colleen bit her lip. "You're going to tell me Cass is dead, right?"

"Well, I can't tell you that either, Colleen. I can't tell you very much, actually. That's why I'm here to ask *you* some questions."

Colleen jumped off the windowseat and started pacing. "Wait a minute. I've done this scene before. *'We're sorry Miss Russell, we know your sister fell a hundred floors off the Hancock, but we just don't know why or how. Is there anything you can tell us to help with our investigation?'* What the hell is with you cops? What *do* you know?"

"I'm aware of your sister Megan's death, Colleen. I wish the department had more to offer you on that investigation, but I happen to know there hasn't been any meaningful leads." Terri walked over to Colleen and stopped the pacing by taking her arm. She guided her back to the sofa, then flipped her folder open again and stared at her notes. "All right, here it is. Six nights ago a 23rd district patrol car responded to a call about a disturbance — specifically, repeated screams — in Graceland Cemetery. The two uniformed officers picked up a cemetery security guard from his office and conducted a search of the grounds, expecting to find evidence of vandalism, or teenage drinking or some other prank. Instead, they found two bodies. An unidentified young female, and an unidentified male. Both were in various states of undress and showed signs of sexual molestation. Both bodies had multiple wounds of an undetermined nature."

Tears cascaded down Colleen's cheeks now. "C-Cass? Murdered in some goddamn graveyard? With... a *girl?*" She wiped her cheek with her sleeve. "So what's with all this 'undetermined' and 'unidentified'? Who was she? Can I see Cass'...that is, do you need to me to go down to...I mean, I've done that before. I've been to the morgue."

Terri Shepherd sighed. She reached across the sofa and took Colleen's hand. "Well, this is where I come in, Colleen. The two unidentified bodies were taken to the Cook County Medical Examiner's facility — the coroner, or the morgue, as you call it — later that night. Unfortunately, it was a particularly hot and muggy night, if you recall, and on nights like that, the bodies start stacking up. Gang fights, shootings, domestics, heatstroke's, you name it. Other than the responding officers' on-site report, no further post-mortem was conducted that night or the following day. The bodies were both photographed, tagged as Jane and John Doe's, and placed in storage. If I'm being too clinical for you, Colleen, just — "

Colleen shook her head.

"Okay, the ME's personnel finally got around to the bodies three days ago. The female is still unidentified, though we have her picture circulating the other precincts, Juvenile Division, runaway hotlines, that sort of thing. The report on *her* confirms that while she was not raped, she was sexually molested, and showed numerous bite marks on various parts of her body. There is some discrepancy about the exact cause of death; she appears to have bled to death, rather than died from the wounds themselves. Though there was a considerable amount of blood found at the crime scene, it was nowhere near sufficient to account for the victims' blood loss."

"And...and what about Cass?" Colleen said. "Same?"

"Colleen, the reason I'm talking to you this evening is that neither the Police Department or the ME's Office can verify how the male victim died, much less if he really was your roommate."

"But he matched my description, is that it?"

"Yes, he did. The clothes, makeup, everything."

Colleen stood up abruptly. "Well, we have to go down to the morgue, right?" She darted around the living room all flustered. "Just let me... uhm...right, let me get my purse. And my keys. I'm always forgetting my keys. Cass is always razzing me about that, just let me — "

"Colleen, stop." Terri flicked the pixie bangs off her face and rubbed her forehead, as if a headache was brewing. "We're not going to the ME's Office."

Colleen halted at the door, with her purse half over her shoulder. "Sure we are. I can do it. I never got to say good-bye to Megan. At least I can say it to Cass."

"No, Colleen, you don't understand. If it was Cass, you can't identify him, or say good-bye to him."

"Why?"

"Because his body disappeared."

✦

Terri Shepherd got Colleen a cold beer from the refrigerator, and opened one for herself as well. Both women sipped their beers right from the sweaty bottles while Colleen led the detective into Cass' room.

"Sure, look at anything you want." Colleen sat on the edge of Cass' bed. The shiny black satin coverlet crinkled beneath her. "But I still don't understand. How could they lose a body?"

Terri set down her beer and her attaché case, then wandered around the room, taking note of Cass' bookcases: an entire row of Children Of The Grave gaming books, Series I through IV; Montague Summers, Bram Stoker, the requisite Anne Rice. Lumley and Brite, they were all there. Neat stacks of magazines: Delerium, Drawing Blood, Dark Parlour, Carpe Noctem, Ghastly — piles of comic books: Vampirella, Crimson, Vamps, Lady Death — whole shelves of them. "Frankly, if the public ever knew just how often it happens, it would be on the front page of the Tribune. But it rarely gets out. Usually occurs with a homeless person, O.D.'s, five dollar hookers — not anyone with a funeral home waiting to pick up the body."

She moved onto Cass' tapes and CD's: all the old standards she expected to find: Bauhaus, The Cure, The Damned. And all the serious stuff too: Dark Heresy, Cradle Of Thorns, Eva O, Black Rose. "That's why I'm investigating this. The Police Department and the ME's Office already started fingerpointing. I guess you could say my job is to make sure the fingers point the right way." She jotted down notes on a small pad while she scanned the top of Cass' dresser: two vinyl monster models, one an imitation Bela Lugosi, the other a half naked femme fatale with a long toothed leer. Pewter rings and gold plated jewelry cluttered the dresser, along with makeup brushes and lipsticks, eyeliner and blush. Terri started to open the top drawer, then glanced back at Colleen, who nodded.

"But wait a minute," Colleen said. "Didn't you say that the coroners office took pictures of these two victims when they were brought in?"

"Yes, they did manage that." Terri tried each of the dresser drawers, and each was stuffed full of mesh undershirts, black silk boxers and briefs, leather and lace gloves of every conceivable type. Socks and countless black T-shirts shared space with coils of nylon rope and a few sex toys, along with stacks of comic books, videos, and a stray pair or two of Colleen's panties that never made it back to her own drawers. Terri shut the bottom drawer and opened her attaché case. "Are you sure you want to see this?" She held out a 4 x 5 snap shot.

Colleen gulped, but she took it.

"Oh." She handed the picture back. "That's the girl."

"Yes. Do you know her?"

"I met her. That night." She got up from the bed and opened Cass' closet for the detective. "She was with Cass' friends. Chrissie, or Jessie...*Chelsea.* That was her name. Chelsea."

Terri scribbled that down on her notepad. "I'm guessing that was an assumed name. I've seen her. She looked pretty young. I'd bet she was a runaway. I'll certainly want the names of any of these other friends you met. I'll want to talk to them."

Gabrielle's face immediately flashed in front of Colleens' eyes. "Good luck. They all made Cass look like a stockbroker." She plopped back down on the bed and took another sip from her beer.

"You'd be surprised what some stockbrokers are really into." Terri flipped through the hangars in the closet: two black satin capes. Some fake medieval shirts and vests, lace and ruffled blouses. Rows of black leggings, black pants, black shirts, black leather. "I've seen weirder things hiding in people's closets." She shut the door and smiled when Colleen reached out with the beer she'd laid down before. The detective took a long swig, then nodded at the window. "Boy, the fog really blows in off the Lake here."

"Yeah. Cass likes that. Or...liked it. Spooky, you know?"

"So, you work for Whitestar Media Group, right Colleen? Charade Magazine?"

Colleen nodded.

"Your sister helped get you the job?"

"No. I started there after she died. It's...it's a long story."

"Well, maybe you can tell me sometime." Terri walked over to the window, opened it, and a puff of fog rolled inside. She stood there, sniffing the Lake breeze. "Charade's hooked up with this whole Gothique hoopla, isn't it?"

Colleen smirked. "If my boss heard you say that, he'd explode."

"Why's that?"

"Oh, he's just kind of fed up with the direction the magazine's taking. All this superficial nightlife and fashion and clubbing scene stuff. And the whole Goth-thing. I kind of see his point. I mean, some of the music's okay, but it is all just soft core S&M for the artsy coffeehouse crowd, in a way. Isn't it?"

The detective laughed. "I wouldn't know. I like my coffee black and in a coffee cup. Not with foam and a bondage manual gussied up like poetry-to-go. Sounds to me like your boss is on the right track."

"Yes, Jeff's all right." Colleen set her beer down on Cass' nightstand. "So?"

"So?"

"So...you're stalling, Detective. Aren't you going to show me the other photo?"

"Are you certain you want to — "

"I have to."

Terri took another snapshot out of her attaché case and handed it to Colleen.

Colleen looked at it, looked up at Terri Shepherd, and handed it right back.

"There's the last part of my mystery, Colleen."

"But — "

"I know. I interviewed the ME's Office staff twice. They insist it's the correct photo." She held it up to Colleen again. "See, their camera automatically prints out the day and time the shot was taken along the top border. I grilled the third shift orderly that actually took the photo, and I believe him. The victim the two officers brought in along with the Jane Doe you're calling Chelsea matches your roommate Cass exactly. And I'm very sorry to have to say that unless the patrol officers had some magic mushrooms with their donuts and coffee that night, your roommate was dead, presumably murdered, and in a pretty gruesome manner. And unless I've suddenly gotten real bad at my job and unless I'm suddenly a bad judge of character, that orderly *was* telling the truth when he claims that he photographed what was surely Cassidy Lumbach's body on that table."

Colleen's beer bottle slipped out of her hands. It rolled along the hardwood floor, dribbling beer into the cracks. "But — there's no body. Terri, there's just an empty stainless steel table on that photo."

"I know." Detective Terri Shepherd glanced at the photo again, then downed the rest of her own beer in one gulp.

SEVENTEEN

The following night, Friday night, and a late Friday night, Jeff Stancheck shut off his computer right after Colleen left. He'd been wading through department-head paperwork since ten. Though staying late on a Friday was normally taboo, he was determined to leave the office *at* the office this weekend.

Not surprisingly, Tim and Ivy bolted at five on the dot. The others filtered out soon after. Usually Jeff counted on Kelly to stick around when the crunch was on, but where exactly *she'd* been these days was another matter altogether; presumably Kelly had decided against buying her tombstone at Charade Magazine. If Colleen hadn't offered to stay, Monday morning would be a train wreck.

That girl had enough troubles and Jeff offered to buy her dinner, even offered her a ride home. But she turned down both, plugged away at her Mac and polished off an entire series of Gothique ads and Charade inserts before she said goodnight.

Whether the other artists knew it or not, Colleen Russell was likely to move into the second-in-command spot pretty soon, despite her short time on the job. It may have been a strange set of circumstances that brought Megan's little sister to Charade, but Jeff knew now that firing Gabrielle was the smartest thing he'd done all year.

And none too soon, as it turned out. Blair Armstrong had been a maniac the last two days, making changes to changes to changes in the September issue, and sending over stacks of job requests for Charade's new 'partner' — posters, ads, mailers, menus, premiums and more. There was no discussing the overload. Whitestar's implicit mandate was made eminently clear.

Frankly, there was no discussing *anything* with Blair the past two days. She and Jeff barely spoke, not since the lunch hour romp in the Park Stratford.

Not since her no-show for dinner Wednesday night.

If anything, her barrage of memos signaled the return of the 'old Blair', the Blair Armstrong that blustered in from Manhattan and Interview Magazine in her four hundred dollar pumps and her Lexus with an over-tweaked resume in her Gucci briefcase. The Blair that Jeff wasn't sure he even liked at first.

Back before they became 'pals'.

He initialed the monthly budget variance reports and tossed them in the outgoing inter-office mail box, then checked his watch before moving on to the September forecasts: just a little after eleven.

He'd checked home earlier. Jacks was off to a sleep-over at her friend Rachel's house, just down the block. If she wasn't, he'd feel guilty about that too — about not being home. But Jacks had eased right back in with some of her old neighborhood friends as soon as she arrived in June, and now that she knew she was staying, she was a regular part of the clique again.

"Dad, why are you treating this like it's a major disaster?" she said when he told her about Elaine's call. 'Coming home,' was how Jacks described it, though Jeff was certain she was covering up a little. Her mother putting another flaky job, 'Calvin' and pyramid scheme seminars in Texas hotel rooms ahead of her had to hurt.

Actually, Jacks was the reason Jeff decided to stay late tonight — so the two of them could hash things out in detail over the weekend, uninterrupted by press approvals and page changes and the usual take-home paperwork that never seemed to get done during the workday. There was so much to do now: arranging to have the rest of Jacks' things shipped from Encino, calls to friends that she wouldn't see this year, transcripts to be transferred, applications to fill out for a school here in Chicago. Jeff mentioned — just *mentioned* — the girl's parochial prep school on 56th and Pulaski, but Jacks' disbelieving look pretty much said it all as far as uniforms and nuns. And no boys.

A cleaning woman wheeled her squeaky cart through the art department just as Jeff finally initialed the last section of the September forecast. He tossed the papers in the outbox and clicked off his desk lamp. His briefcase sat open at his side, and force of habit found him reaching for it, ready to shut it and drag it home. He pulled back, though, actually leaving his hand hovering over the lid for a moment. Proofs, papers and more nestled inside. Right on top lay those damaged disks, the ones the mail room brought up two days ago. The ones his old computer at home couldn't read. Even the department's high powered system couldn't read the disks. Evidently they were ruined.

Jeff stared at the disks, wondering if he should just throw them out.

Instead, he scribbled a reminder on a yellow sticky note: *Send to Media Service Bureau Monday A.M. to salvage files.* He rubberbanded the disks together, tagged them and tossed them in the outbox.

Jeff shut his briefcase, slid it under his desk and grabbed his blazer off a hook on the back of his door. He checked his watch as he shut off the lights: 11:20. Traffic should be light this time of night. The red Trans Am was still filthy from Wednesday's storms and due for a good washing this weekend, but it would have clear sailing to the southwest side. He should be home by midnight. Jeff turned to go.

And then the phone rang.

He halted just outside the office door.

It was bound to be a printer. Or one of the separators — they all worked three shifts. The voice-mail could get it.

On the fourth ring, just before the voice-mail would kick in, Jeff grabbed the phone. "Jeff Stan—"

He didn't even finish answering.

"What? All right, try to calm down...are you sure there's no one there now? Did you call the police...who? A detective? Fine...look, don't apologize...just give me your address." Jeff jotted down the number.

"I'll be there in twenty minutes, Colleen."

✦

The Howard El was a crowded, stifling way to commute to work on any weekday rush hour. With Charade's hectic schedules and interminable overtime, Colleen learned that it didn't get better at night, not even on a Friday.

Her grayed aluminum El car was full when she boarded downtown but it emptied fast with each stop as it sped northwards. Colleen stared absentmindedly at the southbound platforms whizzing by and each was crowded with Lincoln Park yuppies in their faux 60's madras plaids and Gap khakis, heading off to comedy clubs in River North and late night grilled swordfish suppers downtown. The train rumbled further north into NewTown and Wrigleyville, where the seedier twenty-something's were dolled up in affected post-grunge and clogs and carefully unwashed hair, craning their necks over the tracks to wait for *their* southbounds to take them to poetry slams and house parties and pirate rock clubs.

Irving, Montrose, Lawrence Avenues — the platforms were just as crowded, but now with kids decked out in all-too-familiar dyed hair and raccoon eyes, blackberry lip gloss and pewter ankhs, the obligatory black leather pants and skirts, the lace gloves and the mesh blouses and the ubiquitous black tights...a humid 78 degrees at 10:30 notwithstanding. Heading for their occult bookstores and all night gaming jams and fetish parties, or whatever it was they did dolled up like death and dominatrixes.

The clothes, the makeup, the licorice whip legs and black granny boots stomping out cigarettes — Colleen automatically started to think about Cass again. About Terri Shepherd and all of her questions about his friends and his hangouts. About Whitestar Media Group and Charade Magazine.

About Gothique.

Never the praying type, Colleen prayed this whole week that Cass had simply fallen head over heels for some sweet young thing, some other black clad kid with a penchant for Dracula videos and femme fashions and brooding techno-pop music. *Please God, please let him be strung out on the worst drug, let him be hanging out in some sleazy tenement with the lowest lowlife Chicago could muster, let him be turning tricks in some Uptown alley for the money to buy one more of his stupid monster toys. Please God, let Cass be doing anything. Anything but...*

Anything but raped and brutally murdered that very night she left him with those catty ghouls.

Anything but bled to death in a cemetery, like a butchered hog.

Cass — tagged like a cut of meat and left cooling in a coroner's drawer.

Cass — vanished, just a blank snapshot of an empty stainless steel slab.

The empty train screeched to a halt at the Morse Avenue stop, and Colleen shuffled out and down the stairs.

She knew the fridge was empty at home, except for the last two beers she and Detective Terri Shepherd left last night. She knew the kitchen cabinets were empty too. Colleen hadn't been thinking about groceries and shopping these past few days.

It didn't matter. She wasn't really up to eating. And the shops along Morse were all closed for the night anyway.

Colleen trudged along the sticky sidewalk towards Sheridan, T-shirt clinging to her back, bra strap cutting into her skin, legs clammy inside her jeans, feet whining inside their socks and tennis shoes for a rest. The lake breeze helped once she reached Sheridan, even if it was still warm, still humid, still six blocks to go to the apartment. 'Got to get a car,' she suddenly decided. 'Once things settle down, I have to buy a car.' Charade Magazine's money was good. She didn't spend much, just on rent and the usuals, even if she did suddenly have to pay *all* the rent. She slung her purse strap higher on her shoulder and hiked along the edge of Loyola Park, where the waves were spraying the little strip of beach just a narrow block away, and the fog was already aglow under the beachlights. 'Yep, I'll look for one as soon as everything's back to normal.'

Once she turned onto her block, Sheridan's car radios and engine rumbles were immediately muffled by the maple canopy looming overhead and swaying back and forth under the streetlamps. The sidewalk was dappled with bits of moving light and shadow. Barely halfway down the block, and the busy street behind was only a memory. It was quiet as a church, quiet as a graveyard, except for the whisper of the waves ahead, the rustle of the leaves above. Her tennis shoes barely made a sound on the cracked sidewalk.

So what were those footsteps clicking on the concrete?

Colleen clenched her purse under her arm and halted. The footstep sounds stopped.

She started up again, and a moment later, the steady click-click of leather soles on well worn cement started up too.

Colleen Russell was a born and bred city girl. She'd wrestled her purse out of a mugger's hands on the El, kneed a total stranger in the crotch when his fingers got to roaming in an elevator at Marshall Fields. She'd mastered the cold stare that could silence catcalls at construction sites.

She stopped again.

Those footsteps stopped.

She whirled around.

The sidewalk was empty.

Cars glided by on Sheridan, not a hundred yards away, though they were soft-focus-hazy through the fog layer already creeping down Chase Avenue. The trees swayed, the streetlamps tried to shine through the moving branches. The old apartment buildings perched on each side of the street, silent, dark except for a lighted window or two.

There was nothing.

No one.

No white faces.

No raccoon eyes. No blackberry lips cracking into a bitchy smile. No Frostbite or Gem role-playing in the dark gangways. No Gabrielle fingering a jackknife, out for revenge.

Colleen shook her head, wanting to tell herself she was just being silly. All the same, weary legs walked faster till she turned into her courtyard, just not listening anymore, even if she did dash through her building's front door a little faster than usual, even if she did take the stairs two at a time. The mailbox could wait until tomorrow. She slammed her apartment door behind her and carefully locked each and every knob, deadbolt and chain.

No footsteps followed her up the four flights of stairs, she was sure of that. Just the comedown from a fourteen hour day, she assured herself.

She didn't bother with the lights. Didn't bother to open a window, even though the apartment had been baking in the sun all day. Colleen dropped her purse by the door, kicked off her tennis shoes in the living room, unclasped her bra and yanked it out from under her T-shirt in the hallway. She was already wriggling out of her jeans while she walked straight towards her room. She only paused for a second at Cass' open door.

Everything was just the way she left it last night when Detective Shepherd said goodnight. Closet door and dresser drawers closed. Windows shut. Lights off.

With her jeans bunched down around her calves, Colleen shuffled across the hardwood floor to her bedroom. She kicked them all the way off as soon as she flopped on her bed.

Face mashed into the pillows, her eyes slammed shut, she was asleep before she could even drag her legs all the way up on the mattress.

But, not half an hour later, Colleen's eyes popped open.

Her head jerked up, her whole body jerked, and she awoke out of a nightmare.

It was an ugly dream: there was Detective Shepherd, and the grisly photo of that girl, Chelsea. There was Gabrielle and the whole crew from Rimbaud's Cave. There was Cass, and the morgue, that snapshot of the empty stainless steel table, and even her sister, Megan.

And that envelope.

Colleen sat up on the bed, shivering. Her room was hot, yet...

That envelope. The envelope brought in to Jeff two days ago, the envelope that had been buried somewhere in the mail room since June.

And suddenly, Colleen knew whose handwriting was on that envelope.

It was Megan's.

Her sister Megan had hand addressed that envelope to Jeff, maybe on the very day she died.

Colleen glanced at the clock radio on her nightstand: 11:15. Was it too late to call Jeff? To find out what was in that envelope? To tell him who it was from?

Still shivering, she dragged the tangle of sheets and blankets over her and pulled them up to her chin. A draft fluttered the red hair dangling around her face.

A draft?

Colleen's shivering increased when she realized she could distinctly feel a breeze on her cheeks, a cool breeze, a breeze that was thick with the familiar scent of the Lake. She glanced at her bedroom window.

Closed tight.

She drew her knees up to her chin and started rocking on the bed when she realized she could hear the lakewater lapping at the breakers four stories down, just the way she could always hear it...

When the windows were *open.*

She bit her lip when she heard the telltale squeal of paint caked hinges...window hinges.

The window hinges in the bedroom...just down the hall.

And she felt a cold sweat break out all over her skin when she heard a floorboard creak, heard shuffling in that room — *in Cass' room* — shuffling footsteps, like the sound of someone tiptoeing in hard soled shoes.

She heard a drawer open.

Then another.

Colleen's eyes were glued to the pitch darkness hovering outside her doorway. She tried to form the word. She could make her lips move, but no sound came out. She gulped when she heard more shuffling steps, and the closet door opening. Gulped again and worked the air and saliva into her mouth, and then she could finally say it.

"C-Cass?"

The sounds from Cass' room stopped.

"Cass, is that you?"

✦

When Libbie clicked the TV off, Frank Hoelevich woke from a comfortable doze on the lounger. "What time is it?" Sox raised his head from his paws. He'd been dozing too, right beside Frank's chair.

"Almost midnight," Libbie said, shutting off lamps in the living room. "You fell asleep. The Cubs lost in extra innings, the weatherman says hot and humid again tomorrow, and that country singer you like was on Jay Leno."

Frank sat up in the lounger. "You went to answer the phone, and then next thing I know, it's tomorrow?"

"Frank, I got the phone a little before nine."

He shook his head, amazed that he slept for almost three hours. Or more correctly, amazed that Sox *let* him sleep. The dog hadn't been out since before dinner. "So, who called?"

"Stella. Said she was going to give us one more try." Libbie put the TV Guide away and took her late night's snack dishes to the kitchen.

Frank nodded to himself. Stella was Libbie's sister-in-law, calling from Sarasota, where half of Libbie's clan had moved to over the past ten years. Frank and Libbie never followed, but they tried to make it down there each summer for the annual family get-together. Or, Libbie did, at least. Frank had his fill of suntanned senior citizens and their know-it-all kids bugging him to sell the storefront two-flat and buy into one of those shoebox condos. But he knew Libbie looked forward to the visits. After all, just as the young ones kept growing, their own generation shrunk a little each year.

Of course, they missed the bash last year.

Money was tight. A doctor bill here, some medicine there, everything was always going up. Interest on their nest egg, Social Security and the few dollars of GI pension only went so far. It was out of the question this year.

Libbie returned to the living room. "Aren't you coming to bed?"

"Yeah, I guess. In a minute. So what exactly did Stella say?"

"Oh, the same. Reminding me that her granddaughter was getting married, and we'd miss the shower *and* the wedding *and* the family picnic."

"Well, Libbie, maybe we could — "

"Frank, don't be silly. Hotels, meals, it'd be a fortune."

"Well, maybe if it was only the one of us? You could stay with Stella."

"Oh? So you and Father Silverez could play cards and drink beer every night?"

"No, I just meant that it would be cheaper if you went alone, and — "

"Frank." Libbie shook her head. "I checked the airlines. Even a discount fare is more than we could manage." She looked around the living room, seeing the same furniture, the same wallpaper, the same everything she'd seen for years. "I'm going to bed."

"Well, I better let the dog out or he'll be waking me as soon as I get to sleep." Maybe it wasn't the smartest thing to do, but Frank hadn't told Libbie about the incident in the gangway. And he hoped Gil would keep it to himself too. There was no sense in alarming her, since nothing came of it. She rarely went out at night herself and probably just assumed the oppressive weather had kept Frank and the dog from their nightly rounds.

As if he could understand Frank and Libbie's every word, Sox already paced by the back door, sniffing at the leash hanging from the knob. There hadn't been any evening trips to Mike's tap the past couple nights. No evening walks at all, in fact, just a quick scoot down the back stairs and into the yard. *Why* was something Sox wouldn't understand, though even his little sheltie brain could still vaguely remember the scuffle in the gangway, the sharp kick of a boot on his flanks.

And the scent.

Sox remembered the unnatural scent of that mean, black shadow with the heavy boots. He remembered that, all right.

"Let's go, boy," Frank said as they trundled down the back stairs. "But make it quick. It's late."

It was still unpleasantly hot when they got outside. At least there was a breeze, enough to ruffle the dog's caramel and white fur. Frank hovered by the gate, peering into the hazy gloom and the patch of streetlight at the end of the gangway. "Come here, boy," he called once he saw that Sox had done his business and was fastidiously kicking his hind paws, covering it with a pile of grass.

"Gang-bangers or not, I feel like a smoke." Frank clipped Sox' leash to his collar. "Been two days now."

They walked quickly through the dark gangway, but just before they stepped into the lights out front, Frank paused. He poked his head out and looked up and down the street.

Nothing.

Not a single car passed by either way. A black Caddie and a black Mercedes were parked across the street, right under The Palace's marquee, but that was all.

"Nope, shouldn't be calling it The Palace anymore. 'Gothique" now." Frank shook his head as he bent over one of Libbie's potted geraniums. Underneath was a nicked and dented metal case — a watertight canister issued to the GIs the night before they hit the Normandy beaches. Then it contained bandages, sulfa powder and one syringe of morphine. But Frank had squeezed in two Havana Morillos. He took up the stogies in boot camp — anything to make a teenage face look a little older. That canister made it through the war, and he kept it since.

Sox sniffed the flowers while Frank lit a cigar and puffed it to life. "It's hell about Libbie, boy." The dog looked up at him, like he always did when Frank talked, but he went back to his earnest sniffing once he was sure it wasn't talk about food. "God knows *I* don't want to get dragged down to Sarasota. A bunch of old people pretending to be fifty again in their golf carts and their Bermuda shorts. That, or just waiting around to die, and their kids waiting around to get theirs." Frank puffed away on the cigar, letting the warm breeze twist the smoke into spirals around his head. He sat down on the stoop to the first floor doorway and leaned against the burglar bars. *Hoelevich Hardware* was still painted on the glass. There used to be a neon sign in the window, too, but Frank took that down after he closed the business. "But Libbie sure looks forward to that annual shindig. Family, you know. Family's important, boy."

Sox glanced up from the flower bed, then buried his nose back in the plants. Family *was* important, to Libbie and Frank both. Problem was, they couldn't have one of their own. After three miscarriages, the doctor told Libbie to stop trying. Frank mentioned adoption once. But instead, they both just made do by doting on the nieces and nephews, passing out quarters and candy to the poorer neighborhood kids.

"Jeez, I wish I could scrape up the dough." Frank glanced across the street, where the huge theater loomed overhead. Not a single light shined out of the black glass doors or the windows on the three upper floors. But near as Frank could tell, all the windows were painted over black. "But, no use wishing, I guess." He watched twin taillights hover in the foggy darkness just a short hop up Damen Avenue.

Suddenly, Sox jerked the leash, staring intently across the street — ears raised, fur bristling, tail up — his little black nose twitching.

Frank stood up from the stoop, a nervous feeling buzzing along his spine. "What's up, boy?" He looked up and down Damen. The streetlamps lit up wide circles of almost-fog, the next cross street was gray and indistinct. Just those two red taillights glowing down the block...

"Come here, Lassie. Got a special treat for you."

A low growl rumbled out of Sox' throat.

The words came from nowhere, and everywhere at the same time. They just floated in the darkness, a barely-there whisper echoing between the huge theater and the Hoelevich's two-flat. Frank looked back and forth from the theater, to the alley next to it, to those murky taillights, those two red dots glowing in the haze.

"Come on, pooch, come and see what we've got for you."

"Who's there?" Frank dropped his cigar.

Something brushed against his back.

Sox growled and leaped, but Frank yanked him back by the leash.

But there was nothing.

No one on the little patch of front lawn. No one by the gangway. No one down the sidewalk. No one...

"What are you looking for, old man? Come out to see more titties tonight, did you?"

Then another disembodied voice: *"What's the matter, don't like peeking at your woman's old bags anymore?"*

"Who is that?" Frank took a firm step forward. "You come on out and I'll teach you to talk like — "

The words caught in Frank's throat. That's when he noticed that those twin red taillights weren't taillights at all. They were just two glowing points of red light, hovering in the haze over Damen Avenue. Hovering, and drifting closer.

"Where's your buddy, old man?"

"Yeah, bring us the priest, old man. Bet he wants to see titties, too."

Frank jumped. Something brushed past him again. He spun around, tangling Sox' leash around his ankles. The dog growled again, then tugged, uncoiling the leash and spinning Frank around till he almost fell.

"Sox, don't — "

But Sox dashed straight across the street.

And then, Frank saw them.

They were just shadows at first. Just slender patches of black that were darker than the darkness surrounding them. One popped up from behind the Caddie parked across the street. Another eased out from behind the Mercedes. Two more slithered out of the alley next to the theater. More just seemed to appear out of the shadows under the marquee.

Sox shot between the two black cars, barking like a hound on a fox hunt.

But the barking stopped abruptly as soon as he rounded the Caddie.

There was a moment of silence.

Then, a high pitched squeal.

"Sox?" Frank stepped up to his curb. "Where are you, fella? You okay?" He jerked his head back and forth, watching those black figures glide over his way. And out of the corner of his eye, he still saw those two red dots glowing, still drawing closer.

Then — they were gone.

All of them. The red glow, the shadow figures — *gone.* Just as if they'd never been there at all. The street was silent. Even the breeze went still.

But he could hear Sox whimpering.

"Sox?"

Just as suddenly as they vanished, they were back.

Right in front of his face now.

"Jesus Christ, Jes — " Frank would have fallen on his ass right then, but a white hand shot out of the darkness and grabbed him by the throat, cutting the words off along with his breath.

A pale face hovered right in front of his, a face with two wide eyes that glowed red-orange, just like barbecue coals. It was that same kid from the gangway, the same one he and Gil caught pawing that girl.

"Sorry, old man," the kid sneered, his voice all lispy and vicious. "None of that churchy stuff now, okay? Ain't polite."

Frank struggled. He took a wild swing with one fist, but the skinny punk dodged it effortlessly. He still held Frank tight by the throat, held him up high, so Frank had to stretch his legs, almost had to stand on tiptoe just to keep from choking.

And *damn* if that kid's eyes weren't glowing for real. Damn if his face wasn't as white as a clown's, if his grinning lips weren't black as dirty oil, if his teeth...

Frank's mind reeled. *'Holy Mary —* those teeth — *Mother of God, pray for us sinners —'*

"Now, now, old man. I told you. Don't even be *thinking* that stuff. I can still hear you."

One of the shadow figures glided across the sidewalk. Her eyes glowed too, her red lips cracked into a devil's grin, her teeth glistened under the hazy streetlight. "Put him down," she said, and her voice was like something straight out of a nightmare — part windchime, part shattered glass, and all evil. "You'll break the old guy's neck, and then what good will he be?"

It was dawn on Omaha beach all over again. It was December in Malmedy, and the black jackboots were crunching the snow, drawing closer, Lugers drawn and cocked. Frank was sure he'd piss his pants, or worse. But he didn't.

The girl passed under a circle of streetlight, no shadow trailing behind her on the asphalt. It was that same girl — the girl from the gangway, the girl that they tried to help, the girl this other one was trying to...only now she was...she...

She cradled Sox in her arms.

Her long, white fingers poked out of lacy half gloves. Those fingers were tipped with dark nails, and they stroked Sox' fur.

But the dog would have none of it. He thrashed like a trapped weasel, clawing at her see-through blouse till he shredded it, revealing her fishbelly white chest. Sox flung his head back and forth, teeth bared, nipping for her sleeves.

But the girl grabbed Sox by the scruff of the neck and held him out — just like a magician pulling a rabbit out of a hat — all fifty five pounds of the sheltie-and-a-half, dangling from her skinny arm like a paper doll. Sox growled and snapped.

She growled right back at him, her nose wrinkled, her eyes slits, her teeth bared. The dog hesitated — just long enough for her to wrap her other hand around his snout. "There, you little shit." She sidled up to Frank and rubbed against him. "What do you say, old man? Should I have it out with him? Would you like to see what a set of real teeth could do to this mutt?"

Frank kicked at the punk still holding him by the throat. He kicked again and again, as hard as he could. But the skinny kid never flinched.

The other shadows floated across Damen and surrounded them, a circle of pale faces with black eyes and glimmering irises, with black lips and shiny white teeth, all of them decked out in black leather and fluffy shirts and glittering jewelry, all of them pawing at Frank and Sox with their pallid white hands tipped with long painted nails, poking, jabbing, giggling and then poking some more. They circled closer, and even Frank's old nose twitched. They *smelled.* On the surface it seemed like an alluring smell, like a woman wearing too much perfume. The scent was flowery and sweet, smoky like incense.

But a little ripe.

They smelled just like a funeral parlor.

"So, here it is, old man," the one holding Frank said. "Maybe one night your little dog will just disappear while you're sleeping." He leaned his crazy mime face right into Frank's so their noses almost touched, so Frank couldn't ignore those eyes simmering away in their dark sockets. "Or, maybe you can just mind your own business? Maybe you should keep your eyes closed, your blinds down, your mouth shut. If we want a fucking audience, it sure as hell won't be you."

"Better yet, why don't you just go away?" It was the girl again. She kept circling Frank, rubbing against him, and when she did it sent icy shivers down his back. And all the while, she dug her nails right through Sox' fur, and the dog squirmed and whimpered, his snout still locked inside her white hands. "Why don't you just blow away and die? Pack up and leave. We don't want you here. No priests, no old people, see? This is our turf now, and only the young, only the pretty, only the *extremely* cool need apply."

Frank's eyes followed the girl as she circled him, glaring at her with equal parts of anger and terror as her lethal looking nails clawed at Sox. But the punk with the iron grip jerked Frank's head back to face him. "Now you could run off to your friend the priest. But we're not scared of him. Or you could call the cops." A couple of the shadows elbowed each other and laughed at that. "But then, you could find your woman dead some morning, see? Or maybe, maybe she's just like — gone? Maybe the worst part will be wondering for the few years you have left...just how did we off her? Like, was it quick, or was it slow, was she boo-hoo-hooing your fucking name while she died?"

"Or maybe we just make you watch." The girl smiled, then her dark lips parted and she let her even darker tongue loll out and flap obscenely in Frank's face.

"Think about it, old man," the punk said.

And then — he was gone.

Frank fell to his knees, right on the curb. He looked up, and the punk was just — *gone.*

The girl was gone.

All of them were gone. Only the humid haze lingered on Damen, stirring into ghost swirls from a breeze that wasn't blowing.

Sox appeared at his side, panting, whimpering and licking Frank's cheeks till they dripped. "Good boy," Frank said, wrapping his arms around the dog and hugging him tight. "That's a good boy. They're gone now."

Frank stared across the street at the black cars and the empty shadows. He looked up at the dark theater towering overhead.

One window was open now, up on the top floor. A pale light shined out of that window.

And a far away sound filtered out of that window and drifted down to Damen Avenue, where Frank sat on the curb, coughing through his aching throat, clutching his dog like a baby. It was that same, insane, giggling, those same devil-child voices laughing from somewhere inside the bowels of the old Palace Theater.

From inside Gothique.

EIGHTEEN

Optimistic? Naive? Or just plain stupid? Jeff should have known he couldn't possibly make it to Colleen's apartment in twenty minutes.

Between the cars lined up to exit the lot where he parked and the downtown movie and nightclub crowd cramming every on-ramp, it took twenty minutes just to get onto Lake Shore Drive. There he gunned it and the red coupe roared up the northbound lanes, slicing at a dangerous eighty through the fog drifting across the beaches. Altogether, it was nearly an hour before he whipped off Sheridan Road onto Chase Avenue. He immediately saw a squad double parked at the end of the block, light bar flashing an eerie blue and red strobed halo in the haze.

Jeff left his car hanging halfway out of a too-small space, then sprinted to the courtyard. The front door to Colleen's building hung wide open. He took the stairs two at a time.

"And you are?" Two uniformed Chicago cops crowded the little fourth floor landing, sipping coffee from to-go cups. One puffed on a cigarette.

"My name's Stancheck. Colleen Russell called me." Jeff pointed into the open apartment doorway, fearing the worst. "She works for me."

The officer with the cigarette dangling from his mouth just returned a blank stare. His partner offered a similar 'so what?' look.

"So, can I see Colleen? Is she all right?"

Just then, a short young woman stepped out of the kitchen and into the apartment's living room. "What's up, fellas?"

"Some guy. Says he's the girl's boss."

"Well, let him in," Detective Terri Shepherd ordered. "And you guys can go now. I'll follow up on the paperwork with you in the morning.

The two policemen glanced inside the apartment, snickered at the horror movie posters framed on the wall, then clomped down the four flights of stairs.

"Mr. Stancheck? I'm Detective Shepherd." She stepped forward with her hand outstretched.

Terri Shepherd's brown pixie hair poked out porcupine style. Even her long bangs stuck straight out in spikes, like she'd just gotten out of bed. Her face was free of makeup, revealing a hint of freckles on the top of her cheeks and across her long nose. She wore a wrinkled Loyola University T-shirt, sloppily tucked half in-half out of blue jeans that were too long and covering white running shoes.

At first glance, Jeff marked her for a friend of Colleen's.

But there was no missing the large revolver poking out of a clip-on holster. Right next to the plastic Police ID badge hanging from the waistband of her jeans.

Though Terri Shepherd's brown eyes looked a little sleepy, Jeff spotted an intimidating alertness in them too. That, and the fact that they were big and round and richly sienna brown, and suited her thin, long nosed face perfectly. Under the circumstances, he was surprised to find himself reluctant to let go once they shook hands.

She motioned Jeff inside. "Colleen told me she called you at the office. I'm glad you came."

"Then, she's okay?"

"She's fine. But pretty shaken up. She's — "

Colleen came shuffling out of the bathroom. "Jeff, you came." She ran up to him, sobbing, and he instinctively wrapped his arms around her in a fatherly hug. "Oh God, I'm so sorry I called you. But I didn't know what to do. I was just...just so scared. And then, then I - I — "

"It's all right, Colleen. Everything will be all right." Though he wasn't even sure what had happened yet, Jeff did his best to sound as soothing as he could. He had thirteen years of skinned knees and bruised feelings to practice with before Jacks was whisked away to California. He ignored the fact that Colleen was an employee and just held her tight.

"God, I'm j-just so embarrassed," Colleen sobbed.

"Don't be," Jeff said. He led her to the couch.

Hovering across the living room, Detective Shepherd watched Jeff closely. "Colleen phoned me at home," she said. "I was sacked out on the couch with the TV blaring away. Surprised I even heard the phone. I notified a patrol car from this precinct to get right over. Colleen called you while she waited, Mr. Stancheck."

It was all still confusing. Yet Jeff still managed to conclude that Detective Shepherd's smile seemed sincere.

And that he liked it just fine.

She stepped away from the couch. "Well Colleen, any chance there's some coffee hiding in that mess of a kitchen?"

"M-maybe. I don't know. I haven't shopped or — "

"You two talk," Terri said. "I'll snoop." She disappeared into the kitchen.

So Colleen told Jeff everything: her train ride home, the feeling that someone was following her down her block. Falling into bed, the nightmares that followed. And then, the sounds.

The unmistakable sounds of the windows opening in Cass' room. The footsteps shuffling across his floor. Drawers flung open, the closet door squeaking. "I was so scared, Jeff. I've never been so scared in my life. When I could finally get my mouth to work, I called him. I called out Cass' name. And the footsteps just stopped. The drawers opening, everything, it just stopped."

"And then?"

"You'll think I'm nuts." She managed a half smile, and wiped her eyes with her fingers. "Bad enough I dragged my boss here in the middle of the night. If I tell you this, you'll have me in Human Resources Monday morning getting the *'we're very sorry, Ms. Russell, but —'* speech."

"Let's forget I'm your boss for now, okay? Just think of me as a friend."

"I do, Jeff." Colleen twisted her hands in the bottom of her T-shirt. "I really do." She looked over her shoulder, down the hallway leading to the bedrooms. "I'll show you."

Cass' room looked like a tornado had blown through.

The two halves of the large window were completely shattered and hanging by broken hinges. The dresser, the closet, the bookshelves, the bed — everything was overturned and scattered all over the floor. The closet doors were smashed. Lamps lay on their sides. The room was littered with clothes, magazines, books and CD's.

"There was just this — this *sound,* Jeff. A — a *whoosh.* I heard the windows slamming, the glass break, and a noise like a — a big wind or something roaring through." Colleen picked up one of the Goth-rock zines from the clutter on the floor and set it on an overturned bookcase. "I waited a couple minutes in my room. I was too scared to move a muscle. I didn't hear anything more, then. So I ran for the phone."

Terri Shepherd stepped into Cass' room, juggling three mugs of steaming coffee. "Well, it's just instant. I didn't find any sugar, and Colleen — if that's supposed to be milk in the refrigerator, it's gone green."

Jeff and Colleen took the mugs. Jeff sipped his as he stepped over Cass' things flung across the floor. "So what's the story, Detective Shepherd? Why would anyone trash the place like this?"

She raised her eyebrows from behind her mug. "I don't know. But do you notice anything peculiar about the mess, Mr. Stancheck?"

Jeff looked around the room. He shrugged his shoulders.

"Notice how everything's blown off the shelves, off the dresser, out of the drawers, the closet — all in one direction — *out?* Even the windows are blown outward, and hard enough to smash the glass. It's like...something, something powerful, a big gust of wind maybe, just dragged everything out of place, like a vacuum just sucked everything towards the windows."

Jeff shook his head, feeling stupid and looking just as confused. "I don't get it. Who could do all this damage?" He uprighted an overturned bookcase. "Someone had to break in and — "

Terri Shepherd shook *her* head now. "Colleen insists she locked the door when she came in. There's two deadbolts, a lock on the knob, two latches and a pair of security chains. Those uniforms and I checked that door extra close. There's no sign of forced entry."

"It was Cass," Colleen said.

Jeff and Terri both turned to her.

"I'm telling you, it was Cass."

"Colleen, if you really did lock those doors, even someone with a key couldn't get in," Terri said. Obviously she and Colleen had gone over this already. "Not with the latches and security chains. It would take professional burglary tools. And a pretty professional burglar."

Jeff stood by the broken window. He leaned out and looked down four stories to the courtyard below. Lake fog covered the grass. More spilled in across the breakers.

"Well, there's no way someone could get up this wall. The brickwork's pretty worn out, but there's nothing to grab onto. It would take mountain climbing equipment or something like that."

"It was Cass," Colleen repeated.

Terri Shepherd wrapped one arm around Colleen's shoulder and started to lead her out of the room. She turned back to Jeff. "Come on back to the living room, Mr. Stancheck. This may not exactly be according to policy, but perhaps Colleen and I should tell you a little bit about Cass."

✦

The jar of instant coffee was empty a few hours later.

They talked all that time — Colleen and Detective Terri Shepherd explaining the peculiar details about the young man that was murdered in the cemetery earlier in the week, and the even more mysterious disappearance of his body from the Cook County Medical Examiner's facility.

They even showed Jeff the photos — Chelsea's head and bare shoulders, mauled, chalk white and very dead. And a shot of an empty coroner's slab, where what may have been Cass' body lay when the photo was taken.

Jeff listened intently, no matter how strange their story was. He had no reason to doubt Colleen Russell. Though he'd only known her a short time, he was absolutely certain she was an honest, level headed, rational person. And she was Megan Russell's sister — Megan, his partner at Charade for so many years. Terri Shepherd, he didn't know at all. But she spoke professionally, sounded convincing enough. And frankly, she could have told him that little purple men landed in a spaceship on the roof and he would have bought it. Her big, brown eyes nestling under those twisted bangs made him want to believe just about anything she said.

"The disks!" Colleen jumped off the couch. "Jeff, those disks, that's what woke me up."

"What disks?" Terri asked.

"Jeff got this letter at work. It got lost in the mail room, had been there a few weeks. And there were these disks inside."

"It's nothing," Jeff said. "I've tried to open them, but the disks are damaged. I think the files are probably corrupted. Or totally gone."

"Jeff, those disks were from Megan," Colleen said. She turned to Terri. "They were mailed the day after she was killed. I remember the postmark. I couldn't get the handwriting on that envelope out of my mind all week. And then, last night, right before all this stuff happened, I just woke up from this nightmare, suddenly *knowing* that it was Megan's handwriting."

"You still have the envelope?" Terri asked.

Jeff shook his head. "Nope. Tossed it. That envelope's long gone. I have the disks, though. In fact, I was going to send them out to a service bureau Monday morning to see if they could be salvaged. But what if they *were* from Megan? They could just be some copy for the magazine, or a budget report, or some memos or a million other inconsequential things."

"No," Colleen said. "I just have a feeling."

Terri Shepherd locked those brown eyes of hers with Jeff's. "Well, whatever it is, I'd be interested in knowing once you find out."

"Sure," Jeff said. "If you think it's important."

They tried to convince Colleen to go to a hotel for the night. Jeff even offered to let her expense it, and when she turned that down, he insisted she stay at his house over the weekend. But Colleen would have none of it.

So the Lake fog was already backlighting with a subtle, purplish pre-dawn glow when Jeff and Terri Shepherd finally left and crossed the courtyard towards Chase.

"You think she'll be okay up there?"

Terri shrugged. "I think so. I hope so. At any rate, I'm going to call the local precinct again and ask them to send a car over. If they can spare one on a Friday night. For whatever good that will do." They walked past the courtyard gates and onto Chase Avenue. The entire street was still blanketed in a layer of haze. And completely silent, as it could only be in the still time just before dawn. "So, you knew Colleen's sister pretty well?"

"Megan Russell and I went way back. Nothing social, just work. Actually, I never even knew she had a younger sister until after she was...until she died."

"I gather you don't think she simply had an accident?"

"Off the top of the John Hancock building? Hell of an accident."

"Suicide?"

"Not a chance," Jeff said. "So what light can you shed on all that? On Megan, I mean?"

"Well, if you want the official line, nothing. But I'll tell you this. If she *did* jump off that building by herself, she took all her clothes off before she did. Which would be odd, don't you think? And they haven't been found anywhere. Believe me, a thorough search was done in the building, in the whole neighborhood.

Wind, you know. But, as I told you inside, I'm I.D.D., not Homicide."

Jeff looked her in the eye. "But you're definitely not telling me *all* you know, are you?"

"No. I'm not. Anything else I could tell you would be totally off the record, totally unofficial, and would get my butt in totally hot water."

They walked along toward their cars. "So Detective, would you think I was nuts if I told you that Coroner's photo you showed, the one where Cass' body should have been..."

"Yes?"

"What if I told you that's not the only photo I've seen lately where someone who's supposed to be there...well — *wasn't there?"*

She stopped dead in her tracks. "I'm listening."

Jeff told her about the snapshots he took in front of Gothique. And about the aloof, dark haired man in the black suit, stepping out of his chauffeured Mercedes and disappearing into the theater's black glass doors. Jeff told her how the man was right there in the viewfinder when he snapped the picture.

And how he just — *wasn't* — in the pictures once they developed.

"This is like something out of a bad movie," Jeff said.

She nodded. "A horror movie."

They started walking again, and reached Jeff's Trans Am.

"Detective Shepherd, I'm not a suspect in anything, am I?"

She gave him a puzzled look.

"What I mean is...well, I know we've both been up all night. And my daughter should be home from her sleep-over in a few hours." Jeff's keys jingled nervously in his fingers. "But, is there any reason you couldn't grab some breakfast with me?"

She smiled. "None at all."

✦

Libbie woke up promptly at 5:45, just like she always did, whether she stayed up late the night before or not. The Hoelevich's didn't even have a working alarm clock.

She reached over for Frank, but only patted an empty mattress.

Libbie sat right up. Frank's side of the bed was untouched. The blanket was still folded neatly under his pillow.

"Frank?"

No answer.

She slipped on her robe and slippers, then opened the venetian blinds so the pink glow of dawn could wash into the little bedroom. Frank's clothes weren't laying over the chair like they usually were. His shoes weren't beside the dresser like they usually were.

"Frank?" Libbie shuffled out of the bedroom. "Frank , where are you?"

She halted at the living room.

"Frank?"

Frank Hoelevich leaned over the armrest of his lounger, fingers holding two slats of the front window blinds open just a crack. He stared through the narrow opening, stared across the street at the old theater building. Sox sat on his hind legs right next to the lounger, his furry snout poked right up to blinds too, nostrils twitching.

"Frank, are you all right?"

He turned to his wife, and Libbie reached for her chest, feeling her heart actually skip a beat.

Frank Hoelevich looked like he'd aged ten years overnight.

"Frank?"

He clutched a large silver crucifix in one hand.

Illinois Intra-Municipal
Law Enforcement Bulletin AC45GR0097
From: Calumet City Sheriff's Department
Date: 8/21

Notice: Unidentified female body retrieved from Calumet Harbor. For chain and cinder block weights bound to body, see Cal-Cit Exh. #2399. Body discovered by fishermen, statements on file. Status: Unclothed, multiple lacerations, misc. wounds, blood cont. 0%; extended decomp. Description: Late 20's, approx. 5'6", brown hair. Remains shipped to CCMedEx 8/19. For more information, see file number...

Dark Delvings WorldNet
Chicago Chat Room
8/26 11:41 PM CST

MW: ((GGGG)) Yep, I quit that crowd. They just want to play dress up and hang out at the Coven Lord's place watching tapes and stuff./

Cee-Mee: Word is his parents are right there in the basement with you guys./

MW: Accurate! But CL's mom makes beer runs for us, so that's OK.

Cee-Mee: Well, we're three short for next RPG session. Friday night. But I need someplace to change before./

MW: Change at my house. Parents out Fri PM. Count me in. Did you get those new fangs yet?/

Cee-Mee: No. Dentist says he won't without a signed note from the 'rents. Anyway, I need to wait till my braces are off. Think?/

MW: Agreed. So what's the word on Gothique? Hype or gonna happen?/

Cee-Mee: I say hype. But if you get that new inkjet, maybe we can try the ID's again. Let's...

Soirees And Shindigs

NINETEEN

Each had marked their own turf down in the dark chambers, deep below Gothique.

Now some of them had virtually been raised on old black and white Universal horror films from the 30's and 40's, weaned on the Technicolor Hammer gothics from the 50's and 60's — all seen on the Sci-Fi Channel, late night TV and video, of course. So *they* believed each and every word of each and every cinematic superstition. And even though one scriptwriter's mythos rarely matched the next, it had all gone Jungian by the 90's anyway, and long since replaced the old folktales.

So *they* demanded coffins.

Some made do with crude boxes banged together out of pallets and drywall scraps. Others indulged in gleaming metal and tufted satin lined caskets that had been filched from a mortuary out on the west side. One poor slob still napped in a corrugated cardboard refrigerator box, though he did it with such finesse that no one would have thought of laughing at him.

Then there were the others.

They snickered at the superstitious fools and their boxes dusted along the bottom with lumps of crumbly Chicago clay and alley dirt, thought them all hopelessly trite. Now these were the ones that came around by way of the elaborate role-playing games, were lured by the industrial music clubs and fetish parties, the ones who thought reality only kicked in on-line or at the almost weekly comics-fantasy-horror-something-con's.

But even if they didn't lie down in coffins, even if they didn't shield their eyes when they skipped past St. Alstantius' Church, even if they weren't rehearsing faux-Balkan and affected British accents, they jealously guarded their own filthy mattresses nonetheless. Guarded their turf with just as much fervor, and marked their territories by spray painting graffiti on the dingy mortar and brick, plastering posters and CD covers and torn pages from Propaganda and Carpe Noctem and their industrial music zines on the mildewed walls.

Some even talked about striking out on their own, sniffing out some new lair elsewhere in the city. Or maybe in the boonies, where the cemeteries were manicured like golf courses, and the mausoleums were there for the taking, just like model condos. Where rumor had it that the pickings were sweet and clean-veined kids strolled the suburban streets at night, blissfully unaware that death and danger might be lurking in the 7-11 parking lots, behind the dumpster at Dunkin' Donuts or at the food court in the mall.

But it was just talk.

Adolescent rebellion and teenage bravado aside, none of them had the guts to venture out on their own.

Not yet.

So tonight, a warm night in the first week of September, they all awoke at sunset, just like every other night.

Some just bolted upright on their mattresses. Some were slower, yawning and stretching in their coffins, smacking red lips that still tasted from last night's binges. Some were curled up together, nestled in a tangle of their soiled black clothes, or naked — their white flesh squirming in the darkness.

But they all awoke, all with the same sensation, that same cold, gnawing thirst kneading their insides and searing their throats and aching right inside their teeth and their gums.

Some took showers in the communal baths that had been installed down there, for all the good it did. There wasn't enough water in Lake Michigan to wash the smell of death off a cold body that was, after all, dead. They grumbled about dormitory living while the lukewarm water splashed across their pallid skin, or maybe just chuckled at the memory of the bloody attack on the proud plumbers once the last faucet and drain had been sealed, the recollection of the monkey wrenches and the butane torches clinking on the floor — almost, but not quite — louder than the little boy squeals the burly union men made before their throats were dripping like the worst of leaky pipes.

Of course, some just wallowed in their graveyard stink, actually relishing the way the odor marked their turf, like a dog marking its territory in the alley.

The very last traces of pink and lilac disappeared from the western sky outside while they primped and preened. They all doted on their costumes before they came here, and they were just as self-absorbed now. Trunks flung open, duffel bags unzipped, makeshift garment racks plundered — their white hands clawed through musty piles of cast-off's and collective kitsch, and they wiggled into their jett black tights and their clingy leather pants, ripped new slits in their black denims and sleeveless T's, buffed their combat boots and their Capezio flats, shredded and slid on black thigh-high's and leggings and fishnets, lingered over which black micro-mini and which velveteen boustierre and which black lingerie to wear tonight, knotted up their taffeta capes, pulled on their belled sleeve blouses and their black turtlenecks and their leather vests and their bike jackets and their pumps and Cuban heels and spikes. They sounded like an army breaking camp when they slapped on their jewelry, hundreds of chains and rings and necklaces and bracelets clinking into place.

Some still even bothered with makeup, enjoying the needless rituals of painting their clawed nails, flouncing blush into the hollows of their pale, sunken cheeks, carefully drawing raccoon rings around their already black eyes, painting their cold lips with shiny maroon, blueberry and black gloss.

No one rushed.

If anything, they dawdled. After all, they had all the time in the world.

Finally — spruced, pampered, jingling and shimmering in leather and nylon, pewter and lace — the nightmare cliques filed out of their cells, laughing, gossiping, giggling, poking each other in the ribs like children, pausing in silence for just a moment to listen to the moans and whines, the boo-hooing and occasional scream of *Oh-Jesus-God-Mommy-Please-Let-Me-Go* from behind the bolted doors where their 'guests' were kept. But that just started the shattered glass laughter and tinkling crystal giggling all over again, and some of them sniffed along the bottom of the door, some of them licked their red lips with cold pink tongues as they sauntered by. They climbed the dank stairways up to the theater, their black irises flickering red and fiery orange as their eyes sliced through the darkness.

Three months ago, there had only been six of them.

A month ago, fourteen.

Tonight, this warm, early September evening, two dozen of them climbed the stairs. Two dozen children of the streets and the clubs and coffeehouses, two dozen 'children of the night'.

Two dozen kids who'd already forgotten their tedious jobs in copy shops and diners and second hand stores, forgot about hustling in alleys for heroin and sex and money, forgot about the drunken stepfathers stumbling into their bedrooms each night, and the high school jocks that beat them up at the bus stops, and the cops that rousted them from the El platforms, two dozen kids who dreamed and wondered and yearned, who pretended and played dress up night after night, wishing for the movies and the songs and paperbacks and the games to be real.

Be real. *Please be real.*

Two dozen newborn vampires.

✦

Marek lounged in his huge leather chair, swiveling it in circles behind a just as huge desk.

This was the very same room where Nicky Kolitzky had nibbled the barrel of a 9MM Mauser just two and half months earlier. The smeared bloodstains from the back of Nicky's blown away head were long gone though.

In those two and a half months the room had been transformed, just like the rest of the old theater building. Dingy wallpapered walls and sun bleached linoleum floors had all been redone. Now the long room on the fourth floor above Damen Avenue was decked out in marbleized paint, sleek neutral carpeting, framed prints appropriated from one of River North's most exclusive galleries. A sculpted black leather sofa and easy chairs formed a conversation pit in one corner. Trim micro-mini blinds covered the tall windows.

Across the room, Arianne ignored Marek, annoyed with the way he played with his new chair like a toy.

She stood at one of those tall windows with the blinds raised. Though the glass was painted over — like all the others throughout the entire building — this window was open and the September evening breeze washed over her. Warm wind blew her long, black hair away from her pale face. It teased the colorless chiffon dress that hung on her slender frame, swirling flimsy fabric around her thin legs. Barefoot, she idly pawed her toes in the carpet.

That breeze was thick with the scent of Lake Michigan, just two miles due east. But Arianne's acute senses detected so much more in the air: autumn's imminent approach, the yellowing of the grass, the browning of the little patches of backyard gardens, the subtle aromas of leaves starting to turn. Warm as the breeze was, and full of day-long baking city smells, she could feel a shift, felt how it was laced with a hint of northerly crispness.

Summer would quickly vanish. Fall would flit through this city and a bitter midwestern winter would descend in the blink of an eye. She never wanted to come to Chicago in the first place. That had been Marek's idea. She wanted someplace warmer. Monaco. Rio. Miami, perhaps. "So, when is the gala opening?" she asked, still gazing out the window at the darkness falling over the city. "Aren't you just a tad off schedule?"

Marek stopped spinning the chair and leaned over his desk, hands folded on the immaculate surface. No papers, no pens, no calculator, no computer. Not even a phone. "Soon enough. We've had a few delays."

"When?"

"Two weeks, I should think. Three, perhaps."

Arianne didn't look back at him, but she shook her head, a barely there smile curling at the very ends of her red lips. Outside, lamps flicked on in hundreds of shaded windows in the walkups and the four-flats and mid-rises stretched out below the open window. In the two flat above the shuttered storefront directly across the street, the blue light from a television set flickered behind the blinds on the second floor. Arianne narrowed her dark eyes, wondering if she saw those blinds move, if she saw a pair of eyes staring back at her.

Neither Arianne or Marek talked for quite a while. In fact, neither of them even moved. If it wasn't for the breeze tugging at her black hair, the whole room could have been a store window display, or a museum diorama. Just mannequins in a theater set, their features as perfect, as rigidly breathless, as lifeless looking.

Finally, Marek broke the tortuous silence. "So, you don't approve?"

"You know I don't."

"Why?" He sounded exasperated. "Why won't you go along with this?"

She did turn around now, and her black eyes bored into his. "I've done nothing to stop you."

"Nor anything to help."

She opened the window a little more. It was a tall, old wood-framed unit, caked with countless coats of paint, hanging on seventy year old rusted hardware. But she raised it with barely a flick of one long nailed finger. Arianne eased onto the narrow window sill, curled up there and drew her legs up to her chin, looking more like a teenage girl in a frilly cotillion gown than a bewitchingly beautiful demon. "I haven't interfered."

"They can sense discord, you know. *That's* hindrance enough. They may all be young, but they're alert. They detect things."

She shrugged her white shoulders, and the lacy strap of her dress slipped off on one side. "So? Let them."

"Arianne — "

"You've gone too far." Her eyes glared at him from behind her folded arms. "All of this — this *circus* you're building. It's too much. And your little minions?" She smirked, her white teeth catching the moonlight. "They'll bring you down, Marek. They'll bring us both down."

"I admit, some of them are a little impetuous, but — "

"They'll destroy us," she spat back at him. "They're too young. Too bold. They're out of control."

"Together, we can easily control them."

"Really, Marek? Are you so sure?"

He pondered that for a long while. Long enough for city lights to form a hazy canopy over the buildings outside Arianne's window. Marek rose from his chair, came around the desk, his suit as black as the enameled wood. "Well, what about your little escapade in that cemetery? Bodies left behind for the police? Hardly what I'd call discreet." He paused at the edge of the desk and leaned back against it. "Anyway, this was all your idea, originally."

"My idea?" Arianne waved her thin arms dramatically. "*This* was my idea?"

"Yes, if I recall — "

"No." Arianne slid her white legs off the sill. "No, it was supposed to be something small. Clandestine. Something quiet and out of the way. A refuge. A quiet little nightspot, someplace to hide, to call home for a while."

"Someplace dark where pale faces don't seem quite so — white?" Marek said sarcastically. "Someplace like...oh, say, a back alley bohemian cafe in Prague?"

"Yes." Her dark eyes filmed over with a far away look. "Like in Prague."

"Yes. Prague," he said. "But it's not the 30's anymore. Times have changed." Marek walked across the long room to her side. "And as I recall, once the Gestapo arrived, they rousted your little den of iniquity in short order. Threw your Jew waiters into the camps. Threw your precious little bloodsucking whores out into the sunlight, if I remember correctly."

They'd both received a long list of errands, and had to get along well enough tonight to do them together. There was so much to be done, and not a lot of time. Marek laid down the law: Gothique's grand opening would be back on schedule, or someone would suffer. And neither Joey or Gabrielle had any intention of being that someone.

The meeting in Marek's office had been longer than usual. It was more unusual still for everyone to be there at the same time. Marek usually handled affairs like a Mafia Don, his orders whispered to one set of ears at a time. But tonight, even Joey and Gabrielle crowded into his fourth floor office with the rest of the...the *gang*.

The smell of almost thirty bodies that should have been dead and buried was stifling, all ripe and funeral and mortuary sweet. There were sounds of an occasional tongue licking dark lips, of sniffing around the two mortals in their midst, and it left Joey desperate for the meeting to end, his mouth watering for a cigarette and a stiff drink. Gabrielle, on the other hand, seemed to like it all just fine, gazing into the pairs of black eyes and wallowing in the implied danger, like standing at the very edge of the lion pit at the zoo.

Everyone of them was assigned a job. There was some grumbling at first, and Arianne seemed to find that funny, smirking all aloof from her perch on the windowsill. But a red-eyed glare from Marek silenced any complaints quick enough.

Some of them had marked time as waiters and waitresses before, like the inept barmaid from Rimbaud's Cave who joined them just last week. They'd hold the same jobs now, whether they liked it or not, and pocketing tips was going to be strictly forbidden.

Some had been in garage bands, some had been drama majors, some had been artist-wannabe's short on skill, and these would all help with the entertainment, lining up bands and booking performance artists and staging elaborate role-playing game sessions. Some had been computer geeks, spending their days and nights websurfing for soulmates that liked to masturbate over blood and plastic fangs, and they could program the sound systems, the video screens and the lights. Some had been thugs and hustlers, and they'd work the door and security.

Some had just been utterly ambitionless lumps, lazily part-timing as clerks and cashiers while they gauged just how far government grants and Daddy's goodwill could be stretched while they pretended to work on associate degrees at junior colleges. Like it or not, they'd be housekeeping.

A job for everyone, a regular little commune. But even Marek agreed that they'd have to recruit more, and that was 'job one' for the next few nights.

It was the one job they all embraced with sheer delight.

Joey and Gabrielle watched the Caddie pull away, watched them all vanish into the haze on Damen Avenue. Then they both got into the Mercedes. "Sitting in that fucking room with all of them gives me the creeps," Joey said. "Doesn't seem to bug you."

Gabrielle shrugged her shoulders and lowered the passenger window. The wind tugged on her tangle of dyed hair. "Nope. I liked it."

"You would."

"Don't you just get off on all that power, Joey? Don't you want to be just like — "

"No." He turned off Damen onto Diversey and headed west. "You know, you're fuckin' nuts, Gabrielle. Seriously. Me, I'm in it for the dough. And the chicks. I get enough and then I'm outa here. Dangerous? Maybe. But at least it makes some sense. But you?" He reached over and grabbed the half pint of vodka and took a swig. "You know what they are, and you still dig 'em. I mean, they're all fucking *dead,* Gabrielle. Dead."

"Not exactly," she said, staring out the open window at the Gen-X couples strolling past Diversey's coffee bars and antique shops. "Anyway, what's the big deal? Why is everyone so turned off with the whole death thing?"

"Gee, I don't know," Joey said. "Maybe something to do with not being alive anymore?" She didn't answer. He handed the vodka back to Gabrielle. Pausing at a red light, Joey asked, "So, you're not pissed about tagging along? You usually don't go in for this kind of drudge work."

Gabrielle lit up a Gitane and blew the smoke out her nose. "Sure, I'm pissed. I thought I could hang out with Arianne tonight. I mean, when the hell is she finally going to do me, you know?" She leaned forward and played with the radio till she found a station she liked, then flipped the volume up full throttle. "But you heard Marek."

"Yeah," he said. "Big plans. Big deals. Pretty heavy stuff."

Gabrielle took another gulp from the vodka. "They're going to need a lot more cots and handcuffs."

TWENTY

"I don't know how to describe it, Jeff," Colleen said. "It's like a *ping-ping-ping,* then a rumble."

Jeff turned away from his computer screen and the center spread of Charade's October issue *(A Free Gothique Poster Inside!)*. "Sorry, Colleen. It's like I told you last week when your air conditioning blew hot air: you get what you pay for." He motioned to one of the visitors' chairs on the other side of his desk, and Colleen took a seat. "I'd have been more than happy to go car shopping with you, but you wanted to do it by yourself. So what have you got now? A Korean econo-box. And a dealer demo, at that. Give me good old Detroit iron any day."

Colleen snorted. "No offense, but your hot rod's probably half foreign parts. Ever hear of the global economy?"

"Yes, but let me maintain my illusions, Colleen."

"Well, they gave me the whole warranty."

Jeff nodded. "Yep, and you're going to need it."

"You're probably right. I'm usually not that impulsive, but the El started to creep me out after...Well, I was just looking over my shoulder a lot."

"I know, Colleen. Look, if you think the Panmunjon-mobile can hobble down to the south side, why don't you bring it around Saturday, and I'll take a look at it."

"Oh, would you, Jeff? That'd be great."

"Don't get too excited, Colleen. I know cars. Tuna cans with lawnmower engines, I don't know so well."

"Still. I trust you." She tossed her jean jacket over her shoulder and stood up. "Anyway, sorry I'm late. Again."

Jeff glanced at his Timex. "Five minutes doesn't exactly qualify as late in this department." He nodded towards his office door and the empty cubicles beyond. "Notice?"

"Guess you're right. Well, I better get to work." Colleen headed for the door. "Jeff, is everything okay? You look a little...well, preoccupied."

Jeff shook his head. "Actually, I'm a little pissed."

"At me?"

"No, not at all." He pulled a Charade Inter-office Memo from his in-box and handed it to Colleen. "Blair's struck again."

Colleen quickly scanned the memo. "Wait a minute, she's assigned Charade's Annual Chicago Graphics Review to...Arnold Gateys? Isn't he like a...well, a — "

"A third string free lance hack writer?" Jeff nodded. "Your sister Megan and I always did the Annual Graphics Review together. Megan knew it was my baby, so she always wrote the copy herself."

"I know," Colleen said. "I read it every year. Man, you two would really rip into some of the competition sometimes." Colleen smiled, then thoughts of her sister made the smile fade. "No way Arnold Gateys will write anything readable. I've laid out some articles for his stuff. It's regular tabloid sleaze. And crappy tabloid sleaze at that."

"Oh, Arnold's a writer for the ages all right."

"Uh-huh. Between six and nine." She handed the memo back to Jeff. "Nothing against Blair, but she sure is doing some wacky stuff to Charade. Kind of a different magazine than it was just...well, just a few months ago. What's with her?"

"Blair?" Jeff shrugged his shoulders. "Blair's kind of an acquired taste. You have to try to understand her. I know on the outside she's all designer suits and Rolexes and trendy clubs. But on the inside she's really..." He paused, stared at the memo, then tossed it back in his in-box. "Come to think of it, maybe on the *inside* she's just designer suits and Rolexes and trendy clubs." Jeff nodded to the Art Department outside his office door. "Looks like the troops are starting to file in. Go on and let me brood."

Jeff watched Colleen head off to the Art Department, where Tim and Ivy were just waltzing in, then turned back to his monitor. A two page, four color spread filled the 20" screen: a bone-thin ballerina made up so her pale skin looked dead, cold and blue, standing *en pointe* on the top of a fake tombstone. Flashbox cables could still be seen in the shadows behind the tumbleweed and dead treebranch props. He'd shoot the file over to one of the staff for some digital retouching once they all ambled in. Anytime between 9:15 and 9:45 seemed to be fair game these days.

Jeff knew he shouldn't even bother. No one would notice the cables. They'd be too busy gawking at the stageblood dribbling from the fake wounds on the ballerina's throat, a glistening streak of red running down her white leotard and tights, all the way down to her satin toe shoes.

Too busy ogling the Gothique logo, lasered into the tombstone prop.

"Got a sec?"

Blair Armstrong stood in his doorway, all black leather and velvet.

"Sure, Blair. Come on in."

"So, the October issue's on track?"

"If you'll stop sending over changes to changes, we'll make it," Jeff said.

"We always do."

"'Course you will, Jeff. You're the one guy I can count on in this place." She wobbled over on impossibly tall, black suede spikes and peeked over his shoulder. "So, what are you working on? Oh, the center spread. Cool."

He started to look back over his shoulder at her, but only raised an eyebrow instead. "'Cool'? You finally take over, and your first issue's got to have a centerfold? How soon do we start the scratch and sniff's?"

Blair playfully punched Jeff's shoulder. "Oh, get with it. It's — artsy. This is going to make my first issue a collectible."

Jeff did turn around now. He stared at Blair. Her trademark Channel suits, Ungaro pumps and all her Michigan Avenue finery had been replaced with head-to-toe black from Near North boutiques. Still pricey, he figured, but more in keeping with Charade's new look. 'Haute Couture Goth', if that was possible.

"Artsy? Blair, the whole goddamn issue's a Dracula magazine." He clicked off the center spread and scrolled through more completed pages. "Let's see here, a tour of hip Chicago cemeteries. The film review section's a retrospective about Italian Giallo cinema. A profile on the Black Lyceum Gallery. The music column's a feature on Velvet Noir and an interview with Robert Smith."

"Well, he was in town. And it's not 'Dracula' stuff, Jeff. The word Dracula isn't in there once. It's a little more sophisticated than that."

Jeff clicked back to the pullout poster center spread and pointed at the screen.

"Oh come on, Jeff, it's just a gimmick to sell magazines.

"It's a Gothique ad. The whole magazine's a goddamn Gothique ad."

"Jeff, today it's Gothique, next year it'll be some other fly-by-night trend, and something else the year after that. It's just a magazine, you know. Just a bunch of pictures and bullshit articles we need so we'll have an excuse to sell ads. This is *Charade,* Jeff. Not the New Yorker."

Jeff just shook his head. "No. It's not." He clicked on the title bar box and closed the spread. "So, what brings you down here anyway? Slumming?"

"No. Just visiting." Blair plopped into a visitors chair. "Did you happen to get my memo on the Annual Graphics Review?"

"I seem to recall seeing something about it, yes. Thanks for screwing up that piece."

"Jeff, I know Megan Russell used to handle it, but I just don't have time to write a whole article these days."

"By the way, congratulations. I haven't seen you since the announcement came out."

"Thanks. Megan leaving...well, dying...is a hell of a way to get the Managing Editor job, but —"

"But it's what you wanted."

"Oh, that's nice." Blair fussed with her hair, moussed, gelled and pouffed, and wildly framing an over made up face. Jeff had always liked that face, always thought that someone half-nice lurked underneath all the overpriced department store goop. Now, there was just that much more layered on top.

"Actually Jeff, the real reason I popped in was...well, I was hoping you could be a pal."

Jeff squirmed in his chair. "Blair, I don't know, I — "

"Don't worry, I'm not talking about a nooner at the Park Stratford. Not that it doesn't sound like fun." She peeled back her black velvet sleeve to peek at her Rolex, then faintly shook her head as if she was trying to figure out if she really could squeeze in a quickie. "No, actually I need an escort tonight."

"What's up?"

"Oh, just a little soiree at Roberta Whitehead's." Blair waited for her announcement to elicit a reaction. She wanted a raised eyebrow, a look of surprise or a smile of approval. But Jeff's face didn't budge. "She's throwing a little cocktail party up in the penthouse to celebrate my appointment to Managing Editor. Be a good opportunity to hobnob with the movers and shakers."

"No thanks."

"Jeff, don't worry, you don't have to rent a tux or anything." She glanced at his clothes and fought an urge to frown. Jeff wore his trademark denims, boots and button down shirt. His well-worn blazer hung sloppily over the back of his chair. "You could change, though. A suit, at least, I suppose, or — "

"Not interested, Blair."

"Don't suppose you'd changed your mind if I told you that some of those elusive Gothique folks are rumored to show up?"

"Nope."

"Come on, Jeff be a pal."

He glared at her.

"Okay, bad choice of words."

"Blair, things are hectic enough already right here. And then Jacks has just started at a new school, and — "

"Jacks? I thought your kid was back in California?"

"There was a change in plans. I'd have told you, but you haven't exactly been around lately."

"Hmmm, I detect some hostility here," Blair said, trying to sound flip. "This wouldn't be about my promotion, would it? Everything's okay when I was the Assistant Managing Editor, but not anymore now that I'm in charge?" Blair looked over her shoulder and out Jeff's door. Colleen Russell stood by the laser printer waiting for some outputs. Blair turned back around and smiled at Jeff. "'Pal-ing' around with someone else these days?"

"I'll ignore that. Colleen's young enough to be my daughter. Make that my considerably younger sister."

"Well, it's just I've heard some gossip. Part of the boss' job, you know. Sounds like you two have gotten pretty chummy."

Jeff's eyes narrowed. "You know as well as I do that kid's had a load of troubles. I've tried to help out. Is there anything in the Whitestar H.R. Policy against that?"

"Not a thing, Jeff." She stood up from the visitor's chair. "You know, I didn't mean to stand you up that night. I got corralled into dinner with Roberta and some advertisers. I really did mean to call."

"It's okay, Blair."

"I mean...well, it's just that whole daughter thing. And that hokey blue collar bungalow scene on the south side. I mean, you're the Art Director for the coolest magazine in town, but you just insist on being this...this..."

"It's *okay,* Blair."

"Sure you won't change your mind? Couldn't hurt your career to brown-nose with the elite for one night. Might even be fun. You could finally find out if the Gothique people are really the boogie-men."

"It's not for me, Blair."

She sashayed towards the door, audibly swishing leather, nylon and velvet. "Still pals, Jeff?" Just out into the hallway, she stopped and turned around. "Let me rephrase that. Still friends?"

"Still friends, Blair."

✦

The passable polish with mustard and onions that Jeff picked up at the carryout off St. Clair had already oozed grease through the wrapper and the bag. The gyros-with-everything he carried in his other hand dripped sour cream and mystery meat juice. He sprinted through the Lake Shore Drive underpass near Ohio, then scanned the lunchtime crowds sprawled out on the lakefront park just north of Navy Pier. Secretaries sunbathed in the last of the summer sun. A group of junior executive types had a volleyball game going, sweat staining their French cuffed shirts while they awkwardly lunged for the ball in their wingtips. Couples filled park benches and picnic blankets.

"Need something to drink with those, buddy?"

Jeff whirled around, and there was Detective Terri Shepherd, a jumbo soda in each hand.

"Orange or root beer," she said, smiling. "Take your pick."

Jeff took the root beer and handed over the drippy gyros bag. "With everything, right?" he said.

She nodded, and peeked in the sack. "It's not a real gyros without sour cream and onions, is it?" She pronounced it *ji-roe.* "Hey, it's still warm. Come on, there's an empty bench over there by the breakers."

They ate their lunch right at the shoreline, with the blue-green water splashing four feet below and Lake Shore Drive high rises casting creeping shadows across their backs under the late summer sun. Terri Shepherd deftly handled the sloppy gyros without getting a drop of sour cream on her navy skirt. Jeff knocked off his passable polish in four giant bites. Charade's schedules bred fast eaters.

"This gyros is a lot better than the one you got last week," Terri said through a mouthful of lamb and pita bread. "I told you that joint on McClurg was a dive. Never trust a place where the uniforms eat. Their tastebuds are all mummified from too many donut shop coffees."

"I'll keep that in mind," Jeff said, mimicking a Jordanesque free throw with his cup and wrappers. The cup tipped into the trash basket six feet away. The wrappers missed and scurried away across the grass. "Maybe you'll let me buy you a real lunch some time."

The last bite of her gyros disappeared into Terri's mouth. "Maybe. Or maybe I'll cook you a dinner some night?" She slurped loudly on her straw. "As soon as I learn how to cook." She stuffed her garbage inside the empty soda cup and tossed it over her shoulder. It landed dead center in the basket.

"Show off."

"Nope. Accident," she said.

"Your aim as good with that thing?" Jeff pointed at the gun poking out of the holster under her camel blazer.

"Better. Tops in my class at the Academy."

"I'll keep that in mind too," Jeff said. "Ever have to use it?"

"People always ask that."

"Most people have never shot a gun."

"Actually, I've never even drawn it in the line of duty. The Inter-Departmental Division's usually busting some bureaucratic scam. You know, a crooked building inspector hooks up with a crooked cop. Precinct Captain shaking down tavern owners, some clerk pocketing valuables at the morgue." She stood up from the bench. "Not exactly your gun toting gangster types. Come on, let's walk."

They strolled along the shore, leaving the high rises further behind. As the park's trees and shrubbery covered their path, they could barely hear the engines and horns blaring on Lake Shore Drive just a couple blocks back.

Terri quizzed Jeff on how Jacks was settling into the new school. Jeff quizzed her back on the wall papering job she was doing in her northwest side apartment's bathroom. She'd brought him four rolls of samples to choose from at their last lunch a few days before, and two swatch books a few days before that. Naturally she rolled her eyes at his choices. *'And you're a designer?'* she'd said then, laughing.

They circled the park and were headed back towards downtown when the small talk faded, so they just walked along in silence for awhile, enjoying the sun and the blue sky. And each other's company.

"It's really pretty here," Terri said, gazing up at the skyscrapers rising over the trees. "Hard to believe what's really going on in this city."

"So you *do* believe there's something rotten going on?" Jeff said.

She laughed. "There's always something rotten going on. Two murders a day, minimum. That's just the ones we know about. And we're all tooting our horns over how the homicide stats are down by half. Jeff, right now, somebody's getting stabbed somewhere. Some girl's getting raped, some store's getting robbed. A hundred dope deals big and small are going on this very moment. This is Chicago. There's no shortage of rotten."

"Terri, you know what I mean."

Her smile faded. "Yes, I do. And yes, there's something rotten going on."

"But you're not going to tell me what it is."

"Nope." They reached the edge of the park and headed under Lake Shore Drive. "Cemetery murders. Missing bodies. That incident at Colleen's." She looked Jeff in the eye. "Best I don't tell you what I think."

Out of the underpass, they plunged back into the office and apartment building canyons.

"Bet I know what you're thinking," Jeff said. "I bet it's the same thing I'm thinking, even though I know it sounds crazy. You think that — "

"No, don't even say it. I don't want to hear it. Because it *does* sound crazy."

They walked east on Ohio, close on the crowded sidewalk, their hands brushing every few steps. By the time they turned onto Fairmont Court and saw the Whitestar Media Group building looming overhead from the next block, their fingers slipped into one anothers'. Just a few steps more, and they were holding hands. Neither said a word about it, afraid the other might pull away. They walked north on Fairmont that way, hand in hand.

"So, any luck on those disks?" Terri asked.

"Disks? Oh." Jeff shook his head. "None. They came back again yesterday afternoon. That's the third service bureau I tried. The things must be ruined."

"Colleen still thinks they were her sister's, though?"

"That's what she says. But even if they were from Megan, that doesn't mean they were anything important."

"Still, I'd love to know what was on them. Especially if Megan Russell was going to mail them the day she died. Why don't you give them to me? Our computer nerds might be better than yours."

"Oh, we'll get into them."

"I could just take them. Evidence, you know." She scanned Jeff's face but he didn't seem to react. "Well, just keep me posted." They slowed their pace as they approached the front entrance to the Whitestar building. Neither of them was ready to let go just yet. "Well, I didn't have any luck either," Terri said. "With that ex-employee of yours. Gabrielle?"

"She wasn't tied up in any of this? I thought Colleen said she was there the night her roommate disappeared."

"Probably was. But we can't find her. She hasn't been back to her last job, hasn't even been back to her apartment. The landlord's been selling off her stuff, what there was of it. So she's just vanished too."

"Well, I never was a big fan of hers, and what Colleen told me made me like Gabrielle even less. But I hope nothing's happened to her." Jeff gazed up the skyscraper's green marble and glass sides, all the way to the twenty seventh floor and Roberta Whitehead's penthouse offices. From the outside, they just looked like another layer of sandwiched stone and reflective windows. "So, do you really think Charade Magazine's tied up in all this?"

"I'm not saying," Terri said. "But I think you should keep your eyes open, Jeff."

"Oh?" He laughed. "Asking me to do a little private investigating for you?"

She gripped his hand tighter. "No. *Definitely* not." She pulled him a little closer, and her sudden seriousness startled him. "I'm asking you to be careful."

"Okay, okay." Jeff's smile faded. "You know detective, I think one day soon, you and I have to talk seriously. With no secrets."

"You think so, huh?"

"I do. Why not over dinner? Say this Saturday?"

"Jeff, I told you I can't cook. I mean, maybe I could — "

He pressed a finger to Terri's lips to silence her. "No, but I can. Why don't you come around in the afternoon? I'll barbecue something. Nothing fancy. Colleen might even be there. I'm supposed to take a look at her car." He paused. "And you can meet Jacks." Jeff watched her eyes, waiting to see if he'd just scared Terri Shepherd away.

"Okay." Terri's brown eyes sparkled. "With your daughter and Colleen there, you'll have to behave." She smiled. "I mean, then it's not like it's really a date."

Jeff sighed. *Was the 'pal' speech coming now?* "Actually, let's say it really is a date. Still want to come?"

Terri nodded, her smile widening. "Yep."

"Saturday then," Jeff said, reluctantly slipping his hand out of hers.

But she pulled him back and completely surprised him with quick peck on the lips.

Then Terri Shepherd spun around and headed off down Fairmont. "Saturday," she called out.

Jeff watched her short, slender figure disappear into the crowds on the sidewalk, the feel of her hand still warm on his, the taste of her lips — lipstick, gyros, sour cream, onions and all — still there on his, even though the kiss lasted no more than a second. Finally, he turned to face the Whitestar Building, and headed back inside.

✦

Baggie jeans dragging on the pavement, Jacks strolled down Archer Avenue, her backpack loaded to the brim with schoolbooks. Rachel — another new senior and Jacks' friend from way back in the old days — was right alongside. Rory, Rachel's younger brother and apparently Jacks' newest admirer, tagged along right behind them.

"So where are you guys headed?" Rory asked, swinging his own back pack — half empty except for some CD's and magazines. "Going to McDonald's?"

"Maybe," Rachel said. "Why?"

"Maybe I'll join you, that's why."

"It won't matter," Jacks said.

"But I'll treat. Honest."

"Still won't matter, Rory." They waited for the light to change at the busy intersection of Archer and Pulaski. Madame Curie High School stood behind them, the huge seventies style brown brick blob they'd all raced out of just ten minutes earlier at the 3:00 bell. Hundreds of other kids spilled out along with them, crowding at the bus stops, and cutting across traffic into the bungalow blocks just across Archer.

"Cool it, Jacks," Rachel said in a fake whisper, loud enough to make sure Rory heard. She cocked her head, swirling long, straight brown hair. "If he wants to treat, let him. Trust me, it's an event."

Rory quickened his pace till he joined up with the two girls, sidestepping a lamp post to sidle up next to Jacks. "Give me a break, sis." He turned to Jacks. "She's never going to let me live down that one time you went out on a date with me."

"It did *not* qualify as a date," Jacks said.

"So I thought paying our own way was, like, proper etiquette these days. I'm supposed to know you're an old fashioned girl?"

"Rory, you're a junior, I'm a senior. I drove. I paid. Not a date. End of story."

They cut across a bowling alley parking lot and headed for the Golden Arches. "Oh, you're just hurting from the tragic breakup," he said.

Rachel reached around Jacks and knocked her brother on the back of the head.

Jacks laughed, elbowing Rachel away. "Rory, you want to treat, go for it. But I'm telling you, it's still not going to make a difference."

"Aw, come on, Jacks. You know you can get us in. You're connected."

"Give up, Rory."

He raced in front of them and held the door open, bowing dramatically as the two girls slipped past.

Armed with shakes and jumbo fries, they settled into a booth. Rory made good on his promise and paid, but he was carefully counting his change before he sat down. Rachel took advantage of the delay to slide in on Jacks side before her brother had a chance to.

"Why don't you stop hassling her?" Rachel said with a handful of fries aimed at her mouth. "She's told you a million times she can't help."

"Because I don't take rejection easily," he said, plopping down on the other side of the booth and ripping into one of the greasy bags.

"For real? Jeez, I hadn't noticed." Jacks sucked on her chocolate shake, while she swirled a french fry in her ketchup with disinterest. "Look, you guys, this is the last word on the subject. My Dad can*not* — and *would* not — get us passes. And even if he could, there's the little matter of being under age."

Rory rolled his eyes. "No prob. I have fake ID's. And they never card girls. Ask my sister, here."

From behind her shake, Rachel exchanged a guilty look with Jacks. *"One* time. And just at that shot-and-a-beer joint on 47th and Kedzie. Not at a real club or anything."

"Hey sis, I've seen you all decked out," Rory said. "You can pass for twenty one easy." And she could. Rachel was teen-model pretty, with shampoo ad hair, a rail thin figure, and big eyes made for mascara ads. "Trust me," he said. "The shorter the skirt, the sheerer the shirt, the less they look at your ID's."

"Always works for you, does it?" Jacks said, cracking up till she snorted her chocolate shake. She lunged for a napkin. "Look, maybe Rachel can get away with it, but I wouldn't stand a chance. They don't make skirts that short. And I wouldn't wear one if they did."

"Then how about the sheer — "

"Rory!"

"Too bad."

"Rory, I've got a sneaky feeling the bouncers at Gothique might be a little tougher than a south side corner tap. Think?" Jacks quit playing with the fries she hadn't really wanted and slid them across the table to Rory. He plunged right in. "And as for you, Madame Barfly..." She turned sideways in the booth and pinched Rachel's arm. "Isn't that place, like, a biker bar or something? At least it was, before I moved to Encino."

Rachel tried to disappear behind her shake. But she wasn't quite *that* thin. "I told you it was just that one time. Anyway, things change in four years. It's not *too* Harley Davidson anymore. More like greaser-gearhead-deathmetal."

"Oh well, fine then. *What* possessed you to go there, Rach?"

"Well..." she hesitated. "There was this guy...and..."

"'Nuff said." Jacks slurped the last of her shake from the bottom of her cup. "Come on, I have to get going. Boynton dumped a load of homework on us. Why I signed up for Advanced Computer Programming, I don't know."

Crossing Archer Avenue, Rory still wouldn't surrender. "So what's your old man got against Gothique anyway? I thought he worked for them?"

"Hardly," Jacks answered, shifting her overstuffed backpack to the other shoulder. "He works for Charade Magazine."

"Yeah, well — same thing, isn't it?"

"Jacks' dad would pop you one for that remark," Rachel said. She turned to Jacks. "But seriously, what *does* he have against it? I mean, it's just a nightclub."

"Try *the* nightclub," Rory said. "Make that, 'Entertainment Complex'. Make that the coolest scene to hit cow town since...well, since forever."

Jacks ignored him. *"I* think my Dad's bummed about the way this whole Gothique thing kind of took over Charade Magazine. Guess it's too trendy for him." They turned on to Karlov. "You have noticed that my Dad's not exactly on-line with trends."

"I think he's cool," Rachel cooed. "You ever want to trade, holler. He's too good looking to be a real dad."

"Well, trust me," Jacks said. "He's a *real* Dad. A real dad who'd ground me for life if I tried to sneak into Gothique. Or any nightclub."

"Aw, he's just too old to do the whole darkwave scene, that's all," Rory said. "Come on, he's probably like The Who and Zeppelin and VH-1 and stuff, right?"

They came to Jacks' corner and hesitated there.

And as they did, the black Mercedes that had been shadowing them since they stepped out of Curie High eased into a vacant spot a few houses back on Karlov.

"Bite me, Rory," Jacks said. "Maybe *I* like The Who and Led Zeppelin."

"Hel-loo, welcome to this century, Jacks. Time to unload the 8-tracks at the garage sale."

Jacks took in Rory's head-to-toe black get up. He had the ripped jeans and the Doc Marten's, the Propaganda T-shirt and the pewter jewelry. He had the hair cut right with the buzzed sides and the long and shaggy top, though Rachel'd told her their father kept threatening to shave it all off some night while Rory was asleep.

The raccoon eyes and the lip gloss — *those* Rory skipped.

Some things the south side just wasn't ready for yet.

"Look, some of the music's okay," she said. *"I* like some of the bands. *I* read some of the magazines. *I* surf some of the sites." She glanced at Rachel: black platform boots, jett black tights, black skirt, black sweater. Makeup layered on a little heavier than a naturally pretty face needed. "But I'm just not into the whole...*scene* the way you guys are."

Rachel shrugged her shoulders. "Well, it's that, or take up house music and acquire a taste for *cerveza fria.* Face it, Jacks. Those are about the only scenes there are these days. Unless you want to hang with the grunge crowd." She curled her dark red lips. "But that's just so...retro."

"Nothing in between, huh?" Jacks said.

Rory and Rachel both shook their heads. "Well, since you take Advanced CP with Boynton, you could always join the Cyber-Geek Club," Rachel offered. "But then we'd have to disown you."

Jacks checked her watch. "Fear not, gang. Thought I might check out the Intramural Ping Pong Team, though. The captain's kind of cute. Nice shorts." She paused. "I'm *kidding.* Jeez." She backed away towards her house. "Gotta go, guys. Call me tonight?"

"Absolutely," Rory said, beaming.

"I meant Rachel."

"Nine-ish, Jacks. Like always. We can bad mouth V-boy here." Rachel play-punched her brother and started to drag him away.

"Thanks for the treat," Jacks called while she fished in her purse for her keys.

"Skip the thanks, just get those Gothique passes," Rory hollered back.

"The Grand Opening night." Rachel punched him again, and not so playfully this time. "VIP passes'll do. Get us into one of the private lounges they're pitching, okay? Oh, fuck it, any night, okay? Jacks — "

Rachel clipped Rory across the back of the head and finally shut him up.

Jacks looked over her shoulder, laughing at the two of them. Then she took the front stairs two at a time and opened the front door to the brown bungalow that matched each and every other one up and down Karlov Avenue.

As she locked the front door behind her, the black Mercedes pulled away from the curb on the next block and slowly, very slowly, cruised by the Stancheck house.

TWENTY ONE

Across town, Father Gil Silverez double timed it up Montrose Avenue. Not yet five o'clock, the rush hour traffic was already heavy. But Montrose tie ups wouldn't slow him down. After all, Gil didn't have a car. Hadn't had one in years, his last a '78 Chevette he bought third hand in '84, and that had been more rust and repaints than sheetmetal. Some priests did well on their pastor's salary. But at St. Alstantius — classified 'middle-middle class' by the Archdiocese — someone always seemed to need a couple bucks just that much more than the parish.

Out all day on parishioner visits, Gil still had two more stops before he could head home for supper. There was Mrs. Heullarta, who hadn't been out of the house in months since her third mugging of the year; she needed Communion. Then Augie Lachowicz's daughter called this morning to say that old Augie'd taken a turn for the worse. Gil didn't know if he'd be stopping by to give the old man a pep talk or the Last Rites.

A few doors up Montrose he saw the green and white shingle of the storefront Chicago Public Library branch. Gil halted, actually slapping his forehead as it suddenly dawned on him that there were four library books back at the Rectory, each a couple weeks overdue. Marian, the little wisp of a librarian — neighborhood girl, just a kid actually, fresh out of grad school and all proud of her Library Sciences degree — that Marian would give him holy hell. Oh, she might let him slide on the overdue fines. Priests got away with little things like that all the time. But one of the books was that latest terrorists-taking-over-a-nuclear-sub bestseller, and everyone was probably looking for it.

Gil stepped aside to let a group of kids squeeze by on the narrow sidewalk. And once he did, he spotted a familiar pile of caramel and white fur napping right in front of the library door. There was Sox, leashed to the bike rack. The dog raised his head as Gil approached, furry tail wagging before the big brown eyes even opened all the way.

The priest reached down to scratch Sox behind the ears. "Now what are you doing here, boy?" Gil shielded his eyes with his hand and peeked in the library's window.

There was Marian, cute and fresh faced, wire rimmed glasses hiked up over short hair, wearing her trademark long skirt-and-Peter-Pan-collared-blouse. Sometimes Gil teased her that she was too young and too pretty for those prim looking outfits, told her she picked them just to look more like a 'real' Librarian. Sometimes he teased her about switching to contacts, that it was a shame to hide those pretty eyes of hers. Sometimes Marian teased Gil right back that she'd call the Archdiocese on him. And sometimes she just blushed and Gil could tell she loved hearing it all, even if it only came from a priest.

Marian was leaning over the tiny library's one computer station, lending a hand to a patron. Gil felt his cheeks flush, suddenly afraid the young Librarian would look up, spot him and chase him down for the overdue books.

There was Marian leaning over the computer station all right, guiding the mouse and pointing at the screen.

And there was none other than Frank Hoelevich himself, sitting at the terminal, looking all befuddled and shaking his head. The two of them were flanked by towers of books.

Silverez glanced down at Sox to make sure it really *was* him and not some other caramel and white sheltie. Then he looked in the library window again. Since the day he and Frank shared their first beer and card game at Mike's Tavern, he'd never seen the man touch a book, not once.

And now, computers?

Sox yelped for another pet. Gil obliged, ready to stop in the Library. But he checked his watch first. Mrs. Heullarta expected him a quarter hour ago. And there was no telling how long old Augie was going to hold out. "Sorry buddy, got to run," the priest told the dog. "But I'd sure like to know when Frank took up reading."

Gil peeked in the library window one last time, then hustled off down Montrose.

✦

Mrs. Heullarta kept Father Silverez for a good hour. Kept him trapped, to be precise, positioning her rocker inside her apartment door so there was no easy escape. Oh, she needed Communion, all right. But it was communion with another human that she needed much more than the sacrament. Her six flat was a den of gang-bangers, illegal immigrants, drug dealers and the stray hooker or two, the hallways an odorous stew of piss and garbage and worse. Gil dutifully chatted with the old woman, listened to her retell the story of each of her three muggings in gruesome detail, promised to find someone in the parish to help with her shopping, then even agreed to return next week.

'When you can stay awhile', as she put it.

It wouldn't have mattered if he left Mrs. Heullarta any sooner, as it turned out. Augie Lachowicz passed on in the afternoon, fortunately in his sleep. His daughter was just on her way out the door to the undertaker when Gil arrived. He walked with her, offering what little solace he could to a forty-five year old woman who'd been sponge bathing her own father, had been cleaning bed pans and pus and vomit for the past seven years while she let her own life slip away. She should have been relieved.

Instead, she just seemed lost.

Gil left her, feeling a little purposeless himself.

So it was close to 7:00 when Father Gil Silverez backtracked down Montrose towards the rectory, wondering if there was still anything edible in the refrigerator — St. Alstantius' budget had no room for a housekeeper or a cook, so Gil made do with a bi-weekly cleanup by Ladies Sodality volunteers. Maybe just a trek down Damen to Mike's Tavern for a burger or a slice of microwaved pizza? He was still mulling over his menu options when he approached the library.

Sox was gone.

Gil peered in the window.

But there was Frank Hoelevich standing at the front desk, while Marian checked out a stack of books for him. Sox cooled his heels at Frank's side, tail on an autopilot wag the moment Gil opened the door.

"Don't tell me that pooch even has a Library Card?"

"Sox?" Frank smiled. "No, he only reads the sports pages. Marian here, she let him in. I didn't even know it till the dog was sniffing my pants cuffs over there at that damned computer."

"Some kids were teasing the dog out front," Marian said, inserting a due date card into one of Frank's books. "I thought it'd be safer for him in here. The heck with the rules."

"So what brings you here, Gil?"

"Thought I'd ask you that," Silverez said. "The wife's out of town, so you've taken up reading, that it?"

Marian closed the cover on the last of Frank's books and slid the pile across the counter. "And here I thought he's been hanging around the library because he had a crush on me. Frank, I'm devastated."

Frank blushed a little as he wrapped his big hands around the books and tucked them under his arm. It was quite a load. "Where are you headed?"

Gil shrugged his shoulders. "I was trying to decide just that when I passed by. Back to the rectory for a baloney sandwich and a beer, or down to Mike's."

"Well, I'll do you one better," Frank said. "I got a Dutch oven of kielbasa and kraut been simmering on the stove all day. Come on over and eat with me."

Gil shook his head. He turned to Marian. "Get this guy. Wife's out of town for three weeks now. And how does he live it up? The girlie shows on Western? Running off to the track? No, he's sneaking heart attacks in a sausage casing."

"Well, are you interested or not?" Frank said. "Sox is probably hoping you're not. More for him that way."

"Of course I'm interested." Gil reached for the books under Frank's arm. "Here, let me have a couple of those, old man, and we can — "

"No." Frank pulled away, his smile suddenly fading. But it returned, just as quick. "No Gil, I got them. They're not heavy." He reached for Sox' leash. "We can go as soon as Marian's locked up. I said I'd walk her to her car."

"Oh, get out of here, the both of the you," Marian said. "I'm a big girl, I think I can find my car on my own."

"No, Marian," Frank said. "I'd feel better if we waited."

"There *are* a lot of crazies running around the neighborhood, " Gil added. "I've just come from Mrs. Heullarta's. You know she's been mugged — "

"Three times this year," Marian said. "Yes, Father, I know." Reaching under the counter, Marian grabbed her purse and pulled out a small, black aerosol can. *"Urbane Guerrilla Spray.* Can drop a bear at twenty yards, you know."

"Black bear, or a grizzly?" Gil asked.

"Black or...well, how should I know?"

"Well, you'd know it was a black bear if you sprayed him and he ran."

"And how would you know it was a grizzly?"

"You wouldn't. You'd already be dead. He'd be chomping that can for dessert."

"Nice," she said. "Hunted a lot of grizzlies in your time, have you, Father?"

Gil shook his head, smiling. "Never seen one in my whole life, Marian. Not a one."

"That's it." Marian came around from behind the desk. "Out with you both." She took Silverez and Frank by the arms and guided them to the door. Sox followed along on his leash.

"Marian," Frank said, "You really need someone to wait and — "

"What I really need to do is get you guys out of here so I can finish my work and go home. I happen to have a date tonight, gentlemen, and I'd like to get home and change."

"Good for you, Marian," Gil said. "But what do you have to change for? You look great as always."

"Well *you* aren't supposed to be noticing, *Father* Silverez. But thanks anyway." She shoved the threesome out on the sidewalk.

"You lock up right away, " Frank called as they headed off down Montrose. "Right away, Marian."

She waved from the Library doorway. "And you tell the Padre there that if he doesn't bring those overdue books back tomorrow, I'm going to take the fines right out of Sunday's collection basket."

"Right away, Marian," Frank repeated. "You lock that door." He didn't turn around until he saw her close the door and lock it.

Frank stared ahead at the western sky as they walked away.

Summer was fading fast.

Evening came so quick these days.

✦

It was nearly eight by the time Marian finished the filing, shut down the computer, then re-shelved all the books that had been left out on the six round tables that made up the reading area in the little storefront Library. Finally she slung her purse over her shoulder and headed for the backroom.

She'd fibbed to Frank and the priest.

Not about the date. That was real enough. Her sister had fixed her up with a guy from work, *'Bob, kind of a computer geek, but cute'* she'd said. Maybe not the best endorsement, but Marian hadn't had a date in almost a year, and she'd been reading more books and renting more movies in that time than she could count. Lately, she was starting to count how often she found her hands creeping inside her pajamas at night. And she didn't like the number.

But what she'd fibbed to Frank and Father Silverez about was going home.

Her cute computer geek date, Bob, wasn't really picking her up at home. Actually, he was going to meet her right here at the library at 8:30. Then they were heading to Lincoln Park for dinner — Italian, and Marian *lived* for Italian food. So she was just going to change here at the Library.

Frankly, she wasn't even sure *why* she fibbed.

Unless she felt a little self-conscious, just a little funny about the outfit hanging on a hook back on the bathroom door. Unless she hoped that new outfit might make Bob the cute computer geek find her more intriguing than just Marian the Librarian with the always pressed, round collared cotton blouses, and the freshly polished loafers, and the sensible just-over-the-knees skirts. Unless tonight she wasn't thinking of herself as Marian the Librarian, but Marian — a woman — and a desirable woman at that. Or at least, that's what she wanted to be, that's really, really what she wanted to be, really what she wanted Bob to think.

Marian set her purse down on the backroom floor, then lifted the hanger off the bathroom door and raised the plastic garment bag, uncovering a shiny, black velveteen jacket and a matching short-short skirt. She'd bought the outfit two nights ago in a swanky store in Water Tower Place, splurging on shoes and a quarter ounce bottle of real designer label fragrance. Two and a half short hours in the glass and brass downtown mall ate up two and a half weeks' salary, but as far as she was concerned, Marian the Librarian was ready to re-shelve herself in a new section...starting tonight with Bob the cute computer geek. She hoped it would be *his* hands creeping inside her pajamas tonight.

Or, somewhere.

Marian reached for a shopping bag she'd tucked behind the bathroom door just as she heard the front door open.

"Bob? Is that you?" She called out. She reached into the bag and pulled out the new brushed suede demi boots, still fragrant of fresh leather and dye, then a brand new, shrink wrapped package of slinky black nylons. "I'm in the backroom, Bob. Have a seat. I'll just be a few minutes."

Marian kicked off her penny loafers. "You're early, Bob. Hope you don't mind waiting. I have to change. You can read a book if you like." She chuckled to herself. "We happen to have a few."

She reached behind her waist to unzip her skirt. Just starting to step out of it, Marian suddenly stopped.

'Wait a minute, what am I doing? I don't know this guy. And here I am undressing, with him just...'

With the skirt bunched around her ankles, Marian shuffled over to the backroom door and quietly turned the little lock on the knob. *There, now she felt better.* Her hand still on the knob, Marian kicked the skirt off her legs, while her other hand worked the top button on her Peter Pan collar.

But then, Marian stopped again.

Froze, actually.

Her breath caught in her throat.

Her hands suddenly went slick with a cold sweat, her fingers sliding across the little lock on the doorknob...

"B-Bob?"

No answer.

...the little lock on the door knob...

...The big lock and the deadbolt on the Library's front door.

The door she locked up tight an hour ago, with Frank Hoelevich looking on from the sidewalk.

"Bob?"

No answer.

She'd read this chapter a dozen times in a dozen books on all those dateless nights. Seen this scene in a dozen bad slasher movies she'd rented.

Yet, here she was, about to do it herself, even while her mind kept screaming *'No, you idiot, lock yourself in the bathroom, hide behind the shelves, NO!'*

But instead, as quietly as she could, Marian's sweaty fingers unlocked the back room door.

Even quieter, at least to her ears, she slowly turned the knob. Slowly and silently, then just as quietly, just as slowly, she inched the backroom door open.

"Bob?"

Marian flipped her wire rimmed glasses down off the top of her head. They flopped onto her nose crooked, while she peeked one eye around the half open door.

The library was dark as a cave.

Someone had shut off the lights.

She heard a tinkly, crystal sound up front, and her eyes jerked that way.

Dark as it was, she could make out the shattered glass on the front door.

Dark as it was, she could see that the front door hung wide open. She immediately thought about Mrs. Heullarta and the three vicious muggings.

She heard the tinkly, crystal sound again, thought it might be the sound of broken glass. Wanted it to be. Wished it could be only that and nothing more. But deep down inside, she knew it wasn't. She knew it was the grating sound of soft, otherwordly giggles floating out there in the darkness.

And that's when Marian the Librarian saw the silhouettes of the figures sitting in the dark, at the six round library tables.

✦

All the way to the storefront two flat, and all through the dinner of kielbasa and kraut, Frank and Gil kept to small talk.

They debated the Cubs' and the White Sox' slim chances of pulling off an upset in the last few weeks of the season. They held out high hopes for the Bears, even though they already lost their first two exhibition games. They agreed to wait for the Bulls to save face for the city, Jordan-less or not. They never even bothered with the Blackhawks.

After dinner, Frank washed while Gil dried, with Sox chipping in to pre-clean the plates before they made it to the sink. With the kitchen cleaned up, though not quite to Libbie's standards, Sox got a rawhide chew — a rare treat, since they were going for $1.99 a pop these days — while Frank poured three fingers of Crown Royal into two glasses, and Gil grabbed two more cold beers from the fridge. They made themselves comfortable in the living room, Gil on the sofa, Frank on his recliner, Sox gnawing away at his rawhide on the floor right beside him.

"So, Libbie ever coming back, Frank?"

"Seems to like it down there, though I can't imagine why. But she'll be back in another week or so."

"Not to pry, but have you been visiting that bookie on Hermitage on the sly or something?"

"Why?"

"Well, train tickets, three weeks in Florida," Gil said. "I know you didn't have the money."

"Libbie's staying with her sister. No hotel bills, no eating out every day. It's not that expensive."

"Still."

"Let's just say Sepp Deitrich paid Libbie's way," Frank said.

"Sepp...huh?"

Frank hefted himself out of the recliner and wandered off to the bedroom. When he returned, he tossed two military medals in Gil's lap.

"Purple Heart," Gil said. "D.S.C. I don't get it."

Frank plopped back into the recliner. "I took those medals over to that Military Surplus store on Ashland, thought they must be worth something." He knocked back a good sized gulp of the Crown Royal, then washed it down with a sip of beer. "Twenty five bucks each, the guy tells me. I tell him, 'Hey buddy, that's a goddamned Purple Heart, from the Bulge no less.' He just shrugs his shoulders and says 'Okay, thirty bucks'."

"I'm not following you, Frank. You didn't sell them. Good. So who's Sepp Deitrich?"

"Come on, Padre. Didn't they make chaplains read anything other than the Good Book in the Marines?" Frank sipped at his beer, his eyes glossing over with a distant look. "Sepp Deitrich was the Nazi son of a bitch that led one of the Panzer columns in the Ardennes the Christmas of '44. Could be that one of his goddamned tanks machine gunned down half my squad, two of those green kids already climbing up out of the snow with their hands raised to surrender. Could be one of them goddamned tanks got a bazooka shell right in the ass where it could do some good. Could be one of them got a grenade lobbed right down the hatch. Could be one of them had a big old red and black and white swastika battle flag hanging on the radio antenna, big as a bed sheet, the thing was. Could be I tucked that goddamned flag in my pack — *after* I unloaded two clips right through the hatch, with one of those black suited bastards staring up at me with a regular 'Fuck You, Yankee' face. Could be that flag made it through the Bulge, made it all the way home with me, even though we weren't supposed to keep souvenirs."

Frank Hoelevich gulped down the rest of his glass. His other hand gripped the sweaty beer bottle so tight the glass was ready to break. "Finally got that Military Surplus guy up to fifty bucks each for the medals, then told him where to stick his money. But he told me if I had any German shit, come on back and we'd talk." Frank's grip finally loosened on the bottle, and he took a sip. "Thirty five hundred dollars for that goddamned flag. Thirty five hundred, Gil, can you believe it?"

Gil was nursing his own glass. He'd felt a quick shiver run down his back when that sudden, far away coldness appeared in Frank's eyes. He'd seen that look before, in the eyes of terrified kids returning from combat zones during his chaplain stint. He knew that look meant they'd seen things God never meant for his children to see. "Big collector's market for that stuff."

Frank nodded. "Collectors, all right. The guy tells me he's selling the stuff to the artsy-fartsy crowd these days. Those black leather fruitcakes. They buy up all the Nazi crap he can lay a hand on." He pulled a cigar out of his shirt pocket and lit it up, blowing a tire sized circle of blue smoke around himself while he got it going. "Sick little shits. I'd like to see one of them laying there in the cold, watching your buddies' guts exploding all over the snow, listening to them cry to their mother, cry to God, begging not to die, not there, not like that, watching that look on their faces just before they fell, that look that told you they knew they were never going to see home again, knew they were dead. I'd like to..." Frank rolled the cigar around in his mouth. "No, actually I wouldn't like one of those little dopes to know. Better they never know." He slowly exhaled a long stream of smoke. "Libbie can enjoy all the fresh orange juice and palm trees and sand she wants, Gil. Long as she wants to stay. We earned it."

"Amen."

Frank leaned over the side of the chair and raised the venetian blinds halfway. He slid the window open, and a cool September breeze crept in. While it did, Frank and the priest both felt their eyes drawn to the window, and to the building looming overhead right across the street.

Gothique stood there, an immense hulk of dark stone and darker windows.

Frank let the blinds fall, and he turned back to Gil. "So?"

"So...what?"

"So, go on and say it. You think I'm nuts."

"Frank, what are you talking about?"

"I know you saw the kinds of books I got at the library." Frank gestured towards the console TV, where the books were stacked on top, right next to his and Libbie's wedding photo.

Montague Summers.

Devendra P. Varma.

Olga Hoyt.

Bram Stoker.

J. Gordon Melton.

Anne Rice.

"Marian's been ordering them for me from the Main Branch downtown. I've been going to see her there at the library since I put Libbie on the Amtrak. Now that Marian, she's a cool one. She *does* think I'm nuts, I'll bet. Told me as much today when she helped me figure out the computer. Showed me how to search newspaper files. Even had me on the damned internet, *me,* can you believe that?" Frank glanced back at the closed venetian blinds. "Lot of strange things in the world, Padre."

"Frank, they're just books. Just stories. You can't take them seriously."

Frank nodded. "Those books? Yep, they're just stories. Mostly, I guess. But there's been a lot of bad stuff happening around town. You wouldn't really notice it, just reading the paper, just watching the ten o'clock news. You wouldn't connect one ugly story with another. Hell, there's so many ugly stories in this goddamned city." He leaned forward in the recliner and locked eyes with Father Silverez. "A murder here, a disappearance there. One more runaway on the lam, one more hooker sliced up in an alley, one more junkie washing up on the beach, some snafu down at the county morgue, a burglary at a funeral home. Happens every day, right? But once you start looking, once you start putting two and two together...well, then they aren't just 'stories', Gil."

"Frank, I know what you're hinting at, and you're right, it's nuts. The cops would get wise. They'd 'put two and two together'."

"Maybe they're in on it. Or some of them, anyway. You called the cops the night that freak attacked that girl right outside this house, remember? Or have you been trying to forget, Gil?"

"No, I remember."

"Remember what the cops told you?"

Reluctantly, Gil nodded his head. "Couple of kinky kids playing rough 'n tumble kissy face in the gangway. Nobody hurt, mind your own business."

"Right. Kissy face. Gil, that weirdo was biting the girl's breasts. Biting them so she was bleeding. And *she* loved it."

"But that doesn't mean..."

"The hell it doesn't. You know, Gil, I didn't think you'd be the skeptical type. Being a priest and all. Me, I never had much religion. Except maybe back in those foxholes in Europe. Seems to me that spotting the devil would be right up your alley."

"Or right up on Damen Avenue, that it, Frank?" Gil set his beer down on the coffeetable in front of the couch. He leaned forward, big hands folded in an unusually priestly manner for him. "I like to think I am pretty good at spotting the devil. And kicking him in the butt too. But he's that crack dealer that tried to set up shop out in front of the public school on Irving. He's that sleazeball that opened that massage parlor on Montrose. He's that gang banger that spray painted the front of Mike's tavern last week. He sure isn't some spook with hooves and horns and a pitchfork."

"Maybe not," Frank said. "But, how about fangs?"

"Definitely *not* fangs."

"That the official line, Father? The Church turning the other way too?"

"Frank, we don't 'turn the other way'. Not ever. We turn the other cheek."

They glared at each other for a moment. Finally, Gil broke the silence. "There's a lot of sick people doing a lot of sick things. You don't want to hear what I listen to in the confessional Saturday afternoons. But those kids — well, they *were* just kids. Kids do all kinds of crazy stuff. You know, I read too. And I've read all about this stuff. You can read it yourself. Pick up a copy of Charade Magazine, it's right in there. 'Goths', they call it. Ethereals, New Romantics. Gamers. All hepped up on Dracula stuff. Weird music, weirder clothes. But it's just another kids' fad."

"Fad my ass, Padre." Frank took another gulp from his beer. Then he reached over and yanked the cord on the blinds again. They shot up noisily. Even Sox looked up from his rawhide chew.

Now the windows were opened in Gothique. Lights glowed in each one. Dark figures glided back and forth inside. It looked even more menacing than before.

"It's got something to do with that place," Frank said, pointing out the window. "I don't know why, but they're in there. Right now. And they're bad, Gil. Real bad. Not like gangbangers or pushers or pimps. They're *evil.*" He turned back to the priest. "They're vampires, Gil. For real. Vampires are in there, in that place they're calling Gothique now."

"Frank, come on, you can't — "

Frank pulled the blinds closed as noisily as he opened them. "Let me tell you about something that happened to me a couple weeks ago."

✦

The old man was losing it.

That's all Gil could conclude as he walked up Damen towards Montrose.

But it didn't add up. Frank Hoelevich was one the most sensible men he'd ever met. He respected Frank. Moreover, he *liked* Frank. Liked him too much to accept that Alzheimer's could already be softening his brain, or that the loneliness of a childless marriage, or a wife gone for too many weeks, and too many silly books lying around the house had driven him batty. Or that the unimaginable terrors of an evil war over fifty years before had him imagining new and even more frightening evils in his own front yard.

No, he couldn't accept that about Frank Hoelevich. Or wouldn't.

Red eyes glowing in the fog on Damen Avenue? Black figures with ghost-white faces materializing out of the darkness?

Fangs?

Vampires lurking in that old hulk of a theater, that place that was scheduled to open any day now as 'Gothique'?

All the same, Gil stepped up his pace, glancing over his shoulder every few steps as the tall, ugly building merged with the darkness behind him. Damen Avenue was deserted tonight. Quiet as a church at night.

Quiet as a graveyard at night.

Not that Frank wanted to let Gil leave. Not that he wanted him to walk home by himself. He pleaded with the priest to call a cab, to stay the night. But St. Alstantius didn't pay for priests to flit around town in taxis. And there was no missing the 7:00 AM weekday mass for the before-work crowd. Gil waved good-bye to Frank at the back door, while Sox quickly did his business in the back yard. He left Frank swearing at himself for inviting the priest to dinner, for keeping him so late, for letting him leave after dark.

And as Gil waded through the darkness of Frank's gangway and as he first turned onto the sidewalk on Damen, the sight of that ugly eyesore of a theater-now-nightclub gave him the chills. That, and the memory — maybe the repressed memory — of that grinning kid with the strangely white teeth and the even stranger white skin, locking eyes with him that night, locking his black-no-red irises with Gil, then shoving him aside and vanishing into the darkness. Gil remembered that sure enough. There *was* no repressing it, even though he'd gotten down on his knees and prayed every night since, trying to forget it.

Up ahead, a squad car sped by on Montrose, light bar flashing, siren wailing. Then another.

Gil almost heaved a sigh of relief when he turned off Damen and waited at the Montrose stoplight. Traffic whizzed by in both directions, out of tune motors chugging, radios blaring, horns honking. Even over all that noise, Gil glanced up at the sound of a jet high overhead, lining up with the Kennedy Expressway and beginning its descent to O'Hare. He could see two more banking into line behind it up in the night sky.

The stoplight, the cars, the planes — they were all somehow...reassuring. They were all concrete. Normal. Reality. He walked up Montrose towards St. Alstantius and the rectory, relieved to leave the darkness of Damen Avenue, and Gothique, and Frank's demons, behind.

But reality turned ugly quick enough. Like it so often did. And then it crumbled altogether for Father Gil Silverez.

He saw the two squads' blue and red lights flashing up ahead, joined by even more. There was an ambulance wedged between them.

All blocking traffic a block up on Montrose Avenue.

Right in front of the little storefront library branch.

Gil started to run.

He was wheezing when he sprinted through the library's front door.

The glass was shattered on the floor.

The deadbolt was torn right out of the doorjamb.

A uniformed cop blocked his way, till another came forward. "He's okay," the cop said. "That's the priest from St. Alstantius." He turned to Gil as the other policeman stepped aside. "Not much you can do here, Father. But you can go back if you want to."

Gil walked towards the back of the Library. Other policemen and women were filling out forms, taking pictures. Off in a corner, a skinny, clean cut young man in jeans and a blazer sat on a kiddie chair, his face a blank, nodding like a robot to a policewoman asking questions and jotting down notes. The entire place was a mess. Tables overturned, chairs broken, books spilled out of their shelves and all over the floor. Gil walked towards the backroom. Walked — he wasn't sprinting now, he wasn't even sure he wanted to see what might be back there.

Who might be...

"Who are you?" A plainclothes cop stopped Gil from stepping through the doorway to the backroom. "Not much for you to do now, Padre. We're almost done here. Medical Examiner's going to take her away in a minute."

Father Gil Silverez stood there in the doorway, trying to keep the bile from churning up his throat, trying desperately to keep his legs from buckling. The plainclothes cop kept on talking, but Gil wasn't really listening anymore. "Yeah, we figure she went around eight, maybe, but the ME will know for sure. Gang shit, probably. The Latin Princes, maybe. They've been raising hell around here lately, haven't they, Father? Say, you knew her, Father? Then did you know this..."

No, Gil wasn't listening.

Gil was staring, eyes wide, mouth gaping open, hands trembling with anger and fear and revulsion.

There were Marian the Librarian's wire rimmed glasses on the floor, lenses smashed, frame twisted.

There was the Peter-Pan-collared-blouse and the penny loafers and the sensible over-the-knees skirt, there were her underthings, all scattered on the backroom tile. All shredded, all torn.

All stained with blood.

And there was Marian.

Hanging upside down.

There was Marian, not five feet away, her blue eyes a sickly, pale hue, staring wide open and blank and very dead. She was stripped naked, her skin a pallid, cold looking white.

Except for the wounds.

Except for the neat pairs of holes on her wrists and her thighs. Except for the bruised, rough edged gashes on her breasts. Except for the ugly, ripped flesh on her throat. Those were red. Dark, congealed blood dribbled out of the wounds. It was smeared around them, like it had been slobbered all over by drooling lips and hungry tongues.

Marian's delicate hands hung a foot off the floor, tied together with a knotted pair of beige pantyhose.

Marian's naked, mauled body hung upside down, her bare feet tied together like her hands, with another pair of nylons — black — looped around a utility pipe suspended from the ceiling.

"Padre, you knew this girl, huh? Any chance you know her boyfriend, that geeky kid out there? He's the one found her. Says he didn't know her. Blind date. We think he's clean, but you never know." The plain clothes cop took Gil by the arm and guided him out of the back room. "Nah, that squirt's too much of a pussy to do something like this. He never could have hoisted her up on that pipe anyway. No, must've been gangs. Right, Padre? Now these Latin Princes, they — "

"It wasn't the Latin Princes!" Gil jerked his arm free from the detective's hand. "No God damned gang could do that!"

"Whoa, Father, watch the French."

"Are you insane, officer?" Gil shouted. "Are you blind? Or are you just stupid? You see those wounds on...on...on her." He started to sob. "On — Marian."

"Yeah, so?" the cop said. "Lot of the gangs go in for that ritualistic stuff. Seen a lot of it lately."

"Those were *bites,"* Gil seethed. "They *bit* her. With teeth. With *fangs!"*

The detective drew himself up and half-guided, half-shoved Gil against the wall. "I didn't see nothing that looked like any bites. And this is Chicago, Father. There's no animals around with 'fangs'. And there sure as shit aren't any that can tie a girl up with her own stockin's and hang her upside-fucking-down either." He pushed his face close to Gil's, brows rippled up over a threatening glare. "What I am seeing is a parish priest who smells like he's had a few too many tonight. Maybe they'd like to know that down at the Archdiocese, huh? So you didn't see any 'bites' in there, got it? You didn't see anything like that, Father. And you sure as hell aren't going to tell anyone you did, are you?"

The policeman stepped back, and his whole face softened. "Hey, Shepherd. You're about done there, aren't you? What do you say you give the good Father here a ride to St. Alstantius? I think he's feeling a little lightheaded."

"Sure thing." I.D.D. Detective Terri Shepherd got up from one of the wooden library chairs and slipped a notebook back in her pocket. She motioned for Gil to follow her. "Come on, Father. There's nothing you can do here now."

"Say, Padre." It was the plainclothes cop again, calling from the doorway to the backroom. Gil paused by the front door. "You remember now. Don't compromise our investigation." Right behind him, Marian's naked body hung obscenely, all white skin and red wounds. "Some things only us and the perpetrators should know, right?"

The detective winked at him.

Gil said nothing. All of Frank's cryptic warnings suddenly were swimming in his head. He let the young policewoman usher him out of the little Library.

TWENTY TWO

Unlike the Whitestar Media Building's regular elevators, which always whisked the worker bees back to their offices and cubicles with rapid efficiency, the private elevator to the penthouse suite up on the twenty seventh floor was engineered to move at a tortuously slow pace. Roberta Whitehead herself had specified that the machinery be adjusted to do precisely that. It was just one more in a long list of her affectations. The slow ride built anticipation for the invited and enhanced anxiety in those about to be browbeaten, fired, or worse.

Right now the elevator's slow crawl was having its intended effect on Blair Armstrong.

She fussed with her over teased hair, fidgeted with her dress and her satin gloves, even sneered at her reflection in the elevator's floor to ceiling mirrors. This had been the sixth outfit Blair tried on, all of them brand new, black and sinfully expensive. Of course, she'd been up to Roberta Whitehead's palatial office before. Even dined out with the Queen of Whitestar several times, including the last, when Roberta had promoted her and told her about the raise that now kicked Blair comfortably into the mid-100's.

But she'd never been to Roberta's private suite, that rumored labyrinth of grand salons, plush parlors and interconnected bedrooms that shared the twenty seventh floor with her equally opulent office. Blair'd never been, but she heard about it. Chicago's trendy club scene was full of beefcake models, up and coming photographers, account exec's, DJ's and TV reporter wannabe's who'd had the tour, more often than not naked, sometimes at the end of a dog collar and leash with spoonfuls of cocaine stuck up their nose to make the junket more bearable.

All of Chicago's media elite who were 'in the know' knew about Roberta Whitehead's penchant for entertaining.

The elevator crept up from twenty three to twenty four. Blair tugged at the hem of the short, black jersey dress with slick gloved hands, trying to keep the flimsy thing from riding over the tops of her dark stockings. Short was in, but 'in' was usually awkward. Suddenly, Blair decided she absolutely hated the dress, couldn't believe she'd left that multi layered black chiffon number on her bedroom floor, couldn't believe she'd gone with these blasé satin pumps, couldn't believe she'd chosen the platinum bike chain necklace instead of the faux ebony studded choker, couldn't believe her makeup or her hair, couldn't believe she...

The elevator door slowly slid open.

A pasty faced kid of unknown gender stood there in a tuxedo.

"Ms. Armstrong? Follow me."

Blair followed the skinny androgyne through a twisting maze of marble floored hallways, all dimly lit except for occasional overhead spots zeroed in on neo-expressionist paintings adorning the walls, objets d'art perched on pedestals.

It was cool in the penthouse suite. Cooler even than it had been outside. Even so, Blair felt a trickle of nervous perspiration slide out from behind her ear and down along her neck. These new shoes chafed her feet. The elastic buried in her stockings' lacy bands cut off the circulation in her legs. Her purse was all wrong, she'd sprayed on too much perfume, her damned underwear kept riding up her butt.

The drop of sweat trickled down onto her shoulder. Blair wiped at it with a gloved finger, wishing once again that she could have prodded Jeff into coming.

She felt naked.

Not just because her breasts threatened to bob out of the flimsy bodice, or that the air conditioned coolness had her nipples rock hard and poking through the fabric like nubby appliqués, or that the ridiculously short dress rode halfway up to her ass. She felt naked walking into Roberta's soiree without an escort, someone to dump at the bar once the mudslinging heated up and the gossip got good and juicy. Sure, Jeff could be a dud sometimes. And he'd probably have dressed all wrong.

But at least he was an arm to hang onto, long enough to make an entrance.

No, just as well, Blair decided. Jeff would've been asking for a Stroh's and haranguing someone about Nascar stats, drywalling tips, or something...*Jeffish* like that. Jeff just didn't fit up here on the twenty seventh floor. Now that she was finally out from under Megan Russell's thumb, now that Blair was finally on the fast track, now that all the dues were finally paid after clerking in the classifieds at the Times, sucking ass in the copy editing department at Elle, fetching sandwiches at Interview Magazine — *now,* Jeff Stancheck just...didn't...fit.

Period.

"In here, Ms. Armstrong." The butler or usherette or whatever it was opened an imposing set of double doors and stepped aside.

Blair stepped in.

Roberta Whitehead's 'informal little cocktail party' was all Blair expected it to be.

And more.

The room was huge, all shiny marble and glass and buffed leather, two stories tall, with floor to ceiling windows looking south and east onto the downtown skyline. Tuxedoed boy-girls with dyed black hair and retro 80's Siouxsie And The Banshees makeup flitted back and forth with silver trays of hors d'ouvres, champagne flutes and iced vodka shots. Guests huddled in seemingly earnest conversation. They pretended to admire Roberta's collection of Schnabel's and Fischl's, they huddled in powder sniffing cliques around marble coffeetables.

Blair recognized the photographer who'd shot last month's Charade cover stretched out on a leather sofa with two cloyingly pretty models, both of them nibbling his ears. A local anchorman, famous for his inflammatory right wing commentaries, played kissy face with the beefy, bearded owner of a string of X-er themed restaurants. Two well connected state legislators were competing for the attention of an anorexic chocolate skinned jazz chanteuse, their wives presumably off at more socially acceptable shindigs for the night. Pretty girls and prettier boys, dandied up in their Oak Street boutique and Boul-Mich knock off's of goth-rock street clothes, mingling with tuxedoed swells and portly power brokers and boorish city bureaucrats, sharing glasses and white lines and sloppy tongued kisses along with the repartee. New age style darkwave music hummed innocuously in the background.

Blair took a deep breath there in the doorway.

"I'm home," she gushed out loud.

✦

Frostbite and Gem had been standing at the bus stop on Armitage for twenty minutes now. Frostbite clutched his guitar without a case. Gem held tight to her knapsack, overflowing with sheet music she couldn't read, scrawled lyrics she could never memorize, and stacks of floppy disks that ran her digital keyboards.

"I'm not so sure the Armitage bus runs after 10:00," Frostbite said, craning his neck to stare down the street. "Come on, let's just take a cab."

"Sure, Diamond Jim. Then you can five finger discount our dinners till Monday."

"Look, with transfers for the El the bus will be, what? $3.80? A cab can't be more than five bucks."

"Well, maybe if you didn't insist on drinking so much, we'd have another five bucks right now."

"Gem, how was I supposed to know the drinks weren't free for the band?"

She narrowed her eyes till the caked-on eyeshadow and mascara started to flake. *"The band?* It was Open Mike Night, Frost. We weren't 'the band'."

Gem set her sack down, then sat herself down beside it on the curb. But she still wrapped the knapsack's handles around her hands. This far west on Armitage, all the trendy 'WestTown' and 'Wicker Park' and 'Ukrainian Village' gentrification labels evaporated into one big long stretch of urban blight, where the low riders and Latino gangbangers might slit your throat for your bus money as soon as look at you. At least, that's what she heard. Gem had never actually been this far west into the bowels of the city, or away from the hip 'hoods hugging the Lakefront. From where she sat, though, all she could actually see were shuttered gas stations, dilapidated row houses and boarded up factories. One of those just a block west was where she and Frost just finished their 'gig', booed right off the stage halfway through the set they'd rehearsed for two weeks straight now.

"This was an absolute, total bust," Gem whined. "That was no fucking Goth club. Darkwave-ethereal, my ass. It was fascist industrial head slammers all the way. Fucking Nazis." She nudged a crushed Slurpee cup aside with the pointy toe of her scuffed, black granny boot. A car whizzed by, the Mexican family inside eyeing the two of them up. From the back seat, two dirty faced grade schoolers hollered "Los Vampiros!" But Gem held her head high, the evening breeze tickling her pudding bowl hairdo, and flipped them off with a pale finger poking out from the long, lace cuff of her black dress.

"Everyone said Dark Echoes is the next big spot," Frostbite said. "Like, I'm supposed to know it's not Gothique."

"Not Gothique?" Gem rummaged through her knapsack and retrieved a crumpled cardboard Dunhill Menthols box. There was one cigarette left inside. She lit up with a plastic disposable painted over with nail polish runes, then tossed the carton away to join the Slurpee cup on the street. "Like we're ever going to play someplace like Gothique." Gem dragged on the Dunhill. The white filter tip came out of her mouth coated with a ring of purple lipstick. "Fuck Gothique, too. That place is never going to open anyway."

"Next week, I hear," Frostbite said."

"Like you heard that Dark Echoes was a Goth club?"

Frostbite sat down on the curb beside her, stretching his long black leathered legs out onto Armitage, his battered Strat across his lap. "Look, don't let tonight get you down. We just have to practice some more. Write some new songs. I can borrow my buddy's four track again. We can make another demo. You just have to be patient, Gem."

She looked up at him, brown pupils glaring from inside her raccoon ring makeup hollows. "Frost, I put the wrong fucking disk in on the second song, for Chrissakes. No wonder they booed us off the stage. We were playing two different songs."

"Well, actually...three, I think." He leaned closer and stole a drag from the cigarette dangling in Gem's fingers. "I'm not complaining, I mean, it almost sounded kind of cool, but I think you had the program in for *Renfield's Lament* but you were singing *Death In A New Vein.*"

"And what were you playing?"

"Coffin Games. You couldn't tell?" Frostbite stood up and stared down Armitage again.

"Sorry," Gem said. "Well, what do you expect? Using the house amps and that other band's keyboard — who the hell could figure out that piece of shit." She dragged on her cigarette and played with the smoke rolling out of her mouth, letting it rise up into her nose. "We really need a fucking P.A."

"Yeah, so when you win Lotto, you let me know." He tapped Gem on the shoulder. "Well, at least a bus is coming."

"Figures. I just lit a cigarette." She hefted herself up and saw the unmistakable shape of a CTA bus just a couple blocks down. "Well, no way I'm putting it out."

The bus driver had no intention of starting up with these two ghouls sharing a cigarette in the back seat. They took the bus to the Armitage El station. Frostbite tried to cajole Gem into hiking the few blocks over to Rimbaud's Cave, just to see if anyone was around. But she reminded him that no one had been around for ages. Gabrielle. Fitch. Brandon. Cass. Chelsea. All...gone. She also reminded him that after the busfare and transfers, they had exactly four dollars in change between them. Enough for a pack of generic cigarettes. Maybe they could splurge and split a Hostess fruit pie.

They rode the El all the way north to Uptown in silence, getting off at the Lawrence stop, where crowds of kids were waiting for southbound trains to take them deep into the city for a night of clubbing and concerts. Frostbite and Gem trudged down Lawrence, jealous and glum.

"Man, it really sucks," he said, finally breaking the silence.

"What? Everything, or something particular tonight?"

"Not having money, that's what sucks."

"Well, we could go straight. I'm betting that's what all our missing cohorts have done," Gem said. "Bleach out the old hair dye, do some time MasterCarding in a mall. How about it? A cute little Cameron Diaz look for me, maybe a nice sportcoat and tie for you. What do you think, would I make a good legal secretary? I took a court reporting class in high school, you know. Maybe clerk in The Gap or something? I like costumes, I could wear yup-yup threads with the best of them. "

"Get serious. You know what I mean. It's all just so unfair. We work so hard on our music and your lyrics — "

"Poetry."

"Poetry, right," Frostbite corrected himself. "Why do the suits get all the money, and all the real artists have to suffer?"

"Don't go all Van Gogh on me now, Frost. Anyway, payday's a comin'. I have a feeling."

Gem steered Frostbite into the corner liquor store just up the block from their walkup apartment. They spent their four dollars on a pack of generic menthols, but were thirty cents short of the fruit pie once tax was added on.

Hiking the rickety stairs to their apartment, Frostbite was still complaining. "Crappy jobs, crappy paychecks, that's all we ever get. And no one's in tune enough to even understand what we're trying to do. Musically, I mean. *Creatively,* you know? It's bitches like that fag hag friend of Cass', the ones who are willing to sell out their souls for a few scraps from the great and glorious Corporate America, *they're* the ones that get all the bread. I'll bet she's raking it in. And I'll just bet she cocksucked and muff dived her way through Personnel, I'll just bet."

"Who?" Gem said once they reached their door. "Oh, right. Colleen, or something. Just shut up and get the keys."

"No money," he kept on mumbling as he fumbled with the lock." "No fucking money for anything."

"Maybe." Gem grabbed Frostbite by the arm and spun him around just as the door opened. She smashed his mouth with her purple lips and pushed him inside the dark apartment. "But fucking's still free, isn't it?"

✦

Roberta Whitehead's soiree was already thinning out barely an hour after Blair Armstrong arrived.

Half the guests made showy farewells with a profusion of bussed cheeks and promises to meet for brunch or drinks. A few slipped out quietly, champagne and vodka bottles tucked under jackets, chafing dishes of cocaine not so discreetly dumped into designer purses.

Not that Blair paid much attention to them. Oh, groups of media leeches swished by periodically to congratulate Blair on her promotion to Managing Editor. The models and photographers and freelance writers made a special point of hovering for a moment, ready with lunch invites and eager offers to pop down to their cars to bring their new portfolios up.

But one and all, they only hovered for a moment.

Because at best, Blair responded with a disinterested smile. Most she just ignored.

She was too engrossed in her conversation with Marek. Had been since the moment he introduced himself, handed her a champagne flute and guided her to a huge black leather chaise in a secluded corner of the vast and overdecorated salon. She didn't know why, but she followed the tall and imposing figure in the crisp black suit and even blacker silk shirt as if he led her by a leash.

Across the room, Roberta Whitehead waved *Ta-ta* to another group of guests, sent a mime faced usher scurrying off for a double vodka, then waltzed over to plop down on the chaise beside Blair and Marek. "So, I see you two have met?" she said, reaching down and tugging off her strappy black glitter sandals. "Now, *that's* better. Piccilomino may have a flair for design, but he really has to stop using third world sweatshops. They cobble them together like hobnail boots." Roberta's double vodka on ice appeared, and she waved the usher off. "So Blair, I assume Marek's been charming you? He seems to do that with everyone he meets." Roberta edged closer to Marek and draped a territorial arm over his shoulder.

Marek slowly turned away from Blair and glared at the Queen of Whitestar.

Roberta shivered. She slid her arm back to her side and took a nervous gulp from her glass.

Blair pretended to miss the little exchange. But she filed it away for future reference while *she* inched a little closer to Marek on the opposite side. "Actually, he was tattletelling about some of Whitestar management. Now he's got my head spinning from all his plans for Gothique and Charade." She held up her half empty champagne flute, smiling at the handsome yet pale face next to hers. "Well, that and the champagnes he keeps handing me. You know, Marek, I don't think a man with eyes like yours needs to get women drunk."

"Oh, sometimes we all need to be a little drunk," Roberta said, gulping down the rest of her glass.

"Shouldn't you be seeing to your guests, Roberta?" Marek said.

"My 'guests' are mostly gone. Anyone left is too busy trying to get laid."

He glared at her again. Blair watched Roberta Whitehead's fingers tremble around her empty glass. Watched her seem to shrink right before her eyes, then sheepishly pick up her sandals and slide off the sofa. Roberta slinked away and settled in with a little clique starting up their own Gold Coast version of a teenage petting party across the room.

"How *do* you get away with that?" Blair said, laughing. She slid still closer. "Promise you'll teach me?"

"Oh, there's much I can teach you," he said.

"I'll bet. But let's start with manipulating the boss."

"Roberta? She's been very...useful." Marek looked around the room, located Drake, who was huddled in a dark corner with a pretty woman from one of the local television news shows. As if he'd been tapped on the shoulder, Drake immediately looked up to lock eyes with Marek. Some unspoken message was relayed. Drake abruptly walked away from the newswoman and vanished through the servants' doorway.

Marek turned back to Blair. "I wouldn't worry too much about Mrs. Whitehead. *You* strike me as an ambitious woman. I can sense your... enthusiasm. Perhaps you already hunger for more than Roberta's little empire can offer. Am I correct?"

Blair leaned back into the chaise, her head practically on Marek's shoulder, her legs stretched out in front of her on the marble floor. She didn't appear to care about her ridiculously short dress creeping up over the tops of her stockings anymore. "Slow down. I just made Managing Editor at Charade. Let me enjoy this for awhile." She sipped her champagne, eyes raised coyly from behind the glass and searching his. But whenever their gaze met, it sent a strange shiver right up and down her spine. The man's irises were as black as his pupils, or she was drunk. "Anyway, don't tease. Who exactly's going to move me up and out of Whitestar's little fiefdom? Correct me if I'm wrong, but it was my understanding that Roberta's been bankrolling Gothique."

He smiled at her. It was a cold, knowing smile that sent more tremors quivering through Blair's whole body. "Gothique? Yes, Roberta has been helpful with that. But I assure you, it's only a small part of what I have in mind." Marek's hand settled on Blair's leg, his cool fingers lightly stroking back and forth across the silky nylon, the lacy band, up to the bare flesh of her thigh.

"Like I said, you don't have to get me drunk." Blair's words came out all breathy and tense. Those cold fingers on her skin made the shivers come one after another now, and she felt her hips start to roll into the soft leather chaise, her thighs clench tightly together. "And you don't have to try to mesmerize me with little hints about my next rung up the ladder. I told you, Marek, those eyes of yours are enough on their own."

"Yes. So I've heard." His cool fingers slid under the filmy hem of the jersey dress.

Blair drained her champagne flute and let the glass slip from her hand. It shattered on the floor, where her shoes were already pawing the marble. Those cool fingers still crept up her thigh with agonizing slowness, till they teased at the edge of her panties. She nuzzled into his suit, sniffing his strange cologne, all floral, all ripe, and a little too strong, like carnations and old fruit and...

"Y-you know...mmmmm..." Blair buried her face in his silk shirt, her lips brushing the hard, cool skin of his chest beneath the open collar. "Marek, why don't...why don't we just s-say goodnight to Roberta...and..." One cold finger slid inside her underwear and traced a path through her soft patch of hair. "M-Marek, come on, I don't know if I want to be making out in front of the...mmmmm...the boss."

"I hardly think she'll notice," he said, his finger sliding into the sudden warm wetness between Blair's legs.

"Maybe...b-but the others, they..."

Marek's finger stopped its little dance. "The others? I believe they're a little preoccupied right now."

Blair raised her head from his chest, blinking like she just woke up. She looked down at herself, splayed across the chaise, her legs spread, one shoe crunching shattered glass on the floor, the other fallen from her foot, at Marek's pale hand thrust deep under her dress. With his other hand, he gripped Blair's chin and lifted her head higher.

"See for yourself." He still held onto her chin.

Firmly.

Till it hurt.

"Look."

✦

Still crushing her purpled lips on Frostbite's mouth, Gem maneuvered him inside their dark apartment and kicked the door shut behind them. Finally, she pulled away, their mouths separating with an audible smack.

"I guess the best things *are* still free, huh?" Frostbite dropped his Stratocaster on the floor and reached for her again, but Gem skipped right into the dark front room.

"I said that *fucking's* still free. I'm charging for the kisses," she said, giggling while she snatched the new pack of generic menthols from her knapsack, then dropped the huge bag on their Salvation Army Outlet couch. The faded maroon lump of stuffing and broken springs matched all their other cast-off's, alley treasures and repainted junk. It suited them and the roaches they shared their cluttered Uptown flat with.

Gem glided through the dark apartment, pausing at the bathroom door. "I'm washing some of this makeup off first. But I expect you to be all ready with a heroic hard-on when I get out."

"Promise," he said, wandering through the darkness to the kitchen. "Care to put on that nifty corset thingie you got at Flash & Trash last week? I'll help you cinch it up."

"Dream on. I've had enough costumes for one night, Frost." She could hear him rummaging in the refrigerator.

"Hey Gem, we still have a whole bottle of wine in here."

"Cool. Be like a regular little party, huh? Celebrate our impressive debut, what do you think?" She heard him stumble, and then something tumbled over on the kitchen linoleum. "Frost, are you okay?"

"Yeah, just knocked over the garbage. I'll get it in the morning."

"The mice'll get it first." Gem closed the bathroom door and flicked on the light. As she turned to the dirty mirror, there was another smash, and a bang. She flung open the door. "Frost, are you — "

"Yeah, yeah," he called, from the bedroom now. "Goddamn, there's a lot of shit in here. We really have to straighten up some day, you know?"

"Right. I'll tell the maid." She shut the door again and turned on the faucets. Rusty brown water flowed for a minute till the pipes cleaned out, then a steady stream of gray filled the chipped sink. Under a bare bulb fixture's harsh glare, she stared at her face for a moment, then lathered up with a sliver of Ivory and started to scrub the thick layers of mascara, eyeshadow, rouge and foundation.

It took a while.

Little colored specks still clung to her skin as she dried her face in a towel stained and restained with makeup residue, so much so that no bleaching would ever get the threadbare terry cloth clean. As she reached for the faucet, Gem heard another crash and boom from outside the bathroom door. "Turn on a fucking light, Frost, will you?" she muttered to herself, and started to work on the dozens of buttons, clasps, Velcro strips and iron-on tape that held her black outfit together. She'd made it herself, patching together Amvets $20 bridesmaid gowns and fabric shop remnants, soaking the mismatched bundle for two days in a bath tub full of black Rit dye.

Gem dropped the lid on the toilet and sat down to unlace her granny boots, then yanked them off. She glanced into the tub; the bottom half was permanently stained gray from the dress' dye job, but then, it really wasn't all that darker than the rusty rings the cracked porcelain wore when they moved in. *As if they'd ever get their security deposit back when they finally left this dump anyway.* She smirked, reached for the pack of cigarettes and lit one up.

The bohemian lifestyle really was *tres chic.*

Her legs ached from standing around Dark Echoes, from walking to and from bus stops and El stations. She stretched them out on the rim of the dirty tub, idly puffing away, savoring a moment's peace and the generic tobacco aroma.

Tranquillity was shattered by another series of bumps and crashes from outside the bathroom door, punctuated by a loud grunt, and one last, loud *thump.*

God, that Frostbite was a klutz.

But they'd been together for two years now, sharing the apartment for the past eight months, and Gem supposed she loved him, whatever the hell that meant. At any rate, she planned to stick around as long as this Goth thing was *the* thing.

The cigarette dangled from lips still dark with traces of purple lipstick as Gem hefted herself off the toilet seat, peeled off her tights and underwear, suddenly feeling all gooey-sentimental for that lovable geek with the bleached white shag and the pale pencil dick that worked magic inside her every time, and his not entirely melodic way with a Stratocaster's strings. 'Frost and all his big time Darkwave music dreams,' she thought to herself, smiling and shaking her head. Gem flicked off the bathroom light, and let the tiny orange glow of the cigarette tip lead her through the dark hallway to the bedroom.

Uptown's stoplights, headlights and blinking signs cast their murky, multicolored gleam into the shadowy room.

"So, ready with that heroic hard-on I requisitioned?" She struck a sexy pose in the bedroom doorway — one hand planted on her hip, the other stroking the triangle patch of hennaed hair between her legs, the glowing cigarette dangling from her lips.

"Frost?"

A pale shape squirmed under the bedsheets.

Frostbite moaned.

"You better not be jacking off. I'm taking you for a ride anyway." She dropped out of her sexy pose. "Frost?"

Gem reached for the wall switch beside the door, and flicked on the lights.

The cigarette slipped out of her lips.

A scream rumbled up her throat.

But she never quite finished it.

Someone shut the lights off again, plunging the bedroom and Gem's muffled shriek back into darkness.

✦

Whatever 'guests' remained were squirming on the floor now or lolling across sofas and stretched out over tables. Some were naked. Some were stripping. Fashion models, fat financiers and buffed junior execs clutched each other, pawed each other, went down on each other, fucked each other, with Roberta Whitehead right in the middle of one group, getting it from behind from a pretty boy from MIS while she grabbed for the breasts and darted her tongue into the blonde fur of a senior analyst from Whitestar's accounting department.

And standing in a circle around the room were the pasty faced ushers and hostesses, winking to one another with their kohl-black eyes, one or two licking their deep red lips. Drake stood with them, looking back at Marek. Waiting for a command.

Without a word, Marek gave it.

Drake and the ushers all exchanged conspiratorial whispers. Then, giggling like hopped up teenagers, they slowly stepped forward.

"Marek?" Blair leaned forward on the chaise. "What's going on?"

One of the hostesses tore off her tuxedo jacket, skirt and blouse, then scampered across the room half naked. She dived onto a lipstick lesbian couple noisily sixty-nining on a sofa.

Two ushers with black Duran Duran hair and whip cream skin pounced on a trio of naked male models writhing on the floor. Others leaped into Roberta Whitehead's little orgy, one of them hopping right up on Roberta's back, smacking her liposuctioned butt cheeks and riding her like a hobby horse. Still others dropped their hors d'ouvres trays, flung their glasses of champagne and chilled vodka to the floor, climbed out of their tuxedoes and black minis and skipped hand in hand over to couples and groups — leering, drooling, laughing, their dark eyes sparking with red fireworks.

Drake waited and watched till every one of the 'servants' that he'd hand-picked for Roberta Whitehead's little soiree had joined the guests. Only then did he cross the salon towards the TV newswoman he'd left moments before. She still stood by the two story floor to ceiling windows with the city skyline sparkling behind her — panting, terrified, but anxious and eager all the same. She'd heard all about the wild times at Whitehead's parties, heard about the dark secret making the rounds in Chicago's media cliques and culture clubs. With Drake slowly drawing closer, she unbuttoned her see-through blouse, flung it off and held up her full breasts like melons for sale at a fruit stand. Once Drake reached her, he buried his head between them.

Blair saw one of the ushers raise his pale face from between a boy's legs, and his lips were...were so...

"Marek, what the hell — "

The boys lips were so...*red.* They shined. They glistened.

They dripped.

She looked at another group. A hostess who'd stripped down to her tights and boots lifted her head up from the throat of an alderman's mistress that everyone knew and everyone had at one time or another.

The hostess smiled. And that smile...that smile...that smile dribbled blood.

"Marek...what the — "

Drake stepped back from the newswoman, glared at her, and she nodded, then frantically stripped off the rest of her clothes, still standing there right in front of the twenty seventh floor windows for all of Chicago to see. Those full silicone implant breasts oozed red trickles. Once she was completely naked, Drake slammed her against the glass. He looked over his shoulder at Marek and Blair, and his pale face was twisted into a hungry snarl, lips smeared with hideous streaks of dark red. Then he lunged for the newswoman's throat.

"I don't under-understand," Blair stammered. "Marek, w-what's — "

But now that cold finger danced between Blair's legs again. Marek's other hand gripped the front of Blair's dress and tugged. The flimsy jersey shredded like tissue. He lowered his head and kissed one nipple. Then the other, holding onto the hard nub of flesh with his teeth.

"Marek, tell me, what the hell's....mmmmm...." Blair squirmed on the chaise, her head swirling from too much champagne, from the fire and ice touch insistently probing deep between her thighs, from the pleasure-no-pain-no-pleasure igniting the tips of her breasts, from the sensory overload of the highbrow orgy nakedly squealing and squishing all over the salon. She could barely talk. "M-Marek, what in God's name are they doing?"

"Slowly, he raised his head from her breasts. "This is hardly in *His* name, my dear.." Marek looked at her and smiled.

Blair sucked in her breath.

His grin revealed his shiny, white teeth. They glimmered like pearls, especially the two, sharp fangs protruding over his lips. A thin, red line dribbled down his white chin.

Blair looked down at her torn dress and her naked chest. Tiny droplets of blood bubbled up at the tip of one of her pink nipples.

"M-Marek? What is happening?"

He dropped his head to her breast again, lowering Blair down on the chaise.

"Watch," was all he said.

✦

A satin gloved hand clamped down over Gem's mouth, stifling the pitiful shrieks pointlessly echoing inside her throat. Another hand violently twisted her arm behind her back, and yanked till Gem was sure it would break.

But she didn't really feel the pain. Gem was too busy gaping at the thing on top of Frostbite, the thing riding Frost's ass, the thing with its lips wrapped around Frost's wrist.

The thing that was sloppily sucking, sloppily dripping Frostbite's blood all over the bed.

"His name's Fonda," Gem heard from behind her, and it was Gabrielle's voice, she recognized it immediately.

"Ride 'em, cowboy," Gabrielle hollered, while she shoved Gem down to her knees on the bedroom floor.

And Fonda did, he rammed in and out of Frostbite, shaking the bedframe, smashing Frost's face into the tangled sheets and pillows, and all the while sucking, still sucking on Frostbite's wrist, making sickening, giggling, gurgling sounds even though his mouth was full.

Gabrielle kneed Gem flat and face down on the floor, then straddled her. "Honey, you ever hear of locking your door?" she said. "This isn't the Gold Coast, it's Uptown, you know." She grabbed a hunk of Gem's pudding bowl hair and pulled hard. "We were waiting for you in the hallway when you came home, dummy. Maybe your slumlord could spring for a couple of lightbulbs? Guess you were too busy to see, huh? 'Fucking's still free', oh that was rich."

On the bed, Fonda let go of Frostbite's wrist. It fell limply into the sheets.

"Yo, Fonda," Gabrielle said. "Finally done?"

The vampire pulled out of Frostbite's rear with a *pop,* then slithered across the unmoving, naked body. He held Frost's arm like a piece of candy, and licked away the last of the blood splattered across the skin.

"Fonda — gay boy — I think you already got to the chewy flavorful center, what do you say? Fon—"

The vampire jerked his head away from Frostbite's wrist and snarled at Gabrielle, fangs bared, eyes glowing.

"Okay, okay," Gabrielle said. "But he looks like dead meat to me." Beneath her, Gem squirmed, jerked her head free long enough to let out one yelp, then tried to struggle loose. But she only managed to flip herself over before Gabrielle slugged her hard in the face.

"Another move like that, sweetie, and I'll see that it goes really ugly for you," Gabrielle hissed. *"Really* ugly." Still straddling Gem on the floor, Gabrielle punctuated her point with a vicious twist of one of Gem's bare nipples. "I'm taking my hand off your mouth now, precious. Scream again, and Giggle-Boy over there gets you. And he only likes knocking on the back door, *comprende?"* She slowly lifted her gloved hand away from Gem's mouth.

Gabrielle touched her fingers to her rancid raspberry lips and dramatically licked the tips. "Oh, *yum.* Almost as good as you-know-what, Gem. Almost." She leaned down close to Gem's face. "Always wanted to do you, did you know that? But you always had albino-dick hanging around." She planted a wet kiss on Gem's mouth, her tongue trying to force it's way through gritted teeth. Finally, Gabrielle gave up. "Guess *he* won't be a problem anymore now, huh?"

"Ga-Gabrielle, w-what do you want?" Gem choked on her tears and the waxy taste of Gabrielle's lipstick. "What did you do to Frost? Is he...is...?"

"Oh, he's dead, honey. Drained dry. No, no — don't start crying. It makes me so sad, Gem." Gabrielle stroked her satin fingers over Gem's naked chest. "We tried to catch your, uhm, *gig* at Dark Echoes. Just missed you. Heard you were a real smash, though." She started to grind her pelvis into Gem's hips. "We've been tailing you two for a couple nights now. Thought it'd be nice to hook up with all my old...friends. Oh yeah — Chelsea, Fitch, Brandon — they're all dead. Drained dry. Cass, too. But they turned him — don't ask me why — so we figure he's still skulking around town somewhere. Probably spending his days in a dumpster, the stupid fuck."

"Wh-what are you talking about?" Gem tried to lift herself up, tried to see up onto the bed. But Gabrielle just shoved her back down.

"Hiding from the sun, silly. Oh yeah, it's all true. Totally." Gabrielle cupped Gem's small breasts in her gloved hands and squeezed hard. "All for real, can you fucking believe it? After all those stupid role playing games and movies and books and shit. It's finally the real thing."

"No, y-you got me all wrong, Gabrielle. I'm not really into this whole scene. It was Frost, see? He was Mr. Goth, I was just along for the ride, I — "

Gabrielle shook her head at Gem, smiling.

"You — you're crazy, Gabrielle."

"Yeah, and you're fucked. Or, you're about to be. You should've gone with us that night, Gem. Remember? Back in old Rimbaud's Cave? You could've met my friends weeks ago." She nodded towards Fonda on the bed. "Not that *he'd* be interested in you. No, old Fonda there, he only had eyes for Cass. Gave him the blow job of his life...well, so to speak...right there in Graceland Cemetery." Gabrielle looked back down at Gem's terrified eyes, all stained from tearstreaks mixing with mascara residue. She stretched herself across Gem's body, nuzzling Gem's hair, whispering in her ear. "I mean, naturally we'd have off'd your pale little fuck muffin. But you? You, I think, they might have kept. You could've joined up then." Her tongue darted into Gem's ear. "But now? Now, I think maybe you'll just have to die."

"Enough."

The voice came from nowhere, or just from a shadowy corner of the dark bedroom.

Gem jerked her head away from Gabrielle's face and saw a figure that seemed to materialize right out of the darkness. A thin, frail looking young girl floated there, with a thick mane of long black hair, with skin even whiter than the flimsy white dress that fluttered around her in a breeze that wasn't even there. She glided barefoot and silent across the room, hovering beside them

"Why do you insist on torturing them so?" Arianne said.

"I — I'm sorry," Gabrielle stammered. "I just..."

Arianne lay a white, long fingered hand on Gabrielle's shoulder. "Get up off of that girl. Now."

Gabrielle's sarcasm and bravado wilted instantly. She slid off of Gem and skulked behind Arianne.

"Fonda," Arianne said. "I believe you are finished?"

Fonda crept off the bed and zipped up his pants.

Arianne turned back to Gabrielle. "Now help him do something with that boy's body. Then wait for me."

"But I thought — "

Arianne glared at her. Still lying on the floor at their feet, Gem watched in bewildered terror — then just amazement — as Arianne's eyes glimmered with visible red sparks.

"But Arianne, *when?"* Gabrielle whined. "I thought she'd be the — "

Arianne pressed a cold finger to Gabrielle's lips and silenced her. "Go now. Your time will come."

Gem curled up on the floor beside the bed, trying to cover her nakedness, trying to disappear. Her stomach churned, and her head started to swim when Fonda and Gabrielle pulled Frostbite's body off the bed. It hit the floor with a sickening *thud.* She watched them drag Frost out of the bedroom into the darker hallway beyond. A moment later, she heard the apartment door open and close.

She looked up at the thin, white girl standing in front of her. Arianne fingered the slender shoulder straps on her shapeless dress, then slid each of them down her arms. The gauzy garment fluttered down to her feet.

Arianne held out her arms to Gem. Her eyes were black caves with glowing red centers, boring into Gem's head. Her mouth was all rich, red sin and worse, wrapped around sparkling white teeth.

Smiling.

And sharp.

"Come to me, child," Arianne said.

And Gem did.

TWENTY THREE

Jeff Stancheck spent all of Friday morning trying to stay awake during Charade's tediously long monthly budget meeting.

He kept his own report mercifully short, nodding politely when his third monthly request in a row for additional staff was shot down by Finance. There wasn't much else to do while Production, Sales, Administration and all the other departments droned through their presentations.

Editorial was unusually brief this month.

Or more correctly, skipped altogether.

Blair Armstrong simply didn't show up for the meeting.

Which normally would have been a major faux pas, but then Roberta Whitehead was a no-show herself...an event, to say the least. Her fondness for slashing project allocations and department budgets in front of a conference room full of hired help was legendary...even more than her penthouse suite's not so hush-hush hijinks. Everyone knew she loved nothing better than monthly budget meetings. At least everyone who *thought* they knew what Roberta Whitehead loved.

It was past noon when the meeting finally ended. Jeff wandered back to an empty out-to-lunch Art Department, each vacant cubicle glowing with new Gothique screen-savers on the 20" Mac monitors. Outputs, proofs and layouts littered the desktops and draped over partitions in a familiar mess — Colleen Russell's the worst, but then she'd been doing the work of two since Kelly Feeny decided to up and disappear. Jeff checked his voice mails and headed out for lunch himself.

On the way back, a midwest autumn brewed all damp and cool in the winds jetting between the skyscraper canyons along Fairmont. He clutched his corduroy blazer closed with one hand and held onto an extra large carryout coffee with the other, warmth seeping right through the Styrofoam cup into his fingers. Stomach grumbling from a questionable fast-food enchilada — Jeff grumbling to himself about the wasted morning on a busy day in a busy week — he headed back into the Whitestar Media Building's glass and brass revolving doors.

Just as Blair Armstrong slid into the doors behind him.

"Oh God, let me have that." When the doors spun them into the lobby, Blair snatched the cup from Jeff's hands, whipped the plastic lid off and gulped.

"Yow, hot."

"Care for some coffee, Blair?"

"Fine, but what's this crap?"

She didn't look good. Or didn't look right. Or at any rate, didn't look like Blair. No tailored designer suit. No spiky designer pumps. No designer anything from the looks of it. Blair shoved a gray NYU sweatshirt's floppy sleeves up her arms and brought the coffee cup back to her mouth with both hands. The rim nudged huge, opaque sunglasses covering half her face like bug eyes.

"Jeans?" Jeff laughed. *"Torn* jeans? A sweatshirt? And Jesus — running shoes? Where's my camera when I need it?"

"Fuck off."

"Nice."

"Bad morning, Jeff. Come on, walk with me. I have a meeting." She started to shuffle through the lobby toward the elevators.

"If you mean the monthly budget meeting, you're off by a few hours."

"The monthly — that was today? Goddamn it. What did Roberta — "

Jeff shook his head. "You were both no-shows. Must've been one hell of a party last night."

The elevator doors slid open. Jeff stepped in, but Blair still slouched in the lobby, holding that extra large with both hands. Shaky hands. "Last night? Oh, right...the party. Yeah, it was...was...really something."

"Coming?"

"Huh? Oh...right." She dragged herself on to the elevator and the doors closed.

"Blair, you don't look so good."

"Thanks a lot."

"You know what I mean. You must have really tied one on last night."

"Huh? Oh, yeah." She handed the cup back to Jeff. Empty. "Last night... yeah, it really...uhm...drained me."

"Hobnobbing'll do that to you." Jeff eyed her up closely. "So, you got to meet all your Gothique ghouls?"

"What? What about Goth — oh, yes. Sure, some of the, uhm...the people from Gothique were there. They all...that is, I went back to Gothique after the party, and...Jeff, you wouldn't believe..." She paused. "That is, you really missed it."

The elevator doors slid open on the sixteenth floor.

Jeff stepped out.

Blair still leaned against the wall, head drooping.

"Blair, are you sure you're all right?"

She stumbled out of the elevator and aimed herself toward Editorial, leaving Jeff at the Art Department. "Yes, I'm fine. Really." Blair shuffled across the carpet in her running shoes, bumping off cubicle walls. "Oh right — Jeff, I forgot to tell you," she said over her shoulder, never bothering to turn around. "That uhm...that Annual Graphics Review thing of yours. I canceled it."

✦

Colleen hunkered down over her keyboard, but there was no ignoring the shouting and the fists slamming a desk inside Jeff's office. The rest of the department leaned over their partitions and even stood up on chairs, anxious to see if Jeff's door might burst open and the furniture fly out.

"You stood right there just yesterday and acted like everything was fine, Blair. And you knew all along you were going to kill the piece, didn't you? What's the matter? Not 'pals' anymore? Just because I wouldn't go to your little soiree?"

"Oh, move on, will you Jeff? I had to cut that Review thing to make room for something else. No one wants to read that boring crap anyway. I don't know why you and Megan always thought it was so special."

Colleen lifted her head over her own cubicle wall. "Hey guys, show a little class, will you?"

The rest of the department looked at her like she was crazy and turned back toward Jeff's closed door.

"So that's it? You killed it, no discussion? What's up, need room for some new bondage-blood-bar feature? Going to tip in some role playing cards now? God, I can't believe you would just lie to me like — "

"I didn't lie to you. I just forgot to mention it, Jeff. Look, don't make a big thing out of this. I have a hangover. I can't deal with this right now."

"Well, you better deal with it. If the Annual Review is out, then maybe I'm out."

Now even Colleen couldn't help herself. She leaned against her partition and stared at the closed door like the rest of the artists.

"Oh get real, Jeff. Without this job you'd just be another dime-a-dozen middle aged mouse clicker. So let's skip the dramatics."

"I'm serious, Blair. I don't like what's been going on around here. I never signed on for a job at a high brow fetish mag, and that's what Charade's turning into."

"So Jeff, you go with it or you can just...go. Whatever. I have a meeting, I don't have time for this. You got any aspirin?"

Nothing boomed out from behind Jeff's closed door for a long minute.

"So that means you don't then. Fine."

The door opened and Blair stepped out of Jeff's office, sliding those huge black glasses back over her bloodshot eyes. The artists all fell into their chairs just like third graders leaping into their desks when the teacher stepped back into class. All except Colleen. She locked eyes with Blair before those glasses slid back into place. Colleen shook her head and watched as Blair looked over her shoulder into Jeff's office.

"I'll be tied up with the writers," Blair said, already yanking folders out of her shoulder bag. "Try to get with the program, Jeff."

No sooner had Blair disappeared into the labyrinths of cubicles and file cabinet rows, then Jeff burst out of his office, snapping his briefcase shut.

Colleen jumped out of her cubicle to head him off. "Jeff, wait. Are you...is everything okay?"

"No, everything is definitely *not....*" He paused. Closed his eyes and took a deep breath. "Sorry, Colleen. Sorry you had to hear all that."

She followed him to the elevators. "Where are you going? You're not really...*going?"*

"No?" Jeff punched the down button. "I — look, I just — " The elevator doors opened.

Inside, Tim and Ivy broke off a sloppy tongued kiss and looked up smiling at Jeff and Colleen. Their dopey grins drooped immediately once they realized that silence was the password for the moment and slinked out of the elevator, then off to the Art Department.

"I just have to get out of here, Colleen." Jeff stomped onto the elevator. "And maybe you should too."

The doors closed in Colleen's face.

✦

Outputs usually inched out of the large format color inkjet at a snail's pace. This particular two page spread crept out like a snail in a Vicodin haze. Colleen spooled the pages just after 6:30, had been standing beside the monstrous printer since quarter of seven, and still only half an inch of blank white margin peeked out of the rollers. Even though the machine furiously hummed and click-clacked away at *something.*

Friday evening.

Working late.

Again.

The elevator doors had barely closed on Jeff before most of the Art Department shut off their computers and pulled on their coats. If the ever-inseparable Tim and Ivy hadn't both extended their typical two-hour lunch into two-and-a-half, Colleen never would have been able to guilt-trip anyone into staying.

The boss was gone for the day.

The boss was gone for good?

Who knew, but Jeff and Blair's not-so-behind-closed-doors sparring match signaled 'afternoon off' to most of the artists.

"Tim," Colleen called back to the cubicle rows, "Have you had any trouble with the large format today?"

Tim didn't answer, but Ivy's head popped up, multi-colored drapes of blonde/brown/black hair sliding over her partition. "He's in the can, Col. But I hope your pages'll come out quick. I have a couple spooled up behind you." Ivy rolled up a belled and naturally black lace sleeve to glance at her watch. "Tim and I have a da— I mean, we're both thinking of checking out this film fest at 8:00. They're running the whole Hammer Karnstein Trilogy at the Music Box Theater."

Colleen looked up from the printer. "Ivy, I have a bulletin for you. I *know* you two are dating. *Everyone* knows you two are dating. The *whole world* knows you two are dating."

Ivy smiled shyly, ruby red glossed lips sparkling under the fluorescent overheads. "Well, you know, Whitestar HR policies and all that crap."

"I don't think they really care about coworkers dating, Ivy. Practically screwing in the elevator — *that* HR might have a rule against."

Ivy laughed and slid back down into her cubicle. "Say, Colleen," she called from behind the upholstered partition. "You want to come with? Ingrid Pitt. Yutte Stensgaard. Peter Cushing and the Collinson Twins. I'm talking cinema classics."

"Pass." Colleen listened to the inkjet churn and watched the paper creep out another half inch.

Ivy reappeared over her cubicle wall. "Well, if your pages are running so slow, I'm going to see if there's any coffee left. Want some?"

"Nope. Go ahead," Colleen said. "Once this spread decides to appear, I'm out of here."

"'Kay." Ivy slung her purse over her shoulder and headed off towards Editorial and the coffee stations. With most of the lights already shut off in the next department, her head-to-toe black vanished into the gloom.

Colleen watched her go, then watched the glacial speed printout for a moment, but found herself glancing back over her shoulder instead. An early autumn evening was descending outside the floor to ceiling windows that overlooked Fairmont. Her eyes surveyed the usual Art Department Friday end-of-day mess — just left that much messier that much earlier today — and then she inevitably glanced at Jeff Stancheck's office. Door open. Lights still on. She left the inkjet churning along and wandered over.

She looked inside.

Jeff's desk was littered with proofs and reports and copy drafts. His computer was still on. Colleen stepped inside, closed his files and shut the computer down.

She let go of the mouse and her hand brushed three floppies.

Right there, next to the mousepad, half buried under a stack of layouts.

The disks.

The disks.

Colleen grabbed the disks, ran a finger over the bent shields and the cracked plastic. Immediately she thought about that envelope. The letter the mailroom ghoul brought up weeks ago. The envelope addressed to Jeff.

Addressed by her own sister — she was sure of it — addressed by Megan, maybe even the very night she died.

Died?

Murdered?

Colleen shivered and dropped the disks. Cracked plastic and crinkled metal shields clattered on Jeff's desk. Colleen flicked off the lights, slammed Jeff's office door closed and ran back to the printer.

Three more inches of paper made it past the rollers.

"Come on, you..."

The inkjet churned back at her, the only sound in the empty Art Department.

✦

"Tim? Tim, so where are you?"

Wading from one pool of darkness to the next, Ivy took little baby steps through Editorial.

"Tim? C'mon, stop fucking around." Stray overheads only lit up corners of the Department. Office doors were closed tight. "Tim?" Secretarial station desk lamps were all shut off. "Tim, I'm getting pissed off now."

A hand shot out of the darkness and clamped down on Ivy's wrist so fast she never had a chance to scream.

An office door flung open and she was dragged inside.

"Oops, my bad. It's just me, Ivy. Jeez." Tim smiled, suddenly all innocence.

But Ivy was hyperventilating too much to answer. She did manage to smack Tim on the back of the head. Hard. When she finally caught her breath she threw in a good punch to the chest too. "You asshole. What are you trying to do, scare the living hell out of me?"

Tim wrapped his arms around her. "Sorry, babe. Thought I'd surprise you."

"You surprised me, all right. Almost pissed my pants." Ivy tried to wiggle out of Tim's arms, but it was all for show. Finally she settled in and hugged him back. "Who's office is this?" She looked around. "Christ, are you nuts, Tim? This is — "

He nodded. "The head cheese."

"This is honcho land, Tim. Let's get out of here now."

"Why?" Tim said. "You saw Blair today. She was three sheets from the wind. Or two sails from the gibbet, or — "

"She was hungover."

"Yeah. That."

"Tim, this is creepy. Let's get out of here. Colleen's still working. She finds us in here, we're screwed."

"Screwing sounds good," he said, leering a little as he let go of Ivy and plopped into Blair Armstrong's huge leather swivel chair. "Could kind of get us in the mood for those flicks tonight." He spun the chair in a half circle till he faced Blair's windows, looking out on the downtown skyline, a sea of tiny lights against deepening blue.

"Get us in the mood?" Ivy slowly ambled around Blair's desk. "Oh, I get it. Sorry, mister. Colleen Russell's too straight for me. And I'm too straight for...*that.*" She stepped between the huge windows and Blair's chair, easing herself onto Tim's lap. "Tired of me already?"

Tim shook his head. His hands stroked the cobweb patterns on her black nylons and disappeared under her skirt.

"Hey, save it for later, Tim." Ivy brushed his hand away with about as much conviction as she'd wiggled out of his arms a moment before. Tim's hand shot back under her dress and tugged on the hose. She leaned back against him and sighed. "Well, my last pages won't be out of the printer for a while anyway."

Both of them stared at the wall of high rises hovering outside the giant windows. Stared at their reflection in the glass, haloed by those twinkling silhouettes and the violet sky. Tim slid Ivy's cobweb nylons and then her panties down past her knees, while she reached back and groped for his zipper.

"You...know," Ivy said, her words breathy and halting as Tim's fingers buried themselves between her legs. "We get...caught in...here...and..."

"I — I — know," Tim said. Ivy's hands finally managed the zipper on his jeans. "We...get...caught...in here...and..."

They both heard the door squeak open.

They both saw it reflected in the window glass.

But that's all they saw. Just the door swinging open.

Ivy spun the chair back around to face the door.

"Yeah...caught...and...we're..."

"Dead?"

Tim and Ivy saw them then. Ivy fell off Tim's lap, flat assed on the floor. She scrambled halfway under Blair's desk, clutching her nylons, starting to pull her underwear back up her legs. But she froze. They both *saw,* but didn't really *believe.*

Until the vampires lunged at them.

✦

Colleen's printout still had another inch to go, but she ripped it out of the printer anyway. The machine churned one last time, reluctant to let go. "Mine's out, Ivy," she called on the way back to her cubicle. She clipped a routing slip to the output and set it on top of a mound of proofs. "I'm out of here. Hope you guys make it to your film fes — "

She stopped next to Ivy's cubicle.

It was empty.

Colleen looked over the partition to Tim's.

Empty too.

"Coffee. Right." She wanted to be mad, but smiled instead. Maybe Tim and Ivy wouldn't nab any raises or promotions, but at least they were together. Content. She envied them.

Colleen shut down her computer and grabbed her jean jacket and purse. She could hear the inkjet churning again as Ivy's pages started to inch out. "Farnstein-Marnstein-Karnstein trilogy, whatever," she said out loud, still smiling. "I'm thinking you guys'll be late for the show." But the film fest name rang a bell somewhere in the back of her head, and she automatically thought of

Cass and all his crazy videos and books and games. And her smile immediately faded. Colleen slipped on the jacket and stepped out of her cubicle.

Just as the lights went out.

Only the eerie glow from Tim and Ivy's monitors kept the Art Department from going totally black.

"Hey," she called out. "Still working up here."

No answer.

"Ivy?"

Colleen felt her way along the tops of the cubicle walls towards the elevators. "Tim?"

Still no answer.

She made it to the hallway by the elevators. Felt along the wall. Bumped into a potted plant and knocked it right over.

"Who's there?"

Security?

Maintenance?

A breath breezed past her, cold and fetid.

"W-Who's — "

A hand brushed her face and vanished back into the shadows.

Colleen yelped and jerked away. She stumbled through the darkness and patted the wall for the elevator. She spotted the little illuminated Up and Down buttons just ahead.

Saw a shadow bleed over them and then disappear.

"Who's there?" Colleen fought back the fear in her voice. "G-Goddamn it, who's there?"

She heard the giggling then.

And the voices. If that's what they really were.

Behind her.

'Is that her?"

In front of her.

'Looks like the one.'

All around her and flitting back and forth in the darkness, circling her in the shadows.

'What's so special about her?'

And drawing closer.

A click.

A spark.

Another. And then a lighter flashed, a small circle of yellow light, barely illuminating the elevator hallway, but shining brightly on a smiling face draped in a frizzed-out cape of black hair. "Hi there, Red."

Colleen gulped. Blinked, tried to focus. "Gab-Gabrielle?"

The lighter flame raised closer to Gabrielle's face while she lit a long, black papered cigarette. Gabrielle sucked hard and then blew the smoke straight at

Colleen. "None other."

The lighter clicked off, plunging the hallway back into darkness.

"Gabrielle? How'd you get in here?"

There was that giggling again. And those voices, just whispers really, like the fuzzy flutter of wings. Like long nails dragging across velvet, like breathy obscene phone call sounds in Colleen's ears.

She saw the orange tip of Gabrielle's cigarette raise and lower. Heard her drag on the cigarette, saw the orange flare brighter, illuminating that smiling face. Heard Gabrielle exhale the smoke again.

"Oh, we just pretty much come and go where we please, Red."

"W-we? Gabrielle, how the hell did you...what do you want?" Colleen slowly inched along the wall towards the elevator buttons till she stood in front of them, her back to the wall. She reached behind her. Pressed down on one of the buttons as quietly as she could. She didn't really care which one it was.

"So, how's the old job going, Russell? Or should I say, how's *my* old job going? Seems to me we still have a little unfinished business to settle. All by your lonesome tonight?"

"Uhm, no, actually. Colleen thought she heard the distant whir of machinery from behind the elevator doors. Thought she did. Hoped she did. "There's a whole bunch of us working late tonight. Look, I don't know how you got up here, Gabrielle. But they'll all be back soon, so you better get out of here now. Before they call security. And Tim, he's — he's a pretty big guy, he — "

Gabrielle's laughter cut Colleen off. That, and the insane giggling sounds emanating from all around and deep in the shadows.

"Tim, huh? You mean that little weasel we found with his hands in the cookie jar. So to speak." The orange glow from Gabrielle's cigarette hovered there in the darkness, but appeared to be drawing closer now. "You forget. I was here first. I remember when Tim and Ivy both started. 'Pretty big guy'...oh please. Anyway, I have a feeling Timmy boy's a little busy right now. Him and that other little intern slut too. She tried to run, but that's kind of hard to do with your skimpies around your ankles, you know?"

Colleen listened to the icicle giggles tinkling all around her in the dark. Listened to the sounds from behind the elevator doors.

"Methinks they're dead, Red. But don't be sad, they went happy. And they'll be together all the time now, forever and ever."

The cigarette glow drew even closer. Just a few feet away now. Colleen pressed her back against the elevator doors. The metal vibrated and the machinery revved behind them.

"Look," Gabrielle said, "Much as I'd like to watch you do the wide-eyed stuttering thing all night, time's a wastin'. We have things to do, places to go, people to see, that kind of thing. So what do you say, Colleen? Going to come easy? Or would you like to do it the hard way? Me, I'm really hoping you'll go for the hard way."

Colleen felt a thump from behind the elevator doors. Heard one of those voices that weren't really voices hiss. Heard another one sneer, *'What's that?'*. Heard the whir and spin of metal and machinery.

A little bell rang in the darkness.

The elevator doors slid open behind her.

And the rest? The rest was just a blur.

Those doors slid open and Colleen fell backwards and inside.

Light spilled out of the elevator and into the hallway. Colleen saw Gabrielle standing right there, not ten feet away now and diving straight at her. Saw three figures hovering at the edge of the light. In familiar head to toe black. But their faces, their eyes, their mouths — those weren't so familiar.

Then ice cold hands gripped Colleen's shoulders and dragged her all the way into the elevator. The doors hesitated and then started to slide closed with agonizing slowness.

"Get her!" Gabrielle shrieked.

The figures leaped out of the shadows, eyes flaming red and mouths gaping open.

The elevator doors slammed on Colleens' legs. Gabrielle lunged, one black gloved hand reaching out for Colleen's leg, the other grabbing one of the doors. The shadow figures with the white faces and the red eyes and the even redder hellmouths seemed to fly right through the darkness. And straight for Colleen.

She screamed. Kicked frantically till she knocked Gabrielle's hand off the elevator door. She heard her wail. But Colleen also felt those cold hands again, heaving her backwards till her feet slipped past the elevator doors.

They finally slammed shut.

And the elevator began to descend.

But she could still hear the shrieks and screams right through the thick metal. *"I'll get you. I'll get you, you little bitch..."*

The cold hands on her shoulders finally let go.

Colleen started to get up. She stared at the polished brass and mirrored elevator doors and saw nothing but the back wall, the hand rail, the floor.

Herself.

She stood, knees weak, legs ready to buckle.

It may have been the hardest thing she ever did, but Colleen Russell slowly turned around.

And once she did, her legs *did* give out. She fell back against the elevator door and started to slide right down to the floor.

But those same cold hands grabbed her again and held her up.

Pulled her close.

Hugged her tight.

"Is it really you?" Colleen just went limp. "Oh, Cass. Cass..."

TWENTY FOUR

Gabrielle kicked the elevator door. "Turn on a goddamn light."

"Why?" one of the vampires asked, genuinely puzzled.

Gabrielle kicked again and again, denting metal and knocking the door right off the tracks. "Because *I* can't see a fucking thing."

"Oh."

Gabrielle didn't even know the kid's name. He was just another one of the newcomers that popped up every couple nights now from the lower levels beneath Gothique.

"So? Don't you want to go after them?" Another nameless one. "This big creepy crawly stakeout, you do the whole chatty villain routine and then we just let her go?"

The lights switched on by the elevators and back in the Art Department. The two vampires still in the hallway instinctively backed towards the wall, almost cowering. "Boy, that redhead just oozed girl-power, didn't she?" one gushed.

"And who was that waiting in the elevator?" the other said. "Looked to me like he was one of us."

"Listen, just go get the others," Gabrielle said, puffing furiously on her black cigarette. "Tell them to hurry up with those two weasels in Editorial."

"Sure." One vampire turned to go. Then stopped. "In where?"

"In — forget it. I'll get them."

"Good, I'm thirsty. You said we'd get — "

"Oh, just shut the fuck up and come on." Gabrielle ground her cigarette out in the hallway carpet, then stomped through the Art Department towards Editorial and Megan Russell's — make that Blair Armstrong's — office. The newborns tramped along behind her.

They found Drake leaning against a file cabinet right outside Blair's door.

Licking blood off his fingertips.

"Missing somebody?" he said.

Gabrielle shrugged, but it was all feigned nonchalance. "So, you guys done yet?"

Drake nodded towards the open office door. Gabrielle shimmied past him and peeked inside.

Fonda and another equally skinny and equally giggly androgyne — though this one looked like it had something that would have someday been called breasts had she lived — had Tim stretched out on his back and on the floor. Tim's already pale body was stripped naked now and convulsing on Blair's plush carpet. Fonda's lips fixed on the red, quivering pulp that had been Tim's throat just a few minutes ago. Finally, Fonda pulled away and wiped a wet red smear off his mouth. "Oops, did it again," he tittered, all coquettish and holding his pale hands over his mouth. "Looks like we finished him off."

Tim's naked body wasn't convulsing anymore.

Across the office Gabrielle saw two more vampires working Ivy over. *She* still looked alive. Barely. Cobweb patterned nylons all shredded and dangling off her white legs, panties yanked down around her knees, skirt hiked over her belly, Ivy sighed and swayed as the two vampires ran their cold hands all over her, dragged their cold tongues all over her and lapped up the blood oozing from the wounds on her arms, her thighs and her breasts.

Gabrielle watched them, transfixed, voyeuristic thrilling, feeling her own blood boil in her veins, feeling her head swim, feeling her legs go weak and gooey. She wanted...wanted to...wanted to be like...

"Just leave them be, girlie," Drake said. "I hear you're still supposed to stay in the wishin' and a-wantin' stage." He grabbed Gabrielle by the hair and dragged her out of the office doorway. "So what's with this little commando raid of yours? I'm not so sure we should be fucking around up here anyway. Thought you needed us to help you nab some particular puss you've been after."

"Meow," one of the newborns giggled from behind. "Puss-puss got away."

"Got away?" Drake growled. "She *saw* you and you let her get away?" He glared at Gabrielle, eyes blazing red. "What the fuck are you up to? Marek will have your head on a platter for this. Hell, maybe *I'll* have your head on a platter right now." His lips peeled back from his fangs as he stepped towards her.

"Hold it," Gabrielle said, backing away till she bumped the wall. "Someone helped her, Drake."

"What are you talking about?" He stepped closer.

"It was Cass."

Drake halted. His red eyes cooled to dead black while he worked over the name.

Fonda suddenly appeared in the office doorway, Tim's dead body all but forgotten now and lying naked in the other vampire's arms. That one still licked the last traces of blood off Tim's skin. And the chair. And the desk. And the carpet.

"Cass?" Fonda clapped his hands and danced in the doorway. "Did I hear you say 'Cass'? My sweet little renegade?"

"That's right,' Gabrielle said.

"Ooo, I want my run-run-runaway back," Fonda said.

"Cool down, princess." Drake patted Fonda on the head till he stopped prancing. "Talk fast, Gabby girl, or I throw you to these three." He jerked his head back towards the newborns. "And I doubt they have the hang of just when to stop anymore than Fonda does, dig?"

Gabrielle produced another black cigarette and fumbled with her lighter. Drake reached over, steadied the lighter and lit it for her.

"I'm waiting, warmblood."

"We had her, Drake," Gabrielle said, all her bitchy bravado melting away. She puffed on the cigarette, coughed and puffed some more. "But like, from out of nowhere, there he was. Cass. That little fag hag's roomie. Ex-roomie, make that. And they...they both got away from us."

Drake eyed up Gabrielle long and hard till sweat started beading up all over her face and her mascara and eyeshadow pooled into watercolor puddles on her cheeks. "This is the swish that Fonda was making goo-goo eyes at back in that cemetery? That guy?"

She nodded.

"I don't like loners, man. Especially not when they get in our way. We're gonna have to find that cat and do something about him."

"Oh can we, Drake?" Fonda pranced up and down and clapped his hands again. "I want my Cass back, he was supposed to be all mine."

"Later, freak." Drake stuck his head in Blair's office. "You two. Finish that bitch off or bring her with us. Time to vamoose." He turned back to Gabrielle. "*You* can help them clean up, warmblood. Spit 'n polish so no one knows we were ever here, or I'll wipe that office clean with your face. I have to think about all of this."

Later, they all filed down the fire stairs, two of the newborns glumly carrying Tim's dead body with his bloodstained clothes laid on top and the scent driving them crazy. Two others half walked—half carried Ivy, still stealing the occasional lick off her stained skin.

The others glided down the concrete stairs, Gabrielle right behind Drake.

"All this fuckin' around just to bring back one fresh one. Half drained at that." Drake mumbled to himself as much as to Gabrielle, two steps behind him. "Seems like a lot of trouble just to get back at some bitch that took a job you don't even need anymore."

"She just rubbed me wrong, Drake."

"Or maybe she just wouldn't rub you right, sure that ain't it?"

"Look, that Colleen Russell's one dead bitch," Gabrielle hissed. "If not tonight, then — "

Drake froze.

Gabrielle plowed right in to him, then jumped back two stairs.

He turned around slowly, and now Drake's eyes were blazing red again.

"*What* did you say her name was?"

✦

Once the elevator doors slid open onto the Whitestar Media Building's lobby, Cass and Colleen just ran.

They blew past the guard nodding off — or pretending to — at the security station. Flew through the revolving doors and spilled out onto Fairmont Court, certain the vampires were right on their heels.

But they weren't.

Fairmont and Michigan and all the other streets teemed with the usual Friday night apres-office secretaries dressed up like vice-presidents and junior execs dressed down like beatniks, near-north yuppies and suburban singles all milling around on the sidewalks and heading off into bars and bistros, hailing cabs and hopping out of limo's to size each other up, weigh their options, take inventory for the weekend. And none of them even glanced at Colleen and the tall, good looking skinny guy in the black velvet pants and the black trenchcoat, frantically racing in between the crowds.

They ran the three blocks to the deserted parking lot, Cass practically dragging Colleen when her breath started to give out. It wasn't until her little import sedan was merging onto Lake Shore Drive that she finally calmed down. A little. But she still eyed her rearview mirror more than the lanes ahead, still twisted around in her seat to look over her shoulder.

"What the hell was..." Colleen gritted her teeth and passed two lanes of traffic at an even sixty. "Cass, what the hell..."

Then she let go of the steering wheel and hit him.

She slugged Cass right on the face. "You son of a bitch!" She pounded on him as hard as she could — slaps across the head, fists hammering away on his shoulders and his chest — even if she missed half the time and just banged the bucket seats.

Cass didn't fight back.

Finally she stopped. Colleen took hold of the wheel and twisted the little car back into its own lane. Not that she could see the road all that well. Tears clouded her eyes like rain on a windshield.

"I'm sorry, Colleen."

"Sorry? Sorry!" She balled up another fist but just punched the dashboard this time. "Cass, where the hell have you been? What's going on? Who — what the hell happened back there?"

"You really need me to explain it?"

"Yes, I really fucking need you to explain it. I thought you were dead. That your body was stolen or missing or...What the hell's going on?" She twisted the wheel and cut across to the right towards the Belmont Exit.

"Where are you going?"

"I'm getting off the Drive. We have to call the cops, Cass."

"No. No police."

"Cass, they're looking for you. For Gabrielle." She cut off a car in the right lane and made for the exit. "Tim and Ivy are still up there. And those...they...I just left them up there."

Cass leaned over and grabbed the wheel. "Colleen, just keep driving." He edged the car back to the left. Colleen tried to keep the wheel straight, but there was no fighting him.

"Cass, we have to — "

"No!" It wasn't Cass' familiar voice, wasn't Cass' voice at all. It was some strange other-voice, from somewhere else, somewhere dark and scary. The little sedan swerved into the next lane, just missed a car, and then swerved back. "No," he said, quieter now, calmer. "Don't you get it, Colleen? We can't call the police."

The car shot by the exit.

"Cass, they told me — the police, they told me. That you were murdered. That your body was missing." She looked at him, at the dashboard glow painting him monster-green. But he just stared straight ahead at the rows of twin taillights weaving across Lake Shore Drive. "They told me you were dead."

"Colleen, I am."

✦

Colleen unlocked the rows of deadbolts, opened the apartment door and reached in to turn on the lights. She started to turn around, tried to manage a smile. "Well, everything's pretty much the same as — "

The words froze in her throat.

The living room lights spilled out onto the landing and lit up Cass.

And she saw him. Really saw him now. Not through fear filled eyes like in the elevator. Not by the dim green dashboard glow in the car, or the foggy haze in the courtyard.

Now she saw Cass and knew — *knew* that every single utterly insane thing he'd been telling her all the way up Lake Shore Drive and Sheridan and all the way from the car must be absolutely true.

He looked just like he did on so many nights when she'd watched him primp and preen before going out. *Like* that...but not. Cass' skin was completely drained of color — pallid, translucent flesh stretched too thin over dead, graying muscle. It was repulsive, yet inexplicably alluring. His face was somehow ghastly *and* beautiful at the same time. His eyes were ringed in dark, shadowy hollows, but now it wasn't filched eyeshadow from Colleen's makeup case or costume shop greasepaint. His irises were black, just like opals, black as his pupils, just big round cartoon dots in the center of the whites, and even those seemed to flicker and change from white to see-through diamonds. Cass' lips sliced across his pale face in a blue-red slash, some kind of nightmare clown, an acid trip mime.

And there was simply no ignoring the tiny tips of the two fangs poking out of his mouth, or the way they dented his lower lip. Not plastic, not mail-order acrylic, not some whacked out dentist's hack job. No, they sparkled like pearls in the light, especially the lethal looking needle tips.

Colleen couldn't help herself. She instantly recoiled, stepped back on the landing, her nostrils wrinkling, finally noticing the distasteful scent of dead flowers and rancid fruit and tarnished copper.

"Uhm, no lights, okay?" He clicked the switch and the landing and the living room went dark again. "It'll be better. For both of us."

She nodded and followed him into the apartment. Cass locked all the deadbolts and the chains behind them.

Colleen dropped her purse on the floor. Her jean jacket fell off on top of it. "I need a drink. A major drink." She headed for the kitchen. "Can I get you any — " She stopped. Turned around and looked back at Cass, still standing there by the door. She disappeared into the kitchen, shaking her head.

She returned with a juice glass in one hand and an old and never opened fifth of bourbon that had been lurking in the cabinet over the stove for the longest time. But the living room was empty. Cass wasn't there.

"Cass?"

She crept down the dark hallway, wishing for a moment that maybe it was all a dream, thinking, hoping that none of this had just happened, that it was just a crazy dream, just a nightmare.

Till she stood at Cass' bedroom door. And saw him standing there by the window, the faint city light leaking through the courtyard to wash over him, painting his pale face a powder blue.

"It was you that night, wasn't it?"

Cass didn't respond.

She pointed the bourbon bottle at the window, finally repaired only a couple weeks ago and still smelling of fresh glazing and paint. "You came here, didn't you? Snuck in somehow. And when I called out your name, you just...crashed right out your window."

He nodded.

"Just flew down four stories. Don't tell me. You sprouted little bat wings?"

He smirked.

"Why? Why did you run away?"

He shrugged his shoulders. Barely.

"Cass, what's happened?"

He stepped away from the window. Wandered past his bookcase, his pale fingers dragging along the tops of the paperbacks and video boxes. He paused at the dresser. Picked up a magazine. Looked at the cover, at a garish photo of a teenage couple gussied up in their cinched black corsets and fishnets and dyed black hair. Cass smiled, and his fangs glimmered in the faint light. But the smile faded. He slammed the magazine down on the dresser and gripped his head in his hands, clawing those pale fingers through his own bleached and black hair.

Colleen wasn't certain, but it sounded like he was sobbing.

She sat down on the edge of the bed. Dropped her juice glass on the floor. Cracked the seal on the bourbon. She kicked off her shoes and dragged herself back across the mattress, leaning against the headboard. Colleen shoved that bottle into her mouth and gulped. Gulped some more. "Cass, it's all for real, isn't it?"

He nodded.

"Your books." She ground her fingers into her thighs, clutching the blue denim till it looked ready to rip. "Your videos and all those role playing games. All of it. It's all...real now. Isn't it?"

He nodded again.

"How?"

Cass shrugged.

"And those...those things back at Charade. They were — I mean, you're like them?"

He said nothing. Didn't even nod this time.

"So you...you're a...a vampire?" She slugged down the bourbon again. "For real, you're a vampire? They were all...vampires?"

Cass turned around and faced her. Colleen thought she saw red sparks flicker in his eyes.

"Gabrielle? Cass, is *she* one too?" She shivered, then gulped down more bourbon.

"No."

"Then what was she doing with those — "

"I don't know, Colleen. I guess she just wants...I really don't know."

"Wants? Cass, how the hell could anyone want...Cass, you have to talk to me. You have to explain this to me. You've got to tell me I'm not going crazy. That there are no such things as vampires. That was all just some fucked up game you played, just your clothes and the makeup and the music, just some turn-on, some kinky sex thing you fooled around with. Tell me that's all it is, tell me you're not really — "

"Colleen, I'm a vampire. Those others at your office, they were all vampires. Whoever was with you there — "

"Tim. And Ivy."

"Well, they're probably dead now. And if they're not, they'll wish they were by tomorrow night." Cass sat down on the bed. "Or maybe they won't. Maybe they'll love it. I thought I would. Look, I'm going to tell you all about this. Tonight. Everything. Right now. But then — you have to go away."

"Go away? Are you nuts? No, I can help you. You're my friend." She gulped from the bourbon bottle again and then slammed it down on the nightstand. "You can't just drop this shit on me and then tell me to go away."

"Colleen, I *am* your friend." He shook his head. "No, I *was* your friend. Cass was your friend. But Cass is dead. I'm not Cass anymore. Not really. I'm someone else. Some*thing* else."

"But Cass — "

"Cass is dead!" He leaped off the bed and suddenly his eyes flamed red, actually glowing, sparking. Those blue-red lips peeled back and his fangs slid out, his tongue lapping at the sharp teeth. Cass' hands curled into long, pale claws and reached out for her. Colleen stifled a scream and tried to edge away on the bed, but she was already pressed against the headboard.

And just as suddenly, it was all gone. The red eyes. The groping claws. Gone. He was just...Cass again.

Cass...with two white fangs poking out of his lips.

"Cass—is—dead," he repeated.

"But — "

"No, just listen to me. It all happened that night at Rimbaud's Cave. Or, after Rimbaud's Cave. Or, at some cemetery, maybe. See, I'm not sure, it's all kind of a blur now. And I remember it less and less each night. I keep trying to hold on to it, but everything just gets hazier. Some nights I can't even remember your face, or think of your name. Sometimes I can't even remember *my* name. I spend whole nights right down there in the courtyard, staring up at this window, trying to hold on. But it's slipping away. My memories, everything."

Colleen leaned across the bed and reached out to him, but Cass shifted away on the mattress.

"I've been following you. Not every night. But some nights I do, I wait across the street from your office and watch till you leave. I've even snuck into the building sometimes when you work late."

"Like tonight." Colleen said, still clawing her jeans with nervous fingers. "Why?"

"Why? You saw what almost happened."

"But Cass, how could you know?"

"I didn't. I just guessed. I just wanted to protect you from what's out there now." He turned to face her. *"They're* out there, Colleen. Right now. Dozens of them. And there's more every night. They're bad, Colleen. Real, real bad." He grabbed the bourbon bottle off the nightstand. "I'll tell you the little I know. What I can remember, at least." Cass handed the bourbon to Colleen. "Drink up. You're going to need it."

✦

A lot of people needed a drink.

The merlots and sticky sweet cordials were moving faster than the flavored coffees tonight at Rimbaud's Cave, but then everyone was on edge and had been for days now, so they huddled around their little tables and second hand shop sofas in earnest conversation, checking up on who hadn't been seen in days and who hadn't shown up for work all week, while they all looked up suspiciously from their drinks each time the door opened and a cool blast of exhaust fumed autumn air blew inside, as if the black satin and lace crowd was suddenly closing ranks and almost beginning to wonder if something just a little too real might steal in from the night.

And the $1.50 shots and Friday Night Special 75 cent drafts were going faster than the bartenders could pour them at Dark Echoes, especially for the starstruck young guys who kept racing back to their tables to set the glasses down like offerings in front of the unbelievably beautiful pale skinned chicks that toyed with each drink but never bothered to sip one and instead sent the skinny, horny, leather clad mopes scurrying back to the bar to buy some more because those chicks' almost-too-dark-to-be-real eyes promised backseat of the Bonneville and back in the alley and back on your ass pleasures even the most gender-confused Dark Echoes Goth couldn't resist.

And the fern bars and brass and etched glass watering holes flanking both sides of Division Street and scattered throughout the rehabbed warehouse and gallery lofts in River North did brisk business with their margaritas and screwdrivers and undrinkable-but-so-cool-to-order dark brown ales, where the same secretaries gussied up like vice-presidents and the same junior execs dressed down like beatniks that had stood aside on the sidewalks to let Colleen and Cass blow by earlier now jostled for elbow room in the bathroom queues and tried unsuccessfully to mark their turf on the dance floors, some of them — too many of them, tonight — finding themselves inexplicably sweaty and flushed and all gooey hot inside their colored Jockey briefs and Victoria Secret satin tap pants as they made great big cow eyed *voulez vous couchez avec moi ce soir* looks at the strangers dipping in and out of the crowds with their oh-so-lickable cool white skin and oh-so-kissable red, red lips and perversely enigmatic bedroom smiles that promised so much more than fern bars and too many margaritas had a right to promise.

Down on the southwest side, Jeff Stancheck sat at the kitchen table sipping a warming beer, oblivious to the muffled music booming from behind Jacks' closed bedroom door. She was headed out with her pals tonight, with Rachel and her kid brother Rory, who always struck Jeff as a little weird and all the more so these days the way he'd embraced all that goddamned dyed hair and biker leather in drag clothing, but then all the kids were doing it and Jeff smirked as he reluctantly pictured himself at seventeen, decked out in sleazy lounge rat big hair and rolled up sleeved blazers or arena rock ripped jeans and Molly Hatchet muscle shirts. Jeff upended his sixth beer and emptied it when he finally heard Jacks' music click off, her bedroom door open and close, heard her clomp towards the kitchen. He felt like a hypocrite sitting there with a beer in his hand and five empties on the table while he reminded her about their agreed upon weekend curfew and to call if she was going anyplace other than Rachel's and that drinking and driving never mixed. Once she left, he twisted the cap off his seventh Budweiser, annoyed as hell that he wasn't feeling a buzz yet, and he really needed a buzz tonight to stifle his anger over Blair and Charade and Whitestar and the whole damn job. Jeff just sat there alone in the kitchen, brooding over his bottled Buds and wondering if he even *had* a job anymore.

Blair Armstrong stood in front of her dresser mirror and shimmied a black sheer bra over her breasts. She tugged it one way and adjusted it the other way, frowned at her reflection in the mirror and then just tore the flimsy thing off. She grabbed the chilled bottle of French Chablis off the dresser, started to refill her wineglass, then gulped right from the green bottle instead. She finally set it back down, half emptied. The wine warmed her insides, but she was already glowing. Blair glanced at the clock on her nightstand, blinking 9:15 at her in LED orange. She was going to be late. Was supposed to be there by 10:00. *He'd* told her last night to arrive promptly at 10:00. Told her, even though she never saw his lips move, never heard his voice in her ears, just somewhere distant and echoing in her head, but no less insistent, no less commanding. She flung a dresser drawer open, rummaged through the twisted heaps of underwear inside and pulled out an opaque black push-up number and slipped it on. Reached behind her to snap it closed. Glanced in the mirror again. And frowned again too. The stiff black satin cups barely covered the blue welts on her breasts. She ran a freshly painted nail over a red wound glistening at the center of one of those bruises and immediately sucked in her breath. A strangely sinful kind of lust had her legs squeezed tightly together. Eager anticipation had her pulse racing. Just as utter terror had her fingers trembling as she reached for her dress.

Roberta Whitehead leaned against the cold glass of her twenty-seventh floor penthouse suite windows and stared out at the downtown skyline while the very last traces of purple vanished behind the western horizon, spiked as it was with black silhouettes of high rises, chimneys and antennas. The glass was cold, so she clutched her silk kimono closed over her naked skin. The marble floor was cold too, so she eased her feet back into the satin furred mules. She shivered, her head swirling with jealousy and much scarier notions about deals with the devil. But just then a tentative hand tapped her on the shoulder and she turned away from the window, waltzed drunkenly back over to the carpeted sitting area where tonight's boytoy handed her a double scotch on ice and then helped her lay back into a black leather chaise, while *he* grimaced, gulped and plunged back down between the Queen of Whitestar's thighs and went back to work, a long day in Production Control made longer still by tonight's after hours O.T.

Frank Hoelevich hung up the phone after talking to Libbie (the rates were so much lower after 9:00 PM, she reminded him) and shuffled back over to his recliner by the front window. Sox watched him sit there in the darkness and then lay his muzzle back down on his paws — not asleep, just nervous and puzzled — watching Frank settle into a another night sipping Crown Royal and peeping through the drawn blinds at the theater building across the street, where the huge sign on the marquee was all lit up now and glowing red and right into the Hoelevich's second floor window, reflecting a ghastly crimson reverse *Gothique* on the parlor wall.

Father Gil Silverez washed his one dish and melmac tumbler from dinner, tossed on his trenchcoat and left the rectory, carefully double checking each window and door before he did. He ran full speed across St. Alstantius' cyclone fenced parking lot and into the Church, which was dim and eerie with only the sanctuary lights and votive candles illuminating the cavernous interior. But he heaved a sigh a relief anyway once he locked the door behind him, feeling safe and secure for the first time since the early autumn night had descended. He sat down in the first pew across from the lectern where he gave his Sunday sermons and stared up at the huge crucifix on the sanctuary's back wall, at the flanking alcoves on each side with life size statues of the B.V.M. and St. Alstantius himself, their cold stone features animated and alive from the flickering red and green votive candles. Father Silverez reached into his back pocket and pulled out the pint bottle of rye he'd bought on the way back from his parish rounds, bought and paid for at the discount liquor store on Ashland Avenue where he'd clutched his trenchcoat closed over his clerical collar even though the girl behind the counter recognized him and he'd recognized her perfectly well. He broke the revenue seal and twisted off the plastic cap, cringing when the cheaper-than-cheap rye burned its way down his throat. But it couldn't burn away the vision in his head, the grim and unforgettable vision of Marian the Librarian hanging upside down in the storefront library's back room, tied up to a pipe and stripped bare naked, her pale skin pockmarked with welts and gashes and still-dripping wounds. He swigged from the pint again, but only managed to replace the vision of Marian the Librarian with the face of that fresh faced young Detective Shepherd who drove him home. She'd seemed like a nice kid herself, nice as Marian had been, but she'd held his hand tight when he got out of her unmarked sedan, locked eyes with him and told him to forget what he'd seen that night, just forget all about it, it'd be better that way. But Gil Silverez couldn't forget. He gulped again from the rye and eased down onto the kneeler. Gil started to pray, sipping from the bottle after each decade of the rosary.

And somewhere in the honking horned Friday night traffic buzzing right past St. Alstantius, Joey Fortuna drummed his fingers on the Mercedes dashboard along with a thundering dance mix CD. He paused mid-beat to grab another cold Lite from the six pack beside him on the front seat and flicked the turn signal to make a left onto Damen Avenue. Even two blocks away he could see the red glow on the marquee, and a cold shudder ran right through him. He deftly opened the beer one handed, feeling that itchy feeling creeping up the back of his neck again, that inner voice screaming in his ears, *Just go!* He'd been hearing it a lot lately. *Just take the fucking money and the car and go!*

But the voice silenced as soon as he pulled over to the curb a few spaces away from the theater and saw three of them milling around by the black glass doors, their white faces rearing up and then quickly crouching into the shadows when the Mercedes' headlights bounced off of them. Just the sight of those freaks was enough to silence any thoughts about moving on. And that rebellious voice was instantly replaced with another that whispered tales of torture and death and worse for the ungrateful.

The itchy feeling...that stayed.

He found Marek and Drake standing in the middle of the empty dance floor, surveying the now completely redone interior.

"Joseph, my compliments," Marek said, gesturing around the club. His voice echoed in the huge and empty space. "You really have been...cracking the whip? Is that how you'd put it?"

Drake snorted. "Kickin' ass, more like it. Heard you had some more trouble with the electrical union guys."

Joey dropped a briefcase on the bar and clicked it open. "Trouble taken care of." He stepped behind the bar and poured himself a whiskey. The bar was nearly ready, lined up from end to end with rows of colored bottles, all standing neatly at attention like soldiers ready to attack. All that was missing were the beer kegs and wine casks waiting to be hooked up to the dangling spigots.

"Got some papers for you to sign, Marek. Picked them up from Whitestar Legal today."

"Yes, Joseph? But first you wanted a drink?"

Joey froze behind the bar, his glass an inch from his mouth. More of their mind games, more of their power tripping, more of their fucked up dead guy etiquette. He flinched, unfroze long enough to gulp down the whiskey.

"Very good, Joseph," Marek said, smiling at him. "Well, now you've had your drink. Bring me your papers."

Marek signed the papers without a glance as Joey ticked off each contract's purpose, carefully memorized over and over again throughout the long day's errands. But Marek ignored him and turned back to Drake. "Yes, so you were saying you were at Roberta's tonight yourself? A little trouble? I would have thought you'd know better than to be playing around there, Drake."

"Well, it's like I was telling you," Drake said, his voice revealing more than a little apprehension. "That little warmblood slut of Arianne's, she — well, *she* caused all the trouble. Real mess. But I took care of it." He shot a glance at Joey. "See, the game was to nab some chick she was after. Now get this, Marek, This puss she was after is none other than one Colleen Russell. *Russell.* As in Megan-fuckin'-Russell's little sister." This time Drake shot a sneer Joey's way. "For the uninformed in the audience, this would be the lady your old pal Nicky Kolitzky helped sashay off the roof of the Hancock. Remember him, remember ol' Nicky?" Drake's sneer widened into a white fanged leer. "Oh, 'course you do. Seeing's how it was you that dumped him and his greaser-mobile in the drink."

Joey took the signed contracts and scurried back to the bar. Both vampires watched him closely while he poured another whiskey.

"So what do we do about this, Marek?" Drake's voice got all nervous again. "Megan Russell had a sister. And she's working at Charade now. She might know all about —"

Marek silenced Drake with a glance. Then he smiled. "Do you really think that I didn't know all along about our Miss Russell's younger sister?" He patted Drake on the shoulder. "You and our young gangster friend behind the bar aren't my only resources. Now, don't be petulant. You're very important to me, Drake. But I need many...assistants. Yes, I knew all along that our enterprising Managing Editor had a younger sister, and I was fully prepared to use her if necessary to help convince Miss Russell of the — shall we say — the *consequences* of any attempt to reveal what she'd learned about us. Or shall I say, what we presume she learned, since our Mr. Kolitzky bungled that simple operation rather thoroughly. But then, as you've duly noted, our previous 'day man', Mr. Fortuna's one time associate, was a trifle over zealous and...well, there you are."

Marek kept his arm around Drake and ushered him over to the bar. They both stood across from Joey, now working on his third whiskey. "No," Marek continued, "Megan Russell's little sister can be dealt with any time we like. What actually concerns me is this 'other' that intervened. I don't like the notion of renegades. But then, Fonda's been very callow with his lovers. I suppose I shouldn't be surprised. I'll have a talk with him."

Even Drake shuddered at that.

"So, I presume you've thoroughly questioned that annoying little hanger-on?" Marek asked.

Drake nodded. "I was pretty pissed off. I should've known you were wise to the Russell bitch having a sister, Marek. But, I figured, better safe than sorry."

"Yes." Marek smiled. "Yes, in a way, this is quite good, actually. It's bound to annoy Arianne considerably." He noticed Drake's sudden look of concern. "Now, don't worry. I'll intercede."

The front doors opened and they all turned at the sound of heels clicking across the lobby.

"Well," Marek said, clasping his hands together. "I believe you're both done with your chores for the evening? All work and no play and all that. But just one last little task to please me. Why don't you and Joesph here have another chat with Arianne's pet? As you say, Drake, better safe than sorry." At that, he turned away, effectively dismissing them.

Joey gulped down his drink and followed Drake towards one of the back service doors. He shivered, knowing now that they were headed down into the dark lower levels below Gothique. He paused at the door and turned back to suck in a last breath of clean air.

As he did, Joey saw Blair Armstrong step out of the lobby, dressed to the nines and hovering nervously there by the edge of the empty dance floor. Some unspoken command echoed soundlessly in the darkness, and Blair glided right into Marek's outstretched arms.

✦

"What's the matter, Fortuna?" Drake waited while Joey fumbled with the huge keyring outside the bolted basement door. "I thought you'd be cool with this. One less warmblood to get in your way. Kind of makes you the 'head human', you know?" The lock clicked and Joey opened the door. "As if *that* counts for anything, huh, Joey?"

Drake slid right past him. Joey followed and flicked on the light. The anemic little overhead bulb lit up the chamber and immediately each of the figures on the cast iron cots started wailing from behind their duct tape and filthy rag gags, straining at the handcuffs locked to the bedposts...those of them that had the strength to strain anymore, that is. The others just moaned and lay there helplessly.

Half of the cots had 'guests' tonight.

The two that held Brandon and Fitch only a few weeks before were empty.

Fitch never made it past that second night.

Brandon, on the other hand, was happily out there with his new friends this evening.

"C'mon, bright boy, let's have a chat with Miss dyke-meister." Drake plopped down on a cot and gave Gabrielle a poke in the ribs.

"Jesus Christ, Dra — "

"Watch it!" Drake snarled, and his black eyes instantly flamed hot red. "Save that for your Mama on Sunday mornings, got it?"

Joey clammed up. Seeing Gabrielle handcuffed to the cast iron cot was as good a reason as any to shut up. She struggled uselessly against the sturdy police cuffs, the filthy cot squeaking and shaking right along with her. She was a mess. Her dress was in tatters so that Joey could see the black and blue bruises running up and down her arms. It was one thing to hook strangers to those cots. Hell, they were mostly just a bunch of junkies and hustlers anyway. But Gabrielle...someone he *knew*...even if he hated the bitchy dyke's guts...

"What are you doing, Drake?" Joey finally stepped away from the door and inched between the cots. "This is...she's...Arianne will — "

"Will *what?* You heard Marek." Drake gave Gabrielle another poke and laughed when she tried to squirm away on the cot. He ran a long, filthy nailed finger in and out of her black dress' rips and tears, tickling all the bruises discoloring her skin. Gabrielle shrieked from behind her rag gag and did her best to kick Drake away, but it was pointless.

"Oh, give it up, Gabby girl. If we *do* get all intimate, honey, you'll be way past being offended."

Joey couldn't budge. He hovered there, three cots away, and just stared.

The shoulder holster under his blazer and the pistol inside never seemed useless.

Drake leaned across the cot and yanked on the dirty rags knotted around Gabrielle's mouth. She gasped for air, coughing, her face a clotted mess of mascara congealed over bruises and smeared lipstick. Her upper lip was puffed up like a sausage. "Joey, oh man," she gasped. "Joey! Y-you have to get me out of here. I didn't do anything! I just — Joey, please. *Please!"*

But Joey just stood there, silent. Watching. It wasn't too hard to picture himself hooked up to one of those cots. He didn't know if Drake was using some of that bloodsucker voodoo hypno-shit to make him picture that, or if was just his own ice cold fear.

"Drake...Joey...you have to get Arianne. She — she'll help me out, man." Gabrielle's wide eyed black and blues shot crazily back and forth from Joey to Drake. And got no answer but silent, quaking fear from Joey...and something infinitely worse from Drake.

"Dr-Drake, what the f-fuck is all this about?" Gabrielle was crying as much as talking now. "What did I do? Why am I — "

"What you did, warmblood, is blow it. Big time." Drake leaned down and flicked his cold tongue over one of the bruises on her chest.

"H-how was I supposed to k-know you guys were looking for Colleen Russell? What the fuck do you want with her anyway?"

"That's on a need to know basis, warmblood."

"Then how c-could I know?"

"You couldn't." Drake chuckled, fangs gleaming in the feeble bare bulb light. "Life's a bitch, ain't it?"

And then he shut his lips over his fangs, but let his clawed fingers fly instead. The blows echoed off her skin in the dark cellar.

So Joey just stood there until Drake was done. And that took quite a while. Drake was good at what he did and liked doing it too. Joey just stood there and cringed till he finally heard Gabrielle's last plaintive "Joey, *pleeeease!"* before Drake stuffed the filthy gag back in her mouth and cinched it tight around her head.

The vampire bounced off Gabrielle's cot, gazed around the room and licked his red lips into a huge grin. "You ain't in any big rush, are you Fortuna?"

Joey just shook his head.

"Good." Drake ambled over to another cot, where Ivy was still half undressed and weakly twisting and moaning deep inside a nightmare. Drake draped himself over her and nestled his head at her throat. Joey looked away, looked away from Drake and Ivy and Gabrielle and all the other pale, weeping, squirming figures on the cots, but even when he slammed his hands over his ears he could still hear the wet, slippery sucking sounds.

Finally, Drake sat up, wiped his mouth clean on his arm. He led Joey out of the cellar, clicking the light switch off and leaving Gabrielle and the others yanking on their handcuffs, twisting on their cots and screaming behind their duct tape and rags in the darkness.

The cellar door slammed shut and the locks clicked closed.

"Guess you'd like to call it a night now, Fortuna?" Drake slapped Joey on the back and shoved him back up the dark hallway. "Gee, you look like you could use a drink, yourself."

✦

Cass stood at the window — at *his* window — or what used to be his window. He'd been talking non-stop for hours and Colleen hadn't interrupted once. She just sat on the bed slugging away at the bourbon till the bottle was half empty.

Cass stood at the window and noticed the telltale gleam of violet coloring the eastern sky over Lake Michigan now, backlighting the fog that swirled around the courtyard and out on Chase Avenue. "And I guess that's that, Colleen. I know something's coming. Once that place opens, all hell could break loose. How many more are going to die? And they're after you for some reason. That's why you have to get —"

He turned when he heard the bourbon bottle tip over on the hardwood floor.

Colleen was stretched out across the bed. *His* bed. Or what had once been his bed. Had been Cass' bed.

That other Cass.

She was asleep. Knocked out, actually. Half a bottle of bourbon'll do that. He glanced out the window one more time and then lifted Colleen off the bed, held her easily in his arms like she was just a toddler. He carried her to her own room.

Cass grimaced as he lay Colleen down on the bed. Grimaced and bit right into his lip.

Her scent...

Her aroma...

Her smell...

Her soft skin and supple flesh. Her beating heart and the pulsing, throbbing red heat in a thousand veins and a million capillaries screamed at his ears and his nose and his fingertips. He felt his eyes burn, knew they were glowing bright red, felt the thirst twisting his insides into knots, gnawing at his tongue and his lips, aching inside his gums and tingling in his teeth.

Cass fell to his knees.

Leaned across the bed.

Across Colleen.

Saw cold steam puff from his own mouth and settle like graveyard fog on her face. He reached...

Colleen stirred. Rolled over on the comforter and nestled into the pillow. She mumbled something and then drifted off into drunken, sleepy snoring.

Cass yanked his hand back.

Fell back on the floor and scrambled away from the bed till he slammed against the wall.

He ran out of Colleen's room.

Fled back to his old room. He halted by the window and punched himself in the face and the chest, pounding his cold body till the thirst went away, till the hunger stopped its freezing, aching agony inside every single cold, dead cell. But it never *really* stopped. It was always there. Would always be there. For ever and ever. Just like he always dreamed and wished and wanted.

Until he found out what it really was.

The hard way.

Cass looked out the window and saw the violet haze brightening further, saw the Lake fog thinning down in the courtyard.

They were out there. Everywhere. Still running through the dark alleys, scurrying through the vacant lots and dodging between the tenement rows. All streaming back towards the old theater on Damen, like wolves returning to the den after a hunt. Like rats diving back into their nests.

They'd been out there all night.

And just like him, they'd been thirsty. Real thirsty.

They'd all needed a drink.

Cass dragged the drapes closed tight.

TWENTY FIVE

"Heads up, Dad."

Jeff Stancheck looked up from the red Trans Am's wheel well just as Jacks lobbed a plastic bottle of Armor-All his way. He neatly caught it and returned to the front tire. "You're all done on that side?"

"Showroom new, Dad." She tossed a rag over her shoulder and blew a stray lock of wet hair off her forehead. "Tell me you're *not* going to inspect this time?"

Jeff smiled and sprayed the front drivers side tire, taking care to keep the stream away from the alloy wheels and the edge of the freshly washed and waxed body.

"Dad, anyone ever tell you it's a little unnatural the way you keep this car so — "

"Clean?"

"Actually, I was going to say obsessive-neurotic pristine. But clean'll do."

Jeff buffed the vinyl conditioner into the front tire till the rubber shined like it was fresh from the mold. "Uh-huh. An Illinois license in your wallet makes you a little more attentive, does it? Seems to me you've been pretty cooperative about keeping her washed since you nailed the drivers exam."

Jacks stepped around to his side of the car, picking up stray sponges, brushes and towels. *"Her?* Dad, you call our car *her?"* She emptied a bucket into the alley sewer. "You don't think *that's* just on the scary side of normal?"

Jeff moved on to the rear tire, still smiling to himself. "When exactly did this become 'our' car?"

Jacks ignored that question and carried the bucket and rags in through the open garage door. A boom box on the work bench buzzed with a familiar classic rock tune while she put each item back precisely where Jeff always kept them. She knew a misplaced chamois or wheel brush would be as unthinkable as leaving the front door unlocked at night. "Well, it is 'our car' tonight," she called out from inside the garage.

Jacks turned up the volume on the radio as the last chords of a Van Halen song crashed to an end. "Tonight, remember? 'She' rides with me. No eleventh hour backing out?"

"No backing out."

"Cool." It was more a sigh of relief. "And on that note, I'm heading to the showers, coach."

"Hey, I thought you were going to saddle-soap the seats."

"Dad, *obsess,* why don't you?" Jacks stood in the middle of the garage with her hands planted on her skinny hips. "Look, it's almost four o'clock. Do you think I'm meeting this Detective Terri Shepherd looking like this?" She tugged on her drenched T shirt and bibs for emphasis. "And you better be right in line behind me, mister. I know it's the weekend, but I think shaving might be a plan, Dad."

"I plan on shaving, Jacks. Actually I clean up pretty good sometimes. Almost presentable."

"Don't suppose you tried on that new shirt I bought for you at the mall last weekend?"

"Don't suppose *you* still have the receipt so you can return it? I don't think I'm ready for collarless silk shirts just yet."

"You'd look mega-cool in that shirt. I hear cops are very into silk shirts."

"*I* hear police detectives don't like to be called 'cops' and that shirt looked more like a blouse, Jacks." He looked over the fender at her. "I'll dress myself tonight, okay?"

"Uh-huh. And that would be the white button-down or the powder blue tonight? Oh wait, it's a Saturday night date. Polo shirt, right?"

"What was that about hitting the showers? Get going, Jacks. We can do the seats tomorrow."

"Oh, good. Something to look forward to." Jacks headed for the service door to the backyard. "I'll start the grill on the way in. You call it quits in fifteen, Dad. No more."

"Check, honey."

"Promise?"

"Go!"

Jeff smiled again as Jacks disappeared into the little bungalow's even littler backyard. He finished off the rear tire and then Windexed the windows. The late afternoon sun was already dipping below the maples that draped over backyard cyclone fences, but then the maples were already starting to thin. The sun warmed the alley all day, keeping the brisk autumn breeze at bay while he and Jacks washed and waxed the Trans Am. He'd lost himself in the mindless scrubbing, buffing and detailing for hours, just happily downing Cokes and listening to the radio, listening to Jacks motor-mouth on about this class and that teacher, this clique of girls and that couple and some other guy. He never kept any of the names straight, but it didn't really matter because it was all music to his ears. It was precisely the kind of Saturday afternoon he used to relish years ago, back when Jacks motor-mouthed about different classes and different kids, the kind of Saturday afternoon he'd dreamt about during those empty years after Elaine hauled Jacks to Encino.

If it wasn't for some traces of a beer hangover from last night's kitchen table Budweiser binge, Jeff could have forgotten all about the office, ultimatums, Blair and Charade.

Windows done, he fired up the Trans Am, smiled like he usually did when the chromed double throat pipes roared and vibrated his seat. He backed the car into the frame garage that matched all the other frame garages lining the cleanly paved southwest side alley. Jeff just sat there and let the back alley potpourri of carnauba wax, Windex, Armor All and tuned exhaust tease his nose. Finally, almost reluctantly, he cut the engine.

"So, this must be Gasoline Alley." Terri Shepherd stood there in the open garage door.

She held her hands behind her back, pretty as a picture in penny loafers and snug Levi's, nearly disappearing inside a huge white cableknit sweater. The lowering sun shot dappled highlights across her pixie hair and face, lighting up her smile. "I bear gifts." She swung both arms from around her back and held out two six packs of imported beer. "I know some kind of snooty wine's the thing to bring to a dinner invite, but somehow I took you for a beer kind of a guy."

Jeff hopped out of the car, wiping his dirty hands on his dirtier work pants. "I am."

"Good. I'm a beer kind of a girl."

"You're an early kind of a girl."

"I know. Sorry."

"No, I'm glad you're here."

Terri strolled around the Trans Am with admiring glances. "So, I get to scoop out the hot rod up close. '79?"

"Say, pretty good. '78, actually. The last of the authentic Pontiac 400 cubic inch four barrel V-8's. Real duals. Before GM switched to generic engines and the emissions crap came along and ruined things."

"Okay, you already lost me on the first 'four' thing. I'm done."

Jeff looked down at his filthy sweatshirt and pants. "Hey, sorry about...well, Jacks and I were working on the car all day and — "

She held up her hand to stop him. "I'm the one who showed up early. And actually, you look cute. In a grease monkey kind of way."

He smiled, embarrassed. "Let me just get inside and clean up." He took one of the six packs from Terri and led her into the backyard. The Weber Grill was just starting to smoke.

Terri sniffed as they walked past it. "So where's Colleen? Thought you were going to be working on *her* car?"

Jeff shrugged as he opened the back door for her. "Good question. Guess she chickened out about my cooking. She called a couple hours ago to cancel. Frankly, I was getting kind of worried."

Terri followed Jeff up the back stairs. He opened the porch door to the kitchen and stepped aside to let Terri in. "Welcome to the Stancheck house. Such as it is."

Terri stepped inside —

Just as Jacks stepped out of the bathroom right down the little bungalow's hallway, long hair dripping and a bath towel loosely wrapped around her.

"Yikes - oh, uhm," Jacks stammered, clutching the towel tight. "So, uh...hi there. I'm betting you're Terri."

"Sorry," Jeff and Terri both said at the same time, laughing.

"Terri, this is my daughter, Jacqueline."

"That's Jacks. And like, could we do the introduction thing later?" Jacks scampered into her bedroom and slammed the door.

"Well, like I said, welcome to the Stancheck house."

Terri took the six pack from Jeff's hands. "What do you say I put these in the fridge and you get in the shower yourself. Should I expect you in just a towel too?" She leaned closer and pecked Jeff on the cheek. "Hmm. Shaving would — "

"Would be a plan, yes, I know." Jeff smiled and headed for his bedroom as Terri took one of the beers for herself and put the others in the refrigerator.

✦

Colleen Russell stood in the doorway to Cass' room.

She'd been standing there for a long time.

She hadn't even woken up till noon. Bolted upright in her bed and immediately called out Cass' name. But a half drunk bottle of cheap bourbon sent her plummeting back down into the pillows. And the hard liquor haze made her think for a moment that last night had all been just another bad dream. She'd had so many bad dreams for so long now.

Finally she crawled out of bed, pounding head clenched in her hands. She shuffled to the bathroom, downed a handful of extra strength pain relievers like they were candy and sat down on the edge of the tub for a minute, as if the pills would magically make her hangover headache vanish the moment they slid down her throat.

They didn't

The headache didn't vanish anymore than last night's all too vivid memories. Those were no bad dreams: Charade, Gabrielle, those...those things.

And Cass.

Head still banging, she hefted herself off the tub and trudged down the hallway to Cass' bedroom.

The room was dark.

The drapes were shut tight. But even in the darkness she could make him out. She could see Cass lying there on the bed. Absolutely still. Like a corpse. Like he was dead.

Which he was.

Or, at least that's what he'd told her. And after everything that happened last night, Colleen had no reason to think it wasn't true.

So she hovered there at Cass' doorway. Fifteen minutes? Half an hour? However long, the pain relievers were starting to take effect when Colleen slowly inched her way into the darkened room. She stood at the side of his bed, bare inches from Cass himself. He was still fully dressed in his black velvet pants and silky shirt and that black trenchcoat, his face and hands rude splashes of pale white against his clothes and the black bedspread. It wouldn't be the first time she'd seen him like this, asleep on the bed in the middle of the day with the drapes shut tight, face all made up with darkened eyes and purpled lips. Sleeping off a whizbang hangover, curled up on the bed in his clothes and smiling to himself with secret dreams of smooth skinned guys and dark bar whispers and the night before's hijinks.

But now, Cass looked different. Even in the darkness he looked different. He lay absolutely straight, absolutely rigid on his back, completely still, with his pale hands folded on a chest that never rose or sank with deep sleep breaths, just like a body laid out in an opened casket. And the nightmare colored face wasn't makeup this time, she knew that now.

Colleen reached down and stroked his hair. Even like this — even with that pale skin and those dark eye hollows and those blue-red lips — Cass was still beautiful. In a strange and unsettling way, he was even more beautiful than ever. Her fingertips drifted off his hair and gently slid across his cheek.

Colleen jerked her hand away.

He was cold.

Dead cold.

She backed away. Stood in the middle of his room for a long time, staring at him, her body shaking, her breath struggling out of her mouth and her nose in nervous gasps.

Then Colleen turned and went to the window. She looked back at Cass lying on the bed. Looked at the window.

She grabbed the edge of one of the drapes.

Inched it aside and watched a ribbon of afternoon sun shoot right into the room and across the bed.

Across Cass.

She shrieked. And yanked the drapes closed again.

Steam oozed off of Cass' body. Foul smelling steam, rank with the scent of bad things and dead things and worse things she couldn't even name. Cass' body twisted on the bed. His mouth fell open and those ugly fangs champed at his lips. His fingers hooked into claws, ripping the bedspread.

Finally the steam dissipated. Cass' body lay still again.

And Colleen ran out of the room.

✦

Jeff carried another plate of burgers in from the backyard grill, pausing on the stairs to listen to Terri and Jacks talking and laughing inside the kitchen. He smiled to himself and stepped in. "Well, these are the last. Any takers?"

Terri Shepherd wiped her mouth with a paper napkin. "Not me, Jeff. But that was one great burger. So, you really can cook."

"Barbecued burgers, sure. Could even get a job at a greasy spoon. Which I may need come Monday."

"I doubt it," Terri said. "From what you've told me it was just another in a long string of arguments. I wouldn't be surprised if this Blair Armstrong's the one apologizing Monday morning."

"Hope you're right. All the same, maybe I better start practicing for some new career options. Paper or plastic, Ma'am?"

"Hey, Charade would fall apart without the Art King there," Jacks said as she stuffed the last of her second burger in her mouth. "Right?"

"Maybe." Jeff held the platter out to Jacks "So how about you?"

She emptied a tumbler of soda, set the glass down and belched. "Ex*cuse* me." Jacks snagged one last rippled potato chip off her plate, flipped it in the air like a coin and neatly caught in her mouth — all as she got up from the kitchen table. "Nope. I'm done."

"Sure?"

Jacks surveyed the table. The potato chips and the dip were nearly gone. Two Diet Coke cans sat empty by her plate. The deli cole slaw tub was half empty. She shook her head. "Yep. Positive."

Jeff smiled. "So, two's your limit, huh?"

She shrugged. "Guess so." Jacks spun on her heel and started out of the kitchen. "Am I on K.P. tonight?"

"No, you can get going," Jeff said.

"Cool." She vanished down the hallway.

Jeff sat back down and sipped his beer. "Two hamburgers with everything in sight ladled on top. Half a family size bag of chips. Most of the cole slaw. Two sodas. And she's skinny as a rail. Teenagers are just food machines."

Terri leaned across the table and squeezed his hand. "She's great, Jeff."

"Jacks?" He nodded. "Yes, she's special."

"I guess I understand better now."

"What?"

"Everything. Everything you've told me about...well, about your ex and the divorce. About letting your daughter go."

He nodded, silent.

Terri shoved her chair away from the table. "Well, let's not go *there* tonight." She picked up her plate and the cole slaw tub. "Come on, mister. Looks like you and I snagged kitchen duty."

Jeff sprang from his chair. "Oh, no." He took the plate and tub from Terri's hands and set them on the counter. "You got one bad intro to the Stancheck house already. I'm not scaring off my date with chores."

Terri stepped closer. "Date, huh? That's right. This *is* a date, isn't it?" She slid her arms around his waist and looked up into his face.

"Yes." Jeff lowered his head to hers. "It is." Their lips drew closer, just a breath away.

"All right, break it up." Jacks burst into the kitchen. "No parental necking till the kid's out of the house, okay?"

Jeff and Terri jerked away from each other. Jeff grabbed the chip bowl and another plate off the table and carried them to the sink. Terri went for her beer glass.

"I was *kidding* guys. Jeez." Jacks bounded over to the sink and tapped her father on the shoulder.

He wrinkled his face at her outfit again but knew enough by now to shut up. Even if she wore more makeup than he cared for and the skirt was too short and the top too slinky and it was all head to toe black. Jacks tapped him on the shoulder again, harder.

"What?"

"Keys, Dad."

"You have your own — oh, right." He left the kitchen and came back in a moment dangling his key ring, the two silvery Pontiac keys gleaming at the center of the ring. "No drinking, right?"

Jacks held up one hand and lay the other over her heart. "I solemnly swear."

"Not just you. No drinking in the car — period. Not anyone."

"On my honor."

"Or..?"

Jacks dropped her hands and did her best to assume a fatherly stance. "Or you're permanently grounded, kid," she mimicked in a bad 'Jeff-ish' falsetto. "Not just till you're out of this house and away at college. I mean permanent. For life. Even after you're married. Even after you have your own kids. And they'll be grounded too."

"Okay, okay, " Jeff said. He turned to Terri. "I don't really sound like that, do I?"

She just shrugged from behind her glass.

"All right. Have that car *in* the garage and your butt in the house by midnight, Jacks."

He tossed the keys and she caught them one handed. "Thanks, Dad." Jacks skipped over Jeff's way and smacked him on the cheek. "And I'll be home at one." She raced for the door.

"Midnight!"

"One, Dad." And then she was gone out the back door, boots clomping down the back stairs. The door opened and slammed closed. Jeff still stood by the kitchen sink till he heard the Trans Am roar to life and peel out of the garage.

He took a deep breath. "I wish I could've just frozen her at thirteen. Make that twelve. No, eight."

Terri Shepherd put her beer glass down and came over to his side. "No you don't."

"No. I don't." Jeff smiled. "I wouldn't trade a single moment of this."

Terri drew closer and slid her arms back around him. "You're a lucky guy."

He nodded.

She pulled his head down till their lips were back where they started a few minutes earlier. "Now where were we, Jeff?"

He kissed her gently on the lips. "You're right." Jeff kissed her again. "I *am* a lucky guy." They wrapped their arms around each other and kissed for real this time.

"So," Terri asked when their lips finally parted. "How long exactly till Jacks comes home?"

✦

It's not as if Colleen was thinking about the movie *Psycho* as she shoved her face under the shower nozzle and let the hot water massage some of her headache away.

Not as if she kept lifting her head out of the spray to listen for the bathroom door, to hear if it opened, not as if she waited for the shower curtain to suddenly slide open, not that she expected to see Cass' pale, black eyed, red lipped monster face materialize out of the hot water steam, not as if she was waiting for anything like *that* to happen. No, not at all.

No, just because there was a vampire lying cold, stone still on his bed right in the next room.

A vampire.

Colleen rinsed the last of the shampoo out of her hair and the soap off her skin, then shut the water off. She stood there in the tub...listening. But only hearing the steady metronome trickle of the last waterdrops leaking out of the shower nozzle and splashing around her feet.

A vampire.

There was a vampire sleeping in the next room. A goddamn vampire.

Cass was a vampire. There were vampires running around the city.

The water finally stopped dripping, but Colleen still stood in the shower, still listening.

Listening to nothing.

A vampire.

Her dripping skin finally started to chill. She shook her head, grabbed hold of the shower curtain. Sucked in her breath and...yanked the curtain open.

The bathroom was empty.

Just filled with steam.

But it *was* just steam. Wasn't it?

Just steam, not graveyard fog. Not some horror movie mist swirling around her wet legs. It was just hot water steam misting the bathroom mirror and condensing on the cracked porcelain tiles.

Colleen stepped out of the shower and toweled off. She opened the window above the toilet to let the steam out. Wrapped the towel around her long, dripping red hair. As she squeezed out some toothpaste and brushed away the last of the bourbon hangover's cotton mouth, her mind started working double time.

Oh, Cass had talked to her last night. Talked all night, almost, or at least till she finally fell out from too many unbelievable stories and too many sips from the bourbon bottle. He'd told her about everything. As best as he could figure. As best as he could remember.

He'd told her about the night at Rimbaud's Cave. About a ride to the cemetery with Gabrielle's friends. About the nightmare in the graveyard, about that girl — Chelsea — ripped, raped, mangled and drained dry. About being held down by cold dead hands and feeling the searing pain in his throat, about his life draining away, about wanting it — wanting it more than anything he ever, ever wanted in his life. He'd told her about everything going hazy and black till he felt — till he tasted — that cold, cold hellblood dribbling onto his lips and seeping into his mouth and then all of it just going...blank.

And he told her about waking up the next night, all zippered up inside a plastic bag in a cold metal locker. About sneaking out of the morgue over on the West side.

He'd told her about wandering the streets night after night, about crawling into crack dens and hiding in the utility tunnels under Wacker Drive, about sleeping the days away in dumpsters and rat filled burnt out basements. About hiding in the shadows in the sleazier gay bars till some slumming suburban whitebread married slob sidled up next to him and cooed whispered invites in his ears till they stole away into even darker corners or into the john or out into whitebread's minivan or company car where no eye contact was the rule — and that was good because he quickly learned that his eyes burned red when the thirst was on him — and then the zippers yanked open and pants rolled down around knees and if the sucking was hard enough and the bites went unnoticed, the blood would come along with the come. And if sometimes it didn't go unnoticed, if sometimes the screams started, then Cass told her all about leaping out of the backseats or shoving his way through the bar crowds to disappear into the darkness.

Cass told her all about lurking in the alleys and the shadowy gangways along Halsted and Broadway and all around NewTown, where the hustlers flapped their tongues at the passing cars and happily slipped into his arms and let themselves be led off into the darkness where he could nip their hairless chests and lick their nipples and nibble their throats till the blood oozed, till it poured out and filled his mouth and drove away the cold, at least for a little while. About how they never complained because they were mostly too strung out on junk that made their blood sour, and about the few, the very few who were just like *he* used to be and how *they* loved it, adored it, begged him not to stop and jerked and spasmed and came and squealed when the blood flowed into his cold, dead mouth.

Cass told her about Gothique.

How they all went to Gothique. Like the wee children of Hamelin traipsing after the Pied Piper. How he watched them all go there, how they lived there. Like day camp, like some Adams Family Values summer retreat where they taught you all you needed to know.

How they were growing. How there were more of them every night.

Colleen rinsed off her toothbrush and then plugged in her blowdryer. The machine roared to life and evaporated the last of the steam clinging to the bathroom mirror. She started on her hair, blowing it, roasting it, roughly clawing her fingers through the long red clumps while she stewed over what to do.

Yes, Cass told her a lot.

But not enough.

She couldn't just let this go. Couldn't just dry off, get dressed, slip into her tennies and pop out for a pizza and a beer down Sheridan. Couldn't just calmly chat up scouting out a new apartment for the two of them. A nice garden job maybe, a basement flat, someplace nice and dark.

People were disappearing. People were...dying? Were Tim...and Ivy...were they dead? Or were they...?

She had to call...who?

Jeff?

No, she'd already called him, already begged off on the cozy southwest side backyard barbecue and putzing with her car. And the detective would be there. Detective Shepherd. She'd know, she'd have to report it all. She was a cop — she'd have to.

Colleen finished drying her hair and reached for her clothes. *Tell Terri Shepherd?* The cops could check it out. They could go to Gothique. They could look for Tim and Ivy. They could find Gabrielle. They could...

They could do...*what?*

Colleen climbed into her jeans.

They could get Cass.

They could put him away. Lock him up. Hook him up to a bunch of tubes and machines and try to study him. Publish papers about him. Show him off on the prime time news magazine shows, and the head bonesaw would write a book about it and shill it on the Home Shopping Network and Oprah.

They could...kill him.

No.

She couldn't let that...wouldn't...

Colleen threw on a T-shirt. When she opened the bathroom door, the last of the hot water steam puffed out along with her. She headed straight for Cass' room.

But the bed was empty.

"Cass?"

The drapes were open. The window was wide open. A damp breeze sifted in and clung to her skin. Outside, the courtyard was dark. The sky darkened to violet blue and faded right into the darkness of Lake Michigan itself. "Cass?"

Colleen raced through the apartment. "Cass!"

But the apartment was as empty as it was dark.

It was evening now.

And Cass was gone.

TWENTY SIX

No parental necking, Jacks had said.

But Jacks was gone now. And parental necking — or rather, just plain old necking — was precisely what Jeff and Terri were up to.

They were sprawled out on the living room sofa, half on and half off actually, and had been there since dinner. It all started with those innocent pecks on the cheeks and lips in the kitchen, continued with more kisses as they walked arm in arm to the living room where Jeff punched the power button on the CD player and the pre-loaded ten disk changer lilted innocuous soft rock out of the speakers. The kisses got more intense then as they cuddled up on the sofa. A Shania Twain CD ended and a Moody Blues CD queued up, and by then Terri's brown penny loafers were off and on the floor and she curled up like a kitten in Jeff's arms, her hands stroking his chest under his polo shirt. Each time their lips parted, they smiled at each other but said nothing, as if both knew they'd been thinking about this during their lakefront lunch hour walks and middle of the day phone calls and quick meets for coffee after work, and had been thinking about just this for a long time. Since they first met, maybe, regardless of the circumstances.

Another long kiss ended and Terri leaned back, taking a breath. "So, how long exactly till Jacks comes home?"

"I think you asked that already."

"I know." She smiled softly and ran her fingertips under the shirt, teasing, tickling, pressing down into the warmth. "It's just...well, it's a little weird. I'm waiting for her to burst in the door and — "

Jeff touched his finger to her lips. "It's weird for me too. Weirder, maybe. But Jacks won't be home for a few hours." He held his watch up and turned it to the window so the streetlight caught the dial. "Five and a half hours, to be exact. *If* she gets in on time. Which she better."

Terri slid her hand out from under Jeff's shirt. "You worry about her a lot."

Jeff shrugged. "She's a teenager. In a car. With a bunch of other teenagers. Of course I worry. But I can't lock her in her room. I can't pretend that she's not going to end up making out in the dark at some basement party or trying a joint, sneaking a couple beers. I did. And a lot more, not that I'd let on."

"We all did." Terri leaned forward and brushed his lips with a brief kiss. "Still do. Speaking of which, is any of that beer I brought still left?"

Jeff hopped off the couch. "Coming right up."

The kitchen was dark and still a mess. K.P. could wait till the morning. Jeff opened the refrigerator and squinted at the bright light. He grabbed two of Terri's imported beers, twisted off their caps and headed back to the living room.

He didn't see Terri at first.

Then Jeff's eyes locked on her empty jeans lying right beside her loafers on the floor.

Terri stood by the front window, a passing car's headlamps briefly bouncing off her to flash miniblind striped light on her white cableknit sweater, lighting up her pixie hair and girl-next-door pretty face and white socks and her not so girl-next-door bare legs.

He paused there. Drank it all in. Yes, it was what they'd both been thinking of through those lunches and calls and coffees. Jeff brought Terri's beer over and stood beside her.

They both sipped for a few minutes, saying nothing. Finally Terri set her bottle down on an endtable. "So, am I being too presumptuous here?"

Jeff shook his head. "No. Not at all." He wrapped his arms around her and one of Terri's bare legs coiled around his, pulling him close, pressing them together.

"That's a relief. Climbing back into those jeans while you stammered through an 'I'm not ready for this kind of intimacy' speech would be a little — "

"Uncomfortable?"

"I think 'mortifying' would be more accurate."

They kissed long and hard now, a serious, sexual kiss that was hungry and eager and honest. When their lips parted this time, Jeff led Terri toward his bedroom. She halted at the doorway. "So, how long *exactly* till Jacks comes home?"

"Long enough, Terri. Long enough."

✦

The Stancheck's red Trans Am glimmered under the streetlights just off the corner of 61st and Harding. Jacks parked it carefully in a long open space where no trees drooped over the street. Rachel fidgeted impatiently in the front seat beside her, doing a last touch-up on her makeup then clicking her compact closed. Rory was already trying to climb out of the backseat before Jacks even shut off the ignition. But damn if she'd get tree sap and bird crap all over the car after babying it all afternoon.

Kids lounged on the beige bungalow's front stoop, chess club geeks and student council goody two shoes, jocks and hard core scenesters, all indistinguishable from one another now in their apres-class uniforms, the nerdy guys all leather-macho in bike chains and mesh muscle T's, the class reps slutted down in shredded fishnets and peekaboo tops, the jocks femmed out in velour and eye makeup. But they all shivered in the autumn evening breeze. Music, incense and cigarette smoke filtered out of the house's half opened basement windows. Behind the shrubs flanking the brick and concrete porch, one sad-sack clutched the wall while he gagged on beer and pizza downed only minutes before.

"Party!" Rory hollered as he shot out of the car. Jacks gave the Trans Am one last look and followed after him. Rachel did her best runway model strut past the guys on the front steps, fighting back a smile as she heard their conversation pause, felt their eyes on her, almost smelled the high school horny testosterone rush in the air.

"Yo, sis," Rory called. "Save the Kate Moss routine for practicing in your bedroom mirror, okay?"

"Fuck off, little brother." She glided past the porch, long legs parting her black trenchcoat like flapping wings. "You're not even supposed to be out tonight, child. Grounded was what I heard from Dad."

"And Dad's bowling tonight so you and Jacks luck out."

He raced down the gangway to the bungalow's back door. Jacks and Rachel followed, squeezing past a tight threesome sharing a pipe and another couple making out on the dewy backyard grass.

As they descended the back stairs, the music grew louder. Jacks had to tap Rachel's shoulder to get her attention. "So who's party is this again?" A thick wall of incense and smoke engulfed them the moment they made it to the basement.

"That guy I told you about. You know — Trent."

"Trent? Trent *who?* Oh right. That's the guy that took you to the Junior Prom last year, right?"

Rachel smirked. "Well, I never exactly made it to the Junior Prom last year. I made it to Trent's car in the parking lot, but not quite to the Prom."

The music took over and they plunged into a crowd of bodies. Rory made a beeline for a keg in a washbasin by the laundry room. Someone shoved a joint in Rachel's hand, someone else lobbed a can of beer to Jacks. She looked it over longingly, then handed it to Rachel. "Designated, as in driver," she shouted over the thundering bass. Rachel stuck the smoking joint between clenched teeth, grabbed the beer and popped the top with one finger.

Two girls shoved past, a blur of black mascara, jersey and chiffon. "Who said you could borrow that top, skank?"

A CD ended.

"Who said *you* could fuck my boyfriend, slut?" They glared at each other for a moment, then laughed hysterically and vanished into the crowd, arm in arm.

Another CD queued up: a live cut of Bauhaus' *Bela Lugosi's Dead.* Some kids wandering the tiled basement floor ended up in a circle, fingers tapping along with the fast paced cymbals, nodding their heads as the electric bass lines oozed out of refrigerator sized speakers, in their center an ethereal Stevie Nicks-as-Rhiannon clone went into a self-induced or largely feigned trance, showing off her best strip mall ballet school moves. Off in a corner, one group of the deathband T-shirt and ripped nylons crowd lounged across a sofa and some pillows and each other, glassy eyes glued to a big screen TV where some teeth-and-tits cable vamperotica played with the sound off. Across the basement the pool table sat idle, cues and balls all lined up uselessly while another clique made room for a pocket mirror decorated with six neat white powdered lines. Back in the dark corner behind the furnace one couple ignored the crowd and slow-danced their hips into one another, black fingernails clawing each others unbuttoned shirts. Another was already sliding down against the wall till they ended up on the tile floor, the girl's black stretch bells already peeled down around her knees. Just this side of the keg, Rory took his plastic cup of flat beer and ambled over to a little paneled den area, where half a dozen kids huddled around a big box discount store PC. Two savvier surfers pointed and ooooh'd at the Chicago Coven Scene site, guiding their mouse across a Disney character pad with all the earnest reverence of a planchet gliding across a ouija board.

Jacks folded her arms across her chest, sensing her seemed-risqué-when-she-tried-it-on-at-home black tank, skirt, tights and boots were as happening as a poodle skirt and Mary Janes. "Rachel, I thought you told me this Trent was a jock?" Jacks found a lonely six pack of Cokes on a sticky topped card table and helped herself to one.

"Ex." Rachel leaned in close to Jacks ear. "He was," she shouted over the music. "Guess he got religion, finally."

Jacks spied an equally lonely and totally ignored Tupperware bowl of pretzels. She palmed a handful. "You never mentioned anything about getting back together with him."

"I didn't, 'cuz I didn't. As in, we didn't get back together. He went out with that whore Julie Scott the very night after the Junior Prom. The very night."

"Check. And...?"

"And...nothing. Look, I don't do jealousy. It's just so...so pornographic picturing your guy doing some other girl, you know?"

Jacks rolled her eyes and nibbled on a pretzel. Rachel winced as she burned her lips on the tiny butt of the joint. She dropped it on the tile and ground the glowing tip out with her boot. "Look, Trent made goo-goo eyes at me a few times this week, okay? He's not so varsity anymore, and he was having this party and it's been two weeks since I had a decent date that didn't end up barfing in my lap or squirting in his pants before I even got mine unzipped, so..." She slugged down her beer. "Wait a minute. What am I explaining myself for?"

Jacks shrugged. "And let me add a major *Eeeewwww* for the explain."

"Look, kiddo," Rachel said, suddenly gone all big sister, "When exactly did you declare the fun embargo? You have to get your head out of the books and your legs in the air. Let loose, girl, will you? Just a little. Just for tonight? For me?" Rachel jabbed her finger at Jacks' soda can. "Want me to scare up something to spike that up a little?"

Jacks shook her head. "I said I'm desig - "

Rachel slammed her hand across Jacks' mouth. "Designated driver, I know." She guzzled the rest of her beer, crunched the can and tossed it over her shoulder. "Well, I'm going to cruise the room a bit. Coming?"

Jacks scanned the sea of smoke, black lights, black clothes and bobbing heads of dyed hair. "I'll catch up, okay?"

Rachel frowned, a petulant little pouty face.

"I'm cool," Jacks said, screwing herself up into a femme fatale pose that simply didn't sit well on her. "I'm just going to wait here for the right man to come along."

"Uh-huh. Alternate plan: Have a ball with all the wrong ones in the mean time." Rachel shrugged. "Suit yourself." She spun on her heel, trenchcoat flapping, and started towards the crew by the pool table. "Keep an eye on little brother, Jacks. Too many trips to that keg and he's going to be barfing in your Dad's car all the way home."

The Bauhaus song faded and some painfully loud and distorted industrial started up. The basement crowd gravitated towards the center of the dark basement and slam danced each other off the furniture and the faux-wood walls.

✦

'It's like a ping-ping-ping, then a rumble.'

That's how Colleen had described it to Jeff. It seemed so long ago now.

'Korean econo-box, tuna can with a lawnmower engine, and a dealer demo, at that.'

That's what Jeff had called her car when he invited her over for a Saturday barbecue. A little tinkering under the hood in the alley. Burgers and beers. His daughter and Detective Shepherd. It all seemed so safe, so nice, so innocent, so long ago. So far away.

But Colleen's compact did more than just 'ping-ping-ping-then-a-rumble' as she shot down Sheridan now. The little car sputtered and coughed and shifted in and out of gears with a mind of its own as she weaved in and out of lanes. She passed rows of Saturday night cars filled with Saturday night couples on Saturday night dates and Saturday night girls singing along with Top 40 tunes and checking out their Saturday night makeup in the visor mirrors, and Saturday night cars full of Saturday night guys chugging schnapps and head slamming to thrash metal CD's as they played NASCAR oval on the tight southbound S curve at Hollywood, where Sheridan flipped on to Lake Shore Drive.

Colleen almost wished she was crammed into one of those cars herself, laughing her ass off in the backseat over some date-from-hell story and anxiously anticipating a night of mindless club flirting. But her car coughed some more and ground the gears when she nursed it up to sixty-five to bypass a speeding taxi. She hoped the little shitbox would make it.

Make it where?

Where *was* she headed?

Southbound on the Drive. The north end of Lincoln Park whizzing by in a dark green velveteen blur on her right. The Lake just an opaque wall of darkness that bled right into the night sky on her left. She shot past the Foster Avenue Exit.

Where was she headed?

To find Cass.

She passed the Lawrence Avenue Exit.

To find Cass...*where?*

Colleen flicked her turn signal, cut off a car and sped off the Drive at the Montrose Exit.

She knew perfectly well *where* she was headed.

The compact wheezed some more but held steady as she negotiated the crowded traffic on Montrose. Colleen sat impatiently at the light at Kenmore, right across from the El. A carload of rowdy Latino kids revved their lowrider's engine on her right, but somehow the econobox muscled up enough self respect to shoot off the line at the green and Colleen flew through the viaduct, bursting out and under at an even forty five. But she yanked her foot off the pedal the moment she did. Hit the brakes, in fact, and the low rider smoked past her even as the cars behind all blared their horns.

Graceland Cemetery lay at the edge of the sidewalk on her left, all dark and foggy behind a long stretch of wrought iron fence, turn of the century tombstones poking up like pale fingers clawing out of the earth.

A car passed her, the driver swearing at Colleen loud enough for her to hear him through her closed window. She shook her head, turned away from the cemetery and continued west on Montrose, just barely making the yellow at Clark where she left the dark cemetery behind in her rearview mirror.

Just a few blocks later Colleen cruised under the Ravenswood El viaduct, then cooled her heels at one more light, where she stared at the tall spires of an old Catholic Church on the north side of the street, an illuminated statue of St. Alstantius perched beside the wide front stairs and looking ghostly instead of pious under the passing headlamps. The light changed, Colleen gunned it and sped two more blocks to Damen Avenue, her hands clammy on the steering wheel now, perspiration congealing on her forehead now, cold sweat materializing on her arms and face and all over her body inside her clothes. She just made the green, hung left and turned south onto Damen.

And as soon as she did, she immediately saw the red glow two blocks ahead. Saw those faux gothic script letters pulsing off an old movie theater marquee, red like hellfire, red like glowing eyes, red like spilled blood, red and beckoning to the wishers and the dreamers and the foolish.

And the damned.

Gothique.

Colleen slipped the compact into half a space just this side of the alley next to the theater building. She sat there with the engine idling — coughing and sputtering again, and loud enough to wake up the dead, and just that thought skipping through her mind made her laugh, laugh right out loud before she shut the car off. Colleen stepped out and felt the cold, damp air latch onto her damper skin, her bare arms, crawl right inside her T-shirt.

The sign bled Damen Avenue and the two flats across the street all crimson. The huge building loomed high overhead, garish and out of place and out of time on any Chicago street, more like some medieval fortress in a Hollywood horror movie set. The autumn breeze whistled in and out and around the fake gargoyles and phony turrets cluttering the exterior. Lights shined out of half opened windows on the upper floors over the sign. Faint shadows hovered in the darkness below the marquee and by the doors, shadows that were blacker than black and capped with white ghost faces, Cass faces, faces that suddenly looked up.

Faces that turned her way.

And those shadows oozed out from under the marquee. Out onto the sidewalk. Leaked like stained oil across the concrete and slowly, slow-motion-slow, crept towards her.

✦

"I had no choice," Jacks said, laughing.

She leaned in closer to the boy's arm where it draped over the back of the recliner they shared. He slid deeper into the faded plaid upholstery, and she felt him — *what was his name again? Billy? Bobby? Something with a 'B'* — felt him all warm and lean and liked the way his torn black denims huddled against her legs and chafed across the taut fabric of her tights. His arm dropped off the back of the recliner and across her shoulders, fingers hovering a mere inch that was actually a mile of anxious apprehension above her breast. Jacks felt her nipple harden inside her bra, as if it was straining to rear up and touch his long fingers.

"Well, I had to. Rachel's brother thinks he's in love with me, but he's just in lust with anything female right now. Hormones, you know." She laughed again, realized how shrill her giggle was and stifled it with another gulp from the screw-cap wine bottle nestled in her lap. "So I decked him. Knocked Rory's ass right over the keg."

Billy-Bobby-Something-with-a-B hugged her tighter and after hours of hovering around her with idle chit-chat and still more of deep meaningful conversation on the recliner, his fingers finally breached that inch that was a mile, dancing across Jack's tank, settling warmly and firmly on her small, heaving breast. "Remind me not to mess with you, Jacks."

"Not likely." She smiled, coyly, a foreign kind of grin for her but it seemed right somehow just now, what with half the bottle of cheapy wine warming her belly and something else warming the rest of her, what with her boots on the floor and her toes tucking themselves inside the cuffs of his jeans and this amazingly cute guy's soft hands on her breasts. He leaned down and brushed her lips with his, tasting of alcohol and spearmint gum and cigarettes and tasting just fine, thank you. She kissed him back, harder, and their lips parted and the tips of their tongues danced and Jacks didn't feel one bit self conscious when his hand fell into her lap and she set the wine bottle aside, not one bit embarrassed by all the other kids milling around in the dark as she felt her legs ease apart on the cushions and his hand slide under her skirt, massaging her through her tights.

She hesitated for just a moment. Felt some alarm instinctively go off in her head, felt her mouth ready to unlock from his lips so she could mumble some well-rehearsed *'no, please, we just met, I'm not ready'* speech, but Mom never really ever got around to that one back in Encino and Dad probably thought she was ten years away from even needing to know the lines. Jacks hesitated for just that brief moment, just long enough to pull her moist lips away from his, to catch a breath and glance over the arm of the recliner.

Rory wasn't in sight and was probably off mooching the last of the beers the unattached hoarded somewhere while they bad-mouthed the stuck-up chicks and two-timing guys. The grinding guitar grunge and the semi-danceable Goth rock were gone now. Whoever handled DJ chores tonight had switched to a Projekt Sampler and set it on repeat so the dreamy darkwave dirges fit in better with the basement lights turned off and only the big screen and the PC monitor to light up the tangled bodies on the sofas and couches and area rugs. Rachel hadn't been back since she ground out that first joint, vanishing into the crowd hours before, and Jacks figured she was getting the guided tour of 'Trent's' room upstairs — eighth grade model airplanes, Nine Inch Nails posters, multi-colored rubber collection and all (or whatever it was senior guys had in their rooms).

Jacks gulped down one more breath, scanned the dim basement and the couples who didn't give a hot damn and were half naked, sixty-nining on a sofa, peeling blouses down over mall store lingerie shop bras and fumbling with damnably tough leather pants zippers. Another director's cut horror flick glowed from the big screen, all soft focus blood and boobs but the crew by the TV were munching each other's necks and were going to be wearing high collars for a week to hide the hickeys. The group by the PC still furiously clicked away with the mouse and gazed at the screen: a black background bleeding to red as a gothic script logo appeared and morphed on the screen, GOTHIQUE glowing red across all their made-up faces.

But then those gentle fingers made Jacks close her eyes and sigh, and the couples on the couch and the floor and by the TV and the computer just vanished into darkness. Those fingers hesitated at the edge of the waistband of her tights and then found their way inside her underwear and suddenly Jacks felt a few things she'd only felt on some very rare occasions by herself, and she forgot all about Rory and Rachel and flung herself at Mr. Something with a B, smashing her lips into his and groping her own hands across his jeans, hunting for a flap of denim, yanking on his zipper, and slipping her own hands in —

"Well *there* you are."

Jacks' hand jerked away and she nearly leaped off the recliner, but bounced back with the boy's hand still tucked inside her tights, hers inside his pants.

Rachel stood beside the chair with her hands planted on her hips, a sly smile spread across her face. "So...fun embargo lifted?"

Even in the dim blacklight glow, it was obvious Jacks' cheeks kaleidoscoped between several shades of red. "Oh, uhm...yeah, I guess it did. Uhm, Rach, this is...this is..."

"It's Brad."

"Right, this is Brad, and, uhm, we..."

Brad slid his hand out from underneath Jacks skirt and held it out to Rachel.

She took half a step back. "Some other time, okay?" She turned to Jacks. "Hate to spoil the fun, girl, but have you seen the child anywhere? High time we hightail it for home."

"Home?" Jacks eased back into Brad's arms. "Rory? Nope, haven't seen him since — oh wait, isn't that him over by the surfers?"

"So it is. Well, I'll pry him away from the naked lesbian bimbo vampire websites if you can pry yourself out — what was your name again? Oh right, Brad. Well, why don't you and Brad do the good night kiss thing and we can get rolling."

"Wait a minute." Jacks sat up on the chair. "Why are we going? I'm not ready to —"

Rachel's black trenchcoat parted and Jacks — and Brad — saw that her legs were bare and her blouse was ripped wide open. Shredded nylon somethings dangled out of her purse. "Well, ol' Trent's sleeping it off upstairs for one thing, and only the losers like little brother are left looking for love now, so I'd say it's time. That, and the fact that I think you already blew your curfew by an hour, and — "

Jacks flew off the recliner and rummaged in the dark for her boots.

" — and unless you and I plan on going back to bus rides, what do you say we get Daddy's hot rod back in the garage pronto?" Rachel spun around and headed for the clique still huddled around the computer. "Not that you don't know the drill, Jacks, but just in case, give him your phone number."

✦

Terri Shepherd stopped caring about how long it would be before Jacks came home once Jeff waltzed her into the darkness of his bedroom.

In fact, she and Jeff both pretty much forgot about how long it would be before Jacks came home once the weeks of wondering and daydreaming turned into reality and they found themselves making love, slowly, almost cautiously at first, then eager and hungry, but with a warmth and a tenderness that Jeff hadn't felt in years. Maybe really never *had* felt. Not in the hot and frenzied clutches with Blair Armstrong, not with the humdrum marital bed routines with Elaine, where warmth was always cooled by unspoken resentments.

And though they didn't mean to, that's how they fell asleep: tenderly, warm and in each others arms. Comfortable and at ease with their nakedness, with one another. And not worrying one bit about when Jacks might come home.

As it turned out, it was nearly two when Jacks finally dropped Rachel and Rory off at their house a few blocks away. Rachel had to lug her younger brother all the way to the front steps because he'd done his misguided best to impress Jacks and then anyone else by chugging beers and anything else available, which *didn't* impress and was decidedly unimpressive when he doubled over the front banister to blow it all out, Rachel turning away while she fumbled for her keys.

So Jacks never noticed the black Mercedes that killed its headlights when it slipped into a parking space a few doors down from Rachel's house.

She turned onto 49th street and then onto Karlov, gunning the Trans Am, suddenly aware of the time and convincing herself that midnight had mysteriously turned into one and then almost two somehow by accident. Jacks pictured her father scowling at the back door, grabbing the Trans Am's keys right from her hands and she brooded over that and cursed herself for letting the night get away from her, never noticing the black sedan half a block behind on Karlov.

And she still never noticed it when she turned into the alley and punched the garage door opener, never spotted the black car letting its lights go dark again as it hovered at the end of the alley. Waiting. Watching, while she pulled into the garage and the door slowly closed. Never noticed — not even when she scampered across the backyard to the door — that the Mercedes watched her from the alley now, just fifty feet away, and then roared off once she shut the back door behind her.

She unlaced her boots right inside the back door, slipped them off as quietly as she could, then tiptoed up the back stairs and into the kitchen.

Jacks frowned when she saw the plates and glasses still littering the table and the counters. She'd still get K.P. tomorrow morning and wouldn't be able to weasel out of it, not after coming home this late. Not unless she could make it to her room quietly enough. She tucked her boots under her arm and stayed on tiptoe, halting with a held breath as each and every one of the old bungalow's creaky floorboards conspired against her. Out of the kitchen, past the bathroom, creeping as fast but as soft as she could and straight for her bedroom.

She paused by the living room.

Saw the two half empty bottles of Terri's imported beer on the endtable by the sofa.

Saw her father's bedroom door closed.

Saw Terri Shepherd's shoes on the floor.

Smiled when she saw Terri Shepherd's jeans crumpled on the floor right beside them. *'Shot and a goal, Dad,'* she thought to herself, actually cutting the words off when she almost said them out loud.

Jacks pirouetted on tiptoe to head straight for her room.

And spun *smack* into Jeff.

"And midnight," he said, his voice soft but fatherly-menacing anyway, "That just got ignored tonight because...?"

"Dad...I...uhm — "

Jeff leaned in close and sniffed.

"Dad, I only had a little bit, and — "

He held out his hand.

Jacks pulled the car keys from her purse and glumly handed them over. "Dad, really, I — "

"We'll talk about it in the morning."

"All *three* of us?"

Even in the dark, she could see the anger boil up behind his eyes.

"Sorry, Dad. That was out of line."

"You've got that right."

Jacks skulked off to her room and shut the door.

And Jeff returned to his bedroom to find Terri slipping her arms into her bra.

"What's this?"

"Jeff, I'm so sorry."

"Wait...what?" He sat down on the bed beside her while Terri rummaged through the blankets and found her underwear. "Terri, what's the matter?"

She slipped the panties on and then went looking for her socks on the floor. "Jeff, I didn't mean to fall asleep. I'm so sorry. I mean, your daughter, and — "

"Terri, it's okay."

"No, it's not. I'm the one asking you when she's coming home and then...then I just fall out and she *does* come home and...oh jeez, my pants are still out there, aren't they?"

Jeff found her socks hiding in the blankets. She reached for them but he yanked them away, smiling. "Yep. Your jeans are still out there."

"And Jacks...she saw them, she — "

He nodded, still smiling.

Terri flopped down on the bed. "Oh, man."

"Terri, it's okay. Really." Jeff pulled her back into his arms. "Listen, I'm a parent. I have a daughter. Either you can handle that or...or we have a problem. And I don't want any problems. Not with you."

"I don't want any problems either, but — " She paused, and they both listened for a moment to the muffled sounds from outside the bedroom door: Jacks' door opening, feet scampering across the hardwood floor, the bathroom door, the faucets and the medicine cabinet, the toilet flushing. Feet scampering back across the floor and Jacks' door quietly closing.

Terri moaned and fell back on the bed. She grabbed Jeff. "You have to go get them"

"Get who?"

"My jeans. Go on." He didn't move. Terri punched him on the arm. "Now."

"All right, all right."

Jeff returned with the jeans but held them behind his back. "Terri, it's late. You're tired. I don't want you driving back to the north side like this."

"I can take care of myself, you know. I *am* a policewoman." But in the minute he was gone, she'd cuddled back into the blankets and looked awfully comfortable now.

Jeff lay the jeans across the dresser. "Terri — "

"Well, do you have any pajamas at least?" She was smiling now. And reaching behind her back to unsnap her bra.

Jeff shook his head. "Boxers. T-shirts. That's about it."

She threw her bra at him and then dove back under the blanket. "Well, then at least get me a T-shirt, will you? And put those jeans *right* by the bed."

✦

Colleen Russell froze.

The trek down Sheridan and Lake Shore Drive was all high speed determination. Right down Montrose too — even when she passed Graceland Cemetery — her hands clutched the steering wheel like she was possessed.

But now?

Now that she was standing here, standing in the street next to her little car, feeling so small, so alone, so exposed, blinking from the marquee's blood red glow — now she didn't feel so brave.

In fact, she didn't even know what the hell she'd meant to do.

Go knock on the door?

Barge right in?

Ask where they kept the vampires?

Look up the one who did Cass, who made him a monster?

Give 'em all a good talking to?

Tell them to get out of town by sundown?

Sunrise?

Now she just stood there by the car, her feet frozen to the asphalt. Cold sweat breaking out all over.

What...*now?*

Now that the shadows lurking under the marquee and in the darkness by the huge old theater's black front doors seemed to move. Seemed to seep right out onto the sidewalk and slowly creep her way.

Now that she could hear...something. Voices. Or not voices, just whispered nightmare sounds and faint giggles and evil little hisses that could just be — ought to be — just the cold wind whistling in between the theater's old bricks. Or could be...

The shadows lunged.

And it was all a blur.

Shapeshifting ink blots reached out of the darkness cloaking the theater, with long pale fingers lengthening into paler white claws. Ghost faces appeared out of the gloom and lit up with leering red eyes and even redder, hungry mouths.

They bled across the sidewalk. Oozed over her little car, reaching out for her. But she was just frozen there, wanting to run but unable to move, just like in a nightmare.

Colleen felt the cold wash over her and it wasn't the wind, it was just a sudden iciness that stank of sex and graveyards and rotting flowers.

She smelled a fetid breath drown her face.

Felt cold fingers touch her arm, tease her hair.

Felt a chilled hand brush hers.

Saw one of the shadows materialize into a girl, another into a boy — white faced and red eyed and grinning white fanged smiles as they gingerly stepped towards her, just a few feet away now, just another few steps till they...

She screamed

And then the dog barked.

"Come on!"

And a hand *did* grab her, but it was warm and firm and Colleen was yanked right off her feet.

She screamed, but Frank Hoelevich started dragging her across Damen, Sox barking and growling Sheltie-and-a-half fury all the way.

"Come on. Now!" The old man had appeared out of nowhere and now he hauled her across the street, pulling the little dog on the leash along with them.

But the shadows followed.

"Run, damn it!"

Finally Colleen snapped to and ran alongside the old man and the dog.

They sped down a dark gangway, feeling the cold creeping right behind them, hearing those sneering whispered voices echo between the two flats. Frank kicked the back door open and shoved Colleen inside. Sox slipped in just as Frank slammed the door shut.

But they could feel the unearthly cold seeping right through the wood.

"We'll get you next time, old man."

"Yeah, and your little dog too."

Fists pounded the door, and damned if Frank Hoelevich and Colleen Russell didn't see frost spreading on the inside.

"Next time, old man. You too, red."

And then they were gone. The voices. The cold. Just gone.

Deadbolts and chains clanked into place.

"Who...?" Colleen tried to catch her breath. "Who are you?"

Frank bent down to unclip Sox' leash. "Come on upstairs. I don't think those damn things'll try to get in here. At least, they haven't yet. And I'm sure as hell not inviting them in."

Colleen followed the old man and the dog up a back stairway. He led her into a tidy little kitchen on the two-flat's second floor. The lights were on here. Bright. Normal. The kitcheny aromas of home cooked meals and perking coffee assaulted her.

Reality.

"Here." Frank pulled a chair out from the kitchen table while Sox trundled off to his water bowl and slurped noisily. "I'll get you some coffee." He took an old fashioned metal coffee pot off the stove and got a cup from a cabinet. "Or maybe you'd like something stronger?"

Colleen shook her head and fell into the chair. Sox finished his drink and sat down by her feet, warm caramel fur settling right on top of her tennis shoes.

"What the hell were you doing out there?" Frank brought a steaming cup of coffee to the table and set it in front of her. "Are you crazy?"

Colleen didn't answer. She reached for the cup but her hands were shaking too much. She sloshed coffee on the table.

"You're not one of those nuts that's trying to get in there, are you?" Frank sat down at the table with a cup of his own and took a sip. He pulled a cigar from his shirt pocket. "Mind?"

Colleen shook her head.

Frank lit up. "The wife's away for a while. She'd kill me if she knew I was having one of these. Probably smell it the minute she comes back home and walks in the door." He turned then and stared off into the darkness that lay beyond the kitchen. *"If* I let her come back home." He looked down the hallway and into the parlor where a faint red glow seeped through the venetian blinds. "No, you don't look like one of those nuts. The ones that *want* to go in there, I mean. Oh, they're out there most nights now. Knocking on the goddamned theater doors, whining, begging to be let in." He turned back to Colleen and exhaled a blue cloud of cigar smoke. "And *they* let 'em in. Yeah, they let them in, all right."

Colleen lost it then.

She just broke down and cried. "Y-you mean, you know about them? A-about what's going on in there?"

"Of course I know," Frank said. "They're right across the goddamn street."

He exhaled a big cloud of smoke and followed it with his eyes. "I've seen them."

Colleen looked up and wiped her tears away with the back of her arm. "Me too."

Frank reached over with that big bear paw of an old hand, the hand that hefted cases of gallon paint cans and cast iron pipes in the hardware store downstairs, the hand that gripped a Garand M-1 in the mud and the snow in Europe, the hand that heaved the backdoor closed against all those things just a few minutes before. He reached across the little kitchen table and took Colleen's so much smaller hand in his and it felt better and safer and more comforting than anything she'd ever known.

With his other hand he stuck the cigar in his mouth then slid the coffee cup closer to Colleen. "Talk to me, kid."

TWENTY SEVEN

Even the worst bumper to bumper rush hour traffic couldn't phase Jeff this Monday morning.

Chilly as it was, he drove with the window rolled down, arm hanging out, his fingers tapping along with morning drive classic rock tunes. That minivan with the turn signal blinking steadily for two miles? He ignored it. The Malibu with the lady juggling a Starbucks and her lipstick, eyes on her visor mirror while she swerved in and out of lanes? He barely noticed. The suit in the Jaguar with the cellular and the laptop, the one that cut him off at Kedzie Avenue?

Jeff didn't even blink.

He just smiled and waved the Jag into the lane.

He wasn't even thinking about work, certainly wasn't brooding over bouts with Blair Armstrong or canceled articles or Charade's none too subtle revamp into a soft-core fashion-sleaze mag. Hell, he wasn't even thinking about whether or not he really had a job there anymore.

All Jeff Stancheck thought about was Saturday night.

Or more correctly, Sunday morning.

Sunday morning — waking up with Terri Shepherd lying next to him, all warm and snuggling under the blanket, one bare leg entwined with his, one small hand on his chest, softly snoring while the sun peeked through the blinds and striped that adorable pixie face with muted morning golds.

Sunday morning — Terri waking up, the both of them saying nothing, only smiling, then gently making love in the autumn sunshine, stifling sighs and moans into soft breaths of quiet pleasure. Terri heading for the bathroom and a shower after, clutching her jeans and the rest of her clothes protectively as she crept past Jacks' bedroom door.

Sunday morning — as a contritely sleepy eyed Jacks shuffled into the kitchen an hour later and quickly woke up to the smell of Terri's bacon and eggs.

Sunday morning — as the three of them sat around the table till noon, gabbing and sharing the Sunday Tribune over a second pot of coffee. Jeff couldn't even stay mad at Jacks for rolling in past curfew the night before. Or for drinking, and he knew for sure she had been. He was simply too content listening to the sounds in that kitchen, the three of them talking, laughing and enjoying each other's company. As if they'd spent a thousand Sunday mornings together just like that one.

Like a family.

As if the little brown brick bungalow on Karlov finally came alive, like a home. Like it was supposed to be. Like it hadn't been in so many years.

Maybe never had been.

But now Jeff's Trans Am crawled off the Stevenson Expressway and onto Lake Shore Drive. Lake Michigan hovered on the other side of McCormick Place and Meigs Field, summer blued water gone gray now for autumn. The breeze got chillier here, so he reluctantly rolled up his window. He inched closer to the downtown skyscrapers looming over the wide green expanse of Grant Park and just the sight of them made the Sunday morning 'round-the-kitchen-table idyll vanish for a moment. Pointlessly honking horns and dingy clouds of exhaust fumes lingered behind the slow moving cars, dragging his silly grin down into a frown.

Straight ahead, the Whitestar Media Building poked up through the spiked rows of steel and glass towers.

While he parked the Trans Am and briskly walked that familiar walk to Michigan and Fairmont Court, Friday afternoon finally all came back to him. Charade Magazine, Blair Armstrong, closed door fights and ultimatums, they all came back to him. His Sunday morning smile vanished completely as he spun through the Whitestar Media Building glass doors and headed for the elevators.

But he never got past the security desk in the main lobby.

"Mr. Stancheck?"

Jeff halted as two uniformed guards stepped out from behind their desk, faces anxious, almost excited, as if they finally had something officially security-like to do. "You're wanted right away on the fourteenth floor."

Jeff's smile returned, but it was as an ironic grin now. "Fourteen? Human Resources, I'm guessing?"

"Yes, sir. And could you please hand over your Whitestar ID please?"

✦

Cradling the kitchen wall phone in his shoulder, Frank Hoelevich brushed sawdust off his burly arms. "Yes, hon. I know they're not as expensive as we thought. You told me last week." But Libbie wasn't going to be dismissed that easy. She'd been on Frank's case with each call from Florida, telling him how her sister had been taking her around town, how the garden homes weren't really *that* expensive, how the condo's were practically a bargain, how the property taxes were so much lower down there, how the southern sun was warming it up to a balmy seventy five, autumn or not.

"Lib, can't we hash this out some other time? Huh? No, you're not interrupting anything. No, no, there's no wild poker party goin' on in the kitchen." The linoleum floor was dusted with beige sawdust now, forming a neat circle where it sifted off his workshoes. "Libbie, it's just the rates are so expensive this time of day. You should call after nine, like you been doing. Okay, hon. Yes, I miss you. You know that. You have fun, there. Yes, Lib, you stock up on all the realtors' brochures you can. Bye, sweetheart."

Frank hung up the wall phone, promised himself to mop up the sawdust, then headed for the back stairs. He found Sox waiting right where he'd left him when Libbie called.

"Sox, will you quit chewing on that stuff? You'll be crappin' sawdust for a week."

The caramel and white sheltie-and-a-half looked up at Frank, seemed to smile some kind of a doggie smile and then plunged back into the pile of wood shavings littering the floor. Trips down to the two flat's shuttered hardware store were an adventure for the dog. Libbie never went down there anymore. Frank rarely made the trek himself, only to knock off half a stogie when subzero snowy weather made his nightly 'walking the dog' ruse a little too transparent.

Stark white fluorescent light shined down on the old store's dusty shelves, most of which were empty. Frank had sold off most of the inventory to a flea market gypsy when he finally closed Hoelevich Hardware and that guy went for the stuff his Swap-O-Rama clientele favored: the gallons of Glidden and Pittsburgh Paints, the Snap-Lock and Stanley tools, the Black & Deckers and the expensive electrical fixtures. The old store was left half naked with rusty old shelves littered by the scattered remains of a once thriving family business: a stack of copper pipe in one corner, some old moldings in another, wall paper remnants and repair parts for toasters and percolators no one even made anymore. The big pipe threader, the glass cutter, the paint mixer and the too-heavy-to-haul lathe in the back, those Mr. Swap-O-Rama and his tired looking truck passed on.

Sox lay in the pile of wood shavings at the feet of that damn-near-a-ton lathe right now, merrily nibbling on curly-cued rasps heaped as high as his furry head. The dog hadn't liked the lathe's motor screech one bit and barked like holy hell the whole time Frank ran the footpedal, slicing a stack of inch and a half pine dowels and old oak closet rods into manageable two and three foot lengths, then switching to the old lathe's sanding wheel.

The machine made quick work of it, sharpening the tips of those rods into wickedly lethal points.

✦

"Dad, are you going to be okay?"

Jeff tore the cap off another beer and stared straight ahead into space.

Jacks sat down across from him at the kitchen table and dropped her backpack on the floor. "Dad?"

"Hmm?" Jeff gulped from the beer. Two empties sat on the table in front of him.

"Are you just going to sit there guzzling beer all day, Dad? Don't you want to talk or anything?"

Jeff didn't answer.

Jacks reached for a big cardboard box in the middle of the table, the familiar Whitestar Media Group logo emblazoned on top. She peeked inside. "So what's all this?"

"Hmm? Oh, that. My stuff. My personal things. Security let me keep all of that. Some Human Resources nebbish must have packed it up early this morning. They're very efficient about those kinds of things. They don't call it firing anymore. I had an 'exit interview' this morning. They're 'moving the creative staff in an alternative direction', they said. 'Focusing on new cultural megatrends and targeting niche markets that can maximize emerging cross channel synergistic marketing initiatives'. Or some shovel full of crap like that. Jesus."

Jacks nodded, watching her father work his way through half the beer in another gulp. "Have you talked to anyone? That girl in the department? Russell?"

"Tried. She didn't show up for work today. Maybe my little brouhaha with Blair scared the department off. But good for her. Hope she quits. Maybe I can find her something. Something normal." He worked on his beer. "After I find myself something."

"What about your girlfriend? You know, she looks like a pretty sturdy shoulder to cry — I mean, I bet Terri would be glad to shoot over tonight. Talk and stuff, you know?"

Jeff finished the beer, shaking his head. "Maybe I'll call her later. But not now. I'm in a...a..."

"Mood?"

"You could call it that."

"Well, what do you say I whip up something special for dinner tonight, huh? Something to — "

"Don't bother, honey. I'm not hungry."

"Just thirsty, that it?"

His brows knitted together. "Don't push, kiddo."

"Check." Jacks slid the Whitestar box her way. "Well, why don't I unpack this stuff for you, at least." She stuffed the carton under one arm, grabbed her backpack with her other hand. "I'm going to hit the books then, okay? Got a history test tomorrow. And Boynton's stuck us with this godawful CP project." But Jacks could see her father wasn't listening. Not really, even though he kind of nodded. She spun on her heel and out of the kitchen.

✦

Colleen Russell couldn't have taken any calls from Jeff.

At least not at the office. She hadn't gone to work this Monday morning. Couldn't really imagine going there ever again. Couldn't imagine looking into Tim's or Ivy's empty cubicles and pretending like nothing happened, like they were just off hiding again for a midday makeout session.

She didn't even have the guts to return to the apartment. Wasn't really sure what she'd find there.

Cass?

Cass all cold and dead — but not dead — lying on his bed?

Or Gabrielle and a pack of monsters waiting for her in the living room?

No, since dawn Colleen aimlessly cruised the city streets in her sputtering little compact. She'd been up all night in Frank Hoelevich's kitchen, hearing nothing but horror and telling him nothing but the same.

Colleen's eyes got heavy around noon.

By the time the sun already started sliding down behind the taller buildings, she couldn't keep her eyes open anymore and pulled into a sleazy no-tell motel far north on Lincoln Avenue. She was too sleepy to pay much attention to the crack deals going nonstop in the parking lot, the hookers working the afternoon trade in the adjoining rooms. Colleen got herself a single, locked herself inside, fell on the bed and was out like a light.

✦

Frank left the sharpened dowels and closet rods stacked beside the machine now. And Sox settled back into the wood shaving mess when Frank shut the noisy sanding wheel off. Frank looked up from his chair behind the counter, started to tell the dog to leave the wood shavings alone again, then stopped. "Oh, go ahead, fella. Guess you can use your fiber too, huh?" Sox dug into a fresh pile.

Frank returned to the eleven and half pound slab of blued steel and well worn dark brown wood on his lap.

He shoved the last of the .30 caliber cartridges into the top loading, self-ejecting clip. He'd loaded up ten of them now, 8 rounds apiece. That's all he could scrounge from that military surplus mope on Ashland Avenue, and they'd cost him a pretty penny. Hell, he didn't know if the old shells would fire or just blow the whole damn thing up in his face.

With the last cartridge loaded into the clip, Frank picked up the GI issue 1943 model Garand M-1 and blew into the empty chamber, hefted the rifle up in his arms and sighted it, aiming at a dented can of Glidden Eggshell White across the empty store. He pulled the freshly oiled trigger, heard the metallic click...

...And shivered.

A thousand ugly memories danced before his eyes. Fifty year old sights and sounds trembled through every old bone, and Frank Hoelevich suddenly felt older. He dragged himself off the chair and trudged to the empty hardware store's front window. Rifle still in hand, he remembered long icy marches, freezing wet nights, bloodshed and dying buddies in far away places they never came home from. But as he approached the window and reached for the shuttered blinds, he also remembered last night.

He remembered that kid.

Colleen, her name was.

Colleen Russell, she'd said. Sat and talked all night with him till the sun came up over the Lake. And then she left. She didn't even know where the hell she was going and wouldn't listen when he'd begged her to stay, when he told her about good old Gil Silverez at St. Alstantius and how they'd figure something out together. No, she just left and walked across Damen Avenue — all pink with the dawn by then, all pink and safe for awhile — got into her little import and drove away to who knew where. Frank remembered her face as she turned back to wave good-bye before she pulled away from the curb. It was as scared and lonely and just as grim as his buddies' faces had been at St. Vith and in the Hurtgen.

Frank yanked the window blinds open now and thought about that kid, that lost and lonely and scared shitless kid, scared just like thousands of GI's on the cold wet beaches at Omaha and in the cold wet snow of the Ardennes. Frank glared out the front window at that monstrosity across the street — black, ugly and malevolent, brooding over the whole street like hell come to earth. He yanked the cord and the blinds slammed shut.

Frank Hoelevich walked back to the counter, his step a little firmer now. Even Sox looked up and cocked his caramel furred head at the icy, resigned glare in the old man's eyes.

Frank clamped an eight shot clip into the Garand M-1 and ran an oil rag over the barrel once more.

✦

Jacks polished off her second tuna fish on toast and shoved the paper plate away on her desk. A World History textbook lay open under her desklamp. Boynton's Computer Programming notes were spread across the other side just as pointlessly. She couldn't focus on either. Not with her Dad in the kitchen and onto his second six pack. Not with Saturday night on her mind, like it had been since Brad's hand first slipped inside...

She slammed the textbook closed and bounded off her desk chair. Out in the hallway, she peeked towards the kitchen. The lights were out. The early autumn evening drenched the room in darkness already. But she heard a twist cap pop, heard a bottle slam down on the table and knew her father was still in there brooding.

Jacks tiptoed to his office, the bungalow's little third bedroom stuffed with a desk, file cabinets, computer station, drafting table and taboret. She went straight for the Whitestar box and cracked it open. The better part of an entire career unloaded in series of innocuous junk: some desktop knickknacks, framed design award certificates. Three Charade Magazine Employee Of The Year plaques. Some letters and books, imprinted pens and premiums. A manilla folder full of official looking Whitestar dismissal forms, signed and countersigned. Jacks put each item away as best she could.

Nearly buried in between some envelopes and papers she found three floppy disks rubber-banded together. They'd seen better days. Cracked plastic cases. Bent metal shields. They were unlabelled, but had a sticky note with her father's writing attached: *Disks shot — toss or send to Terri.*

Jacks put the rest of her dad's things away, shut off the light and returned to her room.

She waited for her computer to boot up, fingering the bent metal shields on the disks.

✦

Colleen burst out of a nightmare and had to stifle a scream when her eyes flung open.

She leaped up on the bed, head darting each way as she tried to remember where she was.

The dark and dingy motel room flickered with diffused, blinking lights that seeped right through the frayed curtains: Lincoln Avenue headlights, the motel's own neon sign. A 'gentlemen's club' marquee glowing from across the street, most of its letters missing

She ground her fists into her eyes. Slapped her cheeks till she fully awoke. Nervously inventoried the room's colored shadows for darker than black shapes, for white mime faces, for red eyes and leering monster mouths. But the room's shadows were just shadows. She eased off the lumpy bed and shuffled to the window.

Colleen barely edged the curtains open. Up close, they stank like hell from dusty mold and cigarette smoke. But then the whole room stank of cigarettes and spilled booze, of barf and the dried remains of sordid sex.

She peeked out between the barely opened curtains. Looked out on Lincoln Avenue at the cars buzzing by under the streetlamps. At the two hustlers working the corner in their leather chaps and biker caps, grabbing their crotches, flapping their tongues at the yuppie sedans sliding by. She watched two hookers wrestle over the bus bench; prime turf, she guessed. Watched a nerdy North Shore grad school type in a Volvo station wagon hand over a fistful of cash to a skinny, herky-jerky high schooler, watched the Volvo peel away after the crack vials disappeared inside the driver's side window. Watched two cars wheel into the parking lot, shut their lights off, watched a fat gray haired suit and a chesty short skirted bimbo race into the next room.

Colleen let the curtains close just as the thumps and moans and squeals started to muffle their way through the cracked drywall from the room next door.

She crossed the room, flicking on the TV as she passed by. The picture was more snow than image, but the early edition 9:00 news chattered on with some all important just-breaking news from Halas Hall on the latest Bears trade. She kept on walking, shuffling into the bathroom with the sudden need to pee. She hit the wall switch even as she yanked her jeans down and a bare bulb fixture lit up the grimy wall and floor tiles. She kicked her jeans off and left them on the floor under her feet, then sat there listening to the news, listening and wondering how the hell anyone could be chattering on about football and the Bears and joking with the anchorwoman, like everything was fine, just fine, like everything was normal, like it was just another autumn evening, like nothing was going on, not a goddamn thing was going the least bit wrong in town.

No, nothing...nothing but vampires taking over the whole damn city.

She washed her hands in the scummy bowl, looked at the dirty towels and thought better of it. Colleen wiped her hands dry on her jeans and left the bathroom. First she went to the motel room door and checked the lock again. Then the window, which didn't open anyway. Then she returned to the bed. Flopped back onto the mattress, kicked off her tennis shoes and yanked off the white socks she'd been wearing for a day and half now. Her feet ached. Her head ached. Her whole body ached. Her mind and heart and soul ached with sickness and with terror for Cass, for herself, for Tim and Ivy, for the old man called Frank, for the whole goddamn city.

She curled up in the musty bedspread, staring blankly at the TV.

Another murder. Another rape. Another robbery. Everything was fine in Chi-town tonight. Everything *was* normal.

Except if you put it all together. Saw the strands connecting one crime to another, just like the old man had told her. Just like Frank Hoelevich had said last night. A murder here, a missing person there. Colleen watched the preening reporters on location as they mugged for the camera. She listened to the news stories: investigations continuing on the brutal slaying of a young librarian right in a north side branch's backroom. A murder here, a suicide there, just another unimportant death, one a county liquor license commissioner's daughter — drug overdose the likely cause. Runaways, missing persons, one a bedroom suburb teen queen gone three days now, her latest wrong-side-of-the-tracks squeeze nowhere to be found either. A rape here, a mugging there, the latest a series of break-ins and assaults in the trendy Lakeview neighborhood, newscam video of one of the victims showing off a glassy eyed preppie chick who sounded more thrilled than violated. Marauding gangs rampaging through the subway last night, thrill-kill packs doing slice 'n dices down the ivy halls of the UC campus in Hyde Park, a westside mortuary supply warehouse vandalized, a rash of carjackings in the drug bazaars on North Avenue by the Kennedy Expressway ramps.

Just put it all together.

Her own sister Megan, Charade Magazine's Managing Editor — Charade, the city's new bloodsucker newsletter — her own sister doing a swan song somersault off the top of the Hancock Building. Sorry, no reliable leads at this time, Ms. Russell.

Right.

Just put it all together.

Just like the old man told her.

He'd figured it all out and *he* didn't even have a vampire for a roommate. Or ex-roommate. Or...

No, he just had the whole damn nest of them right across the street.

✦

Jacks fiddled with the flimsy, wafer thin magnetic plastic circle and gently placed it inside a pried-open floppy disk case. She snapped the case closed, felt along the seam, then picked up the other one she'd just completed the very same operation on. They looked okay. She popped one in her computer, waited for what seemed like forever as the tiny digital clock face spun on her Mac screen. Finally, almost unexpectedly, it stopped. She double clicked her mouse. The disk opened and a long list of files appeared on the screen. Just as she slid the cursor on top of one and double clicked again to open, she heard the phone ring in the kitchen. Heard a chair slide away from the kitchen table. Heard her father grumble a half-sloshed hello.

She looked back at her monitor: *This file cannot be opened. Resave in another format and try again.*

In the kitchen, Jeff took the phone with him as he fell back into his chair. He reached for another beer bottle. "No, I'm here, Terri. Yes, I'm okay."

"You don't sound okay, Jeff."

"All right, I'm not exactly okay." And he launched into the whole story.

When he was done, the phone was silent for a long minute. Finally, Terri offered, "Jeff, I don't even know what to say. I can't believe they let you go. Just like that. And over some stupid article."

"Well, believe it. And it wasn't just some stupid article. Oh hell, it wasn't the article anyway. It was more than that. I just didn't fit with the new Charade. Didn't fit with the new Blair. I'm just royally pissed off that she didn't have the guts to do it herself. That she let the HR gnomes do her dirty work for her."

"Sure this is about the job, Jeff?"

"Am I sure this...what do you mean?"

"Sure it isn't about something else?"

"Like what?"

"Or *who?*"

"What are you talking about, Terri?"

"Are you sure this isn't also about you and Blair?"

"Yes, I'm sure. Damn sure."

"Good. Well then, the hell with them, Jeff. They don't know what they lost, if you ask me. And they'll find out soon enough when you land somewhere else. Somewhere better, I bet."

"You're pretty good with this pep talk stuff, detective."

"Jeff, I could come over, if you like. Wouldn't take that long to get there. We could talk, we could — "

"Better not, Terri. I appreciate the offer, honest. But to tell you the truth, I'm half drunk already. I don't think I'd be very good company tonight. Things will look better in the morning. *I'll* look better in the morning."

"You sure, Jeff?"

"Positive."

"Okay, but we're going out tomorrow night. Count on it. Or I'll come over there. Or something."

"Sure, Terri, sure. We can talk about it tomorrow when I can think straight."

Back in her room, Jacks closed the first file and then opened another. This one appeared, for all the good it did. She got another opened — equally nonsensical. And she opened five more, at first just pleased with herself for salvaging the disks and trying to figure out if there was any valid way to use this miracle save for one of Boynton's CP projects. But then she found herself intrigued by the seemingly disconnected bits of information on the files.

Just whose were these?

And what were they all about?

There were county comptroller's records on some property in the city, somewhere on the north side. Whatever it was, the place changed hands half a dozen times in just as many years.

Then: what looked like transcripts of phone conversations. Cryptic conversations with someone who sounded like a low level street hustler. Initials: N.K. Only much further in did she finally locate his name.

Nicky Kolitzky.

Reformatted e-mails from some European government agencies. German, maybe. No, they were from Austria. And some more from...Slovakia? And the Czech Republic.

There were some snippets of what appeared to be Whitestar corporate financials. Columns of meaningless dollar figures. Transfers from this budget to that account.

The next few files just opened up into gibberish, just pages full of raw binary character chains. Jacks converted, saved and resaved in half a dozen different formats, trying every high school hackers trick she'd been honing to snag a solid 'A' in Boynton's class. She finally got a couple more to open.

And now it really got interesting.

One was a timeline on the history of the Palace Theatre. And Jacks — and every other kid in school, probably in all of Chicago, knew what The Palace Theatre was.

It was a little place called GOTHIQUE.

✦

"Colleen."

She stirred on the bed, her face buried in the mildewed pillow case.

"Colleen. Hey, come on. Open up, will you?"

She bolted up on the bed.

It took her a second to get her bearings. Then she remembered: the dingy motel room on Lincoln Avenue. Colleen squinted at the clock radio bolted to the nightstand: 4:36.

A.M.

"Colleen, please." It came from outside the door. Through the draped windows she could see...something. A shadow? A silhouette?

Just a dream?

Another nightmare?

Cass?

It had to be...*had* to be Cass. She slid off the bed. Stepped towards the door, felt a clammy chill in the room, damp cold licking at her bare legs and feet. She looked back in the dark towards the bathroom, where she left her jeans.

"Colleen, hurry up."

"Hold on." She grabbed the yellowed sheet off the bed and wrapped it around herself. "I'm coming."

Colleen shivered inside the sheet as she fiddled with the locks. With just the little twist knob on the door handle to go, she paused. Peeled the drapes aside just an inch, but she couldn't really see outside the door.

"Colleen, come on!"

She clicked the knob and slowly opened the door.

"Cass?"

Nothing.

There was no one there.

Colleen leaned her head outside, clutching the sheet tight around herself. "C-Cass?" An icy autumn breeze blew by, whipping her long red hair across her face. She took a step out of the room, cold concrete freezing her bare feet. She looked both ways.

"Who's there? Cass? Cass, is it you?"

Nothing.

Evidently even the hookers and the junkies and the hustlers were tucked in for the night. Except for her own car, the parking lot was empty.

My car...

Little shards of glass twinkled under the streetlights.

The drivers' side window was shattered.

There was someone sitting in her car.

"C-Cass, is that — "

The car's headlamps flashed on, blinding her for just a moment.

And the vampires appeared out of nowhere.

Colleen dropped the sheet and dove back through the doorway, but they caught her in mid-air.

She tried to scream, but a cold, reeking hand clamped down over her mouth. Tried to fight, but more cold hands enveloped her.

She heard them hissing to one another, more voices than she could count:

"You go in there, get her stuff, lickety split."

"Can't you see the sky, man? Let's — "

"Just get it. All of it. Or we'll all be in big —"

"Find her keys, dude."

"Come on now, no fucking around, they want her clean. Just hold tight to the bitch and let's scram."

And they did.

WBBK-TV Evening News
6:23 PM

"...Let's go live now to our Action Newscam Team on North Damen Avenue outside the new nightclub the whole town's been talking about. Mary Anne?"

"Thanks Steve. We're here outside 'Gothique' for tonight's Grand Opening Gala, a special VIP Pass affair that crowds have been lining up for since mid-afternoon. Police are trying to direct the rush hour traffic on Damen since people are now spilling out on the street. As you can see from the renovated theater building and the crowds here behind me, it's a pretty unique place, a unique event, and for a unique crowd. Ma'am, what's your name?"

"My name? You mean on this level of consciousness?"

"Uhm...well, I see you're all decked out for the Gala Grand Opening. Are costumes mandatory?"

"This isn't a costume. These are the clothes I wore when my earlier soul was laid to rest in 1817."

"I...uhm, I see. Well you've obviously taken good care of them all these years. Now your, uhm, your current soul... what's it normally do on this level of consciousness?"

"I'm a stylist."

"Did you have your makeup done professionally?"

"What makeup?"

"Your...well, I see you're wearing a pair of fangs. How did you – "

"These are my real teeth."

"They're your real – "

"Yeah, See. Now how about I use 'em on you right now, you motherfu--Bleep"

"Sorry, ladies and gentlemen, we seem to be experiencing some video problems from our Action Newscam Team. We'll turn to Gail Gordon now for a last look at the weather. And coming up after the evening report, stay tuned for Wheel Of Fortune..."

Gothique: *You'll Just Die...*

TWENTY EIGHT

The darkness emerges and it descends from the east.

Each evening, Chicago's autumn breezes ripen with the scent of decaying leaves, browning grass and summer refuse congealed in the gutters. The night air gets damper, chilling. Feet race faster for taxis and buses and parked cars, more eager than ever to get inside before darkness falls. Though a few, a very few, seem to look up at the darkening sky anxiously, with some kind of inexplicable eager anticipation. But regardless of anyone's reactions, the skyline sparkles through the lake fog a little bit earlier each night.

✦

But in the dayglow brightness of Chicago Ridge Mall, it's perpetual springtime while off-duty Detective Terri Shepherd tries to stifle a laugh. Tries, but fails as she watches Jeff Stancheck chafing impatiently while a sales clerk that's barely older than Jacks guides him to a three-way mirror to get a better look at the navy pinstripe interview suit. A headhunter promised three interviews next week, a fresh start called for a new suit. But Jeff glanced at the price tag. Gulped at $575 and immediately decided to make do with a new shirt and tie to freshen up his trademark corduroy blazer instead.

"How about you pick out the shirt and tie and I'll pick a restaurant?"

"Deal." Terri had three combo's laid out under the men's clothing department's bright lights before Jeff even got back from the dressing room.

✦

It's dimmer, though, back at the Stancheck house on South Karlov. Downright dark where only the monitor glow lights up Jack's small bedroom and Jacks' herself, gangly legs stretched out on her desk, keyboard nestled in her lap along with a bag of nachos, phone cradled by her ear. "Hold on, Rach." Jacks' fingers fly across the keys, hit return and close the file. "There. Saved."

"How can you do homework and talk on the phone at the same time?" Rachel asks, genuinely puzzled. "Make that, how can you do homework *period?"*

"Just multi-tasking, Rach. And that save put me halfway home to

Boynton's CP term project."

"Oh, goodie."

"Hey, this thing all works and I ace his class."

"Oh yeah, this is your mystery file fandango?"

"Actually I was thinking 'Advanced Retrieval Techniques' for a title, but I'll see if I can work in *fandango."*

"Yawning now."

"Hey, I told you this was all some weird background stuff on The Palace Theater, didn't I?"

"Umpteen times, but it all sounds pre-Gothique, Jacks, so I'll just stay in the disinterested mode. Unless your little project involves some magic change of heart on those Grand Opening passes, that is. Time's running out, you know."

Jacks deftly moved her mouse to click and shut down while she tossed a nacho overhead and neatly caught it in her wide open mouth. "Make that 'time's up', I think. Afraid Gala time starts ASAP, as in tonight, and you and I aren't going to be there. Come on, Rachel, no one else we know is going to be there either. Still that little matter of being underage."

"Got the child working hard on that right now in his room. Rory swears he can match an Illinois Drivers license to perfection. Or good enough for bouncers and doormen anyway. Your yearbook photo was looking tres chic on runtboy's last attempt, BTW."

"Ugh, not that...and how did Rory get his mitts on my — "

"Hey, child's in the Geek Club. Or on the Yearbook Committee or something."

Jacks set the keyboard on her desk and dug deeper in the nacho bag. "Be that as it may, Rach, there's still the whole post-party punishment thing."

"Your Dad's still raggin' about that, is he?"

"Rachel, I blew curfew big time. With the car. And I was drinking. Yes, he's still ragging."

"So the car lockdown's lifted when?"

"Dad says when I can buy my own. Like, maybe never."

"Well, there's always the CTA. Orange Line to the Red Line and then transfer to a bus on Montrose or somewhere. Or is it the Green Line?"

"Rachel, you get the color coordination down and then we can talk about it, okay?"

"Hmmm, I'm sensing some give there. Good girl Jacks will *consider* Bad Girl Night? Like once the child gets those ID's mastered we pay the runt off and go for it some night? Next Saturday? This Friday, maybe? A little primp and preen on the sly? Like here at my house and we tell your Dad you're sleeping over so curfew's in the moot point category? A little adventure on the El and then cool time and cool boys and we finally get to see the absolute only fucking thing worth checking out in this town? *This* is what I'm sensing?"

Jacks started laughing halfway through Rachel's run-on.

"Laugh all you want Jacks, but I'm laying odds you and me, girl, will be tripping the dark fantastic at Gothique in short order, so pretty boys look out. Speaking of, no news?"

Jacks laughter stopped abruptly. Even her smile faded. "No."

"Sorry, Jacks. But shit happens. Chad's loss."

"Brad. His name was Brad."

"Same difference. Look, guys take phone numbers, guys fail to use said numbers. It's chronic with them. Like whacking off in the shower."

"Okay, Rachel, that was tonight's *Eeeewwww."* Jacks munched down on the last nacho, crumbled the bag and tossed it in the trash can under her desk. "But..."

"But?"

"But I thought he...well, we...you know, we..."

"Jeez, girl," Rachel shrieked into the phone. "Was your Mom raising you Southern Baptist or something back there in Encino? You think just 'cause his fingers managed to find their way under your skirt, you two are engaged now? Move on, Jacks."

"Rachel, it's not that. It's...well, I really *liked* him."

"Liked him, dyked him. Hey, there's an idea. Next time we bump into ol' Brad, you and me do the Penthouse Pet more-than-good-friends routine for him and he'll be trailing after you like a dog."

Jacks finally cracked a smile again. Rachel never failed her. "Okay, you get two *Eeeewww's* tonight."

"Fine. Now on to biz. I saw you were taking major notes in World History. Any chance I can sort of borrow..."

Jacks' and Rachel's nightly phone check wound down around nine. Dad was out with Terri, stuck in his version of hell on earth: in a mall, shopping for clothes. He said they might catch some dinner after. So Jacks left the back yard light on for them, decided the little bungalow still looked a little too slasher-movie-eerie in the autumn darkness and left the lights on in the kitchen and the living room. She left today's outfit-du-jour in a pile by the closet door and yanked on an oversize T-shirt, then climbed into bed. *'Move on,'* Rachel had said. And she really wanted to. But as she tossed and turned in bed, trying to focus on the sheer impracticality of Rachel's harebrained idea of getting all Goth'd up and then getting into Gothique some night — and getting it all done on the sly — her thoughts kept returning to the basement party, to the snug comfort of that ratty recliner, to wonderfully warm sensations she felt when Brad's hands danced across her shirt and...and...

Jacks smashed her face into the pillow and forced herself to sleep.

✦

Twelve miles as the crow flies. Just twelve miles from 49th and Karlov to downtown's glittering skyscraper canyons. High up on the twenty-seventh floor above Michigan and Fairmont Court, Roberta Whitehead tossed and turned in her bed too, though it was custom made, roughly the size of Jack's entire bedroom and decked out in imported white silk sheets.

Those sheets were still warm beside her, still ripe with the scent of sex and sweat and the lingering smell of the twenty-something toady from — from where? Legal? Accounting? Operations? She couldn't even remember his name, wouldn't even recognize him if she passed him in the halls downstairs tomorrow. Hell, she'd already forgotten the desultory sex, even if the aroma still clung to her sheets.

Roberta lured a different fresh faced yuppie on the make to her suite every night now, had been doing so every single night since that little soiree, the one where Marek and Drake and their brood let loose on the guests, and now what had once been just hush-hush rumors among the Gold Coast glitterati was just another tawdry item on the brunch agendas and cocktail party repartee for all the media elite's savvier scene-makers.

But gossip all they want, none of them knew that had been the last night, the very last time that Marek had *her*. He hadn't even visited — not once — since then. Just sent his own lackeys to get papers signed. Simply couriered the last batch. He hadn't visited, hadn't summoned her, hadn't taken her in his arms and ran his icy cold fingers over her flesh, hadn't licked her throat and her breasts like he'd done so many deliciously devilish nights before, hadn't parted those thin cold lips of his, hadn't bitten down, hadn't drank, hadn't...

Roberta rolled over and untangled herself from the silk sheets. She fumbled on her marble nightstand, shoved aside the bottle of vodka and looked at the antique clock and saw it was barely nine. She knew she should get up, knew she should get dressed and dressed to the hilt, something fabulous, something to turn every head, turn Marek's head, turn it away from that scheming little corporate ladder climbing bitch that had his eye these days. She should get dressed, it was the big night after all. It would hardly do for the Queen of Whitestar Media to be a no show at the big gala, hardly do at all, hardly...

Roberta picked up the priceless antique clock and threw it across the room. She grabbed the vodka, guzzled long and hard and rolled back into the tangled sheets, the bottle clutched tight to her chest.

✦

That scheming little corporate ladder climbing bitch sat at her desk just a few floors below Roberta Whitehead's penthouse suite, unsure about the merits of this latest hop up the rungs.

But damn sure there was no backing out now.

Blair Armstrong stared into a compact mirror, shocked to see a stranger's face looking back at her. She'd dropped five pounds the last few weeks. Her skin was pallid, her eyes sunk in shadowy hollows. But it wasn't anything another dab of makeup couldn't fix, right? A little foundation, a little more blush? She re-lined her lips in glistening red, touched up her lashes with another dollop of mascara. Slammed the compact shut and tossed it into her designer purse. She spun herself out of her desk chair and whisked out of the office, a long drape of glittery black sequins and shiny satin, spiky velvet pumps tapping the tiles as she strode through the dark and empty Editorial Department, struggling with an uneasy mix of disgust, desire and dread.

She was due at nine. Sharp. And it didn't pay to be late. Especially not tonight. He wouldn't like that. No, he wouldn't like that at all. And he had special ways of showing his displeasure.

When she approached the Art Department, Blair halted. She winced at the sight of Jeff Stancheck's closed office door. She'd meant to call him. To see how we was doing. But there was always something else to take care of, something always intervened, always something...

Jeff would be okay.

He'd land on his feet. And, hell, he just as much quit as he was fired, didn't he? Anyway, she didn't have a choice, orders were orders, and she had to find some excuse to let him go. She had to.

Blair turned away from Jeff's office. She glanced at the Art Department.

And shivered.

Charade's new night shift was hard at work.

Printers churned and scanners hummed, cold pale fingers clicked away on mouses and keyboards inside the artists' cubicles. Blair slowly walked through the department, watching the dyed hair heads focused on their monitors. She passed one cubicle and stared at the girl inside. Blair recognized her, knew she'd worked here for — how long now? Months? Yes, the girl disappeared for a few days, but then she came back, came back to work nights, just like Marek suggested, just like the others he said would be showing up now and taking over.

The girl's pale hands halted over her keyboard. She looked over her shoulder at Blair, sending a shudder throughout Blair's whole body. Lifeless black eyes momentarily flickered with a hint of red sparks, then went dead black again. The girl's blood red lips mechanically twisted into something like a grin — if not quite — two short, sharp fangs protruding out of her mouth.

"Good evening, Ms. Armstrong."

"Uhm...evening."

"Leaving?"

Blair nodded, a sickly feeling churning in her belly.

"Well, better get going, then. The big night and all. Sure wish I could be there."

Blair nodded again, then hurried out of the department and towards the elevators.

And Ivy finally let her smile droop when she heard the elevator doors close, then returned to her computer screen and the pages for next month's issue of Charade, still stuck being an intern, even now that she was dead.

✦

The darkness emerges and it descends from the east.

And with the darkness, they awake.

The two of them lounged on a silver Lincoln's trunk.

They'd been there since just after sundown, keeping an eye out, watching the crowds start to form. Sneering, laughing and giggling, mostly. Poking each other in the ribs when someone hustled into the line that queued up by the marquee, someone with a particularly bad outfit, someone clutching a VIP Pass who'd be turned away at the door anyway.

They watched the people milling around outside Gothique, a few anxious ones pointlessly pressing their faces against the blackened glass doors anyway, desperately trying to see inside. By seven thirty the crowd lined the sidewalk four deep and halfway down Damen Avenue. Just after nine now, people were already spilling out onto the street. Taxis and limousines inched through the crowd, disgorging passengers, all of them casually stepping out onto Damen, feigning nonchalance, tossing bills into the drivers with practiced arrogance. But no matter how aloof they tried to act, it showed in their eyes: the buzz, the fever, the eager anticipation. *A wishin' and a wantin'.*

Half the block thronged with row after row of twenty and thirty-something's dolled up in pricey boutique faux-Gothrock knockoffs. Then one clique after another of legit street kids in thrift shop authenticity, mismatched black see-throughs and leathers and dyed gowns and mail ordered rubber gear, carefully put together, every face dripping too much makeup, looking up from seemingly earnest conversations whenever a limo halted in front of the theater, the conversations pausing just long enough to see who would get out.

A few strays nervously huddled in tight knit groups: grunged college kids in mall store jeans, suit and tie account execs wondering if their well rehearsed pickup lines would work on these Goth chicks, uneasy power suit gals wrinkling their noses at the smelly clove cigarettes and the leering Max Factored boys.

"Yikes, look at that one, darling." Fonda shook his head in disgust while he fingered the spaghetti straps of his black lace camisole, two sizes two small and stretched tautly over his emaciated chest. He dug his heels into the shiny Lincoln's trunk lid and giggled. "I mean, you don't dig the drama, fine. But don't go clubbing in a J.C. Penney's suit. *Any* club. *Anywhere.*"

"I hope someone rips it off her thread by thread and fucks her up the ass tonight."

Fonda slapped his knee, his pale hand cracking hard on the black leather. "Oh, that's nice, precious. If I'd known you were this catty before, I'd have gone for you *first.* It's a wonder your old flame put up with it."

Gem shoved her face in Fonda's, eyes glowing hot red, fangs bared. But only for an instant. Her eyes cooled back to black. Her red lips slid back over her teeth.

"That's better, darling," Fonda said. "We're just on patrol here, girl. No need to show the world your charms just yet."

Gem leaned back on the trunk and sneered at a kid she caught staring at her. "Yeah, well, just don't bring up Frost anymore, okay?"

"Quite right, darling. It was rude of me to speak ill of the dead."

Gem patted Fonda on his bony back. "No big. We're still pals, right Pop?"

"Abso-fucking-lutely, daughter."

The two of them were inseparable these nights.

Gem and Fonda. Doting father and darling daughter.

Oh, Gabrielle may have wished and whined all she could for a sip, and Arianne may have rightfully taken the honor of the first taste.

But it was Fonda who got it right later that night back in a deep, dark chamber below Gothique. It was Fonda who'd been glutted almost to bursting on Frostbite, but still had to top off with another drink, Fonda who drained Gem and then bit his own skinny white wrist and let the blood dribble all over her gaping, gasping mouth.

She awoke the next night nestled against Fonda's skinny chest, only to find that her flirtation with the darkwave scene had suddenly take a permanent turn.

Two pretty studs dolled up in their Lost Boys best strolled by. Fonda shivered with dramatic flourish. Gem licked her lips and smiled at them. "File those two away for later," she said. "What do you say? One for each of us? But I'll take the Keiffer Sutherland clone, deal?"

✦

Gabrielle whimpered like a nervous puppy, curling herself into a fetal ball on Marek's immaculate office floor.

She wasn't just whimpering from the pain, though the bruises and the welts had reddened her skin raw. After all, it was only an hour before that they came for her, that they unlocked the handcuffs that had begun to grind her flesh away from her wrists, that they carried her up from the dark basements below the old theater building. No, Gabrielle cried quietly to herself there on Marek's floor because she knew her own miserable little life was being debated over.

And it wasn't entirely clear who would win the argument.

"Your little pet won't bleed on my carpet now, will she?" Marek sneered as much to himself as to Arianne. The question wasn't entirely rhetorical, after all. But Arianne didn't hear it, or simply chose not to reply. She just hiked up her long black skirt and knelt down on the office floor beside Gabrielle. Those long, cool fingers glided across Gabrielle's skin, caressing the bruises, delicately grazing the welts and the wounds.

Marek grunted his displeasure and returned to spinning his massive desk chair in half circles. "At least you could have had her cleaned up some before she was brought up here." He wrinkled his nose. "The whelp smells."

Arianne's long fingers froze. They slowly rose off Gabrielle's black and blue arms. Trembled in the air, then clenched into fists. "You had no right." She said it matter of factly, each word laced with restraint.

"I'm sorry, Arianne? I...come again?"

Arianne looked up from Gabrielle, long hair draping her pale face like a veil. But her black eyes flamed angry red and glowed right through the black curtain. "I said that you had no right. This girl is mine."

"Be that as it may, Arianne. But the little fool could have caused quite a bit of trouble for us."

"Not for *us.* For you. For you and your silly schemes."

"Oh no, I won't be dragged into this argument again, Arianne. Mea culpa for having Drake teach your precious acolyte a lesson in proper discipline. But I can't have her or you or anyone — "

"Silence!" Arianne hissed, a sudden serpentine sound that froze Marek's words in his throat.

Before he could even close his mouth, she leaped clear across the room and landed on top of his desk, her long pale fingers curled into raptor claws, nails bare inches from Marek's throat. "Don't go too far, Marek. Play your mortal games if you wish, till it all comes crashing down around your ears, for all I care. But don't cross *me,* Marek. Don't ever, ever cross me." Her face twisted into a monstrous caricature of her porcelain beauty, lips peeled back and white fangs glistening. "You mistake all your warmblood lackeys and your minions and alliances and your grandiose schemes for power. But you don't really know what power is."

They glared at each other for a long moment, red eyes locked on one another's. Gabrielle scooted across the floor and hid in the corner, afraid to even look at them. And she never saw who blinked first.

But evidently one of them did.

As quickly as Arianne appeared on Marek's desk, she slid off. Or simply vanished like a breeze. One moment Arianne was a lethal demon poised for the kill — the next, she stood in the doorway — small, waifish, her black dress and hair fluttering in a breeze that wasn't there, her pale hands beckoning to Gabrielle, her pale face softened back into a young girl's innocent beauty. But her eyes — Arianne's eyes still glared with hot fury, even as they turned away from Marek and locked onto Gabrielle.

Still sobbing on the floor, Gabrielle looked up immediately. Hopefully.

Then she smiled.

An apprehensive smile. Filled with relief.

And expectation.

Gabrielle crawled across the floor towards Arianne and hid herself as best she could in the folds of the long black skirt.

Marek sneered and plopped back into his chair. "Leaving Arianne?"

"I believe you have guests waiting for you, Marek."

"Yes, several hundreds, I should think."

"So you really plan to go through with this?"

He laughed. "Well, it would be awkward to cancel at this point. The 'Gala Grand Opening' and all." He got up from his chair and left it spinning behind the desk. While Gabrielle clawed her way deeper into Arianne's skirt, Marek strode over to the window and flicked it open with one finger. He looked down on Damen Avenue, where the crowds elbowed for prime spots below the old theater marquee, and hundreds more filled the sidewalks and the street, just gawking.

"Our faithful await, Arianne. All those anxious, pathetic little lambs just begging to be let in, to pretend they're *us* for the evening." He swept his hand out the window and over the throngs. "You will be joining us, won't you?"

"Not likely, Marek."

"It's not like you to be an ungracious hostess."

She hissed at him again.

"Planning on wasting your evening with your little toy, are you?"

"Marek, you think this is all a game, don't you? This — this 'club' of yours. Your plans and schemes." She narrowed her eyes. "Even between you and me. It's all a game, isn't it?"

"Ahh, but it's only opening night. The game's just begun."

"Do you think so, Marek? I think it's the beginning of the end. For you. For all of us."

Marek slammed the window shut. "Oh, enough. Go play with your little whelp. I have business downstairs." He straightened his impeccable black suit and headed for the doorway. But he paused as he approached Arianne. They glared at each other again. But Arianne let him pass.

"Stop worrying, Arianne," Marek said. "I'll have you know I tied up another loose end already. Soon enough any others will be taken care of as well. Go play with your little girl, if you like." His cold white face softened for a moment. "But won't you join me downstairs later? Come see all I've done? It's truly magnificent. See all those silly, sad little children in their ludicrous costumes just begging to give us their money. And their blood. And their souls."

"I don't savor it the way you do, Marek. I never did."

"But you'll join me later?"

She didn't answer.

Marek stomped past her and down the hallway.

Once he was finally gone, Arianne untangled Gabrielle from her dress. She looked deep into the girl's eyes. "You've played some dangerous games yourself, child."

"Oh Arianne, I — I...I thought they were going to...I thought..."

Arianne cupped Gabrielle's cheek in her cool hand. "Yes, well that's all behind you now. But I suggest that you don't cross Marek again. Or any of his brood."

"Arianne, when? *When?* I want it so bad. I — "

Arianne lay a finger on Gabrielle's lips and silenced her. She stared deeper still into Gabrielle's eyes. "You're so certain?"

"Y-yes. It's...it's all I've ever dreamed about. It's all I've ever wanted."

Arianne sighed, shoulders slumping. "Don't you realize...don't you ever think about sin, child? Don't you ever think about your soul?"

Gabrielle just stared back blankly at her.

Arianne shook her head. "Come." She wrapped her arm around Gabrielle, then guided her out of the office and down the dark hallway. "Well, Marek was right about one thing, child. You do *smell.*"

✦

The darkness emerges and it descends from the east.

And with the darkness, they awake.

The children of the dark crawl out of their dens to embrace the night.

He was a bank teller by day.

Liked to go by 'Carravaggio' at night, at least on weekend nights when there was really time to get the outfit and the makeup right. And even though this was a weeknight and he had to pretend he had a wake to attend just to get out of work early, and would still have to be back behind the cash drawer bright and early tomorrow AM, he'd gotten the ensemble just right tonight. All the shopping up and down Clark and back and forth on Belmont was worth it, even if he'd have hell to pay and a lot more than that to pay in plain old money when the Visa bill arrived in a couple weeks. The muslin peasant shirt had belled sleeves and everything, even if it really was just some old 70's-theme thrift shop girl's blouse. In a way that made it feel even better against his skin. But the autumn breeze seeped right inside the flimsy fabric, hardened his nipples against the cloth, so he wrapped his cape tight around himself, the cape he'd drooled over and ogled and begged and haggled and finally paid straight retail for at Dark Mystique, the gorgeous black velour and red taffeta lined cape with the perfect collar and the perfect clasp, the cape that billowed just like bat wings as he briskly walked up Damen, his Dodge Neon parked way back around on Montrose. His boots clicked on the sidewalk just like the staccato sound in all his favorite 60's Italian horror films, the ones with Barbara Steele and all the really bad dubbing.

He saw the crowds up ahead, a whole block away, but there were already so many people lined up in front of the place, so many spilled out onto the street, he couldn't miss them, so he quickened his pace, flushed with excitement, flushed with anticipation, still barely able to believe that all those nights staying up till the wee hours listening to that evenings-only Goth/darkwave station's erratic north side FM reception finally netted him a coveted Gothique VIP Pass.

Just one VIP Pass, but that was okay. He didn't really have anyone to go with anyway.

He was always too shy to actually join the RPG get-togethers and LARP games he saw posted on Dark Mystiques' bulletin boards. Usually just a silent voyeur in the Chicago Clan chatrooms. Never felt at ease in the bars where he normally just hid in the corner and tried to affect his best sexy-brooding look and eyed up the skinny girls in their black tights and ripped chiffon and the androgynous boys in their leathers and mesh tanks while he weaved elaborate fantasies about them, while he chugged tepid drafts, unable to decide which he'd like better — the soft skinned girls or the lean hard boys, but it didn't really matter because he never had either and typically went home a few hours later without dancing once. Without talking to a soul. Went home alone to his way-west of Lakeview 'studio' flat to replay the same tunes on his stereo and preen and dance in front of his mirror till he got all worked up and stripped his clothes off piece by piece and fell to his knees and violently masturbated, picturing himself biting those skinny club girls and being gnawed on by those androgynous dancing boys — did it two, three times, till he could finally get to sleep.

But not tonight.

Tonight he clutched that VIP Pass in his gloved hand, because this was Gothique, for Chrissakes, this was the place, *the* place, and tomorrow night he could log onto the chats with pride and gloat all about it.

He paused under a huge maple shedding its leaves, two of them fluttering right down on his cape, and squeezed his hand into the tight front pocket of his pants. Tugged and finally yanked out the cigarette case with the Coppola Dracula logo on it, fumbled with black gloved fingers and got a cigarette in his mouth, fumbled some more with the matchbook till he got his smoke lit. He took a deep drag, tried to slow his heart down, tried to quell the eager anticipation, the excitement, *Jeez,* he was getting a hard-on wasn't he, *Jeez,* tried to cool down because he was starting to sweat from walking so fast, it would ruin his makeup, it would, *Jeez* —

"Cop a smoke?"

"H-Huh?" He almost dropped his cigarette. He whirled around, tangling himself up in his cape. "Oh, sorry. Uhm, Hi. Sure...uhm...here." He held out the cigarette case.

"Thanks."

Cass stepped out of the shadows beside a shuttered storefront and reached out his pale hand.

✦

Father Gil Silverez stood by the front window in Frank Hoelevich's living room, shaking his head. He peered through the venetian blinds at the cars and the crowds outside and one story down on Damen Avenue. "Frank, I don't feel comfortable leaving you here like this. Not with that...that thing."

Frank shifted on the recliner by the front window and the huge M-1 rifle almost slid off his lap.

Sox wasn't at his usual spot beside the chair. He huddled in a corner, a brand new rawhide chewbone untouched on the floor right next to him. He'd laid there all night, uneasy with the red glow, confused by the noises outside, confused by the funny feeling he'd had for weeks now, a funny something in the air, something he could scent but couldn't figure out. Confused by the two men arguing all evening, ever since the priest first came over.

Just before sundown.

"Frank, do you think I'm just going to leave with you hugging that rifle? I bet the safety isn't even on."

"Sure as hell isn't."

"And those?" Gil Silverez pointed at the two wooden rods beside the recliner. The *stakes* — that's what they were, after all — with their lethally sharpened points. "A fifty year old loaded gun and a bunch of horror show props. I'm afraid if I leave I'll either find you dead in the morning or locked up by the cops."

"So don't go, Gil. Stay the night. Till sunrise at least."

"Can't. Got mass in the AM. And there's two parishioners on their last breaths, I'm just waiting for the call to — "

"Then go home, Gil. Go now. I didn't ask you to come over."

The priest winced. "Frank, I just...I wanted to talk. Frank, I just don't want you to blow your fool head off with that thing. I don't want Libbie to come home to find she's a widow."

Frank ran his old hand along the M-1's wooden stock. "No, I don't think it'll blow my head off. And if it does, that's a hell of a lot better way to go than..." He looked up at Gil, resignation in his eyes. "Better that than Lib finding me holed up in the basement, hiding in a dark corner, waiting for her, waiting to..." He went back to stroking the gun.

"So you're going to take the whole damn lot of them out, that it, Frank? You and your fifty year old GI issue there? You and your closet rods? With Rin Tin Tin over there at your side, that's the plan?"

"What do you suggest, Padre?"

Gil didn't answer. He couldn't.

"You talked to the cops, didn't you? And they just blew you off, didn't they? You said you called the Diocese, didn't you, Gil? Started to tell them what you were thinking? And how'd that go again?"

Gil still didn't answer.

"Told you to keep your trap shut, didn't they? Told you the Church didn't need any pastors screwing up the collection plate any worse than it already is with some cockamamie monster stories, right? Or did I hear you wrong before?"

"They...well, they agreed to see me. Next week, maybe. I have an appointment."

"Yeah. With a counselor. So they can tuck you away in some retreat somewhere. Hell, they're probably in on it too for all we know."

"Frank, no. Not the Church...they wouldn't."

"Why not? You ask me, half the damn city's in on it. Or enough of it, anyway. Wouldn't take much. A few politicians. Few cops. What makes you think the Church would be so goddamn clean?"

Gil stood up from the sofa. "I'm going." He headed for the kitchen and the back door.

"Gil, we both know damn well what's going on, what's living — or whatever — right there across the street. They're vampires, Gil. Goddamn-for-real vampires, just like Bela Lugosi and Count Dracula. Only a lot worse than you or I ever saw in any Saturday matinees."

Father Silverez halted. "I know, Frank. I know what they are."

"So what are we going to do about it, Gil?"

Silverez spun around. "What do you want me to say, Frank? You want me to grab one of those stakes and go marching across the street with you right now? Stick one of them, watch him crumble into dust?"

"No, we'd be better off doing it in the daytime."

The priest shook his head.

"Gil, I don't know what to do either. But I'm not going to let them creep in here one night and start sucking on my neck either. At least I'll be ready for them."

"You're crazy, Frank."

"No crazier than you. Look Gil, you can't go walking back to the rectory after dark, they'll just — "

"Frank, there's a couple hundred people out there on the street right now. Didn't you see the signs?"

"Yeah, I saw them."

"A Gala Grand Opening. Gothique's VIP Night. Hell, maybe the mayor's going to show up and cut the ribbon. I don't think I have to worry about getting back home tonight."

"Still — "

"Come on, old man. Unlock the back door so I can get going. And leave that damn gun by the chair, will you?"

✦

"It's okay," Cass whispered in his ear. "It's okay, okay, you're okay, just lie down now, just ease back."

Cass lay the boy down in the gangway between the storefront and the four flat next door, where the shadows were darker, where the streetlight barely made it through the overhanging maples behind them. The kid was panting, hyperventilating, but Cass ran his cool hands over the boy's cheek and soothed him till his eyes closed. "That's right, sleep. Just sleep." Cass' long fingers traced a line down the boy's cheek, across the jaw, down the throat, where the faint streetlight sparkled on a wet, gaping red wound, on blood trickling down the boy's neck and all across his shirt. "Just sleep, pretend it was just a dream, that's all. Just a dream."

Cass stood up and his fingertips came away wet.

Dripping.

The boy's blood warmed the icy ache inside, but he knew it wouldn't last, never lasted, never did. He sucked on his fingers for a moment, almost retching from the gooey, salty taste, but craving the way the blood still made his lips and his tongue tingle anyway. Cass knelt back down beside the boy. He pried the black and red embossed ticket out of the kid's hands. "You just sleep now. And when you wake up, you go find another hobby, got it? Ask some girl out. Knock her up. Get married. Go buy a split level and breed hordes of kids, mow your lawn and take up golfing, you got that? But you forget about this. Please just forget about all...this."

He rose and looked up Damen. Saw the crowds moving into Gothique. Saw them shuffling past the doormen. Saw Fonda and...saw *Gem.* Damn them, they'd got Gem. Saw the two of them slither off the Lincoln's trunk, shove their way through the lines and disappear through the glass doors.

"Sorry about this." Cass clutched the Gothique VIP Pass. "But I kind of need this tonight. Got a job to do."

Cass hiked his black trenchcoat collar up around his pale face.

He headed for Gothique.

TWENTY NINE

Marek stood on the mezzanine balcony, gazing out on the dark sea of bodies below.

His masterpiece lay before him. The first of many, if all went according to plan. Strobe lights and gelled spots washed over the cavernous interior of the old Palace Theater, transformed now into "GOTHIQUE: Dance Club Extraordinaire", entertainment complex, dark cultural center, mecca for all the city's vapidly vampiric children of the night. C.D. Hall's classic Hollywood horror sets couldn't outdo the club's outrageous architecture. It had been completely rebuilt into an immense haunted castle, crumbling stone walls aglow with backlit stained glass windows, complete with video lightning bolts flashing behind the cracked panes. The ceiling was a honeycomb of Gothic arches and naves, the pillars and balustrades wrapped in thorny vines and dead tree branches. If it tried to emulate the gloomy Nordic mysticism of Caspar David Friederich's haunted abbeys or the English Graveyard School poets' ruined castles, it did so in a uniquely Walpole-esque 'Strawberry Hill' kind of way.

Even if it was all plywood and sheetrock, plexiglass and molded plastics.

At the long main bar, the lucky ones who first made it through the doors snatched the bar stools and weren't likely to give them up for love or money...or a dance invite or even a trip to the bathroom. The boys at the bar were decked out in their Tom Cruise/Brad Pitt/Antonio Banderas best, with elaborate velvet capes, leggings tucked into mail-ordered knee high boots, peasant shirts and velour vests, sipping at colored cordials (at $12.50 a pop), their countless skull and ankh and devil head rings clinking on the tiny glasses while they surveyed the crowds with aloof detachment. Unless they were making eyes at the girls at the bar, the girls who shimmered in shiny black gowns and creaked in constricting leather corsets, Morticia clones and vampire-dominatrixes elegantly flicking their long dyed tresses over and over for dramatic come-hither effect, criss-crossing their skinny legs so their satin and taffeta skirts parted, so their fishnets and translucent black lycra's dangled right into the throngs passing by.

Fog machines oozed stinky clouds onto the dance floor, where two hundred bodies gyrated and swayed — men and women, boys and girls, boys and boys, girls and girls, curious transgendered mixtures of both and no shortage of strays swaying by themselves, each in their own dark little world for the moment, entranced by the place, the music, the crowd, the clothes, the sights, the sounds and the smells, eyes closed and mouths open, enraptured, as if they hovered on the brink of orgasms. It was a sea of bobbing black, where each and every dancer had so obviously fretted and fawned over their outfits for hours, matching this black shirt with those black pants and this black blouse with that black skirt, hair this way, hair that way, combat vs. Beatle boots, stillettos vs. ballet slippers, tights vs. garters, leather vs. denim, chains vs. dog collars, lace gloves vs. blood red nails, just so many choices but all capped off with gallons of makeup, the eyeliner and red lipstick, the mascara and blush and smoky eyeshadow all done to perfection, done to death, done in each and every dancer's own special style, and all of them in the aggregate looking shockingly and depressingly alike.

In dozens of alcoves, couples, foursomes and little cliques of the more jaded clubbers and the hard-core party crowd — the models and the media elite and the youngish Gold Coast dilettantes with too much time and too much money on their hands and too much cocaine up their noses — sipped little shots of iced vodka and snifters of brandy, trying to act above it all, as if they just dropped in to scope out the new place but didn't really care, not really. But for all their feigned disinterest they were dressed for the scene in Neiman Marcus, Saks and Fields black on black, their drunken drugged out eyes taking inventory of the lithe young bodies sashaying past them, unable to hide their highbrow hedonist fantasies of three-ways and silk scarves knotted around wrists and ankles and razor blades fresh from coke mirrors knicking at tender flesh till the blood flowed for flavor and fun and what the hell, it was something new for this tedious farm-futures hole some had the gall to call a city.

Goth rock videos flickered on immense screens, Hammer Horror, cable-ready soft core and underground 8mm fake snuff flicks played on countless TV monitors. Non-stop non-descript music thundered out of a maze of speakers dangling from the walls and the ceiling and in every corner. Up on the stage, half naked Go-Go-Gothic girls and boys danced choreographed routines. Small groups stood transfixed in front of safety glassed cells where actors played out little tableaus: Torquemada's Inquisition vignettes, bathtime in Castle Bathory, DeRais and DeSade hijinks and plain old unvarnished vampire sex and bloodletting that almost seemed quaint by comparison. In darker corners couples groped each other behind the prop shop cobwebs and beneath the fake gargoyles and plaster buttresses, shirts ripping, skirts falling, pants bunching around ankles, their tongues entwined, their hands inside blouses and zippers, pale flesh nipped and sucked as the heady atmosphere let down the last of whatever few of their inhibitions remained, the pretend 'n play heating up till a few slid right down to the floor and humped and bit away at each other with abandon. So little crowds formed around them, reasonably assuming it was just more of Gothique's great big show.

Throughout it all, in and out of the crowd or standing mutely behind the bar and beside the service doors, the vampires watched.

Watched and struggled mightily to keep their thirst in check, to keep their black eyes from glowing red, to keep their lips clenched tight over fangs that ached with agonizing desire — kids in a candy store, junkies in a pharmacy, thieves let loose in the treasury, black lipped mouths unavoidably drooling at the sight, the scent, the imagined taste of all these eager, desperate, deluded mortals around them.

And the hopelessly hapless, happy humans just gazed at the waiters and waitresses and bartenders and bus boys and the actors and bouncers and wondered how they got their makeup down so pat, so perfect, so good you could barely tell it was even there.

Marek stood up there on the mezzanine balcony, gazing out on that sea of bodies below.

And he smiled.

✦

For three hours now, Cass hovered by various doors. Flanking the stage, at the ends of the long bar, by the actors' cells — but each one was watched. Oh, the dancers and the drinkers and drugged out dilettantes might not notice. But he did. He could smell the guards even when he couldn't see them.

The two at the main door eyed him for an uncomfortably long moment when he tried to blend in with the anxious crowd shuffling in, some fellow newborn — maybe just days old, maybe too young to even scent him — and a human in a tacky black blazer and jeans, a pistol grip poking out from under his jacket. But they finally took his just-stolen VIP Pass and let him in. Cass helped himself to a discarded glass of merlot and he was tempted to taste it, but knew he'd be doubled over in a moment, spitting it back up. He held onto the glass for a long time, tried to keep to the shadows, but the club was *all* shadows actually. So he'd probed one doorway then another, biding his time.

But time was running out.

She's here. She's in here somewhere.

Sure, he fled the apartment. Had to. Too dangerous. Colleen so close, drinking herself to sleep on his bed. It was all he could do to keep himself from —

No.

She hadn't been back to work. Hadn't been back home. All her clothes were still there. Her things. Her checkbook, her secret cash stash in her underwear drawer that never really was a secret between them. She hadn't split. She should've but she hadn't cut out. No, not Colleen. Goddamn ballsy take-no-shit Colleen would've come right here, knocked right on the front fucking doors, that's what Colleen would've done.

They must've snatched her. She's in here somewhere.

He didn't know *how* he knew. He just *knew.*

A foursome that commandeered a cabaret table all night finally were too drunk to stay in their chairs. Ushers appeared out of nowhere and quietly helped them back into their coats, slipped purses over their shoulders, all close-mouthed smiling courtesy with every solicitous move. Then the vampires dragged them away through one of the service doors.

And no one paid them one bit of attention. The few people watching immediately dove for the table and flung their own capes, coats and purses over the seats.

Cass dropped his merlot glass and quickly helped the newcomers into their seats. He fussed with the table, gathered up the left behind glasses and acted as interested as he could while he took drink orders. Then he spun away in his mincy best, palming an empty tray along the way.

Try it. Just go for it. Do it now, or you'll never get in.

He headed straight for the door that the vampires hustled the drunks through. Balanced his tray of glasses, grabbed the knob, mind racing, wondering what to do when he would inevitably find it locked.

They've got her. You've got to find her, got to help her, got to...

The door opened.

He walked right through as purposefully as he could.

And no one batted an eye.

No one.

No one, except Gabrielle.

✦

She'd been standing at the mezzanine railing a long time herself. Safely across the way from Marek, but he was so busy gloating over his sea of acolytes that he never even glanced her way.

Gabrielle slugged down the rest of her drink and grabbed another off a tray as a vampire waitress scuttled by. The dead girl never even noticed. Gabrielle took a deep gulp from this glass too and looked back down onto Gothique's main floor. Glaring.

Brooding.

Anyone passing by would've thought to themselves that this low key chick in the plain black shift and shawl and shoes was doing the whole steely-eyed vampire mistress thing a little too-too.

But she had a good reason to glare. A damn good reason to brood.

After they'd left Marek's office, she let Arianne guide her to her own private suite, Arianne's own lair, and even Gabrielle had never been there before. She let Arianne pour her a bath, full of fragrant oils and puffy clouds of bubbles, let Arianne soap her and sponge away the filth and the crusted blood. Let Arianne wrap a luxurious towel around her, hug her tight and pat her down. Gabrielle watched Arianne ruffle through trunks and closets of dresses till she finally selected one, a simple black sheath. Then a plain pair of black flats. An unadorned satin shawl. She let Arianne brush out her knotted hair, let her hold the dress up in front of her and smile approval. "Here, try this on, child. It's a little big on me, but I'm sure it will fit you.

But Gabrielle just dropped her towel and stood there naked, shampooed hair all fluffy and straight, cascading over her makeup-free face, hair still damp and tickling her bare shoulders, curling around her full breasts. "Arianne, I don't want a dress. I want...I..."

"Yes, child?"

"I can't take this anymore, Arianne." Gabrielle fell to her knees. "Please, I'm begging you. I'm pleading, can't you see? How long will you torture me, Arianne? How long will you make me wait? Why won't you stop playing these mind-games? Just do it!"

Arianne lay the clothes on the sofa. She took Gabrielle by the arms and pulled her up off the floor. "Just 'do it'?"

"Yes. Just do it, Arianne. I'd do anything for you. I bleed for you." Gabrielle held up her arms to show off the small wounds on her wrists and on the insides of her elbows. She threw back her hair and ran her fingers over her throat, pockmarked with raw gouges. Then ran her hands over her breasts, where the nipples were edged with crescent-shaped gashes. "I bleed for you. I'll die for you. I *want* to die. I want to die with your lips on my skin, with your teeth in my flesh, with my blood in your mouth. I want to die...with *your* blood in *mine.* I want...I...I...oh, damn it all, just-fucking-do-it."

Arianne stared at her for a long time without moving. Then she took Gabrielle's hand and guided her to the sofa. Slid the dress and the shawl and the shoes aside and lay Gabrielle down.

"Oh, yes, Arianne. Do it. Please, oh please, do it."

Arianne slithered on top of her, all soft icy skin, just like cool, creamy velvet, her long pale fingers stroking Gabrielle's flanks, her belly, then drifting lower. Arianne's lips brushed Gabrielle's, then traced cool moist circles down her throat, her shoulders, her breasts. Her cold tongue licked circles around Gabrielle's nipples, then chose one and settled her whole frigid mouth on it, sucking hard, till the semi-circle wound re-opened and the warm blood began to flow. Gabrielle sucked in her breath, arched her back and felt her hips begin to rock in circles as Arianne's cold fingers danced through the dark hair between her legs, till it moistened, till it glistened, then they dove inside and stroked back and forth and around and around and all the while Arianne sucked on Gabrielle's breast, sucked at the rich red warmth oozing out. When Gabrielle finally came, it was with a scream, her legs slamming the sofa, her fingers clawing right through the tufted fabric.

Arianne sat up, licked the red smears off Gabrielle's chest, then wiped her own lips and chin clean with her hand.

"N-no, don't stop Arianne. Take it all. Drink it all, drain me, then — "

Arianne slid off the sofa.

"No, Arianne! Take it. Kill me! Kill me, please, damn it, you have to kill me, you have to bleed me. You have to!"

Arianne backed away.

"No, you can't do this. Arianne, bleed me, bleed me now. Let me drink from you, let me...oh, man, oh man, you have to, you just fucking have to, oh God — "

Arianne shrieked, clamping her hands over her ears. "Enough!"

Arianne picked up the black shift, the shawl and the shoes. "You'll never, ever use His name in here again, do you hear me? It's blasphemy. My ears burn at the sound." She threw the clothes at Gabrielle. "Dress yourself, child. Go down to see Marek's circus."

"But I don't want — "

"Do it. It's as much your world as it is his. It's certainly not mine."

"Arianne, I — I — but I thought you were going to...I thought...Arianne, please don't make me beg. I need it, I — "

"Never."

Tears started to form at the edge of Gabrielle's eyes.

"I will never 'do it', child. Never."

"B-but...why? Oh, fuck, no-No-NO! Why?"

"You think it's so simple, child. Pick a new dress, move to a new apartment, choose a new lover. 'Kill me, Arianne.' 'Bleed me.' You see all of Marek's lackeys scurrying around in the filthy basements, giddy with their deaths, savoring what they've become, flagrantly welcoming others into their fold every night. Wantonly murdering more and more, night after night."

Gabrielle was sobbing now. "Y-yes, I see it. And I love it. I want to be a part of it all. I want to be one of them. I want to be like them. Like you."

"You could never be like me, child."

"But — "

"I didn't ask for this, you fool!" Arianne paced back and forth now, pounding her pale fists on her sides. "How could anyone ask for *this?* Don't you realize that we're all going to burn in hell for eternity for this? Don't you realize that all of them have forsaken their souls for this? Why? Because of a fashion? Because of some films, some dreadful music? For a fad, for some pathetic little sexual thrill, for some imagined sense of power? And they're all going to burn in hellfire for eternity for it. *We'll* all burn."

"I...I don't believe in all that. And even if it's all...even if that's true, I don't care." Gabrielle's tears soaked her cheeks now. "I don't give a damn. I want it. I want it anyway. It's all I've ever wanted. I know you're old. You look like a kid, look younger than me, but I know you're...what, hundreds of years old? *You've* killed hundreds. Thousands, maybe. So don't tell me to think about sins and souls and devils."

"Devils? Child, *we're* the devils."

"*You've* killed."

"Yes. I've killed."

"So kill *me.* Kill me now, damn it. Do it. Turn me, Arianne. I know you can do it. I know you've done it before."

Arianne nodded, her dark eyes a deeper black than Gabrielle had ever seen them. "Yes. I've done it before. I made Marek. To save myself. Our little bargain: eternal life for him, just to save myself. He happily bargained his soul for this. Though I imagine Marek's soul was sold — and cheaply — long before his stormtroopers and brownshirts raided my little...well, that was all a long time ago. These are things you'd know nothing about. Things you don't need to know about."

Arianne walked to the door, head bowed, shoulders slumping. "Yes, I have killed. Many times. Over centuries, child. *Centuries.* Think on that for a while. And each and every life I took haunts me through all these years. Can you imagine that, little girl?" She halted at the doorway, turned back to Gabrielle. "I've 'made' one vampire, child. And that was Marek. Through him I've mothered more evil and pain and terror than I myself could have hoped to do in all these hundreds of years. I've done it once, but I'll never, ever do it again."

She walked out the door. "And certainly not to a heartless, vicious little killer like you, child."

✦

Yes, Gabrielle had a damn good reason to glare at the crowds down there. Had a damn good reason to brood.

Yes, she saw him lurking there by one of the service doors. Ol' mincy wincy Cass himself, the reluctant vampire. *Him* they turned. Him!

So...

So what if Cass was pretending to be a waiter just now? So what if he slipped through a service door? So fucking what?

Gabrielle looked across the mezzanine. Marek still stood there, smiling down on his dark carnival.

Then a shadow fluttered behind him, and Arianne appeared at his side.

Marek held out his arms, beaming. They spoke to one another, or at least their black eyes did. Arianne glanced over the mezzanine railing. Her eyes widened. She shook her head and backed away into the shadows she came from. Then she was gone.

Marek slammed his fists on the railing. He knitted his brows, focused on the crowds. And a moment later Drake came running up from downstairs. Marek whispered something in his ear, Drake nodded and was off running again.

But he returned moments later, dragging Blair Armstrong. She stumbled, lost one of her designer pumps, dropped her glass, dropped to her knees at Marek's feet. Marek nodded a dismissal to Drake, then stared at Blair. She hesitated for a moment, then nuzzled into him.

Marek's smile slowly returned, and he swung his gaze back and forth across the club.

Gabrielle slunk back from the railing before he looked her way.
So goodie two shoes Cass was sneaking around. So...So what?
So-fucking-what?

✦

Cass could still hear the music and the video soundtracks and the combined roar of hundreds of giddy voices all the way down here.

Gothique was packed with wall to wall Goths and darkwave death-heads and clubbers and more. But back in the hidden hallways, the place was absolutely deserted.

He wasted two good hours creeping around the back rooms, the upstairs hallways, the offices and storerooms on the upper floors. But he never saw anyone, never scented anyone, never sensed a single soul.

He crept down into the lower levels. Passed the reeking chambers where the newborns slept, ripe with an odorous stew of mildewed clothes, old blood and death and worse. He didn't have a watch, didn't need one anymore, but even deep down here in the sub-basements below the old theater building, he could sense that the night was almost gone, that the sky over Lake Michigan had already brightened from murky black to a brighter indigo. How much time was left? An hour? Maybe that, maybe an hour before the first hints of violet would light up the horizon, till splashes of bright pink would brush across the waves.

He came to a metal door, shut tight, padlocks and chains in place. Cass pressed his ear to the metal, heard the heartbeats, heard the labored human breaths puffing out of bruised lips and from behind filthy rag gags and duct tape. Heard the crying, the plaintive screams, the blood drained pleading, the pointless *Oh God, oh Jesus, oh mommy, daddy, oh please won't someone help me, someone help me pleeeeaaassse* begging. His pale fingers clawed the metal, carving little furrows in the door's surface. His nostrils flared. He sniffed the moldy air. But he knew she wasn't inside.

He just *knew.*

There were three more cells just like the first. Each with its own hellish symphony of desperately futile pleas echoing from behind the locked doors.

But she wasn't in any of them. He just knew.

The dark, damp labyrinth twisted off into even deeper darkness. His eyes narrowed, irises flickering with red sparks.

There was one last door.

"Colleen?"

His whisper echoed off the concrete and quarrystone.

"Col?"

Just a whisper, and barely that, but it sounded like a roar down here in the oppressive silence.

"Colleen?"

He heard —

Something?

"Colleen?" Cass raced for the last door. "Colleen!"

The door was locked. Chained.

Cass grabbed the chain, tugged, grunted, fangs slicing right into his lower lip. The half-inch links groaned.

Twisted.

Snapped, links clattering all over the wet concrete.

Cass grabbed the door handle. Yanked, grunted again, skinny arms flexing, empty veins throbbing, then roared from the strain, his eyes burning like hot coals now.

The handle ripped right out of the door.

He clawed it open.

It was a small cell. Pitch black, dark even for his eyes. Water dripped somewhere.

He squinted, scanned the darkness.

"Colleen?"

Something moved.

"C-Cass?"

Cass leaped into the shadows and fell on his knees.

And there she was.

Colleen curled into a ball in the corner, half naked, trembling, shivering in huge seizure shakes just like a junkie two days off a fix. She was covered in bruises and cuts, her T-shirt shredded, soaked with filth, cold sweat and blood. Her underwear, her socks — the same. "C-Cass? Is it...is it really...?"

Cass cradled her in his arms. She shook uncontrollably. Her legs flopped on the floor, her arms dangled at her sides. She felt so limp, so weak, so cold.

"C-Cass..."

"It's okay, Col." He struggled out of his black trenchcoat and wrapped it around her. "Everything's going to be okay." He held her tight, tried to warm her, tried to stop the shivering. "Come on, we have to get out of here."

'N-no. I-I —"

"Come on, Col. We have to go. *Now."* He tried to help her up, but Colleen just fell back in his lap.

"Colleen?" He grabbed her chin. Turned her face to his.

"Colleen?" She didn't answer. "Colleen, come on, we have to get out of here now. There's not much time left. *I* don't have much time left. Colleen?"

Colleen's eyes flung open.

And even in the darkness, Cass could see.

Didn't want to see, but he could, he could see...

"Oh...no. Oh...Colleen, no..."

Colleen Russell's eyes were just dead black opals.

Just like his.

Like...a vampire's eyes.

"No, Colleen, no, no..."

Her mouth fell open and he could see...see the two short, sharp fangs.
"C-Cass?" Colleen's black irises flickered with weak red sparks.
Cass flung his head back and shrieked. "Colleen, no! Nooooooo..."

THIRTY

Jeff had just grabbed his suitcase when the front doorbell rang. He shot Terri an exasperated look and dropped his bag. "So much for beating the rush hour traffic." She just smiled back at him and set her own two pieces of luggage down on the living room floor.

The doorbell rang again.

"Jacks, I think you're pizza's here."

She called from her room. "Dad, I'm right in the middle of — wait, I'll...damn it, lost it."

Jeff shook his head and opened the front door. He took the pizza and the six pack of Cokes and handed the delivery man a twenty. "Keep it."

Jacks bounded into the living room just as Jeff pushed the door closed. "Oh, cool. This must mean you're treating?"

Jeff plopped the pizza box and the sodas in her arms. "No, that comes out of next week's allowance."

"Thanks a lot," she said. "Big tipper on my dough, huh?" She headed for the kitchen, popping the carton open with one hand and palming a slice.

"So you're sure you're okay with this?" Jeff said, following behind, with Terri right behind him.

Terri piped in. "Really Jacks, if it's too weird for you, I mean, we can... "

Jacks' cheeks were stuffed like a chipmunk's. She gulped and swallowed the entire first slice and was already reaching for another while she grabbed a plate from the cabinet. "Can *what?* Will you two relax?" She hopped up on the counter. "Terri, you've been working some kind of twenty four-seven lately, right? Dad's been mooning around here like a lovesick — well, a lovesick something. And his head's swimming with three megabucks offers." She turned to Jeff. "They are megabucks job offers, right Dad? Like, it's not time for a yard sale yet is it? I mean, I'm not having the neighbors pawing through my things for fifty cents a pop."

"They're good offers, kiddo. All three of them."

"Cool. So there." She hopped off the counter and wiped tomato sauce off on her jeans. "So you guys need this little getaway. A little wine, a little song, a little...well, that's a little more than I care to go into."

Terri laughed. Jeff gave up trying to look parental and laughed right along with her. "All right," he said, "But are you sure you'll be okay here all weekend? You got the number where we can be reached?"

"Check, Dad. The Galena Arms B&B. Sounds all bed and breakfasty. Number's on the fridge."

"And Rachel's staying over tonight?"

"Check again. Maybe tomorrow night, too. Her Dad's out on some male bonding let's-blow-Bambi's-head-off deer hunt thing. I don't know what her Mom's up to. And Rory's supposed to have his gang over at their house Saturday night and I'd say that's enough to send her packing."

"And the two of you are staying put? I mean here. Alone. As in no 'guests'."

"I think he means boys, Jacks," Terri said, smiling.

"Yeah, he's so subtle, isn't he?" She turned to her father. "Relax, Dad. You think Rachel would be doing the gals sleepover thing if she had a date this weekend?" She threw her hand over her forehead, all faked anguish. "Sadly enough, the main plan is to wrap up Boynton's CP project. That's what I was working on and a mis-save on that same 'that' was the reason for the 'damn' you so kindly ignored, Dad." She took them both by the arm and ushered them back to the living room. "Enough, you crazy kids. Vamoose. Hit the road. Burn some rubber. You were supposed to be halfway to Galena by now."

Jeff and Terri grabbed their bags and stepped out on the front porch. Jacks hovered in the doorway, waving. "Now don't do anything I wouldn't...well, let's ignore that, okay guys?"

Terri waved good-bye and walked down to the curb to Jeff's Trans Am. Jeff made it halfway down the front walk, halted and then hurried back up the porch. He opened the door, pecked Jacks on the cheek and shoved two twenties in her hand.

"Cool, Dad. I'm thinking video fest tomorrow."

"Just hold on to that for an emergency." He turned, then turned back once again. "That's a Dad thing."

Jacks waved good-bye till the car pulled away. She stepped out on the porch and looked up Karlov, wondering if Rachel was already on her way over. But the autumn breeze had been doubly chilly since the sun fell below the rooftops. She scurried back inside.

✦

Cass looked over his shoulder, made sure no one was watching, then ducked down the alley off Montrose.

Most Chicago alleys were brighter than the streets. But this one was smack in the middle of no-mans land between the Latin Kings and some hillbilly hoods that had been making moves on their turf. The alley lights had all been stoned into shattered glass months ago. He counted three garages then paused by the fourth, the burnt out one with the plywood haphazardly nailed in place over the windows and the door. Looked over his shoulder once more, saw no one, sensed no one, *smelled* no one and slipped inside.

Colleen still lay right where he left her over an hour ago.

Right where he'd set her down nights ago, with the sky flaming a searing orange, with a long and desperate race from Gothique behind them, or at least it seemed long, as long as their feet could carry them with the sun starting to rise, with the acrid smelling steam rising off their bodies. He'd stuffed some old rags and newspapers into the gaps in the boarded up windows then, kicked more trash into a makeshift pile and they both fell to the floor just as sleep overtook them.

And here they'd stayed these past few nights. How many? Two? Four? Cass wasn't sure. He only remembered that the first night he made do with a couple of alley rats, determined not to leave her side. Last night he couldn't fight it anymore and hustled out to the street, hustled up a strung out hustler for himself.

And each night, however many it had been, it went the same with her.

Colleen just shivered on the filthy floor, clutching her arms around herself, clawing her nails into her flesh, teeth chattering non-stop, her fangs shredding her lips. Colleen's skin had gone from pale white to a sickly, ugly ashen gray. She stank, stank like hell, like death, like *real* death, and Cass figured that's what they all really smelled like...without the blood to work its little dark magic.

But Colleen wouldn't drink.

Not the rats, not the inquisitive tomcat that snuck in the garage and just made it out before Cass got a hold of him. She wouldn't join him on the street — couldn't maybe, she was so damn weak — wouldn't have taken a taste from that little hustler if her life depended on it. Which it did. Or whatever the hell this was.

He didn't know what to do, didn't know what would happen. After reading and re-reading all those books and comics and knowing all those songs and seeing all those movies, he didn't have a clue about what would really happen. About what happened to a vampire that wouldn't drink blood.

He was gone a little longer tonight. At first it looked like he would strike out. The streets were empty — not a hustler, not a hooker, not even a stray junkie in sight. Until the Audi cruised the block a second time, until it slowed to a stop at the curb, till the forty-something suburban white collar type smiled and started some inane small talk through his open window, like it was the most natural thing in the world to do with some black clad pale faced filthy creep hanging out on a dark street corner at night in Uptown.

But he did the dope anyway. It was warm in that Audi and the stereo sounded so cool and the leather was so soft, even if Mr. Shirt & Tie — who probably had a wife and some kids at home — was a little soft too. But Cass' cool lips finally did the trick, so the 'trick' was grateful as hell and even asked if Cass would be back on this corner any other nights while he counted out a twenty and ten from his wallet.

Cass didn't feel too bad about slugging the guy or about emptying his wallet. Well, almost emptying it. He left a fiver. But Cass pocketed over two hundred bucks — and just who the hell carried around two hundred bucks at night in Uptown — then Cass scared the dope into utter silence when he leaned over and casually licked the blood running out of his busted nose. Cass lunged then, and settled into climate controlled surround sound calfskin comfort as he greedily drank from forty-something's throat. He left the mope dozing with his head on the steering wheel, engine idling right there at the curb, just waiting for a cop to check him out. Him and his pants around his ankles right there in the drivers seat.

"Colleen, I struck gold. Two hundred bucks. Maybe more. Colleen?"

His eyes quickly adjusted to the darkness inside the garage. He saw her there on the floor, damp newspapers and a black plastic garbage bag pulled on top of her. She still wore only that bloodied T-shirt, the filthy socks and underwear. He could see that her bruises were fading. But *she* was fading too.

Cass tore off his trenchcoat and threw it on top of her. He dropped to the floor and lay beside Colleen, cradling her in his arms. "Money to burn, Col. We can get you something to wear. Maybe get a room for a couple of days, buy some time, figure out what to do, where to go. There's an SRO over on Sheridan. It's not too far. We could make it. Colleen, I'll carry you if I have to."

Colleen didn't answer. She just shook her head.

"Colleen, you're going to have to...why won't you...Colleen you — "

"No."

She had another seizure then, a whole body shaking fit of uncontrollable shivering, eyes rolling back in her head, even the whites kaleidoscoping between black and red. Finally it ended and Colleen hacked up some vile black ooze, some last decayed drop of mortality. She fell back into the trash pile.

"No."

✦

"Want some pizza? It's still hot." Jacks held the front door open for Rachel.

"Just let me in, it's freezing out here." Rachel brushed past, a huge overnight bag in one hand, a garment bag tossed over her shoulder.

"You moving in?"

Rachel dropped the bags on the sofa. "No, but I need something for tonight and something normal for tomorrow and something borrowed and something blue and — "

"Check. Thought you'd never show. So your Mom's really going to put up with Rory and his friends without you to referee?"

"Are you kidding?" Rachel kicked off her shoes and plopped down on top of her bags. "Dad barely pulled away with his beers 'n buckshot buddies and Mom was already dabbing the ol' Chanel No. 5 on her wrists and out the door for 'dinner with a friend'. Rory doesn't have a clue — well, that's not exactly breaking news — but I'm thinking the 'friend' is that insurance salesman who's always hanging around. So I'll expect Mom to roll in about ten minutes before my Dad Monday morning."

"Oh. Uhm...sorry."

"Don't be. Look, you haven't been playing this parent thing right all these years. Mine are still together, in some twisted way, but the guiltier they are the less they hassle me and the child."

"I guess. Well, come on while I shut down."

Rachel followed Jacks to her room where the desk was littered with printouts and the computer monitor glowed. Jacks' boombox hummed with the latest Razor Kutz CD. Rachel headed right for it, twisting the volume dial till the speakers were shaking.

"Well, that's where we're headed, I guess." Jacks pointed to the screen.

Rachel shrugged. "Inside your computer?"

"No, stupid. That's Gothique." She pointed at the screen again. "Or at least as best I can figure." Jacks sat down at her desk chair. "See, these files I've been reclaiming are all some background information on the Palace Theater and how it changed hands like, I don't know, maybe a dozen times. Till finally it was bought for back taxes by some subsidiary of Whitestar Media Group, as in Charade Magazine, only then it changed hands again into some dummy trust that sounds totally bogus, and there's this person called 'Marek' only he doesn't have a last name as best I can figure, or maybe that *is* his last name, and he's on the deed and then he's like suddenly gone and it's — "

Rachel slammed her hand over Jacks' mouth. "Shut-up-and-savor." She whipped out two little laminated cards and dropped them on the desk.

Jacks yanked Rachel's hand away. "Wow." She picked up one of the fake Illinois Drivers Licenses. "My photo sucks eggs, but — *wow.* Major compliments to Rory. These look absolutely real. How old am I? Twenty four? How the hell am I going to pull off twenty four? Let me see yours." She scanned Rachel's. "Twenty six? Who are you kidding? And BTW, how did *you* get such a cool photo? Had some glamour shots done on the side?"

"Perks for the purveyor, pal. Just perks." Rachel leaned over Jacks, spun the mouse around on its pad and closed the file on the screen. "Shut this puppy down while I get my stuff. Time's a wasting, Jacks. We have some major primping to do." She spun on her heel and raced out the bedroom door. "And I expect rights of approval on whatever you're planning on wearing."

Fifteen minutes later the computer had already cooled, the Razor Kutz CD was traded in for a Two Witches maxi-single set on repeat, and Jacks' bedroom, the bathroom and the entire hallway in between were draped in considered-but-rejected combos from Jack's closet and Rachel's bags. Rachel hunched over the bathroom sink in her bathrobe, hips swaying in time to the music, fingers delicately lining the rim of her lips with a darker shade of deep red. Jacks appeared at the doorway, holding up another hanger with a short black cotton dress in front of her T-shirt and jeans. "How's this?" she yelled over the music.

Rachel shook her head. Dabbed one last touch of lip gloss and smacked her lips. "Nope, too Gap."

Jacks returned with another attempt.

"No, too Elvira. Think cool, not camp."

Jacks sat on her closet floor when Rachel finally waltzed in, her face a picture perfect fashion vamp, good enough for any Charade cover. "Tres chic, Rach. A little less 80's Siouxsie Sioux than I expected you to go for." Jacks grabbed a pair of black velvet leggings, looked them over, sneered and threw them to the back of the closet.

"Hey, we're on the hunt tonight, Jacks. I'm not out to scare guys away. I'm looking to reel 'em in." She sat down on Jacks' bed and unzipped her garment bag, upended her duffel bag and emptied everything out on the comforter. "We have this whole house to ourselves for the weekend. Just consider this look my good-time-till-Sunday guarantee." She slipped off her robe, stood there naked and pawed through her things, sorting them into piles.

Jacks looked away and rummaged through her closet some more. "Slow down, Rach. I'm still teetering on the edge of chickening out on this whole deal. You're up for the hunt, I'm on-line with that. But we're leaving it to flagrant flirtation, slow dances — maybe — and trading phone numbers and leaving. Alone. No strange guys are being invited back here for an apres Gothique-adventure party."

"Uh-huh." Rachel hiked her underwear up her legs, smoothed them in place, stuck her thumb inside the waistband and gave them a loud snap.

"I'm serious, Rachel." Jacks threw a sequined black pullover into the growing pile at the back of her closet. She looked over her shoulder and saw Rachel snapping the multiple clasps on a black Merry Widow, all lace and rigid stays with garter straps dangling from the bottom. "And seriously, have you been MasterCarding through the Frederick's Of Hollywood catalog or something?"

Rachel fell back onto the bed. "What, this stuff? Bulletin: this thing's my Mom's, though what the hell she's doing with this I don't know. No, check that. Maybe she has this kind of stuff for her 'dinners with a friend'. You know, she actually borrowed one of my tops tonight? I mean, Mr. Life Insurance and my *Mom* in one of my tops. Mr. Life Insurance and my Mom *out* of one of my tops...ugh. Too gross to contemplate." Rachel grabbed a flat shrink wrapped package from her pile and tore it open. A pair of delicate black stockings fluttered out and across her lap.

Jacks turned around on the floor. "Oh come on, you're kidding right?"

"What?" Rachel rolled up one stocking, carefully dipped her foot inside and then slowly eased it up her leg. Jacks climbed up from the closet floor and plopped down on the bed beside her.

"I'm up for batting my eyelashes for a free drink, Rachel, but what's your game?"

"Don't go Amish on me." Rachel smoothed the black stocking across her thigh and fumbled with the unfamiliar garter clasp. It took a few tries to get it right, a few more to get the one in back. "Guys like these things, you know. You think those girls in the movies and the skin mags pick out their own wardrobe? And anyway, if you think about it, I mean, like, picture the mechanics and all, there are some practical, like... advantages. I mean, like...in the clinch."

"I'm picturing and all I'm seeing is 'slut beacon'."

"I was thinking 'cabaret-decadent', and anyway, if what we saw in the Trib from the Grand Opening is a clue, there'll be as many guys wearing these as gals. It's that whole Rocky Horror nostalgia thing." She rummaged through her pile and produced another package. "Here. 'Nighttime Noir'. It's your shade. Go or it." She tossed the package to Jacks.

Jacks caught it one handed and looked at the model's photo on the front. "Think not." She tossed it back.

Rachel did her other stocking just as carefully and fumbled with the garter just as clumsily. "Your call." She stood up and checked out her long, slender legs. Stood up on tip-toe for effect. "Kind of cool, you know. Can't imagine the olden days though, like *having* to wear this rig all the time." She found her shoes in the pile of clothes scattered across the bed — shiny black pumps, all heel and pointy toes — and slipped them on, wobbling for a moment as she got used to them and to being four inches taller. "Youch. I hope to God that El Stop isn't too far from Gothique or I'm going to be holding onto these suckers just to dance."

Jacks picked up one blouse and another skirt from the pile and tossed them back down with a grunt.

"Oh, enough, girl." Rachel grabbed Jacks' hand and dragged her to the bathroom. "Come on with me and let's at least get your face done."

The maxi-single was on its third repeat as Rachel finally finished Jacks' makeup. "There, all done." She grabbed Jacks by the shoulders and turned her around to face the mirror.

"Rachel, *it's...wow."* Jacks stared at her reflection and couldn't help but smile. It was as good as Rachel's, maybe better. Smoky gray eyeshadow three shades darker than she'd ever risk on her own. Thick mascara and eyeliner turning her big eyes into something lethal. Delicate brushes of blush across her cheeks to make her face more slender, more vampish, and complimenting the deep, shiny red lips perfectly. "I look...I look..."

"Beautiful, kiddo if I say so myself." Rachel leaned over Jacks' shoulder and mugged in the mirror at her side. "Couple of cool vampire chicks on the prowl, huh?"

"Grrr-owl!"

"Now you got it, girl. And since the house rules say no boy-toys welcome back at the bungalow tonight..." Rachel leaned closer and planted a kiss on the corner of Jacks' lips. "Well..."

Jacks jerked away. "Cut it, Rachel. You're creeping me out."

"Oh come on, I'm just kidding." She grabbed Jacks hand and pulled her away from the mirror. "Come back to the bedroom."

Jacks froze.

"To let me pick something out for you to wear, for chrissakes." Rachel tugged and Jacks followed her down the hallway. "Jeez, loosen up, Jacks. Anyway, I'm just saying that the whole scene is kind of transgender ooh-we're-all-so-darkwave-decadent, you know, lezzie chic or gaily-goth or whatever."

"Rach, you're — "

"I'm kidding, kidding, kidding, kidding..."

✦

The El, the subway — those were north side things.

For the most part, trips on either were an adventure for the average Chi-Town southwest sider. It was only a few years ago that the city built the Orange Line out to Midway Airport. Rachel may have been born and bred in Chicago, Jacks spent most of her life here except for the last few years in Encino and they'd both done their share of CTA bus rides. But neither had ever set foot on the El or the subway.

An adventure.

Rachel sprawled out across the last El car's slightly sticky backseat, her black trenchcoat flung wide open so her long legs could stretch out, one shiny black pump lazily dangling off her foot. At least that's how she made it appear. Actually she had to flex her toes just-so to keep the shoe hanging there, but she seemed to enjoy the leering looks she got from the two Latino boys at the front of the car. She shifted in her seat as the train sped on a northeast diagonal through the city, leaving the bungalow belt and Bridgeport behind, cutting through Chinatown now. When she moved, her long black dress parted further. She felt the air kiss her thigh's bare skin, knew immediately that the dress peeled back from the tops of her stockings, maybe was showing off the garter clasps... yep, it was. She could tell by the Latino boys' stares.

"Yo, Rachel." Jacks had to wave to get her attention. "Tramp Alert!"

"What?"

"Close the dress, will you? I don't want vice picking us up before we even get downtown."

Rachel frowned and flapped her dress back over her legs, but that didn't interrupt the boys' staring. The train took a tight turn, making a beeline due north now and both Jacks and Rachel pressed their faces against the dark windows, watching the downtown skyline grow taller at forty miles an hour.

They changed trains in the Loop, Jacks ogling State Street and the glittery skyscrapers till Rachel dragged her down the stairs to the subway. That train shot underneath the rest of downtown and emerged on the Near North side, speeding through Old Town and Lincoln Park with quick touristy glimpses of Armitage and Diversey, Fullerton and Belmont and a lot of other street names that telegraphed where-the-action-is to a couple of overly made up, overly anxious south side teenagers out on a lark. Some gangbangers hopped on at North Avenue but were gone at Fullerton. Two darkwave cadets ambled on the car at Belmont, their backpacks full of books and magazines and CD's spilling all over the seats when they sat down. They nodded to Jacks and Rachel, who both beamed back, like they *belonged,* like they shared something, like it was some really ultra-elite club and they'd just been given the secret sign to get in.

The train deposited them at Montrose and Ravenswood. Rachel scampered down the platform steps, as best as her spiky pumps allowed. Jacks followed a little slower, suddenly overwhelmed by the train and traffic noises, by the narrow, crowded north side streets and the honking horns and rows of garish storefront tavern and peep show signs, by the panhandlers and the hustlers working the curb under the El. They passed an old church, a lonely St. Alstantius statue perched out front in darkness, its floodlights evidently burnt out. Crossed Wolcott, Winchester, came to a stop by the light at Damen. A car full of jocks slowed, the boys hanging out the window, flapping their tongues at them. *Hey, look at Lady Dracula!*

Come on and bite me, ladies.

Yeah, wanna bite on this, girls?

Jacks flipped them off.

Fuck 'em, they're just dykes.

Her mind raced for a comeback, came up empty, so she flung her leg around Rachel, grabbed her chin and planted a sloppy kiss on her lips. Jacks looked back at the boys and smiled, her glossy lips gleaming — their stupid smiles gone now, their mouths hanging open.

"Gee," Rachel said, "I *was* just kidding before, Jacks."

"Oh, shut up." Jacks pulled away and flipped the jocks off again. Rachel struck a hooker pose and was already reaching down to pull her gown open, till Jacks elbowed her. "Rach, better turn it off before they get serious boners."

The boys sped off as Rachel waved good-bye, the cold breeze that coursed down Montrose blowing her coat and the long slit dress open and off her legs anyway. "Just testing the ammo, Jacks."

The light turned green and they crossed the street, heading south on Damen Avenue. "I still say you should have tried those 'Nighttime Noir's', Jacks. And that corset doohickey I borrowed from Amy Wilson, as if *she'd* ever have any place to wear it."

Jacks shoved her hands in her pockets and pushed her leather bike jacket closed. "Mind major if I keep my underwear *under* my clothes tonight. Rach?"

Rachel shrugged. "I'm just saying. Fear not, you look killer. Conservative killer, kind of milk 'n cookies killer. But killer."

And Jacks did. The bike jacket almost reached the bottom of her skimpy dress — a flimsy little wisp of black silk chopped down from Rachel's junior prom gown and left looking more like a slip, a short and startlingly revealing slip at that. As they continued down Damen, she felt her nervousness fade away, felt it replaced by eager, anxious anticipation, felt better, felt one with the night, felt cooler, walked taller, a monochromatic swatch of black, the leather jacket and the little dress ebonied out with black opaques, Rachel's suede stiletto boots, and a studded doggie collar around her throat, compliments of Rachel's collarless-for-the-weekend pup, Sparky — all her makeup and an extra helping of Caron Nocturnes on her wrists and her throat and her chest mostly masking any telltale aroma of poodle.

Halfway up the first block, they caught the unmistakable red glow ahead, pulsing right through the canopy of thinning maples. The immense red gothic letters seemed to float there in the darkness, silhouetting the crowds that milled around below the marquee.

GOTHIQUE.

Rachel stepped up her pace. "Fuck if these shoes aren't going to kill me."

"So slow down."

"Like hell."

The doormen eyed up their fake licenses for a long time. But they finally smiled — leered more like it — and Jacks and Rachel stepped in. They parted with their twenty five dollar covers, the bills sticking in Rachel's fist till one of the bouncers pried hers loose.

"Fear not, Rach. Dad gave me an extra forty just before he and Terri left. For emergencies."

"Broadcast that, why don't you?"

They shuffled through the lobby in line with the rest of the crowd, already feeling the thundering dance music, bass lines rumbling right through the floor and their shoes and up their legs. Already sniffed the fog machine odors, mingling with countless colognes and perfumes and the scent of black leather and sweat and grass and —

And something else. Jacks wrinkled her nose. Smelled something underlying it all, something not so enticing, something musty, something just a little...*off.*

But she forgot all about that the moment they stepped through the doors and into the main hall.

Jacks' jaw dropped wide open. "Oh...my...God."

The guy just in front of them flipped his cape over his shoulder and looked back at her. "God, my dear, has absolutely nothing to do with *this.*"

Rachel's eyes jerked back and forth across a sea of bodies, dancing, drinking, smoking, kissing, snorting, posing, groping. "Want to bet?" She spotted two guys slow dancing, oblivious to the fast paced dance mix, their hands shoved deep inside one another's pants. Fixed on a long haired Goth boy in a dead-on Brad Pitt right down to the colored contacts and translucent blue vampire veins, then locked on another in a picture perfect Edward Scissorhands — fortunately, sans the scissors. "I have died and gone to heaven, Jacks."

✦

They checked their coats and purses, Rachel stuffing some bills in the top of her Merry Widow, Jacks slipping some money in her boots.

Jacks wanted to scope out the performance art cells but Rachel dragged her to the bar, bought two shots and goaded Jacks till they downed them on the count of three, Jacks hacking as soon as the liquor hit her throat. Then Rachel ordered sloe gins for the both of them and dragged Jacks by the hand around the whole dance floor till she'd emptied her glass and stole sips from Jacks'...till *her* glass was empty too.

For the next hour they danced non-stop, first with each other because that was practically a habit if not an actual rule, then with a steady succession of boys and girls or sometimes just by themselves, halfway across the huge dance floor from one another, lost for the moment in their own little worlds. The music never paused, though Rachel finally did and left Jacks dancing away with two skinny but cute black leather boys while she limped back to the coat room and checked her pumps. She was back in a flash, though, sliding across the dance floor in her stockinged feet and picking up where she left off without missing a beat. She pulled one of the leather boys closer, closer still, till their faces touched, their breath steamed in the small space between them, their chests rammed into one another, their legs entwined.

One song stopped, another seamlessly started, but Rachel suddenly pulled out of the boy's embrace. "Come on, I need a breather." Jacks followed her off the floor, leaving the two guys dancing with each other.

"That one was cute but if he stamped on my feet one more time I was going to have to emasculate him. Man, Doc Marten's are real shit stompers."

They waited in line at the bar — the line three deep from end to end — and tried to look interested when they got in the middle of a dreadfully earnest 'Johnathan Frid-Old Dark Shadows' vs. 'Ben Cross-Prime Time Remake' debate, but finally gave up and just stole two drinks when some backs were turned. They ran away from the bar, giggling.

Jacks sniffed her drink. "Yech. This smells like gasoline."

"Looks like whiskey. I'd say scotch."

"Oh, enough with the woman of the world routine. Remember, I knew you when you peed your pants in second grade recess."

Rachel sipped her drink. "Now that's Merlot. That much I *do* know. Here, trade you." They exchanged glasses and Rachel gulped her drink. "Nope, not scotch. Bourbon. And the reason I pissed my Minnie Mouse cottons, Missy, is that you had me laughing so fucking hard when Jimmy Jiankowski spit his Oreos on you. And speaking of pissing my Minnie Mouse's, I'm going to powder my nose."

Jacks shot her a look.

"Figuratively, Jacks. Jeez. Coming?"

"I'm cool. I want to check out those little one-acts behind the glass there."

"Meetcha in ten, then." Rachel glanced at the line winding out of the hallway from the ladies room. "Make that twenty."

She scampered off, chugging down her drink and dropping the glass on a tray as a white faced tuxedoed waiter whisked by.

The crowd at the performance art cells was deeper than the one at the bar. Jacks stood up on tip-toe, catching a glimpse of some pale Goth kids in black monk robes doing a garish Grand Guignol, some kind of ceremonial sacrifice, all bared breasts and black candles and stageblood spilling everywhere. She wandered down the line to the next one and jumped up a few times till she could see over the heads, barely able to make out two amazingly beautiful guys doing some free form ballet in a foggy graveyard set, fake blood splattered all over their white dancers' blouses and tights.

She sipped at the Merlot, decided it wasn't half bad, a lot better than the cheapy wine she shared on that recliner with Brad. And just that thought brought it all back, Brad and the basement party *and Brad* and the scene on that Lazy-Boy chair *and Brad* and the distinct memory of the weird but not at all unpleasant sensations of his hands and his lips and...

The crowd moved on to the next cell, but Jacks stayed, sipping the Merlot, watching the two guys dancing behind the glass, watching them cavort around a huge Styrofoam tombstone, moody blue stagelights shining down on their pale faces and their gorgeous hair *(and Brad)* and their flouncy shirts and their long, slender muscular legs *(and Brad)* and they didn't look fruity in those tights, no, not one bit, they looked kind of sexy *(and Brad)* actually they looked major sexy (and Brad) and with her face pressed right up against the glass, Jacks decided that if she had a couple more of these yummy Merlots in her she'd ask Brad if he'd be game for a little pretend 'n play dress up like those two, if only he was here right now, yes she'd ask him only he wouldn't have those things on for long, yes if only he was here right now, if only he —

"Hey there, stranger. You're going to fall right through the glass."

Jacks froze. *No, come on, did I just wish him here. Did I just —*

She spun around, spilling wine out of her glass.

"Brad?"

✦

Actually it was half an hour before Rachel made it inside the ladies room, not that a single stall was open when she got there.

And after half an hour of listening to the Goth chicks trying to out-Goth each other with their painfully relevant details of this novel or the inside skinny on that band and who had their tattoos done for real and who was too chicken and only sported the wash away kind and who had their dentist make real fang caps vs. who had their incisors redone permanently and some utterly ridiculous argument that sprang up between two catty gals over the comparative merits of Don Calmet's vs. Montague Summers books and which was more accurate while the Anne Rice-only clique kept asking 'who's this Montague guy, he sounds kind of sexy' — after half an hour of *that*, Rachel was ready to pull her hair out. She borrowed a smoke from one girl, copped another from still a different woman, though this one was menthol but she smoked it down anyway just to pass the time. When she finally made it inside the bathroom, but was still waiting for a stall to open, Rachel finally went postal after the three *Nadja* clones to her left got ready to toss punches over which one of the *Subspecies* series was the better flick.

"Goddamn," she hollered. "Don't any of you care about *anything* other than fucking vampire shit?"

Her words still echoed off the fake stone walls, and already Rachel wanted to shrink into a little piece of ladies room lint and just roll away. The entire room went dead silent, two dozen pairs of mascara and eyeliner rimmed eyes glaring at her. But Rachel puffed up her chest, Merry Widow straining, and tried to save face. "I mean, this is all just for laughs, you know? Just some bitchin' bands, just a little dress up time, just to make the dancing cooler and get the guys to wear something other than baggies and backward baseball caps, isn't it? Just something to, like, to give the makeout sessions a much needed kinky edge, you know?"

Every single woman in the bathroom stared at her like she was from Mars. Or maybe from the Evangelical Pentecostals, because of few of them were kind of into UFO's and the X-Files along with the Goth 'n horror, so that Mars thing would've been kind of interesting.

Just then, a stall door flung open and a girl stepped out with the back of her skirt still caught in her pantyhose. A guy stepped out behind her, hiked his iridescent pants up around his skinny hips and zipped up his fly, a smirking 'yeah, bet *you* wish you just got some' look on his face.

Rachel cut ahead of the line before anyone could react and dove into the empty stall. She ignored the yelling and the spike heels kicking on the door. In fact, she took her sweet time, which wasn't entirely intentional, what with her panties getting tangled up in the garter clasps while she tried to keep her shoeless feet elevated off the way-too-wet floor. But Rachel had herself a leisurely time once she was done and fumbling again with the underwear rig, figuring the crowd might change over by the time she got out so she wouldn't have to face the incredulous Goth contingent that heard her little outburst, and maybe she could at least start clean with a fresh group.

When she stepped out of the stall, she was relieved to find the faces looking unfamiliar, though amazingly alike and even more depressingly like her own, if maybe a notch or two less pretty. She rinsed off her hands at the long row of sinks, checked her makeup in the ridiculously tiny oval mirrors over each bowl, standing up on tip toe here because the floor was soaked and it was probably just water here by the sinks, but *still.*

"I agree."

"Huh?" Rachel turned away from the little mirror, satisfied that her makeup was still intact, her purse a long hike back in the coat room and all. "I'm sorry, were you talking to me?"

"Yes." A girl with reddish page boy hair leaned against the wall. She was a little dressed down for Gothique, just a black tuxedo jacket and matching pants. She wore a black silk bow tie around her bare neck; she wasn't wearing a shirt under the jacket. She had the same pale-faced dark-eyed red-lipped look every woman in the club had, though hers seemed all the more smooth, more...*right.*

Rachel did a double take in the little mirror behind her, thinking she saw something, or that she saw *nothing,* but thought nothing of it in the end. "Sorry, I didn't catch what you — "

"I said that I agree with you." The girl smirked, running a pale hand through her pudding bowl of hennaed hair. "Like, what you said before. I mean, *come on* already, everyone. I'm cool with the scene, I dig the bands, but let's get a life, right?"

Rachel smiled. "Absolutely. Hey, *I* didn't get all slutted up just to stand around in the can debating ancient dead guy authors, you know."

The girl nodded, smiling. A bright smile, beguiling. Beckoning.

"So you, uhm, went with kind of a formal wear look?" Rachel said. "It's cute."

"This?" The girl fingered her tuxedo lapel. "Uniform. I work here."

"Oh, *very* cool."

"It's a job. Has its perks. Like meeting some way cool people. Sometimes."

"Better than a donut shop," Rachel said, starting for the door.

But the girl intercepted her. "Hey look, I'm on break for a while. You want to sidestep the literary discussion groups, why don't you come with me? There's a private party going on down in the lower level."

"Lower level?"

"Yeah, I can get you in, if you like. Perks, like I said. You never know if someone big time famous is hanging out there."

Rachel's eyes lit up. "Excellent, that would be — " She frowned. "Well, I don't know, I'm kind of here with someone."

"So you can catch up later. Or just check it out and if you like it you can bring him down and — "

"Her. I mean, I'm here with a her. I mean, my friend. I mean, we're just friends, I don't mean that I'm here *with* her, I mean — "

The girl laughed and the sound was so enticing. Hypnotic little bells, a windchime tingling right inside Rachel's head. "I think I know what you mean. Whatever. You can bring your friend down there if you like the scene. The more the merrier." She slipped one arm in Rachel's, guided her out of the ladies room and past the long line of impatient women staring hopefully at the door. "Cool with you?"

"Cool with me." Rachel extended her other hand. "The name's Rachel."

"Rachel. That's nice." The girl lay her hand in Rachel's.

It was so cold, Rachel flinched and pulled hers away. But the girl just clutched Rachel's arm tighter, ushering her past the crowd.

"I'm Gem."

✦

They'd danced for an hour at least.

Then Jacks and Brad toured the club, twice around and up to the mezzanine where they could look down on the main bar, the dance floor, the entire scene. Brad brought them both more drinks and they leaned over the balcony railing, gazing out across the club's huge interior.

"You know, I really shouldn't drink this," Jacks said, sipping the Merlot anyway. "It's my fourth. And on top of that shot and the gin I started out with...man, I'm...I think I'm getting a little drunk. Nope, check that, I *am* drunk." She swayed away from the railing. But Brad wrapped his arms around her waist and held her tight. He spun Jacks around to face him, their heads close, their lips almost touching. "Uhm...like I said, Brad, I'm pretty...drun-mmmmmmm..." Jacks leaned into his kiss, soft and warm but not stopping there, their mouths opening, their tongues touching, dancing, and it went on and on for what seemed like forever, while the music and the crowds and the scents and the sounds and the absolutely wonderfully warm feeling of Brad's lips and hands swirled around in her head.

Finally they broke away. *"Whew,* have to catch my breath." She gulped more wine. "So, uhm...how'd you get in anyway? Who did your ID's?""

"Don't need any. Not fake ones." Brad shrugged. "They just let me in. I was here last night too. And, uhm...before that."

She nodded, impressed. But not surprised. To her he certainly looked mature enough to pass muster at the door. His plain black suit and black T-shirt seemed so crisp and elegant compared to the cartoonish he-vamps in drag prancing all around the club. Tonight, Brad seemed like a man, not a boy. Not like he did that night at the party, not like all the other guys at school — they were just kids, just little boys, like Rory. Brad was...different. Classier, cooler, only his tousled brown hair and his smooth-as-silk skin giving him away. She reached up and stroked his cheek, savoring the feel of that smooth-as-silk right now. "So, like, what school do you go to? I never even asked you...the last time. You don't go to Curie, I know that." She blushed. "I checked. Kennedy? Bogan?"

He looked past her and down on the dance floor.

"Then, where do you go, Brad? Wait, you're not in college already, are you?"

"So Jacks, where's your friend? The one you came with. That one from the party?"

"Rachel." She spun around and scanned the dance floor. "Rachel? Where the hell *is* Rachel?"

But Brad twisted her back to face him, planted another kiss on her lips and guided Jacks away from the railing.

"Oh well, I guess we'll catch up," Jacks said. "If I know Rachel, she probably fell deeply in lust with somebody on the way back from the john." She finished her wine, left the glass on a table as they passed by. "So where to now?"

"Come on, Jacks. Let's check out those parlors over on the other side of the hall."

"I'm thinking those are like *private*. Isn't that what the 'VIP Lounges' signs are for? Like for hot shots and stuff?"

"And who says *you're* not a hot shot? You are to me, Jacks."

And that was enough for her. She hugged him close and walked right along. "Maybe we'll spot Rachel on the way." Jacks snuggled still closer when his arm coiled around her waist. "It'd be just like her to snag some celeb. Wouldn't surprise me if we find her in one of those VIP Lounges. As if they're going to let *us* in." But with Brad at her side, it almost seemed possible.

They circled all the way to the other side of the club. Medieval arched doorways led off into little parlors, barely glimpsed from the other end of the mezzanine. Each door was flanked by two pale faced, dark eyed, tuxedoed ushers. Jacks halted. "Brad, maybe we should just go back downstairs. We're never going to get in there."

"No, come on." He held her tight and they walked right into one of the parlors, neither usher at the door batting an eye at them.

"Hmmm, not much happening here." The room was dark, lit only by sparse little strings of tiny red lights and a couple of dim fixtures dangling over some creepy paintings that looked awfully old and awfully expensive and, to Jacks eyes, awful. But other than the feeble sparkle from those little Italian lights and the faint glow around the paintings, she couldn't see a thing, not really, but then she didn't really care much either because Brad led her to some kind of fancy tufted chaise — some antique maybe, because it smelled even mustier than the rest of the club. He sat down and pulled her down beside him.

"I don't see any celebs, Brad. Actually I can't see any — " But he was all over her then, kissing her, fingers deftly working the zipper on the back of her dress. Before she knew it, Jacks was spread across the chaise with Brad half beside her and half on top of her, her dress peeled back off her shoulders, one of his hands working the clasp on her bra, his other hand working her dress from the other end as it slid up her thigh.

And for one glorious, breathless moment, she liked it.

Liked it just fine. No boy-toys back to the bungalow for an apres Gothique-adventure party?

Like hell.

In that brief, glorious, passionate moment, Jacks decided that maybe tonight her old bed — the same one she cuddled up in with her Winnie The Pooh when she was five and endured the measles in when she was eight and got her first period in when she was twelve — that ol' bed was going to get christened tonight.

So to speak.

Till her eyes began to adjust to the dark.

Till —

Till the room — and what was in the room — came into focus like a photograph slowly developing, ghosts emerging from the blackness.

Ghosts with scary mime faces.

Ghosts with stark white faces buried in the necks, between the breasts, between the legs of half a dozen half-naked and still some more all-naked bodies. There were guys sprawled across other couches with their shirts hanging by threads, their pants yanked down below their knees. There were girls flopping around on the floor, elaborate black dresses still wrapped around one leg, underwear shredded. There were men and women slammed up against the fake stone walls, stark naked.

And every one of them moaned and sighed in ecstasy as one of those white mime faced things pawed them, licked them, humped them, beat them, fucked them.

Jacks' eyes widened into circles. She broke their kiss, a trace of saliva dribbling down her chin. "B-Brad...what..."

"Oh Jacks, come on," he murmured, his hand working its way under her dress. "Come on..."

They were all bleeding.

All of them — *they were bleeding.* Or being bled. The skinny wraiths that slithered all over them were biting them, lapping up the blood flowing from their throats and their breasts and their wrists and their...

"B-Brad?" This was no performance art skit. This —

Jacks suddenly realized that the darkened room wasn't lit by strings of little red Italian lights at all. The tiny glowing dots were eyes, the glowing eyes on each of the...the...

But, no. No, it had to be the wine. She was drunk, that's all. Had to be, had to. Still...

"Brad," she whispered. "Let's get out of here. *Now.*"

Brad sat up. "What's the matter?"

She looked at him like he was crazy.

He casually smoothed his suit jacket. Looked around the room while he retrieved a slender silver case from his breast pocket. "What?"

She just sat there, stunned, watching Brad leisurely flip open his case, take out a little vial and lay down two neat white lines of cocaine on the lid. He sucked one up his nose then held the case out to her. "Come on, get with the program."

Jacks suddenly felt like she was sitting next to someone else, a stranger. A stranger she didn't think she liked anymore. A stranger she suddenly didn't trust. She felt her eyes start to tear. Felt days and nights of pleasantly naive dreams cruelly melting away. She wanted Rachel, wanted Rachel real bad and right now, right at her side as the two of them got right the hell out here and got right back home as fast as they possibly could.

"You don't want any?" Brad shoved the coke in her face one more time. "Well, then, gotta blow."

And he did.

Brad blew right into the metal lid, spraying the coke right in her face.

Jacks screamed, wildly waving at the sparkling powdered cloud.

When it finally dissipated, Brad was gone.

She sat there alone on the couch. Started to reach behind her to zip her dress back up.

Till she glanced across the shadowy room again.

And saw that everyone was staring at her.

✦

"No, don't! No, oh God, no! I'm afraid of the dark, I — Don't...*don't* —"

"Someone shut the little bitch up or I'll rip her tongue out."

Rachel kept on screaming as the vampires dragged her through another door, down another dark and filthy staircase.

"P-please, oh God, *please!* I w-won't tell, I won't. Just let me go, I don't want to go down there, I don't — "

A pale hand shot out of the darkness and cracked her hard across the face.

Rachel struggled, but there were four of them on her: Gem laughing hysterically as she clawed her nails into Rachel's arm. Fonda, giggling insanely and licking his lips, his skinny fingers coiled around her other arm like a bony vise. Two others, one in front and another right behind, licking their chomps just like they all had been doing since the moment Gem led Rachel through the service door, since the moment they pounced on her, clawed at her dress, pawed her skin, licked her throat till she shivered, tore her clothes till she began to cry — all of them snickering at her in her shredded teenage grindhouse gear — then bit down on her wrist, bit down hard on her leg, her breasts and her neck...till she screamed.

"Please, no, let me go let me go, let me *gooooo!*"

"Sorry honey," Gem cooed, flashing her bloodied fangs in Rachel's face. "But we don't 'care about anything other than fucking vampire shit'." She laughed at that and yanked Rachel along.

They turned down another dark, stinking, hallway. One of the vampires ran ahead and unlocked a door, flung it open and stepped aside. The others dragged Rachel, their cold hands gouging her slick, blood smeared skin. They halted at the doorway. Grabbed her hair and forced her too look up. Rachel saw the cell, the cots, the rows of half naked figures pockmarked with horrible wounds, awash in their own blood and filth.

Gem leaned in close, her white face deep in Rachel's hair. "Let's go, sweetheart," she whispered, then flicked her icy, serpentine tongue in Rachel's ear. "The more the merrier."

Rachel screamed again, and kept on screaming till her throat couldn't scream anymore.

✦

"Girlie? Come on, girlie. Let's wake up."

Jacks' eyes reluctantly fluttered open. "Huh?"

"Come on. We're here."

"Here?" She slowly raised her head, and as soon as she did the pounding started. "Where?"

"Jesus Christ, girlie. 49th and Karlov, just like you said."

Jacks sat up. Tried to focus, then peered through the taxi's dirty rear window. She saw her house a few doors down from the corner.

"You okay? You're not going to get sick in my cab are you?"

She jerked her head back and saw the driver's hand stuck over the seat, palm open.

"And that's $49.50, girlie. I hope you got the money."

Her head exploding with the start of a monstrous hangover, Jacks pawed through her purse. She dropped some crumpled bills in the driver's hand, saw him frown, and remembered the money in her boot. She fumbled with it till she slipped it off, dug out another twenty and handed it to the driver without even looking back. The bill fell on the front seat as she got out of the cab.

She stood there on the corner, trying to clear her head. The taxi roared away and then everything was absolutely silent.

Jacks looked over her shoulder, saw the sky brightening a little behind her. *Damn, what time is it?* She tucked her boot under her arm and hobbled to her house.

She'd only made it in the front door, only dropped her purse and the one boot on the floor when it all came back. Gothique, the crowds, the videos, the music, the liquor —

And Brad. *Brad...*

The lounge, those — those people. They were crazy, they were screwing and drinking each other's blood. They were —

She kicked the other boot off. Stumbled towards the bathroom — *Brad* — hands grinding into her pounding temples. She paused at the bathroom door — *Brad, oh Brad, how could you* — wondered if she was going to be sick, then felt it pass. Wondered —

"Rachel!" She shouted it out loud, and then it really hit her, then it *all* came back to her.

Fleeing from that horrible room, those horrible people.

Searching for Rachel, racing through the entire club once, twice, again, and on that third trip seeing some of those very same faces from the VIP Lounge, seeing them grinning at her, leering at her. licking their lips and flapping their tongues at her.

'Where are you going little girl?'

'Come on back upstairs, little girl.'

Getting her things from the cloak room, waiting in the lobby while the Goths and the gamers and the skinheads and the hard core club crowd finally filed out, waiting while the lights flickered, while the tuxedoed ushers carried the drunks and the drugged out the door and just flung them out on Damen. Waiting out there on the street for Rachel, crying the entire time, not even remembering the right trains to get home. Finally hailing a taxi and climbing in and...

Rachel.

Jacks stumbled to the kitchen. Checked the answering machine and saw one message.

"Thank God." Rachel had gone and done it again. Snatched up some guy with a good enough line or a good enough car and made the most of gals sleepover night. *Goddamn, they were going to have it out when she finally got here.* Jacks punched the answering machine button and fell into one of the kitchen chairs while it queued up.

'Hi Jacks. Just checking in...'

Not Rachel.

Her father.

'Terri and I are here, so I just wanted to give you our room number in case you need to reach me. It's 208. And by the way, where exactly are you? It's after ten so this better just be a video run. Call if you need anything.'

Jesus, Jesus Jesus...she started chanting as soon as the answering machine beeped off. She returned to the bathroom, climbing through the heaps of discarded outfits they left behind, shucking her black clothes into the piles along the way. When she flicked on the light over the sink, she almost shrieked. Her hair was wild mess, her face was streaked with black stripes from the all the tear-stained mascara. Her lips were smeared in a halo of red from Brad's urgent kisses...*Brad, you jerk, how could you...*

Jacks scrubbed it all off, grinding away at her face with her fingers and a washcloth and bar soap till her skin was raw.

She shuffled to her room, ripped off the last of the black clothes and fell back on the bed. She curled into a ball as brightening violet bled through the window. Her head still pounded, a sudden fit of uncontrollable shivers started. Jacks wrapped herself in the comforter, the tears starting to flow again.

"Rachel, where the hell are you?"

THIRTY ONE

4/17: Met N.K. again. Did his usual macho-gangster bit, suggested I keep my nose out of this. No longer a reliable source.

P.S. First time ever he actually scared me.

4/19: Lunch meeting/Spago/Roberta Whitehead. Rambled on (drunk?) about Gothique and Whitestar's involvement. Name dropping. Obvious that Gothique crew have something on her. More: All of Charade up on R.W.'s notorious bedroom hijinks, especially all those poor interns and young MBA's new to the job. But looks like she's all ga-ga over some guy in the Gothique gang now. 'Marek' — first name/last name? Alias? Same name that appeared on Palace Theater deeds and property transfers? Note: Job out background check on this 'Marek'.

Jacks turned away from her computer. She reached for the reheated slice of Friday night's pizza, but left her hand dangling in space over the paper plate because she felt the tears brimming up at the edges of her eyes again.

The hangover was finally gone.

Oh, it was there full force when she finally woke up around noon. When she raced to the phone, checked the answering machine again.

Nothing.

Her head pounded like a cannon when she nervously dialed Rachel's house. When she sighed with relief at the sound of Rory's voice. Yep, their Dad was still away on the hunting trip. No, their Mom didn't come home last night from her 'dinner with a friend', not that he expected her to. "So how was it, Jacks? Was it as cool as they expected? I bet my sister thought she died and went to heaven. Let me talk to her. Hey, can I come over? And Jacks, you guys owe me major for those ID's..."

Rory hadn't heard from Rachel either.

The digital clock on her screen switched from 10:02 to 10:03.

P.M.

Wherever Rachel was, she'd been gone all Friday night and all day Saturday and now into Saturday night.

Rachel was a flirt. Bottom line: a party chick. She wasn't past conveniently losing a friend for a few hours or even the rest of the night for a good time or for the right guy. But not like this. She would've called. Rachel would've checked in. She wouldn't just disappear like this, not for a guy, not for a party, not for...anything. They were best friends. She wouldn't —

Jacks gripped her mouse and scrolled further down this last of the mystery disks' files that she could open, trying, but not succeeding too well at focusing on the screen.

5/13: On the news last night: Steve Fornton found murdered. Gothique's agency Account Manager. Missing a week, body found in condemned CHA high-rise. Sun-Times article hints he was tortured. Cops looking at organized crime, drugs, sex stuff for motive. Note: this makes two agency staffmembers dead in last six weeks. Both on G. team.

5/21: Dinner/La Tour/R. Whitehead/'Marek'. R.W. and 'Marek' practically doing it in the duck l'orange. Marek very creepy fellow. Foreign? Some trace accent. Handsome, yes, but in a slimy way, like a pompous old movie villain type. R.W. obviously wrapped around his little finger. Note: Marek has health problems? Pale, cold hands, ate nothing. Pretended to drink, but 'pretended'...glass never emptied, never even went down an inch. Who does this guy think he is, Dracula? Big talk all evening about Whitestar and Charade tie-ins, sponsorships, etc. with Gothique. Cabbed home, let R.W. leave in limo with Marek. Boo!

5/24: Editorial summer interns start tomorrow. Put to work on background checks, etc.

5/26: Prelim. reports: CBT, CSM and Wall Street sources have no records. No registered U.S. state corporate ownership's, boards, directorships, etc. Checking international sources...

✦

At least she was cleaner now.

No sooner had Cass checked them into the scuzzy two story motel on Sheridan then he'd whisked her into the tub and bathed her himself. Scrubbed her down from head to toe and every place in between, and Colleen wasn't embarrassed, not one bit, even though all the time they lived together he'd never seen her naked, but then Cass wasn't likely to play peekaboo on a naked girl. Anyway, after he'd been wiping up black bile oozing from her mouth and her nose and everywhere else for all these nights — *how many nights?* — it was pointless to start getting modest now.

She was a little past embarrassed.

She was dead, after all.

He disappeared for a little while, took her filthy T-shirt, underwear and socks with him and left her buried under sheets and blankets on the lumpy bed, the TV on with the sound off. But he came back quick enough with a brown paper bag full of clothes from some thrift shop on Broadway. She just lay there while he laid them out on the dresser, and if she was up to it, if she was her old self, *if she was alive,* Colleen would've frowned at all the black clothes: black jeans, black socks, black shoes, black shirt, black jacket. But she wasn't her old self, wasn't up to it, *wasn't* alive, after all. So she just laid there while Cass set the clothes out, while he prattled on to break the silence, telling her how it'd be better in black, how they might be on the lam, might have to hide, how they could melt right into the shadows if they had to.

And then — he was gone again.

Colleen lay there on the bed, wondering if she had the strength left to get up, if she could crawl to the door come morning. Could force herself to just walk outside when the sun came up and roasted her into a little pile of ashes on the parking lot, or whatever it was that really happened to vampires when the sun got 'em, and it seemed to her from the few occasions Cass made her sit through his movies that it was going to hurt like hell, but maybe that was the only way to stay out of there.

Hell, that is.

But it was a moot point.

Colleen Russell could barely roll out of bed to shut the stupid TV off, much less crawl all the way out of the room, with Cass probably trying to stop her.

So at least she was cleaner now.

At least she didn't stink like weeks-old food and swamp muck.

But a fresh soap and shampoo smell didn't do one damn thing about her insides. Her cold, dead insides that were aching and freezing and aflame all at the same time.

It could've been an hour, could've been two when Cass came back.

He wasn't alone.

The guy Cass brought back was one of them.

Not one of *them,* but one of the still deluded, still naive night fiends, decked out in black jeans and shirt, fingerless black gloves, countless piercings connected by little chains and Dave Vanian makeup and dyed hair, done to early eighties post-punk perfection. Just like Cass used to do every weekend.

Colleen just lay there with the blankets tangled around her, silently watching, watching Cass and the guy silhouetted by the parking lot lights, kissing in the doorway, all smacking lips and tongues, urgent hands inside shirts and pants, till Cass kicked the door closed and waltzed him into the room, into the dark, where only the blue flicker from the TV screen lit up their monster faces...one carefully applied in front of a mirror before hitting the streets. The other — all too authentically unreal. The boy pushed Cass away, then smiled coyly and wiggled his pants over his skinny hips and down his legs, tugged off his boots and socks, his erection all pink and pulsing and poking up from his skimpy bikini briefs.

And she could hear him.

Colleen could hear his anxious breaths puffing past his lips, out of his nose, actually hear his nostrils flare with each pensive breath.

But she heard more, could hear his heart beat, hear the blood pulsing in his arteries and his veins and every one of his countless capillaries, hear it gorging his hard-on, hear it pumping, bubbling, screaming out to *her.*

She slammed her hands over her ears but she could hear the kid anyway, hear him unbutton his shirt and tear it off, hear his underwear peeling down, the fabric catching in tiny little whispers on his leg hairs. Colleen smashed her cold hands against her head but it didn't help, she could still hear him, hear *them,* hear Cass fall on his knees, hear them both on their knees, then down flat on the floor, hear their bodies scrubbing the tattered carpet, hear the kid wince and then *ooooh* and then sigh and then she could hear the sucking sounds ...entirely different sucking sounds than he may have come here for, though he was obviously loving every sinfully sweet sensation infinitely more.

Colleen burrowed deeper into the mattress, hands still clamped around her ears, mumbling to herself, singing to herself, anything to blot out those sounds, the sweet, succulent sucking sounds.

Suddenly, the blanket was ripped off of her.

She felt-smelled-knew Cass lay down beside her, stroked her hair, stroked her cheek and her back and she smelled him, smelled it, smelled...

Blood.

"Come on, Colleen. You have to."

"No."

"Colleen, you *have* to. I don't know what'll happen if you don't. It won't hurt him, I swear. He wants it. He —"

And then it was right in her face.

Cass rubbed his fingers all over her mouth and nose, fingers wet with warm blood, smeared all over her face, tingling in her nostrils, sizzling on her lips.

Her tongue.

Her fangs.

It came from somewhere deep down inside. Somewhere she didn't even know existed inside her.

A growl.

A low, rumbling animal sound, all predatorial and hungry and instinctive.

Colleen's hands fell from her ears.

Her fingers curled into claws. Her eyes burned, flamed fiery red as she pulled herself up on the bed. Climbed over the pillows and the blankets. Fell onto the floor.

She crawled across the carpet, crawled through the flickering TV light and quivering shadows, crawled with her mouth hanging open, her fangs slicing right into her bloodless blue lips, crawled to the naked, shaking, wheezing naked body, pallid flesh awash with his own blood, smeared all over his throat, his chest, his belly and his legs.

She hovered over him, the scent drenching her, igniting something inside her, hovered there for just a moment's last indecision till raw hunger overpowered her and she dove down on the boy, her naked gray-white body smothering his, her mouth fixing on the gaping wound in his throat. Her fangs plunged into the pulsing flesh, the fiery wet warmth bubbled up and into her mouth.

Colleen Russell drank his blood.

She drank, and drank and drank some more and when his throat stopped oozing, she slithered across his belly and sank her fangs into his thigh and drank some more, the boy's heartbeat thundering in her ears and blotting out everything else, everything but the blood, but the blood, everything but the blood, but the...

Enough!

"Colleen, stop! You've had enough."

She jerked her head away from the wound, a nick of flesh clinging to the tip of one of her fangs and then flying off into the darkness. Colleen hissed at Cass and then plunged back down.

But Cass yanked her away. She went flying right across the room and crashed into the bed. Immediately back on her feet, she bared her fangs, snarling.

"Enough, Colleen," he cried, words choking in his throat, something like tears clouding his dark eyes. "Enough."

The boy sat up, dazed. Tried to stand, fell once, then finally made it to his feet. He stared wide eyed at the two monsters on opposite sides of the room, their hands twisted into vicious claws, eyes burning, fangs bared, animal growls rumbling out of their throats.

The kid grabbed his pants and his shoes and ran for the door. Fumbled with the knob till he flung it open and ran out into the night.

The glow faded from Colleen's eyes and they went dead black. Already her lips reddened beneath the cold skin. Her gray flesh flushed into a pallid imitation of life, all cool marble white.

"Colleen, you had to stop. You would've...you could have killed him." He turned away. "I — I'm so, so sorry, Colleen."

Her mouth closed over her fangs. Her fingers untensed. She fell to her knees. Raised up her hands, her bloodied hands, and stared at them. Looked down at her naked chest and belly and thighs — all smeared with blood, stark and horribly dark red against her white skin.

Colleen started to shake.

Then she screamed.

Shrieked some horrible hellish anguished wail that was never meant to be heard on earth or in heaven and she shrieked over and over, shrieking in tormented agony and pain and utter damnation.

✦

5/30: Working at home for holiday weekend. Interns dug up reams. Files copied; see Marek/Interpol 1 & 2, Marek/Czech Republic Securiatat Archives, Marek/Prague Holocaust Museum E-mail downloads 1, 2 & 3 for actual text and translations. Topline: German ex-patriot, reasons for expulsion hazy. Multiple citizenship's: Austria, Czechoslovakia, Hungary. Ties to pre-W.W.II Czech and Hungarian Nazi Party groups, Nazi German S.A. (Brownshirts, 'Night Of The Long Knives' etc.). Doesn't make sense. None of this makes sense. Can't possibly be same person. More: Female name keeps popping up in multiple files along with Marek. 'Arianne'. Various surnames/aliases: Arianne Stephanovich, Ariadne Stedtmeinster, Anne Stephan, Arianne Stevens, etc. etc.

Jeff slammed the phone down and stomped back into the living room, right past the suitcases and little bags of souvenirs laying forgotten all over the floor.

"They're still not home," he said, shaking his head. "I called their neighbor. Rory's going to stay there for the night unless his parents come back." He turned to Jacks, a curious mixture of fear and disappointment and anger twisting up his entire face. "Why? Why, Jacks? Why in the world would you lie like that? Why would you two do something so stupid?"

But Jacks was still crying. Curled up on the couch, wrapped in Terri's arms, and crying.

Crying just like she had been since the moment Terri and Jeff came back from their weekend trip, bustling in through the front door all smiles and happily hollering *'Jacks, we're home'*.

Crying hysterically like she had been ever since, crying since she broke down and told them all about the Friday night trip to Gothique, about waiting for Rachel, about Brad and the strange room, about waiting by the phone all of Saturday for Rachel to call, and all of Saturday night. And Sunday morning.

And afternoon.

And evening.

Terri eased Jacks back on the sofa and then stood up. "It's not quite 48 hours yet, but she's a juvie. Jacks, is your friend 18 yet? Jacks? Well, whatever, I'm going to make some calls. But I don't know what good it will do. This is a big town. A kid wants to get lost, wants to hook up with some bad crowd, there's no telling where she could be." Terri started for the kitchen, but stopped beside Jeff. She lay a hand on his shoulder. "Don't be too hard on her, Jeff. She's scared. She needs you right now."

He nodded as she left for the kitchen.

Jeff sat down next to Jacks. She looked up at him. Looked away, shame blushing her already reddened cheeks a darker red.

Jeff reached out. Paused. Then wrapped his arms around her and Jacks melted right into him.

"Oh God, oh God, I'm so sorry, Dad. I'm so, so sorry. We never thought...I never...and now, now I don't know if she's just off somewhere in over her head in some scene or if she's really in trouble, and all that sick stuff going on there at Gothique and t-th-then all that stuff I found on th-those files, and..."

"It's all right, honey. Everything's going to be all right. I promise."

Jacks looked up at him again, her face filled with hope, and to Jeff's eyes she could just have easily been six years old and crying over a broken toy, a skinned knee, a spill from the monkey bars. He hugged her tighter still, seeing the sudden certainty in his daughter's eyes, the absolute confidence that everything really *would* be all right, that he could make it all better, that he could fix it, fix everything because that's what father's did.

Only he didn't have a clue what to do or even the slightest hint where to start.

"Now Rory said their father's off on a deer hunt. Up in Wisconsin or somewhere. That there's no phone in the hunting lodge. Did Rachel tell you anything different? *Any* way we could get a hold of him?"

"No." Jacks wiped her eyes and her cheeks. "We just didn't talk about it."

"Okay. Now her mother went out to dinner Friday night and she's still not back on *Sunday?* Jacks, it's after nine PM, I mean — "

"Dad, Rachel's mother didn't go to 'dinner with a friend'. Best as Rachel can figure she's having an affair or something. She could be anywhere, Dad. They're...it's not like here, it's not like us."

He nodded.

"All right, now all this other stuff. These files. Jacks, honey, why the hell didn't you tell me you had them? Didn't you know Terri wanted these? That they could be something important? These were Megan Russell's. You know what happened to her. She may have been murdered. Those disks could be important evidence, something the police could use. Honey, didn't you think?"

She shook her head and the tears started flowing again.

"All right, well...still, I don't get it. What has you so upset with those files? I glanced at some of it, but it's all just — "

"W-what did you look at, Dad?"

He shrugged his shoulders. "I don't know, some property tax records, transcripts of deeds. Reports Megan had someone working on. It's pretty weird stuff. I'm more certain than ever that Charade and Whitestar have been tied up in some shady deals."

"Guess y-you got out just in time?"

Jeff nodded. "Guess so. But — "

"You have to see the rest, Dad. Terri too."

She dried her eyes, took Jeff's hand and led him back to her bedroom.

Jacks sat down at her desk, clicked the mouse and scrolled through the files she'd opened Saturday. Jeff read from over her shoulder, still disinterested at first, still more worried about Rachel and how to find her parents and just how close Jacks might have come to serious trouble. He was still confused as they scrolled together through Megan Russell's notes.

6/4: Whitestar VIP tour of Palace Theater renovations. Roberta Whitehead (on Marek's arm the whole evening), EVP's from broadcast media division, SVP's from new entertainment subsidiary, Charade Operations, Whitestar Legal, Finance and MIS. Turning theater into some kind of horror show theme park, reminds me of the old Limelight club on Ontario and Dearborn. All for the Goth Rocker scene? (Is there any money in that?) News: Marek has whole entourage, each creepier than him. All obviously heavy into Goth scene by the look of it. Halfway through tour, young girl makes an appearance, obviously surprised Marek (who's normally very in control). M. very agitated. They argued, girl ignoring all of us, Marek very embarrassed. Tour ended immediately, all of us ushered out. Except Roberta.

Girl's name: Arianne. (!!!!)

6/15: At office till 10:30. Last copy routings for current issue, pizza & proofing meeting with Jeff. Had late night visitor after Jeff left. Arianne! Same Arianne from Gothique. And now I know. Same Arianne from international info interns dug up. All confirmed — Marek, his entourage, they're all...No. Too much to believe. Can't write now. Note: Tell Jeff about this?

"My God," Jeff said. "She *was* in trouble. Megan was in trouble and she didn't tell me. Or didn't get a chance to. My God."

Terri appeared in the doorway. Jeff and Jacks looked up hopefully.

"Well, I called in a couple favors. Juvenile Division. Missing Persons. I've checked in with Central and Hom — " Terri paused. She stepped into Jacks' room and sat down on the bed. "Well, I checked in with Homicide too. Nothing. Or at least nothing on anyone even remotely resembling Jacks' friend. At least that's good news." She turned to Jacks. "Honey, didn't Rachel say *anything*, anything at all that might clue us in on where she could've gone to?"

But Jacks just stared at the computer screen. "No. I've called everyone I could think of, all our friends, every guy she dated in recent history. Rachel — well, Rachel's kind of good time gal, you know? I mean, she could have hooked up with someone, headed off to some party, went for a ride with some guy, sure. But not for two days. No way."

"I believe you," Terri said. "Well, some cops will start checking the hospitals. Check some of the suburban police departments too."

"Send someone over to Gothique." Jeff reached over Jacks and scrolled the mouse down another page. "Why can't you just send some cops over there right now?"

"Why there?"

"Why *there?* Because that's where they went. Because that's where Jacks last saw Rachel."

Terri shook her head. "And do what? Jeff, there could have been a thousand people there Friday night. More, I bet. And another thousand there last night. A bartender's going to recognize some teenage girl's photo? Which, by the way, won't look anything at all like she actually looked Friday night?" Terri paused, looked like she was trying to collect her thoughts. Trying to assume a professional air.

"Look, these two were probably decked out like the rest of the Goth crowd. No one's going to remember one kid out of two thousand. But you're ignoring a hundred much more likely scenarios. Jacks' friend fell for some guy, and she's off making the most of it, stretching the weekend since her parents are away. Or she bumped into some friends, got whisked off to some weekend long house party and is sleeping off one hell of a big hangover across town right now. Look, I and every other cop would like to get our mitts on kids like her and spank their asses till they can't sit down till college and then ground them in their rooms till they're married off. Jeff, you have to understand, this stuff goes on all the time."

Jeff digested all that. Reluctantly. Then he pointed at Jacks' computer. "You're probably right. I hope you're right. But have you seen any of this?"

"Some." Terri sat up at the edge of the bed and looked at the screen. "I sure wish I had this stuff to turn over to the Megan Russell investigation weeks ago. I should have taken these disks right at the start."

"How? We couldn't open them at the office, Terri. My best service bureaus couldn't tap into them. Your people wouldn't have done any better. Took a high school hacker to get somewhere. But Terri, just look at this stuff."

6/17: Nicky Kolitzky calling all day. Threats on voice mails. Says Marek wants to see me. They know I've been investigating. Two summer interns working on this haven't shown up for work for four days now. No answer at their apartments. Arianne warned me two nights ago — to stop. To go away, leave town, go underground immediately. Could take no responsibility for what happened if I don't. Doesn't make sense — she's just a kid, or looks like one at any rate. 18? 20? No older than the interns. But...if it's all true, if—

Detective Terri Shepherd drew closer and closer to the screen as she read each word. Till she grabbed the mouse from Jeff's hand and scrolled back and forth through the pages on her own. "Damn. I knew it."

"Megan was murdered, Terri. Wasn't she?"

Terri nodded.

"You knew all along, didn't you?"

"Jeff, I've told you a million times. I'm not Homicide. I'm I.D.D. I heard things, sure. Damn it, I should've taken these disks right away. I knew I should have."

Jacks started crying again, harder.

Jeff shook his head. "Advanced Computer Programming project. Jesus."

"But guys, look at this stuff," Jacks said. "You haven't seen the weirdest. Or the worst. Just read it."

6/18: Already trashed all files in office computer. Will trash all in laptop after copying all files onto disks. No, no time. Will copy essentials only. Leaving town tonight. Send disks to — who? Cops? D.A.? A priest, for God's sakes? Heading to L.A., vanish there for a few weeks. Watch what happens via papers, internet. Maybe will blow over. Someone else has to see what's going on. I can't be the only one, can I? Send disk, send disk to...to Jeff! He'll hold onto files. Contact from L.A. Can trust Jeff.

It's all true. Everything I was already guessing, everything Arianne told me. They're vampires, for God's sakes. Fucking fangs and capes and coffins vampires. Gothique will be a front for them. Hide behind the whole Goth Rocker scene. They have Roberta Whitehead, they've been building their ranks for months now since they arrived in Chicago. They're VAMPIRES!

Jeff, if you're reading these files, I haven't gone crazy. Get them to someone official, someone in law enforcement, SOMEONE YOU TRUST. I can be reached at A&M Arms Motel, 233 Yomeda Blvd. L.A. till next Thursday. After that, I'll get in touch with you.

THEY ARE VAMPIRES. For real! Copying now, then have to go.

Vampires...

The three of them sat there in silence for a long time, staring at the screen, staring at that word, just eight innocuous little digital Times Roman letters. But together, they looked ugly. Malevolent. With Charade and Colleen and Rachel and Gothique and all of it put together, the word just looked like pure Evil.

Vampires...

"I knew it," Jeff said. "I swear, I knew it. I just thought it was too damn crazy, but inside, deep down inside, I knew it."

"Dad, it *can't* be. It's crazy, it's — "

"Your Dad's right, Jacks."

Jeff and Jacks both spun around and stared at Terri.

"He's right." She plopped back down on the edge of the bed. "Well, he's partially right."

"Terri, what the hell are you talking about?"

"About Gothique. And everything you see there in Megan Russell's files. Whitestar, shady deals, blind trusts and the Palace Theater, all of it. Enough stuff's gone on there to put half of Whitestar senior management away for years. The police, the D.A., the state's attorney, the Feds — they just could never get the goods on them. Or people high enough up got enough payola to turn the other way. Maybe with some of these files to heat things up again they can finally make something happen."

"Right," Jeff said. "But...*vampires?*"

Terri shrugged. "Oh, Jesus, not *real* vampires. Not like ghosts or anything. No, but this Marek person, his little entourage — they're all vampires, all right. S&M freaks, blood fetishists or a cult or something like that. Homicide's absolutely certain that at least some of them are responsible for some unsolved murders. And not just here in Chicago. There's stuff dating back a way in other states — hell, back in Europe too. But they've never been able to link anyone directly to a specific crime."

"No, there's more to it than that, Terri." Jeff started to pace the little room. "That business with Colleen Russell's friend. Cass. His photo from the morgue. And that snapshot I took of that man going into Gothique. Christ, that could've been this 'Marek' guy." He shivered. "And people just...just disappearing. Gabrielle. Kelly Feeny. Colleen's roommate. Even Colleen now. She hasn't been to work in days. Hasn't answered at home. And now Rachel."

"Terri, you weren't there," Jacks said. "You didn't see those people. In that horrible room. A cult? I don't know." She sucked her breath in. "My God, I might have...and Brad, he led me right in there, left me with them." Jacks jumped off her chair. "Rachel! What if they have Rachel, what if...oh my God, they — "

Jeff started to respond, but the doorbell rang and all three of them bolted from the room.

"Dad, maybe it's Rachel, maybe she — "

Jeff got to the door first. He looked out the little window, but couldn't see anyone there on the porch.

Terri raced up behind him. "Jeff, who is it?"

"I don't know."

He opened the front door slowly. Scanned the darkness. Reached behind him for the wall switch and flicked on the porch light as he eased open the screen door.

'Turn that light off. Please.'

"Who's there?" Jeff opened the screen door all the way. Terri shoved Jacks aside and tried to grab Jeff, but he already stepped out onto the porch.

'Please, Mr. Stancheck. Turn the light off.'

That voice...he'd heard it before. Heard it and...

'Jeff?'

Another voice.

And this one he recognized right away, even though it sounded different.

Very different.

'Jeff, please. Turn the light off.'

"Terri, turn the porch light off."

"Jeff, I don't think — "

"Do it!"

She turned the light off.

The porch went black again. The cool night breeze blew a whiff of something musty and floral, something old, something ripe across the front steps and right in the front door.

A shadow emerged out of the darkness. A face appeared. Pale, dark eyed, huddled inside a black trenchcoat's upturned collar.

Jeff flinched. His mind raced, knew he recognized the face — or almost did, because it was different now. Knew he recognized it though from a long night at a Gold Coast Funeral Parlor, months ago, standing beside Megan Russell's closed casket.

"Cass?"

The figure nodded.

Terri shoved Jacks back inside the door and ran back to Jeff's side.

And then that other voice spoke. The one Jeff knew, the one he immediately recognized no matter how different it sounded now.

Another shadow fluttered down at the foot of the steps. The darkness swirled like black fog, barely audible footsteps brushed the concrete stairs. Long, wavy red hair blew back in the breeze to reveal a shockingly white face, a pair of perilously dark eyes and a glistening red mouth, the tips of two sharp fangs protruding just over the lips.

Jeff grabbed Terri's hand, uncertain for a moment if his legs would buckle, if he'd go tumbling down off the porch and right into the darker than dark shadows.

"Jeff, I...I'm sorry we came here. But...well, we have to talk. I didn't know who else to go to."

"Colleen?" Jeff's head swam, but Terri gripped his arm and he steadied himself. "Colleen, is that you? Oh, Jesus no, Colleen..."

✦

He was consumed with guilt.

Plain old fashioned Catholic guilt, the worst kind there was, the kind that reeked of Venial and Mortal Sins and Penance and took truckloads of Sanctifying Grace to cleanse away.

Father Gil Silverez sat in the back of the Clark Street Bus, his parka pulled up tight around his neck to hide the telltale priest's collar. Bad enough the bus driver and the few night shift cleaning ladies glared at him while he slugged down huge gulps from the pint bottle of no-name whiskey. They didn't need to know he was a priest as well.

The bus inched along north on Clark, stuck in the middle of bumper to bumper traffic. Cars double-valet-parked in front of trendy restaurants and watering holes, cars stopped right in the middle of the street while the drivers bartered through their windows with the prostitutes, cars slammed on their brakes to avoid the teenage hustlers and junkies, some pausing instead to conduct a little quick business.

That it was *Sunday* night only held some small measure of irony for Father Silverez. No one else seemed to care.

Of course he'd meant to be safely back in the rectory by dinner time.

Or by sundown, to be more accurate.

It was his own fault that it was nearly eleven now and here he was stuck on this bus, with a long walk down Montrose still ahead of him. His own fault — no one *made* him step into the little tap room on Chicago Avenue after his meeting at the Archdiocesan Offices behind Holy Name Cathedral. That meeting was brief enough, though the message was also clear enough. The little Diocesan ferret — probably just two years out of the seminary, probably never dug into his own pocket for a sawbuck for a parishioner, probably never baptized a premature baby that wouldn't have a chance to see morning, probably never held an old lady's hand through the last rites and tried to get her to pray through two more hours till the next morphine shot arrived while the cancer slowly ate her insides out, no probably not — that little ferret sat there behind his desk and told Gil in no uncertain terms that they'd received several less than complimentary reports on him. That they'd heard about his sermons, about his warnings to the parishioners to stay inside after dark, to keep their windows locked, to never, ever answer the door after sundown. That they'd read his memo on the librarian's murder and an incident in a gangway (when he was on his way back from a tavern card game no less — oh, they knew all about those little details) and about the new nightclub that opened up in his parish. That the memo had been passed along to the Diocesan Rehabilitative Ministry, which Gil and the ferret both new meant the Church's hush-hushed exurban nut house.

Gil let the little punk trot out all the entries in the dossier, then smiled and assured him he'd pray for the strength to get his parish and his own act together. Then he fled from the Archdiocesan Offices and down Chicago Avenue to the little tap room, where he shared the no-stools bar with a depressing delegation of drunks, delusionals and derelicts, each as absorbed in their own little world as he was. The Bears Sunday Game was on, but Gil never paid attention to it, no more than the others at the bar did, and he finally bought himself the pint of unknown-origin booze for the ride home once the post game show started.

But the shots in the tap room and the slugs from the pint didn't do a damn thing to solve his own little personal crisis of faith. Anymore than the nightly novenas and repeated rosaries on bended knee before bed time. Litanies or liquor, they both left him confronting the same thing: the starkly terrifying image of a middle aged priest trudging down Damen Avenue to knock on the door of that awful place, a lonely hopeless priest standing under Gothique's marquee in his Sunday best Chasuble and Alb, Holy Water sprinkler loaded, Cereborium full of blessed Hosts all ready. A lonely and not-too-nimble-anymore priest standing there quaking with sheer terror till the white faced monsters woke up and dragged him inside and down into some black pit of pain and perdition.

But he knew he had to do it.

If not tonight, then tomorrow. Or the next day. He couldn't keep putting it off. Couldn't wait till he found Frank Hoelevich drained and cold dead in the two flat's second floor kitchen. Till some other sweet and hopeful librarian — or a store clerk or one of the streetwalkers or a school teacher — was hung up like a carcass and tortured and bled to death. Till who knew how many more kids died, how many more souls were condemned to an unbelievable and ugly nighttime existence that they might have thought mighty cool in their stupid books and their ridiculous movies, but was really just leaving one foot on earth while the devil held onto the other down in hell.

He had to do it.

But not tonight.

No, not tonight. He was drunk. Or close enough. And it was dark already. They were all awake now.

No, not tonight. Not yet. Dear God, not yet.

Father Gil Silverez repeated his own special 'God give me strength *(Dear God, not tonight, not yet)*' litany from the Clark Street bus stop, and kept on repeating it all the way down Montrose after the pint was emptied and tossed in the trash.

The night was cold, the breeze was brisk. Enough to send all but the most determined of Montrose's hustlers and dealers into the round-the-clock diners, donut shops and taverns. None of them ever hung out in front of Gil's Church anyway, as if the benevolent but stern face of St. Alstantius — just carved out of marble, of course — kept those couple hundred feet of Montrose Avenue marginally sleaze-free. So the street was deserted as Gil stuffed his hands in his parka pockets, the chilly wind already clearing his head of the alcohol haze, as he looked up from the sidewalk and approached the wide front staircase and huge twin steeples of St. Alstantius Church.

They were waiting for him.

His feet froze.

There they were, waiting for him.

Right out in front of the Church. *His* Church.

There'd be no lonely priest shivering in fear under Gothique's marquee now. No Holy Water sprinkler ready to be lobbed like a grenade, no Cereborium full of holy ammo. And no more need for rye or no-name whiskey or novenas to beg God to delay another night.

Time's up.

The battle was on whether he was ready or not.

There they were.

The vampires hovered just outside the streetlamp's halo, huddled there in the darkness, dodging the occasional flash of light from a passing car. They saw him, and he saw them, and they stepped across the sidewalk, smirking.

"God, give me strength."

Father Gil Silverez started walking again. His first couple steps achingly, tremblingly slow. Then surer. More deliberate. "God, give me strength." He took his hands out of his pockets and they instinctively tightened into fists. Gil walked right towards the Church, wondering for a moment — the way a condemned man's mind might wander as he took those last few steps — what the Archdiocesan ferret would do now.

As he approached, he caught a flash of something at his side, and noticed two more of them stepping out of the shadows behind the St. Alstantius statue. Those two fell into place right behind him.

Finally Gil halted in front of the church's wide staircase. "God, give me strength."

"Aw, you'll need more than that, padre."

Two more. Gil recognized them immediately. From that awful night — it seemed so long ago now — that night in Frank's gangway. There was that very same boy. And the girl too. She was one of them now. Of course she was. She probably had been begging for it that night. They both lounged there on the top stair, the girl's head in the boy's lap, both of them smiling, leering, their blue-red lips peeled back from long, ugly fangs.

"Don't you dare defile my Church. Get off of there right now."

The girl slid off the boy's lap and started down the stairs. But the boy grabbed her and yanked her back.

"*Your* church, huh?" The boy got up. The other vampires closed ranks around Gil.

"Maybe we don't feel like going anywhere, padre. We kind of like it here. This big old building going to waste with just one little priest? Doesn't your church keep up with things? Times is tough, old man. You got your poverty, your addicts, your jobless, your homeless. I'm thinking you could squeeze quite a few in here." He took a threatening step down the stairs towards Gil. "I'm thinking *we* could fit quite a few in here."

"Get away from my Church!"

"Oh come on, padre, why don't you stop kicking and just join up? Everyone is. Well, practically. I personally guarantee you all the altar boys and school girls you could want. I mean, with the little plaid skirts and knee socks and the whole routine. That is what you'd want, right? Don't all priests — " The vampire paused. Sniffed the air. "Oh, I get it, got yourself a different little habit, do you? Well, we know all about habits and addictions and stuff. Really, you got yourself a big ol' thirst, we can satisfy that. I mean, maybe not booze, but we have something lots better. What do you say, padre?"

"Never! Get out of here. I'd rather burn in hell for all eternity."

"Maybe we could arrange that too, padre."

Gil ripped open his parka and the top of his shirt, his white priest's collar flying off into the darkness. He dug inside and grabbed a little crucifix from around his neck, tore it off the chain and thrust it out at them.

"Get out of here!" He waved the tiny crucifix at them. The group on the sidewalk almost fell over themselves as they dove for the shadows. "Get out of here and await God's judgment for your sins. All of you." The two vampires behind him flung their hands up and hissed, but they held their ground. Gil backed away, made for the steps, first thrusting the cross at the two vampires following behind him, then at the boy and the girl at the top of the staircase. When he made it halfway up the stairs, the girl screamed, leaping off the stairs and tumbling down onto the sidewalk. Gil shoved the crucifix at the boy —

And he just smiled.

"Oh, padre, you've been watching too many movies."

Gil gripped the tiny cross tighter. "Don't try to deceive me, devil. I know what you are." Gil made it to the top step, keeping a wide space between him and the vampire, then backed towards the church's front doors. "I've seen your movies. I know all about it. This Cross — it may just be a symbol. It does nothing without faith. But I have faith."

"Yeah, padre. I seen that one too." The vampire casually leaned back against the railing. "Pretty cool flick, didn't you think? But I think they lifted that 'gotta have faith' thing from some novel. Stephen King maybe. Whatever."

Gil continued backing towards the church's front doors till he bumped right into them and dropped the crucifix.

The vampire lunged, but Gil did too and caught the cross before it even landed. He held it out at the vampire, then fumbled in his ripped parka for his ring of Church keys. Reached behind him and fumbled with the door handle.

"Hey, not bad. For an old guy. And an old guy that's been tossin' back a few today by the smell of it. Almost had you there, padre." The vampire paced in predatorial half circles, just a few feet away. Two others held back just a few stairs down. "Look *Fadda,* some of us have a lot of respect for all that stuff." He jerked his head back towards the group still huddling in the shadows, and then at his girlfriend, skulking down at the bottom of the stairs. "Cases in point. I'd say they take it all pretty goddamn seriously. The bread and wine and the incense and the saints and all of it. Crosses and holy water — hell, you name it, padre."

Working his hands behind him, Gil got the right key in the lock, fumbled some more, then unlocked one of the front doors. "All of you, get back! Go back to your dark holes and wait for God's judgment!"

Two of the vampires down on the sidewalk dutifully turned away and started down Montrose, their smiles gone, their eyes darkened. The girl slithered off into the darkness.

Gil inched the door opened behind him, still holding out the crucifix.

"Yeah, padre. Like I said...cases in point. Hell, you could've told them to shove a fuckin' stake up their ass and they probably would've done it, you holding that cross and all." The vampire stopped circling. He just stood there, and he wasn't even smiling now. "But see, some of us, well, we were deprived kids, you know? Our parents never took us to church like they should've. Or sent us to Catholic School or CCD or Sunday school or nothing. Too busy screwing the neighbors and sleeping off their Sunday morning hangovers, I guess."

Gil opened the door all the way and slipped inside. The familiar fragrance of blessed incense washed over him immediately like a protective mantle. Faint colored light from the banks of vigil lights and the sanctuary candles behind him spilled out onto the staircase. "Leave now, devils. Vampires! Leave before you finally incur God's wrath!" He stepped inside the vestibule and slammed the door shut in the vampire's face.

"I wasn't through, padre." The vampire's voice still came through the door. "All that 'gotta have faith' business? See, I'm thinking it works both ways. *You* may believe it all, but what happens if *we* don't?"

Gil felt a chill on his neck, smelled something awful mixing with the fragrant incense.

"Sorry, padre."

He whirled around.

And saw vampires rise like black wraiths from between the pews.

THIRTY TWO

"This is so stupid."

Terri eased into the Montrose exit lane and guided her unmarked police issue white Caprice off of Lake Shore Drive. Fog rolled in from Lake Michigan, obscuring the park and the beaches on their right, swirling around the cars backed up at the stoplight ahead. "This is just so stupid, Jeff. We have to leave this to the professionals."

Jeff fidgeted beside her in the passenger seat, never comfortable in someone else's car, with someone other than himself driving. Even if that *was* Terri, a police detective and in her own cruiser. *"You're* a professional."

"I know that. But it's not like I'm a regular cop, Jeff. I'm just — "

"Inter-Departmental Division, yes, I know, Terri, I know. But you're as close as we've got to a 'professional' right now. And no one else in this whole goddamn city seems to get it. Or care."

The stoplight went green and the traffic slowly edged forward, turning left into the Montrose underpass and then vanishing into the fog. They inched forward, just in time for the light to go yellow, then red again once they reached it. "Damn." Terri slammed the wheel. "This is just so stupid."

"She's right, Jeff."

Colleen spoke up from the back seat. And just the sound of her voice made Jeff shiver. It sounded like an echo from some dark, frigid cavern instead of the back of the car. All the way up the Stevenson Expressway and Lake Shore Drive, neither she nor Cass said much. Jeff could have almost forgotten they were sitting there in the back seat. He'd figured out by now that a glance in the rearview mirror revealed nothing. No reflection. Nothing. Which was enough to deflate Terri's assurances that this 'Marek' and 'Arianne' and the whole ugly Gothique coven were just a cult, just blood fetishists, just S&M freaks.

As if everything Cass and Colleen told them back at Jeff's house wasn't enough.

Colleen leaned forward, her pale hands on the front seat. And though he hated doing it, Jeff involuntarily flinched. She pulled her hands back and fell back into her seat.

"Jeff, Terri's right. What do you think we're going to do?"

"Look around? Ask around? I don't know."

"Jeff, you can't imagine how huge the place is. Rooms upon rooms, basement on top of sub-basement. We told you about the cells, where they've got all their...victims. Who knows how many they have there now? Do you think they're just going to let us waltz right in to look for your daughter's friend?"

The light changed to green just as Jeff spun around in his seat. "Do *you* think I can just leave that kid there? That's where she is, I'm sure of it."

"We don't know that, Jeff," Terri said as she turned the car onto Montrose.

"So we don't know it. So we go find out. How could you — a policewoman — just do nothing about it? Every goddamn cop in the city ought to be storming the place with assault rifles and SWAT teams right now."

"Jeff, have you ever heard about a few little things like the Constitution? Bill Of Rights, due process? Reasonable cause? Miranda? Search warrants?"

"That stuff just doesn't apply here."

"I don't have the authority to send in SWAT teams, Jeff. Hell, I don't even know who to call to get a hold of a Swat team. I don't even have the authority to go nosing around Gothique as it is. I'm going along here strictly as a civilian."

They inched along on Montrose for a block and stopped behind traffic at Halsted.

"Look," Terri said, reaching across the front seat to pat Jeff's hand, "At least we finally got a hold of the kid's parents. The uniforms are there now, they're going to get some photos, get it all in the system and get the proper divisions working on it. Maybe we'll be lucky. Maybe this Rachel will turn up drunk or stoned at some house party and the worst she'll have to worry about is her parents screaming her."

"Or maybe she's already dead." It was Cass. He leaned forward in his seat, his dark eyes locking with Jeff's, then glaring at Terri Shepherd. He sat back then, still eyeing the detective, still not sure he and Colleen belonged here in this police car, still waiting to pull up in front of a police station, still waiting for a horde of cops to surround the car and yank them both out. "Or maybe she's already one of them."

"Cass, don't," Colleen said.

Jeff twisted around in his seat again. "I hadn't even thought of that." He hated looking at the two of them in the back seat. Hated seeing Colleen like...like...like this. But it was better than it had been back at his house, back in his living room. With the lights on, seeing their pale faces and their black as night eyes, seeing the tips of those fangs denting their bottom lips. But he stared into the darkness of the back seat now. "My God, what if they...what if she...what the hell would we do then?"

"Well, depends on your preference," Cass said. "Line up a nice long wooden stake on top of her little teenage boobs and then hammer it right down deep into her flesh while she's screaming, pleading, begging you to let her live. Or cut her head off, you up for that Mr. Stancheck? Or you could burn her, douse her with gas or something and just toast her. Or maybe just wait for morning and drag her out into the sunrise, see if your daughter's little friend just explodes. Or — "

"Cass, stop it!" Colleen shouted, and the sound was enough to rattle the cruiser's windows. "Just stop it."

"I'm not trying to be an asshole," Cass said, the sarcasm gone from his voice now. "I'm trying to make you — make all of us — stop and think about what we're doing here. This is utterly insane." He lunged forward and grabbed Jeff's shoulder, his fingers digging in like talons. "We're vampires, Mr. Stancheck. *Vampires.* Do you understand that? *Really* understand that? Colleen and I are dead. We were murdered. They drank our blood and just before we died they made us drink their blood. And we rose from the dead as motherfucking vampires. Just like the books, just like the movies." He grabbed Jeff's hand and slammed it against his chest. "Feel that? Nothing. Nada. No heartbeat. No breathing. Nothing. We—are—dead. Colleen is dead. I'm dead. And that place is crawling with a lot more dead things. Only they're not 'friendly' like we are. They're not 'good' vampires." He let go of Jeff's hand. "I can smell you right now, Mr. Stancheck. You too, Detective. I can smell the blood flowing in your veins. I don't want to. But I can. So can Colleen. She won't admit it, but she can. If we wanted to, we could yank you both back here one handed and rip your throats out before you even managed to scream. We'd drink your blood, and we'd love every fucking minute of it. But we're 'good vampires', so we'd feel awful afterwards. Oh yeah, there'd be a great big remorse thing going. We'd feel real, real bad.

"Cass, stop, stop, stop!" Colleen was crying now, or something vaguely like it.

"Colleen, they have to understand. They have to see that what we're doing is insane. There's probably a bounty on my head. And yours. Every goddamn vampire in there is probably looking for the two 'renegades'. We can't just walk into Gothique and ask to pop down to sub-basement B so we can get some little teeny bopper home before curfew. They'll slaughter us before we make it past the door and everyone out front would just think it was part of the fucking show."

"Jesus," Jeff said under his breath. "I — I — Terri, those two cops. Those cops you left at my house, they — "

"They're the best I know, Jeff. You have my word. They're off-duty and armed to the teeth and do quite a lot of...well, 'special assignments'. Jacks is safer there than anywhere else. Those two would take a bullet before they'd let anyone get to her."

"Maybe...maybe we..." Jeff shook his head. "Maybe I shouldn't have left her.

✦

Frank Hoelevich woke up on the recliner.

He rubbed his eyes, let them adjust to the bright red glow seeping in through the blinds from the marquee across the street. He glanced across the front room to the little clock on top of the TV. 1:20 AM. Another uncomfortable night on the recliner. But he hadn't meant to fall asleep. Better to catch a few catnaps during the day. At night, he wanted to be ready. Awake. Alert.

He sat up and the M-1 fell off his lap and banged onto the floor. "Damn." That's all he needed. Shoot his goddamned foot off, just like Gil said he would. He carefully set the gun against the chair and wondered if he'd left any coffee on the stove. Wondered if any of the Danish from the bakery over on Ashland were still left. He shuffled off to the kitchen.

"Sox?" That dog loved a good Danish as much as Frank did. Or even a two day old bad one. But as Frank recalled, they'd already knocked off the cheese, the apple and the poppyseed during the dinner time news. Only a prune and an apricot left, and damn if he was going to let Sox chow down on a prune Danish so he could clean up crap five times a day in the yard the next week.

"Sox?" The dog was usually right at his side by the recliner. Maybe that awful red glow finally got to him. Wouldn't blame him one bit if he decided to bed down in the bedroom or the kitchen. Jeez, if Libbie knew the dog had been sleeping on her bedspread while she was away, there'd be hell to pay.

"Sox?"

Frank stepped into the kitchen and flicked on the light. He turned the gas on under the coffee pot and took the plate of sweet rolls out of the cabinet. "Midnight snack, boy. Well, 1:22 snack. Sox? " The dog had been tired from the afternoon's long rounds: bakery and deli on Ashland, groceries down Damen, a quick stop at Gil's but he was gone somewhere, probably off on parish business. Hell, they were both tired when they finally got home, and just in time too, just before sunset, just barely in time to let the dog do his business in the backyard before they got inside and up the stairs in a rush with the sun falling below the garage roofs. Just made it in before sunset and already those goddamn creeps were lining up out on Damen, parking their cars all over, pissing on the front lawns and barfing in the gangways and raising hell up and down the block, waiting to get in, waiting for goddamn 'Gothique' to open. On a Sunday, for Chrissakes.

"Sox?" Sure, they were both tired. No other reason why he fell asleep on the recliner. "Sox?" But it wasn't like Sox to sleep so soundly that he didn't come prancing in at the very sound of the kitchen cabinets opening. Hell, Frank rarely made it to the cabinet door. The damn dog knew the sound of each and every floorboard leading to up the cabinet doors. That, or he was psychic.

"Sox? Where the hell are — "

Frank's eyes shot to the kitchen door.

Almost closed.

Almost closed.

No.

No goddamned way. Sure they were tired, sure they were in a rush when they came in, sure he was juggling two armfuls of groceries and the leash but —

The door wobbled an inch from some unseen draft.

And then he heard it.

Far away, downstairs. A muffled yelp. A kind of squeak, just like Sox made when you accidentally knicked his paw with your foot.

"Damn!" Frank raced to the front room as fast as his old legs could carry him, and ran back with the M-1, twisting the khaki canvas shoulder strap around his arm. "Damn, damn, damn."

He flew through the kitchen door and took the steps two at a time. When he reached the bottom landing, he saw the back door was open. Wide open. A little bit of fog coated the backyard, and a little more crept inside.

He heard another sound — just a shuffle, just a whisper — and raised the rifle high. Took the next few steps to the shuttered hardware store on the first floor slow and easy, old eyes suddenly alert...

...Patrol's just up ahead. Over the rise. In those trees. Four of them. Rifle squad, Frankie. Black uniforms. Goddamned Waffen-SS. Careful, Frankie, be careful...

He heard it again.

A shuffle, a giggle, whispered voices, a muffled yelp.

Frank pressed the rifle barrel against the door to the old store. It creaked open.

The store was completely dark.

But he still heard the sounds.

Frank edged in, rifle ready. "Sox?"

He carefully took one hand off the M-1 and reached for the wall switch. Turned on the overheads.

The room flooded with harsh bright light and Frank immediately sucked in his breath as four vampires were all lit up, cowering for a moment.

But they composed themselves quick enough and stood up all cocky and proud.

One of them held Sox tight, though the dog squirmed and clawed at the monster's arms, struggling against the cold, pale hands wrapped like a vise around his snout.

Frank tried to keep his grip on the rifle. "How'd y-you get in here?"

"Tsk, tsk, old man." A vampire girl wearing a long black cape over her mini leisurely wiped some dust off an empty shelf. "What are you, some kind of hick or something?" She hopped up on the shelf. "Don't you know you ought to lock your doors at night?"

Frank leveled the gun at her, then swung it back and forth from one to another: the blond haired boy in faded denims and a bike jacket and no shirt over his flat, fish-belly white chest. Another girl with haphazardly cut multi-colored hair and a skimpy little black dress over her black tights and combat boots. And the boy, the one gripping Sox, a tall, creepy looking punk with long black hair and black cowboy gear . Frank aimed the M-1 at each of them, but didn't pull the trigger. Couldn't. He kept one eye on Sox. "What do you want? Let my dog go. He can't hurt any of you."

"No, we kind of like him," the girl on the shelf said as she fussed with her cape, arranging the long folds over her legs. "So what are you going to do with *that?*" She pointed at the rifle with her long skinny finger, tipped with a longer still black nail. "You know that can't do anything to us. Why don't you put your pop gun down, old man and play nice. Don't want your little dog here to get hurt, do you?"

Frank lowered the gun for a moment, then raised it back up, the barrel pointed right at her. "No. No, I think I'll hold onto this. N-now, you let my dog go."

"Say please? Pretty please with virgin blood on it? No?" The girl's fangs glittered in the overhead light as she spoke. "The way I hear it, you were warned already. Get out of Dodge and all that. So your old woman's gone, but you and micro-mini-Lassie here are still hanging out. I thought we told you. You're—not—wanted."

"Y-you're not wanted," Frank said. "You don't belong here. You don't belong anywhere. Except in your own graves. Now get out of here. And leave my dog alone."

The girl shook her head and slipped off the shelf. She sashayed over to the boy holding onto Sox and ran her long black fingernail along the dog's back. "Mmmmm, nice 'n meaty, this one is." She spun around and glared at Frank, eyes glowing and fangs bared. "Maybe we want a mascot, old man." Her voice dropped, echoed from somewhere else than just her mouth, somewhere dark and ugly. "Maybe we want the pooch for a snack. I don't know about them, but I haven't had a good hot dog since...well, *since."*

The vampire girl in the skimpy dress stepped forward, but kept out of the way of the Frank's gun. "Gee mister, we're not all so bad, you know." She laughed to herself then. "I mean, some of us are just absolutely *evil,* sure. But some of us are still kind of sweet." She traced her gloved fingers across her chest and played peekaboo with the top of her dress, revealing the ugly gouges and bites from where they'd taken her only a week before. "Well, I am, at least." She left her hand splayed across her chest. "I don't want any trouble. I don't want to kill anyone that doesn't *want* to be killed. Don't get me wrong, when they *want* to be killed, when they really, really want to die, well, I just fucking adore it, you know? But other than that, I'm really kind of nice."

The other girl gave Sox a jab in the ribs and turned to Frank."What Pollyanna there means is we could drain you before you even pulled the trigger. But who wants to? Not me. Who needs some watered down stale old blood when there's a whole fucking city full of sweet, young, bitchin' beautiful boys and girls just waiting to drop their pants and hike up their skirts and bare their tender little throats for us. Look outside, old man. They're lining up for it. They're fucking paying twenty five buck covers for it."

Frank gripped the gun tighter. "So then...just go. Leave me and mine alone. Just go, and leave my dog."

The girl in the gown shook her head. "Not so easy, old man. We hear things. Even when we're sleeping, we hear things. Maybe we can't do anything about them then, but we do hear. Like big old noisy machines, like that one back there, I think." She pointed at the lathe. "Aren't there, like, noise ordinances or something? Are you zoned light industrial, old man? And what's with all those thingies over there?" She pointed to the pile of sharpened wooden stakes. "Planting some tomatoes maybe? This late in the fall? I'm thinking not."

The boy holding onto Sox stepped forward then. "Here's the deal. Nice and simple. Last warning, final round: time for you to move on, old man. Just blow. Vanish. Like disappear. When we wake up tomorrow evening, some of us are coming over to pay a visit. You're still here, then we kill you. Not nicely. But first we'll make you watch while we eat your fucking little dog. One bite at a time. Starting on each paw so you can listen to him squeal while he dies." He smacked his blue lips. "Yum."

The girl in the multicolored hair came up beside him. "But if you're like gone, then we'll just let little Sparky or Bowser or Foo-Foo, or whatever the fuck this mutt's name is, we'll just let him go. No joke. No trick. 'Course, he'll have to do one of those G rated family film deals and go cross country to find you, but what the hell, he'll be alive. And so will you."

"You give me my dog back now." Frank tightened his hands on the M-1 but he knew his aim was off. Tears were starting to cloud his eyes. "Y-you let him go right now or I swear I'll shoot. I'll shoot you all like —"

"Like what, old man? Like *dogs?"*

Everything was a blur then, and it wasn't the tears in Frank's eyes. One of the vampires leaped for the wall switch and plunged the empty store into darkness. There was a whoosh, a flutter of clothes and footfalls and a lot of giggling as Frank was knocked flat on his ass, the rifle clattering to the floor. He heard a last laugh, heard a last muffled yelp from Sox and then the doors slammed shut.

Franks hefted himself up off the floor up and turned the lights back on. But the store was empty. They were gone.

Sox was gone.

He went back to pick up the rifle. Stood there in the middle of the empty store, clutching the gun.

Then he fell to his knees and cried like a baby.

✦

Jacks bolted up in her bed, cold sweat soaking her T-shirt.

It was the fourth time tonight she jerked awake like this from another nightmare. Hair plastered against her forehead and cheeks. Pillow soaked, sheets soaked, like she had a raging fever. Only she *didn't* have a fever.

She was just plain scared.

"Dad?"

But no, he wasn't there. He was headed for Gothique, maybe in there right now. With Terri. With that guy and that girl, only they weren't really just a guy and a girl, were they? They'd all sat there in the living room just a few hours ago, arguing, plotting, listening to Colleen Russell and her friend's stories. Listening to two *vampires* tell how they died, how they came back, what they'd become.

And then — gone.

Gone into the night, gone to look for Rachel. Gone to Gothique.

Jacks whipped the damp comforter off and climbed out of bed. The floor was cold on her bare feet. She splashed her face in the bathroom sink, toweled the sweat off her arms and her neck and her legs. Then crept into the living room. To the front windows. She peeked through the mini blinds.

Karlov was dark. The wind twisted the maples and shook leaves all over the lawn and the street. Her eyes followed one of those leaves down into the streetlamp glow, down to the front walk, to the front steps, where it landed at the feet of a tall, dark figure.

She felt a shiver run right up her spine, then relaxed. Jacks saw the big belted holster wrapped around his waist. The huge pistol poking out, the radio, the flashlight, the bulky bullet proof vest. The familiar shape of a cop's hat capping the whole silhouette. It was just one of the two off-duty cops Terri had called over. Standing guard. Watching over her.

Headlights appeared at the end of the block.

A car slowly — too slowly — crept up the street. Jacks saw the dark figure immediately tense, saw one of his hands immediately whip the radio off his belt, the other hand shoot straight for the pistol grip.

The car just continued slowly past their house, turned on 50th and vanished into the darkness, trailing a litter of fallen leaves in its red taillight glow.

Jacks watched the figure untense, then lean back against the front porch.

She stepped away from the window. Felt a little better, knowing he was out there. Knowing there was another just like him in the backyard, guarding the back door. She tried to ignore the bungalow's symphony of furnace whispers and floorboard creaks while she shuffled back to her room. Tugged her T-shirt down around her bare legs and sat down on the bed.

"Oh Dad, just get back here. Just come home."

She climbed back under the comforter and waited for sleep to come again. And the inevitable nightmares.

Outside, the off-duty cop's radio light flashed. He clicked the transmitter. "What's up?"

"Nothing back here. I'm heading up front."

The cop from the backyard came up the gangway and crossed the front lawn. "Anything?"

"A car went by, just a minute ago."

"And?"

"That's all."

They stood there in silence for a long time.

Then they both turned when headlights appeared at the end of Karlov again.

Both of their hands shot to their gun belts, hovered there like wild west gunslingers, waiting to draw.

The headlights crept slowly up the street, the glare almost blinding them.

The car slowed as it approached.

The two cops' hands relaxed.

They looked at one another.

Nodded.

And then they walked away.

Walked straight to the corner, got in their own car and drove off.

The headlights went out. The black Mercedes quietly eased up to the curb in front of the Stancheck's bungalow.

✦

"Okay, so now what?""

Terri Shepherd's unmarked Caprice idled behind a taxi and two limousines letting their passengers out in front of Gothique.

"Jesus," Jeff said, staring out the window at the crowds lined up and down the sidewalk, spilling out onto the street.

It was like the last few issues of Charade magazine came to life.

A line three people wide snaked under the huge marquee, their pale made-up faces painted red from the glowing Gothique letters overhead. Little groups in dowdier getups huddled on the sidewalk and by the alley entrance, passing around bottles crunched in brown paper bags and lighting each other's long colored cigarettes. Couples leaned against lampposts and pawed each other. A group of medieval costumed kids were caught up in some frightfully serious role-playing game. A few stray straights in jeans and warm-up jackets shared quarts of beer and watched the black lycra and greasepaint circus.

"I told you, Jeff." Terri beeped her horn pointlessly at the cars ahead. "It's a zoo. We're not going to accomplish anything here. Not now. Not tonight."

The limousines finally pulled away. Terri inched the car along, nudging careless she-vamps and Dracula's-on-drugs out of the way till she squeezed into a sort of space just past Gothique's front entrance.

One of the men in black by the door immediately hustled out from under the marquee and headed straight towards them. He squinted at the car, looked it over long and hard as Colleen and Cass shrank into the back seat, while Jeff felt sweat building up on his palms. Eventually, the doorman seemed to recognize the car for what it was: an unmarked police car. A pretty obvious one at that, to anyone who knew what to look for. He turned away and went back to his post at the club doors.

"Let's get out of here," Cass said from the back seat. "You want to go in there, fine. Go. Tomorrow. In the daytime. And bring as many cop friends as you can gather up. Blow the place up if you want to. But not now. Not at night. Don't you get it? It's *night* time. They're all in there. Awake. Ready. Thirsty."

Jeff shook his head. "I don't know. I can't just leave. I — " He spun around in the seat and pointed out the rear window. "Hey, what's going on over there?" They all turned to look.

Across Damen Avenue, some kids hopped off the cars.

The role playing group scampered out of the streetlights.

A Goth couple making out against a mailbox stopped suddenly and ran down the block.

"So what's got them so uptight?" Terri said. "They don't look like they'd scare easy. They — "

Colleen jumped up in the backseat, face pressed against the window. "It's — oh no, look. It's Frank!"

She grabbed the door handle and jumped out.

"Colleen, wait!" Jeff and Cass almost said it together and then both of them jumped out of the car too.

Terri followed. And they all ran right down the middle of Damen Avenue. The crowds parted for them, but the crowds were parting anyway.

They were making room for the old man stumbling across Damen.

The old man with a big brown rifle slung over his shoulder. The old man with a long wooden stake gripped tight in each hand.

The old man shuffling along with tears running down his wrinkled cheeks.

"Oh cool," one of the Goth brigade cooed even as he hustled out of the way. "Watch, I bet they're going to do a show right out here on the street. Man, this place is just so fucking cool."

"Frank! Frank, what are you doing?" Colleen reached him first. "Where do you think you're going?" She grabbed Frank Hoelevich's arm but he jerked it loose, dropping one of the wooden stakes on the asphalt.

"Get away from me. I just want my...just get away from me unless you want — " Frank stopped. He turned and stared at her. "Oh, sweet Jesus. Oh, little girl, little girl. They got *you?* They goddamned got you after all?"

Cass and Jeff ran up then. Terri walked up behind a little slower, more tentative, her eyes fixed on Frank's rifle.

"Vampires? All of you?" Frank spat it out along with the tears, then he dropped the other stake and brought the M-1 around, his finger on the trigger in a flash. "No, I see. Just the two of you. Well, get out of my way, all of you." He stared at Colleen sadly, then had to turn away because he couldn't stand the sight of her eyes, those perilously black eyes. "I don't want to hurt you...Colleen, right? I remember you, little girl. Colleen, I don't want hurt you, I just want my dog back. Now let me by."

Recognition suddenly hit Jeff like a hammer. Standing across the street on Damen, snapping the Polaroid's of Gothique, of the man in black getting out of the car, the man that never appeared on the photos. An old man and his dog, a not-so-little sheltie. *This* old man. *His* dog. 'Mister, you can't go in there. They'll...they'll..."

"They'll what? Kill me? They're going to kill me anyway. But they have Sox. They have my dog and I'm going in there to get him and anyone that gets in my way gets a bullet in the head or one of those stakes in the heart."

Terri pushed through them. "Sir, I'm a police officer." She pulled her badge out of her coat pocket. "I can't let you do that. I have to ask you for that gun now, or I'll have to call some other officers here."

Frank whipped the M-1 up and pointed it right at Terri's head. "Lady, I don't know you. I know this little girl here, but she's one of them now. And this guy here...yeah, you look kind of familiar, but that doesn't mean a goddamn thing. All I know is you're here with two vampires now. And I'm going in to get my dog. You're a cop? Fine. You stop me. If you think you can."

Terri and Jeff exchanged glances. But before anyone could say another word, Colleen and Cass leaped. Suddenly Colleen was holding Frank's rifle, holding it out like it was a bomb ready to blow. Cass scooped up the wooden stakes.

"What the — Goddamn you, give me my...my...oh, Jesus, oh sweet Jesus H. Christ..." Frank Hoelevich's knees started to give as the tears flowed again.

Jeff grabbed him and threw Frank's arm over his shoulder. Colleen tossed the rifle to Terri and took Frank's other arm. "Frank? Frank, I know what you think you're seeing here. I know what...what I've become. But I swear to you, I swear...to...swear *to God,* we won't hurt you."

Colleen stepped around in front of Frank and stared into his eyes. "Frank, look at me. I'm telling you the truth. We want to stop all of this as much as you do. We want to help. Do you believe me, Frank?"

The crowds decided it wasn't a show after all and went back to their own conversations, their own games, went back in line, went back to Gothique.

"Frank, do you believe me?"

"Th-they took my dog. My little...my..." Frank looked from Terri to Cass to Jeff and then back to Colleen. "Yes. Little girl, I think I do. I believe you."

"All right. Come with us, okay?" Colleen motioned to Jeff to help Frank to the car. "Tell us what happened to you. And we'll tell you what we know. And maybe we can figure something out. Together. All of us. Together, Frank, okay?"

✦

Jacks didn't bolt awake from this nightmare. She slowly drifted out of it.

Rachel and the bar and the crowds and the beautiful pale boys dancing in a graveyard stage and Brad and the people in that room groping and kissing and nipping and bleeding and Brad...everything fading in a cloud of white powder blown in her face...

"Brad, why'd you...Oh Brad, why?"

She tossed and turned in the tangled, sweaty sheets and comforter, rolled over and there he was — there was Brad lying right beside her. In her bed. Right beside her. His head on the pillow, that beautiful head lying right on the pillow beside her...

Jacks blinked.

That beautiful head on the pillow right beside her...

She wiped the sleep from her eyes and tried to make them focus in the darkness.

That beautiful head on the pillow...

"B-B-Brad?"

Just that beautiful head.

She edged away across the bed, kicking at the twisted sheets.

"B-B-B-Bu-Buh-Brad?"

Jacks screamed.

But they emerged from the darkness then, and Drake lunged at her.

One cold hand slammed across her mouth, the other grabbed Jacks by the hair and hauled her right out of the bed. "B-B-Bu-Buh-Brad? What's the matter, kid, you have a stutter or something?"

✦

"We have to get Gil."

They all huddled in Terri's cruiser, Frank stuffed in the front seat between Jeff and the detective, his rifle and the two stakes tucked between his legs. Colleen and Cass were in the backseat again, by themselves.

Terri pulled away from Gothique and drove down Damen Avenue. "Who?"

"Gil Silverez. Father Silverez. He's the pastor over at St. Alstantius."

"Oh great." Cass hissed. "First a cop. Sure, now let's get a priest. Why don't I just take one of those stakes and shove it in my own chest now."

"Cass, stop it." Colleen leaned forward. "Frank, why do you want this priest?"

"Gil knows everything. He's seen them. Just like me. Back in the summer. And then he saw...he saw Marian. In the library."

"The librarian?" Terri turned at the next corner. "The girl who was murdered at the library branch on Montrose?"

Frank nodded.

"I met him," she said. "The priest. I gave him a ride back to his rectory. But she was murdered. Gangs or something."

Frank glared at her. "Lady, if you're really a cop then you're either really stupid or you're covering something up just like the rest of the goddamned city. That

Marian was murdered, all right, she was murdered by the vampires. Hung up like a piece of meat and tortured and drained dry and who knows what else. Gil told me all about it." Frank twisted around in the seat. "Where are we going?"

"Let's go back to my house," Jeff said. "I can't leave Jacks alone like this. We can figure out what to do there, we can..."

"We might as well," Terri said, turning again and heading back north now.

"No," Frank said. "First we stop at St. Alstantius and get Gil. If we're going to do anything, we're sure as hell going to need a priest. We get Gil or you can let me out here."

"Why not?" Terri shrugged. "Let's see how much crazier this can all get."

A few minutes later, the Caprice eased up a deserted Montrose Avenue and stopped in front of St. Alstantius Church. Lights glowed multi-colored through the stained glass windows.

"I'll go 'round to the rectory and get him," Frank said. "You'll all wait here?"

Terri looked at Frank's rifle. He still carried it, along with the two stakes. "Any chance I could convince you to leave that thing here with me?" She saw his face, saw his answer. "Okay. We'll be waiting right here."

"Just hurry," Jeff said. "Please? I want to get back home as soon as we can."

Frank disappeared down the side walkway, passing right by the St. Alstantius statue.

Jeff and Terri, Cass and Colleen, they stood there on the sidewalk, saying nothing, not even looking in each other's eyes. As if none of them wanted to confront what was really happening.

A few minutes later, Frank came back. "There's no answer. Lights are on in the church, though. Maybe he's inside."

"Sounds like a good place to be," Jeff said as he started up the front steps.

The others followed. But Cass froze. "I - I can't go in...there."

Colleen grabbed his hand. "Cass, what's the...oh." She looked up at the church, at the twin steeples towering overhead. At the crosses perched on top and glowering down on her. She waited for something to happen.

But nothing did. She stepped forward as the others watched her. Set her foot on the first step.

Nothing.

"Cass, come on. It's all right. Nothing's going to — "

"No. I can't."

She shrugged and followed the others up the stairs.

But they *all* froze just a few steps up.

They saw one of the huge front doors open just a crack. Saw the sliver of colored light slice into the shadows.

"Gil?" Frank puffed as he took the steps two at a time, rifle and stakes still in hand. "Gil? He flung the door open and light spilled out all over the staircase. Cass leaped into the darkness beside the steps.

"Gil? You in there, buddy?" Frank ran inside the church. "Gil, are you — "

"Frank, what is it?" Colleen ran up the stairs, Jeff and Terri followed behind her. "Frank, what's wrong?"

They stepped inside the door and halted there in the vestibule. Saw the flickering lights from the banks of vigil candles and sanctuary lamps silhouetting Frank Hoelevich, saw him standing there in the center aisle, saw him drop the stakes, first one then the other, then the rifle too. Saw him stumble forward up the aisle.

They stepped inside the church and stared, wide eyed, disbelieving, speechless. Stared at Frank holding onto one of the pews, then saw him plunge to his knees. Saw him, and then heard him wail, heard him let out a hoarse and utterly terrifying shriek of despair.

And they saw what he saw, and they felt the same sense of despair, the same sense of futility, the same sense of defilement. Felt the same absolute and total fear that sheer *evil,* that raw unfettered malevolence was toying with them, sweeping them all into its dark embrace and that there simply was no hope left.

Felt all that as they looked up at the sanctuary, as they saw the life size statue of the crucified Christ that had been ripped from the cross, shattered into pieces all over the floor.

And saw Father Gilberto Silverez' lifeless body hung upside down on that huge cross on the wall behind the altar.

Saw his body spiked to that cross, spiked hand and foot and covered in a maze of horrible bloody wounds, spilling blood all over the clean white linen covered altar.

✦

Drake held Jacks up by the hair, her legs kicking empty air. "Gee, I thought this was what you wanted? Thought you'd been dreaming about getting pretty boy in the rack all this time. Anyway, that's how *he* told it." He tightened his other hand over her mouth. "Sorry only part of him could make it tonight."

Jacks' eyes spun crazily behind Drake's hand. She kept on screaming even though the sound was lost in his cold palm, till she started to gag on the vile stench of death oozing in her nostrils, gag from the sight of Brad's head, Brad's bloodless, mangled stump of a neck nestled in her pillow.

"Yeah, the little fuck thought we were going to make him. Probably would've, I mean, shit, who cares, right? But he blew it, big time. Wasn't supposed to let you vamoose next time he caught up with you. Oh, am I bursting some bubbles here, sweetheart? You thought it was true love? Hell no, girlie. That punk has been trailing your ass for weeks. Took him fuckin' long enough, and then he let's you slip right through our fingers. Well, best you learned this little lesson now. Guys are all liars."

Jacks' eyes shot to the doorway. Two more vampires stood there in the darkness, one holding her computer, the other with her printer and a messy pile of papers in each arm.

"Did you get everything?" Drake said.

Another appeared in the doorway. "Think so."

"Disks, files, *everything?"*

"I said we did."

"Well, do yourself a favor and look again so I don't rip your fucking fingers off for fun, okay?" Drake turned back to Jacks. "Don't barf on my hand, little girl, or I'll make you lick it clean." He let go and Jacks fell to the floor. Hard. "Make a sound, and you'll end up like your little boyfriend." He squatted down beside her. "Tsk, tsk. Little girls shouldn't go poking around with things they don't understand. More than one person's died because of those fucking files. Now what the big deal is, I don't know. Tell the world, I say. Like, who's going to do anything about us now, you know? But orders is orders, and seems like they want to see what the hell that Russell bitch cooked up on us."

Two vampires overturned Jacks' desk, flung everything off her dresser and out of the drawers. Another tore into her closet.

"So...thanks. I guess. For doing that cyber voodoo shit all you kids seem to be so good at these days. Seems kind of geeky to me, but hey, I'm an 80's kind of guy, what do I know?"

The vampires carted armfuls to the doorway. "All clean. Let's load up and go. It's getting late. We're done here."

"Not quite," Drake sneered. He gave Brad's head a shove and it slid off the bed, falling on the floor with a sickening thud, wobbling back and forth. "Take this lump of shit with you. Take the pillow too." He turned back to Jacks. "Wouldn't want to leave a mess, would we? I know just how ooooh-embarrassed a young girl would be about a little bloodstain on the sheets."

One of the vampires grabbed Brad's head and playfully swung it back and forth as he left.

"I know it seems like a lot of trouble, ripping the little shit's head off, creepy crawling in here and plopping it on your bed while you did the whole tossing and turning nightmare thing. That *was* a nightmare, wasn't it? Hate to think you went to bed with impure thoughts. Oh, and for the record, you snore, kid." He laughed, a dreadfully chilling cackle of a laugh. "But man, it was worth all the hassle just to see your fucking little face when you woke up."

Drake grabbed Jacks again and she shrieked.

"Oh quit whining. You'll love it. All those squirmy teenage daydreams about hot love with headless boy? Wait till you see what we have in mind. Just wait till you get a little taste of some *cold* love, kid."

Jacks gagged. "Y-you...you'd have to kill me first."

Drake's clipped her in the ribs with his boot. "Oh no, precious. Not 'first'. *During."*

He hauled her up off the floor. "And now, what do you say we take a little drive? You can leave your fake ID's at home this time. You'll be going in by the back door tonight. But hey, you can play catch up with your little girl friend. She's just been howling your name since we convinced her to stay with us."

Jacks kicked and punched wildly, started to work up another scream. But Drake clamped his icy hand over her mouth again and dragged her out of the bedroom. He paused at the door and looked back. "Hmmm, computer gone, the magic disks gone, room's a fucking war zone. And the little girl is just — gone." He dragged Jacks out of the room, out of the house and right down to the black Mercedes idling at the curb. The other vampires tossed their booty in the trunk and hopped in.

Drake threw Jacks in the backseat and leaped in behind her. "Yeah, I think this ought to make Daddy and the little Hardy Boys gang come 'round soon enough. You think?"

The Mercedes peeled away and sped off into the darkness.

✦

The police were finally finishing up with Jeff.

Two uniforms took notes while a detective hovered two pews back, eyeing him up suspiciously all the while. Jeff repeated the story the third time, the same story Frank and Terri gave, the same story she cooked up before she raced out to her car to call the local precinct.

Colleen and Cass escaped the grilling. They hid in St. Alstantius' parking lot before the squads even arrived, taking Frank's rifle and stakes with them.

The two cops closed their notebooks. The detective gave Jeff one more suspicious glance and then they left the church. Right behind them, the men from the ME's office rolled a squeaky wheeled gurney between the pews. Jeff winced as it passed by, staring at the black vinyl body bag. Remembering how horrible it was when they pried the spikes out of the priest's outstretched hands, when they cursed and twisted and wrung the last one out of his feet, and the whole cross came crashing down onto the sanctuary floor along with his mutilated, blood drained body.

Jeff shuddered, said a silent prayer as the gurney rolled out the church's front doors, not that he remembered any *real* prayers, not really. But he wished to hell he could. He followed the priest's body out the door and saw the old man sitting on the bottom step, shoulders bowed, head drooping. Terri stood by a squad, talking to two plainclothesmen.

"Mister — uhm — "

"Frank."

"Are they through with you, Frank?"

He nodded.

"The priest. He was a good friend of yours, wasn't he?"

"The best."

Jeff saw the old man fiddling with something in his hand. "What's that?"

Frank held up a little crucifix. "Picked it up inside."

"Was it your friend's?"

Frank shrugged his shoulders. "Don't know. If it was then he wore it inside his shirt. Gil, he didn't go in for that real preachy stuff, all that holy roller on the outside thing. Know what I mean? He was just...well, just a regular guy. A good guy." Frank twirled the little crucifix between his fingers. "Do you suppose...you think it could've been his?"

Jeff didn't answer. He just watched Frank tuck the crucifix in his jacket pocket.

The coroner's van pull away. Two squad's followed behind it. Terri finished up with the plainclothes cops and they got into their car and sped off too.

"Well, they want you both in the precinct at one P.M. tomorrow," she said, unclipping her badge and stuffing it in her jacket pocket. "You know the only reason they didn't drag you in now for more questions is that I'm here. And I don't know how much good that's going to do tomorrow. Pretty flimsy story we offered."

"What's the difference?" Frank said, as much to himself as to the others. "They're probably in on it anyway."

"Mr. Hoelevich, I don't think you can — "

"Lady, look at all the crazy stuff that's been happening. Think of what's been going on right in this neighborhood since that place opened up. You think it could all go down without the police knowing all about it?" He stood up. "You and I both know half the goddamn force is probably in on it. Or too damned scared to admit what's happening."

Terri started to answer, but Colleen and Cass emerged from the shadows just then. Cass took the M-1 and the stakes out from under his black trenchcoat and handed them back to Frank.

Colleen took Frank's hand, and at first the old man recoiled. But then another tear slipped out of the corner of his eye, even though he thought he cried every last one over Sox and Gil already. She raised her hands up, tentatively, then wrapped them around the old man. And he fell into her arms and sobbed.

"Look, I don't want to sound like a jerk," Cass said, his voice nervous, his eyes scanning the sky. "But...uhm, Colleen and I have to get going. Soon." He pointed his thumb over his shoulder, back down Montrose. Back east. There, the night sky was already a shade lighter along the rooftops. "I figure we have an hour and a half. Maybe."

Frank pulled away from Colleen's arms, but he patted her shoulder. "Your friend's right, little girl. You have to get going." He wiped his eyes and straightened up, stood taller, gripped the rifle tighter. "We'll figure something out. There has to be something we can do about you. About all this."

"You just have to come with us," Jeff said. "Both of you."

Terri stepped forward. "Jeff, I don't know. Do you think — "

"Jeff, Terri's right," Colleen said. "We can hook up someplace tomorrow night. Maybe we can figure out what to do then."

"No. We have to stay together. It's just like in all the scary movies. Everyone splits up and then they get picked off one at a time. So we stay together until this if finished." Jeff turned to Frank. "You come with us too."

"I don't think you get it, Mr. Stancheck," Cass said. "You can't just fix up a pillow and a blanket on the living room couch for us."

Jeff spun around and glared at Cass. "You think I don't know that?" His fingers tightened into fists. "I don't care what you are or what you can do to me. Don't play games with me, kid. I know what we're dealing with here." His voice rose with every word. "And I've just seen what they're capable of. So now we're all going to get in the goddamn police car and Terri, you're going to drive like hell back to the south side. Because I want to go. *Now.* I want to see my daughter."

They didn't say anything more, didn't dare.

They all climbed back into Terri Shepherd's cruiser, and didn't say another word until the car had already exited the Stevenson Expressway, until the eastern sky was paling into a brighter violet. Terri sped down Pulaski at an even fifty and blasted right through the stoplight at 49th.

"Look, you two," Jeff said, turning around to face the backseat. "Maybe you can find someplace in my garage. No, the basement."

Cass hiked his collar up around his head.

"There's a utility room," Jeff said as the Caprice pulled up to the curb on Karlov. "Laundry, furnace, water heater, you know. It's actually pretty warm. You can shut the door. There's no windows."

Cass nodded.

Jeff looked at Colleen. "You got that? Just follow me right inside and head right downstairs. You'll be all — "

"Jeff?" Colleen wasn't listening to him. She leaped forward in the backseat and pressed her face against the window. "Jeff, wasn't there supposed to be a guard out there?"

Jeff Stancheck's face went white.

He spun around in the seat. Gasped, and frantically started fumbling with the door handle.

Finally, he flung the door open. Fell out of the car and then just stood there on the parkway grass.

Staring.

"Oh God."

Staring at his house. At the porch.

At the front door.

The front door hanging wide open, the metal screen door flapping in the wind.

"Oh God, no. No."

Jeff raced up the stairs, screaming for Jacks.

THIRTY THREE

The sun rose Monday morning, but it only glimmered over the lake for a short while.

Densely gray overcast clouds cloaked the city, so the sun skulked behind them by the time the morning rush hour got underway. The wind blew that much colder, whipping down the skyscraper canyons in the Loop and up the Mag Mile, tearing at morning newspapers and topcoats along the Western Avenue bus stops, heaving trash against the garage doors in Uptown alleys, swirling piles of fallen leaves down the side streets in the southwest side bungalow rows.

The city awoke, almost hesitantly, peering through parted blinds and half raised shades to see what new indignities the day held.

A Pakistani donut shop clerk stacked trays of double chocolates and Bavarian Cremes, wondering when his minimum wage paycheck would leave enough for tuition to finish his masters degree. A hooker stealthily crept out of a Cicero Avenue motel bed, eyeing up the disgustingly fat john and his empty pants and the wallet in the back pocket. A fashion model failure tossed a white smock over her boutique best and dusted off bottles and tubes and Free-With-A-$75-Purchase Made In Haiti designer carry all's at her department store cosmetic counter. A waitress in a diner on the corner of 95th and Cottage Grove endured another pinch in the ass on her way back to the kitchen, carefully counting out her tips to see if they would get her any closer to the overdue car payments before the repo men came a knockin' again. A balding three piece suit gazed out his office door at the pretty twenty-something assistant manager two cubes down and decided her six month raise would get iced indefinitely if she didn't put out after next week's off-site sales conference.

The city awoke and grudgingly started its day. Maybe still a little tired. Maybe even a little scared after another long and eventful night.

A Lincoln Park Gen-X'er gone yuppie hustled between tightly parked cars on Lot Level A-6, already punching the security shut-off on his Acura's key fob, until he dropped his Coach Leather briefcase and upchucked his lowfat bagel and Macadamia Mocha Supreme Dark Brew breakfast all over the asphalt at the sight of the naked body, the body with a starkly white arm sticking out from under his rear bumper, the wrist a shredded mess of torn flesh.

A Belmont district cop tossed his fresh book of traffic tickets and a freshly Xeroxed stack of call reports into the front seat of his freshly washed squad and thought for a moment about the shopping mall security guard gig his brother in law offered him, thought maybe it had to be better than all the sick, crazy, fucked up things he'd been seeing the past few months, thought better of it and pulled out of the precinct's lot for the morning shift.

A Gold Coast dilettante woke up in her Laura Ashley meets Martha Stewart madhouse master suite — heaved a sigh of relief that her futures trader husband was long gone to work and must have been gone already when she finally rolled in this morning — and contemplated the ugly impracticalities of divorce for the five thousandth time but didn't brush it away *this* time, no, not after last night, not after her Prada full of fifties bought her all the pretty boys' attention and a long night of non-stop dancing and then an ushered invite into a private salon where she watched in wild wide eyed and wet pants wonder at a whole new kind of game she'd never seen yet in any of her nightly naughty nihilistic jaunts in New Town and Uptown and in and out of downtown when hubby was working late and the kids were — well, playing or doing homework or *something* — till they invited her to join, to lay down and be laid bare and be laid, oh that was fine but then they slithered and sleazed all over her and when the cold kisses turned into bites and she was shrieking so loud they had to clamp their icy hands over her mouth, she'd decided that it simply had to be either divorce or death, or maybe if everything they told her was really true, then maybe *both* because she wouldn't need any settlement and wouldn't need any maintenance and sure as hell wasn't going to be worrying about child support anymore, not after she moved in there, and after all there was a lot she could do with a lick of paint and bit of wallpaper trim to turn even the dankest sub-basement cell into a little bit of home.

A Halsted hustler brushed his teeth with his fingers in a 24 hour fast food joint's mens room, staring at the mirror, staring and plotting how one more night, just one more night of dusk to dawn tricks could finally get him out of this fucked up town and back to Sheboygan, where he'd never ever have to run for his life again from the red lipped leering monsters that had been cruising New Town all weekend, out for much more than just his mouth, his dick or his ass.

A data entry clerk half an hour late for work snapped the heel on one of her pumps as she raced down the subway stairs and smacked into a sweating, shivering delirious teenage boy, his black leather jacket hanging off one arm, his black mesh muscle shirt ripped open across his skinny chest, his gloved hand falling from his neck to reveal a wicked, ragged gash on his throat, red blood still oozing out of the wound.

A Wicker Park junkie stuffed the last bite of a Twinkie in his mouth as he took the fire escape stairs two at a time up to the abandoned Milwaukee Avenue warehouse's third floor, then froze on the landing outside the broken window, started babbling incoherently and pounding on the jagged shards of glass still clinging to the frame, pointing all the while at the gruesome sight of his needle partner splayed out across the cast iron radiator, neck and chest and arms mauled into a savagely bitten, unrecognizable pulp.

A LARP game Lothario shivered on the park bench by Buckingham Fountain and clutched his homemade black taffeta cloak tighter around his shoulders, setting aside his super Slurpee so he could stroke the face of the shockingly beautiful boy he'd danced with all night, kissed and pawed and sucked on after hours here in Grant Park till they ended up doing each other's arms and chests with double edged razors, spasming and spurting all over each other's clothes as the tiny trickles of blood flowed into their mouths, moaning like alley cats till the sun rose over Lake Shore Drive and they pulled their pants back up and their shirts back on and slept right here for awhile because he was probably fired from his franchise copy shop job anyway after missing work altogether the fifth time in a month, and the beauty said *his* parents would skin him alive — and not in a fun way — for blowing curfew and now classes again, and hell, not even coming home last night.

A pioneer Goth princess knotted the sash on her thrift shop kimono because her Logan Square walkup was positively frigid like it was every other morning, stirring her instant coffee and wishing she had some cream left in the fridge and deciding she didn't care anyway because after thinking she'd seen it all, seen everything there was to see all the way back to when punk and glam and techno merged and went dark, back to the Damned's and Siouxsie's and Bauhaus' earliest London and NYC dates, back to pre-VCR's and pre-netsurfing and pre-RPG's and pre-con's and Christ-a-mighty, pre-*everything,* she'd done died and gone to heaven last night at that place where she wasn't a freak anymore and was one among a thousand just like her and no one seemed to care if she was on the wrong side of forty, least of all the dark fairy girl who was death-dolled-up in that lethally little black dress with gauzy bat wings flapping on her back like some devilishly dangerous cupid, who slow danced with her from midnight on and whose eyes gleamed when the dance floor flirtation turned to talk of black sheets and velvet cords and silk scarves and bedposts and rubber toys, and who thought the botched bargain basement dental job canines were fine, just fine and whispered that she hoped like hell they'd be nipping *her* till the skin broke and the blood oozed out and damn if they didn't work just fine after all so they balled all night and clear through the dawn's early light and that same fairy waif was gently snoring away like a dark angel right now back in the bedroom and it was a shame to wake her up but it was time to untie her, time to wake up and shower and maybe do it some more, but just straight this time, then talk about what to wear tonight since it would be fun to have someone to play Barbie-from-hell dress up with because they *had* to go back, *had* to be right back in line under that black and red marquee right after dark and goddamn, she really *had* done died and gone to heaven last night and maybe if they were both lucky, maybe they could *both* die and go to heaven tonight, maybe, hand in hand, together there, right there on that magnificent dance floor...tonight...maybe...

A DePaul music major rolled over in his dorm room bed and stared at the clock, knew he was missing his Percussion 205 lecture, knew but didn't care and rolled back into the sheets, finally peeling off the black jeans and leather vest he wore out clubbing last night, peeling his underwear off more urgently till he finally ripped them off, lay there naked and ran his fingers over the welts on his chest and between his legs, where he'd been kissed with deliciously cold lips all last night, touching himself now and giggling with sexual delight as tiny drops of blood oozed out of each wound, while he wondered how long it would be before he could get dressed up again, before the club opened again, before he could find that beautifully pale skinned black lace girl he met last night and stay there with her in Gothique forever and ever and ever...

All across the city people went about their mornings, went about their jobs, went about their lives in urban anonymity, and if more than just the usual assortment of CTA car and street corner paranoiacs were glancing over their shoulders, were suspiciously eyeing up strangers, were double checking the car locks and the front door deadbolts and the window latches, were postponing blind dates and rescheduling evening get-togethers —well, then there were just as many anxiously watching the clock, eagerly waiting for morning to fade away, for the grim overcast sky to darken, for evening to return, for the night, the sweet and glorious night, waiting...

Waiting to return to Gothique.

✦

Frank Hoelevich poured two cups of coffee in the Stancheck's kitchen. He hoisted one up to Terri Shepherd.

She tucked the telephone in her shoulder and took the steaming cup.

"No, that's not good enough, Marty," Terri yelled into the phone. "You told me those guys were the best. Now you get me some other numbers, or you call someone yourself, but you just find those two bastards and hold them for me." She took a sip from the cup, burned her lip and stretched to set it down on the kitchen table. "All right, then just transfer me to Tactical. No, Marty, I'm *not* coming in today. I've got a...I have a kind of a situation here I have to deal with. Yeah, Marty, I'll check in. Now just transfer me."

Frank poured one more cup and carried the two coffees out of the kitchen. He passed Jacks' bedroom and looked away, didn't want to see the overturned furniture, didn't want to see the mattress and the sheets hanging off the bed, the clothes and everything else flung all over. He made for the living room, where Jeff sat on the sofa with his head in his hands.

Where he'd been for three hours solid now, barely moving, almost catatonic, where they'd finally calmed him down after he raced through the entire house screaming Jacks' name. Till Colleen and Cass had to leave, had to flee downstairs to the basement utility room and left Terri and Frank to hold him down, calm him down.

"Your lady friend doesn't seem to be getting anywhere." Frank set one of the coffee cups down on the endtable beside the couch and glanced out the front window. The sky was ominously opaque gray, wind kicking the leaves into torrents up and down Karlov. "Why don't you drink some of that?"

Jeff didn't answer. Didn't even move.

"She tried that number you had by the phone. Houston. Your ex-wife. Or the last address and phone you had on her anyway. No luck, son. Guess she'd been gone for weeks now. No forwarding."

Jeff slowly raised his head out of his hands. His eyes were bloodshot. Wide, staring into space in utter disbelief. It looked like he'd gained ten years in the last few hours.

"Drink some coffee, son." Frank nudged the cup on the endtable. "You haven't had any sleep."

"You think I could sleep?"

"Well, we're going to need every bit of strength we got. You want something to eat?"

Jeff shook his head. "So what's happening in there?"

"With the detective?" Frank sipped from his own cup. "Sounds like no word on those two off-duty cops. Guess they weren't as good as she figured. If you ask me, it was a setup. Either that, or they're both dead." He set his cup down. "Hey, that doesn't mean your daughter is...well...oh, Jeez. Look son, we're going to find her. And she's going to be all right. I have a feeling."

"I have a feeling too," Jeff said, his voice seething with pent up anger and frustration now. And fear. "I have a feeling we're all going to be dead before this day's over. But I have a feeling that before I go, I'm going to personally tear that building down brick by goddamn brick if I have to until I find her. And I'm going to send every single one of those freaks straight to hell if I can."

"I'm for that. And the sooner, the better. It's daylight now. We're just wasting time here."

But they still wasted more time there while Terri made one call after another, while Frank slowly sipped one cup of coffee and then another, while Jeff left his chilling on the endtable and endlessly beat himself up for leaving Jacks alone. While he racked his brain trying to figure out why this was happening, why it was happening to *them,* and how the hell they were going to get out of it. How they were going to find Jacks.

Find Jacks.

Find Jacks, that was all he really cared about right now.

Terri finally slammed the phone down and came to the living room. She sat down beside Jeff and rubbed a consoling hand across his shoulders.

"So?" Frank asked. Jeff looked at Terri hopefully.

"So? So...nothing." She shrugged her shoulders. "No sign of those two. My office is screaming for me to get my ass in right now. They'd like to know what the hell I'm doing at murder scenes and messing around in missing juvie cases. And no one wants to listen to anything I have to say. Either they're too scared, or...well, I'm I.D.D., after all. I ought to know better. Either they're scared or enough of them are in on it."

She ran a hand through her windblown hair. Then wiggled out of her jacket and threw it aside. The clip-on holster with the big pistol jabbed her khaki chinos in the thigh as she curled up on the couch, sighing with exhaustion. "Jeff, we need to report this. You have to. *I* have to. We can get the right people working on this, get them looking for her right away. I'll pull whatever strings I can."

He just turned around and glared at her. "Terri, if you can guarantee me that a hundred cops will meet us at Gothique in half an hour, let's call. If you can guarantee me that they'll break the goddamn doors down and tear that hellhole apart till we find my daughter, fine. Then you call. Yeah, you do that."

"Jeff, I'm sorry. I'm so sorry. I don't know what's happening anymore."

Jeff stood up abruptly. "Enough of this. Enough talking about it, enough waiting for the next horrible thing to happen. Let's go."

Frank stood up too. "About time." He reached for his rifle and the two stakes waiting beside his chair.

"Go?" Terri stood up too and looked back and forth from Jeff to Frank. "Go where?"

"To Gothique." Jeff and Frank actually said it at the same time.

"Oh no," Terri said. "What in the world do you think we'll accomplish by going there? Do you think they'll just pop the front door open and invite us in? If everything we've seen is even *half* true, we'll all just wind up dead."

"Could be," Frank said. "So what's your plan then?"

"I don't have a plan. But we wait."

"Right." Frank slung his rifle over his shoulder. "Are you ready?" He tossed one of the stakes to Jeff.

"No, Jeff. Wait." Terri grabbed his arm. "Don't do this. Don't let him goad you into doing something stupid."

"Terri, I've done enough stupid things to last a lifetime already." Jeff rolled the wooden stake around in his hands. "I never once noticed that Megan Russell was in trouble. And now *she's* dead. I let her sister down, let her get snatched by those monsters, and now she's dead." His hands tightened on the stake. "No, something a lot worse than just dead. Megan probably died over those goddamned files and I let them sit around the office, let them sit around *here,* and never did a damn thing about them." The wood actually started to splinter in his grip. "And now I've let them take Jacks. I left her here alone and now they have my daughter. *My daughter,* Terri. Can you understand that?" He searched her eyes. And maybe didn't find the answer he was looking for. "So now I have to go there. It's just that simple. I *have* to find her. I have to get her back. I have to save Jacks, or die trying."

Jeff turned away and started walking out of the living room. Frank followed right behind him.

"Wait." Terri grabbed her jacket off the sofa. "Wait, damn it. We're going together."

Frank halted. Jeff turned around and his face flooded with relief.

Terri pointed at the floor. "But what about those two? Downstairs in the basement?"

"We can't worry about them now," Jeff said. "Colleen and Cass are safe enough down there for now. If this all works out we can figure something out later."

Terri took her keys out of her pocket. "Well, let's at least take my car." She flipped back her jacket, pulled her pistol out of the holster. "I have a few little extras stashed in the trunk that might come in handy." She released the clip from the handle, checked that it was loaded and firmly punched it back in. "Let's go."

✦

Nothing supernatural conspired against them. Just another Monday in the city like any other. A Monday with a semi flipped over, blocking traffic at the light on 43rd and Pulaski. A Monday with the inbound Stevenson down to two lanes, then only one for pothole repairs, traffic backed up solid the moment they got on. Just the normal crush of cars on Lake Shore Drive as it bypassed downtown. Plus two fender benders on the tight S-curves along Oak Street Beach.

The sun hid somewhere behind the overcast autumn skies when Terri's Caprice pulled up in front of Frank's two flat on Damen Avenue. It was afternoon already.

"You two just give me a minute," Frank said as he got out of the car.

"Where are you going?"

"I need some things inside. Just wait."

Frank hustled away and vanished down the gangway.

Colleen and Jeff stepped out of the car and stood there on the sidewalk, staring across the street.

Gothique loomed over them, huge and dark, the low lying gray clouds wheeling over its fake turrets, shadows blinking like black eyes in its alcoves and dark windows. Ugly and malevolent, even more so in the daytime, if that was possible. Now that its secrets were revealed. The cold wind blew crinkly leaves and street trash down the sidewalk and underneath the marquee.

One of the front doors hung wide open.

"Jesus." Jeff gaped at the bank of black glass doors and the even blacker hole behind the one that hung open.

"Doesn't look like we'll have to knock, does it?" Terri stepped around to the back of the car and popped the trunk. "Jeff, come here."

She opened a canvas duffel bag and spilled out the contents. Grabbed another clip for her gun and shoved it in her jacket pocket. Clicked a flashlight on to make sure it worked and shoved that in her other pocket. She pushed aside pairs of handcuffs, a blackjack and a box of plastic gloves. Picked up another pistol, shiny, silver, with a black grip. "You think you could use one of these, Jeff?"

"If I have to, hell yes."

She showed him the safety. Handed it over and he gripped the pistol, held it up, felt the heft.

Frank came huffing and puffing out of the gangway then, a bunch of long wooden stakes tucked under one arm, a brown canvas pocketed belt slung over his shoulder along with the M-1. "Here, take some of these." He handed two stakes each to Jeff and Terri. "You know what they are. You know what we do with these, right?"

Jeff nodded, tucking one stake in his belt, gripping the other tight. "Like the movies. In the heart."

"I suppose so, yeah." Frank wound the canvas belt around his waist. "Military surplus. Just like I had in the service." He opened one flap and checked one of the eight-cartridge M-1 clips inside. "Don't know if I have enough of these. Hell, I don't even know what good they'll do."

They started across the street.

Slowly.

"I just want to get my hands on the sons-a-bitches that took my dog," Frank growled. "I want to look them in the eye when I kick their asses straight to hell."

Terri screwed up her face. "Mister, I don't think that's physically possible."

"Well, if they've done anything to Sox, it will be when I get through with them."

✦

Overcast or not, outside on Damen it was still daytime. Still Chicago on a Monday afternoon. Still real.

But the moment they stepped over the threshold, the moment they filed through that one open door in a wide bank of black glass doors, it was like stepping through the portal to hell.

They only took a few, slow, very tentative steps into the lobby when the wind — or something — gusted up outside and the door slammed shut behind them.

Jeff dropped his stake and it rolled away into the darkness. Terri clicked on her flashlight. She shined it back and forth across still another bank of black glass doors just ahead.

They crept forward. Frank stepped ahead and tried one of the doors. It opened right up, revealing more darkness beyond. They went through.

As their eyes slowly adjusted to the darkness they could make out — barely — that they stood at the entrance to a huge room. They could almost see the pillars and columns and balustrades arching up into shadows high overhead. Almost. Could just make out the row of stools lined up along the bar. Terri's flashlight scooted through the darkness, an anemic little sliver of light in the overwhelming immensity of silence and shadow. The light danced across leering gargoyle heads, half empty bottles and countless unwashed glasses, gleamed briefly on speaker grills, fake cobwebs and spotlight housings. Moment by moment their eyes adjusted more, brought more into focus out of the oppressive gloom.

But there was no adjusting to the smell.

Maybe at night, maybe when the club was crawling with hundreds or even thousands of bodies, maybe then the scent of their sweat and perfumes and colognes and their sex masked the odor. Maybe. But not now. Now the air was thick with a vile odor of musty things and old things. Dead things.

Jeff tried to put a word on it. But all he could think of was the smell of pure Evil.

"All right," Terri said. "So? Now where?"

"I don't know," Jeff whispered. Even so, the sound of his voice echoing in the vast, empty darkness unnerved him.

"Sox? Sox!" Frank shouted and his voice reverberated throughout the shadows.

"Goddamn it, Frank," Jeff whispered. "Why don't you just ring a bell and tell them we're here?"

"Son, they know we're here. *Someone* knows we're here. They left the goddamn front door open for us. I don't think we have to whisper." Frank stepped ahead, outside of Terri's flashlight beam. "I've been here before. Long time ago, when this was still The Palace Theater. But, everything's different now." His voice grew a little fainter, swallowed up in the darkness. "There, I'm off the carpeting now. I'm on tile. Jeez, it's marble."

"Must be the dance floor," Jeff said.

"If I remember, there used to be offices overlooking the street. That'd be right above and behind us." With the echo, it was hard to tell where Frank's voice was coming from now. "I imagine you got to them through the service doors. There were dozens of them. On each side of the screen. Up on the balconies."

"Look, why don't you stay where you are?" Terri said, waving the flashlight back and forth but landing on nothing. "Where are you going now?"

"I'm going to find one of those doors."

"Frank, if you're still on the marble, then that's still the dance floor," Jeff said. "I've seen photos of this place at the magazine. Keep heading straight, you should run into the stage. Where the screen used to be."

Terri grabbed Jeff. "What are you encouraging him for? We need to stick together."

"Terri, I don't want to stand here in the dark like a sitting duck."

"Jeff, we can't see a thing. That old man's liable to blow our heads off with that cannon of his."

"I heard that."

"Jeff, we — "

Jeff pulled his arm free. "Look, we didn't come here to stand around and wait for something to happen. You remember what Colleen and Cass told us. There are lower levels. Basements and sub-basements. That's where they sleep. That's where Cass found Colleen. Where they keep their victims."

"I know Jeff, but — "

"I found a door. Come on, it's straight ahead and then to the right."

"Wait!"

"Frank, wait for us." Jeff turned back to Terri. "That old man's walking right into the mouth of hell for all he knows, just to get his dog back." Jeff started off into the darkness himself. "You think I'm going to stand here while they've got my daughter?"

They heard a door open.

"Frank?"

Heard it close.

"Frank? Frank!"

No answer.

"Terrific," Terri said, seething now. "Just great. So now he's wandering off on his own."

"Maybe he got tired of waiting for us."

Terri flashed her light around till she hit on Jeff, walking slowly through the darkness fifty feet away. He stopped and turned. "So, are you coming?"

She kept the light on him and followed.

Only halfway across the huge dance floor — or as best as Jeff could guess anyway — they froze.

The lights went on.

The whole cavernous room suddenly lit up with overheads and bar lamps and colored spots.

"Come on!" Jeff grabbed Terri's hand and they ran towards the stage, all lit up now and straight ahead. To the right there was a service door, all right. There were three, actually. And just behind some velvet drapery, still a couple more.

They halted by the first group of doors, with no idea which Frank had taken. Jeff grabbed the closest knob and the door opened right up. He ran through, dragging Terri behind.

It was dark inside, and just a few feet in Jeff stumbled on a stair. "This isn't going to any basements." The stairs led up. He still held Terri's hand and started up the steps.

Terri's flashlight tracked each step, a landing and another flight of stairs. They came to another door. Jeff turned the knob as quietly as he could, and as soon as the door swung open, light spilled inside. He stepped through and out onto the mezzanine balcony.

He clung to the wall, Terri right behind him. Jeff let go of her hand and took the pistol out of his jacket pocket. He held it out ahead of him, yanked the stake out from his belt with his other hand. Stood there in a corner, staring out over the balcony railing, staring out at the huge interior, a wave of vertigo briefly swirling over him as he glanced up at the arches disappearing into nowhere, scanned across the huge emptiness above the dance floor and the bar, then tracked back along the balcony, all the way across the club, back here to where he stood —

Back to —

To the man in the black leather blazer.

The man casually sitting at a table, sipping a drink.

And pointing a wicked looking automatic straight at them.

"Hi there, folks." Joey Fortuna waved his glass of scotch at them. "Stop by for a drink? We're really not open till later."

Jeff gripped his gun with both hands, pointing it straight at the man. "Don't move. Dr-drop your gun, mister. Drop it and — "

"Don't think I'm gonna do that," Joey said, smiling. "Anyway, I'm having my drink right now." He drained the glass then slammed it down on the table. "There. All done. So, now..." He started to slide his chair back away from the table.

"I said, don't move, mister." Jeff was on adrenaline now. He took a hesitant step forward and in front of Terri.

But Joey continued, sliding the chair back, standing up, starting for them, his gun aimed right at Jeff.

"I'm warning you." Jeff's sweaty hands squeezed the pistol grip. His finger tightened on the trigger. "Mister, I'm warning you, I'll shoot you down if you take another step. I swear I will."

Joey eased around a table, the big ring of keys on his belt jangling with each deliberate step. He kicked a chair out of his way. "I don't think so." He kept on coming.

"Mister, I mean it, I — I — "

Jeff pulled the trigger.

Click.

He pulled it again.

Click.

Nothing.

He pulled again and again and again.

Click. Click. Click-click-click-click-click...

Joey Fortuna kept on coming, till he stopped just two feet away, his gun barrel pressed right against Jeff's forehead.

Click-click-click-click...

"Oh, give it up, already," Joey said.

But Jeff kept on pulling the trigger, even though his knees felt ready to buckle, his legs ready to give way, even with that icy cold metal barrel pressed hard against his forehead and digging into his skin. He starred at Joey's face, saw his eyes, saw where *his* eyes were looking.

Right past him.

Right at Terri.

And he was smiling. Goddamn, the man was smiling.

No. The stake fell out of his hand.

"Sorry, Jeff."

No. No, no. No-No-No-No-No —

Detective Terri Shepherd slowly walked around from behind him. She wrapped her hand around Jeff's pistol. The gun slipped right out of his hands, but his finger kept pulling on a trigger that wasn't there anymore.

No, no, no —

"Took a chance, Jeff. Didn't think you'd feel the difference between a loaded gun or an empty one." She winked at him. "Sure enough, you didn't."

"Terri...Terri, no. No..."

"'Fraid so, Jeff." She turned to Joey. "You have a smoke? I'm dying for a cigarette."

Joey kept his gun pressed right against Jeff's forehead and reached inside his blazer for his cigarettes. He knocked one out of the pack and handed Terri a lighter.

Terri Shepherd lit her cigarette and hopped up on one of the tables. She dragged long and hard and sighed as she blew the smoke out overhead. "Oh, that's good. That is very, very good." She kept her own gun pointed at Jeff. "Had to lay off of them for a while now and I was thinking that was for the best, I mean, you know what they say about how these things can kill you. But I'm thinking, so what? You know? I mean, what's the difference? As if it's going to matter soon enough. But Marek, oh he just thinks of everything, he does. Figured it wouldn't go along with the little school teacher look he wanted me to have. Figured you'd just melt all over that whole ivy league good girl thing and sure as shit, he was right, damn it. He was right."

Jeff could barely see Terri now. His eyes were glassy, sweat poured off his forehead, dribbled around Joey's gun barrel and dripped right into his brows and his lashes.

"I know this is all pretty goddamn lousy of me, Jeff. But in the beginning, it was almost on the level. Okay, not really. But look, I've been in on this thing pretty much from the get-go. I mean, who's going to sniff out a little chicanery better than an I.D.D. investigator, right? Precinct captains on the take, patrolmen looking the other way, licensing bureaus getting weekly envelopes, city inspectors vanishing like the wind and even the usual syndicate goombah's don't have a clue? And don't even get me started with those mopes at the ME's office." She leaned back on the table and slid the two stakes out of her belt.

"Thought I was going to be busting up some tidy little scam here, but when I found out what's what, when I found out what they're offering...well, a gal in my position can get money any day. But *this.*" She shrugged her shoulders and smiled. "How's a girl supposed to say no?"

"Terri...Terri, you can't, you..."

"Look, at first I was just keeping an eye on things at Charade, looking over some shoulders to see if anything came up about Megan Russell that I could sort of put back down. I mean, *of course* she was murdered, Jeff. As if *that* was ever a question. The way I heard it, she had to strip buck naked at gunpoint right there on the top of the mother-fucking John Hancock building, all boo-hooing away and then got shoved right off. Good ol' Joey, here, his partner did it. Well, ex-partner, right Joey? So what happens? *You* have to hire her little sister. Stick her right in the middle of everything. Hey, Whitestar was all set to give the kid a nice fat check and send her and the fruitcake packing, but *noooo,* you have to give her a job."

Terri put the cigarette out in a candleholder. "Thanks, Joey. That tasted mighty-fucking-good." She started twirling one of the stakes like a baton.

"Terri, why? Why did you...you could've just....just..."

"Just what? Take you and the little redhead out? No, Jeff. They like things a little more low key. At least that's the line they always give. But between us, I think they just like to fuck with people. Wouldn't you say so, Joey?"

Joey just rolled his eyes

"I think they just like to play games," Terri said. "All those long nights with nothing to do, you know?" She tapped the stake in her palm. "So what else could I do? Tell you what was going on? Like you'd go away then? No, you're the good guy type, Jeff. You'd have to try and do something about it. Those disks show up and I'm thinking they're bound to be the Megan files everyone wanted, so I just had to stick close. You're sitting on a snapshot of Marek. Or I should say, a snapshot with *no* Marek. You know, I *am* a cop. I could've taken the disks or the photo any damn time I wanted. And you'd have handed them over without blinking an eye, am I right? So, confession time, Jeff."

Terri held one hand over her heart and looked up at Jeff from beneath her lashes, all contrite and apologetic all of a sudden. "I confess. I got off on it. The games. Toying with you and Colleen and your daughter. What's the fun of being a cop if you can't fuck with people once in a while, huh?"

She smiled now, coyly. "To tell you the truth, it wasn't so bad. You're a nice guy. I was already starting to think like every girl does. Can't help ourselves, you know, doodling Terri *Stancheck* — which, by the way, would not have been an option — and picturing the wedding and all that. I mean, you are pretty easy on the eyes and not a half bad lay, as things go. Figured I could bring you around to my way of thinking eventually. Think about it, Jeff. A whole eternity of nights, together, cruising around in that hod rod of yours, fucking our brains out. But leave it to Marek to set a gal straight. 'Focus,' he said. 'Do your job, and all will be as promised'. "

"But Terri...Jacks. Why Jacks, why..."

"Hey, buddy, that's *your* guilt trip, not mine. You bring a loaded gun into the house, you can't go crying when someone blows their head off. I didn't give the goddamn disks to your kid. But all's well that ends well, and you have to admit, she did a bang up job with them. I honestly doubt the department could've gotten them open. And now they're all safe and sound with us." She slammed the stake in her palm one last time. "Just like *she* is."

Jeff glared at her. "Tell me. You have to tell me. Is Jacks really here? Is she...is Jacks still — alive?"

"Oh, she's here." Terri sat up on the table. "Alive? Well, she *is* a real cutey, Jeff. Young. Pretty. Clean. Innocent. Okay, I'm just guessing on that last one. But I'd lay odds they wouldn't want to just kill her. No, I'd think they'll want to keep Jacks."

Joey started fidgeting with his keys. "How long am I supposed to stand here holding this gun at his head?" He cocked the pistol. "Could you hurry it up with the long winded villain speech? This isn't a fucking movie, you know."

"Easy does it, Joey." Terri hopped off the table.

"Look, I got other things to do today. Let me get him downstairs before they wake up so I can get going."

Terri laughed, and it sent shivers right Jeff's whole body. "Oh no. He deserves better than that." She sauntered over to Jeff, ran her fingers over his sweaty cheek, then pushed Joey's gun away, grabbed Jeff's head with both her hands and kissed him. Hard. She finally pulled away with a *smack.* "You're not a bad guy. Just not the kind of guy I'd want to spend eternity with, as it turns out. But let's remember the good times, Jeff. We'll always have...well, Galena. Tell you what. Joey won't take you downstairs. You *do* know what 'downstairs' would mean, don't you? Not a pleasant way to go. I've watched." She stroked his sweaty cheek. "No, I'll make it nice and clean. One bullet, right to the brain." Terri punctuated that by digging her fingertip into the side of Jeff's head. "You'll never know what hit you."

"Okay," Joey said, stepping back and raising his gun. "Let me do it, already."

"No, wait." Terri's finger still lingered on Jeff's head. "I've been fucking him all this time, the least I can do is clip him myself. But first I have a little unfinished business to take care of."

"What now?"

"Relax, Joey." Terri turned back to Jeff. "A little matter of two renegade vampires dozing away in that stupid southwest side bungalow of yours, right Jeff? And by the way, what is with that hokey house, anyway? I mean, do you even have a clue?" Terri glanced at her watch. "Jeez, it's after three already. Well, no problem. I'll catch the two of them long before they wake up — as in, they're never going to wake up now — and still be back in time to let you see them do your daughter before I do *you.* Deal?"

Terri went back to the table and got the two stakes. "Guess I'll need these. Joey, put him somewhere nice and safe. Then you have your own little problem to take care of."

"What?"

"Well, I'm afraid we brought some company along. That old man from across the street."

"Who, the one with the dog?"

"Well, let's assume 'the dog' is dog chow by now," Terri said. "But yes, that one. Hate to tell you, but the old coot's wandering around somewhere with an old army surplus rifle. I don't think that geezer can cause too much trouble, but you better take him out before Marek wakes up anyway."

Terri tucked the two stakes in her belt, shoved her pistol in her clip-on holster. She walked past Jeff, paused, came back and kissed him on the cheek. "Like I said, Jeff. Sorry." She dug into his jacket and grabbed his keys.

And then she left.

✦

'Frank, where are you?'

'Frank, slow down. The Krauts are right over that ridge.'

'Oh God! They shot my guts out, Frank. I don't want to die here. My God, I don't want to die. Frank, help me. Frank!'

He smacked the M-1 against his forehead. Hard.

Ran his bear paw of a hand over his face, and it came away slick with cold sweat.

Frank Hoelevich waded through the darkness. Slower now. He'd already stumbled halfway down a flight of stairs. But they only led to a locked door. Retraced his steps, wondering all the while where Jeff and the detective went, why they didn't just follow behind him. But then he remembered long cold nights in the Hurtgen and the Ardennes, remembered how absolutely complete the darkness could be, even though the ground was covered with snow and the clouds sometimes parted on the coldest nights to briefly reveal a few stars. He remembered tumbling head over heels into shell holes and smacking right into trees in the dark. Remembered how many times his squad got separated, got picked off one at a time or stumbled into a mine field and half of them watched their legs go flying off into the darkness with each explosion.

Frank backtracked most of the way to the service door he'd first gone through. Or at least he thought it was the same one, but it was hard to tell. The corridors were like a maze. He held the heavy rifle in one hand, wooden stock tucked under his arm and his finger ready on the trigger. Felt along the walls with his other hand, felt his way through the darkness.

He reached another door. Metal. Felt with his fingers and found the knob, then two deadbolts. Then some wires and little plastic boxes. Security system. The door had an alarm. "The hell with it," he said out loud. They were expected all along. It was all a game to *them.* The deadbolts both turned with a noisy *clink.* He tried the knob.

Shoved the door open.

No alarms sounded. Or none that he could hear, anyway.

But light suddenly washed over him, making him squint. Light, and cold, fresh air. The alley. Frank stuck his head out, the stakes tucked in his belt clacking on the door frame. He looked both ways, looked at two overflowing dumpsters, looked up at the sky and saw dark gray clouds boiling overhead. Looked towards Damen and froze.

There they were. Half a dozen of them, there —

No.

No, it wasn't *them.* No, they wouldn't be out and about just yet, would they? It was just more of those stupid kids, two of them leaning against the wall at the end of the alley, one taking a leak against a telephone pole. Two more splitting a pint of something. And all of them decked out already, in the afternoon, all dolled up in their 'Gothic' costumes, or whatever the hell they called them. Frank quietly eased the door closed. Stayed there for a few moments till his eyes readjusted to the total darkness.

He shuffled along in the dark again, listening carefully, hoping to hear a whimper, a whine, a familiar bark.

But he heard nothing. Nothing at all except his own breath laboring with each step, his own heart pounding inside his chest.

He took another stairway, up this time, hit a landing and then went up yet again. Felt his way along another dark corridor, till he found a door. He tried the knob, and it opened. A sliver of faint light seeped out.

Frank stepped through the door and into a parlor. Like a living room, or a lounge, with old looking sofas and chaises tucked along the walls. And an open doorway across from him. The light spilled in from that doorway. And he could see the cavernous spaces above the dance floor and the bars beyond that. All lit up.

Yeah, they were expected all right. They were expected all along.

Frank dashed through the parlor, then halted at the doorway. He fell to his knees so he could hold the gun right, peeked around the edge, then stuck the M-1 out next. He was up on the mezzanine balcony now, he could see that much. He surveyed the huge and empty dance floor. The empty stools along the bar. Nothing. He tracked along the balcony, then froze.

He saw Jeff Stancheck slowly trudging along the mezzanine.

And right behind him, a tall guy in a black leather blazer. With a gun aimed right at Jeff's back.

Frank didn't hesitate, didn't wonder where the detective was or what exactly was going on. He raised the rifle. Leaned in close, squinted. Fifty yards away, give or take. He'd shot from a lot further. The M-1 could pack one hell of a punch at half a mile or more. But that was a long time ago.

He drew a bead on the black leather blazer, finger tensing against the M-1's trigger.

Aimed.

"You're going to wake up the dead with that thing."

Frank whirled around at the sound of a whisper in his ear.

Gabrielle stood up from behind one of the sofas.

"Who are you planning on shooting, old man?" She didn't seem to care that the rifle followed her every step as she slid out from behind the couch and scampered over beside him. "How'd you get in here?" she said, still whispering. "What's — Oh. I get it. Joey, huh? Fine with me."

Frank recoiled as she quietly sidled up next to him. He gave her a quick top to bottom, noticing the all too familiar black hair and clothes. But he felt the warmth from her body too, heard her excited breathing. Knew she wasn't one of *them* but knew she couldn't be up to any good either.

He shoved Gabrielle behind him.

"And who's that with Joey?" she whispered. "Which one are you going to shoot, old man?"

"Shut up."

Frank turned back to the balcony. Jeff was no more than fifty feet away now. Frank quietly raised the M-1 again.

But Gabrielle suddenly stood up and shouted. "Holy shit, if it isn't the old boss man himself." She jumped past Frank and out onto the balcony.

Everything happened fast then.

Frank leaped through the door and shoved her aside. "Jeff, run!" In one graceful motion his old body never should've managed, he spun around and aimed the ten pound rifle.

Jeff dove for the floor and tumbled under a table.

Joey Fortuna wavered for a moment, aiming at Jeff and then swinging his automatic around, first at Gabrielle and then at the old man.

Frank squeezed the trigger.

And then the W.W.II Garand M-1 fired, and everyone's heart stopped for half a beat. The GI's always said that one of the best things about that gun was the goddamndest loud noise it made, like a cannon, that the sound alone might be enough to take you out if the bullet missed.

But it didn't miss. Not this bullet.

Joey screamed like a little girl and the automatic went flying out of his hand.

Gabrielle's eyes went wide. "Awesome."

Joey's knees crumpled first. "Fuck." He went down on the floor, then hauled himself up. "Fuuuuuck!" A big and growing bigger red circle spread out across his shirt. Joey flailed around at his back and his hand came away soaked red and dripping gore. The big .30 caliber M-1 bullet went right in below his stomach and came out his back, dragging half his belly right through the huge hole it tore out of his leather blazer.

Joey hovered there for a moment, quivering, gurgling, blood starting to bubble up out of his mouth. Then he tumbled forward and flat on his face with a *thud.* Smoke still rose off the hole in his back.

Frank finally let out the breath he'd held since he first brought the M-1 up to aim.

✦

'Well, no problem. I'll catch the two of them long before they wake up — as in, they're never going to wake up now — and still be back in time to let you see them do your daughter before I take you out.'

"Not like this I won't." Terri pounded the steering wheel again and then pounded on her horn. "Damn it!" But the traffic on southbound Lake Shore Drive just wasn't moving. She'd wasted over an hour already, and there was still a long way to go.

She reached over to the glove compartment and yanked out the magnetic Mars light. Plugged it into the dash socket, opened the window and slammed the light on the roof. With a flick of a button the light started flashing and her siren blared. She jerked to the right, half on the shoulder and half on the curb and revved the Caprice up and around the stalled traffic.

She sped that way down the Drive and up the Stevenson ramp. Shot around more traffic snarls in the Dan Ryan interchange, but then she hit the construction and the siren and Mars light didn't matter much anymore. There was no shoulder, nowhere to go anyway. So she swore and pounded the wheel some more as the early rush hour traffic did what it could to get out of her way.

When she finally turned off 49th and onto Karlov, she shut the siren off. Grabbed the light off the roof and flung in on the seat. She pulled up in front of the Stancheck house nice and slow, parked careful and easy. Got out and held her jacket closed over the two wooden stakes tucked in her belt.

The house was dark inside. Maybe not the total opaque blackness of Gothiquc, but an ominous horror movie darkness nonetheless. She crept through the first floor to the basement doorway. Flicked on the wall switch and tiptoed down the stairs. Stopped halfway. "What the hell am I doing?" she said out loud. "They're out cold." Terri took the remaining steps loud and two and a time.

She stepped inside the utility room, and there they were.

The basement overheads backlit her, casting Terri's shadow across Cass, curled up in a ball between the dryer and the laundry sink. Colleen was tucked nice and cozy by the water heater, lying on her back, her hands folder across her chest like a corpse laid in a funeral home.

Terri pulled her gun out of the holster. "Well, sorry kiddies. Nothing works out quite the way you'd like." She clicked the safety back on. "If you'd just sat tight, Russell, you could've had a big fat Whitestar check and been on your way somewhere else with a real life. Hell, you could've even taken fruitcake here with you if you wanted to. And what the hell was with *that,* huh?" She flung her jacket back and slid one of the wooden stakes out of her belt. "But now he's dead and you're dead and even if neither of you are *really* dead, you're about to be in a sec. And now Jeff has to die and his little squealy girl's going to get it." Terri climbed on top of Colleen. "Well, hopefully she'll have a clue and get with the program once they're done with her." She nudged Colleen's jacket aside and pressed the stake's sharp wooden tip into the black fabric stretched taut over Colleen's breast. "Hell, maybe I'll take her under my wing once they take care of me." Terri raised the pistol overhead like a hammer. "Teach the kid the ropes. Do that whole gal-pal step-mom thing, what do you think?"

She swung the pistol down at the stake.

✦

Frank slung the rifle over his shoulder. "Jeff, are you okay?" He scrambled across the mezzanine just as Jeff pulled himself up from under the table.

"Yeah, I'm fine. Where'd you — " Jeff saw Gabrielle.

She stood next to Joey. Stared at his body, wrinkling her nose at the acrid smell of cordite and sulfur, burnt leather and skin. And the blood. "Coooool." She backed away. Backed all the way to the balcony railing. "Hey, old man. How about you let me borrow that thing." She turned to Jeff, her eyes narrowed into slits all of a sudden. "I have a little score to settle with my old boss, here."

"Frank, watch her," Jeff said as he ran over to Frank's side. "She's nuts. She's been in on this. She's — "

But Gabrielle bolted away from the railing then. She dove across the balcony and skidded across the floor, just a few feet away from Joey's automatic.

"Frank, watch it, she — "

Frank whipped the rifle off his shoulder, but not fast enough. Gabrielle rolled over and then up on her feet with Joey's gun in her hand. "Gotcha now, Jeffy boy!" She squeezed the trigger and the gun fired, the bullet smashing into a plaster column, showering chunks and dust overhead. "Hey, this thing is wicked!" She fired again and this time Jeff and Frank almost felt the bullet whiz by, then heard it shatter glass far behind them.

"Put it down, girl," Frank shouted as he took aim. "I don't want to shoot you. But I will."

But she shot again.

Frank's finger hesitated on the trigger. "Put it down, kid. I'm telling you, put it down. Now."

"Gabrielle, put it down. Please. Maybe we can help you, maybe — "

She fired again, ricocheting off the table beside them. "Oh, shut the fuck up, Jeff." She pulled the trigger again, but the gun jammed this time. Gabrielle punched the pistol, cursed and then brought it up again. But Jeff didn't wait and lunged across the balcony, somersaulting when he hit the floor and smashing right into her.

Gabrielle slammed into the railing. Hard. And heard the hollow brass screech, felt it snap out of the drywall and faux stonework base.

One second she was clawing at Jeff and trying to pull the trigger again —

— the next, she was halfway through the broken railing, hovering in the air, the pistol flying out of her hand, Jeff grabbing for her.

"I'm falling, oh my God, Jeff, help me!" She screamed and waved her arms wildly, trying to grab onto anything. But there was just empty air between her hands and the broken railing. "Jeff, please! Don't let me fall, don't — "

He grabbed her dress and it tore right out of his hands.

Gripped her legs but they slipped right through his fingers.

Took one last leap forward and wrapped his hand around her ankle.

But he only held onto her shoe.

"Jeffffffffff!"

Gabrielle fell backwards, arms flailing, legs kicking at nothing and went head over heels down to the main floor, smashing right on top of a ringside table stacked high with dirty trays and glasses and bottles. They shattered in an explosion of colored glass and last night's drinks.

Except for one.

Except for the one bottle that drove right in her back and through her heart and burst right out of her chest.

Jeff and Frank leaned over the broken railing just in time to see her body convulse for a second, gasp and then go limp.

Jeff fell to his knees. "My God, I...I — " He lifted one leg over the edge.

But Frank pulled him back. "You didn't do it, son. She did." He pulled Jeff up. "She's dead son. Let's go." Frank hustled over to Joey Fortuna's body and took the huge key ring.

Joey's automatic lay there on the floor. Jeff picked it up, cocked it and this time it chambered just fine. "Give me one of those."

Frank pulled one of the stakes out of his belt and handed it to Jeff. "Where's your lady friend?"

Jeff's look answered that question.

"Well, tell me while we go. It's late."

Jeff sucked in a big breath. "Right. Let's find those basements."

✦

Terri's gun swung in a wide arc, right for the head of the wooden stake pressed against Colleen's chest.

Just as Colleen's eyes flashed open.

Colleen's hands flew too fast to really see, knocking the pistol right across the room and grabbing the wooden stake.

And she snarled. Just like a wolf.

Terri Shepherd held onto the stake and tried to ram it in, but Colleen's hand tugged, twisted and then twirled it in a three-sixty, spinning Terri's hand right along with the stake till her wrist snapped with a loud *crack.*

Terri shrieked and fell back on her ass. She scrambled across the floor, one eye on her gun, her good hand stretched out, just an inch away —

Till Cass' pale hand shot through the darkness and grabbed the pistol.

Colleen stood up and looked at the stake. "So, what's up, Terri?" She whacked the stake across her thigh and it shattered into splinters. "Got religion all of a sudden?"

"Colleen, no...you don't understand, you — "

"We hear things," Cass said, each word a hiss. "You ought to know that. Even when we sleep, we hear things. We can't do anything about them, not then. Oh, but we hear."

"No, you guys, you got it wrong, you — "

Both their eyes flamed an angry, fiery red.

"This room's pretty cozy, Terri. And it's right below the kitchen. And the kitchen phone." Colleen stepped forward, eyes glowing, her lips cracking into a sinister snarl. "We heard it all. Every call. Oh sure, you made a few to your office. For show. But the rest?"

"Got Gothique's private number, detective?" Cass said as he stepped closer too, right behind Colleen. "You set us up. You set us all up, didn't you?"

"No, I — " Terri whimpered, clutching her broken wrist, her hand dangling limp and already swollen twice normal size. "No, I don't know what you heard but I didn't, I mean, th-they made me. You know what they're like. They made me, said they'd — "

"You set them up," Colleen roared. "You've set us all up."

"N-no, I didn't, I swear, I — "

Colleen lunged. She landed on top of the detective. Straddled her hips, and when Terri tried to shove her off, Colleen grabbed her good arm and twisted till the bone snapped and Terri screamed again.

"You lied to me and got me killed," Colleen hissed, peeling her lips back and letting her dark tongue loll over her fangs. "And now you're trying to get everyone else killed too." She grabbed Terri's shirt and tore it open. Clawed her chest with her nails till the blood spurted up in little furrows. Colleen dipped her head and lapped her tongue over the blood, then reared up again, eyes flaming, blood dripping off her lips and down her chin. "You're going to die now," she said, but her voice echoed low and unearthly and vicious and it wasn't Colleen's voice anymore at all. "I'm going to rip your fucking throat out, Terri. I'm going to drink your blood till your heart stops and you die and your ugly little soul goes straight to hell where it belongs." She shoved Terri's head aside and gripped her throat with her nails. "And I swear to God I'm going to love doing it."

"No, you have to believe me, I didn't want to, I — I — "
Colleen drove her fangs into Terri's throat.

THIRTY FOUR

Jeff and Frank lost track of time, lost their way more than once and even lost a couple of their stakes along the way.

But somehow, fumbling through the darkness, flicking on a light whenever they felt a wall switch or a pull cord, they made their way down through the maze of corridors and past the countless doors. Down into the lower levels below Gothique.

The smell was overpowering. It clung to them like clammy hands, thick and odorous and ripe with death.

"Sox?" Frank felt this way through another dark corridor, shoes sloshing through puddles, hands recoiling at the slick, moldy sheen on the walls. "Sox!"

Suddenly, they both halted.

Listened.

No barking. But — *something.*

"Up here, Jeff." Frank waded through the darkness, hands patting the walls. "Here. There's a door."

Frank felt for a knob, a handle, a lock. Fumbled with the countless keys, hearing it clearer now. Crying. Moaning. Muffled and vague from behind the metal door, but clearly human, clearly desperate. Clearly terrified.

"I think...wait, yeah..." The lock clicked. The knob turned.

Frank shoved the keys in his pocket and swung the rifle around. He tapped the door with the barrel and it swung open on squealing hinges.

The rank smell of blood and bodies and worse billowed out.

"Careful, Frank. This could just be another trap."

Frank inched forward, slamming his hand along the inside wall right away to feel for a light switch.

Found one. A weak, cobweb shrouded overhead bulb lit up on the ceiling.

Jeff pushed his way in behind Frank.

They both stood there just inside the doorway and stared.

"Sweet Jesus."

✦

Just holding her leg with one hand, Cass dragged Terri Shepherd's dead body up the basement stairs. Her head bumped and thumped on each step all the way up to the hallway between the kitchen and the living room. He dropped her there.

Colleen stood in the living room, looking out the front window.

"Col, are you okay?"

She turned around, wiping blood off her mouth with her sleeve. "I'm fine, Cass. Just fine."

"I was just...just asking. I mean, you know...you kind of — "

"Went crazy?" Colleen turned back to the window. The streetlamps flickered on out on Karlov. "Went all horror-movie monster on you down there? Seemed like I was getting off on it a little too much, Cass?"

"Uhm, well...yeah. That."

For a moment, Colleen watched the wind rip the last few leaves off the trees outside. "Yeah, well...I did. Way too much. But just laying down in that basement all day, unable to move, hearing her right through the floor the whole time, just listening to her making one call after another, all her cop friends on the take and then right to goddamn Gothique itself, and making like she was really trying to help whenever anyone came into the kitchen. Just setting them all up. Setting us up." She turned back to face Cass. "Yeah, I got off on it, Cass. I got off on it just fine."

"So, now what?"

Colleen pointed out the front window. "That looks like her police car out front. I'm going to pull it around to the alley. You bring her body out and we'll put it in the trunk. We can dump the car somewhere later. Let her cop friends find her."

"Later? 'Later' after what?"

"What do you think, Cass?"

"I know. I know."

"We have to try, Cass. Don't we?"

He nodded. Reluctantly. "But I don't think there's really going to be a 'later'. Do you?"

Colleen shrugged. "I'll get her car."

✦

There were no words for it.

At least none that occurred to Frank or Jeff.

The dank and dingy cell. The rows of iron cots, the horrible sounds of the handcuffs clinking on the frames, the wails and shrieks muted by all the duct tape and filthy rags.

And the bodies.

Naked. Or nearly so.

Pale, drained, feebly straining at their bonds and cuffs.

Bruised, beaten, torn, bitten and bleeding from countless wounds.

Some just lying there cold and dead on the floor like discarded trash, tossed off their cots to make room for new arrivals. For someone alive and kicking. For someone fresh.

"Jacks? Jacks!"

"Have you seen a dog, son? Heard anything?" Frank unlocked another pair of handcuffs, helped another stark naked boy rip the duct tape off his mouth and then helped him off the cot, helped him stand up till one of the others that he'd already released shuffled over and helped to carry the boy towards the door. "A dog, a little brown and white sheltie," Frank called after them. "Pretty big for his...no. No, it's okay, son. You go with the others, now. Hurry."

Jeff still raced from one cot to another. He checked another girl, but she was dead. Had been for days now. Grabbed still another as she shuffled towards the door. But it wasn't Jacks. She wasn't here.

"Jeff, catch." Frank tossed the huge keyring across the room. "They said there's more rooms. Two, maybe. Right next door. Go. *Now."*

Jeff raced out of the cell.

Frank got the last one in here out of the cuffs and duct tape and ushered her to the door. "Just follow the corridors. You can feel your way in the dark spots."

They all stumbled and tripped and half crawled away, crying, stammering, shivering. Some still naked, some wrapped in what used to be their finest black gowns and capes, their sexiest black lingerie, their fetish gear, their silk shirts and leather pants and vinyl skirts and chiffon blouses. All shredded now. All ripped away from their bodies, their bruised and bitten and pale bodies. All stiff and stained with blood.

"You can do it. Stick to your right. You should come out next to the stage. Or somewhere in the main hall. One of the doors is unlocked. You can walk right out. You're free." He knew it was pointless, but he couldn't help himself. "And if you should see...see a little dog, just a...well, get going now. *Go!"*

Frank looked at two kids still standing there in the corridor. The dim light from inside the cell spilled out on them, one skinny bare footed and bare chested boy in only a dirty pair of black jeans, his arms and throat dotted with ragged bites. And a girl, skinnier even than the boy, her black tank dress barely covering her pallid skin anywhere, stockings shredded and dangling off her legs like flaps of skin. She stood crooked on one high heeled shoe. Just the one.

"Go on. Get out of here. *Now.* It's almost night time. It may be too late already. Get going. Stick with the others."

They didn't move.

"Go on, I said."

"No. We...want to help."

"You want to..." Frank nodded. "Well, come on then. Next door." He took them both by the hands, felt their cold fingers weakly holding on, and dragged them to the next cell.

Jeff already had a few loose there. He worked on a teenage girl right now, who cried hysterically and tried to push him away. But the boy in the black jeans ran over, knelt beside the cot and calmed her down. Then helped her up and out into the corridor.

"Jeff, give me that key ring."

Frank peeled keys of the ring and tossed a few to the girl in the torn tank dress. "Here, try these. There should be another cell next to this, right? See if you can get in." Then Frank grabbed a girl shuffling by that looked half alert. "You! You go with her." She followed like a robot at first, then seemed to come alive the moment she stepped through the doorway. "And if you see a dog, a little...oh forget it." Frank went to work on another pair of handcuffs.

A woman from this room stayed to help, trying to hold her shredded dress closed with one hand while she fiddled with another set of handcuffs. And as a steady stream of dazed victims shuffled into the dark corridor from the next room, two boys and another girl broke ranks and helped the ones who were too weak to walk, came running back to Frank — or as close to running as they could manage — and pitched in.

"M-Mr. S-Stancheck?"

Jeff whirled around.

It wasn't Jacks.

But it *was* Rachel.

"Oh God, Mr. Stancheck, th-they...oh my God..." She started to droop, looked ready to fall.

"Rachel! Thank God." Jeff raced to her side, tearing his jacket off and throwing it over her shoulders. "Rachel, you're safe now. We'll get you out."

"Oh God, Mr. Stancheck, they — and then...oh God, I'm so sorry, I'm so...."

"Rachel, have you seen Jacks? Have you seen her? Is she here?"

Rachel tugged the jacket around her torn clothes. Tears flooded over her pale cheeks.

She shook her head 'no'.

"Rachel, you must have seen her. They got her, she's here somewhere, she's — "

The sudden screaming in the corridor stopped the words in his mouth.

Jeff and Frank spun around. Rachel, the woman, the other kids helping — they all spun around too, but *their* eyes were wide with terror, they knew all too well what lurked down here in the dark mazes and cells. They all immediately started to back away from the door.

"Looks like someone left the barn door open."

"Oh no," Rachel gasped. "Oh God, no, no-no-no-no — "

A grinning vampire girl appeared in the doorway, as if she just materialized out of the darkness. Her black eyes surveyed the cell. Then lit up with an evil red hellfire. "And now it looks like all the little piggies are escaping." Her fingers curled into talons. Her lips peeled back over her fangs and she hissed like a snake ready to strike.

Jeff shook his head. Tried to see past the glowing eyes, the fangs, the gray-white skin and the vile, icy odor wafting around her like a stale breeze.

"I-Ivy?"

She lunged.

"Jeff — here!" Frank whipped a stake from his belt and flung it at Jeff.

He caught it just as Ivy leaped at him.

And drove the two foot wooden stake right into her chest.

Ivy's momentum carried her right up and over Jeff's head. She crashed into two empty iron cots, shrieking some unearthly banshee wail and thrashing at the posts and springs.

"No!" Ivy clutched frantically at the stake jutting out of her chest. "Noooooooo!" But her eyes went dead black again as she looked down at the bile bubbling up around the wound. The light went out in them altogether as her entire chest collapsed, as her pale skin wrinkled into an ugly green. Her fingers fell off the stake. Her arms fell limp at her sides. Steam rose off her body, hovered over her like a wraith, then dissipated in some unseen wind.

"Jesus." Jeff stood there gaping. "Jesus, that was — she — that was a girl that — "

But there was no time to mourn the Charade Magazine intern.

Rachel screamed again.

Jeff whirled around and Frank whipped his M-1 off his shoulder.

There were two more in the doorway. Another looming behind them in the corridor. Two more bolting after the kids still shuffling off into the darkness.

It was nighttime now.

It was too late.

They were awake.

✦

The delirious parade snaked its way through the dark corridors and somehow found its way up to the main hall. Some of them crawled, some of them ran — right to the lobby, pounding on the black glass doors till they found one that was unlocked. They stumbled out under the marquee and fell on the sidewalk or wandered in a daze right out into the street, squinting in the last remnants of the sunset's glow.

The eager and the anxious, the just-couldn't-wait kids and clubbers, grinning Goths and all the wishin' and a wantin' darkwave cadets parted on the sidewalk. Certain that this was just another part of the whole experience, another of the Grand Guignol one-acts, *and damn,* weren't those makeup effects real, those bites and the blood — *cool!*

The Gold Coast dilettante ogled the scene from the front seat of her

Mercedes. The LARP game Lothario and last night's boy-toy stared from their cozy perch on an overturned mailbox. The pioneer Goth princess and her little cupid gaped first in awe and then with growing unease from across Damen Avenue. The DePaul music major fainted outright when one of the victims tumbled through Gothique's doors and fell right at his feet.

A few, a very few, decided it was all looking just a bit too authentic for them. They backed off, then walked away and vanished altogether down Damen. But more were arriving every minute, pulling up in taxis and scampering up the block, buttoning up black suitcoats, zipping up leather bike jackets, capes flapping and gauzy gowns shimmering, makeup gleaming, hustling up to the crowd and jumping up and down to see what the hell was going on.

It was night now.

The streets were theirs again.

The show was on again.

Back inside the main hall a few fell out of line with the steady stream clawing up and out of the service doors. "Wait, we gotta help them. Wait!"

But the dazed and the bruised and the just plain terrified shuffled off to the lobby, still howling out the names of their parents and husbands and girlfriends and wives and boyfriends, crying out for whoever they came here with.

"It's night, man, it's fucking night already. We *have* to do something."

"The rest of them'll get slaughtered down there. That old man, that other guy, they're dead meat, man. We have to — "

"What?"

"I can't help them, I can't even walk. I'm fucking naked, look at me, I'm — "

"I don't know, I don't — "

"But we *have* to do some — "

"So what do we — "

"Let's roast them."

That came from a skinny little waifish girl, still standing in the middle of the vast dance floor, the very same place where she'd twirled and spun in sheer abandon only a week before. Or was it...no, she couldn't tell anymore. It all went so dark after she started doing the free form bump 'n grind with that beautiful cat, that tall and slender and dangerously pretty boy in black who nuzzled her ears and her throat while they danced, who kissed her and whisked her off to a secluded room and showed her things she'd only read about and dreamed about and never really thought could be true — not *really* — but she always hoped and wondered and wished. Until they turned dangerous. Until they got all scary and painful and his face changed and his eyes burned and then there were more of them and they were all over her with their cold hands and their cold lips and their cold tongues and their teeth — my God, their teeth slicing into her and biting and it hurt, oh Christ it hurt when they bit, hurt like nothing she'd ever felt before...and then she awoke in darkness with her hands cuffed and a stinky rag knotted in her mouth and they came back night after night and giggled when they did it to her, when they peeled her gorgeous gown away — the same one she'd slaved over and sewn and dyed and tacked together listening to her Black Tape For A Blue Girl CD set on repeat and watching Razor Blade Smile and Daughters Of Darkness and Dance Of The Damned over and over again with the sound down, just getting off on the visuals — they just shredded that dress with their claws and leered at her in her underwear, cuffed to that bed like some sleazy S&M show, picked at her and poked her and did ugly things to her, like she was just a doll, just a toy, just a pet, and they laughed and laughed their hellish laughs when they told her she'd be dead soon and be really dead because she wasn't going to join them, she'd be dead soon, tomorrow night maybe, yeah tomorrow...

"Let's roast the motherfuckers." Her eyes narrowed as she shuffled over to the bar. "I want to see them burn." She kicked two stools aside, climbed up on the bar and jumped right over. She grabbed a bottle and whacked it on the edge of the bar. Whacked again till it smashed, brandy splashing out. She held the jagged bottle up and screamed, "I want them all to fucking burn in hell!"

Two more made it behind the bar and grabbed as many bottles as they could hold.

"My lighter's gone, all my — "

"They took my purse, man, I had matches but they — "

"Fuck, everything's gone, just look — "

"Just look for something. Matches, candles, something — "

"Not the wine, just take the hard stuff. Hurry!"

And with some of the gawkers from out on Damen already peeking in the front door and filtering into the lobby, the little troop of half naked and all-naked men and women and girls and boys clattered and clinked with their bottles of Gothique's best, hesitated at the threshold by the service door, and then plunged back down into the darkness.

✦

Jeff held Joey Fortuna's automatic straight out, grabbed a stake from Frank's belt and gripped it like a spear. He shoved Rachel and the others behind him. Frank leveled his M-1 dead ahead.

The vampires spilled out into the corridor. Some of them yawned and stretched, some slinked along like rats, some laughed and giggled and licked their lips, but each of their dead black eyes lit up alert and hot red once they stumbled into the scene outside their lairs.

Right up front were those two — the same boy and that girl from Frank's gangway, from that night so long ago, the same ones who attacked him and Sox on Damen Avenue. They'd each snatched one of the dazed prisoners before

Frank and Jeff blocked the corridor, held them by the necks now and slapped their faces till they stopped screaming.

"Let them go!" Frank took half a step forward and aimed his rifle at that leering devil that haunted his nightmares ever since that first night he saw them with Gil.

"Oh, sure. Right." The vampire burst out laughing, the chilling sound echoing off the damp walls and into the darkness. "Should've taken you out that first night, old man. You and your shaman friend." He dug his nails into the girl's neck and she screamed again. "But we got your buddy, all right. Got him good. How'd you like that, old man?" The vampire threw the girl aside and another grabbed her. "How'd you like finding the priest hung upside down on his own cross like that, huh? Downright sacrilegious, wasn't it? You should've heard him, old man, should've heard him screaming his prayers when we hoisted him up there, when we pounded the spikes in his hands and his feet, when we bled him. Should've been there."

Frank's hands tightened on the M-1 till they hurt. "You bastard. You — "

He fired.

The bullet hit the vampire right in the chest, spinning him in a full circle and down into a puddle.

The others behind him started growling.

But he got up again.

Slowly, but he got up.

"Damn!" He clutched his chest. "Man, that hurts." Black blood oozed through his shirt. "Oh man, you are going to pay for that." He tore his shirt open and stared at the huge hole. Then looked back up at Frank, evil simmering in his red eyes. "So what the hell is *that* supposed to do? Don't you get it yet, you stupid old shit? You can't kill me. You can't kill *us.* We're immortal. You and your bullets can't do — "

Frank fired again, pulling the trigger now as fast as the cartridges flew out of the top of the semi-automatic M-1, emptying the rest of the eight shot clip right into the monster.

The vampires seethed with anger now, their lips all peeling back over their fangs, growling and hissing like a pack of hungry wolves.

They inched forward.

"Oh, you are going to die so fucking slowly, old man, so fucking slowly and then..." The vampire coughed up a mouth full of black blood. "Then I'm going to make you myself. So I can keep you around and torture you every fucking night for all eternity, I swear, I'm going to — "

But Frank already flipped open a pouch on his belt and had another clip in the M-1. He leaned into the sights, aimed and emptied the whole clip, all eight shots.

Right at the vampire's legs.

And shot them right off at the knees, the big .30 caliber bullets ripping dead flesh and bone away until the vampire crumpled to the floor, the stumps of his legs sizzling and smoking from under his shredded pants.

Jeff leaped forward then.

He landed on top of the vampire and drove the stake right in his chest.

There was an unholy shriek. A flash of smoke and the acrid smell of sulfur and old ashes and charnel house fumes. The vampire's writhing body curled up on itself like a burning leaf, sizzled and then crumpled into a quivering pile of dust and bones and hunks of awful *something's.*

Frank reloaded and leaped to Jeff's side. The girl in the tank dress, the boy in the black jeans, the woman still clutching her gown closed — they yanked stakes out of Frank's belt and took the flank, fear gone from their eyes all of a sudden. Something grim and determined and lusting for revenge replacing it there.

Some of the vampires gawked at the smoldering heap of ashes and bones. Some fled back into their cells. But more were still stumbling out of the lairs.

Gem and Fonda ambled out arm in arm, nuzzling each other and giggling, then freezing at the sight of the crowds in the dark corridor. "What the — what's going on here?"

"Where's my daughter?" Jeff pointed his gun at Fonda, then at another vampire, at Gem and then at another. "Where's Jacks? Just give me my daughter you goddamn monsters and maybe we'll — "

"What the hell are you talking about?" Fonda slithered through the vampires, his perpetual giggling finally pausing, his snotty leer twisting with just a bit of unease. "Who are *you?* What daughter? How are we supposed to know who *your* daughter is? Everyone here is somebody's daughter. Somebody's son. Hell, *I'm* somebody's son, you warmblooded little shit. I hope *your* fucking little daughter's dead already. Or back here with us. Now you better drop your little toys before the others awake and hear what's going on down here or there's going to be one hell of a — "

But before he could finish, the corridors came alive with voices and footfalls, bare feet splashing through the rank puddles, racing as fast as their blood-drained bodies could carry them.

The kids from upstairs stumbled down through the darkness with the liquor bottles clutched to their naked chests.

Fonda looked up. Gem took a few steps back. The other vampires hesitated.

The first bottle flew right over everyone's heads and shattered against the wall.

"What the — "

Another. Then another. A dozen bottles rocketed overhead in so many seconds and smashed against the walls, a couple clipping two vampires in the head, then tumbling to the floor where they shattered.

"Mister!" The girl who started it all up on the dance floor ran forward and lobbed her last two bottles, both fine cognac as it turned out, and then ran back. "Mister, shoot them!"

Confusion reigned as a barrage of bottles smashed against the walls, till the entire corridor was awash in bourbon, brandy, scotch and liqueurs and the vampires crunched broken glass underfoot as they milled back and forth. Some still growling. Some starting to howl with fear.

"Shoot it, mister!" The girl grabbed Frank's arm and shook him. "Shoot the fucking booze already, will you?"

The vampires dropped the two screaming kids and backed away.

"Mister, light 'em up." She grabbed Frank's rifle and shook it. "Roast 'em!"

Frank finally got it just as another bottle sailed overhead. He raised the M-1 and fired.

The bottle exploded in a hail of glass and flame right over the vampires.

Frank slammed Jeff with his rifle, they nodded and both let loose. It was a battlefield roar then as Jeff emptied the automatic's entire clip. Frank fired seven rounds, slammed another clip in as fast as his fingers could move and shot another eight, each bullet sparking off the concrete or catching a bottle in mid-air, igniting explosions of blue and yellow flames.

The entire corridor echoed with the insanely surreal sounds of hell then, the sounds of the deepest, darkest fire pit in Hades as the flames shot up the sides of the walls and fanned out across the floor.

Three vampires leaped out of the fire, their clothes already burning, but the kids were on them like a mob, dragging them down to the floor and plunging the stakes into their chests, the woman who'd been clutching her dress closed letting it fly open now as she straddled one vampire and rammed her stake over and over again into the screaming monster's body, even after the vampire wrinkled, smoked and collapsed into a rotting pile of ashes.

Jeff finally pulled the woman off the sizzling heap and dragged her away. "Run, all of you. Get out of here. Now!"

The flames enveloped the end of the corridor and shot right into the cells. More agonized shrieks echoed out of the open doors as one vampire after another caught fire, flew out only to fall into a deeper wall of flame.

"Get back!" Frank shoved the kids back up the corridor, no longer a dark, black tunnel, the dripping walls a flickering blue and orange light show now.

They backed away, then turned and started to run, with the fingers of flame roiling across the floor right behind them.

Gem clutched Fonda and tried to drag him back towards their lair, but the doorway was ringed with flames. Fonda's back was already on fire, his black mesh shirt disintegrating into little molten nylon balls that seared his white skin. His hair went next and he shrieked some wounded animal sound, wrapped his skinny arms around Gem and the flames enveloped them both. They fell to the floor where a river of fire burned a ring around them and consumed their writhing bodies.

The vampire girl who'd cowered on the steps at St. Alstantius just stood there in a daze, too terrified to move even as a bottle crashed at her feet and splashed bourbon all over her legs. She caught fire immediately and screamed as the flames shot up her legs, melting her black tights and then her dead skin and finally enveloping her.

The vampires that feasted on Kelly Feeny wailed while their flesh simmered, boiled, till they exploded into dust. The crew that hung Marian the Librarian from a storeroom pipe while she was still pleading for her life — they were pleading themselves now in frightened little baby voices, begging and pleading to devils and dark gods and other unlistening ears as the flames pushed them all back into a cell's dark corner where their booty and heaps of stinking black costumes and bloodstained mattresses caught fire and then caught *them* and they all fell in piles of screaming, smoldering gore. The squad that did the commando raid at Charade, the group that kidnapped Colleen Russell from the no-tell motel, the gang that hid in the pews inside St. Alstantius and gleefully nailed Gil Silverez to the cross and bled him — all of them — they all cowered and squealed and shrieked as the flames hemmed them in, as they watched one after another catch fire, melt, explode, or mercifully just go plain and for-real dead.

Another she-vamp flew out of a cell, her black cape already burning along the edges and flapping behind her like fiery wings. "You think you won, old man," she screamed, the fire eating away her long black gown now. "But you lost anyway, you lost, you lost, you..."

And Frank froze as her words transformed into a hellish shriek of pain, turned as her wail faded altogether under the roar of the fire. He dropped his rifle when he heard a sound from behind the flames.

A yelp.

A bark.

Frantic.

Another.

Desperate.

Still another bark. Hopeful this time?

"No."

"You lost, old man, you lost, you lost..."

"NO!" Frank dove forward, but Jeff caught him just before he reached the sea of flames.

"Let me go, damn it, let me — "

The bare chested kid in the black jeans joined Jeff. Another jumped to his side and grabbed Frank's rifle. They pulled him away from the fire.

"No, let me go, let me go! They have him, they have Sox in there, he'll burn, he'll..." Frank shook them off. He grabbed his gun back. Stood there in the corridor as the flames snaked out across the floor and towards his feet. "Sox. Boy, I — I — "

They all heard it then. Another bark. More of a painful squeal, really.

And another vampire somersaulted out of the fire and crumbled into screaming ashes right in front of him.

"Sox, I — y-you were a, a good boy, buddy. You were the best."

Jeff pulled Frank back.

"All right! I-I'm...all right." The old man sucked in a deep breath. Turned to Jeff and nodded. "All right."

They both followed the others out of the basement corridor. Behind them, the moldy concrete and cracked quarrystone walls echoed with a hellish symphony of screams and shrieks from one vampire after another, cowering in the corners of their cells, watching the flames corral them into groups that were swallowed up by the smoke, exploding in gruesome flashes of skin and sulfur, blood and bile, each ugly undead soul careening its dark way from one fire to another, straight down to hell.

THIRTY FIVE

"Don't stop, just keep going!"

Jeff held Rachel's hand tight and dragged her up the last flight of stairs from the basement. Frank was just a few steps behind, puffing and wheezing, eyes stinging and watering from the smoke. And from the sound of Sox' last yelp that still echoed painfully in his ears.

They burst through the service door and out onto the dance floor. Up ahead, a few of the kids that led the fiery bottle barrage already stumbled out of the lobby doors. Some Goth'd up gawkers hovered there. They saw the terrified eyes and the wounds, the bruised and blood drained, half naked walking zombies, saw the tears and heard the cries of pain. Finally saw the smoke start to creep up out of the service door far across the main hall and only then, finally caught on.

Maybe not enough to actually pitch in and help the last of the kids through the lobby doors, that brave barefooted and bare chested boy in the black jeans, or the grim faced girl in the tattered black tank dress, or the wild-eyed woman with the shredded gown flapping open. Not even the little waif who first incited the booze bottle raid. No, maybe not enough to actually help any of them as they tripped and stumbled out the doors, but certainly enough to finally figure out that something wasn't right, that something had suddenly gotten awfully scary here.

Certainly enough to promptly push *their* way through the lobby doors first and hightail it right out of Gothique altogether.

"Frank, come on. Hurry!" Jeff stumbled halfway across the dance floor, practically carrying Rachel now, who cried hysterically and could barely drag her feet along with him.

"Right behind you, son." Frank dug into his cartridge belt as he wheezed along. "Just get that kid out of here!" He looked back and could see a flickering glow through the service door. Thought for an instant he even saw some shadowy figures moving back there. He rammed another clip into the M-1 and realized that there really *was* more than just smoke starting to creep up from the basements. A pale hand clawed the threshold, a smoldering red eyed monster face emerged from the flickering darkness. Frank fired off the whole clip, shooting wild as he ran, only zinging the door and the emptiness behind.

He stopped to reload. "We're not done here, Jeff, we still — "

"I know, Frank. By God, we're not done yet." Jeff scooped Rachel up in his arms, winced, and headed straight across the huge dance floor. "I'll get you out, Rachel. Then I - I have to — " He tripped, went down on his knees, almost dropped her. Got back up on his feet and ran again, his eyes riveted on the lobby doors, still swinging where the last of the victims had just run through, on the one outside door that hung open, at the tiny glimpse of sidewalk and Damen Avenue beyond. "Then I have to come back, Rachel. I have to...have to...find Jacks..."

Another hundred feet, just another —

The outside door suddenly slammed shut.

Jeff skidded to halt. Rachel fell out of his arms and tumbled across the dance floor.

"You're quite right, Mr. Stancheck."

The lobby doors all swung closed, each latch and lock clicking into place on its own.

"You're most certainly not done yet."

Marek stepped out of the darkness.

✦

The white Caprice police cruiser roared up Damen Avenue, hit the brakes and finally screeched to a stop fifty yards past the Gothique marquee in a cloud of burnt rubber fumes.

Cass peeled his fingers loose from the dashboard. "So, I guess we're not going to try and sneak in quietly?"

He and Colleen saw the confused crowds milling around on the sidewalks. Saw the half naked wounded refugees spilling out from under the marquee and falling in between the parked cars.

"Is that smoke?" Colleen pointed down the alley. Wisps of greenish gray spilled out of the stinkpipes and vents.

"We're too late, Col."

"Like hell." She floored it and spun the steering wheel at the same time, U-turning at fifty and clipping a limo that just started to let out a Gold Coast glam couple.

Cass and Colleen could hear Terri Shepherd's dead body thumping around in the trunk as the cruiser bounced off a taxi's rear end, roared right up to the curb in front of the marquee and finally stopped. They both leaped out, took in the scene on the sidewalks and the street. Exchanged the quickest glance and then raced for the one open door, just as two pale kids stumbled through and fell to their knees, coughing and crying.

And then the door promptly slammed shut right in their faces.

✦

He seemed to materialize right out of the shadows.

An arrogant, leering white face, discolored in horror-movie hues from the gelled spots and filtered lights shining overhead, dark eyes taking in the whole scene with apparent disdain. His black suit still was one with the darkness till he strode forward — slowly, purposefully, with deliberate, measured steps that clicked across the marble, swirling little wisps of thin smoke around him.

"No, Mr. Stancheck, I should say you're most definitely not done here. Nor are you, old man."

Jeff helped Rachel up. Fifty feet behind on the dance floor, Frank fumbled with his cartridge belt, suddenly all thumbs as he tried to jam another clip in the rifle. His last wooden stake fell out of his belt. Clattered on the floor and just rolled away into the thickening haze.

"Who are *you?*" Jeff shoved Rachel behind him. "H-how do you know my name?"

"Who am I?" Marek stepped out onto the dance floor and gazed all around him. At his creation: at the plaster cast faux medieval arches, the Styrofoam balustrades, the molded buttresses and plastic gargoyles, the spun fiberglass cobwebs and the backlit acrylic stained 'glass' windows. He stared all around at the club's cavernous interior. He stretched his arms out wide. "I, young man? *I* am the master of this place."

He stared all around at Gothique.

At his masterpiece.

In all its tacky glory.

"You've caused much trouble here today, I suspect. Perhaps we can survey it all later. *Together.* While I have your flesh slowly peeled away inch by painful inch from your living bodies. Hmm? How does that sound?"

"Fuck you." Jeff tried to shield Rachel behind him. "Just tell me where my daughter is. *Now.* While you still can. Where's Jacks?"

Marek massaged his temples. "Yes, I see it all now." He appeared to be deep in thought for a moment as he slowly paced back and forth along one end of the dance floor, where the gray-green haze congealed, floated like graveyard fog and licked at his black pants legs. "I do believe our Mr. Fortuna's dead, am I right? Shot with that rifle, I imagine. And...yes, the little warmblooded monster that made such a nuisance of herself. Gabrielle? Yes, Gabrielle. I do believe you've killed her too?"

"I didn't kill her. She fell. She — "

"Perhaps. But she's dead by your hand nonetheless. How many more of my children have you two 'heroes' destroyed tonight? And now you wish to know where your daughter is?"

"Just shut up!" Jeff shouted. "Where's Jacks?"

"Jacks." Marek seemed to roll that name around on his tongue. "A silly name for such a pretty little thing. Don't you think?"

"Jacks!"

Marek turned away. "Drake?" As he spun around, fingers of smoke rose around him, suspended overhead like groping claws.

"Drake, don't be alarmed," Marek said. "Do bring our little 'guest' out."

Something shuffled in the darkness behind the bar.

Then Drake appeared, his pale arms wrapped tight around Jacks, one white hand clamped over her mouth. She struggled and kicked as he dragged her out and stood beside the bar.

"Jacks!" Jeff leaped forward, but Marek suddenly stood between them.

"I would stay right where you are, Mr. Stancheck. Unless you want to see Drake rip your little girl's throat out right before your eyes. I assure you, he can. Before you could even make it halfway to her. She'll bleed to death before you could do anything about it, And he'd have such a lovely time lapping up her blood. While you watched."

Marek stood beside Jacks. Jeff moaned — Jacks cringed — Rachel fell to the floor and whimpered — as the vampire delicately traced his long nailed finger along her cheek. Down her throat. Across the front of her T-shirt, lingering there, laying his whole, pale white hand across her chest and rubbing. "Ahh, the sweetness of youth. Could anything be finer?" Jacks squirmed. "We seem to be at a bit of a standoff here, gentlemen."

They all turned then when an ugly growling sound echoed throughout the huge hall.

Their eyes all went directly to the open service door, to the thick smoke billowing out over the threshold. To the flickering fire glow brightening inside and down the basement steps.

And to the vampires crawling up those steps, heaving themselves up through the doorway.

One stood up, its entire body smoldering, dead skin peeling off in layers, then disintegrating and falling off like dust. Another weakly clung to the doorway, trying to raise itself up, its clothes and hair all on fire.

Frank shouldered the M-1 and fired off four rounds into one, four more into the other. The impact knocked the dying vampires down, and they tumbled back into the smoke with a horrible wail.

Two more slithered and sizzled out the door and crawled across the floor. But they collapsed in their own puff of acrid fumes, sparks flying off their bodies before they disintegrated.

A velvet curtain flanking the stage started to smolder.

A plastic gargoyle started to sputter, then melt.

A bank of black PA's and speakers began to smoke.

Frank had another clip in hand and already locked in place as he whipped around. "There's no standoff here, monster. Those — those things of yours stole my dog. And now he's dead. Burnt up down in that hell hole of yours.

Now you're going to let that little girl go and we're going to walk right out of here. Or you'll get the same."

Marek laughed.

He threw his head back and laughed, then Drake started laughing too and the horrible, chilling sound made Frank and Jeff and Rachel and Jacks — all of them — made them quake with utter terror, with a shivering, empty feeling of sheer futility as it rang in their ears and echoed all around the pillars and buttresses and even shook the stained glass. Finally, Marek stopped. He raised his hands.

Then he clapped.

Once.

Twice.

"Bravo!" Slowly at first, then rapidly, he clapped in hearty applause. "Oh, bravo, old one. A heroic display. Simply magnificent. You dispatched the mindless monsters to the flames. Really, bravo!"

"Shut up." Frank aimed at Marek again. "Shut up right now or I'll — "

"Wait!" Marek raised one hand.

Frank blinked, trembled, shook his head.

"Wait, old man. Before you shoot, just remember the little girl here."

"Frank, hold it!" Jeff's eyes shot back and forth from Frank to Marek to Jacks. She still struggled in Drake's arms, her terrified shrieks muffled behind a dead white hand. "Just — just wait, Frank."

"Yes, 'Frank'," Marek said, sneering with arrogant malevolence now. "Wait. Your bullets can't kill us. You know that. They may cause as much pain in us as they would in you. But no, they cannot kill us. And I certainly don't really plan to let you launch another attack with my finest liquor. No, just wait, old man." He turned to Jeff. "I have every intention of letting your daughter go free. Much as it would please me to simply take her here and now, before her father's eyes."

Jeff couldn't contain himself and lunged forward.

"Wait!" Marek held his hand up again, and Jeff actually froze in his tracks. "She may go free. *In exchange.*"

"Exchange? For what?"

"Why, for *you,* of course."

Jacks kicked Drake doubly hard then and bit down on his hand. "Dad, no!"

But Drake twisted her arm behind her. Jacks shrieked in pain.

Jeff lurched, then halted. "Talk. Fast."

"Very simple, Mr. Stancheck. You come with us, and she may go free. She can go with the old one, if you like. You can even take her little friend, if you wish, the one on the floor there. She's a mess after all. And I'm told she whines a lot anyway."

"Dad, don't listen to him , don't — "

"Silence, whelp!" Marek never even looked back at Jacks. He just glared at

Jeff, his red lips curled into an evil grin. *"You've* killed *my* children. It's a fair exchange. So, you come with us, Mr. Stancheck. Your life for your daughter's."

"All right."

"Dad, no!"

"Ahh, but let me finish," Marek said, pacing the dance floor again, his malevolent grin widening. "We shall make you one of us. Tonight perhaps. Yes, tonight, the sooner the better, I think. And then you can be at our side forever. For an entire eternity of deliciously dark, hellish nights. Because we will torture you, Mr. Stancheck. We will torture you in immeasurably, imaginatively painful ways that no mortal words could even describe. Forever, Mr. Stancheck. That's my bargain with you." Marek locked his dead, black eyes with Jeff's. His sneering grin was all smug now, more arrogant than ever. "So, do you still agree so quickly? Do you truly love your daughter that much? Will you commit yourself to hell? Do you — "

"Shut the fuck up. I said, all right."

Marek nodded. "Very well. Would it surprise you if I thought you might hesitate? Just a moment? Some brief indecision? Yes, yes, I understand all about love and loyalty and responsibility and 'family'. But then, you let that all come apart on your own anyway. Didn't you, Mr. Stancheck? I thought you might want to mull it over a bit." He held his pale hand out to Jeff. "But I can assure you, you'll have years and years to mull this moment over, as you pay for all you've done here today. You can regret your choice for eons, long after she and any brood of hers are long dead." He stepped through the smoke swirling around on the floor, stepped towards Jeff, one white hand outstretched. "Come, then."

"You let her go, first."

"Oh, no waffling now." Marek was almost on him.

"You tell your boy there to let her go. Jacks goes free. Frank and Rachel, they all leave. Then you can take me."

"Dad!"

"Jeff, don't do it boy, we can still — "

"Enough of this!" Marek growled, his face twisting into long toothed, red eyed horror all of a sudden. "Perhaps I'll just take you all and bathe in your blood right now." Those pale, beckoning hands curled into talons and he lunged for Jeff. "I'll have you and your little — "

But in that instant, the entire room exploded into noise and action.

First — a *crash.* From out front.

Drake growled from beside the bar.

Then another — *crash!* — and the lobby doors shattered in an explosion of black glass. Two dark figures burst through, flew right through the smoke and somersaulted in a hail of black sparkles.

Cass and Colleen leaped to their feet out of the shower of broken glass.

And just as they did, a strange sound echoed throughout the huge hall.

Short.

Sharp.

And *angry.*

There it was again. "Drake!" Marek pointed at the two renegade vampires, already racing towards the dance floor.

Marek whirled this way and that way, took a hesitant step —

Then froze, his black eyes wide and staring at the smoke churning up on the floor.

There was that strange sound again. And everyone froze for just a moment —

Just as a sizzling missile of fifty five pounds of pent up fear, fury and smoldering fur erupted up out of the gray cloud hovering along the floor.

Sox burst up out of the haze, growling, then shot like a rocket right at Drake.

Ears flung back, singed fur raised, muzzle twisted into some kind of instinctive vulpine snarl, the dog's own fangs clamped down on the vampire's face and dug in deep.

Drake howled and tried to shake the dog loose. But Sox' little legs flailed away, sidewalk sharpened claws gouging Drake's arms. He bit down with enraged *kill the bad smelling thing — protect Frank* fury, jaws slicing Drake's face to ribbons.

The vampire tried to pry Sox off.

And let go of Jacks.

"Dad!" Jacks dove through the bar stools, knocking them all over like a row of dominoes.

Drake finally shook Sox loose. The little dog fell to the floor, blackened with soot, fur still smoldering, patches of raw pink skin glistening in the colored lights. But he hefted himself up on his paws and shot right back at the vampire.

And so did Jeff.

He dashed across the dance floor and grabbed Frank's wooden stake. With one leap he was on top of the bar, then sliding right across it, the stake gripped tight and overhead like a javelin.

It plunged deep into Drake's chest in an explosion of black blood, torn flesh and cracking bones.

Drake shrieked, tried to grab the stake, but Jeff just rammed it in deeper, till the point jutted right out of Drake's back. "Marek!" Drake tumbled to the floor, rolled back up on his feet and then started to smoke. "Marek, help me! Marek!" Black bile bubbled up out of his mouth, choking his screams. His skin started to wrinkle, his flesh began to crumble, and after a few moments of sickly, sizzling, cooking sounds, he burst into an explosion of dust and gore.

Sox ran to Frank's side, whimpering. But his almost furless tail wagged with some kind of doggie triumph, waving wisps of smoke off the end like a lit cigarette. "Table's turned, fancy-ass." Frank stepped forward now, the M-1 aimed right at Marek.

"No. No, this can't..." Marek cowered for a moment, red eyes darting around the room. "I won't let this happen. I — "

Frank didn't wait to hear the rest. He fired, right into Marek's legs, just like he did to the vampires downstairs.

Marek screamed. "No, wait! I can give you power, I can — "

"Save it." Four shots into one knee, shredding his pants, ripping right into pallid undead flesh and bone, spinning Marek around like a top.

"No!"

Four more into the other, and the vampire fell to his knees, his face contorted in stunned disbelief. He gaped at them all, eyes wide, flashing back and forth from dead black to furious hot red. Then Marek fell backwards, his shattered legs flopping on the floor uselessly. "No. This can't...not like this. Noooooo!"

The lights flickered and went out. But the immense hall didn't go dark. It just glowed in quivering blue, yellow and orange and green. A row of spotlights sparked high overhead, lenses popping, showers of colored glass careening down to the dance floor. Flames crept up the huge stage, crawled along the edges of the curtains, started on the chairs and the tables, where half full bottles and glasses of liquor flamed, then detonated like countless grenades.

Frank picked up Sox and cradled him in his arms, hugging the dog tight till it yelped. The old man wiped his eyes with his sleeve, and it wasn't because of the smoke now.

Jeff raced to Jacks. She fell into his arms, sobbing hysterically.

Rachel crawled through the smoke and off the dance floor.

Cass followed Colleen.

He followed Colleen as she crunched through the broken glass, swirling smoke that was knee high now. She knelt down beside Marek. Gazed into his eyes. "I remember now," she said. "I remember. In the dark. In that cell. How *you* came to me."

Marek grimaced. "Yes, child. So you must help me now." He jerked his head back and forth, searching the smoke, the shadows, the flames. "Someone help me here. I command it!" He grabbed Colleen's arm. "Help me up, we can — "

"I remember."

Cass stepped forward "Col, careful. He's — "

She spun her head around and the look on her face was as vicious as any ugly, monstrous thing that ever lurked in the dark corridors below Gothique. The words froze on Cass' lips.

She turned back to Marek, pried his hand off her arm and shoved him back down into the smoke, down to the floor. "I remember."

"Yes, yes child." Marek's smug grin was completely gone now. Even his evil eyes were filled with fear. "Someone! I need...I — "

"I remember now," Colleen growled. "I remember who it was that stepped out of the darkness after they'd beaten and raped me. I remember who it was that planted his repulsive cold lips on me, who it was that kissed my throat and plunged his teeth into me. Who it was that killed me."

"Y-yes, child. I gave you my gift, I — " Marek lifted himself up, but she shoved him back to the floor. Hard. Some bone snapped somewhere inside his body.

"You murdered me. You took everything away from me and then couldn't just let me die. You made me drink. Grabbed my head and pried my mouth open with your cold stinking fingers and made me drink from your veins." She reared back and shouted at the ceiling. "You did *this* to me!" Colleen clawed at her chest and arms, as if her own body was something foreign, something evil and repellent. "This, you made me *this!*"

"Y-yes, I — Arianne!" Marek called the name over and over again. "Arianne, please. *Pleeeeease!* Save me, save me!"

No answer came. Only his own words echoing in the cavernous hall. He looked back up at Colleen.

Her lips peeled back, her fangs glistened in the flickering glow.

"Die!"

She lunged for his throat.

The smoke swirled right over them. All anyone could hear was Marek's hands slapping the marble floor, his wheezing attempts at a scream and Colleen Russell snarling like a wild, hungry, rabid animal. Till it all went silent, till all they heard were their own breaths and Sox panting.

Till Colleen finally stood up, her lips dripping black blood. The smoke parted as she stood, and all that was left at her feet was a quivering husk of a black suit and a crumpled, wrinkled caricature of Marek.

Cass yanked the smoldering wooden stake out of the pile of filth that had been Drake only moments before. He threw it across the dance floor.

Colleen caught it. She raised the stake high overhead. Roared with an awful, hellish scream of despair as she felt some last tiny piece of her humanity melt away.

"Go to hell, 'Father'."

The stake plunged down.

Marek's body began to boil. Colleen leaped back, right into Cass' arms. There was a flash, then a puff of green smoke. Maybe they all heard some kind of soulless wail. But the crackling flames growing all around them, the smoke billowing over the entire floor — swallowed everything up.

They stood there in silence for a moment.

Then the smoke started to creep higher up their legs. Rachel was still crying. A siren whined somewhere outside.

"We're done here," Jeff said as he held Jacks tight in his arms. Rachel shuffled up next to them. Frank carefully carried Sox. They all picked their way through the shattered glass and broken doors.

And walked right out of Gothique.

✦

A fire engine and two squads sped up Damen Avenue, lights flashing, sirens blaring. The crowds on the sidewalk and the street stepped back as the hook and ladder stopped and the firemen jumped off. More squads raced up Damen, cops scattered all over the street. Smoke began to seep out of the front windows. A black leather and lace clique ran out of the alley squealing, as a thick cloud puffed out right behind them.

Jeff and Jacks, Frank and Sox, Rachel and Colleen and Cass — they all walked out of Gothique, out from under the marquee.

The gawkers nervously fingered their capes and their dyed hair, fidgeted with their lace gloves and ruffled shirts, the Goth kids and the gamers, the hard core clubbers and the fringe-scene junkies and hustlers, the just plain curious and all the rest — they just stepped aside. Then were shoved aside as the police took over, as paramedics arrived and started to check on the wounded and the delirious and the half naked refugees still wandering around Damen Avenue in a daze.

The six of them all walked across the street.

Stood there in front of Frank's two flat. The darkwave cadets and the clubbers all lined up in front of them, staring at the old theater building. The windows on the upper floors exploded and flames shot out. A huge cloud of smoke erupted through the roof, another billowed out of the front doors. The firemen scurried back and forth with their hoses and extinguishers. The cops swarmed all over the crowds and Terri Shepherd's police cruiser parked half on and half off the curb under the marquee.

The crowd trampled all over Frank's little patch of grass, some smiling at the extravaganza, some no longer convinced that it was just another part of the show. Some stared, some jeered, a few even cried because they never made it in and now it was all burning up and *goddamn, now what are we gonna to do tonight?*

Jeff and Jacks, Frank and the rest, they all stared at the burning building too, watched as the flames rocketed out of every window, crept up the facade, as the huge black and red marquee finally flickered out, the enormous red medieval script began to peel, melt, then cave in on itself, while the cops shoved everyone off the sidewalk.

They just stood there on Frank's lawn, silently staring. Maybe with some grim satisfaction.

All of them, except Cass.

He stared at one of the kids on the sidewalk.

At a slender young thing, just another of the countless black wardrobe warriors. Just another goofy Goth chick at first glance. But beautiful, so very beautiful. Like a porcelain doll, with the darkest eyes, with long black hair whipping around her face in the cool breeze, wearing a little nothing of a black dress and nothing else despite the cold. With a black duffel bag slung over one shoulder.

Arianne stared back at him.

"Cass, what is it?" Colleen tugged on his arm.

Jeff looked up from Jacks, suddenly tensing, his eyes instantly alert again.

"What's up, Cass?"

Arianne approached.

Cass stepped back, dragging Colleen with him.

"Cass, what's — "

Arianne stopped right in front of them. All of them. She dropped her duffel bag on the sidewalk, then stared hard at Cass. "You know me?"

He nodded.

She searched each of their eyes. Lingered on Jeff's and Frank's, on each of theirs. She looked back at Cass. "This one knows me. Knows who I am. What I am." She scanned them all again. "I wish you no harm. Enough has happened here. You've destroyed him. He was mine. I made him, and you've destroyed him."

Frank's fingers were already working the M-1's strap off his shoulder.

"No, leave your weapon where it is, old man. I am not one of those fledglings you destroyed in there. I assure you, you'd all be dead, even with all these people around us, even before your police could intervene." Arianne sighed. "But there has been enough killing here. Marek is destroyed. His madhouse is gone. Perhaps that is better. Perhaps the flames will cleanse everything. Perhaps the evil will leave here. For awhile."

They all just stared at her, no one able to answer, no one able to say a single thing to this slender girl, who looked just like a teenager, just like all the other teenagers scurrying around on the street and the grass. But her eyes silenced them, those deep, dark knowing eyes that simply didn't belong in a pretty, pale, young girl's face.

"I only wish to leave." She stooped and picked up her bag. Slung it back over her shoulder. "I mean you no harm. Forget you've ever seen me. Forget all that has happened here. Forget *me.* I'll never trouble you or yours again. I swear this."

Arianne turned, and walked away.

Jeff shook his head, coughed as the smoke filled the street. Frank wiped his eyes, tearing from the fumes. Rachel plopped down on the grass and started crying that she wanted her mother, and Jacks ran to her side.

But Colleen and Cass still stared into the crowds, stared and saw some of them part down the block, part to let the slender little wisp of a girl in a black dress walk by. The gawkers and the Goth's slid back into place then, jostling for a better view, hollering at the cops, laughing at the firemen.

Arianne was gone.

As if she'd never even been there at all.

"What...who was...?" Jeff looked around like he just woke up.

"No one," Cass said, still staring down Damen. "Like she said. Forget it. Forget about her."

"I want my mother," Rachel whined on the grass. "I want to go home."

Sox yelped then and they all came back to reality. "Look, I have to get my dog inside and patch him up," Frank said. "You all want to..?" He looked at each of them. "No. No, I guess you all want get away from here. Maybe that's best. Me? I think once I get Sox cleaned up I'm going to call my wife. And to hell with the rates." He started towards the gangway. Stopped. Turned back. Looked at Colleen. "Little girl, I-I'm sorry."

Colleen reached out and patted Frank's hand. "It's okay, Frank. It's...well, it is what it is."

Jeff came up beside her and threw an arm around Colleen's shoulder. "Look, we can figure something out."

"Like what, Jeff?"

"I don't know, Colleen. *Something.* There has to be some way we can — "

"Tomorrow night," Frank said. "We can get back together after you...well, after. We can think this all out. Figure out some way to help you. And your friend, too." He looked at Cass now. "I mean it...Cass. You too."

Colleen shook her head. "No, Frank." She turned to Jeff, hugged him and he didn't flinch at her touch. She wiped away something like a tear. "Good-bye Jeff."

Colleen took Cass' hand and they backed away into the crowd. "Don't look for us. Try to forget. Forget about us."

And just like Arianne, just like they'd never even been there, Colleen and Cass vanished into the darkness.

Northtown News
March 21
North Damen Reborn

The Mayor and local dignitaries posed with ceremonial gold spades and took reporters' questions after breaking ground for the $65 million Westlake Centre, which will feature an all new 40,000 square foot state of the art regional Public Library, a senior citizens center, 60 tenant enclosed shopping mall and multiple screen theater complex. The project will be anchored on North Damen Avenue, just south of Montrose, an area dominated for the last decade by row houses and vacant storefronts, as well as the now demolished Palace Theater, which briefly made headlines late last year as...

Chicago Police Department
Juvenile Division
Report #00414
Subject: R/MP Status, 1st Quarter

Confirming MIS preliminary tally, 11% decrease in runaway and juvenile missing persons reports for YTD vs. same quarter last year. Cook County Social Services also corroborates projected stats of 47% decrease vs. 4th quarter last year. CC: HQ Homicide, HQ Vice, HQ Domestic Violence, All Precincts...

Chicago Tribune Business Section
April 12
Last Nails In Whitestar Coffin

Amacom, Inc. released details of last month's FCC auction in which they acquired two local FM radio stations, both the last saleable assets of the now liquidated Whitestar Media Group. Whitestar Media, helmed by controversial CEO and primary stockholder Roberta Whitehead, was dissolved by the Justice Department following the recommendations of the SEC after...

Delightfully Disaffected, Disenchanted And Disenfranchised Again

THIRTY SIX

The darkness emerges and it descends from the east.
And with the darkness, they awake.
Another night, and they awake.
The children of the dark crawl out of their dens to embrace the night.

Winter cloaked the city, burying Chicago in its blizzards and ice storms, drenching it with freezing rain and sleet. And after it all finally melted away, not surprisingly, things looked pretty much the same.

Night after night, they still held court at their chat rooms and websites. Still devoured their graphic novels, their used paperbacks and their ink-jetted 'zines. Memorized their multi-volumed sourcebooks and collected their shared world figurines. Still pounded away on their programmable keyboards, flailed away at their pawn shop guitars and pre-planned their witty interview responses throughout the MTV wet dream garage bandstanding sessions. They still hacked away on their never-to-be-finished software schemes and agonized over their adolescent dreamin' love-is-pain poems and novel fragments, their hand scribbled screenplays, their loose leaf doodled felt tip frescoes and stolen, scanned and bit-mapped digital art for the new ages, all their roads to hopeful hells still paved piece by pointless piece with obscure works in progress.

The rituals hadn't changed. If anything, there was something that much more comforting in them now.

They still mugged in their dresser mirrors and preened in grimy bathroom stalls, still rummaged through underwear drawers for their mail-ordered pewter skulls and batwing rings, their genre-con chromed plastic ankhs, velveteen chokers and studded vinyl dog collars. They still painted their chewed-to-the-tip nails all red, black, then decaled. Still painted their lips all shiny-sexy wet, still ringed their eyes with shadows and mascara bruises, still adored that beguiling heroin chic, haute cocaine couture, that gaunt and painfully pale and oh so creamy-hot-hard-wet, oh so sex-is-death-is-love look.

But for a few, the dreamlike summer and fall had been somewhat of a cathartic experience.

As if they'd whipped their black molded plastic death's head compacts open and stared at their own overly madeup faces in the mirrors — something their folkloric counterparts could never do, after all — something about seeing all the slummers and the weekend-only crowd doing the costumes and the clubs and the games, something disturbingly deconstructivist about it all, something that hollered 'time out', time for some reassessment, if not an outright reality check. So a few — just a very, very few — disengaged, went AWOL, vanished back into the split levels and the subdivisions, swallowed their pride and finally called home to get the money to laser off the tattoos or see a doc about at least a *few* of the piercings, opened the want ads or even begged the step-mom for the scratch to finally finish up that almost completed Associates Degree in Communication Arts.

But though those few proved disloyal, showed their own lack of commitment, cashed it all in sometime in the early winter when the first snow finally blanketed the blackened ruins and the burnt out red and black marquee, the rest...

Well, the rest?

The rest — *they* still wished.

They still wished their dark secret wishes each night, the moment they felt the fingerless gloves against their soft, skinny hands. When they felt the rough sewn seams inside the mall store lace, or their freshly painted nails clawing shiny sleazy nylons into gauzy black cobwebs, when they felt the uniform jett black tights snap into place around their anorexic hips, felt the corset straps slide over their bony white shoulders, felt the Harley Hog leather shimmy over their gangly legs. Because they still loved the sound of artfully shredded jeans and leather pants and vinyl skirts sliding and crinkling into place, the crisp snap their satin capes made when they spun them around in front of the mirror, the somehow reassuring sounds of their jingle-jangle bike jacket zippers, their combat boots and fetish heels clomping below their black lycra'd legs.

Because it *was* reassuring. Because now everything was somehow...*normal* again. The way it should be. They could bask in the scowls from the dopey dismissive straights again, from the sanctimonious suits and secretaries, from the great proletariat unhip. Because finally, the suburban mall rats and Gold Coast dilettantes understood that just tossing on a black mini wouldn't pay the membership fee anymore. Every prep school jock didn't think a smudge of eyeshadow was some kind of badge to flaunt. Because it took more than quoting lines from one or two direct-to-cable boobs 'n blood flicks to buy some goddamn credibility.

So they still congregated in their clubs, their cults, their cadres and covens, in their non-franchise coffeehouses with authentic bare brick walled, mismatched cupped bohemian legitimacy. The elders still argued Bauhaus and Maplethorpe, Shelley and Baudelaire, still preached to the youngsters, who were still all flushed and cyber'd up to the minute with their Brite's and Melton's and the latest RPG reg's.

Dark Echoes may have already gone under and reemerged as a taxi barn.

Rimbaud's Cave may have endured another facelift and reopened as an X-er veggie sports bar. But there were always new and just as dingy converted storefront bars and converted warehouse clubs and yet-to-be-converted gangways and alleys where they could lick the tips of their acrylic dental delusions, lick their lips at each other, lick themselves, lick each other, lick their wounds, their self-inflicted wounds that still bled from the sores of their days' discontented dreams. They could still puff away on their Bi-Di's, still wallow in the stinky, cloying, fruity smoke from the countless colored cigarettes hovering around them like graveyard fog.

Yeah, like fog.

Like graveyard fog — oh, that would be cool.

Because now the lines were redrawn. The way they *ought* to be.

The thirty something drop-in's and the yuppie strays went back to the health clubs and theme bars. The Bloomie's in-store boutique crowd and the Oak Street salon sodalities handed all their black dresses and black suits and black shirts and black tights off to Goodwill along with their barely scuffed Doc Martens and spikes. The cheerleaders went back to the Gap and the jocks went back to mini-mall arcades and the chess club dweebs went back home where they'd belonged all along.

Now everything was back to normal.

Us: here.

The world: *there.*

Because when all was said and done, it just wasn't that much fun to hover on the dark fringe of society when soccer mom's practiced line dancing to a Morphine Angel CD and showed up at the PTA night in Morticia gowns. The fashions and the bands and the 'zines no longer seemed intrinsically subversive when futures traders were getting crown-of-thorns tattoos around their throats and scheduling LARP sessions in between November Hogs prices.

No, now everyone could cool off. Relax, sip a Merlot, savor a Gitane, pull the lace gloves taut, smooth out their fishnets, just ease back into a mustily comfy alley cast-off chaise and browse a good old fashioned fetish mag for an hour or two by electric candlelight without some tourist plopping down next to them and acting all at home.

Like it was *supposed* to be.

Delightfully disaffected, disenchanted and disenfranchised...

Again.

Now — and only if they were really in the mood, only if they already had a few or if they hadn't had enough yet — now they might set the Rimbaud and the Crowley down, might order up a couple liqueurs in those lovely little glasses, might patiently click their three inch black lacquered nails together and stare deep and all serious into a newcomer's eyes and agree to listen to the all too familiar timeless tale. As if this dark and decadent secret was being revealed for the very first time. That breathlessly told tale about desperate waiting and hoping. A wishin' and a wantin'. Hoping for it all to come true.

The movies. The songs. The videos. The paperbacks. The CD's, the comix and the zines, the rulebooks and the games, the websites and chatrooms, the clubs, the con's and the costumes — all of it, *oh please,* if it could only be real, could happen for real, could erase the daylight blandness, could all be true, just be true, be real, oh please, *please* become *real.* Become fog shrouded savage sacrileges, become moonlit crystal goblets of warm-thick-red *real,* be under-my-power, do-my-bidding *real,* welcome to my house, come into my room, climb into my bed, slither under my sheets *real,* be real and touch me — yes, touch me for *real* — there, yes, oh right there and don't stop, there — kiss me there, yes, there — bite — yes, bite me, bite me there, it's okay, bite me, no for real, make it *real,* like that, just like that, oh just like that and be *real.*

Be real.

Be *real.*

Oh, please be...

And then the Goth pioneers and the darkwave savants would nod knowingly, scab another round and draw those newcomers close, and all the better if they were young, if they were pretty, had a few bucks tucked in their black boustierres, had a car, had an apartment, or just had the patience and the respect to sit still and listen.

Because then those newcomers would hear all about what's real and what's not, about the rumors and the facts, told in hushed 'swear to God, my cousin's roommate was really there' third hand accuracy.

Then they were told all about Gothique.

✦

Spring meant sunny blue skies, budding trees and blooming flowers in a lot of places.

But Chicago really only had two seasons most years: a dreary hot and humid summer and an interminably long and frigid winter. This year was no different. Spring arrived by the calendar, but the sunny days were few, the snow only warmed into freezing rain and slush and at that, just barely. The winds still blew out of the north, skies stayed overcast, the lake still churned all gray and choppy and it would all likely stay that way clear through mid-May.

But Colleen hadn't seen any sunny skies in months anyway.

Either had Cass.

The cold wind that gusted through the budless trees and whipped faded winter trash in between the monuments couldn't really chill her much colder than she already was. Scanning the names on the stones, Colleen held her black leather jacket closed with her arms — the nifty jacket Cass bought her at the flea market on Milwaukee Avenue and gave her for a Christmas present, which almost made her cry, even if it wasn't wrapped and especially because she didn't think to get him something too, and even if they spent Christmas Eve sitting out on The Rocks all night at Belmont Harbor, just watching the ice chunks float by. She never took it off. Well, almost never. Only on the very rare occasions when they scraped up enough cash from a random picked pocket or some generous or downright terrified mope who'd been foolish enough to play bedroom eyes with her or with Cass — depending on the mope's preference — foolish enough to stop his car and whistle to them on Broadway, or ply them with drinks in one of the Halsted Street bars, the drinks that were always left untouched. Then they might have enough for a cozy night or two in one of the sleazy motels on North Lincoln or one of the SRO's in Uptown, where they could shower and rinse out their clothes and could huddle together under a real blanket on real sheets in a real bed for a night or two, hugging each other close during the long, comatose daytime sleep of the dead.

"It's over here," Cass called.

Colleen saw him pointing, two rows of tombstones down. She flitted between the monuments, her black eyes scanning the darkness with ease. Halted beside him. Colleen looked down and saw the name carved into the base of the marble tombstone, the garishly ornate pink thing Whitestar had bought and paid for with its laundered corporate blood money.

Megan Anne Russell
Your Legacy Was Love

Colleen knelt down. Opened her jacket and pulled out the crushed little bundle of carnations she'd bought from a guy selling them out of a cardboard box on Hollywood and Sheridan, the last bunch left in his box that late after rush hour. Five bucks a bundle. Just carnations. Some of them already wilting.

She gently lay the flowers down at the head of her sister's grave.

"Funny," Cass said. "I mean, not funny ha-ha. Just funny-odd. You know, with all the time on our hands." The wind whipped his black trenchcoat out like dark wings. "Funny we never came here before. Not since she...well, you know. Since."

Colleen stood up and dragged her long red hair off her face. "*'Your legacy is love'*. I don't know, Cass. I wonder how she'd feel about that? I wonder if Megan would worry that her legacy was all the horrible things that happened? All the people that died. All the kids that are still scarred, ruined for life, bouncing their heads of the walls of some nut house. I wonder if she could have ever known what she stumbled across and what trouble it would cause?"

Cass stood next to her. He leaned his head on her shoulder. "As usual, girl, you have it all wrong."

Colleen smiled. "Oh I do, huh?"

"Yep. It's that old glass-half-empty or half-full thing. You can choose to look on the bright side or choose to look on...well, let's not go into the whole dark side thing."

She elbowed him. "Make sense, boy."

"Megan didn't cause all that. Colleen, your sister isn't responsible for what happened. You might want to consider that she saved a hell of a lot of lives. She dug up the truth, set things in motion. Maybe if she hadn't...well, who knows what could've happened? Who knows how many more would've died before it all came crashing down? So maybe, in some weird way, maybe your sister's legacy *was* love."

"Yeah. And it got her killed."

Cass nodded. "Well, yes. It did do that."

"Didn't do any wonders for me either."

"Dark side, Col. Dark side."

Colleen stepped away from the grave. "Don't imagine either of us are ever going to have one of these."

"One of...? Oh."

"Who's going to bury us? Who's going to buy a tombstone?"

"Hopefully someone who doesn't pick out pink marble with angel statues on the sides."

Colleen looked up at Cass, looked deep into his eyes. "Who's going to put flowers on *our* graves?"

"Precious, you'll be rolling in rose petals in heaven someday."

"Think so, huh? What about you?"

Cass laughed. "Me? Oh, I committed more than a few indiscretions before I even met you, girl. I'll be pricking my fingers on thorns in hell, I guess." He draped his arm around her shoulder and guided her away from the grave. "So, morbid time's over?"

They walked through the grave rows, came to the wrought iron fence ringing the cemetery and hopped right over.

Cass and Colleen headed off into the dark.

They made their way through the alleys and the one way streets, dipping in and out of streetlamp haloes, just shadows, just black wraiths no one would even notice unless a passing car's headlights caught their pale faces or a porch light glimmered on their eyes. They walked for a good two hours from the cemetery, back north into Rogers Park, finally crossing Sheridan at North Shore Avenue, a short tree lined street a lot like Chase, just like their old street. Just a few blocks south of their old digs, in fact.

Neither had mentioned the apartment in a long time. They hadn't been back and it seemed a good guess that the landlord helped himself to their things — which weren't much, after all — once the mail started piling up and the utility bills went unpaid and the rent money just never arrived anymore.

They walked past the rehabbed twenties era four story condo conversions and courtyard buildings in silence. Finally came to the end of the block where a skinny sliver of beach began, a sliver that was more broken bottles and sunbleached Slurpee cups and discarded rubbers than sand, sadly. Lake Michigan churned noisy and black in a cold pre-dawn breeze. The wind whipped Cass' coat all around him, whipped Colleen's long red hair across her face. But she paused just after they hit the sand and yanked her shoes off. Left them there in the sand, walked a little further, then awkwardly hopped on one foot while she tugged at her socks and flung them into the wind, running barefoot to catch up with Cass.

Colleen slipped out of her leather jacket. "Hold this a minute." Cass took the jacket while she unbuttoned her shirt, slipped it off and let it fall on the sand.

"Let me guess," Cass said. "Skinny dipping?"

Her pale arms and shoulders were that much more starkly white against the black sleeveless undershirt. She smiled at him, shook her head 'no' and took her jacket back, flung it over one shoulder as they trudged through the sand. They approached one of the long, ugly corrugated metal and concrete breakwaters jutting out into the lake.

"Okay, I'll bite, Col. Planning on catching a few rays then?"

She stopped. Looked at him, looked Cass right in the eyes, looked long and hard and serious. And sad.

"You are, Col. Aren't you?"

She nodded.

"You knew it had to come someday, Cass. Didn't you?"

He looked away, but she reached up and grabbed his chin, turned him back to face her. "Cass, you didn't think I could just go on like this. Did you?"

He didn't answer for a long time.

"Cass, it's...it's just time."

"Okay." He slipped his fingers in her hand. "Well, let's go, then."

"Wait. I didn't mean for you. Cass, no. You have to go. You don't want to be here when...no, Cass, no."

But he held tight and headed for the breakers.

They walked all the way out to the very end, their black eyes riveted on the horizon, where the line between the lake and the sky was already defining itself by the moment. Where the inky darkness was lightening into violet, then brighter blue with each step they took.

They sat down on the very edge, dangling their feet over the water, the waves practically licking Colleen's toes. "Cass, are you sure?"

He didn't answer.

"There's still time, Cass. Bolt now. Hell, we're only two blocks from our old place. You remember how to jiggle that basement lock to get in the laundry room, don't you?"

Cass just watched the sky going bright blue along the horizon. Watched the clouds catch fire with yellow and orange along the edges.

"Cass — "

"You know, I've had more 'loves of my life' than I can count. But I've only had one friend. One *real* friend. And I don't think I'd like to try to make it through eternity without her. Hell, I don't think I'd want to make it through tomorrow night." He looked at Colleen and smiled, his fangs peeking out of his lips. "Not without you."

She stared at him and saw once again just how absolutely beautiful Cass was. Maybe even more right now, this very moment, with the almost orange pre-dawn glow starting to light up his face. Beautiful. The most beautiful man, the most beautiful person she'd ever seen. Black eyes, fangs and all. Beautiful. Inside and out.

Her fingers crawled across the concrete. Their hands locked together. A sharpening shadow lengthened behind their backs.

"Cass...I'm scared."

He nodded.

"Do you think it will hurt?"

"I don't know, Col. Maybe...or maybe it'll be real quick."

She squinted. Had to shield her eyes with her other hand. "No, it's hurting, Cass. I — can you feel it?"

The sky lit up like fire all along the top of the water.

"Yeah, I feel it, Col. I feel it."

A sliver of hot orange crested the horizon.

"It *hurts,* Cass. It really, really hurts."

He pulled Colleen close, wrapped his arms tight around her, started to wrap his coat around her bare shoulders.

"Oh God, Cass, it — "

Their ears roared as the boiling, ball of fire inched higher.

"Cass..!" She had to shout. The raging inferno blotted out everything else. "I-I...I love you, Cass!"

"I love you too, Colleen!"

They both screamed, but that faded into a far away echo once the flames erupted, once the smoke engulfed them.

Another gust of cold wind fanned the waves. Blew the last of the smoke away.

And scattered their ashes across the water.

✦

No one waited for Spring showers to cleanse all the dirt away.

The blackened, crumbled ruins of Gothique were still smoldering the day after the fire when legions of cops and ME's and investigators dragged in from throughout Cook and DuPage Counties began poking through the rubble.

They didn't find much. What they did only begged more questions, a lot of which no one really wanted asked in the first place, and certainly no one was prepared to answer. But they continued to pick and dig and poke around and cart out boxes of carefully tagged evidence bags. There were press conferences and the TV news trucks set up camp on Damen Avenue and even started to spread out on Frank Hoelevich's tiny patch of front lawn till he and Sox chased them off.

It played pretty big on the news and in the papers for a while. Teenage covens, mixed up montages of witchcraft and vampire cults. Veiled hints of drug use gone haywire, of prostitution rings, kinky fetish cults and anything else unwholesome and titillating that came to mind, but then it was sweeps month, after all. But soon enough the sensational stories went stale and the nitty gritty details of city bureaus and the police department had to be considered, which was all pretty tame for the front page and the nightly news and hell, there were better reruns on Channel Nine at 10:00 and *hey,* most folks just went right to the sports page to see how that latest Bears trade went down anyway. Nonetheless, the spinmeisters worked overtime trying to crisis-manage the whole affair. Till in the end, the proper deals were cut at the proper levels and a suitable number of suspensions, firings and arrests in a suitable number of city departments and in a disturbing number of police precincts were made. But those were all parceled out a few per week so no one much noticed. Carefully peppered with hints about gangs and organized crime and foreign underground's, it all was sanitized into tedium, so no one really paid attention.

This *was* still Chicago after all. A little corruption wasn't news. It was expected.

It didn't take long for the trail to lead back to Charade and then to the entire Whitestar Media Group organization, and finally right up to the top floor. There was some nifty video on that, when the cops hauled a haggard and half naked Roberta Whitehead out of her palatial twenty seventh floor suite in handcuffs, when the last eight weeks or so of boozing twenty four-seven left her largely incoherent, while she was shoved into the back of a squad, mumbling to the cameras that *they'd* come back for her, and the squad door slammed on her obviously insane cackle.

Roberta Whitehead had her holidays in a cozy padded cell, her Christmas Turkey puree spoon fed to her by a burly nurse with whiskers named Wanda, while the Whitestar empire crumbled and the senior managers jumped ship or — in the grisly case of one VP of Legal Affairs — jumped right out the window.

Because by then all those little corporate ferrets that only held onto their jobs by holding Roberta's thighs against their ears on a periodic basis were pretty much left holding the bag. The Attorney General's office got involved. The Chicago Police Department still had a few issues of its own to sort out, so the FBI stepped in. Interpol was contacted for some background matters. The SEC and the FTC, the FCC and the ICC and a whole hell of a lot of other state and federal C's swooped down on Fairmont Court for a closer look and quickly dismantled the Whitestar Media Group, brick by bloodstained brick.

Needless to say, Charade Magazine put out its final issue before the year ended, and though it was quite a collectible among the now temporarily low-key Goth community, the distributors and rack jobbers had a hell of a time hauling back all the unsold returns. As they discovered, naked vampire centerfolds usually didn't do big dollars during the holiday season.

Blair Armstrong got out before the very end, but *just.*

More accurately, she was booted out by the Whitestar board in one of their last official actions. So she endured a particularly chilly winter since she'd always spent more than she made and the fat six figure Managing Editor's salary barely had time to kick in before she got kicked out, and she'd acquired a round the clock taste for the booze and a couple other more expensive addictions during her flirtation with the *inside* of the darkside, but then just coping had been tough through those days and nights. All the fawning, solicitous Chicago media hangers-on that tried to court her only weeks before suddenly turned their backs on Blair, pretty much around the time the fire trucks finally packed up and pulled away from Gothique's smoking ruins. As in, immediately. December was mostly a long string of unreturned phone calls from publishing industry headhunters. January was a longer string of avoiding creditors' calls. February found Blair mailing out resumes on her own. By March she was finally filling out job applications in person, but one finally clicked, thank God, since she was down to portioning out her Happy Meals to cover lunch *and* dinner. Blair landed a job with her name right on the masthead as Managing Editor — a lateral move, on a title basis at least — but only for the *Filtration Products Manufacturers Marketing Bulletin,* only at $25K and only in Topeka, Kansas. Which she relocated to on a Greyhound bus, the Lexus gone with most everything else.

Blair found herself alone in her chilly Topeka studio flat on many nights that winter and on into spring, alone and staring at the phone, trying to work up the courage to call Chicago, to dial up Jeff Stancheck, to check in on her old 'pal'. But despite every stupid, sleazy — if not downright wrong — thing the wunderkind from NYC had done, at least she had the decency to let him alone and move on.

Or she was just too damn drunk to remember Jeff's number.

✦

Jacks stood right behind her father. Close. Like a shadow.

She did that a lot these days, but Jeff didn't mind. It would take time.

And if she was a little clingy here in *this* place...well, who wouldn't be? The cemetery would look grim enough on a sunshiny blue sky day. But this was just another gloomy, gray, overcast afternoon in that wet and ugly stretch between winter and summer, and all the Saints' statues and all the crucifixes capping the tombstones really didn't put either of them any more at ease.

Probably something to do with learning how the dead didn't always stay dead.

Jeff set a bouquet of roses down on Megan Russell's grave, then stood there for a moment saying a silent prayer. But he couldn't concentrate, couldn't remember the right words. He kept staring at a dried and faded bunch of carnations that leaned against the pink marble monument. Wrapped in tissue that had probably been bright green once, but was sun bleached to a yellowed off-white now, torn and picked at by wind and rain. He touched the bundle, and the tissue crumbled. The dry carnation petals disintegrated in his fingers, scattering in the wind.

But he caught one flower in his hand before it flew away. Held it in his palm. Gently tucked it in his pocket.

"Come on, Jacks. Let's go."

Heading for home, they talked about school, about next fall, about college. Jacks knew she was welcome to go pretty much wherever she wanted to. Money wasn't an issue. Jeff started at a pretty good buck as the Corporate A.D. for the northwest suburban Millimark Publications Group, oversaw the design teams for seven different magazines, and already got an extra twenty five grand pat on the back for all the good work in his first two months on the job.

But she'd settled on Loyola University. Right in the city, planned to start out at the downtown campus, right on Michigan Avenue, right next to the Park Stratford Hotel. Teased about trying Fine Arts. Maybe with some kind of minor in Graphic Design, something with computers, but something *fun* with computers. And she planned to live at home. Commute to school. Jacks would go silent, would just get up and walk right out of the room if Jeff even mentioned dorms and student housing. She talked more and more about car shopping, something small but sporty, maybe one of those nifty little import economy coupes and that always got Jeff going. "Hey, old man," she'd joke. "I just got back home a few months ago and you want to kick me out already?"

But Jeff knew it wasn't just that. It had nothing to do with 'being home'. He knew Jacks wasn't ready yet. When he got right down to it, Jacks was still just plain scared. Maybe would be for a long time to come. He wondered when her scars might finally heal. Wondered how many other kids were nursing the same kind of wounds.

Jeff negotiated Lake Shore Drive's narrow lanes, feeling narrower still at rush hour. He switched the headlights on. Then eased the Trans Am to the right as he passed the sign: *Montrose Avenue — Next Exit.*

"What's up, Dad?"

He didn't answer at first. Just swung off the exit and then onto Montrose.

As they rolled past St. Alstantius church, Jacks sat forward in her seat. Looked around. Recognized where they were. Saw the stoplight at Damen Avenue approaching. "Dad, what are you doing?"

"I just..." He hung a left down Damen. "Jacks, I just want to see it. I *need* to see it."

"Dad, I don't want to."

"Maybe you should, honey. Maybe it'll do us both some good."

Jacks shook her head. "Dad, no. I — "

Jeff pulled the Trans Am to the curb, in between two huge and overflowing construction site dumpsters.

Everything was gone.

Every last trace of Gothique was gone. Obliterated. Every plaster buttress, every melted acrylic 'stained glass' window and molded plastic gargoyle. Right down to deepest sub-basement and the last stinking, scorched hunk of quarry stone. The burnt out ruins had been torn down and hauled away to a landfill right after the New Year. The deep pit had been excavated as soon as the ground thawed. To lay the foundations for the new Westlake Centre.

Jeff looked across the street.

Looked at a huge billboard, an artist's rendering of the Westlake Centre development — the library, the seniors' center, the shops, the enclosed mall and the happy shoppers. A charming little chunk of pseudo-suburbia plopped down right on north Damen Avenue.

He gazed at the sign.

The footings stood right where Frank Hoelevich's flower bed had once been, where he hid his GI issue watertight case stuffed with the non-regulation stogies. The top of the huge billboard was just about where Frank's front window used to be, where the old man peered through the blinds and watched the horror looming overhead right across the street. Thirty yards back, a construction trailer perched on cinder blocks. Right where Frank's back yard had been, where Sox had fertilized the grass before their nightly walks.

But it was all gone now.

Damen Avenue was mowed down from Montrose almost all the way to Irving Park Road. Every house, every two flat, every vacant store front. Bought by the developers or eventually condemned by the city and blasted into piles of broken bricks and shingles and hunks of old lathe and plaster walls — some with fragments of outdated wall paper still holding the pieces together in the dumpsters. All gone. A whole neighborhood, a whole big chunk of people's lives, a chunk of the city, another neighborhood knocked down and dug up and about to be rebuilt. But it was better this way. The flames hadn't been enough. The whole evil place and every inch of the street and the sidewalk the demons ever stood on needed to be purged, cleansed, or better yet, just dug up and hauled away altogether.

Jacks stared out the window at the huge, gaping hole in the ground. "It's really gone, isn't it, Dad? I mean, *they're* really gone. *Really* gone."

Jeff nodded.

"And they can never ever come back, can they, Dad?"

Jeff reached over the center console. He grabbed his daughter's hand and held it tight. Squeezed, maybe till it hurt, but she didn't seem to mind. "They can't come back, Jacks. They're gone." He put the car in gear and pulled back onto the street. "I think they're really gone, honey."

✦

They crawled through rush hour traffic on the Stevenson.

Jacks reached up and tapped the little crucifix hanging from the rearview mirror. "Dad, where'd you get that?"

"Frank gave it to me. Frank Hoelevich."

"The old guy? The guy with the dog?"

Jeff nodded. "I saw him a couple times after...after everything."

They were supposed to be in a police station the day Gothique went down in flames. Were supposed to be giving another statement on Father Gil Silverez' bloody murder in St. Alstantius Church. They never showed up, of course.

But they got together a few weeks later, after Jacks finally went back to school.

Jeff and Frank met at Mike's Tavern, shared a few beers and burgers, which were shared with Sox, of course, who was milking his heroics for every stray snack he could, even if his little sheltie mind didn't quite put two and two together. They fabricated some almost plausible stories, but never had to repeat them. Never got called, not even one single inquiry about I.D.D. Detective Terri Shepherd, as if the straight facts were the last thing in the world the police wanted to hear. Not that Jeff actually knew what finally happened to Terri. But he could guess. Oh, he could guess.

They met the last time just before Christmas. Flurries blew outside Mike's Tavern. Jeff gave Frank and Sox a lift home. As they slowly cruised back up Damen Avenue they could see the wrecking ball smashing the burnt out building's walls. They could see the bulldozers heaving ugly piles of scorched bricks and twisted pipes into waiting dump trucks.

They could see the little crowd of black clad kids standing off to the side by the alley. Watching.

"Jesus," Jeff muttered. "It never ends, does it?"

Frank held Sox in his lap and petted his back, where the caramel and white fur was already growing back. "Maybe not. Maybe we never really win. But that's no reason to stop fighting." Frank rummaged in his pocket and pulled out the little crucifix. Handed it to Jeff. "I'd like you to have this, son."

Jeff looked at it and a thousand ugly images flashed through his head — Gothique, St. Alstantius, the priest spiked upside down on the cross, finally racing home and seeing the most chilling sight of all: the bungalow's front door hanging wide open. Knowing Jacks was gone.

"Frank, this was your friend's. Maybe you should — "

"No, I want you to keep it, son. I'll be gone soon. I think you should have it. I think Gil would like you to have it. I hope you'll never ever need it. But at least you'll remember some of the good that came out of everything. Maybe."

Jeff took the crucifix. They shook hands at the curb in front of Frank's two flat. Just shook hands. No hugs, no sentimental words. Somehow he knew that wouldn't be the old man's way.

Jeff bought a little chain that very day and the crucifix had been hanging from the rearview mirror ever since.

✦

Jeff eased the Trans Am off the expressway and waited at the first light on Pulaski.

"Actually, I got a letter from Frank yesterday."

"A letter?"

"Yes, Jacks. A letter. You know, a stamp, an envelope, paper with writing on it. Us old folks still do that sometimes."

"Yeah, I know. Ground mail."

Jeff popped open the console and took out an envelope as the light changed. He pulled out a snapshot and handed it to Jacks.

"Oh, look...Dad they're so *cute.*"

"Yep. Guess Frank and his wife are kind of like grandparents after all."

Jacks smiled at the little photo of Sox sitting proudly beside a black and white border collie. Six not-so-little puppies were piled into a caramel, black and white fur ball in front of them.

"Oh, Dad. Can we have one?"

"Actually, that was pretty much the point of his letter, Jacks."

She handed the photo back. "You really liked that old guy, huh?"

"Barely knew him, honey." They sped through the 47th Street intersection. "Well, at any rate, he seems to like it just fine down there in Florida. Guess he cut a pretty good deal with those developers for his two flat. His wife's near her family now. I never met her, but I bet she's a pretty special gal. Hey, he's even working. Got himself a job, part time in a Sears. Hardware department. He says the kid he reports to is driving him nuts, but I'll just bet he's loving every minute of it."

The Trans Am rumbled down Karlov. Jeff pulled up in front of the little brown brick bungalow. They got out and walked up to the front steps.

Past the realtor's sign on the front lawn.

Marked 'Sold'.

✦

They had to leave the car on the street.

The garage was packed to the rafters with cartons and junk from the basement. The movers would be there at 8:00 sharp tomorrow morning. Loading everything up, hauling it to a tidy little raised ranch out in the burbs.

Calling a realtor was one of the first things Jeff did once he settled into his new job, once Jacks was back in school, once the very sorest parts of both of their wounds had healed enough to focus on day-to-day living.

They shared some reheated pizza in the living room. All the lights on —

Jacks liked it that way these days — even the TV on, though the sound was turned down low. Jeff drained his can of Pepsi. "I'm getting another. Want one?"

"Sure, Dad. Diet." Jacks shot off the sofa. "Wait. I'll come with."

In the kitchen, Jeff popped open her soda and handed the can to Jacks. "So, is Rachel still on for next week?"

She nodded as she gulped and followed him back to the living room.

"Yeah. I warned her it won't be the same as coming back to the 'hood. But I think she's going stir crazy up in Milwaukee." Jacks took another slice and chomped off half in one bite. "Believe it or not, I think she actually misses Rory. But with him off in Colorado with their Dad and her Mom wanting to go...well, go *anywhere* but around here anymore." She saw Jeff staring at her. "Don't worry, Dad. It's just a weekend visit. We won't be going out anywhere. Videos, junk food junket, PJ party. That's it. I think even Rachel's clubbing days are behind her. Forever."

They finished eating. Carried paper plates, paper napkins and empty cans to the kitchen. Jeff wrapped up the last of the garbage and took it out to the alley. Came back in the yard and saw Jacks standing in the back window, watching him.

"Honey, I was just — " He stopped. Just followed her back into the kitchen.

He sat down at the kitchen table then, knocking back the last of the soda from the fridge. Jacks sat on the counter next to the sink, idly swinging her legs back and forth. Or not so idly. Maybe thinking. "Dad?"

"Hmm?"

"Have you really been trying? I mean...you know, you've really been calling and...?"

Jeff set his soda down. How could he answer? What was the right way? How could he tell Jacks how many times the phone rang and he answered it, but there was no one there? How many times he froze, thinking of all the horrible things they'd both been through, but thinking all those times that it really was just Elaine? How could he tell his daughter that...

"Honey, I *really* have tried. A lot."

"And nothing?"

He shook his head. "Not since right after Christmas. When she was in Houston."

"And you didn't tell her anything yet?"

"Honey, I didn't think it was something to do over the phone. Maybe in person. When we all see each other again...maybe then. And maybe you and I can discuss it all first."

"So Mom doesn't know anything about it? About what happened?"

"Don't see how she could."

"Dad, you don't think she's in trouble, do you? I mean, not a single phone call. Nothing since Houston?"

He thought about that one before he answered. "No, Jacks. Look, I don't have an itinerary on where these New Dimensions Ltd. things are held. But I'm sure your mom's okay. She's on the road, that's all. That's what this job of hers is. Seminars in one city, then move on to the next. One hotel after another." But the unspoken question on both of their minds still lingered in the air: *So why hadn't Elaine called?*

"Jacks, any calls will be forwarded to our new number for the next few months. Mail will be forwarded too. And I'm not through checking around." Jeff set his soda down by the sink. "Look, what do you say we both knock off early tonight, huh? Big day tomorrow."

Jacks hopped off the counter and headed for her room. Her new room. She moved into Jeff's converted office room after everything. His things spent the last few months in the garage.

She paused at her bedroom door.

"Dad?"

"Yes Jacks?"

"You know...I mean...well, thanks. I mean, I just want to say thanks for what you did. For everything. You were like...like, heroic or something. And I never really said it, said 'thank you'."

He nodded from his own bedroom doorway.

"And Dad?"

"Yep, kiddo?"

"Well, despite everything, I mean, all that happened, you know. Well...I'm just really glad I came home."

"Me too, Jacks. Me too."

✦

So why hadn't Elaine called?

Elaine Stancheck-now-Porter-again hadn't called for months because, at first, she really *was* incredibly busy managing the New Dimensions Ltd. southwestern region programming.

On the road all the time, holding seminars in one city then moving on to the next, one motel after another. Dutifully coordinating her activities via long distance with Calvin, scrupulously sending all the revenues in to him on time. Calvin was the Dimension Program Director that first got her involved back in Encino, and he made it down to Arizona, New Mexico or Texas once in a while, managed to catch up with Elaine at some Ramada or Holiday Inn to go over the books and to give her a little pep talk, usually late at night, long after dinner and drinks in some supper club along the highway, after Calvin had 'empowered her', so to speak, back in her motel room bed.

Calvin had last pep-talked Elaine back in December, long and loud enough that the guests in the next room were banging on the walls in the Red Roof Inn in the out-outskirts of suburban Houston. From there Elaine worked Dallas, San Antonio, Galveston and a whole string of no-name towns in between. She sent her reports in, always sent the checks and cash and credit card receipts in. But Calvin didn't visit once throughout January or February. Didn't even call in March, by which time she was working her way west from El Paso into New Mexico.

It was during a one week layover just across the New Mexico state line, with no new schedule for the next seminar dates yet, that the cops came calling.

Elaine was hauled out of her no-name motel room in the middle of the afternoon — in handcuffs, no less — and dragged down to the sheriff's office, where the New Mexico State Police and a representative from the Texas State's Attorney General and the California Department of Revenue all waited for her.

But she was released the next day.

Oddly enough, they actually believed her when she told them over and over again that she didn't know a thing about pyramid schemes and off-shore accounts and thousands of earnestly empowered seminar attendees who never got their videos or their booklets or their inspirational audio cassettes. She probably sounded pretty convincing because, after all, she was telling the truth. She *didn't* know a thing about it. Because she honestly believed every single duplicitous word that Calvin told her, and honestly believed all the hokum she doled out in the suburban hotel banquet hall seminars, and was even foolish enough to believe all the promisingly hopeful things Calvin whispered in her ears when they were naked and sweaty and catching their breaths under the sheets.

She had to leave her no-name motel room the next day when the manager curtly informed Elaine that her New Dimensions Ltd. corporate credit card had been canceled, and dropped the chopped up plastic pieces at her bare feet right there in the doorway.

Since then?

Since then, Elaine slowly worked her way west, aiming for Encino even though Jacqueline was back in Chicago with her father, the house had been re-leased to someone new and there really wasn't anything or anyone waiting for her there. But she left the no-name New Mexico motel with exactly four dollars and sixty cents in her purse, having dutifully sent her reports and the money in just the day before, and New Dimensions per-diems being unusually small.

So it took a few stops along the long, long way for some short-lived waitressing jobs and even a temp job as a night shift telemarketer in a little office court outside of Flagstaff — which only lasted one night anyway, which she never got paid for, and which turned out to be a phone sex gig.

By the time Jeff and Jacks were saying good-night and turning in before the big moving day, Elaine-Stancheck-now-Porter-again sat on a sunbleached, wind-worn wooden bench outside the bus station in Tucson, Arizona.

Not the Greyhound Station. Just some little regional carrier that was a few bucks cheaper. She figured she had enough to buy a ticket to get her over the California state line, and could figure out how to get the rest of the way once she got that far, even if she had to wash dishes in a greasy spoon or clean toilets in a fast food joint, because she was sick and tired of the desert and sick and tired of living out of a suitcase and sick and tired of doing her laundry in the middle of the night in some tumbleweed town's wash-o-matic and sick and tired of living on microwaved breakfast burritos and just wanted to get back home. Wherever the hell home would be now.

But all that was largely speculative, about getting back into California, because the bus station was closed till morning, she was only guessing about the ticket price and she'd been fired from the last roadside diner waitressing job before she even got into her uniform, having foolishly started in on the boss about how short the pink and white shifts were and how maybe his customers didn't appreciate the way he objectified women and — well, Elaine got cut off and rushed right out the back door into the alley then, her suitcase lobbed out right behind her.

Hot as it had been all day, it was getting chilly now that it was night time.

No, not chilly. Cold. Damn cold, cold like only the desert could be after baking in the sun all day.

The cut rate carrier simply *had* to stick its station on the rough side of Tucson, as if Elaine would've known Tucson had a rough side and that this would be it. She shooed a hobo away two hours ago. A lowrider full of leering Latino boys slowly cruised by too many times for comfort. Elaine hauled herself up off the bench, hauled her heavy suitcase along with her and headed across the street. She'd been staring at the illuminated sign all evening. Just a tiny little neon thing, overdue for a recharge, anemically flashing COCKTAILS in curlicue pink in a just as tiny storefront tavern's window.

She had no business wasting money on a drink. But Elaine saw the lowrider's headlights at the end of the block again.

She opened the tavern's door.

It was cool inside, but comfortably cool. Cool and dark. Barely lit up with little beer company signs behind the bar and shaded lamps on the tiny round tables.

The place was empty.

Deserted.

No one sat at the tables. There was no one on the bar stools. No one behind the bar, for that matter.

Elaine shrugged her shoulders and dropped her suitcase next to one of the stools.

"Good evening." A voice called out from behind a swinging door next to the bar. "I'll be out in a moment."

"No problem," Elaine called back. She slid onto one of the stools. Looked around, squinting in the dim light. "Excuse me, but do you have a phone?"

No answer.

She squinted some more. Spotted an old pay phone sign way in the back behind the tables. And a wall mounted telephone below that. Elaine slid back off the stool.

Her fingers hovered over the buttons for long time. Finally she punched the number in. Waited for the operator to tell her how much, dug in her jeans for change and dropped the coins in the slot. Waited some more, then heard a 'hello'.

Heard Jeff's voice.

Elaine slowly let the receiver slide away from her ear. She hung up. Stared at the pay phone. Stared and wondered why she'd done it again, done it like she'd done so many times already since everything fell apart. Silently told herself *'No, wait. Wait till you're back on your feet, wait. You can't call him for help, can't go begging for money again, not again.'* She leaned her head against the pay phone, felt tears welling up in her eyes. Fought them back. Wiped her eyes on her sleeve and turned around.

And almost screamed.

The girl stood right there, so close that Elaine almost smashed right into her when she turned around. "Jesus! You scared me."

The girl winced, stepped back. "I'm sorry."

Elaine looked around the little bar again. Still empty. Wondered where the bartender might be. This part of town? There had to be a bartender, someone big and burly with anchor tattoos on his arms. Not this girl. Just a kid. "Are you...uhm, are you open?"

"Of course." The girl stood aside and gestured towards the stools. "Please, have a seat. What may I get you?"

Elaine followed behind her, watching the skinny little thing slowly walk barefoot around and then behind the bar, her short, flimsy black dress and her long black hair fluttering in some cool breeze that shouldn't be there.

"Hmm, I don't know." A place like this? Boiler makers and cans of beer? Shots of hard whiskey and pint bottles to go?

"I have some very nice wine you might like to try. Actually, I have a very lot of it. I don't seem to get much business here."

Elaine slid back on top of the stool and watched the girl take a green bottle of Chablis out of a refrigerator and expertly uncork it, her slender, long nailed fingers working the corkscrew with finesse. "You don't? *You* don't? This place is — "

"Mine, yes. I'm afraid so. I wanted to move to someplace warm. Well, it seems I did." The girl poured the wine. "I found this charming little place, the owner coincidentally decided to leave the business quite suddenly, and I decided it was precisely what I'd been looking for. For a very long time, mind you. But I think I may have made a bad business decision. I never really was particularly good with those kinds of things."

The girl brought a beautiful wine goblet over and set it down in front of Elaine.

The wine tasted good. Chilled just right, condensation already beading up on the glass. Elaine's throat almost sighed *ahh* when the white wine slid down. "Mmmmm, that's nice."

"I'm glad you like it." The girl smiled, and Elaine blinked, suddenly noticing how red the girl's lips were, how white her teeth were, how they sparkled even in this dim light. How pale her complexion was, as if she'd completely escaped the relentless desert sun. Which was pretty tough to do in Arizona.

The girl — woman — however old she may be, the girl was absolutely stunning.

Elaine swung her purse around. "How much is that?"

The girl shook her head. "With my compliments. You are my first customer tonight. And you look like you could use a cool glass of wine and a place to rest for a little while."

"Got that right." Elaine smirked. "Well, thanks."

"You have troubles? I didn't mean to eavesdrop by the telephone, but...a man, perhaps? It's always a man."

"No. It's...well..."

"Perhaps you can tell me while you drink your wine."

Elaine sipped again and eased back into the bar stool. After all she'd been through lately, she could think of worse ways to spend an evening than sipping this wonderful wine and telling her troubles to this pretty but peculiar girl. She looked around at the tiny tavern's interior. Actually, it was almost quaint. In a dingy wrong side of town kind of way. With a little creativity...some little touches here and there...

"By the way, my name's Elaine. Elaine...Porter." She held out her hand.

The girl leaned across the bar and her long black hair cascaded across the varnished wood. Her face hovered only inches away from Elaine's. Her eyes — her perilously dark eyes glimmered in the reflected light from the beer signs and the table lamps. They looked just like dark jewels, like opals, like flawless black diamonds. She slowly brought her arm around, held her own hand out. Slowly, lightly, like the brush of a cool feather, lay her hand in Elaine's.

"I'm very pleased you joined me tonight, Elaine." Her pale fingers wrapped around Elaine's.

"My name is Arianne."

Author's Note

"No, there aren't any old theaters on Damen Avenue just south of Montrose, though Chicago has no shortage of creepy old shuttered neighborhood movie palaces that could stand in for *Gothique* very nicely. Also, "Damen" and even "Karlov" are real Chicago streets and not contrived variations on "Damn" or "Karloff." *Please!*

Though this novel takes a jab or two at vampire enthusiasts and the Goth community (if it's even fair to lump so many different levels of flirtation with any 'scene' into a community), it was all merely in the interest of telling a good story. For the record, I actually applaud the 'delightfully disenchanted, disaffected and disenfranchised' Goth culture as a very rich and diverse fin de siecle update of good old fashioned beatnik bohemia – albeit with a decidedly darker, kinky edge. Nonetheless, I'll always wonder how punk became 'Goth', disco became 'darkwave' and New Age elevator music became 'ethereal' just by dialing the beat down a notch, lowering the vocals an octave and dressing the bands up in regulation black tights and corsetry. It's only the cynicism of age creeping out when I look at any youth subculture – be it the surf-scene, mods & rockers, hippies or even bo-do-di-o-do jazz babies – sensing that it really boils down to the proper apparel and what kind of music one buys, and that all the elaborate ritualism is really just designed to somehow get the most ardent adherents more dates."

Kyle Marffin is a midwestern writer whose 1998 debut novel *CARMILLA: The Return* was nominated for the International Horror Guild Award For First Novel.

STORYTELLERS

Julie Anne Parks

A writer who once ruled the bestseller list with novels of calculating horror flees to the backwoods of North Carolina. A woman desperately fights to salvage a loveless marriage. A storyteller emerges — the keeper of the legends — to ignite passions in a dormant heart. But an ancient evil lurks in the dark woods, a malevolent spirit from a storyteller's darkest tale, possessing one weaver of tales and threatening another in a sinister and bloody battle for a desperate woman's life and for everyone's soul.

"A macabre novel of supernatural terror, a book to be read with the lights on and the radio playing!"
Bookwatch

"A page-turner, for sure, and a remarkable debut." **Triad Style**

"Genuine horror and the beauty of the Carolina wilds. It's an intoxicating blend."
Lisa DuMond, SF Site

1-891946-04-8
Trade pb, 256 pages
$15.95 U.S.

THE DARKEST THIRST

A Vampire Anthology

Sixteen disturbing tales of the undead's darkest thirsts for power, redemption, lust...and blood. Includes stories by Michael Arruda, Sue Burke, Edo van Belkom, Margaret L. Carter, Stirling Davenport, Robert Devereaux, D.G.K. Goldberg, Scott Goudsward, Barb Hendee, Kyle Marffin, Deborah Markus, Paul McMahon, Julie Anne Parks, Rick R. Reed, Thomas J. Strauch, and William Trotter.

"Fans of vampire stories will relish this collection" **Bookwatch**

"If solid, straight ahead vampire fiction is what you like to read, then The Darkest Thirst is your prescription."
Ed Bryant, Locus Magazine

"Definitely seek out this book."
Mehitobel Wilson, Carpe Noctem Magazine

1-891946-00-5
Trade pb, 256 pages
$15.95 U.S.

SHADOW OF THE BEAST

Margaret L. Carter

Carter has thrilled fans of classic horror for nearly thirty years with anthologies, scholarly non-fiction and her own long running small press magazine. Here's her exciting novel debut, in which a nightmare legacy arises from a young woman's past. A vicious werewolf rampages through the dark streets of Annapolis, and the only way she can combat the monster is to surrender to the dark, violent power surging within herself. Everyone she loves is in mortal danger, her own humanity is at stake, and much more than death may await her under the shadow of the beast.

"Suspenseful, well crafted adventures in the supernatural."

Science Fiction Chronicle

"Tightly written...a lot of fun to read. Recommended."

Merrimack Books

"I found myself in the hands of a very good storyteller."

Malice Books

1-891946-03-X
Trade pb, 256 pages
$15.95 U.S.

NIGHT PRAYERS

P.D. Cacek

Nominated for the prestigious Horror Writers Association Stoker Award for First Novel. A wryly witty romp introduces perpetually unlucky thirtysomething Allison Garrett, who wakes up in a seedy motel room — as vampire without a clue about how to survive! Now reluctantly teamed up with a Bible-thumping streetcorner preacher, Allison must combat a catty coven of strip club vampire vixens, in a rollicking tour of the seamy underbelly of Los Angeles.

"Further proof that Cacek is certainly one of horror's most important up-and-comers"

Matt Schwartz

"A gorgeous confection, a blood pudding whipped to a tasty froth."

Ed Bryant, Locus Magazine

"A wild ride into the seamy world of the undead...a perfect mix of helter-skelter horror and humor."

Dark Regions/Horror Magazine

1-891946-01-3
Trade pb, 224 pages
$15.95 U.S.

THE KISS OF DEATH

An Anthology Of Vampire Stories

Sixteen writers invite you to welcome their own dark embrace with these tales of the undead, both frightening and funny, provocative and disturbing, each it's own delightfully dangerous kiss of death. Includes stories by Sandra Black, Tippi Blevins, Dominick Cancilla, Margaret L. Carter, Sukie de la Croix, Don D'Ammassa, Mia Fields, D.G.K. Goldberg, Barb Hendee, C.W. Johnson, Lynda Licina, Kyle Marffin, Deborah Markus, Christine DeLong Miller, Rick R. Reed and Kiel Stuart.

"Whether you're looking for horror, romance or just something that will stretch your notion of "vampire" a little bit, you can probably find it here."

The Vampire's Crypt

"Readable and entertaining." **Hellnotes**

1-891946-05-6
Trade pb, 304 pages
$15.95 U.S.

CARMILLA: THE RETURN

Kyle Marffin

Marffin's provocative debut, nominated for a 1998 International Horror Guild Award for First Novel, is a modern day retelling of J. S. LeFanu's classic novella, *Carmilla.* Gothic literature's most notorious female vampire, the seductive Countess Carmilla Karnstein, stalks an unsuspecting victim through the glittery streets of Chicago to the desolate northwoods and ultimately back to her haunted Styrian homeland, glimpsing her unwritten history while replaying the events of the original with a contemporary, frightening and erotic flair.

"A superbly written novel that honors a timeless classic and will engage the reader's imagination long after it has been finished."

The Midwest Book Review

"Marffin's clearly a talented new writer with a solid grip on the romance of blood and doomed love."
Ed Bryant, Locus Magazine

"If you think you've read enough vampire books to last a lifetime, think again. This one's got restrained and skillful writing, a complex and believable story, gorgeous scenery, sudden jolts of violence and a thought provoking final sequence that will keep you reading until the sun comes up."

Fiona Webster, Amazon

1-891946-02-1
Trade pb, 304 pages
$15.95 U.S.